THE ROUTLEDGE COMPANION TO SUPERHERO STUDIES

This Companion explores the evolution, representation, and meaning of superheroes within the broader popular media and culture landscape, as connected to both contemporary and historical frameworks. The volume proposes itself as a comprehensive resource in the interdisciplinary field of "Superhero Studies," acknowledging it as its own area of scholarly and cultural interest. Superhero Studies brings together perspectives from a number of intersecting disciplines such as comics studies, film studies, television studies, fandom studies, game studies, and beyond. In answer to the evolutionary portrayals of superheroes in our cultures, histories, and narratives, *The Routledge Companion of Superhero Studies* addresses the development, transformation, and meaning of these iconic figures, by taking a transnational, multimedia, and interdisciplinary approach to assessing their importance in our evolving representational contexts.

Lorna Piatti-Farnell (PhD) is Academic Dean at SAE Creative Media Institute in Auckland, New Zealand. She is the Founder and Director of the Australasian Horror Studies Network and sole editor of the "Routledge Advances in Popular Culture Studies" book series.

Carl Wilson is a freelance scholar and author based in the UK.

ROUTLEDGE COMPANIONS

For more information about this series, please visit: https://www.routledge.com/handbooks/products/SCAR30

THE ROUTLEDGE COMPANION TO SUPERHERO STUDIES

*Edited by Lorna Piatti-Farnell
and Carl Wilson*

LONDON AND NEW YORK

Designed cover image: iStock

First published 2026
by Routledge
4 Park Square, Milton Park, Abingdon, Oxon OX14 4RN

and by Routledge
605 Third Avenue, New York, NY 10158

Routledge is an imprint of the Taylor & Francis Group, an informa business

For Product Safety Concerns and Information please contact our EU
representative GPSR@taylorandfrancis.com. Taylor & Francis Verlag GmbH,
Kaufingerstraße 24, 80331 München, Germany.

Trademark notice: Product or corporate names may be trademarks or
registered trademarks, and are used only for identification and explanation
without intent to infringe.

British Library Cataloguing-in-Publication Data
A catalogue record for this book is available from the British Library

ISBN: 9781032433547 (hbk)
ISBN: 9781032433554 (pbk)
ISBN: 9781003366911 (ebk)

DOI: 10.4324/9781003366911

Typeset in Galliard
by codeMantra

CONTENTS

Contents

FIGURES

TABLES

ABOUT THE EDITORS

Lorna Piatti-Farnell (PhD) is the Academic Dean at SAE Creative Media Institute in Auckland, New Zealand. She is the Founder and Director of the Australasian Horror Studies Network and editor of the "Routledge Advances in Popular Culture Studies" book series.

Carl Wilson is a freelance scholar and author based in the UK.

CONTRIBUTORS

Cathrine Avery is a lecturer in Film, Television, and Digital Animation at the University of Hertfordshire. She has previously taught literature at Birkbeck University and The Open University. Her research focuses on gender and agency, particularly in relation to the crime genre. Her previous work has examined the representation of a feminist embodiment within the crime novels of Sarah Dunant, Sue Grafton, Åsa Larsson, and Jenny Siler, all of whom challenge the objectification of the female victim and unapologetically incorporate generic violence as an expression of female agency. She has recently published an article on Nolan's Batman trilogy: "Paternalism, Performative Masculinity and the Post-9/11 Cowboy in Christopher Nolan's Dark Knight Trilogy" in the *Australasian Journal of Popular Culture* (2023). She is finalizing an article that explores the representation of femininity within the audio-visual anomalies of Sebastian Schipper's *Victoria* (2015).

Jason Bainbridge is the Dean of the School of Humanities and Communication at the University of Southern Queensland. He has published widely on comics, film, toys, and merchandising across more than 60 publications and presented nationally and internationally on superhero culture. He has a large collection of well-read comics – and an even larger collection of superhero toys, many of which currently reside in his office.

Matthew Brake is an Associate Professor of Philosophy at Northern Virginia Community College in Manassas, VA. He is the editor of Bloomsbury Academic's *Theology, Religion, and Pop Culture* series and the *Studies in Comics and Religion* series from McFarland.

Sean Patrick Casey, disguised as a mild-mannered librarian for a great metropolitan school district, fights a never-ending battle to assist students in becoming active and responsible locators, users, creators, and evaluators of information, media, and technology. He has a bachelor's degree in Studio Art from St. Olaf College in Northfield, MN; a Master's degree in Library & Information Science from St. Catherine University in St Paul, MN; and has been a library media specialist with Minneapolis Public Schools since 2011.

A collector of comics since 1992 and a published creator of them since 2022, Casey's artwork most recently appeared in the American Library Association's (ALA) Addressing Comics Challenges Community Zine Project. In addition to being a member of the ALA and its Graphic Novels & Comics Round Table, Casey is a member of the Comics Studies Society and presented at CSS 2023 on Todd McFarlane and his use of comics' margins as creative space and at CSS 2024 on "demaking" comics. He most recently attended the 2025 International Comic Arts Forum, where he presented on superheroes, shared universes, and social justice.

Leo Chu is a postdoctoral fellow at the Laureate Centre for History & Population, University of New South Wales. A historian of agriculture and environment specialized in the exchange of development knowledge between Cold War Taiwan and Southeast Asia, he also writes broadly about popular culture such as anime and games. His works have been published in *Agricultural History*, *Extrapolation*, and *Configurations*.

Jo Coghlan is an Associate Professor at the University of New England, Armidale, New South Wales. Her research interests are in popular culture and material culture with an emphasis on gender, politics, fashion studies, death studies, film and TV, and gothic noir. Her most recent publications have appeared in the *Australasian Journal of Popular Culture*; *Clothing Cultures, Film, Fashion and Consumption*; *and Media/Culture Journal*. Jo along with Lisa J. Hackett and Huw Nolan are the founders of PopCRN – The Popular Culture Research Network, Australia's leading research network on popular culture and material studies. Jo, Lisa, and Huw have recently written on *The British Royals in Popular Culture* for "Routledge Advances in Popular Culture Studies" series. Jo and Lisa are also writing the cultural history of the swimsuit.

Chris Comerford is a lecturer in Communication and Media at the University of Wollongong. His research covers digital and screen media developments, fan cultures, serious leisure, and digital pedagogies. His current project is an analysis of television's shifting cultural, social, and industrial boundaries in the streaming era. He is the author of *Cinematic Digital Television: Negotiating the Nexus of Production, Reception and Aesthetics* (Routledge, 2022). Additionally, Chris has published on topics such as the use of superheroes as lenses for legal and moral interventions on jurisprudence, the benefits of video game play in Animal Crossing during COVID-19, and the creation, exploitation, and archival use of fan-made wikis in understanding popular culture franchises.

Cathleen Allyn Conway (PhD) is a poet and scholar. She has previously published on intersections of feminism, race, and the Gothic in *The Transmedia Vampire: Essays on Technological Convergence and the Undead* (2021), *Toxic Cultures: A Companion* (2022), *The Heroic "Final Girl" in Popular Culture: Young Girls as Figures of Resistance and Futurity* (2024), and *Toxic Nostalgia on Screen: Undead Memory in the Twenty-First Century* (2024).

Tanya Cook (she/they) is a Sociology Professor at the Community College of Aurora near Denver, Colorado. In 2019, she was one of the 26 community college faculty who was awarded a research grant from Mellon/ACLS to support sociological research on fandom. Co-authored with Kaela Joseph, *Fandom Acts of Kindness: A Heroic Guide to Activism*,

Advocacy, and Doing Chaotic Good (2023), she helps individuals engage in fan activism. Her paper "'It's a Gift and a Curse': How Covid Reframed our Understanding of Disability as an Intersectional Identity" won the Barbara R. Walters Award from the Eastern Sociological Society in 2022. When she's not trying to find new ways to use popular culture and fandom to democratize the classroom, you can probably find her at Comic Con.

John Darowski received a PhD in Comparative Humanities from the University of Louisville in 2024 with a dissertation analyzing the influence of the Gothic on superheroes. He is the editor of *Adapting Superman* and the forthcoming *Adapting the X-Men* as well as the co-editor of three essay collections on horror and popular culture. He has written several essays on the history of superheroes. His other research interests include adaptation and monster studies.

Jarrod DePrado is a PhD student in English at the University of Connecticut. His area of specialization is transhistorical drama – bridging Shakespeare, 20th- and 21st-century American drama, and musical theater – focusing on adaptation studies and American politics. He received his Master's degree in English and American Literature from Boston University.

Anthony Enns is an Associate Professor of Contemporary Culture at Dalhousie University in Halifax, Nova Scotia. His work on popular culture has appeared in such journals as *Journal of Popular Film and Television*, *Quarterly Review of Film and Video*, *Popular Culture Review*, and *Studies in Popular Culture* as well as the anthologies *Comics and the City* (2010), *Consumerism and Prestige* (2022), and *Digressions in Deep Time* (2024).

Owen Farrington is a historian of media and popular culture, with a particular focus on comic books and the role of superheroes in 20th- and 21st-century society. They are the creator and host of *Owen Likes Comics*, a YouTube series with over 16,000,000 views and 111,000 subscribers. Alongside this, Owen frequently contributes to The Superhero Project, co-hosts the Superhero Project Podcast, and most recently worked as a graduate teaching assistant at Edge Hill University. He has work forthcoming in *Into the Marvelous: Charting 15 Years of the Marvel Cinematic Universe*.

Marco Favaro (1990) is a program manager at the University of Europe for Applied Sciences in Berlin, where he teaches Cultural Studies. He earned his PhD in Cultural Studies and Human Sciences at the Otto-Friedrich-Universität Bamberg in cooperation with the Università degli Studi di Verona. He is the author of *La Maschera dell'Antieroe*; the book analyzes the structures of the contemporary superhero genre and explores its implicit philosophical concepts. In 2023, he co-edited *Batman's Villains and Villainesses: Multidisciplinary Perspectives on Arkham's Souls*, a collection of multidisciplinary studies on Batman's iconic antagonists.

Marco's academic journey began with a degree in Philosophy in Rome, followed by a Master's at the Freie Universität Berlin. Between 2020 and 2021, he taught a seminar on the "antihero" at Bamberg University, and has collaborated with the online magazine *Lo Spazio Bianco* since 2022.

A prolific author of essays and research, Marco has contributed chapters to several collective volumes, including "The Dionysian Clown" for *Joker and Philosophy*, "The Horror vs. l'Indagatore dell'Incubo" for *Horror and Philosophy*, and "Dylan Dog's Nightmares" in *Critical Approaches to Horror Comic Books* (Routledge). Many of his presentations, articles, and academic contributions are available online.

Teresa Fitzpatrick is a lecturer at Manchester Metropolitan University. Her specific research interests are in ecoGothic and speculative eco-fiction, critical plant studies, and gender studies with a focus on narratives from the late 19th to the 21st century. Her doctoral thesis developed a material feminist ecoGothic framework to explore the intersectionality of nature and gender through cultivated plant monsters and their gardeners in speculative fiction of the long 20th century and the eco-social changes this illustrated. She has contributed chapters on exotic flowers as eco-*femmes fatales*; wisteria as a signifier of domestic abuse; fungal horror; and ecoGothic monstrosity to several edited essay collections, has written book reviews for several journals, and has presented her research at various international conferences.

Valerie Estelle Frankel is the author of over 100 books on pop culture, including *Hunting for Meaning in The Mandalorian*, *The Villain's Journey*, and *Star Wars Meets the Eras of Feminism*. Many of her books focus on gender in fiction, from her heroine's journey guides *From Girl to Goddess* and *Superheroines and the Epic Journey* to *The Trans Hero's Journey*. Her *Chelm for the Holidays* (2019) was a PJ Library book, and now she's the editor of *Jewish Science Fiction and Fantasy*.

Lisa J. Hackett is a Cultural Historian at the University of New England, Armidale, New South Wales. Lisa's research examines aviation, fashion, clothing, and uniform in popular culture through a sociological and historical lens to expose the ways popular culture objects define identity and social roles. Her PhD examined the ways that Australian women utilize 1950s style to fashion their identities. Lisa is the co-founder (along with Jo Coghlan and Huw Nolan) of PopCRN, the Popular Culture Research Network which brings together scholars and researchers who share a fascination in the academic inquiry into all manner of mass phenomena. Her current research includes the study of the use of female Second World War pilot's uniforms in propaganda, the history of air pageants, and the British Royal Family in popular culture. She is on the editorial board of *Popular Culture Review* and is Director of Research for PopCRN.

Professor Steve Halfyard is the Head of BMus programs at the Royal Conservatoire of Scotland in Glasgow, UK. Their research is mainly focused on music in horror/supernatural and superhero film and TV, and on television title sequences and end credits. Publications include *Danny Elfman's Batman: A Film Score Guide* (2004), *Sounds of Fear and Wonder: Music in Cult TV* (2016), and the edited collections *Music, Sound and Silence in Buffy the Vampire Slayer* (2010), *Music in Fantasy Cinema* (2012), and *The Palgrave Handbook of Music and Sound in Peak TV* (2024) with Nicholas Reyland. *Music, Sound and Silence* was awarded the "Long Mr Pointy" for the best book in Whedon Studies in 2010 by the Association for the Study of Buffy+ (formerly the Whedon Studies Association), and the chapter on music in *Buffy* in *Sounds of Fear and Wonder* won the "Short Mr Pointy" in 2016. Other essays have appeared in edited collections including *The Oxford Handbook of New Audiovisual*

Aesthetics (2013), *The Palgrave Handbook of the Vampire* (2023), and *The Oxford Handbook of Television Music* (forthcoming).

Chris Hall (PhD, 2021, University of Kansas) is an Assistant Professor of English at the University of the Ozarks in Arkansas. His work articulates formations of identity as the politics of living in modern culture, and his writing on this topic has appeared in *Angelaki*, *Transgender Studies Quarterly*, *Twentieth-Century Literature*, *SubStance*, and is forthcoming from *Criticism*. Previous publications on popular culture and media have also appeared in such venues as *Games and Culture*, *First Person Scholar*, and *PopMatters*. He is currently working on a monograph on the biopolitics of global modernist literature, and he is co-editor of a volume of essays on the "Metal Gear Solid" videogame series, published in 2025.

Forrest C. Helvie (PhD) is a veteran writer in the comic book and criticism community with extensive contributions spanning multiple platforms. He is best known for his time as a contributing writer for Marvel.com and Newsarama where he reviewed comics, wrote think pieces, and interviewed hundreds of comic creators. He served as the editor and a contributing writer for *How to Analyze and Review Comics: A Handbook on Comics Criticism* and forthcoming *The Exceptional American Superhero*. His contributions also extend to creative writing publishing with credits in numerous small press comics and anthologies. He is a long-time faculty member at Connecticut State Community College where he has served as a campus department chair, statewide director of professional development, and English professor.

Mark Hibbett is the Head of Research Information Systems at the University of the Arts London, UK. He has spent 30 years working with research data in arts and science contexts and his current research focuses on transmedia character cohesion, particularly related to superheroes and children's humor comics. He is the co-host of "The Funny Comics Fan Club" podcast, the world's leading academic expert on Doctor Doom, and also the world's only academic expert on Doctor Doom.

Dru Jeffries is a lecturer of Film Studies and Cultural Studies at Wilfrid Laurier University, Waterloo, Ontario. He is the author of *Comic Book Film Style: Cinema at 24 Panels per Second* (2017), editor of *#WWE: Professional Wrestling in the Digital Age* (2019), and has recently been published in *JCMS*. He is currently co-editing an edited collection with Anna F. Peppard on superhero television.

Karl Johnson is a lecturer in Sociology at Queen Margaret University, Edinburgh, a life-long geek, and a Shetlander trapped in the Central Belt of Scotland. He researches and writes about widening access to higher education, social theory and pop culture, and issues affecting the Scottish Islands such as gendered exclusion in Lerwick's Up Helly Aa festival.

In 2022, Karl wrote *The Loki Variations*, a sociological exploration of the mythological and contemporary pop culture interpretations of Loki.

Charles Joseph, an Associate Professor at Le Mans Université, France, completed PhD in North American Cultural Studies. His dissertation, entitled "Being and Writing (from) Los Angeles: Wanda Coleman," analyzes the complex and evolving relationship between the work of the African-American author and the city that has harbored her birth, life, and death. He is looking not only into the practices of the world-renowned entertainment industry based in Los Angeles, and the implications they have had on the city's history, but also in the shaping of its socio-cultural identity. He has simultaneously developed an academic interest in comic book studies, interrogating both the production systems through which they conquered most of the world and the adaptation processes, which led them to become staples of a globalized pop culture. He has published several articles and contributed to book chapters on the matter including "The CW Arrowverse and Myth-Making, or the Commodification of Transmedia Franchising" in the *International Journal of TV Serial Narratives* (2018), "Marvel's Telltale Super-Girls in the Marvel Rising Franchise" in *Genre en Séries* (2019), and "The CW missing link: iZombie" in *The CW Comes of Age* (2022).

Kaela Joseph (PhD) is a queer and nonbinary licensed clinical psychologist and fandom researcher. She is the co-author of the book *Fandom Acts of Kindness: A Guide to Activism, Advocacy, and Doing Chaotic Good*, with additional academic publications on superheroes and other popular media franchises such as *The Boys*, *Supernatural*, and *Barbie*. She has roughly ten years' experience in ethnographic fandom research, with clinical and research specialization in diversity, equity, and inclusion, as well as gender, sexuality, disability, and social movements.

Anna-Sophie Jürgens is a senior lecturer in Science Communication at the Australian National Centre for the Public Awareness of Science of the Australian National University (ANU) and the Head of the POPSICULE, ANU's Science in Popular Culture and Entertainment Hub. Her research explores the cultural meanings of science, the history of (violent) clowns and mad scientists, science and humor, and the interface between science and (public) art. Anna-Sophie has published numerous articles and book chapters on the Joker, Joker science, and science in comics with the aim to better understand how pop cultural narratives about science have affected the public discourse and understanding of science, and thus our science-society relationship.

Devon Keyes is a PhD student in the English Department of the University of Colorado Boulder. His primary field is visual culture; within that field, much of their attention is concerned with comics studies, particularly superhero comics and the ways in which superheroes index both historically and culturally how American audiences define and redefine concepts of heroism and identity through the changing nature of the superhero. They have an additional interest in the ways in which comics storytelling has become increasingly multimodal, also affording a greater interest in video game studies, film studies, and media studies at large.

Orion Ussner Kidder received his PhD from the University of Alberta where he wrote on metafiction in American comics written by British authors. He has since moved home to Vancouver and taken a position with Fairleigh Dickinson University where he primarily teaches composition and media studies, and is Coordinator of the Writing Centre. Kidder has most recently published on depictions of genocide in Russel and Pugh's *The Flintstones* comic book (2016–2017). He lives with his partner, two kids, and two black cats.

Christina M. Knopf is a Professor in the Communication and Media Studies Department, the presentation skills coordinator, and the Assistant Dean in the School of Arts and Sciences at the State University of New York (SUNY), Cortland. She is the author of *Politics in the Gutters: American Politicians and Elections in Comic Book Media* (2021) and *The Comic Art of War: A Critical Study of Military Cartoons, 1805–2014* (2015), along with numerous critical essays on politics and military culture in the popular arts. Dr. Knopf is a co-editor of the "Routledge Advances in Comics Studies" series. She holds a PhD in Cultural Sociology and Political Communication from the University at Albany.

Siobhain Lash is a Teaching Assistant Professor through the Kendrick Center for an Ethical Economy in the John Chambers College of Business and Economics at West Virginia University. Her work has appeared, among other places, in Humanities and Social Sciences Communication, Constitutional Political Economy, Ethics, Policy & Environment, and Public Philosophy Journal. She works at the intersection of political economy, environmental justice, and urban ecology. Her research also focuses on ethics in business and information and AI.

Justin F. Martin is an Associate Professor of Psychology at Whitworth University. His research explores the intersection of moral development and superhero and dystopian media. His superhero scholarship highlights superhero media as a context for generating pedagogical and research activities that examine the relationship between moral and nonmoral social concepts. Recent publications explore Black Panther, Luke Cage, Mr. Freeze, Bishop, Jean Grey, Daredevil, Superman, and *The Walking Dead*. He is the co-editor of *Arkham's Souls: A Multidisciplinary Analysis of Batman's Villains and Villainesses* (2023) with Marco Favaro. He teaches courses in statistics, research methods, developmental psychology, moral development, and morality within the Marvel Universe. He lives with his wife and two kids.

Rob Mclaughlin is a lecturer at Arden University and has a passion for all things comic book and horror related. He has written about Tobe Hooper's Poltergeist, horror in Children's television, Doctor Who, and Deadpool. He has presented papers on Hauntology, the demise of VHS, long-forgotten television, and B-movies.

Paul Mountfort is an Associate Professor in the area of critical media studies at Auckland University of Technology's School of Communication Studies. He writes and talks widely in the area of popular culture studies and fan practices. He is the author, with Anne Peirson-Smith and Adam Geczy, of *Planet Cosplay: Costume Play, Identity and Global Fandom* (UK, 2018).

Patrick Munnelly (he/him) is a faculty member of English and Communication at the Community College of Aurora. He has won awards for his teaching practices and pedagogies, where he incorporates gaming and gamification into his classrooms. He studies queer video games, and all things related to sexuality and play. He has a chapter forthcoming in Routledge about Queer Consent in Gaming as well as a forthcoming journal article about Queer Semiotics in Video Games. He has another forthcoming journal article about Queer

Failure in the writing classroom. He has presented his work at various conferences and continues to advocate for the LGBTQ community.

Angelique Nairn is an Associate Professor in Communication Studies at Auckland University of Technology, where she specializes in teaching public relations. With a deep passion for identity and its role in public communications, her research spans multiple disciplines, from organizational communication and identity construction to rhetoric, artificial intelligence in communication, and the evolving landscape of the creative industries. Angelique's scholarly pursuits are driven by a fascination with how individuals and groups construct, negotiate, and project identities in various contexts. She has explored the intersections of identity, morality, and popular culture, examining how issues like racism, sexism, and technological determinism manifest on screen, particularly in representations of women, creative professionals, and ethical dilemmas in media narratives. Her recent work delves into the sociology of work within the creative industries, scrutinizing the challenges and opportunities presented by artificial intelligence.

Huw Nolan is an Animal Welfare Scientist and Ethicist with a strong passion for science and its portrayal in popular culture. His research investigates the implications of human imagination, beliefs, and intuitions on the welfare of animals and the environment. He is committed to scrutinizing the ethical dimensions of how non-human life is represented in popular media and its subsequent influence on societal attitudes and behaviors, combining his enthusiasm for science with a focus on its role in shaping public perceptions. Huw is a founding member of the Popular Culture Research Network (PopCRN) and is a Senior Co-Editor of the *International Journal of Popular Culture Studies*.

Yael Rachel Novich received her M.Des. degree in Design from the Shenkar College of Engineering, Design and Art in 2021. She received her B.Ed.F.A. degree with distinction in Fine Arts and Education from Faculty of Arts – Hamidrasha at Beit Berl College, Israel, in 2017. She is a New Media artist, with experience in pixel art, video art, and 3D printing. Her current research interests include graphic design, costume design, feminist studies, and film.

Fernando Gabriel Pagnoni Berns (PhD in Arts, PhD candidate in History) works as Professor at the Facultad de Filosofía y Letras, Universidad de Buenos Aires (UBA), Argentina. He teaches courses on international horror film. He is the Director of the research group on horror cinema "Grite" and has authored a book about Spanish horror TV series *Historias para no Dormir* (2020) and has edited books on the Frankenstein bicentennial, on directors James Wan and Wes Craven, on the Italian *giallo* film, and horror comics (Routledge). He is currently editing a book on Dario Argento and another one on Baltic horror. He is the Director of "Terror: Estudios Críticos," the first-ever horror studies series in Spain.

Gwyneth Peaty (PhD) is a research fellow at the Centre for Culture and Technology (CCAT), Curtin University, Western Australia. Her research focuses on representations of monstrosity, Gothic horror, disability, technology, and the body in popular culture and media. She is currently writing a monograph about gargoyles for the University of Wales Press (UWP) "Gothic Literary Studies" book series. Peaty is the review editor for *The Australasian Journal of Popular Culture*.

Anna F. Peppard is an award-winning researcher and public scholar. Her work on representations of gender and sexuality in comics and pop culture is widely published in academic books and journals and on websites such as Shelfdust, Women Write About Comics, The Middle Spaces, and ComicsXF. She is the co-project lead of the social media research project Sequential Scholars; co-host of the podcast Oh Gosh, Oh Golly, Oh Wow!; and editor of the anthology *Supersex: Sexuality, Fantasy, and the Superhero* (2020), which won the Comics Studies Society Prize for Best Edited Book. Her current projects include an anthology titled *Small Screen Supers: Essays on Superhero Television*, co-edited with Dru Jeffries, and a monograph on the Marvel character She-Hulk.

Lorna Piatti-Farnell (PhD) is the Academic Dean at SAE Creative Media Institute in Auckland, New Zealand. In addition, she is the Director of the Australasian Horror Studies Network (AHSN) and an Adjunct Research Professor at Curtin University, Australia. Her research interests lie at the intersection of film, media, and creative industries and include a focus on horror, environmental studies, consumer culture, superheroes, and Disney. She has published widely in these areas, including volumes such as *The Superhero Multiverse: Readapting Comic Book Icons in Twenty-First-Century Film and Popular Media* (editor, 2021), *Gothic Afterlives: Reincarnations of Horror in Film and Popular Media* (editor, 2019), and *Disney Gothic: Dark Shadows in the House of Mouse* (editor, 2024). Dr. Piatti-Farnell is the sole editor of the "Routledge Advances in Popular Culture Studies" book series as well as the co-editor of the *Horror Studies* series.

Ashleigh Prosser, PhD, is a lecturer in Professional Learning at Murdoch University, Perth, Western Australia, who has been working across various academic and professional service roles in the tertiary sector since 2013. Ashleigh holds a BA (Hons-1st) and PhD in English and Cultural Studies from The University of Western Australia, and a Graduate Certificate in Educational Leadership from the Queensland University of Technology. Ashleigh's research interests lie with the study of gothic and horror in literature and popular culture, and the scholarship of teaching and learning. Ashleigh is a Senior Fellow of the Higher Education Academy and Associate Editor of *The Australasian Journal of Popular Culture*.

John Quinn is a lecturer in Screen at the University of the West of Scotland. His research focuses on popular film and television, with a particular interest in representations of masculinity. Quinn's recent publications have explored themes such as authenticity and symbolic identity professional wrestling, and the construction and deployment of liminal criminal identities in the Star Wars universe. His forthcoming works will explore the representation of criminality and urban legends in contemporary media and the aesthetics of predatory capitalism in the Alien cinematic universe.

Sarah Regier is a PhD student in English at Western University in London, Ontario. Her research focuses on colonial and postcolonial dynamics in fantasy literature. She is also particularly interested in issues of identity and representation in fanworks.

Chris Reyns-Chikuma teaches French Cultural Studies and Comparative Literature at the University of Alberta, Canada. He has published over 100 articles, chapters, and special issues on Spirou-Trondheim, manga-anime, manfra (French manga), Kamala Khan (in Muslim superheroes Harvard U.P., 2017), the French publisher Glénat, etc. In the recent ten years, he has been focusing more on Canadian comics. His most recent publications are "PLANCHES, une revue de BD québécoise: entre dynamisme et précarité, 2014–2024," @nalyses 18.2, 2024, p. 63–90, and "Les images dans l'hebdomadaire Le Franco-Albertain [1967–1978]: révélatrices d'un changement radical par rapport à son prédécesseur, La Survivance [1928–67]," *Cahiers franco-canadiens de l'Ouest* 36.2, 2025, pp. 140–167, and, in collaboration with Qian Feng, "Sascha Hommer's In China (2016): masks, animals, learning and identity flux," *Journal of Graphic Novels and Comics* 1–25, 2025, and two co-edited special issues are forthcoming: one on the artistic and literary representations of the historical character Le Chevalier and the other on the representations of AI/IA in French and Francophone cultures (in Alternative Francophone).

Philippe Rioux holds a doctorate in French Studies with a specialization in Book History. His work focuses on the history of comics in North America and, more specifically, on the cultural transfers between the American, Canadian, and Quebecois productions. His thesis received the Best Thesis Award from the Université de Sherbrooke, in 2019, and has been published at the Presses de l'Université de Montréal, in Fall 2022. Philippe Rioux now teaches comic book history and theory at l'Université du Québec en Outaouais.

Christopher Roman is Professor of English and specializes in Comics Studies and the Graphic Novel, LGBTQ+ Literature, Queer Theory, the work of Michel Foucault, and Sounds Studies. His new book *Queering Wolverine in Comics and Fanfiction: A Fastball Special* has been published by Routledge (2023) and examines the bodily and relationship queerness represented by the Marvel character, Wolverine. His previous works in medieval studies include the books *Domestic Mysticism in Margery Kempe and Dame Julian of Norwich* (2005), which interrogates queer family formation in medieval mystical texts, and *Queering Richard Rolle* (2017), which investigates the queer identity of the understudied and important medieval hermit, Richard Rolle. Finally, his co-edited collection, *Medieval Futurity: Essays for the Future of a Queer Medieval Studies* (2021), explores new theoretical directions for queer identity in the Middle Ages. His new work has turned to Comics Studies where he investigates the intersections of queer theory and the superhero, LGBTQ Comics, critical race and ecocriticism in comics and other comics studies projects.

Sophia Staite is the leading English-language scholar of the influential Japanese superhero franchise *Kamen Rider* and its Anglophone adaptations. Sophia's work on *tokusatsu* has led to a visiting fellowship with "The Global Sentimentality Project" at Friedrich-Alexander-Universität in Germany and serving as an invited expert with ACMI, Australia's national museum of screen culture. Sophia's research appears in *The International Journal of Disney Studies, Jeunesse: Young People, Texts, Cultures, The Australasian Journal of Popular Culture, M/C Journal, Children's Literature in Education,* and *Intersections: Gender and Sexuality in Asia and the Pacific.*

Liam Sunner is a lecturer (Education) in Law and Technology. His research explores the intersection of intellectual property (IP) rights and human rights, and how this is centered and shaped by the development of the European Union's External Action Policy. He also maintains an active interest in the related developments surrounding the areas of law, technology, and cultural rights.

Sean Travers has a PhD in English from University College Cork, Ireland. Her research interests include trauma, popular culture, postmodernism, contemporary American culture, horror studies, and naturalism. Her book, entitled *Trauma in American Popular Culture and Cult Texts, 1980–2020*, was published in 2022. She has publications in the *Irish Journal of American Studies* (*IJAS Online*), the *Popular Culture Studies Journal* (*PCJS*), *The Journal of Popular Culture, Fantastika Journal*, and a forthcoming publication in the *Irish Journal of Gothic and Horror Studies* (*IJGHS*). She now works as a project manager for EU-funded projects.

Jorge Traversa is MA in Arts graduated at the Universidad de Buenos Aires. He specializes in the study of comics and horror films. He has a chapter published for *Superheroes and American Exceptionalism*, edited by Forrest C. Helvie (2024) and one on *Aliens: A Companion*, edited by Simon Bacon. He participates on a research group with a grant for researching horror cinema in the Baltic regions.

Eduardo Veteri is MA in Philosophy graduated at the Facultad de Filosofía y Letras (Argentina), Universidad de Buenos Aires. He is a lecturer in Popular Culture and has published in *Iron Man Versus Captain America and Philosophy*, edited by Nicolas Michaud; *Twin Peaks and Philosophy*, edited by Richard Greene; and *Batman's Villains and Villainesses: Multidisciplinary Perspectives on Arkham's Souls*.

Lilia Walsh is a curatorial and collection researcher at the National Library of Australia and holds a Bachelor of Science with Honors in Science Communication from the Australian National Centre for the Public Awareness of Science of the Australian National University. She has also completed a Graduate Certificate of Ancient History from Macquarie University and is an ongoing collaborator for POPSICULE, ANU's Science in Popular Culture and Entertainment Hub. Her research focuses on the depiction of historical alchemical laboratories within superhero films, and she has broader interests in the history of science, ancient sciences in modern popular culture, and the image and visualization of science within popular fiction.

Dingkun Wang is an Assistant Professor in Translation at The University of Hong Kong. His present research focuses on the reception and translation of global entertainment media in Chinese contexts. He has published on subjects related to media localization, fan translations, and Asian digital economies in peer-reviewed journals, including *Translation Studies, JosTrans, Target, Emerging Media, International Journal of Communication*, and *International Journal of Cultural Studies*. He is leading the development of two online testing modules on Traditional Chinese subtitling in Mandarin and Cantonese, as part of the AVTpro Initiative – a professional qualification in media localization.

Michaela Weiss is an Associate Professor in the Department of English and American Studies at the Institute of Foreign Languages, Silesian University, Opava, Czech Republic. She teaches courses on American literature, and Literary Theory and Criticism. Her main areas of interest include American Jewish literature, adaptation, and comics. She is currently working on a book *Community, Geography, and Language in the Works of Irena Klepfisz*.

Carl Wilson is a guest writer for Eisner Award and Harvey Award-nominated Fanbase Press. With Lorna Piatti-Farnell, Carl has guest edited a Superhero Special Issue for the *Australasian Journal of Popular Culture* (2024) and established the Superhero Studies Network (2023). Carl is a superhero and monster scholar with a focus on their representation in video games. He has published work in over 40 edited collections, with chapters on superhero studies including the superheroic origins in D&D; the digital franchising of Spider-Man; Marvel bodies on screen; the depowering of DC superheroes; the representation of women in Batman games; the legacy of various Supermen in games; and the cultural contexts of Catwoman, Aquaman, and Poison Ivy. His current focus is to map the superhero field in video games.

ACKNOWLEDGMENTS

The editors of the *Companion* would like to jointly acknowledge and thank commissioning editor Lucie Bartonek at Routledge for her support of the project and for her encouragement and enthusiasm throughout. Heartfelt gratitude goes to all the contributors in this volume, for their hard work and commitment to the project.

From Lorna:

I would like to thank my friends and colleagues for their continued support and interest in everything that I do. A big "thank you" goes to my family (Evra, Rob, my mamma, my papá, and the super-pups), for all their love and affection.

A huge "thank you" goes to my wonderful and talented co-editor Carl, for his compassion, support, and incredible work ethic, without which this project would never have been completed.

From Carl:

Above all, I would like to thank my wonderful wife, Rebecca. As with Big Barda to Mister Miracle, she has supported me in my cartoonish endeavors with a beautiful depth of character that has always far exceeded my own capabilities.

I would like to dedicate this work to my parents, Garry and Barbara. They're the true comic book archetype: generous, kind, hardworking, most likely to save a dog from a hurricane.

I would like to give minimal thanks to my cat, Kipo the disruptive Anti-Krypto, and maximal thanks to my brother, Garrath, who is more ace than Ace the Bat-Hound fighting Ace of Spades at Ace Chemicals Factory.

I would like to offer appreciation for the many conversations with my fantastic friends who have kept me on the "right" side of the hero/villain divide over the past few years. Thanks especially to Simon Bacon, the MoM Guys, the Anti-Quizwolds, the Old Team Chat, and the ever-mysterious "Line of Duty."

A celestial-sized "thank you" to Lorna – a co-editor who generously shared with me the epic task of balancing entire superhero multiverses within the *Companion* in your hands. I think we just about pulled it off, no "snap" required.

INTRODUCTION

Approaching Superhero Studies

Lorna Piatti-Farnell and Carl Wilson

In the 21st century, superheroes have proliferated and multiplied across the multimedia land-scape. While superhero stories and characters have been continuously tethered to the early years of their narrative development, and the comics context from which they originate, they have also consistently found renewed life in modern and contemporary re-imaginings and re-adaptations, regenerating through iterative retellings, reboots, and cultural readjustments (Grant and Henderson 2019). Indeed, in our contemporary era, superheroes have morphed into truly transmedia entities, switching registers between narrative formats and storytelling frameworks, across in-print and digital platforms (Gilmore and Storke 2014; Taylor 2014; Piatti-Farnell 2021; Sierra 2023). Remaining strong in the world of comics, superheroes are now a constant and recurrent presence in film, television, video games, and online media contexts. They have found fertile ground in the networked and transnational webs of fan-dom, especially through performative activities such as cosplay. They are central and lucrative presences in the industrial structures of toys and merchandise (Brassett and Reynolds 2021). Superheroes have even found transformed life as part of tourism contexts and trans-spatial narratives, as "superhero attractions" at entertainment parks across the world have become increasingly more popular (McCartney and Cheong Su Man 2020; Baker 2022; Condis and Schwiezer 2024). Superheroes are no longer confined to one medium, or even just a few production giants, to ensure their cultural success. While the impact of multimedia produc-tion companies such as Marvel and DC remains unquestioned, superheroes have reached beyond the bounds of traditional narrative forms, and production demands across countries, testifying to their elasticity as popular icons. Here, their iconic status comes precisely from their ability to function as "reflections of their eras," while also continuing to have an ongo-ing impact on the "cultures they inhabit" (Piatti-Farnell 2021, 3).

Taken as emblematic cultural representations, superhero narratives can function as sym-bolic spaces where the diversity of bodies and identities has consistently been foregrounded and positioned alongside socio-historical politics. While there are certain codified expectations and unmissable repetitions that accompany the superhero narrative mystique – including, among other things, highly recognizable costumes, a tragic backstory, over-the-top battle scenes, and the inevitable presence of dubiously motivated supervillains – the intermingling of divergence and conventionality has also been a characterizing feature of storytelling in the

DOI: 10.4324/9781003366911-1

superhero genre (Darowski 2014b; Smith 2016; Pagello 2017). The narratives can be mainstream and countercultural; the settings can be relatable and otherworldly; the characters can be simultaneously heroic and deeply challenging of that very concept. In their multiple incarnations, superheroes can reflect all aspects of humanity: amplified and distilled, aspirational or repulsive. Indeed, superheroes can not only "make us consider who we aspire to be" but can also easily "problematize" seemingly simple "distinctions" between good and evil, "forcing us to develop a more nuanced moral compass to deal with the complexity of life" (Duncan and Smith 2013, xiii).

Seen through evocative examples – such as the cross-media properties of *The Umbrella Academy* (2007), the convergence culture of Batman, the conglomerate hierarchies within Marvel Entertainment, the multiverse publications that enable spaces for an empathic Gwenpool, or a discussion of race with the Green Lanterns – superheroes continue to evolve through the conditions of their production and the cultural discourses that they engender. Superheroes appear across the spectrum of mainstream to indie publications, in both print and digital media formats. Cinematic Universes extend to SVOD platforms such as Netflix and Amazon Prime, while marginalized comic book heroes are reinvented in IMAX spectacles. In their emerging and entangled forms, superheroes engage with changing viewing practices, which, in enabling a wider variety of stories to be told in a multitude of different ways, gives rise to a plurality of voices and perspectives, not just in and about America but also across multiple cultures and continents. Comics featuring the gay hero of *Superman: Son of Kal-El* (2021) share terrain with the Magical Girls of anime television shows such as *Yuki Yuna Is a Hero* (2014). Japanese manga are indeed known to cross-culturally deconstruct the superhero genre, with examples such as *My Hero Academia* (2014–) being particularly salient (Sigley 2022). Superheroes aptly encompass all these swirling points of signification within discursive fields surrounding their costumes, their enemies, their sidekicks, their own bodies, and across their individual and collective histories.

As superheroes have enduringly strengthened their cultural hold on our storytelling practices across media, scholarly attention focused on these iconic figures has also continued to grow. Scholarly explorations of superheroes have particularly proliferated in the past few decades, and the critical focus has been broad and wide-reaching. These have ranged in focus and breath and have included: debates over definitions of what a superhero "is" and what a superhero "does" (Coogan 2006; Arnaudo 2013; Rosenberg and Coogan 2013); explorations of the representation and meanings of superhero bodies, including the impact of their iconic costumes (Brownie and Graydon 2015; Haslem, MacFarlane and Richardson 2018; Wilson 2024); critical conversations focused on clarifying the iconic origins and conventional qualities of the "superhero genre" (Ramgnoli and Pagnucci 2013; Duncan and Smith 2013; Gavaler 2015); discussions over narrative and characterization that uncover the ability of superheroes to engage with discourses of gender, race, and ethnicity (Stevens 2015; Kent 2021; Gary and Kaklamanidou 2011; Darowski 2014a; Nairn 2021); as well as preoccupations connected to issues of morality, trauma, the environment, bio-ethics, science, justice, disability, trans/posthumanism, and, overall, the very concept of what it means to be human (Nama 2011; Rosenberg 2013; Alaniz 2014; Moore 2017; Rayborn and Keyes 2018; Neimeyer 2020; Matthews 2021; Kahan 2021; Chatterji 2022; Piatti-Farnell 2024). In addition, scholarship focused on superheroes has also pointedly explored issues related to the superheroes' ability to find constantly renewed and mutating life across platforms, placing an emphasis on adaptations, reboots, and re-imaginings in the transnational and transmedia landscape (Brown 2016; Darowski 2021; McEniry, Peaslee and Weiner 2016).

Within this, evaluations of what has become known as the "superhero multiverse" have also gained prominence, and drawn attention to the interconnected nature of superhero media across time and space (Kukkonen 2010; Piatti-Farnell 2021; Leonard et al. 2013; Comerford 2024). Collectively, these growing and virtually uncountable instances from the scholarship show the influence that superheroes exert on our social, cultural, and political structures, uncovering the power of popular icons to speak to our identities in evolving media discourses.

In answer to the constantly changing portrayals of superheroes in our cultures, histories, and narratives, *The Routledge Companion to Superhero Studies* addresses the development, transformation, and significance of these iconic figures – as connected to both contemporary and historical frameworks – by taking a transnational, multimedia, and interdisciplinary approach to assessing their importance in our evolving representational contexts. This *Companion* begins with a premise that emphasizes the stakes, so to speak, of our cultural and scholarly investment in superheroes. In particular, the volume sets out to explore and establish not only an ongoing interest in superheroes in our media and culture, but, specifically, also the emergence of "Superhero Studies" as its own separate field. Indeed, the volume acknowledges Superhero Studies as its own interdisciplinary area of scholarly and cultural interest. Superhero Studies brings together perspectives from a number of intersecting disciplines, such as comics studies, film studies, television studies, fandom studies, game studies, and beyond. At the heart of Superheroes Studies is the interpretation of superheroes not as discrete assemblages of tropes, but as central and recurrent vehicles for cultural representation, which carry shared characteristics across different socio-historical contexts.

Indeed, Superhero Studies is not simply a fanciful way of bringing together critical perspectives on occasional and disparate instances of superhero representation across platforms. Instead, Superhero Studies operates as a field precisely because it is focused on unraveling the binding threads and the meaningful networks that make superheroes the iconic figures that they are across media platforms and living milieus. This overarching approach places an emphasis on superheroes as central iconographic conduits for social, cultural, and political representation, reflecting both contemporary and historical perspectives. Incorporating aspects of the superhero in different contexts – from comics to film, from television to online media, from fandom to merchandising, and beyond – Superhero Studies is founded on the understanding that superheroes operate as metaphorically charged figures and maintain a symbolic function across contexts. Their narrative influence can both reinforce and challenge the status quo and invites us to re-examine "the values of our culture" (Duncan and Smith, xiii). As a field, Superhero Studies recognizes that each of these figures is expansive and detailed: it is not simply tied to popular trends but also continues to thrive in subcultural discourses.

While inevitably often focused on representation, Superhero Studies also incorporates and extends its reach into matters of creativity and transmedia transformation, so to explore and uncover the different facets that superheroes take across multiple socio-industrial discourses and ways of life. In doing so, the field also considers the different components of how superheroes reflect our experiences, transhistorically and transnationally. Within this, the focus remains across the board on uncovering how superheroes are able to respond to cultural currents and transformations, while also – and perhaps, most importantly – operating within their own genre iconographies and narrative structures, and how these are significant for understanding the evolutionary nature of human experiences in different contexts. As a field, therefore, Superhero Studies focuses on both similarities and differences but maintains at its core the central idea that these now iconic and highly recognizable figures, while taking on different forms and operating in different narrative formats, continuously engage with our changing identities, as cultural preoccupations mutate, mingle, and merge.

Exploring the Field: This Book

The *Companion* is divided into five main parts, each comprising chapters that explore a particular thematic strand within the field of Superhero Studies: Part I, "Creating and Selling the Superhero"; Part II, "Adapting the Superhero"; Part III, "National Superheroes and Translations"; Part IV, "Superhero Bodies and Identities"; and Part V, "Evolving Superhero Debates and Concerns." In its organization and rationale, the *Companion* does not aim to provide a singular and comprehensive source of scholarship for the field but aims instead to highlight and strengthen the logical areas of connection between different, yet intrinsically connected, areas of interest within Superhero Studies as a field.

Part I, "Creating and Selling the Superhero," includes chapters about the cultural formation of superheroes, including their origin and evolution on the page, across a publication history or "Ages," and in relation to overlapping fields such as science. The varied outcomes of these imbricated developments are then surveyed through chapters that show how creators play with the rules that govern their comic book superheroes, which leads to metafictional heroes, multiverse entanglements, and narrative reboots. From these expansive worlds and destabilizing textual aporias, chapters in this Part contend that alternative heroes can then arise within comics that reflect the divergent cultures of their readership. Yet, as this Part shows, superheroes are also shaped by the variables of commercial priorities and strategies, such as marketing, toy sales, and intellectual property. While these are not necessarily in opposition to cultural imperatives, being themselves a vital part of superhero formations, they demonstrate a complex and negotiated engagement between superheroes on the page and screen and how their (trans)media forms are both created and sold.

Part II, "Adapting the Superhero," engages with the diverse ways in which the superhero has been reformulated while being transferred to media forms beyond their comic book origins. Films, television, and animated series are at the forefront of this Part, being arguably the most popularly pronounced demonstrations of such adaptation. These chapters also consider how the unique properties of the media form itself can color and shape wider conversations around superhero representation. Examinations of video games, the stage, audio plays, and the music within the movies demonstrate how the heroes also continue to evolve in new ways that help mold the core of modern superheroes as they transition into the 21st century, often feeding back into a shared, wider mythos beyond these specific media forms. In this context, the *Companion* also suggests that the superhero genre is not only composed of unimpeachable "official" texts. Part II concludes with an exploration of how through localized instances of cosplay, parodic/homage video, and many volumes of fanfiction, the notion of a stable superhero canon can also be disrupted by fandom, using adaptation to claim and/or refute ownership over the "legitimate" superhero form.

Part III, "National Superheroes and Translations" turns toward constructions of the hero from broad, yet distinct, cultural perspectives, histories, and traditions from across the globe. While World War II is an inciting event for many of the national heroes assembled here, the ways in which they are expressed diverge greatly, coming from vastly different points of cultural orientation. Flying heroes, patriotic heroes, and desperate folkloric defenders, share ground with heroes created in the face of territorial occupation and cultural condescension, which also diverts toward parody as a viable and popular stance. Moving from the traditions of Europe and North America, to East Asia, there is the same sense of countries grappling with their history through superheroic identities, but in the examples selected here, they are tinged with a greater doubt and uncertainty in the national mechanisms behind which their heroes are created and lauded, with the Part concluding with an exploration of how imported American texts can also vary significantly in how they are translated for foreign audiences.

Moving from projected notions of the national body to how the heroes connect with the superhero genre itself, Part IV, "Superhero Bodies and Identities" focuses on aspects that construct heroes across the multiverses and their corresponding multimedia. Chapters here address how the superhero identity is projected by empowered clothing and an inner dialogue with the super "'freak." Identity is contained by the legal aspects of ownership but shared with sidekicks and familial, hierarchical structures, all of which give rise to internal conflicts and pseudo-deistic formations when skewed and questioned or embraced and adored. This Part posits that superheroes can be transgressive or even supervillains, with both groups capable of facilitating change to an order that the traditional superhero often seeks to preserve. The same playful disruption to identity, which often subverts formalized structures of the genre, creates space for unexpected queer redemption narratives, but it can also show how superhero identities reflect real-life identities, and through this how all participants can draw their own power from this recognition.

The chapters included in Part V, "Evolving Superhero Debates and Concerns," look more explicitly at the connections and differences between the superhero as a nebulous ideal or a figure with the potential to enact change and the worlds that they inhabit, which then comment and reflect upon the real-world itself. Here, the rudimentary "good guy/bad guy" dichotomy is exploded when the "guy" is pushed to the back and the contested battleground of the environment is situated in the foreground. Narratives of the Anthropocene are then also challenged in a countercultural turn that deprioritizes anthropocentric anxieties partially through reflexive strategies around the superhero; then, there are conversations around race, which also interrogate assumptions around the technological capabilities of African countries, and the dominant narratives of culture, this being done through an alien other, negotiated through problematic images of government enforcement. Space is then given to a discussion of Militarized superheroes, which starkly highlights the gaps created by superheroes that are based on civil self-mythologizing and direct, combative, intervention. The final chapters in the *Companion* move from the presentation of social concerns in ways that superheroes can uniquely engender to those that reflect the individual. Trauma, morality, empathy, and legacy – these are the emotional corner stones of most modern superheroes, and they are examined here, across multiple media forms, with the intent of showing the great capacity and potential for further conversations as the superhero genre, and our understanding of the field and ourselves, evolves.

Together, these chapters present a multitude of research points around the intersectional superhero field, which has been expressed in a wide range of contexts across the history of the superhero, and provide a directional guide for Superhero Studies, drawing attention to the evolutionary nature and "future of the superhero narrative" (Klock 2002, 17). Indeed, this book does not attempt to be an exhaustive or definitive discussion of all topics, forms, modes, and debates; nor is it designed to cover every superhero from every media form in every country, of which there are countless multitudes. Instead, the editors of the *Companion* have assembled new voices alongside established scholars and have given them all space to weave their own multiverse, one in which fresh and lively approaches resonate with one another to tentatively establish the nascent shape of a superhero field. While defining evolving scholarly views and delineating the porous boundaries of Superhero Studies as a field, the chapters also act as an inducement for readers to individually and collectively go further into this newly emergent critical space and engage more deeply with the superheroes that they encounter across the changing transmedia landscape.

References

Alaniz, José. 2014. *Death, Disability and the Superhero: The Silver Age and Beyond*. University of Mississippi Press.

Arnaudo, Marco. 2013. *The Myth of the Superhero*. Johns Hopkins University Press.

Baker, Carissa. 2022. "From story-based to story-interactive experiences: Layers of narrative application in theme parks and attractions." In *Global perspectives on strategic storytelling in destination marketing*, edited by A.C Campos. IGI Global.

Brown, Jeffrey A. 2016. *The Modern Superhero in Film and Television: Popular Genre and American Culture*. Routledge.

Brownie, Barbara, and Danny M. Graydon. 2015. *The Superhero Costume: Identity and Disguise in Fact and Fiction*. Bloomsbury.

Brassett, Jamie, and Richard Reynolds. 2021. *Superheroes and Excess: A Philosophical Adventure*. Routledge.

Chatterji, Roma. 2022. "Gaia and the environmental apocalypse in superhero comics and science fantasy." *Perspectives – A Peer-Reviewed, Bilingual, Interdisciplinary E-Journal*, 2: 1–30.

Condis, Megan, and Bobby Schweizer. 2024. "Trans-spatial narratives of Disney Imagineering in the society of explorers and adventurers." *Popular Communication*, 22(4): 203–218.

Comerford, Chris. 2024. "The accidental multiverse: Adaptations and reboots and the new superhero content strategy." *The Australasian Journal of Popular Culture*, 13(2): 137–149.

Darowski, Joseph J. 2014a. *X-Men and the Mutant Metaphor: Race and Gender in the Comic Books*. Rowman & Littlefield.

Darowski, Joseph. 2014b. "The superhero narrative and the Graphic novel." *Critical insights: The Graphic Novel*, 1(2014): 3–16.

Darowski, John, ed. 2021. *Adapting Superman Essays on the Transmedia Man of Steel*. McFarland.

Duncan, Randy, and Matthew J. Smith. 2013. *Icons of the American Comic Book: From Captain America to Wonder Woman, Volume 1*. Greenwood.

Gavaler, Chris. 2015. *On the Origins of Superheroes: From the Big Bang to Action Comics No.1*. University of Iowa Press.

Gilmore, James, and Matthew Storke. 2014. *Superhero Synergies: Comic Book Characters Go Digital*. Rowman & Littlefield.

Grant, Barry Keith, and Scot Henderson, eds. 2019. *Comics and Pop Culture: Adaptation from Panel to Frame*. University of Texas Press.

Gray, Richard J. II, and Betty Kaklamanidou, eds. 2011. *The 21st Century Superhero: Essays on Gender, Genre and Globalization in Film*. McFarland.

Haslem, Wendy, Elizabeth MacFarlane, and Sarah Richardson, eds. 2018. *Superhero Bodies: Identity, Materiality, Transformation*. Routledge.

Kahan, Jeffrey. 2021. *Why We Need Superheroes*. McFarland.

Kent, Miriam. 2021. *Women in Marvel Films*. Edinburgh University Press.

Klock, Geoff. 2002. *How to Read Superhero Comics and Why*. Continuum.

Kukkonen, Karin. 2010. "Navigating infinite earths: Readers, mental models, and the multiverse of superhero comics." *Storyworlds: A Journal of Narrative Studies*, 2(1): 39–58.

Leonard, Steven, Jon Niccum, Kelsey Cipolla, and Jonathan Klug, eds. 2013. *Power Up: Leadership, Character, and Conflict Beyond the Superhero Multiverse*. Casemate.

Matthews, Justin. 2021. "Adapting Judge Dredd: Civic guardian or hyperviolent cop?". In *The Superhero Multiverse: Re-adapting Comic Books icons in 21st-century Film and Popular Media*, edited by Lorna Piatti-Farnell, Lexington.

McCartney, Glenn, and Karen Cheong Su Man. 2020. "Batman rides again! the influence of a superhero branded attraction on visitation to a casino-integrated resort in Macao." *Event Management* 24(4): 515–526.

McEniry Matthew J., Robert Moses Peaslee, and Robert G. Weiner, eds. 2016. *Marvel Comics into Film: Essays on Adaptation Since the 1940s*. McFarland.

Moore, Ellen E. 2017. *Landscape and the Environment in Hollywood Film: The Green Machine*. Springer.

Nairn, Angelique. 2021. "Super-heroine Objectification: The Sexualization of Black Widow Across Comic and Film Adaptations". In *The Superhero Multiverse: Re-adapting Comic Books icons in 21st-century Film and Popular Media*, edited by Lorna Piatti-Farnell, Lexington.

Nama, Adilifu. 2011. *Super Black: American Pop Culture and Black Superheroes*. University of Texas Press.

Neimeyer, Robert A. 2020. "Preface" In *Superhero Grief: The Transformative Power of Loss*, edited by Robert A. Neimeyer, Routledge.

Pagello, Federico. 2017. "The "origin story" is the only story: Seriality and temporality in superhero fiction from comics to post-television." *Quarterly Review of Film and Video*, 34(8): 725–745.

Peter, Coogan. 2006. *Superhero: The Secret Origin of a Genre*. MonkeyBrain Books.

Piatti-Farnell, Lorna, ed. 2021. *The Superhero Multiverse: Re-adapting Comic Books icons in 21st-century Film and Popular Media*. Lexington.

Piatti-Farnell, Lorna. 2024. "Transhuman liminalities and the othered body: Exploring disability and superheroes in the marvel cinematic universe". In *The Routledge International Handbook of Critical Disability Studies*, edited by Katie Ellis, Mike Kent, and Kim Cousins, Routledge.

Rayborn, Tim, and Abigail Keyes. 2018. *Jessica Jones, Scarred Superhero: Essays on Gender, Trauma and Addiction in the Netflix Series*. McFarland.

Romagnoli, Alex, and Gian S. Pagnucci. 2013. *Enter the Superheroes American Values, Culture, and the Canon of Superhero Literature*. Scarecrow Press.

Rosenberg, Robin S., ed. 2013. *Our Superheroes, Ourselves*. Oxford University Press.

Rosenberg, Robin S., and Peter Coogan. 2013. "Introduction" In *What Is a Superhero?*, edited by Robin S. Rosenberg and Peter Coogan, Oxford University Press.

Sigley, Alek. 2022. "Next it's Japan's turn: Nation and otaku masculinity in my hero academia." *Mechademia*, 14(2): 77–98.

Smith, Matthew J. 2016. "Superhero comics." In *The Routledge Companion to Comics*, edited by Frank Bramlett, Roy Cook, and Aaron Meskin, Routledge.

Stevens, Richard J. 2015. *Captain America, Masculinity, and Violence: The Evolution of a National Icon*. Syracuse University Press.

Sierra, Juan José Martínez. 2013. "From the page to the screen. Superlópez: Fun superheroes and transmedia." In *Transmedial perspectives on humour and translation*, edited by Loukia Kostopoulou and Vasiliki Misiou, Routledge.

Taylor, Aaron. 2014. "Avengers dissemble! Transmedia superhero franchises and cultic management." *Journal of Adaptation in Film & Performance*, 7(2): 181–194.

Wilson, Carl. 2024. "Digital Avengers, disassembled: Understanding thirty years of changing superhero bodies in Marvel licenced video games across three distinct phases (1982–2012)". In *Superheroes and Digital Perspectives: Super Data*, edited by Sarah Young and Freyja McCreery, Lexington.

PART I

Creating and Selling the Superhero

1

CREATORS AND THE CREATIVE PROCESSES BEHIND COMICS

Forrest C. Helvie

Introduction

The creative process behind the creation of comics is as varied as the stories themselves. For decades, the methods employed by creators have evolved and continue to do so, reflecting both individual talents and broader shifts within the industry. From the collaborative, spontaneous nature of the Marvel Method to the precise and controlled approach of full-script writing, each method offers unique insights into how some of the most iconic four-colored comics come to life. Considering how technology as a whole has shifted over the past five to ten years – let alone since the early 20th century when the comics medium more fully emerged – it's no surprise then that the ways comic creators tell their stories will only continue evolving in how they script, draw, ink, color, letter, and publish their comics. All the same, both academic and general comic audiences will find that having a foundational understanding of the creative process behind making comics enriches their appreciation and deepens their understanding of this medium.

This evolution in the creative process is something I have observed firsthand through my varied roles in the comics industry. In previous works, such as *How to Analyze and Review Comics: A Handbook on Comics Criticism* (2021), I provided readers with tools to dissect and understand the medium of comics beyond the surface level. Moreover, I've published a variety of comics as a writer, collaborating with artists, letterers, and editors to produce both short stories and full issues for independent or self-published comics. These experiences have afforded me a deep appreciation for the intricate processes that underpin the creation of comics and the myriad roles that contribute to storytelling within the medium. My time as a writer for both *Newsarama*, the oldest comics news website, and *Marvel.com* has also provided me with the opportunity to interview dozens of creators from the "Big Two" to across the independent publishing spectrum, including artists, writers, and editors.

In this chapter, I will first establish a foundational understanding of the Marvel Method and the full-script approach, positioning these as two ends of the creation spectrum. Following this, I will provide a brief overview of the various roles involved in the creative process, including writers, pencillers, inkers, colorists, letterers, and editors. Finally, I will draw on insights from well-known creators within the industry to offer a "behind the curtains" look

DOI: 10.4324/9781003366911-3

at how some of today's most celebrated comics are crafted, both in the independent scene and within the major publishing houses of Marvel and DC.

The goal of this chapter is to offer readers a deeper appreciation for the complexity and creativity that drives the comic book industry. By understanding the diverse methods and roles involved, readers will gain a more nuanced perspective on the stories that have captivated audiences for generations, allowing them to better analyze, critique, or even create their own comic narratives.

The Creative Spectrum: Marvel Method vs. Full-Script

For most comics, the process begins with a core idea that eventually finds its way into a script, serving as the foundation for the visual storytelling to come. These initial concepts might originate as rough sketches, character designs, or even thematic explorations, with the artist or writer gradually building the narrative around these early visuals. In other instances, it can begin with a theme or a plot that the storyteller wants to explore and bring to life visually. Regardless of how they start, many comics eventually take form as a script. Yet not all scripts are created equally. The most commonly known approaches for scripting comics generally fall on two ends of a spectrum: the Marvel Method and full script with writers falling somewhere on one side, the other, or somewhere in between.

Although the Marvel Method no doubt found its origins prior to Stan Lee's coining the phrase, it was during the 1960s with the famed writer and publisher of Marvel Comics that the approach took hold and is best known especially across single-issue publications. It opts for a boiled-down, summative approach to describing both the plot points and the major emotional beats for an entire comic issue, often covering the span of less than a full page to around a page and a half. The work of breaking the story down and determining what occurs not only on each page but on every panel is then left to the (line) artist to develop. Once the line art, inking, and coloring were finished, the writer would then go back and review the pages to determine any kind of dialogue, narration, etc., which would be completed by the creative team's letterer. Of course, this doesn't mean that there isn't dialogue between the editor, writer, and artistic team necessitating revisions; however, this approach generally offered a much greater level of creative autonomy to the artists involved, especially the line artist if distinct from the inker, and increased expediency as the artists were not left waiting for a script to be complete before beginning their work. The challenge to this approach, however, is that it leaves even more of the workload of creating a visually driven narrative onto the shoulders of the artists. For more experienced comic artists, this may even be preferable; however, it also necessitates important conversations around co-writing, creative collaborations, and attribution of credit in this creative medium.

On the other end of the comic scripting spectrum is the full-script approach, which takes many cues from television and film script formatting. While the Marvel Method prioritizes artistic freedom and spontaneity, the full-script approach takes a more structured path, placing greater control in the hands of the writer. In this approach, it is the writer who breaks the story down by page and panel, typically including the full dialogue and narration along the way. As a result, the artistic team "has a very complete map of what the story is and how it can be told" (Bendis 2014, 28). Of course, this, too, has its drawbacks. For less experienced line artists or those who are operating under a work-for-hire situation with highly specified publisher outcomes for a given issue, this approach may be preferable given the high-level specificity involved. Yet, that same level of detail can also create a more directive experience for the artistic members of the storytelling team and lead to a less creative and more stifling experience, and thus, perhaps a less inspiring reading experience.

Today, the format for a script varies widely and often depends on both the composition of the creative team as well as the publisher. For many creators (writers, artists, and editors), engaging in dialogue around the flexibility and space for creative input becomes essential when identifying the kind of scripts used and how to best convey the visual narrative to the reading audience. A modified Marvel Method may work best when working with more experienced artists who can operate and flourish under greater autonomy and writers who may be juggling multiple comic titles. Still, a more detailed full-script approach has often proven popular particularly in the hands of creators at the helm of multi-title crossover series that necessitate a significant level of detail alignment. Of course, that is to say nothing of the original graphic novels by single author-artists, who adopt a format that falls somewhere in between.

In order to gain a greater appreciation for what these differences look like, critics, scholars, and general readers alike have access to a number of scripts from well-known creators of all genres within the medium thanks to the internet. For example, the *Comics Experience (CE)* website, run by one-time Marvel Editor and now *CE* publisher, Andy Schmidt, offers a full database of scripts from both widely known and established independent writers (see Bendis n.d.).

Script Synopsis: *The Fantastic Four* (Stan Lee, quoted in O'Keefe 2019).

SYNOPSIS: THE FANTASTIC FOUR
JULY '61 SCHEDULE
STORY #1 – INTRODUCTION: "MEET THE FANTASTIC FOUR"

This story is told in 2 chapters. Chapter one is 6 pages long. Chapter 2 is 15 pages.
There are four main characters:

1. **REED RICHARDS.** *(Mr. Fantastic)* He is a young, handsome scientist. Leader of the four. Invents a space ship to go to Mars. Hopes to be first man to reach Mars.
2. **SUSAN STORM.** *(Invisible Girl)* She is Reed's girlfriend. She's an actress. Beautiful, glamorous.
3. **BEN GRIMM.** *(The Thing)* He falls for Susan but is too gruff, brutish guy. He's a pilot. He is Susan's admirer.
4. **JOHNNY STORM.** *(Human Torch)* He is Susan's kid brother. A teenager. 17 years old. High school student.

Story might open up with a meeting of "Fantastic Four." As meeting starts, caption tells reader that we will go back a few weeks to see how it all began—

Reed Richards tells Susan and her brother Johnny that his space ship is finally completed. He hopes to be first man to Mars, but he needs a pilot. They hire Ben Grimm—Ben is a huge, surly, unpleasant guy who doesn't want any part of project until he sees Susan. He falls for Susan, and she manages to coax him into piloting ship. Ben is a crackerjack pilot, ex-ww war hero, best pilot available.

As the four are about to begin flight, they are warned against it by authorities. Told that no one yet knows what the effects cosmic rays will have on human bodies nor what the dangers are in space. But they decide to go anyway. They fear that if they don't go, Reds may beat us to it.
(NOTE: At the rate the Communists are progressing in space, maybe we better make this a flight to the STARS, instead of just to Mars, because by the time this mag goes on sale, the Russians may have already MADE a flight to Mars!)

So, without clearance from the authorities, in the dead of night, they take off for the nearest star—very dramatically.

In space, on the way to the stars, FOOMP! They are bombarded by cosmic rays which penetrate the ship and which affect all four of the occupants. They sense it—although they don't yet quite know HOW they've changed—they are lucky to land alive. But they are all different now—

Suddenly, they can't see Susan! But they know she's there! They can HEAR her. They realize she has become invisible. She can not become visible again. Later, she will try to make a dress of a fabric like the one she had and she will have to wear that xxxx xxxxxxxx in order to be seen. Her clothes will appear, but she won't seem too sexy in art work. Better talk to me about it, xxxxx Jack—we might change this gimmick somewhat.

As for Johnny, Susan's brother, whenever he gets excited, he bursts into flame. Becomes a Human Torch, and can fly, as his body gets lighter than air. BUT doesn't get excited for more than 5 minutes. At end of five minutes, his flame goes out and he becomes normal. Comics Association will not let us allow flame on him indefinitely—he ignites after he's gotten burns. So—he cannot toss fireballs as the old Human Torch could.

His biggest asset is that he can fly.

In looking at the "Marvel Method," Stan Lee employs here with Jack Kirby, it becomes clear just how much work of telling the story falls on the artist. Many of the high concepts are discussed along with a few of the key story beats; further, Lee shares how he sees Marvel's First Family interacting with one another. Nonetheless, it's up to Kirby to corral these ideas together into a structured story that has a clearly defined beginning, middle, and end that will satisfy readers with the story's conclusion. It's also worth noting that – given the latitude Lee gave to Kirby to actualize this story concept – there is neither dialogue nor sound effects or any sort of captions described at this point. Instead, Lee would go in later and figure that out once the art was finished based on the art on each page. As such, collaboration was a hallmark for those early days of comics publishing – and even today – where the Marvel Method is employed. Of course, Michale Hill from the Kirby Museum contends that in many cases – such as this synopsis from the *Fantastic Four* #1 (1961) – Kirby never received any input from Stan Lee, referring to the previous script saying: "I've never seen it, and of course I would say that's an outright lie" (Hill 2015). What this highlights, more than half a century later, is that the Marvel Method, while effective in many ways for experienced artists and collaborators, creates challenges when it comes to creative attribution for both scholarly and legal perspectives.

Fast forward decades from the time of the first issue of *Fantastic Four* to the Marvel Architects (a name given to a number of established Marvel writers charged with guiding the House of Ideas during the early 21st century), and we can see that Brian Michael Bendis employs a much more full-scripts approach to his comics as seen in his jointly creator-owned comic, *Powers,* with artist Michael Avon Oeming.

Script: *POWERS* (Quoted in Bendis n.d.).

```
POWERS
THE LEGENDS
ISSUE ONE
BY BRIAN MICHAEL BENDIS FOR MIKE AVON OEMING
```

```
PAGE 1-
Three equal sized widescreen panels. Similar images to page one
of volume one.

1- Ext. City- late day
The sky line of our nameless city. Silhouette towers pierce a
gray blue night sky. No flying figures in the sky. Its dull grey,
hazy day.

It looks like Portland in the fall. Lifeless.

2- Ext. Street- Same
As if the camera panned down to reveal this typical looking
downtown intersection. Not street level. About two stories up.

A indiscriminate block of buildings. Each has its own distinct
characters.

People mill about. A peeling FG-3 poster that's faded from two
years of weather beating.
```

```
Ken- this is a perfect place for you to start introducing as
much city type work as you want.
Fill the streets with type and signage. But do remember that
Sony will own anything you put in here so do not put in anything
copyrighted or anything you have invested interest in.

3- Ext. Alley- Same
Panning down. Street level.

Wide of the street. A live crime scene. The alleyway is taped
off. a dozen civilians have gathered, blocking our view of what
is inside.

In the foreground, Police cars, emergency vehicles. Yellow
police tape is up keeping the casual smattering of a crowd at
bay.

A couple of news vans are parked as close as they can get. Cops
mill about. This has been going on for quite a while.

In the foreground right, a nondescript white car has made its
way to the front of the scene.
```

What's interesting to note in this scripting of the first page of Issue #1, Vol. 2 of *Powers* (2009) is the dialogue that occurs not only between Bendis and Oeming, but also to their letterer, Ken Bruzenak with guidance about how to letter the varied art provided in each panel. Unlike Stan Lee's script, Bendis provides guidance on the number and types of panels, with a cinematic like direction in terms of foregrounding, the camera panning, etc. Speaking about his early career as a writer, Bendis makes no secret of learning to write for his artist collaborators: "I wasn't letting them express themselves. I wasn't trusting them…a good writer lets her artists draw" (2014, 83). This translates to the writer recognizing that it's the artist – not themselves – who will be speaking directly to the audience, and so, the script they write needs to be for the artist and to inspire, not direct, them.

The key takeaway for readers of all backgrounds, however, is that since there is no one single way to determining the creation of any given comic, simple assumptions of attribution should generally be avoided while simultaneously recognizing the significance of all members involved in the telling of a story in this medium.

The Roles in the Creative Process

What follows is a broad overview of the various roles involved in the creation of a comic. The responsibilities of each role can vary greatly depending on the context of the project. For instance, in comics produced by Marvel or DC, editorial oversight often plays a significant role, dictating which characters may be used or the extent of their impact on the larger story arcs that have been meticulously planned. Moreover, some creators may take on multiple roles within a story, or the writer and artist might share storytelling responsibilities, further blurring the lines between their contributions.

Given this variability, it's essential to recognize that the boundaries of "who does what" can shift from one project to the next, even when the same creative team members are involved. Despite these nuances, the following breakdown provides a general understanding of the key players in the process of transforming a single idea into a published story.

Whether using the Marvel Method or a full-script approach, drafting the script for a comic generally falls within the scope of the writer. It's important to note, however, that the script is rarely intended for the readers; instead, it serves as a guide for the artistic team, capturing the plot and key story elements (and may include dialogue, depending on the scripting approach used). Famous for his extensive, prose-heavy scripts, Alan Moore urges aspiring comic writers to "fascinate the reader with your first sentence, draw them in with your second sentence, and have them in a mild trance by the third" (Moore 2012, 41). He balances this notion of prose writing, however, with urging that writers think visually to "take advantage of how much information it is possible to convey within an image" and to "bear in mind that the artist will almost certainly have visual sensibilities 50 times more sound and reliable than your own" (Moore 2012, 41). Moore's advice reflects a recognition that while the writer's prose can set the groundwork, it is the artist's interpretation (the choice of framing, visual metaphors, and emphasis) that often transforms and elevates the narrative. And so, it may be that writers capture the plot and dialogue and transfer them into a script, either in a single-page description via the Marvel Method or a page-by-page breakdown through a full script.

All of the details of taking the writer's script are then left to the penciller, inker, and colorist to flesh out and translate the script in ways that will best leverage their visual sensibilities to tell a story that not only conveys the plot but also the larger ideas and themes in the story for their readers. Where there is a heavier editorial hand and a full script, many of these details are provided to the artistic team; when using the Marvel Method; however, one can see just how much more responsibility for storytelling falls on the artists.

In many cases, writers opt for the Marvel Method in specific circumstances. For example, they may be collaborating with professional artists who have an established record of comic storytelling and understand that these artists will be able to adapt their ideas into a visually captivating form that leverages the visual elements of comics to convey the story. Additionally, the writer might be juggling multiple comic titles and simply does not have the time to invest in full scripting. In fact, this was the method Stan Lee used during his tenure as editor-in-chief at Marvel, which led to this style being referred to as the Marvel Method. As a result, artistic collaborators such as Jack Kirby and Steve Ditko were able to inject far more of their own ideas into the stories, contributing to the creation of many of the enduring superheroes we know today, even if it led to complications around creative attribution.

As noted before, regardless of the scripting approach that the writer uses, the script is developed strictly for the artist or artistic team involved in bringing the comic to life. Assuming there is a single individual occupying each role, we can then consider an approximation of how each person engages with and contributes to the process.

Once the script is complete, the penciller is the first to receive it. They review the script and begin translating and adapting it from the writer's prose into the comics medium. The amount of creative flexibility the penciller has largely depends on the nature of the project: Is the artist working under a "work-for-hire" contract with an expectation of directly translating what the writer or editorial expects? Or are they co-creators with the writer, thereby enabled to make creative edits and changes on the fly? Regardless, the penciller is responsible for initiating the shift from prose to visual, selecting panel and page composition, and creating a visually coherent narrative that sets up the story for the desired emotional responses from the reader. Scott McCloud's seminal *Understanding Comics: The Invisible Art* is invaluable for gaining an in-depth understanding of the choices pencillers make with line art. McCloud contends that when text and line art find a sort of harmonizing balance where each "support[s] each other's strengths – comics can match **any** of the art forms it draws so much of its strength from" (1999, 156). The size and composition of panels can establish context or set the scene. Zooming in on a particular panel emphasizes key elements or heightens tension. Additionally, the style a penciller chooses, ranging from abstract and cartoonish to concrete and realistic, can significantly influence the tone of the story. For example, a penciller working on a Batman comic must consider the story's focus and target audience. A more cartoonish style might be appropriate for a children's storyline, whereas a narrative centered on Batman as the Dark Knight Detective, pursuing the Joker's homicidal spree, would benefit from a more realistic and gritty visual approach.

To that end, pencillers will often go through a series of stages before finalizing their work. Line artists often begin with thumbnails, which help provide a rough layout of each page and the work as a whole (single monthly issue, chapter within an original graphic novel, etc.). From a practical perspective, artists can usually "drawn a dozen thumbnails or more in the time it takes to rough in one final page" (Love and Withers 2015, 63). This is particularly important when working as a member of a creative team and not independently, where the editor and writer will often want to provide feedback on the ways in which the scripts find itself being translated from word to pictures.

For many contemporary artists, the ability to work digitally, in part or the whole, can also allow them to make revisions and corrections on the spot without the smudges and stains that traditional pencils and ink often include. Moreover, artists who opt for tighter versus more loose thumbnails (that is, detailed and neat lines versus sloppier and rough line work) also allow digital artists to "enlarge and draw over their final lines immediately" as opposed to having to start over for the final line art (Love and Withers 2015, 66).

For the writer, it might be as simple as describing the scene as a "dark and stormy night," but the penciller must bring that scene to life, making readers see and feel the atmosphere. Fortunately, the penciller isn't alone in this endeavor, as the inker plays a crucial role in enhancing and refining the visual narrative. Historically, inkers often served a more functional than artistic role in the creation of comics. Printers simply could not reproduce the finer and fainter line art from pencils; thus, original line work would need to be inked for it to stand up to mass reproduction. And while this still holds true in many regards even today, one need only look at the ink work of creators such as Tim Sale on his critically acclaimed *The Long Halloween,* Mike Mignola on *Hellboy,* or Becky Cloonan's run on *Conan the Barbarian,* as but a few examples of where inking not only helps the line art to stand out, but also it truly elevates the mood and story as a whole through the sharp contrasts of characters and setting thanks to their highly individualized inking styles.

In the cult classic film *Chasing Amy* (Smith 1997) by noted comic book aficionado and writer Kevin Smith, a character defensively describes his role as a comic book inker: "It's not 'tracing,' alright? I add depth and shading to give the image more definition. Only then does the image take shape." This scene humorously touches on a common misconception that inkers are merely "tracers," a misunderstanding that unfortunately persists among casual comics readers. Despite the tongue-in-cheek jokes about the underappreciation of inkers, the reality is that their work is fundamental to the final look and feel of a comic. A talented inker adds depth, shading, and definition, transforming the penciller's raw sketches into polished, compelling imagery.

As longtime DC inker Scott Williams points out, inkers play a far more critical role in the creative process. Williams, known for his nearly 30-year collaboration with the legendary artist Jim Lee, explains that inkers are often the ones who complete the actual drawings: "…when a deadline looms, inkers often turn into 'finishers' who tighten up drawings, add backgrounds, and even fix mistakes on the page. The truly elite talent often gets asked by editors to salvage a subpar penciling job" (Avila 2020). The value of a skilled inker like Williams cannot be understated, as their contributions are essential in elevating the line art and, in many cases, bringing the entire visual narrative to life.

For comics printed in black and white, this is where the letterer would step in to effectively complete the process of creating the comic. And for many comics, the story being told will dictate whether this will serve the reading experience. However, many comics include still another artistic role that continues to bring the visual to life: The colorist. Discussing the role of colors in comics, *Batman* and *Spawn* artist, FCO Plascencia explains that the key ingredient a colorist brings to the story is mood. He notes that he brings "emotion through color, and that would hopefully help tell the story in a better way" (Helvie 2021, 83). Through a process of "flatting" the pages, colorists take the inked comic pages and "separate the main areas in color in a panel and on the page" (83). Once the main colors have been added to the key elements of a page, the colorist begins rendering the image through the application of shading and lighting that are layered on top of these flats. The intent, as Plascencia points out, is to not just add to the readability of the comic, but also to "guide the readers' eyes through focal points, separating planes and differentiating scenes with different color schemes" (83). It is through this intricate layering of colors onto the inked line art that not only enhances the visual appeal of the comic but also serves as a narrative tool, guiding readers through the story and heightening their emotional engagement with each scene.

While the colorist uses hue and tone to evoke emotion and guide the reader's eye across the page, it's the letterer who adds the final layer of communication of the story to the reader, ensuring that dialogue, sound effects, and narration seamlessly integrate with the art to enhance both clarity and narrative flow. In the pre-digital publishing era, once the colorist completed their part of the collaboration, it was the letterer who took over, "lettering the copy [finished page] and drawing the balloons, captions, and panel outlines in India ink" (O'Neil 2013, 23). Regardless, it's important to differentiate "lettering" from "handwriting" as Abel and Madden note (2008, 88). Unlike handwriting, "letterforms are drawn, not written," making lettering an essential art form in its own right. When executed well, it allows readers to "hear the dialogue as though it's being spoken by the characters" (88).

Conclusion

The creative process behind the creation of comics is not a solitary endeavor but rather a collaborative effort where each role (writer, penciller, inker, colorist, and letterer) plays a crucial part in bringing a single story to life. The choice between using the Marvel Method or a full-script approach often dictates how these roles interact and influence the final narrative. While the Marvel Method offers artists greater flexibility and creative input, the full-script approach provides a detailed roadmap for translating a writer's vision onto the page. These different methods highlight the spectrum of creative control, where no single approach is superior but rather suited to the strengths of the team involved.

Each stage of this process (drafting the script, translating it into visual form, refining the artwork, adding color, and ensuring readability through lettering) builds on the last, creating a layered storytelling experience that is unique to comics. By understanding these creative roles and methods, readers can develop a greater appreciation for the medium's complexity and the nuanced interplay between words and images that make comics such a compelling form of visual storytelling.

Ultimately, this chapter underscores that creating comics is an evolving and collaborative art form. With each role contributing its own distinct expertise, comics are the product of a shared vision that transforms scripts into powerful stories that resonate with readers across generations.

References

Abel, Jessica, and Matt Madden. 2008. *Drawing Words, Writing Pictures: Making Comics from Manga to Graphic Novels*. First Second Books.

Avila, Mike. 2020. "Master Inker Scott Williams on Inking Jim Lee & X-Men Deadline Woes." *SYFY*, October 15. https://www.syfy.com/syfy-wire/scott-williams-on-inking-jim-lee-x-men-deadlines.

Bendis, Brian Michael. n.d. "Powers 1 (Vol.2.) (Word)." *Comics Experience*. Uploaded January, 2017. Accessed October 4, 2024. https://comicsexperience.com/scripts/.

Bendis, Brian Michael. 2014. *Words for Pictures: The Art and Business of Writing Comics and Graphic Novels*. Watson-Guptill.

Helvie, Forrest, et al. 2021. *How to Analyze & Review Comics*, edited by Forrest Helvie. Sequart.

Hill, Michael. 2015. "The Marvel Method according to Jack Kirby – Part One." *The Kirby Effect*, July 25. https://kirbymuseum.org/blogs/effect/2015/07/25/according-to-kirby-1/.

Love, Comfort, and Adam Withers. 2015. *The Complete Guide to Self-Publishing Comics*. Watson-Guptill.

McCloud, Scott. 1999. *Understanding Comics: The Invisible Art*. Turtleback Books.

Moore, Alan. 2012. *Writing for Comics*. Panini Comics.

O'Keefe, Matt. 2019. "Making Comics: The Ever-Evolving Marvel Style of Storytelling." *The Beat*, May 9. www.comicsbeat.com/marvel-style-marvel-method-comics/.

O'Neil, Dennis. 2013. *The DC Comics Guide to Writing Comics*. Watson-Guptill.

Smith, Kevin, dir. 1997. *Chasing Amy*. View Askew Productions.

2

THE FLASH AND THE AGES OF SUPERHEROES

Racing through History

John Darowski

There are myriad histories of superheroes, organized by medium, country, publishing company, characters, etc. Yet, examining creative, publishing, and social trends, there also appears to be a paradigm shift in the characterization of American comic book superheroes approximately every 15 years; these become retroactively identified as different "ages." One character stands out as a particular exemplar of these transformations: DC Comics' The Flash. From his first appearance in *Flash Comics* #1 (cover date January 1940), the many incarnations of the Flash have become trendsetters for the ages; something that is indicated by the different characters who take up the mantle. This historiography of superheroes will demonstrate how the Flashes and their adventures are representatives of the majority of the tropes and conventions from each age.

The ages of superheroes are defined by changes in artistic and narrative styles and content resulting from numerous factors, which form a complex negotiation among creative collaborations, reader consumption, market practices, technological advances, and social conditions, dominated by the "big two" publishers, DC Comics and Marvel Comics (both have operated under other company names during their histories). Fans, retailers, and academics then create historiographical taxonomies based around their own ideological projects and diachronic perspectives. The first published reference to such a taxonomy is attributed to Dick Lupoff in the fanzine *Comic Art* #1 (Spring 1961), stating that comics "came in the thirties, their golden age was in the forties. They declined in the fifties" (quoted in Darowski 2014, 94). This was reified in a letter by Scott Taylor in *The Justice League of America* #42 (February 1966): "If you guys keep bringing back heroes from the … Golden Age, people 20 years from now will be calling this decade the Silver Sixties!" (quoted in Schelley 2013, 151). From these observations, the chronological designations of comic book superheroes in the 20th century became modeled on the ages of man from Roman poet Ovid's *Metamorphoses* (8 CE): Golden, Silver, Bronze, and Iron.

While the years bracketing the Golden (1938–1955) and Silver (1956–1970) Ages are generally agreed upon, Bronze (1971–1985) and Iron (sometimes called Dark; 1986–1999) have less consensus. The dates and naming conventions of the new millennium are open to interpretation; suggestions include Renaissance (1997–"present" [Coogan 2006, 221; Morrison 2011, 267]), Postmodern (1999–"present" [Rhoades 2008, 6]), Diamond

DOI: 10.4324/9781003366911-4

(2000–"present" [Pinchuk 2010]), and Blue (2010–"present" [Resha 2020, 67]). I designate the first age of the 21st century as Baroque (2000–2016). There is a tendency to label whatever the present era is as "Modern" (2016–"present"), which I will perpetuate as there is not yet enough perspective to label it. Significantly, the bracketed dates are not meant to be concrete but porous. Sometimes, there are precursors to significant trends and other times it may take a few years for the conventions to become widespread. With the Flashes as guides, let the race through the ages of superheroes commence.

The Golden Age (1938–1955)

The Golden Age is defined by the introduction of the superhero genre, their explosive growth during World War II (1939–1945), and their waning popularity into the 1950s. The first appearance of the Flash in late 1939 (cover dates indicated when the issues were to be taken off sale, so issues were published one to four months before the cover date) came almost a year-and-a-half after the introduction of the world's first superhero on the cover of *Action Comics* #1 (June 1938): Superman (Clark Kent). However, the Man of Steel, created by writer Jerome "Jerry" Siegel and artist Joseph "Joe" Shuster, would only have been a novel science fiction character unless the key conventions of the new genre, which comic book writer Kurt Busiek identifies as superpowers, costume, code name, secret identity, heroic ongoing mission, and superhero milieu (2013, 133), could be proven imitable with variation. Most of those tropes had appeared in films, comic strips, pulp magazines, and radio shows in the preceding years, but their combination in the comic book medium created something unique. Batman (Bruce Wayne), created by artist Bob Kane (née Robert Kahn) and writer Milton "Bill" Finger for *Detective Comics* #27 (May 1939), proved the superhero concept was imitable. With *Action Comics* featuring Superman selling close to a million copies (Daniels 1995, 22), the floodgates opened as every comic book publisher wanted their own superheroes.

The first Flash (Jay Garrick) was essential in making the superhero a unique, stable genre, including the establishment of a superhero milieu with supervillains and a metropolitan cityscape. *Flash Comics* #1 was published by publisher Maxwell Gaines and editor Sheldon Mayer, who partnered with Detective Comics, Inc., to start All-American Publications in 1939 (Mitchell and Thomas 2019, 26). The issue not only introduces the Flash by writer Gardner Fox and artist Harry Lampert, but also Hawkman (Carter Hall) by Fox and Mayer. The simple concept behind the Flash is explained in the introductory panel: "Faster than the streak of lightning in the sky…Swifter than the speed of light itself…Fleeter than the rapidity of thought…is the Flash" (Fox and Lampert 1940, 1). College student Jay Garrick receives his extraordinary powers after inhaling hard water vapors during a smoke break in the school laboratory (2–3). Inspired by the Roman god Mercury, Garrick fashions a costume consisting of a winged helmet, red shirt, blue pants, and lightning bolt motif. During the Golden Age, superheroes didn't become heroes by doing good; they did good because their heroism was an a priori assumption (Maverick 2021, 160). The Flash provides variation to the genre not only by his power set but through his use of humor and that his girlfriend, Joan Williams, is privy to his secret identity (Mitchell and Thomas 2019, 27).

Part of the Flash's importance in the medium achieving a critical mass of superheroes is evidenced in his role as a founding member of the first superhero team: The Justice Society of America. Conceived by Sheldon Mayer, written by Gardner Fox, and drawn by Everett E. Hibbard in *All Star Comics* #3 (Winter 1940), the Justice Society united characters from

All American Publications and Detective Comics, Inc. The Crimson Comet soon added the solo series *All-Flash Quarterly* (June 1941), which became the bimonthly *All-Flash* with #6 (October 1942). Though chemist Jay Garrick received a deferment from military service (Mitchell and Thomas 2019, 142), the adventures of superheroes, with their message of American exceptionalism and patriotism, soared during World War II.

But that popularity waned after the war as other, newer genres came to dominate sales. *All-Flash* ended with #32 (January 1948) and *Flash Comics* finished with #104 (February 1949). Jay Garrick's last Golden Age appearance was alongside the Justice Society in *All-Star Comics* #57 (February/March 1951), which was subsequently retitled *All-Star Western*. In addition to the genres of Westerns, war stories, science fiction, funny animals, and teen humor crowding the newsstands came romance, crime stories, and horror. By 1952, approximately 25% of the comics sold were horror titles (Schelley 2013, 54). But all of these subversive stories soon came up against the burgeoning Cold War consensus culture to bring an end to the Golden Age.

Local political, civic, and religious groups had attempted to regulate comic books throughout the 1940s, but the movement would enter the national stage in the early 1950s. With teenagers becoming recognized as a new social group, there arose a juvenile delinquency scare alongside the Red Scare. Even though there was no statistical increase in juvenile delinquency (Schelley 2013, 32), a flashpoint nonetheless arrived for the comic book industry with the 1954 publication of Dr. Frederic Wertham's *Seduction of the Innocent* and his subsequent testimony before the Senate Subcommittee on Juvenile Deliquency in April of that year, when he accused almost all comic books of promoting criminal or deviant behavior. Though the Subcommittee ultimately concluded "that juvenile delinquency essentially stems from the moral breakdown in the home and community and, in many cases, parental apathy" (quoted in York 2012, 111), the damage to the comic book industry's reputation was done; almost half of publishers closed shop by 1957 (Schelley 2013, 117). In August 1954, the publishers joined forces as the Comics Magazine Association of America (CMAA) to establish a self-censoring set of content rules: the Comics Code. Almost all comic books were to be reviewed by the Comics Code Authority (CCA) and receive their seal of approval before being sold. The Code was particularly stringent when it came to horror. But some saw the Code's strict morality as an opportunity to reintroduce superheroes to a new generation of readers, beginning with the Flash.

The Silver Age (1956–1970)

The Silver Age was inaugurated with the introduction of a new Flash (Barry Allen) in *Showcase* #4 (October 1956). This superhero revival, marked by deeper characterization, world-building, and continuity (Smith 2014, 111), played out against the backdrop of the Cold War (1947–1991), where the moral certainties of superheroes and supervillains aligned with the political narrative of the democratic and capitalist West versus the Communist USSR. The emphasis on the science, especially radiation, in the arms race and the space race influenced the science fiction origins and stories of several new characters. Editor Julius Schwartz's, writer Bob Kanigher's, and artist Carmine Infantino's origin for the new Flash involved police scientist Barry Allen being bathed in chemicals when struck by lightning, granting him super speed. Inspired by Golden Age issues of *Flash Comics* #12–13 (1940–1941), Allen takes up the code name and crafts a sleek red bodysuit with lightning bolt motifs and winged cowl and boots to fight crime (Kanigher and Infantino 1956, 2–13). But, as the consensus culture of the 1950s gave way to the baby boomer counterculture of the 1960s, DC's status as the leading publisher of superheroes would be challenged by a new company who would come to define the Silver Age: Marvel Comics.

After three more try-out issues in *Showcase*, the Flash received his own title, picking up the numbering where the previous series left off with #105 (October 1958). He was soon followed by other Silver Age incarnations, such as Green Lantern (Hal Jordan) in *Showcase* #22 (October 1959) by writer John Broome and penciler Gil Kane and Hawkman (Kotor Hol) in *The Brave and the Bold* #34 (March 1961) by Gardner Fox and penciler Joe Kubert. Both as superheroes and often in their secret identities, DC's new heroes were protectors of the status quo: Barry Allen is a police scientist; Hal Jordan is a test pilot who, as Green Lantern, becomes a member of an intergalactic police force; Kotor Hol is a police officer on his native Thanagar, though he works as a museum curator when he comes to Earth. The Scarlet Speedster even began modeling the nuclear family with his marriage to Iris West in *The Flash* #165 (Nov. 1966) by writer John Broome and Carmine Infantino. In working as agents of the state, DC's superheroes reinforced the Cold War consensus culture.

In *The Flash* #110 (December 1959), John Broome and Carmine Infantino introduced a teen sidekick, Kid Flash (Wally West), in an attempt to appeal to the teenage Baby Boomer audience. But in this appeal, DC was soon supplanted by rival Marvel Comics. Writer/editor Stan Lee and artists Jack Kirby and Steve Ditko revitalized the industry with their fresh take on superheroes introduced in titles such as *Fantastic Four* #1 (November 1961), the Amazing Spider-Man in *Amazing Fantasy* #15 (August 1962), and *X-Men* #1 (September 1963). Marvel stories emphasized the personal problems of its heroes, not just their battles with supervillains, in an intertwined storyworld where reading every book in every series could matter. Unlike the staider Flash and Kid Flash, in the Marvel Universe, teenagers could be superheroes in their own right. This allowed Marvel to better reflect and explore the countercultural trends of the 1960s, such as civil rights and the anti-Vietnam War movement.

By the end of the 1960s, most publishers were chafing under the strictures of the CCA. In 1970, The U.S. Department of Health, Education, and Welfare asked Marvel to publish an anti-drug storyline as part of the new "War on Drugs," but the Code forbade any mention of drug use (Sacks 2014, 45). Lee published the story, with pencils by Gil Kane, without the CCA seal of approval in *Amazing Spider-Man* #96–98 (May-July 1971). The CMAA swiftly modernized the code, loosening restrictions so that the cover of *Green Lantern* #85 (September 1971) showed Green Arrow (Oliver Queen)'s sidekick Speedy (Roy Harper) using heroin (O'Neil, Adams, and Kane 1971, 1). The shift away from black-and-white morality to a focus on social issues helped usher in the Bronze Age, though the Flash labored to keep apace.

The Bronze Age (1971–1985)

The Flash struggled to stay in the race amongst the social and comic book industry upheavals of the Bronze Age. This era saw an influx of new creators who had grown up reading comics within the counterculture bring fresh perspectives, including a growing awareness of social and political issues. As the U.S. dealt with the consequences of its police actions in Vietnam (1955–1975) as well as the fallout of the Watergate scandal (1972–1974), several superheroes turned introspective to examine the repercussions of their actions. In addition to Speedy's drug use, across longer, multi-issue storylines, Captain America (Steve Rogers) quits due to his loss of faith in a corrupt government, in *Captain America and the Falcon* #176 (August 1974); Iron Man (Tony Stark) deals with alcoholism, in *Iron Man* #120–128

(March-November 1979); and Spider-Man (Peter Parker)'s girlfriend Gwen Stacy dies, in *Amazing Spider-Man* #121 (June 1973). DC tried making the Flash more hip by dropping Barry's signature bowtie and letting his hair grow long instead of trimmed into a crew cut, but these superficial changes proved divisive among fans and he soon returned to his trademark conservative appearance (Lee 2019, 74–75). Peter W. Y. Lee states: "In a countercultural tug-of-war, the fastest man alive remained standing still, his social consciousness nothing more than a flash in the pan" (2019, 78). Cold Warriors were needed less in the time of thawing international socio-political tensions known as détente.

The comic book industry struggled not only to appeal to readers of the "Me Generation," but with a rapidly changing marketplace. The traditional newsstand market struggled to support many titles amidst stagflation (the combination of economic stagnation and inflation), which resulted in higher cover prices, lower page counts, and even mass cancellations; most notably, the DC Implosion when the company canceled 24 titles (Sacks 2014, 248). Retailer Phil Seuling found a solution in 1973 by cutting out the middleman of magazine distributors and instead having the companies sell their comics to specialty shops through the direct market (Sacks 2014, 120). These comic book shops were supported by a devoted fanbase, which also allowed independent and alternative presses to break into the market as they could be profitable with smaller print runs as well as bypass the CAA.

Even though *The Flash* survived the DC Implosion, the Scarlet Speedster seemed to be running in place through a series of long, melodramatic storylines. One story which highlights this trend also closed out the Bronze Age. In *The Flash* #275 (July 1979), by writer Cary Bates and penciler Alex Saviuk, archenemy Reverse Flash, A.K.A. Professor Zoom (Eobard Thawne), kills Barry's wife Iris. When Reverse Flash returns to murder Allen's new fiancée Fiona Webb in *The Flash* #324 (August 1983), by Bates and Infantino, the Flash kills his foe, leading to the two-year long *Trial of the Flash*. The storyline alienated readers and sales dropped precipitously (Dallas 2013, 134). *The Flash* #350 (October 1985), by Bates and Infantino, ends the era with Barry reuniting with Iris in her native 30th century.

The Iron Age (1986–1999)

Barry Allen returns to the present only to sacrifice himself to prevent the Anti-Monitor from destroying all life in the multiverse in *Crisis on Infinite Earths* #8 (November 1985), by writer Marv Wolfman and penciler George Perez. After all of the multiverse is condensed into a single universe (now including the Golden Age Flash, Jay Garrick), in issue #12 (March 1986), Wally West takes up his mentor's mantle, declaring: "I am no longer Kid Flash. From this day forth – the Flash lives again!" (40). West becomes a new Flash for a new generation in a new age.

Crisis on Infinite Earths was part of a comic book trend in deconstructing the superhero genre. This creative paradigm shift into the Iron Age was crystalized by two key texts: *Watchmen* (September 1986-October 1987), by writer Alan Moore and artist Dave Gibbons, and *The Dark Knight Returns* (June-December 1986), by Frank Miller. These texts deconstruct the motives, morals, and purposes of superheroes and ushered in an era of darker, more complex works that elevated the medium while targeting audiences outside of the established comic book readership. This period is also called the Dark Age due to the popularity of grim-and-gritty violence perpetrated by hypersexualized characters in a style-over-substance aesthetic. However, as Christopher Maverick points out, calling the age Dark can be reductive by focusing only on what has come to be viewed as the negative aspects of best-selling titles (Maverick and Wise 2023). Though the Iron Age saw some of the comic book industry's lowest lows, it also witnessed some of its highest highs.

Following *Crisis on Infinite Earths*, DC introduced a streamlined, new-reader-friendly continuity. For some characters, such as Superman and Wonder Woman (Diana Prince), this was an opportunity to reinvent their history. *The Flash* vol. 2 #1 (April 1987), by writer Mike Baron and penciler Jackson Guice, continued the story of Wally West as the Scarlet Speedster. With the Flash becoming a legacy identity, he represented a demographic shift from Baby Boomers to Generation X readers; this move was further cemented by the introduction of Wally's own teen sidekick Impulse (Bart Allen) in *The Flash* vol. 2 #92 (July 1994), by writer Mark Waid and penciler Mike Wieringo. This also served as a precursor to the kind of identity crisis several superheroes would undergo after the end of the Cold War in 1991. Events such as *The Death of Superman* (1992) and *Batman: Knightfall* (1993–1994) saw the traditional heroes replaced with more violent incarnations, reflecting not only the popular aesthetics of the times but also the interrogation of American identity and the country's role in the world following the dissolution of the USSR. While traditional values and secret identities were often restored, some characters like Wally West or the new Green Lantern, Kyle Rayner, stuck around to seemingly fulfill their roles permanently.

The event storylines surrounding the deaths and replacements of heroes were part of the boom-and-bust cycle of expansion and contraction that the comic book industry experienced in the 1990s. At the height of the boom period in 1991, with buyers hoping that each issue would become high-priced collector's items, seven superstar artists walked away from Marvel to found Image Comics. The new company gave creators creative control and more financial rewards for their creations. Image quickly became a major competitor with Marvel and DC. More new publishers followed, each with their own superhero universes; most of these companies faded or moved into other genres when the collector bubble burst mid-decade. The characters and concepts which have endured from the period belong to auteur creators rather than editorially-driven companies.

After the speculator bubble burst in the mid-1990s, which resulted in Marvel declaring bankruptcy in 1997, DC and Marvel began to move away from the excesses of the Iron Age. Randy Duncan and Matthew J. Smith describe this as a transition from an era of ambition to one of reiteration, reemphasizing the classic elements of the superhero storyworlds (2009, 75–79). As usual, the Flash had raced ahead. Writer Mark Waid's approximately 100-issue run on *The Flash* (#62-#162 [March 1992-May 2000]) became a model of classic storytelling for the late 20th century, including Wally West's marriage to Linda Park in issue #142 (Oct. 1998), with co-writer Bian Augustyn and penciler Pop Mhan.

The Baroque Age (2000–2016)

The Flash never settles down during the Baroque Age, running through multiple iterations of the character. The superhero reconstruction which began in the era of reiteration continued in the new millennium through an influx of new creators, most notably writers Geoff Johns at DC and Brian Michael Bendis at Marvel, who emphasized decompressed storytelling and wide-screen artistry to create stories better suited for trade collection in the bookstore market. The age also saw the slow demise of the CAA, which began with Marvel abandoning the Code in 2001, opting for in-house guidelines, and ended with DC leaving it in 2011.

The Baroque style in art history (1600–1750) is defined by complexity, ornamentation, and excess, which the Flash reflects through continuity convolutions with at least four permutations of the character featuring multiple deaths, erasures, and returns. The hallmark of the Baroque Age is an increasing cycle of editorially-driven crossover events, with one event leading into the next. Each tie-in issue, marked by ornamental banners on the covers, form part of the labyrinthine path through the story. Few paths were more twisty than that of the Flash through these years. Wally West and his wife, Linda, and children, Irey and Jai, escape to an alternate reality during *Infinite Crisis* #4 (March 2006), by Geoff Johns and multiple artists. Then Bart Allen takes up the Flash's mantle until he is killed in *Flash: The Fastest Man Alive* #13 (June 2007), by writer Marc Guggenheim and penciler Tony Daniels. But the DC Universe was not long without a Flash as Wally and his family return to Earth-Prime in *Justice League of America* vol. 2 #10 (August 2007), by writer Brad Meltzer and penciler Ed Benes. This was soon followed by the return of Barry Allen in *Final Crisis* #2 (August 2008), by writer Grant Morrison and artist J. G. Jones, as well as the resurrection of Bart Allen as Kid Flash in *Final Crisis: Legion of 3 Worlds* #5 (September 2009), by Johns and penciler George Perez. In the 2011 Flash-centric event *Flashpoint* by Johns and penciler Andy Kubert, Barry attempts to stop the murder of his mother and creates a harsh, alternate timeline. When Barry corrects the past, it results in a new DC history. In the *New 52* reboot, Barry Allen is the only Flash, erasing Wally West and Bart Allen; Jay Garrick is shunted to Earth 2. Barry is eventually joined by an African American Kid Flash (Wallace "Wally/Ace" West) in *The Flash* vol. 4 Annual #3 (June 2014), by writers Van Jensen and Robert Vendetti, and pencilers Brett Booth and Ron Frenz. The *New 52* proved to be a bold yet flawed initiative and the previous DC continuity was soon restored, beginning, again, with a Flash.

Conclusion: The "Modern" Age (2016–present)

DC Universe: Rebirth #1 (May 2016), by Geoff Johns and multiple artists, launched the sixth age of superheroes by restoring parts of DC's legacy continuity as part of the *DC Rebirth* initiative, which began with the return of Wally West. Though there has not been enough historical perspective to name this age, certain themes are emerging. One is trauma, reflecting concerns about mental health in the wake of numerous collectively traumatic events such as the COVID-19 pandemic. This is reflected through Wally; though he was restored, his family was not. In his grief, he lashes out with the speed force (the source of the Flashes' powers) and seemingly kills several other heroes in *Heroes in Crisis* #8 (June 2019), by writer Tom King and artists Mitch Gerards and Travis Moore. Though the slain heroes and Wally's family, including infant Wade West, eventually return, he has still had to process his post-traumatic stress disorder (PTSD). Similarly, Jay Garrick has recently had to cope with the return of his forgotten daughter and sidekick, the Boom (Judy Garrick), after they reunite in *Justice Society of America* vol. 4 #6 (November 2023), by Johns and artists Mikel Janin and Marco Santucci.

In July 2024, DC announced a new publishing initiative: the Absolute Universe. This sibling storyworld would see DC's most iconic characters reimagined as though they were created in 2024 with fewer resources on a darker Earth. Though *Absolute Flash*, by writer Jeff Lemire and penciler Nick Robles, features a Wally West that will not join the line until March 2025, it is undoubtable that the Flash will become a key part of this new universe. The Flash, whoever is behind the mask, will continue to race ahead, defining this modern, as well as future, ages of superheroes.

References

Baron, Mike, and Jackson Guice. 1987. Reprinted in 2019. "Happy Birthday Wally." In *The Flash* vol. 2 #1. DC Comics. *DC Universe Infinite.*

Bates, Cary, and Alex Saviuk. 1979. Reprinted in 2019. "The Last Dance." In *The Flash* vol. 1 #275. DC Comics. *DC Universe Infinite.*

Bates, Cary, and Carmine Infantino. 1983. "The Slayer and the Slain!" In *The Flash* vol. 1 #324. DC Comics.

Bates, Cary, and Carmine Infantino. 1985. Reprinted in 2019. "Flash Flees." In *The Flash* vol. 1 #350. DC Comics. *DC Universe Infinite.*

Broome, John, and Carmine Infantino. 1959. Reprinted in 2019. "Meet Kid Flash!" In *The Flash* vol. 1 #110. DC Comics. *DC Universe Infinite.*

Broome, John, and Carmine Infantino. 1966. Reprinted in 2019. "One Bridegroom Too Many!" In *The Flash* vol. 1 #165. DC Comics. *DC Universe Infinite.*

Busiek, Kurt. 2013. "The Importance of Context: Robin Hood Is Out and Buffy Is In." In *What Is a Superhero?*, edited by Robin S. Rosenberg and Peter Coogan. Oxford University Press.

Coogan, Peter. 2006. *Superhero: The Secret Origin of a Genre.* Monkeybrain Books.

Dallas, Keith. 2013. *American Comic Book Chronicles: The 1980s.* TwoMorrows Publishing.

Daniels, Les. 1995. *DC Comics: Sixty Years of the World's Favorite Comic Book Heroes.* Bullfinch Press.

Darowski, Joseph. 2014. "The Improbability of Assignment: Arriving at the Golden Age of Comic Books." In *Critical Insights: The American Comic Book*, edited by Joseph Michael Sommers. Grey Publishing House.

Duncan, Randy, and Matthew J. Smith. 2009. *The Power of Comics: History, Form, and Culture.* Continuum.

Fox, Gardner, and Everett E. Hibbard. 1940. Reprinted in 2019. "The First Meeting of the Justice Society of America." In *All-Star Comics* #3. DC Comics. *DC Universe Infinite.*

Fox, Gardner, and Harry Lampert. 1940. Reprinted in 2019. "The Flash." In *Flash Comics* #1. DC Comics. *DC Universe Infinite.*

Guggenheim, Marc, and Tony Daniels. 2007. Reprinted in 2019. "Full Throttle: Conclusion." In *The Flash: The Fastest Man Alive* #13. DC Comics. *DC Universe Infinite.*

Jensen, Van, Robert Vendetti, Brett Booth, and Ron Frenz. 2014. Reprinted in 2019. "Slip." In *The Flash* vol. 4 Annual #3. DC Comics. *DC Universe Infinite.*

Johns, Geoff, Mikel Janin, and Marco Santucci. 2023. "Young Justice Society Chapter One: A New Dawn." In *Justice Society of America* vol. 4 #6. DC Comics. *DC Universe Infinite.*

Johns, Geoff, and Andy Kubert. 2011. Reprinted in 2012. *Flashpoint.* DC Comics.

Johns, Geoff, and George Perez. 2009. Reprinted in 2019. "Book Five." In *Final Crisis: Legion of 3 Worlds* #5. DC Comics. *DC Universe Infinite.*

Johns, Geoff, George Perez, Ivan Reis, Phil Jimenez, et al. 2006. Reprinted in 2019. "Homecoming." In *Infinite Crisis* #4. DC Comics. *DC Universe Infinite.*

Johns, Geoff, Ivan Reis, Gary Frank, Ethan van Scriver, et al. 2016. Reprinted in 2019. *DC Universe: Rebirth* #1. DC Comics. *DC Universe Infinite.*

Kane, Bob, and Bill Finger. 1939. Reprinted in 2019. "The Case of the Chemical Syndicate." In *Detective Comics* vol. 1 #27. DC Comics. *DC Universe Infinite.*

Kanigher, Bob, and Carmine Infantino. 1956. Reprinted in 2019. "Mystery of the Human Thunderbolt!" In *Showcase* #4. DC Comics. *DC Universe Infinite.*

King, Tom, Mitch Gerard, and Travis Moore. 2019. Reprinted in 2020. "Alive." *Heroes in Crisis* #8. DC Comics. *DC Universe Infinite.*

Lee, Peter W. Y. 2019. "Barry Allen's Social Awakening in the 1970s." In *Ages of the Flash: Essays on the Fastest Man Alive*, edited by Joseph J. Darowski. McFarland & Company.

Maverick, Christopher. 2021. "No Tights, No Flights: How *Smallville* Put the 'Human' in 'Superhuman.'" In *Adapting Superman: Essays on the Transmedia Man of Steel*, edited by John Darowski. McFarland & Company.

Maverick, Christopher, and Wayne Wise. 2023. "Episode 254. A Primer on the Ages of Comics." *The VoxPopcast*, February 20. Guest John Darowski. Podcast, MP3 audio, 1:13:10. https://voxpopcast.com/wp/2023/02/20/e254-a-primer-on-the-ages-of-comics/.

Meltzer, Brad, and Ed Benes. 2017. Reprinted in 2019. "The Lightning Saga Final Chapter: The Villain Is the Hero of His Own Story." In *Justice League of America* #10. DC Comics. *DC Universe Infinite*.

Miller, Frank. 1986. Reprinted 2002. *Batman: The Dark Knight Returns*. DC Comics.

Mitchell, Kurt F., with Roy Thomas. 2019. *American Comic Book Chronicles: The 1940s–1940–1944*. TwoMorrows Publishing.

Moore, Alan, and Dave Gibbons. 1986–1987. Reprinted 1995. *Watchmen*. DC Comics.

Morrison, Grant. 2011. *Supergods: What Masked Vigilantes, Miraculous Mutants, and a Sun God from Smallville Can Teach Us About Being Human*. Spiegel and Grau.

Morrison, Grant, and James G. Jones. 2008. Reprinted in 2019. "Ticket to Blüdhaven." In *Final Crisis* #2. DC Comics. *DC Universe Infinite*.

O'Neil, Dennis, Neal Adams, and Gil Kane. 1971. Reprinted in 2019. "Snowbirds Don't Fly." In *Green Lantern* vol. 2 #85. DC Comics. *DC Universe Infinite*.

Pinchuk, Tom. 2010. "Is This the 'Diamond Age' of Comics." *Comic Vine*, last updated May 25, 2010. https://comicvine.gamespot.com/articles/is-this-the-diamond-age-of-comics/1100-141229/.

Resha, Adrienne. 2020. "The Blue Age of Comic Books." *Inks: The Journal of the Comics Studies Society* 4, no. 1 (Spring): 66–81. https://doi.org/10.1353/ink.2020.0003.

Rhoades, Shirrel. 2008. *A Complete History of American Comic Books*. Peter Lang.

Sacks, Jason. 2014. *American Comic Book Chronicles: The 1970s*. TwoMorrows Publishing.

Schelley, Bill. 2013. *American Comic Book Chronicles: The 1950s*. TwoMorrows Publishing.

Siegel, Jerry, and Joe Shuster. 1938. Reprinted in 2019. "Superman, Champion of the Oppressed!" In *Action Comics* vol. 1 #1. DC Comics. *DC Universe Infinite*.

Smith, Matthew J. 2014. "The Silver Age Playbook: Minting the Modern Superhero." In *Critical Insights: The American Comic Book*, edited by Joseph Michael Sommers. Grey Publishing House.

Waid, Mark, Brian Augustyn, and Pop Mhan. 1998. Reprinted in 2019. "Get Me to the Church on Time." In *The Flash* vol. 2 #142. DC Comics. *DC Universe Infinite*.

Wolfman, Marv, and George Perez. 1985. Reprinted in 2019. "A Flash of Lightning." In *Crisis on Infinite Earths* #8. DC Comics. *DC Universe Infinite*.

Wolfman, Marv, and George Perez. 1986. Reprinted in 2019. "Final Crisis." In *Crisis on Infinite Earths* #12. DC Comics. *DC Universe Infinite*.

York, Rafiel. 2012. "Rebellion in Riverdale." In *Comic Books and the Cold War, 1946–1952: Essays on Graphic Treatment of Communism, the Code, and Social Concerns*, edited by Chris York and Rafiel York. McFarland & Company.

3

THE CREATION OF SUPERHEROES AND SUPERVILLAINS THROUGH ALCHEMY, SCIENCE ACCIDENTS, AND VIOLENT SCIENTIFIC DELIGHTS

Lilia Walsh and Anna-Sophie Jürgens

Science and visions of scientific advancement, "[t]he chief marker of American epistemic progress", has shaped superhero stories since the 1930s, and characters such as "the original Human Torch, Flash, Captain America, and the Shield were the result of scientific innovation" or experiments (Mills 2014, 40), whether accidentally or intentionally. Early superhero comics propagated both the idea that science could solve all human problems and, drawing on much older tropes, that science could be used irresponsibly for evil in the service of criminal villains. Atomic energy, radioactive substances, and cryogenic weapons, created by (pseudo-)technology and (pseudo-)science, or magic and fantasy, respectively, made prominent appearances in such stories across the DC and Marvel Universes (Jürgens et al. 2024; Regalado 2015, 186–188; Mills 2014, 116). In attempting to create a working definition for the superhero genre, Richard Reynolds posited that in comics, science and magic are applied "indiscriminately" (1992, 16). In the shared continuity of comic universes, superheroes created by magic must coexist with those created by science (Locke 2005; Reynolds 1992). Furthermore, science and scientific terminology in comics exist primarily for storytelling and artistic purposes: "to create atmospheres and fill in background artwork", creating a loose realism of science in superhero comics wherein "the prevailing mood is mystical rather than rational" (Reynolds 1992, 16). Conversely, the vast commercialization of the modern superhero film genre brings with it several production pressures, which in turn affects the depictions of science within these films. Popular films typically predicate storytelling over scientific realism, and accurate portrayals are not a primary focus of science in fictional media (Brewer and Ley 2022; Kirby 2011). Instead, filmmakers adjust scientific accuracy to "significantly enhance enjoyment or impact plausibility" and authenticity of a story rather than to portray the most realistic depiction of science (Kirby 2011, 112). Budgetary limitations and assumed audience expectations, for instance, significantly factor into portrayals of science in popular films (Kirby 2011), including superhero comics adaptations.

The intersection between science and magic is at its most fundamental in a super-protagonist's origin, this being the transformation that gives them superpowers. Using the definition of an origin as "the initial *moment of transformation*" (Locke 2005, 32), the science origin emerges from a distinct, catalyzing moment from human to superhuman. The metamorphosis of the human into the superhuman is a concept that long predates the advent of superhero comics. As creators search for avenues to merge contemporary science with magic to create an origin, they draw, whether intentionally or not, on the long history of Western esotericism, in which transformation of the human into superhuman was a central concept (Ross 2019; Kripal 2019, 2011; Knowles 2007). Western esotericism is a mystic tradition spanning multiple millennia which does not separate science from religious and supernatural power. It was these cultural dynamics which emerged again in 1930s America, where, as Chris Knowles argues, "science, philosophy, religion, and the occult all merged in a general yearning to overcome intractable human problems and improve mankind's future" (2007, 112). In seeking to bridge the gap between science and magic and strengthen the realism of a superhero story, creators often unknowingly rely on the cultural precedent found in alchemy and occult sciences. Drawing on films and comics, this chapter examines some of the most iconic and popular super-protagonists in this context, with the aim of better understanding the stories we tell about science, magic, and the occult in mainstream pop culture, and what they teach us about the cultural power of science.

Super Pseudo-Science – Can Alchemy Give You Superpowers?

Alchemy and occult sciences have particular relevance in superhero media, as alchemy is culturally associated with extreme transformation and superhuman power. One of the core philosophies of alchemy claimed that all matter had an inner divinity equated with incorruptibility, perfection, and knowledge trapped within the corruptible flesh (Abraham 1998; Maxwell-Stuart 2012). Alchemists also believed that the experimental process of metallic transformation was mirrored in the alchemist, as "each metal was … a microcosm of man" (Browne 1948, 17). In the laboratory, not only would metals mature into perfection but so too would the alchemist. Alchemy is the progenitor of the idea that science can be used to achieve spiritual and human perfection, creating a cultural belief that practitioners acquired dangerous, superhuman powers. Throughout history, alchemy was ascribed a number of extraordinary abilities such as immortality (Maxwell-Stuart 2012), the creation of homunculi (Newman 2004), and the ability to defeat the Antichrist (DeVun 2009). These supernatural abilities were transmitted into science fiction through *Frankenstein* (1818) and Victor Frankenstein, who describes alchemists, the inspiration behind his work, thus:

> these philosophers, whose hands seem only made to dabble in dirt, and their eyes to pore over the microscope or crucible, have indeed performed miracles. … They have acquired new and almost unlimited powers; they can command the thunders of heaven, mimic the earthquake, and even mock the invisible world with its own shadows.
>
> *(Shelley [1818] 1992, 46–47)*

By the 19th century, popular culture insinuated that alchemical experimentation could grant a supernatural, divine power to their users. Popular culture, however, does not remember the alchemist kindly, perceiving their research as transgressive and echoing "perennially convincing patterns of horror, mystery, and evil" (Haynes 2007, 29). Mythical and fictional

31

alchemists like Frankenstein are some of the first science superheroes (Knowles 2007), using both occult magic and science to acquire power. Yet they are also symbols of the danger of crossing the limits of science and the negative consequences of blurring this line. The question thus arises as to what extent these sinister connotations of alchemy appear in superhero comics, especially the depiction of science origins.

Before we can identify alchemy in superhero media, however, we first must establish what popular culture considers to be alchemical. Considering science in comics typically has an artistic function to set the scene (Reynolds 1992, 16), and that comics and film adaptations are highly visual, the aesthetics of alchemy are one of the most useful points of reference for alchemical themes in superhero media. Of particular relevance is the alchemical laboratory, as one of the most prominent instances of ostensibly plausible science origins comes in the common trope of the laboratory science accident (Koole et al. 2013, 144). Visual portrayals of the laboratory in popular media retain clear influences from alchemical laboratory aesthetics and iconographies (Straub 2016; Schummer and Spector 2007a,b). Almost 40% of chemistry-related movies, for instance, are consistent with an alchemical laboratory setting (Weingart 2006, 37). Of the various iconographies that appear within popular culture, there is a distinctive catalogue of equipment and aesthetics associated with alchemy. Historical elements of alchemy include "bubbling gases and variously shaped glass flasks and vials" (Straub 2016, 55), as well as vibrant colors emblematic of the stages of alchemy like the "yellowing" and the "reddening" (Kasmire [2019] 2021; Fraser 2018). Art trends in the 17th century linked alchemical laboratories with cluttered workspaces (Hill 1975). Once the alchemical laboratory enters popular fiction, it becomes associated with electricity and machinery through early films like *Metropolis* (Lang 1927) and *Frankenstein* (Whale 1931) (Hoesterey 2001; Holmes 2008), as well as staged photography of "quasi-alchemical" figures such as Nikola Tesla (Straub 2016, 55). Where historical laboratories typify oddity, staged and fictional laboratories have a menacing atmosphere, with "fizzing electrical generators, sinister bubbling vats and violent explosions" (Holmes 2008, 335). This vast canon of iconographies embodies alchemy's "sociocultural associations and connotations" (Schummer and Spector 2007b, 213), including the prominent occult science theme of transgressive transformation into the superhuman. Applied to superhero media, these iconographies act as cultural signifiers of supernatural-scientific origins, carrying with them an underlying notion capable of stretching the limits of science into the realm of disbelief. By examining these alchemical images within superhero science, especially science origins, we can understand the underlying interactions between science and the occult in superhero media.

Spiders and Sinister Science on the Silver Screen – The Many Lab Accidents of the Spider-Man Films

The relationship between magic and science in film adaptations is markedly different to that shown in comics. Where comics had reveled in the fantastical nature of their medium, superhero films emerge in a period where the general belief is that in a modern, rational society, audiences struggle to suspend disbelief to properly appreciate the fantastical tropes of the superhero film (Ornes 2015; Koole et al. 2013; Kirby 2011). Stray too far from realism, and audiences are no longer able to properly enjoy a film. Superhero films of the 2000s and early 2010s instead seek to defend themselves from audience skepticism through "(superficially) believable scientific terms" (Koole et al. 2013, 144). The "Einstein-Rosen Bridge", Jane

Foster's term for the magical Bifrost in *Thor* (Branagh 2011, 00:33:34) comes to mind, as the writers thought "wormhole", the more recognizable synonym, sounded "too 90s" (Ornes 2015, 939). In *Thor's* new non-magical framework, it comes as no surprise when Foster later quotes Arthur C. Clarke: "magic is just science we don't understand yet" (01:01:00). While this period of films still equates science with magic, the mood has shifted in the opposite direction of the comics: the rational trumps the mystic. Amidst the superhero film boom, science origins, especially ostensibly believable ones, are suddenly more common than ever. When it comes to science origins in superhero films, there is no larger pool to draw from than the various film franchises of Spider-Man. Consider the multiversal crossover *Spider-Man: No Way Home* (Watts 2021). Of the main cast, there are seven victims of lab accidents in the one film: five supervillains and (at least) two Spider-Men. In addition, Spider-Man is the most successful superhero at the global box office, with the highest grossing film franchise led by a singular hero (Bebakova 2024). When it comes to examining the science accident trope on the silver screen, there is no better superhero nor rogues' gallery to put under the microscope.

As one might expect, alchemy has an almost ubiquitous influence on this origin trope in the live-action Spider-Man franchise, as laboratories where transformations occur are consistently depicted with alchemical iconography. Even from the first such transformations in *Spider-Man* (Raimi 2002), especially within the Oscorp Laboratory of Norman Osborn, there are clear stylistic elements that resonate with alchemical iconography, most prominently in the active agent of the transformation sequence, the Goblin formula (and its gaseous form in a large glass chamber) (00:16:32). Replicating alchemical colors, gases, and the vessels they were seen in, which were as much a symbol of transformation as they were an effect of the alchemical process, emphasizes the alchemical influence on this particular science origin. Alchemical iconography also appears in the broader set-design of the Oscorp Laboratory: the metal table with straps (00:15:53) is highly reminiscent of *Frankenstein* (Whale 1931), and the palette of sickly green lighting and dull greys walls contributes to the overall gothic aesthetic of the sequence (00:14:55). When Oscorp Laboratory is first introduced earlier in the film, however, very few of these alchemical elements are present, appearing only as the accident approaches. This progressive introduction of alchemical iconography into the set establishes a sort of development for the space itself, morphing itself from a modern laboratory into an alchemical one, and thus visually associating alchemy with laboratory accidents. *Spider-Man* (Raimi 2002) also establishes a conventional style for how the Green Goblin transformation site appears within the franchise, with the visual design of both The Goblin's Lair in *Spider-Man 3* (Raimi 2007) and the Secret Projects Laboratory in *The Amazing Spider-Man 2* (Webb 2014) sharing iconographic similarities to the Oscorp Laboratory. Across all Goblin transformations in the broader franchise, alchemical aesthetics are a defining feature.

This connection between alchemical laboratories and lab accidents is not restricted to the Green Goblin transformations. Octavius' laboratory in *Spider-Man 2* (Raimi 2004), for instance, initially divorces itself from the common features of alchemical laboratories, presented instead with a well-lit, positive, collaborative environment. As the plot progresses toward the lab accident, the lighting dims, switching the camera's focus onto the strange, looming machine at the center of the sequence (00:35:26). Throughout this scene, the laboratory transitions into aesthetics typical of the alchemical laboratory: powerful machinery and darkness, building suspense for the inevitable failure of the fusion machine. The internal progression to the alchemical laboratory is completed when arcs of electricity reminiscent of *Frankenstein* (Whale 1931) strike Octavius and fuse the metal appendages of Doc Ock to his spine (00:38:39). The visual development of the genetics laboratory in *The Amazing Spider-Man* (Webb 2012) also mirrors that of the lab accident sites of the Raimi trilogy. Although initially presented as open and collaborative, the lead-up to the transformation of Curt Connors introduces alchemical iconography into the space. Around the laboratory, glass containers filled with green and orange liquids introduce the colored liquids of the alchemical laboratory into the scene (01:03:39). With no major sources of light, the space becomes lit with gothic green undertones, in sharp contrast to the bright white lights seen earlier in the film (01:03:46), and the vibrantly-green Goblin formula returns as the Lizard serum (01:03:42), once again with stunning transformative power. Like the Oscorp Laboratory in *Spider-Man* (Raimi 2002), alchemical iconography creeps into the space throughout these sequences, culminating in the science accident. The visual progression of these laboratories further cements the connection between alchemical iconography and the lab accident within the franchise.

Other sites of laboratory accidents in the films are instead immediately presented with varying degrees of alchemical iconography. The least "alchemical" site of a lab accident in the franchise is the Columbia University laboratory of *Spider-Man* (Raimi 2002), where Peter Parker is bitten by a spider. This lab is not necessarily "alchemical" in the sense of the bubbling beakers iconography. There is, however, one prominent iconographic feature that this laboratory shares with alchemy: the cluttered, chaotic workspace. Despite an overall lack of alchemical iconography, the one existing symbol – chaos – is what facilitates the accident: in the disorganization of the lab, one missing spider goes unnoticed. Alchemical elements to a lesser extent appear in Sandman's transformation in *Spider-Man 3* (Raimi 2007), which features disorganized, harried scientists and a large dangerous machine at the super collider facility that transforms, and Electro's in *The Amazing Spider-Man 2* (Webb 2014), with colored liquids in conical flasks that seem out of place in a zoology lab, as well as notable arcs of electricity. While the site of a laboratory accident in the Spider-Man franchise is not always the most conventional alchemical laboratory, alchemical iconography is always present at the transformation moment: the origin (Locke 2005). Not every laboratory in superhero films is fully alchemical. It is, however, the symbols of alchemy that herald and, in most cases, facilitate these accidents.

The ubiquity of alchemical iconography in these accident sites suggests that the alchemical laboratory is the defining visual feature of the laboratory accident, exploiting thematic associations between alchemy and extra-ordinary transformative power. Superhero laboratory accidents are extreme events of significant negative consequence (Muscio 2023, 7) and thus require deliberate consideration of the way in which they bridge science and impossibility. Alchemy, especially the alchemical laboratory, is the seemingly-scientific mask that superhero films use to make the laboratory accident plausible. Using alchemy as a cultural shorthand allows creators to strengthen the plausibility of their films without sacrificing entertainment for scientific authenticity. Spider-Man films legitimize the dangerous transformative power of the laboratory accident not with science nor magic, but rather the cultural intersection of the two: transgressive occult science.

"Psychology. Technology. #%&*ology". – Occult Joker
Super-Science in DC Comics

Science is rocket fuel not only for Marvel's protagonists, but also for DC's superheroes and supervillains. From Dr Harleen Quinzel (aka Harley Quinn) to Dr Pamela Isley (Poison

Ivy), science drives the development of characters, identities, and plots (see, e.g., Santos and Jürgens 2023; Kinsella and Jürgens 2024), but it also "creates" them in the first place, either by (criminal) accidents or out of malicious ambition. The "plant-based" scientist-super-protagonists of Dr Jason Woodrue (The Floronic Man) and Dr Alec Holland (Swamp Thing), two former biologists/botanists, are splendid examples of "science gone awry" (Pasko et al. 2021, 247), resulting in confused, but super-abled human-plant hybrids. Not a plant, and less confused, Bruce Wayne/Batman of the same universe is quite the scientist, and what a transdisciplinary polymath! Science defines his Batman identity. He states to have "sampled and tested [Joker's] blood dozens of times!" and to have "created nearly a **hundred** cures for Joker toxins over the years. – antitoxins, antibios, steroids" (Snyder and Capullo 2015, emphasis in the original). He even tests Joker venom on himself to fully understand how it works ("I need to know how it feels", Hine and McDaniel 2011; see also Morrison and Daniel 2010). In addition to being a virologist, biochemist, and biologist, Batman uses methods and approaches that characterize him as a data scientist, forensic scientist, microscopist, engineer and, overall, a thoroughly scientific person, as he explains in *Batman: Bloodstorm*: "My life is **founded on deduction**" (Moench and Jones 2016, emphasis in the original) and scientific reasoning. Unsurprisingly, his Bat Cave, whose original design was inspired by magazines such as *National Geographic* and *Popular Science* (Andrae 2011, 77; Kane 1989, 103), resembles a laboratory, with flickering computer screens, lab equipment, and never-before-seen quaint scientific machinery (see, e.g., Brady 2020). From time to time, he borrows a corpse from "Gotham U's science department" for his studies (Zdarsky et al. 2024). While Batman's endeavors in and beyond the Bat Cave-lab are anchored in Bruce's scientific knowledge and reasoning, his arch-nemesis, the Joker, is not only associated with science themes and tropes (Jürgens et al. 2022; Jürgens et al. 2024), but at the origin of what Batman studies through scientific means, blending "Illusion. Psychology. Technology. #%&* ology" (Morrison and Van Fleet [2007] 2014).

In some stories, the origins of the Joker character themselves are linked to a lab accident (see "This one'll kill you, Batman!") or dark science machinations, as in *Batman: Nosferatu* (1999), where "the miraculous **Laughing Man!**" (Lofficier et al. 2017, 155), aka the Joker, is "painstakingly **assembled**" from corpses in "The Cabinet of Dr. Arkham" (156) and animated by a psychomancer-scientist for violent purposes of the murderous kind. With Bruce Wayne's mother pointedly commenting from her seat in the audience: "Now science adds to the population" (Moench and Jones 2000, 12), in *Batman: Haunted Gotham* (2000), a dubious scientist also reanimates a corpse in a public science show, which becomes the "patchwork joker" (87), another soulless killer clown creature. These versions of the Joker are created by occult lab scientists tapping into alchemy (see above); and in *Batman Volume 7: Endgame* (2015), it is again a scientist who unleashes the full potential of an antediluvian substance hidden in Joker's spine, which is capable of altering basic life patterns "like some reverse Frankenstein" and transforms into an uberpotent virus that even Batman struggles to combat. The Joker is thus not only his own chemistry kit, the origin of viral life, but he is also framed and celebrated by a scientist as a twisted superhero, as "Gotham's own Dionysian man – Dionysus, the god of madness and tragedy … associated with rebirth" (Snyder and Capullo 2015). So perhaps the Joker is, as we read in Morrison's *Clown at Midnight* ([2007] 2014), more of "a new human mutation"? And more than just

bred of slimy industrial waters, spawned in a world of bright carcinogens and acid rains. Maybe he is the model for 21st-century big-time multiplex man, shuffling selves like a croupier deals cards, to buffer the shocks and work some alchemy that might just turn the lead of tragedy and horror into the fierce, chaotic gold of the laughter of the damned.

(Morrison and Van Fleet [2007] 2014)

In recent comic book stories such as *Batman: Europa* (2016) or *Batman & The Joker: The Deadly Duo* (2023), the Joker and Batman are forced to work *together*, which includes uncovering a clownifying virus bioengineered with the Joker's DNA, as STEM cell research meets synthetic biology, which results in "an entirely **new** organism". This again points to the Joker's biological contribution to regenerative science and "genetically engineered superbeings" (Silvestri and Prianto 2023). All of this raises an interesting question: If the Joker is at the origin of regenerative science and scientifically enhanced superbeings, and superheroes are by nature larger than life (Wolk 2007, 92), which includes having super abilities, powers, or capacities (e.g. regenerative ones), does this not bring the Joker closer to the realm of superheroes?

While the Joker may not have the superpowers of the Green Goblin or the Lizard, he nonetheless warrants a place amongst the great science villains of the comics world. He also, along with other science-adjacent DC characters, is a curious contrast to the archetypal Marvel "science experiment gone wrong" origin story. Consider the mad scientist as portrayed by both the Green Goblin and the Joker. Even in the opening minutes of *Spider-Man* (Raimi 2002), Marvel's Norman Osborn is introduced as "something of a scientist himself" (00:05:08), framed as professional and methodical if somewhat ambitious. This (mostly) moral approach contrasts his "mad" Goblin persona that explicitly results from subsequent experimentation on himself (00:17:37). In Marvel, science and scientists precede and even cause madness. It is here that the need to navigate this transformation from methodical to mad arises through the cultural shorthand of occult science. In DC comics, however, the Joker's madness is his defining trait, not his science. His madness itself can also transform others: as Batman asks psychologist-turned-villain Harley Quinn in "Dr. Quinn's Diagnosis" in *Legends of the Dark Knight 100-Page Super Spectacular #1* (2014), "Are you a naive *victim* of the Joker's madness or did you become this by choice?" (Zubkavich and Googe [2014] 2015, 173). The Joker's madness precedes and even motivates his science. Science in DC, particularly occult science, is rather a tool of fantastical, near-superhuman power for those already mad. Joker science and transformation, like the science in comics with a primarily aesthetic function (Reynolds 1992, 16), exists not to explain but to entertain and enhance storytelling. In the spirit of this chapter, perhaps this difference between Marvel and DC is best explained in terms of an (occult) science experiment. If Marvel's "scientist gone mad" archetype is the alchemist, the man transformed by pushing science to its bounds, science-adjacent characters in DC like the Joker are Philosopher's Stones: the supernatural catalyst born from occult science which causes further transformation.

Science and Super-Protagonists – Conclusion

This chapter discusses the relationship between science and magic within superhero comics through the lens of occult science and alchemy. Alchemy and the alchemical laboratory in popular culture are associated with distinct visual iconographies identifiable in a wide range of superhero media. In Marvel, as exemplified by the Spider-Man film franchise, alchemical features signify and legitimize the extreme transformations caused by laboratory accident origins. In DC, through a number of examples, mainly from the Batman-Joker universe, we have uncovered different ways in which science, laboratories, and science-related origin stories come together: these include different ways of doing science, experiencing science, using and abusing science, being "scientized" or "becoming" science, discovering and experiencing oneself through science, and science as a shared (dubious) identity. The various appearances and applications of these sinister science dimensions in superhero media emphasize the underlying influence that the occult continues to have in popular culture. This continuity of occult sciences within superhero media offers key insights into historical and cultural influences that shape popular depictions of science. There is a general belief that the alchemist/mad scientist stereotype is becoming less common in the 21st century (Kirby 2017; Haynes 2014), despite an alchemical "pre-occupation" in popular media (Weingart 2007, 279). Even as the mad scientist character falls out of favor within popular culture, the alchemical laboratory is thriving in conventional tropes of the most popular film genre of the past decade.

Comics invite "leaps of imagination" as they are "full of enticing blank spaces, in both space and time, for readers to decorate in our minds" (Wolk 2007, 133) and also provide characters that can be understood as bold metaphors for ideas that readers care about, fear, and hope for. The sinister power embodied by occult science provides a canvas for creators to explore the extreme and often horrifying consequences of superhero science. Much like Spider-Man's origin story is subject to changes in popular science discourse (what was once a radioactive spider becomes a genetically modified one [Locke 2005, 43]), superhero media use alchemy and the occult to highlight our fears about science unknowns. Yet, it also uses their fundamental presence in the cultural narrative of science to bridge the gap between imagination and doubt (Haynes 2007), combating skepticism and disbelief with the familiar unfamiliarity of occult alchemy. As superhero science expands beyond the bounds of authenticity into the realm of the fantastic, so too must our understanding of how science is represented in superhero media, and subsequently in popular culture as a whole, acknowledge the historically indistinct relationship between science and magic.

References

Abraham, Lyndy. 1998. *A Dictionary of Alchemical Imagery*. Cambridge University Press.

Andrae, Thomas. 2011. *Creators of the Superheroes*. Hermes Press.

Bebakova, Timea. 2024. "These Are the Highest-Grossing Movie Franchises of All Time." *MovieWeb*, January 2. https://movieweb.com/highest-grossing-movie-franchises/.

Brady, Matt. 2020. "Batman and Exponential Growth: Contagion and SARS-CoV-2." *The Science Of*, April 30. https://thescienceof.org/batman-contagion-and-sars-cov-2/.

Branagh, Kenneth, 2011. dir. *Thor*. Paramount Pictures.

Brewer, Paul R., and Barbara L. Ley. 2022. *Science in the Media: Popular Images and Public Perceptions*. Routledge.

Browne, Cornell A. 1948. "Rhetorical and Religious Aspects of Greek Alchemy." *Ambix* 3 (1–2): 15–25. https://doi.org/10.1179/amb.1948.3.1-2.15.

DeVun, Leah. 2009. *Prophecy, Alchemy, and the End of Time: John of Rupescissa in the Late Middle Ages*. Columbia University Press.

Fraser, Kyle. 2018. "Distilling Nature's Secrets: The Sacred Art of Alchemy." In *Oxford Handbook of Science and Medicine in the Classical World*, edited by Paul T. Keyser and John Scarborough. Oxford University Press.

Haynes, Roslynn. 2007. "The Alchemist in Fiction: The Master Narrative." In *The Public Image of Chemistry*, edited by Joachim Schummer, Bernadette Bensaude-Vincent and Brigitte Van Tiggelen. World Scientific Publishing Co. Pte. Ltd.

Haynes, Roslynn D. 2014. "Whatever Happened to the 'Mad, Bad' Scientist? Overturning the Stereotype." *Public Understanding of Science* 25 (1): 31–44. https://doi.org/10.1177/0963662514535689.

Hill, Christopher R. 1975. "The Iconography of the Laboratory." *Ambix* 22 (2): 102–110. https://doi.org/10.1179/AMB.1975.22.2.102.

Hine, David, and Scott McDaniel. 2011. *Batman Imposters*. DC Comics.

Hoesterey, Ingeborg. 2001. *Pastiche: Cultural Memory in Art, Film, Literature*. Indiana University Press.

Holmes, Richard. 2008. *The Age of Wonder*. Harper Press.

Jürgens, Anna-Sophie, Stefan Buchenberger, Laurence Grove, and Matteo Farinella. 2024. "On the Visual Narratives of Ice in Popular Culture: Comics on Ice, Icy Villains and Ice Science." In *Communicating Ice through Popular Art and Aesthetics*, edited by Anne Hemkendreis and Anna-Sophie Jürgens. Palgrave Macmillan.

Jürgens, Anna-Sophie, Anastasiya Fiadotava, and David Tscharke. 2024. "The Cheshire Clown: Joker's Infectious Laughter." In *Moral Dimensions of Humour: Essays on Humans, Heroes and Monsters*, edited by Ben Nickl and Mark Rolfe. Tampere University Press.

Jürgens, Anna-Sophie, David Tscharke, and Jochen Brocks. 2022. "From Caligari to Joker: The Clown Prince of Crime's Psychopathic Science." *Journal of Graphic Novels & Comics* 13:5, 685–699.

Kane, Bob, and Tom Andrae. 1989. Batman & Me. Eclipse Books.

Kasmire, Julia. (2019) 2021. "Managing Balance: Pursuit of Equilibrium Permeates the History of Science and Influences Contemporary Investigations." *Humanistic Management Journal* 6: 133–146. https://doi.org/10.1007/s41463-019-00066-6.

Kinsella, Aisling, and Anna-Sophie Jürgens. 2024. "Gender and Terror Tangled in the Weeds: Poison Ivy between Eco-Feminism and Eco-Terrorism." *Journal of Graphic Novels and Comics* 1–16. https://doi.org/10.1080/21504857.2024.2392601

Kirby, David. 2011. *Lab Coats in Hollywood: Science, Scientists, and Cinema*. MIT Press.

Kirby, David. 2017. "The Changing Popular Images of Science." In *The Oxford Handbook of the Science of Science Communication*, edited by Kathleen Hall Jamieson, Dan M. Kahan and Dietram A. Scheufele. Oxford University Press.

Knowles, Chris. 2007. *Our Gods Wear Spandex: The Secret History of Comic Book Heroes*. Red Wheel/Weiser.

Koole, Sander L., Daniel A. Fockenberg, Mattie Tops, and Iris K. Schneider. 2013. "The Birth and Death of the Superhero Film." In *Fade to Black: Death in Classic and Contemporary Cinema*, edited by J. Greenberg and D. Sullivan. Palgrave Macmillan.

Kripal, Jeffery J. 2011. *Mutants & Mystics: Science Fiction, Superhero Comics, and the Paranormal*. University of Chicago Press.

Kripal, Jeffrey J. 2019. "Can Superhero Comics Really Transmit Esoteric Knowledge?" In *Hermes Explains: Thirty Questions about Western Esotericism*, edited by Wouter J. Hanegraaff, Peter J. Forshaw and Marco Pasi. University of Amsterdam Press.

Lang, Fritz, dir. 1927. *Metropolis*. Parufamet.

Locke, Simon. 2005. "Fantastically Reasonable: Ambivalence in the Representation of Science and Technology in Super-Hero Comics." *Public Understanding of Science* 14 (1): 25–46. https://doi.org/10.1177/0963662505048197.

Lofficier, Randy, Jean-Marc Lofficier, and Ted McKeever. 2017. "Batman: Nosferatu." In *Elseworlds: Justice League Volume 2*. DC Comics.

Maxwell-Stuart, P. G. 2012. *The Chemical Choir: A History of Alchemy*. Continuum International Publishing Group.

Mills, A. R. 2014. *American Theology, Superhero Comics, and Cinema: The Marvel of Stan Lee and the Revolution of a Genre*. Routledge.

Moench, Doug, and Kelley Jones. 2000. *Batman: Haunted Gotham*. DC Comics.

Moench, Doug, and Kelley Jones. 2016. "Batman: Bloodstorm." In *Elseworlds: Batman Volume 2*. DC Comics.

Morrison, Grant, and Tony S. Daniel. 2010. *Batman R.I.P.* DC Comics.

Morrison, Grant, and John Van Fleet. [2007] 2014. "The Clown at Midnight" (originally *Batman* #663). In *Batman and Son*. DC Comics.

Muscio, Alessandro. 2023. "The Ambiguous Role of Science and Technology in Marvel Superhero Comics: From their 'Golden Age' to the Present-Day." *Technological Forecasting and Social Change* 186: B: 112149. https://doi.org/10.1016/j.techfore.2022.122149.

Newman, William R. 2004. *Promethean Ambitions: Alchemy and the Quest to Perfect Nature*. University of Chicago Press.

Ornes, Stephen. 2015. "Science On-Screen and behind the Scenes." *Science and Culture* 112 (4): 939. https://doi.org/10.1073/pnas.1421546111.

Pasko, Martin, Tom Yeates, and Jan Duursema, et al. 2021. *Swamp Thing: The Bronze Age Vol.3*. DC Comics.

Raimi, Sam, dir. 2002. *Spider-Man*. Sony Pictures Releasing.

Raimi, Sam, dir. 2004. *Spider-Man 2*. Sony Pictures Releasing.

Raimi, Sam, dir. 2007. *Spider-Man 3*. Sony Pictures Releasing.

Regalado, A. J. 2015. *Bending Steel: Modernity and the American Superhero*. University Press of Mississippi.

Reynolds, Richard. 1992. *Super Heroes: A Modern Mythology*. University Press of Mississippi.

Ross, Susan L. 2019. "Who Put the Super in Superhero? Transformation and Heroism as a Function of Evolution." *Frontiers in Psychology* 9: 2514. https://doi.org/10.3389/fpsyg.2018.02514.

Santos, Dan, and Anna-Sophie Jürgens. 2023. "From Harleen Quinzel to Harley Quinn: Science, Symmetry and Transformation." *Journal of Graphic Novels and Comics* 15:2: 283–297.

Schummer, Joachim, and Tami I. Spector. 2007a. "Popular Images versus Self-Images of Science: Visual Representations of Science in Clipart Cartoons and Internet Photographs." In *Science Images and Popular Images of the Sciences*, edited by Peter Weingart and Bernd Huppauf. Taylor & Francis Group.

Schummer, Joachim, and Tami I. Spector. 2007b. "The Visual Image of Chemistry: Perspectives from the History of Art and Science." In *HYLE – International Journal for Philosophy of Chemistry*, edited by Joachim Schummer, Bernadette Bensaude-Vincent and Brigette Van Tiggelen. World Scientific Publishing Co.

Shelley, Mary. [1818] 1992. *Frankenstein or The Modern Prometheus*, edited by Maurice Hindle. Penguin Books.

Silvestri, Marc, and Arif Prianto. 2023. *Batman & The Joker: The Deadly Duo*. DC Comics.

Snyder, Scott, and Gregg Capullo. 2015. *Batman Volume 7: Endgame*. DC Comics.

Straub, Verena. 2016. "Science in Pictures: A Historical Perspective." In *New Laboratories: Historical and Critical Perspectives on Contemporary Developments*, edited by Charlotte Klonk. Walter de Gruyter GmbH.

Watts, Jon, dir. 2021. *Spider-Man: No Way Home*. Sony Pictures Releasing.

Webb, Mark, dir. 2012. *The Amazing Spider-Man*. Sony Pictures Releasing.

Webb, Mark, dir. 2014. *The Amazing Spider-Man 2*. Sony Pictures Releasing.

Weingart, Peter. 2006. "Chemists and their Craft in Fiction Film." *HYLE--International Journal for Philosophy of Chemistry* 12 (1): 31–44. https://www.hyle.org/journal/issues/12-1/weingart.pdf.

Weingart, Peter. 2007. "The Ambivalence towards New Knowledge." In *Science Images and Popular Images of the Sciences*, edited by Peter Weingart and Bernd Huppauf. Taylor & Francis Group.

Whale, James, dir. 1931. *Metropolis*. Universal Pictures.

Wolk, Douglas. 2007. *Reading Comics: How Graphic Novels Work and What They Mean*. Da Capo Press.

Zdarsky, Chip, Guiseppe Camuncoli, Andrea Sorrentino, et al. 2024. *Batman: The Joker: Year One*. DC Comics.

Zubkavich, Jim, and Neil Googe. [2014] 2015. "Dr. Quinn's Diagnosis." In *Batman: Harley Quinn*. DC Comics. Originally published in *Legends of the Dark Knight 100-page Super Spectacular* 1by DC Comics.

4

EXPERIMENTATION AND CONTAINMENT

The Metafictional Superhero

Orion Ussner Kidder

Metafiction is almost a defining feature of the superhero. While an example of the genre can be recognizable without metafiction – because all it really takes is a colorful costume and a mission to "fight crime" – metafiction has been a key ingredient of the superhero since very soon after its conception. There are two specific expressions of metafiction that emerge from the way the superhero is created and disseminated into the world: shared universes and analogue heroes. Both are a product of the superhero publishing industry, but they are also a product of the creativity and imagination of artists, writers, editors, and other creators of superhero stories. Superheroes engage with all the other forms of metafiction that are available, such as self-consciousness and comedy, but these two arise directly from the superhero as a generic figure. The pattern that emerges from these two forms of metafiction is that creatives engage in narrative experiments, often marketing stunts, and these experiments have a potentially destabilizing effect on the internal reality of the fiction. However, those same experiments are subsequently contained by the genre and within the industry, thus converting them to stabilizing effects. The pattern even holds for superheroes in other media, specifically film and television, where superheroes have found a second home. This is, of course, a familiar cycle in the history of art, philosophy, politics, and culture in general: the rebellious avant-garde becoming the establishment that the new avant-garde rebels against. Superheroes are one small genre that experiences this cycle, although is important to note that the metafictional experiments that appear in that genre rarely qualify as truly rebellious. This is not a story of creatives in conflict with executives, as though one experiments while the other only contains. Creatives are, by and large, just as interested in selling comics as executives, and executives in superhero comics are almost always former or practicing creatives. It is not a battle between art and commerce. It is the result of the fact that superheroes are a commercial genre. To understand how universes and analogues work, we need a theory of metafiction, one that is flexible, far-reaching, and allows for open-ended interpretations of a given example.

Methodology

Metafiction has been thoroughly studied, as have metacomics. Most recently, Roy T. Cook's (2017) chapter on metacomics in *The Routledge Companion to Comics* summarizes several

DOI: 10.4324/9781003366911-6

taxonomies of metacomic practice, specifically M. Thomas Inge (1995), Matthew Jones (2005), himself (Cook 2012), and Jesus Gonzalez (2014). To this list, I would add my own work on the subject, published in the same period as Cook's survey (Kidder 2008, 2010, 2012, 2016; Kidder and Gifford 2018). Cook has already covered most of this ground, so we need only review a few concepts within the scholarship on metafiction/metacomics to help organize and understand the metafictional devices that are specific to the superhero. Two core concepts will suffice: play with frames and the "poles" of metafiction.

Patricia Waugh's theory of metafiction, from her influential work *Metafiction: The Theory and Practice of* Self-Conscious Fiction (1984), is extremely practical for identifying what a given metafiction might be doing, and thus what meaning it constructs, if any. Waugh defines metafiction in terms of how it interacts with the *frame* of a given text (1984, 31). Waugh describes the frame as the super- and substructure of the fiction, that which keeps it both contained and upright, like the frame of a house: e.g., genre tropes, narrative rules, industry practices, and the like. By that logic, the frame is also the limits of a given text, the conventions that define the lines that the story cannot or should not cross: e.g., between fictions, between layers of fiction, or between fiction and so-called reality. This parallels Linda Hutcheon's assertion from *A Poetics of Postmodernism* (1988) that metafiction "first establishes and then crosses" its frames (1988, 109–110). That is to say, it has to build its frames in order to play with them. The point is that all fiction is framed but most fiction actively avoids calling attention to its frame. The window into its fictional world is structured for readers to look through it, not at it. Metafiction is the opposite. It makes a spectacle of interacting with the frame(s) of the text: foregrounding them, displaying awareness of them, demonstrating their limitations, crossing them, or destroying them all together.

Waugh also places metafiction on a spectrum that illustrates two extremes of how it tends to play with the frame: the *structural* and the *radical*. This distinction will become useful to the process of mapping experimentation and containment below. Structural metafiction "accepts a substantial real world whose significance is not entirely composed of relationships within language" (Waugh 1984, 53). Thus, this type of metafiction ultimately strengthens the frame. At the other end of the spectrum is radical metafiction, which "suggests there can never be an escape from the prisonhouse of language and either delights or despairs in this" (53). This can have the effect of performing the destruction of the frame, or collapsing ostensibly separate frames into each other. The point, for the purposes of examining the metafictional superhero, is to underline that not all metafiction is radical. In fact, a great deal of it is quite the opposite. Rather than questioning or critiquing the frame, it reinforces the frame. There is also nothing inherently better about radical metafiction than structural metafiction, though. They are equally capable of entertaining audiences and/or offering critiques. The examples of metafiction that follow will be analyzed in large part with regard to how they interact with their frames and, thus, where they sit on that spectrum of supporting to demolishing those frames.

Crossovers, Universes, and Multiverses

Shared superhero universes first appear as a side effect of *crossovers*. In crossovers, a character who was already a protagonist in their own right *crosses over* into another character's comic book. These are, of course, marketing stunts meant to sell more comic books, but they also imply that not only do these characters suddenly live in the same physical space with ostensibly a shared set of rules and history but that they always have. A new "fact" about the setting asserts itself in an early example of retroactive continuity. In Waugh's terms, each crossover calls attention to the frames that had existed separately around each individual character, and then it encloses them within a larger frame: a universe. Crossovers are, thus, structural meta-fictions because they strengthen rather than deconstructing the internal reality of the narratives they contain. This is neither new nor unique to the superhero, of course, but it becomes indelibly associated with the superhero. The first superhero crossovers happened in 1940 (see Sundell 1940a, 1940b; Everett 1940; Fox 1940), only a year after the first appearance of Superman (Sullivan 1938). They also immediately give rise to *super teams*, a frame that combines individual heroes into a group frame that is, itself, located within the universe frame. That said, these initial comic-book crossovers happened before there was a universe frame and thus would have had the metafictional effect of drawing attention to their individual frames because audiences had no reason to assume these characters lived in shared universes. Once shared universes were established as a part of the genre, though, their metafictional power was neutralized. This is possible in no small part because superhero comics are serially published, so there is always an opportunity to contain a story after it has been published. Shared universes are, therefore, also *brands*, training audiences to buy anything from a given universe/corporate owner rather than following specific creators or character. This is how shared universes become an inherent part of the genre and are subsequently contained by it.

On top of shared universes are multiverses. To put them in Waugh's terms, a multiverse is the frame that is created when universes overlap, just like a universe is a frame that is created when individual character frames overlap, and these individual universes are quite often the result of purchasing the intellectual property of a rival publisher. Superhero comics did not invent the concept of the multiverse. As with so many other tropes that arrive in them, multiverses were already flourishing in science fiction and fantasy. That said, multiverses have been an integral part of superhero comics since the early sixties, largely because they had to be implemented in only two shared universes in order to become the structure that governs the vast majority of superhero stories: DC Comics (owned by National Periodicals) and Marvel Comics (formerly called Timely/Atlas). Thus, by the 1990s, independent publishers created their own multiverses to mimic the content of those two dominant publishers in their attempts to enter that marketplace: e.g., Image's comics "aleph" (Moore and Veitch 1993) and Wildstorm's "snowflake" (Ellis and Green 1996). This is consistent with the manifest fact that multiverses started as sales gimmicks, crossovers between universes, but also the fact that the artistic motivation to both experiment and contain experiments is inseparable from the profit motive. DC Comics provides an extreme illustration of this pattern, one that requires a little bit of explanation to fully appreciate.

DC's corporate-owned multiverse begins with *Showcase* #4 (Kanigher and Infantino 1954), which introduces a retooled version of the Flash, whose comics were canceled in 1949. In a tip-of-the-hat to that original character, the first panel of the story features the new version reading a comic book featuring the old one. Before this reboot, the original character had been published by a rival company, All-American Comics, whom National had purchased in 1946, so multiverses are very much a product of acquisitional corporate policy at National Comics – a policy that continues to this day. There is no indication that this first panel in *Showcase* was intended as more than a gag, but it is nevertheless a radical metafiction, a device that Waugh calls a *mise en abyme*: a text that is nestled within itself (1984, 53). That one panel, showing the new character holding a comic book, thus calls attention to the same physical act that the reader is engaged in at the very moment of reading, and it implies a second shared universe, belonging to the new version of the character, in addition to the old shared universe, but a new universe that has access to the same comics that readers did just a few years earlier, thus raising the possibility that the new character lives in the reader's world, which is obviously impossible, but nevertheless intimates that "reality" might be just another universe on top of the two that now exist within that comic book. This jumble of implications is not immediately resolvable, as crossovers were, and it requires positing layers of reality in addition to the ones it directly depicts, two of which are not immediately distinguishable from each other, one of which might very well be "reality," depending how we define that concept.

This radical moment is contained, however, within just a few years when DC organizes its multiverse into separated, named universes (see Fox and Infantino 1961; Fox and Sekowsky 1964a), including those that represented rival publishers that National had by then acquired (e.g., All-American Comics and Fawcet Comics), thus normalizing them within DC Comics. The apotheosis of this containment occurs in a contrivance masquerading as a miniseries called *Crisis on Infinite Earths* (Wolfman and Perez 1985), in which DC collapses its multiverse into a single universe, one that would, once again, contain all the new characters it had acquired between the 1960s and the 1980s (e.g., Charlton Comics). Infinity, though, turns out to be very hard to contain because once they are a trope, multiverses are extremely easy to create. Thus, they reappear so quickly and with such regularity that DC's editorial feels the need to recontain them every few years in a new miniseries "event": *Zero Hour* (1994), *The Kingdom* (1999), *Infinite Crisis* (2005), *Final Crisis* (2008), *Flashpoint* (2011), *Convergence* (2015), *Rebirth* (2016), *Flashpoint Beyond* (2022), and *Dawn of DC* (2023). Even this list is arguably only partial given that there are other series from DC that are connected to this recontainment cycle. Thus, that cycle becomes embodied by multiverses and becomes extremely closely associated with the superhero genre to the point where, for example, *Marvel 1602* claims that the nature of superheroes is to obey the laws of storytelling (Gaiman and Kubert 2003), or DC's *The Kingdom* presents a model of superheroes that is so metafictional that it explicitly includes the audience's reality (Waid et al. 1999).

This apparent inability to contain infinity becomes its own form of containment, though. Comics that collapse, explode, or explain their multiverse eventually become just another sales gimmick, as evidenced by the sheer frequency of DC's recontainments, above. They become a recognizable trope, a standardized narrative that reenforces the known and expected nature of corporate-owned superhero comics: that they exist in fluid multiverses with metafictional implications. This trope has become so expected that when superheroes travel to other media, they frequently take the trope with them and with results that will be explored in more detail, below. Thus, while multiverses are narratively radical given that they render their shared universe unstable, they are economically structural given that they create a flow of money. Creators and audiences can "delight" in this fluid space all they like, to use Waugh's term (Waugh 1984, 53), just so long as Warner Bros. Discovery, Inc. and The Walt Disney Co. see the resulting profits. This experimentation/containment cycle occurs in analogues in a similar fashion.

Analogues and Variants

The analogue has been theorized already by Matthew Wolf-Meyer in "The World Ozymandias Made" (2003). He defines them as "characters [who] resemble other established superheroes, both in costuming and abilities" and thus "in their presence they make reference to the original[s]," but they also "have their own lives, their own continuity, and their own costumes" (2003, 504). An analogue therefore "allows the authors to partake of a particular aspect of the discourse of superhero comics, providing their readers with familiar iconography" (504). Warren Ellis (2005) sums up the same idea, claiming analogues are "about the audience's relationship with old characters." That said, analogues are analogous, not identical. Alan Moore describes them as "just taking [the originals] a step to the left or right, just twisting them a little bit" (Kavenaugh 2000), in reference to the cast of *Watchman*. The upshot is that analogues by definition contain differences from their originals and stand in juxtaposition with them. It is the gap between the original and the analogue that can create a commentary on those originals and, by extension, on the genre itself. To put that in Waugh's terms, Wolf-Meyer's analysis means that analogues interact with the frame of genre rather than of narrative or diegesis. Variants, on the other hand, are analogues created by the rights-holder of the original character, so they can include legally owned elements such as names and logos, and they are approved by the owners. They otherwise function the same as analogues, although they are less likely to contain a genuinely critical commentary on their originals.

Certain types of characters lend themselves to analogues based on popularity and sheer age, which makes it easier to achieve an instant emotional relationship with the audience. The *iconicity* of superheroes also makes creating analogues of them relatively easy. Peter Coogan's definition of the superhero – comprising mission, powers, and identity/costume (2006, 30–33) – points us toward those iconic qualities. Each superhero contains a core collection of traits that are associated with that character (e.g., power sets; costume colors; animal totems; the elements; symbols such as letters, images, and flags). Superman, being the oldest and most widely recognizable of all superheroes, is singularly representative of the genre as a whole. Almost any flying character in a cape cannot help but evoke him in viewer's minds. He functions as a synecdoche for the superhero and is a go-to character to use to articulate a commentary on it, which is usually what analogues do. Superman, thus, has a huge number of analogues and/or variants, many of them containing just one discreet change in identity (e.g., female, Black, talking animal) or a moral inversion (e.g., tyrant, criminal, Nazi, Communist), but many others are simple knockoffs (e.g., Captain Marvel, Captain Atom, Supreme, Mr. Majestic). Wonder Woman, Batman, and Captain America have similarly long lists of analogues and variants identifiable by the characters' main traits: godlike woman warrior, non-powered vigilante billionaire, and nationalist super-soldier, respectively. Alternatively, characters who are less well known, even if they have similarly identifiable traits, have relatively few analogues, for example, the Green Lantern, a character that is just as old and has just as many highly recognizable traits. There is a pattern of containment in analogue characters that is especially visible in analogue teams.

Analogues and variants of whole superhero teams achieve their effect by depicting groups of heroes who individually resemble pre-existing characters or who reference a particular team dynamic or theme. The Umbrella Academy, for example, does not resemble the X-Men but reference them by virtue of having highly varied powers and a mentor/father figure who treats them like his children and/or students (Way and Bá 2008; Blackman and McKeown 2019–2024). Because the superhero is now popular and lucrative outside of comics, there are today far more analogue teams in media than in decades past, so a lot more people recognize the references. Analogue teams are distinguishable from each by the kinds of critiques they offer (or do not offer). Some analogue teams only evoke an emotional response in the viewer, such as a Justice League analogue being murdered in *Invincible* (Kirkman and Walker 2003; Racioppa 2021). Others are parodies, such as the League of Honor in *The Pro* (Ennis and Conner 2002). Simple villainy is displayed by the original Squadron Supreme (Thomas and Buscema 1971) and the Crime Syndicate of America (Fox and Sekowsky 1964b). Finally, in *The Squadron Supreme* (Gruenwald and Hall 1985), *Watchmen* (Moore and Gibbons 1985), *The Authority* (Ellis and Hitch 1999), *The Ultimates* (Millar and Hitch 2002), and *The Boys* (Ennis and Robinson 2006; Kripke 2019), superheroes are immoral figures by definition because of the authority they presume to possess for no reason other than the violence they wield, hence for example, the team name "the Authority." These highly critical analogue teams are, however, not difficult to contain.

In all the above cases of critical analogue teams, except for *The Boys*, the characters/narratives slowly shifted from stories of corruption to simple power fantasies, no longer critiquing superhero violence but rather indulging in it. This happens if and when they become popular enough that they are turned by their publishers into ongoing characters and/or are absorbed into their respective multiverses and universes. The Authority and Squadron Supreme, for example, have both been absorbed into the main universes of their respective publishers, both reduced to just another superhero team (see Aaron 2021; Morrison and Janín 2021). This is analogue containment; stories that start as critiques of the moral underpinnings of the superhero eventually transform into yet more saleable superheroes. Ironically, the most successful critiques are often the ones that make the characters the most popular/profitable and, thus, most likely to be contained. Conversely, Warren Ellis' *No Hero* (Ellis and Rep 2008), a scathing critique of the superhero, has never been contained because it did not make a particularly big impact. The upshot of all of these examples is that analogues (and variants) cease to have a critical impact once they become characters in their own right, much like crossovers cease to be metafictions once they are just another part of the genre. Containment normalizes what was previously metafictional, thus negating it. This pattern in superhero comics holds for superheroes in other media, as well.

Film and Television

When superheroes travel to other media, they bring their genre tropes with them, including shared universes and analogues. There have been multiple failed attempts at shared universes before the present popularity of superheroes in television and film (see Corey 1988; Bixby 1989; Schumacher 1997), and two successful if short-lived attempts in animation: e.g., *Spider-Man* (Richardson 1995), and *Superman: The Animated Series* (Masuda 1997). The first crossovers/shared universes in live action, however, occur in Marvel Studios films and Berlanti Productions television shows, respectively (see Favreau 2008; Berlanti 2013), and just like superhero comics, multiverses soon follow in both cases (see Waldron 2021; Berlanti 2016). Berlanti Productions even recreated DC's *Crisis on Infinite Earths* as a series of episodes from five separate shows (Queller 2019; Dries 2019; Wallace 2019; Guggenheim and Schwartz 2020; Klemmer and Shimizu 2020), thus collapsing their own multiverse into a single, shared universe. This mini-series also features dozens of cameos in which actors reprise their roles from various other DC Comics television shows and films: for example, Burt Ward as Dick Grayson (Queller 2019), Ashley Scott as Helena Kyle (Wallace 2019), and Ezra Miller as a variant of Barry Allen (Guggenheim and Schwartz 2020). These cameos retroactively assert that all television and movies based on DC Comics exist within a shared multiverse going back at least to the 1960s and including every live-action DC Comics production in the present. What this means is that Berlanti Productions did not just fall into the same pattern as the comics on which they are based but rather gleefully reproduced it, thus demonstrating just how deeply that pattern has become a part of the superhero genre. The live-action *Crisis* also provides an example of a kind of metafiction that is nigh unique to TV and film: stunt casting. While comics sometimes draw characters to resemble actors who have played a given character – e.g., Gary Frank's cover art for Superman #700 (2010) makes Lois Lane and Superman look more than a little like the late Margot Kidder and Chris Reeves, respectively – stunt casting embodies metafiction through an actor's physical presence, and given that there are a great number of working actors who have played superheroes and related characters, especially in relatively low-budget television, the barrier to hiring those actors to reprise those characters is low.

The most radical example of metafictional stunt-casting occurs in *WandaVision*, in which Evan Peters plays Pietro Maximoff, the ostensibly dead brother of the lead character, Wanda Maximoff (Shakman 2021). When that brother died, however, he was played by Aaron Taylor-Johnson in a Disney/Marvel Studios film (Whedon 2015) while Peters played a variant of the same character in two 20th Century Fox films that were, at the time, not connected to Marvel Studios (Vaughn 2011; Singer 2014). The two versions of the same character appearing in contemporaneous films was a result of ambiguous contract language that meant that both film companies held the rights to him (Jasper 2021), but between his death in that Marvel/Disney film and the *WandaVision* television show, Disney had acquired Fox, which meant that Marvel Studios could use every version of the character that had appeared on film to that point. Therefore, when Peters enters a scene set in the Marvel Studios shared universe, claiming to be Wanda's dead brother but costumed and styled more like the Fox variant, his very presence calls the audience's attention to a great number of frames: Marvel Comics, Marvel Studios, 20th Century Fox, X-Men comics, X-Men films, Avengers comics, and Avengers films, as well as the sitcom frames evoked by *WandaVision*, itself a bewilderingly metafictional production. The sum total effect of casting that actor to play that character in that scene is that it puts the audience in the same position as Wanda: neither they nor Wanda can be certain that that *is* her brother. A character in the show, watching all of this unfold on a television screen and thus acting as a stand-in for the audience, even asks, "They recast Pietro…?" (Shakman 2021). This is a moment of radical metafiction in that the only explanation that accounts for all those frames is outside of the show, in the world of publishing, casting, production companies, and intellectual property rights. It makes sense only in metafictional terms. The show does eventually try to contain this moment, offering the in-story explanation that this version of Pietro is actually a random neighbor who was controlled by an outside force to act like Wanda's dead brother, thus side-stepping the implication of a multiverse in which the Fox variant of Pietro traveled to the Marvel Studios universe, but given that Marvel Studios introduced its own multiverse soon after (see Waldron 2021), there is no other plausible explanation for casting that actor in the role than for the sake of a metafictional stunt. It is *at least* a tease of things to come, a wink directly from Marvel Studios to the viewer. No matter which way we look at it, then, this containment is weak at best, and it remains a moment of radical metafiction. But it also does not carry any particular critique of the superhero itself. Radical metafiction simply does not have to.

Metafiction is inherent to the superhero as a genre, specifically in the form of shared universes and analogues. They were introduced almost immediately following the widespread popularity of superhero comics, and they have flourished in that genre ever since. Shared universes and analogues are so deeply embedded in superhero stories that rival publishers recreate them and superheroes carry them into other media. Both shared universes and analogues are marketing stunts designed to sell comics. The shared universe develops out of the crossover and blossoms into the multiverse. Analogues are a way to capitalize on the popularity of a character by making a copy of the character. Both of them are also creative experiments though, not just crass exploitation: they routinely threaten the structural integrity of the stories in which they appear. Superhero comics are published serially, though, so there is always an opportunity to later contain that threat. Superheroes in live-action are serialized as well, so the pattern holds. The multiverse is contained by making it part of the superhero genre, and analogues are contained by becoming characters in their own right. In both cases, containment means making them saleable commodities, a state that they only ever flirted with escaping to begin with. Thus, the superhero is an inherently metafictional genre: threatening but rarely succeeding at overturning itself.

References

Aaron, Jason, and Ed McGuinness. 2021. *Heroes Reborn* #1-#7. Marvel Comics.

Berlanti, Greg, showrunner. *Arrow*. Season 2, episode 5, "League of Assassins." Aired December 4, 2013, on The CW.

Berlanti, Greg, showrunner. *Supergirl*. Season 1, episode 18, "Worlds Finest." Aired March 28, 2016, on The CW.

Bixby, Bill, dir. 1989. *The Trial of the Incredible Hulk*. Bixby-Brandon Productions.

Blackman, Steve, and Jesse McKeown, showrunners. 2019–2024. *The Umbrella Academy*. Netflix.

Coogan, Peter. 2006. *Superhero: The Secret Origin of a Genre*. Monkeybrain Books.

Cook, Roy T. 2017. "Metacomics." In *The Routledge Companion to Comics*, edited by Frank Bramlett, Roy T Cook, and Aaron Meskin. Routledge.

Cook, Roy T. 2012. "Why Comics are Not Films: Metacomics and Medium-Specific Conventions." In *The Art of Comics: A Philosophical Approach*, edited by Aaron Meskin and Roy T Cook. Wiley-Blackwell.

Corey, Nicholas, dir. 1988. *The Incredible Hulk Returns*. Bixby-Brandon Productions.

Dries, Caroline, showrunner. *Batwoman* Season 1, episode 9, "Crisis on Infinite Earths Part Two." Aired December 9, 2019, on The CW.

Ellis, Warren, and Bryan Hitch. 1999. *The Authority*. Wildstorm Productions.

Ellis, Warren, and Juan Jose Rep. 2008. *No Hero*. Avatar Press.

Ellis, Warren, and Randy Green. 1996. *Sword of Damocles* #1. Wildstorm Productions.

Ellis, Warren. 2005. "I Distrust Your Joy." *Bad Signal*, October 17. E-mail column.

Ennis, Garth, and Amanda Conner. 2002. *The Pro*. Image Comics.

Ennis, Garth, and Darrick Robinson. 2006–2012. *The Boys*. Wildstorm Productions.

Everett, Bill. 1940. *Marvel Mystery Comics* #8-#10. Timely Comics.

Favreau, Jon, dir. 2008. *Iron-Man*. Marvel Studios.

Fox, Gardiner, and Carmine Infantino. 1961. *The Flash* #123. DC Comics.

Fox, Gardner, and Mike Sekowsky. 1964a. *The Justice League of America* #21. DC Comics.

Fox, Gardner, and Mike Sekowsky. 1964b. *The Justice League of America* #29. DC Comics.

Fox, Gardner. 1940. *All-Star Comics* #3. All-American Comics.

Frank, Gary, cover artist. 2010. *Superman* #700. DC Comics.

Gaiman, Neil, and Andy Kubert. 2003. *1602*. Marvel Comics.

Gonzalez, J. A. 2014. "'Living the Funnies': Metaficiton in American Comics Strips." *The Journal of Popular Culture*, 47 (4): 838–856.

Gruenwald, Mark, and Bob Hall. 1985. *Squadron Supreme*. Marvel Comics.

Guggenheim, Marc, and Beth Schwartz, showrunners. *Arrow*. Season 8, episode 8, "Crisis on Infinite Earths: Part Four." Aired January 14, 2020, on The CW.

Hutcheon, Linda. 1988. *A Poetics of Postmodernism: History, Theory, Fiction*. Routledge.

Inge, M. Thomas. 1995. *Anything Can Happen in a Comic Strip: Centennial Reflections on an American Art Form*. Ohio State State University Libraries.

Jasper, Gavin. 2021. "A Tale of Two Pietros: Explaining the MCU X-Men Problem With a Mutant Speedster." *Den of Geek*, February 11. https://www.denofgeek.com/movies/a-tale-of-two-pietros-explaining-the-mcu-x-men-problem-with-a-mutant-speedster/.

Jones, Matthew T. 2005. "Reflexivity in Comic Art." *International Journal of Comic Art*, 7 (2005 Spring/Summer): 270–286.

Kanigher, Robert, and Carmine Infantino. 1954. *Showcase* #4. DC Comics.

Kavenaugh, Barry. 2000. "The Alan Moore Interview." *Blather.net*, October 17. http://www.blather.net/articles/amoore/alanmoore.txt.

Kidder, Orion Ussner, and James Gifford. 2018. "Alan Moore and Anarchist Praxis in Form: Bibliography, Remediation, and Aesthetic Form in *V for Vendetta* and *Black Dossier*." In *Working-Class Comic Book Heroes: Class Conflict and Populist Politics in Comics*, edited by Marc DiPaolo. University Press of Mississippi.

Kidder, Orion Ussner. 2008. "Show and Tell: Notes towards a Theory of Metacomics." *The International Journal of Comic Art*, 10 (1): 248–267.

Kidder, Orion Ussner. 2010. "Useful Play: Alan Moore et al. 's *Supreme* and Warren Ellis/John Cassaday's *Planetary*." *The Journal of the Fantastic in the Arts*, 21 (1): 77–96.

Kidder, Orion Ussner. 2012. "Self-Conscious Sexuality: The Queerness of *Promethea*." In *Sexual Ideology in the Works of Alan Moore*, edited by Todd A. Comer and Joseph Michael Sommers. McFarland and Company.

Kidder, Orion Ussner. 2016. "'Everybody's Here'. Radical Reflexivity in the Metafiction of *The Sandman*." In *Neil Gaiman: Critical Insights*, edited by Joseph Michael Sommers. Salem Press.

Kirkman, Robert, and Cory Walker. 2003. *Invincible* #7. Skybound Entertainment.

Klemmer, Phil, and Keto Shimizu, showrunners. *Legends of Tomorrow*. Season 5, special episode, "Crisis on Infinite Earths: Part Five." Aired January 14, 2020, on The CW.

Kripke, Eric, showrunner. 2019. *The Boys*. Amazon Prime Video.

Masuda, Toshihiko. 1997. *Superman: The Animated Series*. Season 2, episodes 16–18. Warner Bros. Animation.

Millar, Mark, and Bryan Hitch. 2002–2004. *The Ultimates*. Marvel Comics.

Moore, Alan, and Dave Gibbons. 1985–1986. *Watchmen*. DC Comics.

Moore, Alan, and Rick Veitch. 1993. *1963 #6: The Tomorrow Syndicate "From Here to Alternity."* Image Comics.

Morrison, Grant, and Mikel Janín. 2021. *Superman and the Authority* #1-#4. DC Comics.

Queller, Jessica, showrunner. *Supergirl*. Season 5, episode 9, "Crisis on Infinite Earths: Part One." Aired December 8, 2019, on The CW.

Racioppa, Simon, showrunner. 2021. *Invincible*. Amazon Prime Video.

Richardson, Bob, dir. 1995. *Spider-Man*. Season 2, episode 4, "The Mutant Agenda." Aired on September 30, 1995. Marvel Entertainment Group.

Schumacher, Joel, dir. 1997. *Batman and Robin*. Warner Bros.

Shakman, Matt, dir. 2021. *WandaVision*. Season 1, episode 5, "On a Very Special Episode…" Marvel Studios.

Singer, Bryan, dir. 2014. *X-Men: Days of Future Past*. 20th Century Fox.

Sullivan, Vincent A., ed. 1938. *Action Comics* #1. DC Comics.

Sundell, Abner, ed. 1940a. *Pep Comics* #4-#5. MLJ Magazine Inc.

Sundell, Abner, ed. 1940b. *Top Notch Comics* #4. MLJ Magazine Inc.

Thomas, Roy, and John Buscema. 1971. *The Avengers* vol 1. #85. Marvel Comics.

Vaughn, Matthew, dir. 2011. *X-Men: First Class*. 20th Century Fox.

Waid, Mark, Ariel Olivetti, and Michael Zeck. 1999. *The Kingdom*. DC Comics.

Wallace, Eric, showrunner. *The Flash*. Season 6, episode 9, "Crisis on Infinite Earths: Part Three." Aired December 10, 2019, on The CW.

Waugh, Patricia. 1984. *Metafiction: The Theory and Practise of Self-Conscious Fiction*. Methuen.

Way, Gerard, and Gabriel Bá. 2007–2009. *The Umbrella Academy*. Dark Horse Comics.

Whedon, Joss, dir. 2015. *Avengers: Age of Ultron*. Marvel Studios.

Wolf-Meyer, Matthew. 2003. "The World Ozymandias Made: Utopias in the Superhero Comic, Subculture, and the Conservation of Difference." *Journal of Popular Culture*, 36 (Jan): 497–517.

Wolfman, Marv, and George Perez. 1985–1986. *Crisis on Infinite Earths*. DC Comics.

5

WHAT THE KIDS WANT

Superheroes and Shared Universes

Sean Patrick Casey

The stories that rose to the top of newsfeeds following the 2024 San Diego Comic-Con reveal a passion for superheroes and shared universes on the part of fans and creators that shows no signs of stopping or even slowing, despite claims of "superhero fatigue" from some corners. The biggest and most surprising announcement from the event was arguably actor Robert Downey Jr.'s return to the Marvel Cinematic Universe (MCU), not to reprise his role as Tony Stark, but as villain Victor von Doom. Headlines like "A Marvel fan thinks they've worked out how Robert Downey Jr. will return to the MCU as Doctor Doom, thanks to *Deadpool and Wolverine*" evidence intense enthusiasm among superhero fans for shared universes and their tangle of textual threads (West 2024). While the reveal of Downey Jr. as the man behind Doom's mask was happening on stage in Hall H, the reunion of Ryan Reynolds and Hugh Jackman on screen in the aforementioned *Deadpool & Wolverine* (2024) was dominating the box office with what would become the sixth-largest domestic film opening of all time (McClintock 2024), inspiring such similar stories and speculation as "Is *Deadpool and Wolverine* part of the MCU? Its ties to canon, explained" (Salmon 2024). There was a lot for fans of superheroes and shared universes to see in the summer of 2024; the same was true in 1992 when Todd McFarlane declared that with Image, the new company he had co-founded as a creator-owned alternative to DC and Marvel, "we're going to give the kids exactly what they want to see. They want to see superheroes, they want to see a shared universe, and that's what we're going to give them" (Thompson 1992, 9).

While Image may have been an alternative option for creators, it wasn't providing an alternative product for consumers. Superheroes and shared universes are what the "kids" have wanted since comics' earliest days. Fifty-two years before McFarlane made the above statement, the first crossover between superheroes the Shield and the Wizard appeared in MLJ's *Top Notch Comics* #5 (1940); the first battle between the Human Torch and Namor, the Sub-Mariner, characters from what would become the Marvel Universe, happened in *Marvel Mystery Comics* #8 (1940); and the inaugural meeting of DC's (and comics') first superhero team, the Justice Society of America, arrived in *All Star Comics* #3 (1940). As a result of these momentous meetings, just two years after Superman first leapt over tall buildings and off of the cover of *Action Comics* #1, "what had been individual… stories following separate heroes had now come together into shared universes" (Friedenthal 2022, 4).

DOI: 10.4324/9781003366911-7

Being what Roz Kaveney refers to as "the largest narrative constructs of human culture" (Kaveney 2008, ix), the DC and Marvel Universes have rightly received the majority of the attention that has so far been paid to shared universes by scholars such as Andrew J. Friedenthal (2019, 2022). This chapter, however, calls for further study of the superheroes populating the so-called "lost" universes of independent publishers. Following from the work of Vincent Tran (2024), Mark J. P. Wolf (2012), and Patricia Monk (1990), who provide blueprints for building imaginary worlds and frameworks for understanding shared universes across media, this chapter will use McFarlane and his co-founders' Image Universe as a case study.

Inside Image

Image Comics is the third-largest direct market comic book publisher and has been ever since it burst onto the scene, and, while it has never achieved the commercial or critical success of the MCU or even the DC Extended Universe, the Image Universe is arguably the third most popular superhero shared universe, both in terms of initial interest based on the record-setting sales of its launch titles as well as on longevity; the Image Universe continues 32 years after its creation. Despite the impact of Rob Liefeld, McFarlane, and the other Image co-founders on the comics industry both at the time of Image's creation and today, "comics studies has done very little to directly address their work" (Peppard 2019, 321). Indeed, Anna F. Peppard, Bart Beaty, and Benjamin Woo are three of the only scholars to have done so. While researching a chapter on Liefeld for *The Greatest Comic Book of All Time*, Beaty and Woo encountered "a complete absence of the artist from the literature on comics" (Beaty and Woo 2016, 73). As Peppard rightly concludes, however, the Image co-founders' "recording-breaking popularity and wide-ranging influence on not only the superhero genre but the shape of the American comic book industry itself would seem to make them worthy of serious consideration" (Peppard 2019, 321).

While they may be absent from academic literature, there is a wealth of material on Image Comics and its co-founders in the fan press and even the mainstream media; too much for *The Comics Journal*'s Scott Nybakken, who complained of the creators' "crowing in… cover story after cover story about the dawning of the Image Empire" (Nybakken 1992, 34). This rich archive of resources should not be distastefully dismissed, however, as it offers scholars a rare behind-the-scenes view of the birth of a superhero shared universe. As the DC and Marvel Universes approach their 100-year anniversaries and with the majority of their originators now deceased, the relatively recent founding of the Image Universe can still be reconstructed from the pages of publications such as *Comics Scene*, *Hero Illustrated*, and *Wizard: The Guide to Comics*. In this way, one can bear witness to the process of how a superhero shared universe is born. Serious consideration of the birth of the Image Universe, in all its splendor and squalor, is provided below by way of example.

A Brand-New Rob Liefeld Universe

After creating the characters of Cable and Deadpool and launching the series *X-Force* (1991) for Marvel, Liefeld did it again, but this time for Malibu, a small, independent comic book company. According to publisher Dave Olbrich, Malibu had "a couple of things" going for it that Marvel did not, however; the most appealing of which to Liefeld was that "creators retained complete ownership of their work" (Khoury 2007, 144). In exchange for Liefeld bringing "his latest creation directly to Malibu," they in turn "created a whole full color imprint [for] the most eagerly awaited independent comic book of the year: Rob Liefeld's *Youngblood*" (Mason 1992a, 1).

The "most eagerly awaited independent comic book of the year" quickly became the best-selling creator-owned comic book of all time, as initial orders for *Youngblood #1* (1992) totaled more than 300,000 copies (Mason 1992c, 1). At the conclusion of the three-issue miniseries, Malibu reassured readers that while "*Youngblood* may be ending…it's only the beginning of a brand-new Rob Liefeld Universe" and recommended that fans stay tuned for future announcements about "a series of upcoming projects that involve not just Rob but some of the biggest names in the industry" (1). The first of those announcements came in the following issue of *The Malibu Sun*, and the next big name mentioned was one that had not been seen in comics since the publication of *Spider-Man* #16 some eight months prior: Todd McFarlane, making his triumphant return to the medium with a new character called Spawn. This announcement also stated that *Youngblood* and *Spawn* were the beginnings of what Malibu was now referring to as the Image Universe, "an exciting idea that rivals the creation of the Marvel Universe more than three decades ago," and that readers should "look for further details of the Image Universe, and upcoming titles by Erik Larsen, Jim Valentino and others as the weeks progress" (Mason 1992c, 1).

At the first Image Comics press conference on February 1, 1992, it was revealed that those titles by Larsen and Valentino would be two additional series focused on single characters (*The Savage Dragon* and *Shadowhawk*) and that the "others" mentioned by Mason were Jim Lee and Marc Silvestri, whose contribution to the Image Universe would be two more titles featuring teams: *WildC.A.T.s* and *Cyberforce*, respectively. The excitement among these creators and for Image Comics was immediately evident, an excitement that Liefeld compared "to that of a roller coaster ride" in the pages of *Supreme #1* (Liefeld and Murray 1992, 23). Liefeld continued, "Unfortunately, with a lot of comics these days, it's [hard] to maintain [what made them] so exciting in the first place. It starts to seem like you're going on the same ride over and over again." With Image, "you finally get the chance to [get] on at the beginning of the ride" (23). Larsen agreed, complaining that companies like Marvel "seem to maintain the status quo forever… and that's what we all want to [avoid] with the Image Universe, [where] there's a great flexibility… and more of a feeling that anything can happen" (Mason 1992d, 20). "I never had that feeling when I was creating stuff for Marvel," said Lee,

> because it always had to fit in the Marvel Universe. They have certain rules about what can be done, what can't be done. Creating stuff for the Image line has brought me back to the time when I was a kid, when I would create on the fly. That's cool.
>
> *(Chun 1992b, 33–34)*

From a Rob Liefeld Universe to a Shared Universe

Lee, Larsen, and company quickly found that there were limits to what could and couldn't be done at Image as well, however. Because Liefeld "had the first team concept with Youngblood, [who are] government agents and celebrities," Lee stated, "I tried not to duplicate his ideas, so I decided to do a secret team with a hidden agenda" (Johnson 1992, 33). "My book had to be tailored to the things Rob is establishing," he confessed, concluding that "it does make things a little difficult" (Chun 1992a, 11). Similarly, Larsen, who had first conceived of the Dragon 20 years earlier in 1972, and who had self-published the first stories featuring the character in 1982, shared that he

> originally envisioned going back to those days when Dragon was married, had a kid, and led a government team… but [now Rob's] got the government team [and Todd's] got Spawn, who's married with a daughter, [so] I don't want to do that.
>
> *(Cunningham 1994, 45)*

As a result of this difficult but necessary negotiating and compromising, the still-forming Image Universe now met the first of Vincent Tran's criteria for creating a shared universe: it was transfictional, which he defines as simply sharing "common characters and settings" (Tran 2024, 12).

Following the finalization of their individual identities and the publication of their first appearances, the Image characters almost immediately began moving back and forth between titles. Crossovers were common in the initial series set in the Image Universe, perhaps nowhere more so than in Valentino's *Shadowhawk* (1992), where they occurred in two of the miniseries' four issues. The Image Universe was now not only a transfictional textual environment, but one which occurred between discrete texts, which Tran defines as being formed "when different protagonists of different works come into relation with one another" (Tran 2024, 7).

The mere presence of even multiple crossovers is not necessarily an indication of the existence of a shared universe, however. "One-off appearances in which the texts moving forward do not acknowledge the crossover at all do not help in convincing that the texts exist within the same storyworld," explains Tran. What is needed to accomplish this is an "attempt to establish a history between their texts that seems real" (Tran 2024, 8). Liefeld and McFarlane attempted this with a crossover that would provide the answer to the question "who killed Spawn?" Foreshadowed in the series' very first issue, Spawn's killer was confirmed in *Spawn* #12 (1993) to have been Youngblood's Chapel, a character created (and owned) by Liefeld. "It was always confusing to me at the beginning because, like, 'Hey, let's do this thing where your characters are involved in the origin of my characters,'" reflected Lee. "There was just not a complete understanding of the legal issues involved" (Khoury 2007, 55). Legal concerns aside, Image now had the "sense of history that sets apart the shared universe from one-of-a-kind crossover occasions" (Tran 2024, 8).

From Stories to Worlds

Whether or not one of their characters should have been involved in the origin of another's was not the only part of the creative process that was confusing to the Image co-founders. "We didn't have anything figured out," said Larsen. "We were… making up the rules as we went along… and like, you're sitting there trying to build a house and there's no foundation" (Khoury 2007, 31–32). While all of the Image co-founders were accomplished artists, they had wildly varying levels of experience with writing; Larsen and Valentino had been writers/artists since the beginning of their careers, and McFarlane had been allowed to write *Spider-Man* (1990) in an attempt to prevent him from leaving Marvel earlier than he eventually did, but Liefeld, Lee, and Silvestri recruited friends and relatives to help them build the Image house: "a new guy named Hank Kanalz… a friend of [Lee's] named Brandon Choi," and Silvestri's brother Eric (Chun 1992a, 11).

Lee revealed at the aforementioned press conference that Choi had actually been helping him to plot the stories that he told in *X-Men* (1991) following long-time writer Chris Claremont's departure, but neither Kanalz nor Eric Silvestri had prior professional writing experience, a fact that became quickly and painfully obvious to the readers of *Youngblood* and *Cyberforce*. "It sounded like a great idea to… keep it in the family," reflected Silvestri, but "it didn't quite gel" (Khoury 2007, 120–121). *Youngblood* #1 also "didn't turn out the way that it was supposed to," Liefeld later admitted. "I had [a] friend write it, and I thought, 'Hey, cool! This is just like comics when you're doing them as a little kid,' but the end result… was a disaster" (Grant 1993, 71–72). Reviewer Scott Nybakken agreed, writing for *The Comics Journal* that *Youngblood* was "the worst comic book I have ever read" (Nybakken 1992, 33). The "laziness and disinterest" that Nybakken felt were on display in *Youngblood* #1 "renders the concept of a 'shared universe'… somewhat beside the point. The characters in *Youngblood*… are such mindless generic ciphers that [they] could cross over into any universe." He concluded by condemning *Youngblood* to "that particular Beckett-like purgatory where worthless collectors' items endlessly wait for someone—anyone—with some hint of a coherent narrative structure to rescue them" (Nybakken 1992, 34).

Nybakken wasn't much kinder to McFarlane's *Spawn*, writing in his review of the first issue of that series that "the problem with the story in *Spawn* isn't that it's non-existent, like in *Youngblood*. The problem is that it's completely mediocre" (Nybakken 1992, 34). The first seven issues of the series, written by McFarlane, were examples of what Mark J. P. Wolf defines as an "early world" which had grown out of the stories McFarlane was telling in it; a world that entirely "depended on those stories for [its] structure" and where "only the elements needed to tell the story appeared" (Wolf 2012, 154). *Spawn* would soon be rescued from the purgatory of McFarlane's mediocre writing by a pair of stories set in Heaven and Hell, appropriately enough, written by two authors with much more than a hint of coherent narrative structure to their names: Neil Gaiman and Alan Moore. As reported in *Wizard*, Alan Moore "will be guest-writing the eighth issue of Spawn, and will be followed by award-winning writer Neil Gaiman in issue #9" (McCallum 1992, 12). The announcement also made sure to mention that McFarlane would still be providing pencils and inks. "Since McFarlane would be drawing the [two] issues, he would get to work closely with the [two] scripts, perhaps picking up little bits of craft along the way," Greg Carpenter observes of McFarlane's decision to allow the two British authors to "invade" his series so soon after its start. "And there was always the possibility that the writers might wind up contributing… something McFarlane would be able to build on" (Carpenter 2016, 353).

In his issue, Gaiman's primary contribution was the character Angela, an angel and hunter of Hellspawn. "Since stories involve time, space, and causality," writes Wolf, "every story implies a world in which it takes place" (Wolf 2012, 29). The early world implied by the first seven Spawn stories was one "where angels have to be pretty tough," according to McFarlane, who acknowledged that it was Gaiman who "gave life to all that" (Beatty 1996, 33). With the introduction of antagonist Angela, "Gaiman reverses the notions of good and evil," continues Carpenter, which provided *Spawn* "with a more complicated concept to drive many stories in the future" (Carpenter 2016, 355), such as a follow-up *Angela* miniseries (1994) where Gaiman would further develop the character and define the hierarchy of the Heavenly host.

What Gaiman had done for Heaven in the Image Universe, Moore would do for its Hell. "Todd invited us to contribute whatever we wanted in terms of ideas," Moore said of the arrangement that McFarlane had made with the guest writers, "so… I sort of came up with some of the background for Todd's mythology" (Darnall 1994, 93). One of Moore's ideas was to shift the focus away from Spawn, and "in his place, Moore gives us something he's more comfortable with—taking us on a journey through Hell" (Carpenter 2016, 354). With his issue and his decision not to tell a story featuring series protagonist Spawn, Moore demonstrated an understanding and a skill absent from McFarlane's writing: that "storytelling may be a part of [a well-made work], but less often acknowledged is the draw of the world itself" (Wolf 2012, 16). While Hell was a world that Moore had built once before while writing *Swamp Thing*, unlike the version that he had imagined for the DC Universe, "Moore's tone here is more … humorous" (Carpenter 2016, 354). Another of Moore's ideas for *Spawn* was to puncture "the ponderous tone of the series" as Jackson Ayres puts it (2021, 116). "Moore mocks the *Spawn* mythology as much as he celebrates it," agrees Tim Callahan (2012): "though, as the creator of four of the [five] Phlebiac Brothers … he's responsible for expanding the mythology exponentially."

Exponential expansion was something to which Liefeld was no stranger, as his first "disaster" of an offering, *Youngblood*, was soon followed by an onslaught of additional miniseries and ongoing series including *Brigade* (1992), *Supreme* (1992), and *Bloodstrike* (1993), among others; almost none of which Nybakken or Wolf would call well-made, as, like *Youngblood*, they were severely lacking in world as well as story. "As I look at the number of books you have [published] in the first 12 months of Image's existence," Patrick Daniel O'Neill observed in a conversation with Liefeld, "it seems that, instead of allowing *Youngblood* as a title to build … you kept tagging on new titles … before there was any chance to develop a central core to what you were doing." Liefeld agreed that O'Neill's assessment was "valid," stating that the initial expansion phase of his Extreme Studios line (the "Youngblood family of books" or "the Youngblood corner of the Image Universe") had now ended and that its next phase would be marked by quality rather than marred by quantity (O'Neill 1993, 70–72). "When Todd started hiring writers, I was like, 'Wow!'" exclaimed Liefeld of the increased acclaim (and attention) that had been brought to *Spawn* by Gaiman and Moore (Hyland 1995, 66). Feeling that he and Extreme Studios Editor Eric Stephenson had taken their many titles "as far as we can take them," Liefeld declared that "we need to go out to the rest of the creative community and ask them if they want to jump on'" (Fielder 1995, 80).

From Shared Megatext to Franchised Megatext

Like Gaiman, Moore would find future stories for Spawn in the concepts he had created, delving further into the depths of Hell in a three-issue *Violator* miniseries (1994) as well as a four-issue *Violator vs. Badrock* miniseries (1995), this being a crossover between McFarlane's character and a member of Liefeld's Youngblood which also provided Moore with a point of entry into Extreme Studios; an entry which Editor Stephenson was only too happy to help facilitate. "We've been talking to Alan Moore about writing *Supreme* for some time," Stephenson stated in *Supreme* #41 (Moore et al. 1996). 40 issues prior, Liefeld had provided readers with his rationale for creating the character:

> I've always wondered what a person with a tremendous amount of power at their disposal would be like … chances are [they] would be motivated more by ego than by honor or sense of duty. Which … is how I came up with Supreme.
>
> *(Liefeld 1992)*

Supreme, "in both visual design and powers, [was] patterned on Superman … but, in keeping with the era's sensibilities … was originally characterized as an unrelenting, aloof, brutal, and even lethal anti-hero," according to Ayres (2021, 110). "It [was] so obvious that it [was] a Superman knock-off," agreed Moore. It was "somebody who thought, 'Right, gritty realistic superheroes; that's the thing to do. How do you do that? Well, you take someone like Superman and make him a psychopath' … and so he'd done that, and it wasn't very interesting" (Khoury 2003, 176).

What was interesting to both Moore and Stephenson were the Superman stories of the Silver Age. "Alan and I did a good bit of talking about … the sense of majesty and wonder inherent in [those] classic comics," Stephenson said, and Moore "agreed to write *Supreme* on the condition [that] he be allowed to inject his stories with the same elements that made those comics … so wonderful" (Moore et al. 1996). It was a situation that Moore found familiar: "a once-popular character that had never been fully defined … was now being turned over to Alan Moore" to revise (Carpenter 2016, 369). Moore articulated his strategy for accomplishing this definition and revision in a later proposal for reinventing another Liefeld character: Glory, an equally obvious Wonder Woman knock-off.

> Go back to the 'parent' character … and try to analyze all of the elements … that made the initial character tick in the first place. [Then], change them around slightly so that they have the veneer of novelty returned to them.
>
> *(Moore 1999)*

The elements that Moore incorporates into his *Supreme* stories "are not based on an actual textual past [because] the textual history of *Supreme* extends back only to 1992," argues Hyman. But by returning to Supreme's "parent" character Superman, "Moore … treats Supreme as if the character's history were co-extensive with that of the superhero" (Hyman 2017, 69). As Geoff Klock concludes, in a section about Moore's *Supreme* in *How to Read Superhero Comics and Why*, superheroes and shared universes "are invigorated by interaction with their history" (2002, 191).

The house that the Image co-founders had been attempting to build was what Patricia Monk terms a shared megatext, this being a textual environment with "loose … constraints, created by a group of writers, using a pool of characters in common, each writer having 'creator's rights' over particular characters, and producing linked but independent short stories" (1990, 24–25). However, after the hiring of Alan Moore and the entry of Extreme Studios into a phase of "implosion" rather than explosion, Liefeld's newly lean and reinvigorated line was thus transformed into a franchised megatext, which as Monk explains "resembles the shared megatext in taking the form of interlinked stories, but differs in having the invited contributors participate in a megatext created and controlled … by a single writer" (25).

While Liefeld and Stephenson were turning creative control of *Supreme* and eventually *Youngblood* and *Glory* over to single writer Moore, the other Image creators were doing the same for their increasingly isolated wings of the Image house. McFarlane's wing was now called Todd McFarlane Productions, Larsen's was Highbrow Entertainment, Valentino's was Shadowline, Lee's was WildStorm Studios, and Silvestri's was Top Cow Productions. Following Liefeld's lead, they too franchised their families of books and corners of the Image Universe to established writers and world-builders, including Kurt Busiek, Warren Ellis, Garth Ennis, and James Robinson. "It's all intended to help build a better, [more] cohesive Image

Universe," said Stephenson. "The more unified we can make our particular end of the Image Universe, the easier it will be to fit in with the rest" (Johnson 1994, 29).

Each studio's franchising of its megatexts may have made them easier to fit together in theory, but in practice, as each end of the Image Universe became more unified, the formerly shared universe itself became more divided. "It's a legitimate criticism that each one of the studios seemed to be having their own sub-universe," observed Image Comics' Executive Director Larry Marder, whose position was created in 1994 in part to correct this problem:

> They've understood this was happening and asked me to coordinate more ... crossovers and to work on a timeline of events for the Image Universe ... they've entrusted me with this. If we don't have a fully integrated Image Universe in a year, I'll have failed.
> *(Kurtz 1994, 77)*

Megatext as Game

Through no fault of Marder's, the Image Universe "failed" in that it did not become fully integrated after his hiring but instead shattered when Liefeld and his Extreme Studios sub-universe exited Image in 1996 and when Lee sold his WildStorm Studios sub-universe to DC in 1998. "Creator-ownership can come with many freedoms and those freedoms don't always mix perfectly within a shared universe," reflects Joe Casey. "Creators fell away and took their creations with them, [and] what was once a robust, evolving continuity was left fractured and confused." Youngblood and WildC.A.T.s were "essentially—and more importantly, legally---excised from the Image [Universe, which now has] a significant-sized hole in it" (Casey and Fry 2024a).

The accumulation of these confusing continuity problems, "combining to inhibit the reader's imaginative participation in the fiction, suggests that the texts of [shared universes] should be unreadable," states Monk. "Nevertheless," she continues, "they have been and still are widely read by a great many readers;" an observation which causes her to conclude that "imaginative participation in the fiction is replaced by imaginative participation in something else ... the megatext as game" (1990, 33). This is a game played by and between writers and readers, and this social dimension provides "at least part of the attraction" of the shared universe according to Monk (33–34). Indeed, this "interactive energy of speculative readers and writers" is so attractive that frequently "fans may begin as readers only, but a very high proportion of them attempt to become writers, and many of them succeed" (10).

Three such success stories include Robert Kirkman, Tim Seeley, and the aforementioned Joe Casey, each of whom are co-players in the Image Universe megatext turned co-authors of it: Kirkman in *Invincible* (2003) and *Image United* (2009); Seeley with *Local Man* (2023), a "superhero flashback into the depths of the Image Universe" (Image Comics n.d.); and Casey with *Blood Squad Seven* (2024), a series that also looks back at "those initial years of the Image Universe" but set in the present day (Casey and Fry 2024a). Far from being inhibited or confused by three decades' worth of continuity problems, Casey feels that "some of the 'problem solving' aspects that go along with a series like [*Blood Squad Seven*] end up being a big part of the fun we're having in creating it" (Casey and Fry 2024b). They are a big part of the fun that fans are having reading it as well. Echoing the headlines quoted earlier in this chapter, reader Dylan Robinson asks in the pages of the "Bloodsquatting" letters column, "Could we ever see the Guardians of the Globe [a superhero team from Kirkman's Invincible sub-universe] make an appearance?", and reader Martin wonders, "Since [they are] taking a similar approach, will [*Blood Squad Seven*] share any continuity with *Local Man?*" (Casey and Fry 2024b). If, as reader Brian Thomer posits, "one of the fundamental components of a shared universe is participation" (Casey and Fry 2024c), or, the playing of the megatext as game, as Monk would put it, then perhaps the success and continued status of Image as the third most popular superhero shared universe is due less to its founders and more to the writers to whom the founders franchised their creations like Gaiman and Moore; to co-players who have become co-authors like Kirkman, Seeley, and Casey; and to current readers and potential future writers like Robinson, Martin, and Thomer.

Conclusion

Whether in 1940, 1992, or 2024, what the "kids" have always wanted are superheroes and shared universes. While the cinematic and extended iterations of the Marvel and DC Universes continue to excite fans, and while their comic book worlds have been written about by scholars such as Friedenthal, this chapter calls for an application of Tran, Wolf, and Monk's blueprints for building imaginary worlds and frameworks for understanding shared universes across media to the medium of comics and for further academic study of the superheroes populating the smaller shared universes of independent publishers, many of which have recently been reintroduced to readers in *The Overstreet Comic Book Price Guide to Lost Universes* (2022, 2024). As Robert M. Overstreet states in his "Publisher's Note" to the first of these two volumes, and as this chapter strongly agrees, "this is your invitation to discover worlds you might have missed or even dismissed previously, and this is a call to remember that in comics there are always new worlds to discover" (Overstreet 2022, 14).

References

Ayres, Jackson. 2021. *Alan Moore: A Critical Guide*. Bloomsbury Academic.

Beatty, Scott. 1996. "Earth Angel." *Wizard: The Guide to Comics*. Wizard Entertainment, December.

Beaty, Bart, and Benjamin Woo. 2016. *The Greatest Comic Book of All Time: Symbolic Capital and the Field of American Comic Books*. Palgrave Macmillan.

Callahan, Tim. 2012. "The Great Alan Moore Reread: Spawn." *Reactor*, June 4. https://reactormag.com/the-great-alan-moore-reread-spawn/.

Carpenter, Greg. 2016. *The British Invasion: Alan Moore, Neil Gaiman, Grant Morrison, and the Invention of the Modern Comic Book Writer*. Sequart Organization.

Casey, Joe, and Paul Fry. 2024a. *Blood Squad Seven* #1. Image Comics, May 22.

Casey, Joe, and Paul Fry. 2024b. *Blood Squad Seven* #3. Image Comics, July 24.

Casey, Joe, and Paul Fry. 2024c. *Blood Squad Seven: Strikefile* #1. Image Comics, October 30.

Chun, Alex. 1992a. "Image Comics." *Wizard: The Guide to Comics*. Wizard Entertainment, May.

Chun, Alex. 1992b. "Image Enhancement." *Amazing Heroes*. Fantagraphics, June.

Cunningham, Brian. 1994. "Dragonsayer." *Wizard: The Guide to Comics*. Wizard Entertainment, March.

Darnall, Steve. 1994. "Alan Moore's Interview from Hell!" *Hero Illustrated*. Warrior Publications, January.

Fielder, Joe. 1995. "Brave New Order." *Hero Illustrated*. Warrior Publications, January.

Friedenthal, Andrew J. 2022. *The World of Marvel Comics*. Routledge.

Grant, Paul. 1993. "100% Liefeld." *Hero Illustrated*. Warrior Publications, October.

Hyland, Greg. 1995. "The Punk." *Hero Illustrated*. Warrior Publications, May.

Hyman, David. 2017. *Revision and the Superhero Genre*. Palgrave Macmillan.

Image Comics, n.d. "Local Man." *Image Comics*. Accessed February 25, 2025. https://imagecomics.com/comics/series/local-man.

Johnson, Kim Howard. 1992. "WildO.N.E.s." *Comics Scene*. Starlog Group Inc., December.

Johnson, Kim Howard. 1994. "Extreme Settings." *Comics Scene* Starlog Group Inc., May.

Kaveney, Roz. 2008. *Superheroes!: Capes and Crusaders in Comics and Film*. I.B. Tauris.

Khoury, George. 2003. *The Extraordinary Works of Alan Moore*. TwoMorrows Publishing.

Khoury, George. 2007. *Image Comics: The Road to Independence*. TwoMorrows Publishing.

Klock, Geoff. 2002. *How to Read Superhero Comics and Why*. Continuum.

Kurtz, Frank, ed. 1994. "Image Prepares to Meet Its Marder." *Hero Illustrated*. Warrior Publications, May.

Liefeld, Rob, and Brian Murray. 1992. *Supreme* #1. Image Comics, November.

Mason, Tom. 1992a. "Rob Liefeld, Youngblood and the Creation of Malibu Comics!" *The Malibu Sun*, February.

Mason, Tom. 1992b. "The Return of Rust." *The Malibu Sun*, April.

Mason, Tom. 1992c. "Spawn: Created by Todd McFarlane!" *The Malibu Sun*, May.

Mason, Tom. 1992d. "Enter the Savage Dragon." *The Malibu Sun*, June.

McCallum, Pat, ed. "Moore & Gaiman on Spawn." 1992. *Wizard: The Guide to Comics*. Wizard Entertainment, November.

McClintock, Pamela. 2024. "'Deadpool & Wolverine' Box Office: All the Records Broken (So Far)." *The Hollywood Reporter*, August 4. https://www.hollywoodreporter.com/movies/movie-news/deadpool-wolverine-box-office-records-1235961235/.

Monk, Patricia. 1990. "The Shared Universe: An Experiment in Speculative Fiction." *Journal of the Fantastic in the Arts* 2, no. 4: 7–46.

Moore, Alan. 1999. "Alan Moore's Glory Notes." *Alan Moore's Awesome Universe Handbook*. Awesome Entertainment, April.

Moore, Alan, Joe Bennett, and Keith Giffen. 1996. *Supreme* #41. Image Comics, August.

Nybakken, Scott. 1992. "Too Rare for My Taste." *The Comics Journal* #151, July.

O'Neill, Patrick Daniel. 1993. "Liefeld & O'Neill: Round II." *Wizard: The Guide to Comics*. Wizard Entertainment, May.

Overstreet, Robert M. 2022. "Publisher's Note." In *The Overstreet Comic Book Price Guide to Lost Universes*, edited by Robert M. Overstreet, Jack C. Vaughn and Scott Branden. Gemstone Publishing.

Peppard, Anna F. 2019. "The Power of the Marvel(ous) Image: Reading Excess in the Styles of Todd McFarlane, Jim Lee, and Rob Liefeld." *Journal of Graphic Novels and Comics* 10, no. 3: 320–341.

Salmon, Will. 2024. "Is Deadpool and Wolverine part of the MCU? Its ties to canon explained." *GamesRadar+*, July 25. https://www.gamesradar.com/entertainment/marvel-movies/is-deadpool-and-wolverine-part-of-the-mcu/.

Thompson, Kim, ed. 1992. "Marvel Artists Go Independent." *Amazing Heroes*. Fantagraphics, February.

Tran, Vincent. 2024. "Introduction: Televisual Shared Universes." In *Televisual Shared Universes: Expanded and Converged Storyworlds on the Small Screen*, edited by CarrieLynn D. Reinhard and Vincent Tran. Lexington Books.

West, Amy. 2024. "A Marvel Fan Thinks They've Worked Out How Robert Downey Jr Will Return to the MCU as Doctor Doom, Thanks to Deadpool and Wolverine." *GamesRadar+*, July 30. https://www.gamesradar.com/entertainment/marvel-movies/marvel-fan-theory-how-robert-downey-jr-can-return-to-the-mcu-as-doctor-doom/.

Wolf, Mark J. P. 2012. *Building Imaginary Worlds: The Theory and History of Subcreation*. Routledge.

6

OUT OF THE MULTIVERSAL CLOSET

Alternate Realities, Reboots, and Transmedia Coming Outs

Charles Joseph

Several years ago a California psychiatrist pointed out that the Batman stories are psychologically homosexual. Our researches confirm this entirely. Only someone ignorant of the fundamentals of psychiatry and of the psychopathology of sex can fail to realize a subtle atmosphere of homoerotism which pervades the adventures of the mature 'Batman' and his young friend 'Robin.'

(Wertham 1954, 159–60)

In his infamous *Seduction of the Innocent* (1954), Fredric Wertham vilified comics and the alleged harmful influence they had on a supposedly susceptible American youth. Taking Batman as a herald of sexual perversion, Wertham argued that homosexual behaviors were at least encouraged, if not incited, by such comic book titles. His crusade against comics led to the implementation of the Comics Code Authority (also 1954), which clearly stipulated in its "Marriage and Sex" section that "illicit sex relations are neither to be hinted at nor portrayed," that "violent love scenes as well as sexual abnormalities are unacceptable," and that "sex perversion or any inference to same is strictly forbidden." (Nyberg 1998, 166). Anything that alluded to something other than heteronormative standards was to be censored under the code. As showcased in anthology collection *No Straight Lines* (2012), edited by Justin Hall, LGBTQ+ comic book representations found their way into underground titles such as *Come Out Comix* (1973), *Gay Comix* (1980–1998), or *Dyke Strippers* (1995).

Superhero comics have appealed first and foremost to a male readership, and the trope of the secret identity is one that has had deep relatable impact on young gay boys in the United States and around the world, who followed religiously these continuing episodic illustrated storylines of athletic men accomplishing incredible feats in their skin-tight costumes. Superheroes have resonated for decades in the lives of generations of gay men, and manifestations of that now well-established cultural interweaving are more and more perceptible.

Running from 2000 to 2005 on Showtime and Showcase, the TV series *Queer as Folk* was the first American gay-themed TV series to be broadcasted in the country, and its cultural impact on the gay community which was becoming more and more accepted and visible in the United States was incommensurable. One of the series' main characters, Michael

 DOI: 10.4324/9781003366911-8

Novotny, is introduced as a comic book fan and starting from the second season onwards, he opens his own comic book store and creates *Rage*, his very own comic book title whose superhero is gay. The whole narrative thread of the series is interlinked closely with that of Michael's comics as the events that feed his imaginary are the ones unfolding around him with gay bashing and disease, as analyzed in great detail in Monica Michlin's article "Recurrence, Remediation and Metatextuality in Queer as Folk" (2013).

The fan-favorite LGBTIQI+ reality TV series *RuPaul's Drag Race* (2009–) has also repeatedly shown how the gay community (and more particularly the world of drag) and the comic book world collided. In the many seasons of the series, drag queens have been asked several times to create comic book-inspired looks and narratives to fit with their drag personas. RuPaul herself has stated many times that drag queens are the superheroines of the gay community. Creating an entirely new character, drag queens build their own armor with make-up and clothes to become the spearhead of an entire community, empowered by irreverence and over-the-top visibility to fight for equal rights. To that end, we can mention the casting of Dax Exclamationpoint, self-titled "queen of the nerds," who in *RuPaul's Drag Race* season 8 (2016) showcased a merging of common cultural influences and practices as her entire aesthetic is rooted in the world of cosplay and comic books. In *RuPaul's Drag Race All Stars* season 2 (2016), Phi Phi O'Hara decided to create a runway look inspired by Marvel's Nebula in the "the future of drag" challenge. This merging of comic book culture and drag solidified even further with the release of the animated series *Super Drags* on Netflix in 2018. Created by Anderson Mahanski, Fernando Mendonça, and Paulo Lescaut, the animated series was produced in Brazil, not the United States, even if an English-dubbed version was made available on the platform. Not only did this short-lived animated series illustrate how superhero narratives have circulated around the world, it also showed how they found a global echo with the gay community.

Earth LGBTQI+: Queer Readings and Fan Fictions

Queer readings of superhero comics have been made ever since these stories started to be published, putting into action Stuart Hall's encoding/decoding methodology with a readership that became older and better educated as time went by. Even with the Comics Code Authority in full effect, the storylines of mainline publishers like Marvel and DC Comics were streamlined, but it did not stop people from reading into them what they sought out to find. Robert Lang's "Batman and Robin: A Family Romance" (1990), Will Brooker's "Hero of the Beach: Flex Mentallo at the End of the Worlds" (2015), or Dorian Alexander's "Faces of Abjectivity: The Uncanny Mystique and Transexuality" (2018) are very good examples of such interpretations. But one group of superheroes in particular seemed to welcome and support queer readings better than the rest: the X-Men.

Created by Stan Lee and Jack Kirby in 1963, the X-Men were the comic book reflection of the ongoing civil rights movement at the time, mirroring the African-American struggle with that of mutants in the comics. The X-Men became the most used superhero team to deal with issues of discrimination by introducing strong women, African-Americans, Hispanics, Asians, and much later on, LGBTIQI+ characters. Plenty of queer readings of the X-Men universe have been published over the years, such as Ramzi Fawaz' *The New Mutants: Superheroes and the Radical Imagination of American Comics* (2016), or Mikhail Lyubansky "Prejudice Lessons from the Xavier Institute" (2008). In this chapter, Lyubansky observed the propensity of the X-Universe to be used as an allegory for oppression, but he also noticed that "the analogies are not always adequate" (2008, 77). Borrowing from Susan Fiske's analysis of the perception of "outed" minorities indexed on both warmth and competence, Lyubansky reached the following conclusion:

> While this study did not include mutants in their list of out-groups, X-Men fans know that mutants tend to be regarded by humans with little warmth but are perceived to be high in competence. This combination would place them squarely into the envious prejudice category, far from most African Americans today and farther still from how Black Americans were perceived during the fight for civil rights in the 1960s.
>
> *(2008, 84; see Fiske et al. 2002)*

Lyubansky further questions how Mutants would be aptly placed on Fiske's "Perception of Out Groups" chart as enviously prejudiced because of their super-powered skills, since their powerful nature does not imply the political power to put an end to their own oppression. As such, mutants would fit better a bit lower on Fiske's competence scale, placing them closer to gay men, blue collars, and migrant workers than to black professionals, businesswomen, or feminists. Substituting or mirroring discrimination is not as clearly set as some might read it in X-Men, and having African-American characters facing racism is not entirely similar to a mutant being forced to a cure. The biological and medical condition of mutantkind that the writers heavily relied on from the very start intrinsically linked the X-Men with issues of the LGBTQI+ community, especially as the world faced the AIDS epidemic of the 1980s, or when conversion therapy to turn people straight is still happening to this day. It is thus crucial to have out-and-about characters in comic book pages, combining their superheroic specificities with other personal attributes such as being gay, lesbian, or transgender. But introducing a major new LGBTQI+ character that could rival the superheroes people have come to know and love over the past 80 years or so, without them being relegated to the background as a new quota addition to the mix, seems a rather impossible task. With the many resetting story-arcs that have occurred in the past couple of decades in the comic book publishing industry, reinventions have become the new normal but these emerging LGBTQI+ characters do not have the same role to play.

Yet before multiversal inventions and actual reinventions of superheroes as gay, lesbian, or transgender, it was the LGBTQI+ fans that started to imagine what gay, lesbian, or trans superheroes could be like. In the afterword to *Fandom: Identities and Communities in a Mediated World* (2007), Henry Jenkins highlights the fact that the online fan communities were becoming more and more proactive in, and with, the media that they are drawn to and thus invested "in specific media properties or platforms, and often create new content by appropriating, remixing, or modifying existing media content in clever and inventive ways." (Jenkins, 358) The rise of the internet facilitated the circulation and sharing of many fan practices that have remained niche or underground for decades.

Over the decades, superhero narratives have triggered a level of engagement from readers that had not been seen on such a scale. Interactions between the superheroes and their readership were countless on interpersonal levels, but it was also something that was encouraged by the industry itself. The most famous example being DC's 1988 "Death in the Family" telephone poll which urged Batman readers to call the hotline in order to choose whether the character of Jason Todd should die or not. The readers had a very strong input in the story which further cemented the bond between these fictional characters and their readership. But with the rise of digital media, superheroes truly became a property that would transcend the capitalistic boundaries that were, until the late 1990s, seemingly insurmountable. Fanzines existed long before the internet did, and they were the interpersonal space in which fans could engage narratively with their favorite characters, sending fan fiction of their own making to the publishers for everyone to read. In the 1960s, *Xero* (1960–1963) and *Alter Ego* (1961–) were the two biggest comic book fanzines before DC and Marvel took the matter in their own hands and launched their own fanzine magazines, *The Amazing World of DC Comics* (1974) and *FOOM* (1973), both of which ceased publication in 1978. These regulated fanzines featured occasional fan fictions, but none were slash fiction, a specific fan fiction category also born in the 1970s, which focused on same-sex relationships of existing characters. No publisher for a medium such as comics would allow same-sex fan fiction to be included, when the LGBTQI+ community was still under much pressure in the country.

Superhero-related slash fiction still existed back then, but it circulated in very confidential and restricted circles, and very few traces subsist to this day. It all changed in the late 1990s and early 2000s when internet blogs and forums enabled fans to share their slash fiction without the editorial lens that the fanzine had back in the day. Fanfiction.net, adultfanfiction. net, and livejournal.com were amongst the biggest websites used, as well as many others that were made and administered by fans themselves which were very often hosted on Angelfire and Geocities. As analyzed by Gareth Schott and Gemma Corin in *From 'Ambiguously Gay Duos' to Homosexual Superheroes: The Role of Sexuality in Comic Book Fandom* (2009), Pandora's box suddenly opened, and even if there are moderators on these forums to edit (if needed) the content, the fans were free to engage in any issue that they wished to tackle without taking the risk of going too far and being censored. Coupled with the success of the superhero genre in Hollywood blockbusters in the early 2000s, the number of slash fiction narratives about superheroes exploded over the web with discussion threads that could finally address sexuality out in the open.

In doing so, fan fiction through slash fiction promoted same-sex relationships between well-established characters, usually two men, following the narrative pattern of the sidekick or that of the nemesis: Batman and Robin, Superman and Jimmy Olsen, Wolverine and Cyclops, Green Lantern and Sinestro, Iron Man and the Mandarin, or Charles Xavier and Magneto. These popular same-sex romantic pairings of slash fiction are notably found on one of the world's most popular fan fiction websites, archiveofourown.org (AO3). For the pairing Charles Xavier/Magneto, there are more than 17,600 works available on AO3, and for Jason Todd/Dick Grayson, both of them Robins at some point, more than 8,400. Neil Shyminsky's "'Gay' Sidekicks: Queer Anxiety and the Straightening of the Superhero" (2010) explores how the sidekick in superhero narratives can be read as performing alternative modes of masculinity in an attempt to "straighten" the superhero he is attached to, while Gareth Schott's "From Fan Appropriation to Industry Re-Appropriation: the Sexual Identity of Comic Superheroes" (2010) clearly retraces the ownership of LGBTQI+ representation in comics to the fans who did it first.

What such profusion of LGBTQI+ fan fiction means in the long run is that readers are looking for content that they can relate to, and since they do not find it in the pages of the comic books they are buying, it is up to them to create their own storylines in which to revel in. Because such a (pro)active LGBTQI+ comic book community has developed online since the late 1990s, the comic book publishers had to lend an ear to this more and more visible minority. The arrival of Midnighter in *Stormwatch* (1998) released through the WildStorm imprint, and giving him center stage in *The Authority* (1998) is proof of that. But gay couple Midnighter and Apollo, as charismatic as they can be, could hardly rival in popularity with the likes of Batman, Superman, or Thor. The industry then knew that they had to include LGBTQI+ superheroes in another way than creating new additions to an already over-crowded list of characters, where these new additions risk fading into the background as soon as they appear. The longevity of the genre rests upon its unbeatable icons, none of which were created as gay, lesbian, bisexual, or transgender.

Coming Out(s) of the Multiverse

As the rules of the Comics Code Authority were increasingly disregarded by authors, artists, and editors alike throughout the late 1970s and the 1980s, it ultimately became somewhat obsolete in the 1990s until its dissolution in 2011. Because the LGBTQI+ rights movement started in the U.S. with the Stonewall riots in 1969, a clear input toward queer representations in comics truly started to emerge in the late 1990s, pacing its integration in the panels alongside the growing LGBTQI+ visibility and acceptance in American society. Northstar is the most often quoted example of the first mainstream character to ever come out as gay in *Alpha Flight* Vol.1 #106 (March 1992), in what looked like a narrative stunt that took the character's narrative in a completely different direction. Created in 1979, it took 13 years for the character to suddenly reveal his homosexuality. To that extent, Gareth Schott reviewed in detail Northstar's coming out and stated that "his (Northstar) notoriety as a candid character, willing to challenge the expectations of the superhero is sadly not based on a venerable sequence of positive storylines as a gay superhero, but on an uncharacteristic outburst" (Schott 2010, 22). The convoluted plot points of the character are linked with the deleterious political and health climate of the early 1990s with AIDS at its core, and Northstar's coming out of nowhere is undoubtedly linked to that. What is striking is that other LGBTQI+ characters existed before Northstar's big announcement in 1992, but the climate in which it was made has established him as the first out major LGBTQI+ comic book character.

Alpha Flight was canceled in 1994, and Northstar was killed off in several other dimensions before being resurrected in the main Marvel continuity in 2002, when he joined the X-Men. The abruptness of the announcement in 1992 had to be forgotten in order for genuine romantic story arcs to emerge for him in the panels of the early 2000s. At that time, writers were faced with the dilemma of providing their readership with mainline LGBTQI+ superheroes that they could relate to, but creating such a character in an already overcrowded catalog could be perceived as tokenism. What if they didn't need to create a new character? What if other versions of these said-characters were the way to go? This "what if" tagline is precisely what many comic book writers have relied upon over the years, giving birth to one of the genre's most complicated aspects: the multiverse. For both Marvel and DC Comics, the term has now become synonymous with editorial reboots in order to create coherent storylines for readers to follow, entertaining long-time followers as well as providing point of entries for newcomers. The vocabulary associated with the very concept of the multiverse can sometimes feel convoluted, relying on concepts of realms, timelines, pocket dimensions, the omniverse, and a cosmos. The editors will occasionally insert a page to explain as clearly and as succinctly as possible these concepts. According to Karin Kukkonen:

> The multiverse is a set of mutually incompatible storyworlds. In principle these story-worlds can be viewed as counterfactuals; changing particular elements of the characters' situations, they relate to one other as "what if"-versions. But because a baseline

reality is often difficult to discern within this constellation of worlds, the multiverse poses considerable processing challenges. On the one hand, the iconography of super-hero costumes provides readers with something of a shortcut, helping them identify and distinguish between different character versions. On the other hand, reader sur-rogates take paths through storyworlds that, in conjunction with explanatory models they (and thus readers) acquire along the way, enable interpreters to connect these worlds into the larger whole of the multiverse. As the narrative unfolds, readers can, with the help of surrogates, construct a more or less continuous mental model of the multiverse, incrementally moving through its different parts and sets of possibilities.

(Kukkonen 2010, 55)

In describing the multiverse and how its narrative threads are interwoven within the reader's imaginary, Kukkonen also points to the fact that readers nurture a special bond with the superhero whose adventures they follow. The term "reader surrogate" emphasizes that inter-connection between one specific character and its readership. Within the infinite possibilities opened by the very useful tool of the multiverse, LGBTQI+ reinventions became fair game for writers who saw a way to provide representation, leading readers to sometimes discover incredible reinventions.

DC Comics uses multiversity to re-invent several characters as LGBTQI+, which provides them with new symbolical significance. If the re-invention of Catman as bisexual in the Prime Earth continuity in 2015 did not have much of an impact, the re-invention of Alan Scott as gay was much more meaningful. Re-introduced in the *Earth 2* title in 2012, Alan was already known to many as the original Green Lantern when the character was first created back in 1940. Only this time, Alan Scott was an out gay man, the first time that a founding member of the Justice League was portrayed as such. Scott's return in the Green Lantern role lasted until the Convergence storyline of 2015 in which he played a pivotal role, but this reim-agination deeply impacted the way a key LGBTQI+ character could be portrayed alongside the likes of Aquaman, Superman, or Batman. Another symbolically charged re-invention was Grant Morisson's Red Racer which he wrote into his Multiversity storyline. As another re-invention of a founding member of the Justice League of America (JLA) as a gay hero, The Red Racer is Earth 36's equivalent of the Flash, here a gay comic book nerd who was touched by the speedforce. Other reimaginings of existing superheroes as LGBTQI+ include the DC Bombshells universe version of Kara Zor-El, a.k.a. Supergirl, who is portrayed in a romantic relationship with Eloisa Lane; or that of Hal Jordan, iconic Green Lantern, who is depicted as evil in the Antimatter universe and in a relationship with Thaal Sinestro. First appearing in a 2021 storyline, one recent multiversal transformation is particularly interest-ing as it also includes gender bending: on Earth 11, Raven is no longer a young woman but a young gay man in a relationship with Donald Troy.

Marvel publications also make use of the multiversal narrative trick to reimagine sev-eral characters as LGBTQI+, but this mostly happens with the X-Men (and women of the X-Men). Mariko Yashida, the Sunfire of Earth 2109 in the *Exiles* (2001) title, was reinvented as lesbian when in the original universe, Mariko was a love interest of Wolverine. In the *Exiles* storyline, Mariko was instead the lover of Spider-Woman who was none other than Mary-Jane Watson, another LGBTQI+ reinvention of Peter Parker's legendary love interest. In *Exiles* Vol.2 (2009), Hank McCoy a.k.a. Beast, a founding member of the X-Men, was reimagined as gay on Earth 763, where he is portrayed in a happy relationship with Wonder Man, also re-invented as gay. The elusive mutant Mystique has always been a complex character to read in terms of her sexuality, probably reinforced by her shape-shifting ability, but in the *Age of X* (2011) miniseries unfolding on Earth 11326, the pair of Raven Darkholme and Irene Adler (Destiny) is unequivocally portrayed as a married couple.

The Ultimate Universe storylines launched back in 2001 allowed for reinventions and, once again, the X-Men took center stage for LGBTQI+ representation. In it, Piotr Rasputin a.k.a. Colossus was reimagined as gay and in a happy relationship with Northstar. The X-Men have been the most fertile ground for LGBTQI+ reimagined characters, and Greg Pak did not shy away from that in *X-Treme X-Men* Vol.2 (2012–2013). Catapulted to Earth 12025, the comic book depicts James Howlett a.k.a. Wolverine in a gay relationship with fellow superhero Hercules. These LGBTQI+ reinventions did hold a significant importance within the overall process, because the authors specifically chose Colossus, Wolverine, and Hercules, three major superheroes that have been depicted as the epitome of strength and (borderline toxic) masculinity in their original versions. Outside of the mutants, very few LGBTQI+ reimaginations have taken place at Marvel, but three are worth noting. Elektra was portrayed as lesbian in the *Punisher Max* series of 2011, and so was Valkyrie from Earth 22681 who, in *Exiles* Vol.3 (2018), expressed her romantic interest in Rebecca Barnes. Finally, a very brief multiversal cameo of Reed Richards (Mr. Fantastic) and Jack Storm (Human Torch), both coming from Earth 93563, was included in *Fantastic Four* #563 (March 2009) which depicted the two as a married couple.

Comic Book Events and the Rise of New Canons

Comic book events, reboots, and limited runs, while not strictly nor systematically relying on multiversity, have also been used as opportunities for greater LGBTQI+ representations in comic books. Ron Zimmerman's take on the *Rawhide Kid* Vol. 3 (2003) and Vol. 4 (2010) are perfect examples of that. As a popular character in the 1950s and 1960s, the cowboy was reimagined as a very open and very forward gay man in these explicit comics. Volume 3 even had a "Parental Advisory" warning on the cover. Here, it was the creative team's decision to create these very limited series of only four issues to provide representation as well as mock the conventions that expected specific masculine standards when the character was created. As a route sometimes taken by both Marvel and DC, outing an existing staple character as bisexual was an easy way of moving toward greater LGBTQI+ representation. Deadpool's pansexuality was first alluded to in *Cable and Deadpool* Vol.1 (2004) even though the character had been around for 14 years. Appearing for the first time in 1985, John Constantine was outed as bisexual in Brian Azzarello's *Hellblazer* #170 (March 2002) when it was written that he had been involved with men as well, the readers just had never seen it. Constantine was seldom seen with men after that until the New 52 reboot of DC Comics in 2011 which, moving forward, truly integrated that facet of the character into the comics' narrative arcs. These major publishing events were the moments when comic book editors could become more hands on and make use of a convenient multiversal "anything goes" rulebook in order to bring forth greater changes.

DC's "52" comic book mini-series (2006–2007) which served as liaison between the multi-comic events of Infinite Crisis (2005–2006) and One Year Later (2006) was positioned at the crossroads of both the multiversity and the reboot. In it, Geoff Johns, Grant Morrison, Greg Rucka, and Mark Waid all participated in the reimagining of Katherine Kane, a.k.a. Batwoman, who was (re)introduced as a lesbian superheroine. Doing so, it put a clever spin on the original Katherine Kane who first appeared in the panels of *Detective*

Comics #233 (July 1956) and who was integrated into the narrative to be Bruce Wayne's new romantic interest in order to quench Batman's alleged homosexuality. *Batwoman* Vol.2 became one of the cornerstone titles of the New 52 relaunch of the entire DC title slate after the events of Flashpoint (2011). Being multiversal in nature, Flashpoint was the perfect opportunity for DC Comics to reinvent some of its characters without ostracizing its loyal base of readers. With Batwoman leading the way, and after several multiversal reimagination of LGBTQI+ superheroes, DC's ambition was to create a constellation of LGBTQI+ characters, with women leading the way.

After a very dense series of events with Flashpoint and Convergence (2015), DC Comics branded their Rebirth event in 2016 as the beginning of the publisher's new era. Creating a new combination of sorts from old and new multiversal timelines, DC became very outspoken about its most iconic superheroines, outing Selina Kyle, Poison Ivy, Harley Quinn, and Wonder Woman as bisexual. While the first three did not stir any controversy with innuendos made for years about their sexuality, Wonder Woman did. Wonder Woman's creator William Moulton Marston, and Robert Kanigher, the Silver Age author who revamped her origin story, have both made it unclear as to whether one should read the character as a lesbian or bisexual, notwithstanding that Themyscira is an island populated strictly by women. However, as stated by Tim Hanley in *Wonder Woman Unbound*: "in the light of Marston's other work and Kanigher's later interviews and references to Sappho, it's fairly reasonable to interpret Wonder Woman as either bisexual or lesbian" (Hanley 2014, 141). Grant Morrison's *Wonder Woman: Earth One* Vol.1 #1 was published in April 2016 followed by *Wonder Woman* Vol. 6 which started in June 2016 helmed by Greg Rucka, as well as Jill Thomson's one-shot *Wonder Woman: The True Amazon* (Nov. 2016), all tackled the Amazon's origins under a very clear queer reading. But in an interview he did with Comicosity in September 2016, Rucka argued that the adjectives gay, lesbian, or bisexual were somewhat inadequate (McMillan 2016). According to him, from the outside world looking in, Themyscira is indeed a lesbian utopia, but for the Amazons themselves, lesbianism is not a concept they even grasped because prior to the arrival of male intruders, the female-only island is all that they had ever known. Yet this intradiegetic pirouette allowed Rucka to take a firm stand on Wonder Woman's queerness, without completely upending the character's sexual orientation when it came to the history of her romantic endeavors.

DC's Rebirth multiversal event impacted secondary superheroes to their core and radically changed a superhero's sexuality without tying it to the character's journey. Jackson Hyde was introduced as a straight young man in an on-and-off relationship with his girlfriend Maria in 2010, and when Aqualad was reintroduced as the new Aquaman after DC's Rebirth, he suddenly became an out and proud gay man. Establishing or affirming new sexual proclivities was something that Brian Michael Bendis took further in *All New X-Men* #40 (April 2015). Not a multiversal reimagining per se, the *All New X-Men* made use of the title's central storyline, which revolved around the chronological displacement of the five original X-Men (namely, Cyclops, Beast, Jean Grey, Iceman, and Angel) into the future, to out Bobby Drake as gay, something that fans of the comics have read into for decades. The younger versions of the original X-Men thus interact in the present with their older selves. In *All New X-Men* #40, Bobby is literally outed by an intrusive teenage Jean Grey who cannot help but know his secret because of her telepathic abilities. Things were taken to another level in *Uncanny X-Men* #600 (January 2016) when the younger Bobby, now embracing his homosexuality, confronted his older self in the present narrative timeline, stating that if he is gay, then his older self must be as well. This conversation with himself revealed what the Iceman readers have always known; he has always been gay, but he preferred to keep it a secret over the years in order to not be mutant *and* gay.

Taking on the Mantle over the Rainbow Bridge

The longevity and serialization of superhero narratives made it so that it has been rather difficult to integrate high-profile LGBTQI+ representation in the medium. The multiversal reimaginings allowed for short yet significant stepping stones toward better inclusion, and as time went by, new superheroes were created with their LGBTQI+ identities written into their characterization. The Young Avengers' Wiccan and Hulkling as well as America Chavez are very good examples of Marvel's intention on that matter, while DC took the legacy road in order to introduce a new generation of superheroes who embraced their queerness. Within less than a year, Tim Drake a.k.a. Robin and Jon Kent, also known as the Superman of Earth, both came out as bisexual in *Batman: Urban Legends* #6 (October 2021) and *Superman: Son of Kal-El* #5 (May 2022).

With the success of comic book adaptations into film, series, or animated features, multiversity has now taken on a transmedia quality at both DC and Marvel. Marvel has remained rather shy in their adaptations and the possibility of queer reimaginings, alluding to Loki's bisexuality during the first season of *Loki* (Disney+ 2021–2023) and making Phastos gay in *Eternals* (Chloé Zao 2021). In *The New Mutants* (Josh Boone 2020), 20th Century Fox went further in reimagining queer-coded comic book characters Dani Moonstar and Rahne Sinclair as lesbians. But DC is the superhero franchise that has taken the most advantage of the full potential of LGBTQI+ reimaginings in multiversal transmedia. In the animated feature film *Superman: Red Son* (Sam Liu 2020), Diana Prince turned Superman away, letting him know that she was lesbian, and the *Harley Quinn* animated series (2019–present) revolves around Harley's romance with Poison Ivy. It is, however, The CW's Arrowverse television shows that undoubtedly championed LGBTQI+ representation for DC superheroes. It adapted existing LGBTQI+ comic book characters, Anissa Pierce (Thunder) and Grace Choi in *Black Lightning* (2018–2021), John Constantine in both *Arrow* (2008–2020) and *Legends of Tomorrow* (2016–2022), Maggie Sawyer in *Supergirl* (2015–2021), Raymond Terrill (The Ray) in *Arrow* and Kate Kane in *Batwoman* (2019–2022); but it also reimagined non-LGBTQI+ comic book superheroes. As such, Curtis Holt (Mr. Terrific) is gay and Nyssa Al Ghul is lesbian in *Arrow*, Nia Nall (Dreamer) is trans in *Supergirl* and Leonard Snart (Captain Cold) is gay in *Legends of Tomorrow*. The Arrowverse also invented some central LGBTQI+ characters to maximize representation with Alex Danvers (Kara's adoptive sister) and Kelly Olsen in *Supergirl*, William Clayton (Oliver Queen's son) in *Arrow*, and Sara Lance in *Arrow* and *Legends of Tomorrow*. Because of Ruby Rose's departure from the role of Kate Kane in *Batwoman* after only one season, the production created the character of Ryan Wilder to succeed her as Batwoman, a character that was then translated into comic book format in *Batgirl* Vol. 5 #50 (December, 2020).

Whether it has been used as a narrative loophole to reset its narratives or as an attempt to make sense of decades of sometimes conflicting story arcs, multiversity is also a practical tool of inclusion for out and proud LGBTQI+ superheroes in the pages of comics. Now, about 20 years after the first multiversal coming outs, the integration of leading LGBTQI+ characters in the pages of mainline comic book continuities seems to have become the new normal. Queer representation no longer needs to find convoluted pathways to exist, as comics can now use queer coding to signify LGBTQI+ allies rather than hinting at hidden queer identities, as showcased by David Marquez' variant cover for *Thor Annual #1*, released at the end of May 2023, right on time for Pride Month, on which the God of Thunder is walking peacefully toward the readers on a rainbow Bifrost road.

References

Alexander, Dorian L. 2018. "Faces of Abjectivity: The Uncanny Mystique and Transexuality." In *Gender and the Superhero Narrative*, edited by Michael Goodrum, Tara Prescott, and Philip Smith. University of Mississippi Press.

Boone, Josh, dir. 2020. *The New Mutants*. 20th Century Studios.

Brooker, Will. 2015. "Hero of the Beach: Flex Mentallo at the End of the Worlds." In *Superheroes and Identities*, edited by Mel Gibson, David Huxley, and Joan Ormrod. Routledge.

Fawaz, Ramzi. 2016. *The New Mutants: Superheroes and the Radical Imagination of American Comics*. New York University Press.

Fiske, Susan, Amy Cuddy, Peter Glick, and Jun Xu. 2002. "A Model of (Often Mixed) Stereotype Content: Competence and Warmth Respectively Follow from Perceived Status and Competition." *Journal of Personality and Social Psychology* 82, no. 6: 878–902.

Hall, Justin. 2012. *No Straight Lines: Four Decades of Queer Comics*. Fantagraphics Books.

Hanley, Tim. 2014. *Wonder Woman Unbound: The Curious History of the World's Most Famous Heroine*. Chicago Review Press.

Jenkins, Henry. 2007. "The Future of Fandom." In *Fandom: Identities and Communities in a Mediated World*, edited by Jonathan Gray, Cornell Sandvoss, and Lee Harrington. New York University Press.

Kukkonen, Karin. 2010. "Navigating Infinite Earths: Readers, Mental Models, and the Multiverse of Superhero Comics." *Storyworlds: A Journal of Narrative Studies* 2, (Jan.): 39–58.

Lang, Robert. 1990. "Batman and Robin: A Family Romance." *American Imago* 47, no. 3–4 (Fall/Winter): 293–319.

Liu, Sam, dir. 2020. *Superman: Red Son*. Warner Bros. Animation.

Lyubansky, Mikhail. 2008. "Prejudice Lessons from the Xavier Institute." In *The Psychology of Superheroes: An Unauthorized Exploration*, edited by Robin S. Rosenberg. Benbella Books.

McMillan, Graeme. 2016. "'Wonder Woman' Comic Writer Confirms Hero Is Bisexual." *The Hollywood Reporter*, September 29. https://www.hollywoodreporter.com/movies/movie-news/wonder-woman-is-bisexual-writer-933809/.

Michlin, Monica. 2013. "Recurrence, Remediation and Metatextuality in *Queer as Folk*." *TV Series* 3. https://doi.org/10.4000/tvseries.725.

Nyberg, Amy Kiste. 1998. *Seal of Approval: The History of the Comics Code*. University Press of Mississippi.

Schott, Gareth. 2010. "From Fan Appropriation to Industry Re-Appropriation: The Sexual Identity of Comic Superheroes." *Journal of Graphic Novels and Comics* 1, no.1: 17–29.

Schott, Gareth, and Gemma Corin. 2009. *From 'Ambiguously Gay Duos' to Homosexual Superheroes: The Role of Sexuality in Comic Book Fandom*. VDM Verlag.

Shyminsky, Neil. 2010. "'Gay' Sidekicks: Queer Anxiety and the Straightening of the Superhero." *Men and Masculinities* 14, no. 3: 288–308.

Wertham, Fredric. 1954. *Seduction of the Innocent*. Rinehart & Company.

Zao, Chloé, dir. 2021. *Eternals*. Marvel Studios.

7

PUNCH-UPS ON PARADE

Celebrating and Marketing Queerness in Marvel and DC's Pride Month Anthologies

Anna F. Peppard

The first issue of Marvel Comics' Pride Month anthology, official title *Marvel's Voices: Pride* #1, was published in 2021. Similar to the *DC Pride* special launched the same year, *Marvel's Voices: Pride* includes a selection of stories spotlighting LGBTQ+ characters written and drawn by LGBTQ+ creators. Issue #1 opens with a vignette written and illustrated by Luciano Vecchio in which the superhero Prodigy, who identifies as bisexual and possesses the mutant ability to absorb knowledge, relays the queer history of Marvel comics. This history begins with the French-Canadian superhero Northstar rocketing toward the reader with an outstretched hand while exclaiming, in large, bold text: "**I am gay!**" This is a retelling of *Alpha Flight* #106, written by Scott Lobdell and penciled by Mark Pacella. That comic was originally published in 1992, two years after the Comics Code Authority was revised to include "homosexuals" alongside the CIA and FBI on a list of "recognizable national, social, political, cultural, ethnic and racial groups" that should be "portrayed in a positive light" (CBLDF n.d.). *Marvel's Voices: Pride* #1 reprints a portion of the original comic as its final item.

Prodigy's retelling elaborates: "Everyone remembers this moment. A cornerstone. **Northstar** was the first superhero to come out to the public – it was an activist statement, bringing awareness, starting discussions, and inspiring others…." Prodigy, or, more appropriately, Vecchio, then proceeds to recount key moments from what we might call the pre-history of queer Marvel, in that some of the examples remained subtextual for decades and others substantially pre-date the company's existence. For instance, Vecchio cites the examples of Hercules and the Valkyrie Rūna, who have "been around since mythical times," as well the X-Men franchise characters Mystique and Destiny who, in Marvel comics lore, have been a romantic couple since at least the late 19th century.

This introductory history encapsulates several ongoing debates about what queer representation is or should look like within the context of popular stories with lucrative corporate IP that have, for most of their history, focused primarily on appealing to a narrow subset of cis, straight men, and boys. Because some of these fans have organized aggressive backlashes in response to the development of more diverse content (Scott 2019, 3), and because the present cultural moment finds social and political gains for LGBTQ+ folks being met with similar backlashes, Marvel and DC's Pride Month specials are both excitingly disruptive

DOI: 10.4324/9781003366911-9

and, inevitably, compelled to negotiate competing demands. As Bryan Bove observes, within mainstream comics, "Greater representation leads to more inclusive stories. But it also creates a battleground of tension for creators and fans, particularly when it comes to perceived 'changes' in the continuities of established characters" (2021, 527). This is exactly what makes Marvel and DC's Pride Month specials an excellent place to ply one's wares as a scholar trying to do better analysis of better representation. Which is what this chapter is about – namely, the ongoing struggle we face, as pop culture scholars and comics scholars, to move beyond discussing representation in binaries of "good" and "bad."

Within such binaries, good representation is often associated with the capacity to educate and/or proffer idealized versions of minority or minoritized demographics, while bad representation is often associated with bigoted misinformation and/or simplifications that are distilled into stereotypes and caricatures. When dealing with egregious misrepresentations, such as the overt homophobia of the infamous story "A Very Personal Hell," appearing in *Hulk!* #23 (1980), in which a cadre of outrageously gay-coded men threaten to sexually assault Bruce Banner in a YMCA shower, such binaries can be useful. But analyzing representation in texts like the Marvel and DC Pride specials, wherein marginalized creators are trying to do good within corporate structures that often limit creative freedom in the interests of maintaining brand integrity, requires considerably more nuance. In general, and because they include many different perspectives on identities across the LGBTQ+ spectrum, the Marvel and DC Pride specials cannot be reduced to binaries of good and bad representation. Instead, they must be analyzed as webs of possibility in conversation with a variety of stakeholders, including diverse readers and creators as well as corporate overlords, all of whom must be understood as responding, in their own ways, to rapidly changing social contexts. As Sarah Panuska observes, we have arrived at a time wherein "the sheer number of LGBTQ heroes should no longer be a measure of progress. Rather, it is the *quality* of LGBTQ representations in comics that now needs to be evaluated" (2020, 131). Using the 2021 and 2022 Marvel and DC Pride Month specials as case studies, this chapter attempts to reckon with questions of quality, taking stock of current approaches to diversification within mainstream comics while modeling analysis of representation that meets the needs of the moment.

Analysis of representation is also inevitably affected by the positionality of the person doing the analysis. To that end, I will confess that as a queer-affiliated superhero comics fan who also professionally studies representations of gender and sexuality in superhero stories, I was mildly shocked by the recontextualization of Northstar's coming out story in the first Marvel Pride Month special. I have always known *Alpha Flight* #106 as a regrettable, embarrassingly stereotyped example of queer representation. While plans to have Northstar die of an AIDS-related disease were ultimately nixed (Wegner 2022), *Alpha Flight* #106 does feature Northstar adopting an orphaned baby girl who is HIV positive. Admittedly, the story uses the little girl to emphasize that HIV/AIDS can affect anyone. Yet, this baby, whose nameless mother dies off-panel, is more plot device than character, existing primarily to facilitate Northstar's emotional growth. In addition, Northstar declares his gayness in a thoroughly melodramatic and deeply uncomfortable fashion: in response to being violently beaten and choked by an older male superhero named Major Mapleleaf, who is bitter about the AIDS-related death of his gay son and blames Northstar for worsening the epidemic by remaining in the closet. But perhaps, the greater misrepresentation of this story in *Marvel's Voices: Pride* is the suggestion that Northstar's coming out inspired a wave of change. Gareth Schott observes that following *Alpha Flight* #106, "Northstar's sexuality was subsequently suppressed in an attempt to comply with social attitudes and responses to the disclosure"

(2010, 28). Indeed, Northstar would largely disappear from the pages of Marvel comics for most of the next decade and would not have a canonical boyfriend until 2009, the same year Marvel featured its first on-panel kiss between two named male characters, Rictor and Shatterstar (*X-Factor Vol. 3 #45*, 2009). As such, Vecchio's queer history of Marvel comics elides a 17-year period in which the company offered very little canonical queer representation of any kind. Vecchio, or more appropriately Prodigy, also fails to mention that by 2021, the writer of *Alpha Flight* #106, Scott Lobdell, had been largely blacklisted by the mainstream comics industry in the wake of allegations of sexual harassment (Grunewald 2020). Instead, the first Marvel Pride special spotlights *Alpha Flight*'s openly gay assistant editor, Chris Cooper, who is interviewed elsewhere in the anthology.

Yet, I also find myself sympathetic to the revisionist history being performed by Vecchio/Prodigy, which can be viewed as a form of reparative reading. Coined by seminal queer theorist Eve Kosovsky Sedgwick, reparative reading is the inverse of paranoid reading. Paranoid reading anticipates the harmful effects of imperfect representations. In its broadest terms, it describes what we often do when we analyze issues of representation in literature and popular culture: identify bad things for the good of real lives badly affected by those bad things. For the purposes of this chapter, a key aspect of Sedgwick's theorization of reparative reading is her contention that "paranoia for all its vaunted suspicion acts as though its work would be accomplished if only it could finally, this time, somehow gets its story truly known" (2003, 138). In other words, there is a presumption built into many analyses of representation that the act of pointing out bad stuff is not just good enough but actually good, as in, enough to inspire change. At its most extreme, paranoid reading neglects the possibility of joy, and with it, a firm sense of what positive change might look like.

In contrast, reparative reading sees the bad but hopes to contest it. Writes Sedgwick:

> Because there can be terrible surprises… there can also be good ones. Hope, often a fracturing, even a traumatic thing to experience, is among the energies by which the reparatively positioned reader tries to organize the fragments and part-objects she encounters or creates. Because the reader has room to realize that the future may be different from the present, it is also possible for her to entertain such profoundly painful, profoundly relieving, ethnically crucial possibilities as that the past, in turn, could have happened differently from the way it actually did.
>
> *(2003, 146)*

Though not always referred to as such, reparative reading is widely adopted within queer-affiliated fandoms. This is evidenced by, among other things, the slash and genderswap sub-genres of fan fiction and fan art,

> which [make] adhesions between gender, sex, sexuality, and national belonging visible by showing how the meaning of a story changes when, for example, the representation of America's strength becomes physically female, or when a male-embodied Captain America becomes sexually open.
>
> *(Kustritz 2020, 317)*

Stories and images that queer ostensibly patriarchal, heteronormative superhero source texts often draw inspiration from the queer potential of stories about spandex-clad mutants forming found families to heroically fight with/for a world that hates and fears them. But these stories and images also tend to imagine queerer pasts, presents, and futures than mainstream producers are apt to allow. In effect, Vecchio writes Prodigy as a queer fan performing reparative reading, which is itself an act of visibility, sanctioning queer world-making by integrating it into the self-making of the superheroes who make up the Marvel Universe. This goal is quite explicit in the concluding sentences of Prodigy's history lesson, in which he says, "We honor history to appreciate the present. We treasure the past to dream of the future." This resonates with Kate McCullough's assertion that comics are especially adept at reparative world-making. McCullough writes, "Opening up registers of queer time not available in purely prose or purely visual form, comics offer a unique opportunity for the enactment of a queer temporality" (2018, 401).

And yet, Prodigy is not real, and Vecchio is not simply a fan. He is, instead, a work-for-hire creator writing and drawing under the auspices of a queer editor who is ultimately under the auspices of a corporate entity that is not just interested in representing queerness but selling it. As such, without neglecting the specificity of individual vignettes or the creative diversity of Marvel and DC's Pride Month specials, it is appropriate to investigate these specials for marked trends in representation. Such trends may reflect the types of queer stories a publisher and its corporate overlords are interested in prioritizing within the present cultural moment and as a reflection of their respective brand identities.

One trend in all the anthologies, but most visible in Marvel's 2021 anthology, is the purported goal of educating the public about LGBTQ+ identities. This goal is laudable, but the execution of this educational mission often raises questions about which members of the public are being addressed. Marvel's 2021 Pride Month anthology includes two stories in which trans women educate cis straight characters about LGBTQ+ experiences and politically correct terminology. In the first story, "Something New Every Day," written by Lilah Sturges and illustrated by Derek Charm, Elektra confronts and then aids Dr. Charlene McGowan, who is using a villain's abandoned lab to develop technology that would allow trans women to "manufacture their **own** hormones without taking **pills** every day." When Charlene and Elektra are attacked by other villains looking for the Mutant Growth Hormone drugs the lab had previously produced, Charlene complains that the male villain is not listening to her. To which Elektra quips, "Welcome to womanhood." While dodging explosions and mixing chemicals for a counterattack, Charlene offers this rejoinder: "You know, telling a trans woman 'welcome to womanhood' is actually kind of condescending? And it implies that we aren't 'real' women until or unless we transition." Off panel, Elektra exclaims, "I apologize! I was not aware of that!" Later, Elektra buys Charlene a drink to, in her words, apologize again and thank her for the lesson.

In a second story from Marvel's 2021 Pride special, "Totally Invulnerable," by Crystal Frasier with art by Jethro Morales, another trans woman, Jennifer Harris, cosplays as She-Hulk and gets mistaken for the real deal by She-Hulk's nemesis Titania. Harris subsequently relays her story about discovering personal empowerment through her fandom of She-Hulk, prompting Titania to insist, "Hey, I did not know any of that when I attacked you! I swear! I'm totally cool with the… the gender people. Is that how you say it?" "No," replies Harris, sporting a knowing smile, "But it's cool. It takes time to learn. Nobody's perfect." For some readers, these will no doubt be valuable teaching moments. Jeffrey A. Brown neatly summarizes the historical presence and absence of trans identities in superhero comics: "The superhero genre routinely depicts body swamps, gender-switch alternatives, and gender-crossing shape-shifters that metaphorically evoke trans conditions. Problematically, the existence of these trans allegories has allowed the genre to sidestep actual representations of trans characters" (2022, 139). But it is notable that in two stories in Marvel's 2021 Pride special, new trans characters who will not appear again, in this or any other comics, are introduced in part to teach established Marvel characters who will appear again how to be more inclusive. We can, as such, read into these stories an aspect of exploitation, in which the experiences of marginalized folks – including both the characters within the stories and the creators of the stories – are being used to signpost the allyship of corporate IP without having to meaningfully change the makeup of that corporate IP.

Significantly, the DC Pride specials are more likely to spotlight higher profile characters associated with globally popular transmedia brands. This includes LGBTQ+ versions of Robin, Superman, Green Lantern, and the Flash. Notably, none of these characters represent the most recognizable version of their popular monikers. The Robin who appears most prominently in the Pride anthologies is Tim Drake, not Dick Grayson; the Green Lanterns are Alan Scott and Sojourner Mullein rather than Hal Jordan or John Stewart; the Superman is Clark Kent and Lois Lane's son, Jon Kent. However, the Jon Kent example is notable for how explicitly and extensively it allies Superman with the goals and symbols of Pride. DC's 2022 Pride special opens with the story "Super Pride" written by Devin Grayson with art by Nick Robles, starring Jon Kent and the Damian Wayne version of Robin. The first line of the story is a caption box representing Jon's interior monologue, indicated by its branding with the Superman logo. "Symbols are powerful," thinks Jon, and indeed, this is the theme of the vignette, in which Jon must decide how to present himself at the Metropolis Pride Parade. Jon continues, "[Symbols] take complex concepts and translate them into a simple image that bypasses the human brain and speaks straight to the heart." This is not unlike Scott McCloud's theory that comics are especially good at soliciting empathy through a technique he calls "amplification through simplification" (1994, 30). Many critics and scholars have made similar arguments regarding the superhero genre's ability to distill identity into symbols (see Burke et al. 2019). Grayson and Robles' vignette is thus a metatextual rumination on the power of symbols, including both the Superman logo (owned by DC Comics, who are owned by Warner Bros., who are owned by Discovery Inc.) and Pride's rainbow imagery (most of which is free for public use but deeply commodified by rainbow capitalism and vilified by the political right-wing).

More specifically, "Super Pride" is a rumination on the complicated but potentially powerful relationship between the Superman logo and Pride imagery. In the story, Jon's boyfriend, Jay Nakamura, gifts him a Superman cape lined with a patchwork of Pride flags, including the standard Gilbert Baker rainbow flag as well as the bisexual, asexual, transgender, and lesbian flags, among others. In response, Jon confesses, "I wasn't planning to attend **Pride** as Superman… I'm not sure how my **dad** would feel about my riding on a Pride float as Superman." In effect, Jon's dialogue stages the conflict between a supposedly older generation of presumptively cis, straight, white male superhero fans, and a supposedly newer generation of presumptively more diverse and inclusive fans. Damian contests Jon's hesitancy, saying, "Your dad would **love** it. It would be you being **you** – which is **exactly** what he told you he wanted." The choice to have Damian, a canonically straight character, assure the reader that the original Superman would "love" Jon combining his own identity as Superman with his identity as a bisexual man and queer ally, attempts to resolve the supposed generational conflict by saying it does not exist. Of course, the original Superman, an alien refugee compelled to lead a double life in order to either/both protect his loved ones from harm and himself from exploitation, would understand and support Pride, or so Damian tells us; so do many scholarly arguments regarding the inherent queer potential of superhero metaphors (see Scott and Fawaz 2018; Stein 2018; Taylor 2007).

The story's conclusion, in which Jon smiles at the head of the Grand Marshall's parade float with the Superman "S" on his chest and his cape of many colors proudly unfurled behind him, cheered on by a bevy of civilians and other LGBTQ+ superheroes, hammers home the inclusivity of the Superman brand. Jon's monologue reads: "For me, [the Superman 'S'] signifies everything I hope to live up to. Today, here, right now, I want it to mean that I **see** you. That I **am** you." The final caption, "That I **am** you," is accompanied by a close-up of Jon's face in which he is looking directly at the reader, with both the Superman and Pride iconography cropped out. In addition to underscoring the clear-eyed acceptance of Superman the character and DC the company, this creative choice conveys universalism. Superman can be anyone; anyone can be Superman. On the one hand, associating Pride with the world's first and arguably most iconic superhero can be read as a powerful rebuke of the contention that mainstream superhero comics have only recently become political or incorporated allegories about race, gender, or diversity. As Asher Elbein (2018) documents, these charges are commonly recited by the bigoted #Comicsgate movement. The implication is, if Superman supports LGBTQ+ rights, then superhero comics have always done so (or at least, have always had the *potential* to do so). On the other hand, we can question who benefits most from associating Superman with Pride. In "Super Pride," even as the Superman logo legitimizes Pride, Pride imagery legitimizes Superman, and thus DC Comics (and Warner Bros. and Discover Inc.) as supportive of inclusion. And as often occurs within rainbow capitalism, and similar to the Northstar example discussed above, inclusion seems to be predicated on the exclusion of histories of exclusion.

But what should inclusion look like, anyway? This is a question at the heart of the Marvel and DC Pride specials and contemporary LGBTQ+ existence in general. Academic conceptions of queerness typically link it to subversions of the hegemonic status quo. Case in point, in his oft-cited *Making Things Perfectly Queer*, Alexander Doty describes the act of queer reading thusly:

> the use of the term 'queer' to discuss reception takes up the standard binary opposition of 'queer' to 'nonqueer' (or 'straight') while questioning its viability, at least in cultural studies, because… the queer often operates within the nonqueer, as the nonqueer does within the queer (whether in reception, texts, or producers).
>
> *(1993, 3)*

In other words, queerness is not reducible to the fact of sexual orientation but instead describes an oppositional stance contra straight culture. This understanding of queerness as oppositional informs critiques of the rise of homonormativity. Popularized, within a critical framework, by Lisa Duggan, the concept of homonormativity describes

> a politics that does not contest dominant heteronormative assumptions and institutions – such as marriage, and its call for monogamy and reproduction – but upholds and sustains them, while promising the possibility of a demobilized gay constituency and a privatized, depoliticized gay culture anchored in domesticity and consumption.
>
> *(2003, 50)*

As Duggan's emphasis on neoliberal consumption suggests, homonormativity is deeply intertwined with rainbow capitalism. It also includes the integration of LGBTQ+ subjects into wellness and self-improvement discourses. Michael Lovelock argues, "To be happy has become an overwhelming imperative for contemporary gay men," with "an urgent need to 'celebrate gay happiness'… [crystallizing] into a pervasive cultural script in which to be gay and *not* happy amounts to a failure of existential proportions" (2018, 549–550). Certainly, celebrations of queer joy represent an important counterpoint to decades of books, movies, and comics depicting queerness as shameful or tragic. Yet Lovelock argues that within contemporary mainstream representations, becoming "a 'proper' homonormative subject" often involves a form of happiness "which is demarcated as attained by individualized processes of embracing and 'getting over' one's difference to the norm" (2018, 551). In other words, gay happiness can be weaponized to disavow institutional and social barriers to inclusion, a danger that is especially pertinent when such happiness is linked to homonormativity.

Marvel's Pride Month specials reflect this trend, often situating the happiness of LGBTQ+ characters within homonormative frameworks emphasizing domesticity and long-term monogamy. Case in point, in Marvel's 2021 Pride special, the first feature after Prodigy's history lesson is a splash page vignette called "The Vows," starring the characters Wiccan and Hulkling. Written by Allen Heinberg and penciled by Jim Cheung, who created the characters of Wiccan and Hulkling in their 2005 *Young Avengers* series, "The Vows" depicts its feature characters chastely cuddling while surrounded by snapshots of their wedding ceremony and the full, lengthy text of their wedding vows. This emphasis on a married gay couple is understandable given the centrality of gay marriage within the gay rights movement in the US. Yet, it is nonetheless significant that Marvel's first Pride anthology chooses to open with these particular characters presented in this particular way. Esther De Dauw strongly criticizes the characters of Wiccan and Hulkling as historically "[perpetuating] homonormativity and its conservative, heteronormative gender roles" (2021, 93). Other scholars, such as Keith Friedlander (2020), have offered alternative ways to read the couple, as performing important symbolic work related to queer identity. However, this foregrounding of Wiccan and Hulkling's lifelong monogamy (they became a couple as teenagers and have not canonically dated any other characters) presages a trend.

Eight out of the 12 stories in the first Marvel Pride special focus on married couples, depict monogamous partners on dates, or attempt to orient queer characters toward monogamous dating. In addition, two separate stories in the first Marvel Pride special take significant steps to domesticate the sometimes villain, sometimes antihero Daken, son of Wolverine. Historically, Daken is a mass-murdering assassin motivated primarily by money and vengeance. In depictions of Daken as a villain, the character's bisexuality is sometimes mobilized as part of that villainy. Case in point, in *Dark Avengers* (2009–2010), Daken consistently flirts with the reluctant, ostensibly straight character Bullseye, at one point forcing a kiss, partly as a ploy to intimidate and manipulate the rival assassin. This association of bisexuality with villainy – and specifically, villainous duplicity – can be a homophobic trope. However, sexually deviant villains can also be used to challenge the status quo, including heteronormativity. As Ross Murray argues of the villainous Mystique: "Female; lesbian; mutant; villain, Mystique evokes ideas of flow, grotesqueness, abjection, and otherness – the classic marginalized female/feminine other. She is alluring, openly sexual, and enigmatic, inciting ambivalence" (2011, 55). Though Mystique often falls victim to misogynistic and homophobic tropes, her ambivalence endures and informs her queerness. The version of Daken who appears in the 2021 Marvel Pride special is considerably less disruptive. In the story "Man of His Dreams," written by Steve Orlando with art by Claudia Aguirre and Luciano Vecchio, Daken experiences a thoroughly realistic psychic dream in which he lives an entire idyllic, seemingly monogamous life with a male partner, a newly created gay mutant named Somnus. And in the story "Good

Judy," written by Terry Blas with art by Paulina Ganucheau, Daken is presented as the perfect safe queer elder to initiate the shy, awkward teenage boy Anole into the gay dating scene. While the desire to distance Daken from homophobic tropes is understandable, it is worth questioning whether there might be a middle ground between his previously aggressive disruptions of the status quo and his Pride Month domesticity, which is specifically mobilized to promote homonormativity.

Marvel's first trans superhero, Escapade, introduced in the 2022 Marvel Pride anthology in the story "Permanent Sleepover" by writer Charlie Jane Anders and artist Ro Stein, is also centrally defined by lifelong monogamy. Escapade, aka Shela Sexton, is presented in a long-term relationship with her childhood best friend, a non-binary fellow mutant named Morgan, whose home she also shares throughout childhood after being rejected by her biological family. In effect, Shela and Morgan have been partnered for most of their lives, first as friends, then as siblings, then romantically. Shela's relationship with Morgan is also a key aspect of her hero's journey. As Anders summarizes in an interview:

> Shela and Morgan were happy pulling off heists together, until Emma Frost and Destiny showed Shela a terrible vision of the future: she's going to lose control of her powers and cause the death of Morgan. She's determined to do anything to change that fate.
>
> *(Hassan 2022)*

Shela rejects a life of crime and pursues superheroism in an effort to save Morgan, and by extension, her relationship with Morgan. "Permanent Sleepover" can represent the queer joy of found family, which is a central aspect of the X-Men franchise's queer coding; tellingly, Escapade joins the X-Men franchise in *New Mutants* Volume 4 #31 (2022), in an arc written by Anders. Moreover, Escapade's mutant power to temporarily "switch situations" with others, which often functions unpredictably, strongly resonates with queerness by playing with transformation and the nature of identity. The decision not to make Escape an overtly sexual or sexualized character is also understandable to the extent that, as Eliza Steinbock observes, popular representations of trans identities are often hypsersexualized in scopophilic ways. Steinbock writes, "Visual representations of trans people are always already coded as sexual due to the socio-cultural reduction of gender identity to the sexed status of genitals" (2017, 24). Yet the lifelong, foundational monogamy of Shela and Morgan also ensures that for the time being, Marvel's first trans superhero will never be romantically or sexually involved with any pre-existing cis characters. Consequently, while integrating a new trans superhero into the Marvel comics universe is a step forward relative to past representations of trans characters as mere tangential observers of that universe, an element of marginalization endures, wherein queer characters exist separately from straight ones, minimally upsetting the status quo.

On balance, the DC Pride specials are less focused on relationships and more focused on investigating the concept of queer identity and its applicability to superhero metaphors. For instance, the first story in DC's 2021 Pride anthology, "The Wrong Side of the Looking Glass," written by James Tynion IV and illustrated by Trung Le Nguyen, uses superhero metaphors to explore connections between gender deviance and sexual deviance. This is enacted through Batwoman/Kate Kane's relationship with her more feminine-presenting sister (who, in previous comics, died mysteriously before returning, years later, as an Alice in Wonderland-themed supervillain). This story additionally concludes with a tongue-in-cheek subversion of normalizing impulses. Kate gives a speech, directed at the reader, about finding joy and acceptance through queer community, explicitly identifying the power of feeling **"proud** of who you are." This is followed by Kate's sister clocking a supervillain and saying, "It's a nice sentiment, dear sister, but some people would rather break a mirror than look themselves in the eye." "Fair point," replies Kate. In addition, while a majority of art in the Marvel and DC Pride specials prioritizes the clean, shiny aesthetic of contemporary "Big Two" house style, Nguyen employs a more distinctive, challenging style, using fine lines and highly aestheticized, expressionistic layouts that compel readers to sit with the images rather the proceeding easily from one action spectacle to the next. Recurring mirror imagery as well as overlapping panels and interweaving images further reflect (literally) the story's complex negotiations of identity and encourage readers to participate in navigating Kate's perpetual state of flux.

The DC Pride specials also feature numerous stories exploring types of queerness that challenge the bounds of homonormativity. This includes the 2021 story "To the Victors," written by Steve Orlando with art by Stephen Byrne, which involves a team-up between Extraño and Midnighter to prevent a bigoted vampire from "straightwashing history." The story ends with Extraño attempting to turn down a sexual overture from John Constantine – and not quite succeeding. When Extraño points out he is married, Constantine replies, "Then bring him along." Extraño elaborates, "He's **all** but a **werewolf**." This does not dissuade Constantine, who concludes the story by saying, "It's all but **settled** then." In addition, while Mariko Tamaki and Amy Reeder's Harley Quinn and Poison Ivy story "Another Word for a Truck to Move Your Furniture" from the 2021 Pride special features the characters committing to monogamy, their appearance in the 2022 Pride special, in the story "The Hunt," written by Dani Fernandez with art by Zoe Thorogood, shows that monogamy does not extinguish the characters' penchant for gender and sexual deviance. Amid a playful (if cartoonishly violent) game of hide and seek, Ivy quips, "Your fingers are pretty slippery." Harley counters, "Don't get cocky, babe. We know I always come out **on top**." Further down the page, Harley says, "Come and get me, sugar! Or you could give in… It's okay to **submit** sometimes." To which Ivy quips back, "Well **you** would be the expert in that, huh?" The ways Harley and Ivy playfully switch between connotatively masculine and feminine roles throughout this exchange both sexualizes and romanticizes deviance, preserving the subversive threat these characters already present to the status quo as queer women who vacillate between heroism and villainy. The story "Think of Me" from the 2022 DC Pride special, by Ro Stein with art by Ted Brandt, directly reckons with the social pressure to find a monogamous romantic and sexual partner. This story stars Connor Hawke, son of the original Green Arrow, who possesses romantic impulses but identifies as asexual. Within the story, Connor's feelings of alienation, which he partly ascribes to society's **"cacophonous"** celebration of "the **sexual aspect** of love," reflects Nicholas E. Miller's argument that "sex-normative assumptions undermine our ability to represent asexuality positively in comics" (2017, 355).

Because of the diversity of the material on offer in the Marvel and DC Pride specials, and because this chapter addresses a rapidly changing cultural landscape, this essay's conclusions are necessarily inconclusive. One thing, however, is certain: at both Marvel and DC, inclusion remains contested and provisional. Critic and writer Zoe Tunnel (2021) argues that Marvel's apparent indecision about including Loki on the cover of their 2021 special highlights how the company's Pride marketing tends to sideline more high-profile LGBTQ+ characters, such as Kitty/Kate Pryde, Star-Lord, and Psylocke, who happen to appear in big budget feature films. In contrast, DC's Pride specials do highlight intersections between comics and popular transmedia adaptations. For instance, DC's 2022 special includes an introduction by trans actress Nicole Maines, who portrayed the trans character Dreamer on the *Supergirl* TV show (2015–2021) and also wrote Dreamer's appearance in the 2021 Pride special. It then concludes with an autobiographical comic written by long-time Batman voice actor Kevin Conroy, describing how the bigotry and isolation he endured as a gay actor informed his performance as the Dark Knight. However, in a June 2023 tweet responding to the #ComicsBrokeMe hashtag, writer Andrew Wheeler, who contributed to the 2021 DC Pride special, argues that paying LGBTQ+ creators to appear in one special issue per year is not enough to signal a commitment to inclusion. "If you can't put a 'diversity' book together with creators you're actually working with," observes Wheeler, "you're not actually supporting creators of that identity, you're exploiting them" (Johnston 2023). In several cases, such as the example of Anders and Escapade discussed above, Marvel and DC do employ LGBTQ+ creators to tell queer stories beyond Pride Month, but Wheeler's comments highlight the rarity of such support. Moreover, Marvel's recent (at the time of this writing) preview of their 2024 Pride Month material evinces continued tentativeness around the company's willingness to promote LGBTQ+ characters. According to a Marvel press release, eight Pride Month variant covers will be released under the theme of "Pride Allies": "Each piece teams up LGBTQIA+ characters with one of their fellow icons, showcasing both the spirit of Pride Month and exemplifying the importance of strong allyship" (Arrant 2024). To be fair, this campaign does employ LGBTQ+ artists. In addition, pairing lesser-known superheroes such as the X-Men character Rachel Summers with better-known superheroes such as Daredevil may sell more comics. But subtly shifting the focus to straight characters during the one month of the year Marvel overtly spotlights queer characters and creators cannot help but suggest yet another instance of negotiated inclusion.

Ultimately, it is our job, as scholars, to remain both vigilant and empathetic regarding the ongoing diversification of mainstream comics, and to seriously reckon, in our analyses of such diversification, with what we want representation to do. For my part, I find Marvel and DC's Pride Month specials compel me to question whether subversion can survive inclusion. Does queerness inevitably become less queer when it is sold the way superhero comics have traditionally been sold – as capitalistic entertainment that obeys the wills of the market? I cannot answer that question, in this chapter or a book of chapters. But I think it is important to keep asking. And I value Marvel and DC's Pride Month specials, and the many talented LGBTQ+ creators involved in making them, for forcing the issue.

References

Anders, Charlie Jane, Christopher Cantwell, Danny Lore, et al. *Marvel's Voices: Pride* 2022. Volume 1 #1. Marvel Comics.

Arrant, Chris. 2024. "Marvel Celebrates Pride Month 2024 by Focusing on LGBTQIA+ Characters & Straight Allies." *Popverse*, March 22. https://www.thepopverse.com/marvel-pride-month-2024.

Ayala, Vita, Terry Blas, Crystal Frasier, et al. 2021. *Marvel's Voices: Pride (2021)*. Volume 1 #1. Marvel Comics.

Bove, Bryan. 2021. "'Bobby… you're gay.': Marvel's Iceman, Performativity, Continuity, and Queer Visibility." In *The Routledge Companion to Gender and Sexuality in Comic Book Studies*, edited by Frederick Luis Aldama. Routledge.

Brown, Jeffrey A. 2022. *Love, Sex, Gender, and Superheroes*. Rutgers University Press.

Burke, Liam, Ian Gordon, and Angela Ndalianis, eds. 2020. *The Superhero Symbol: Media, Culture & Politics*. Rutgers University Press.

CBLDF. n.d. "Comics Code Revision of 1989." Comic Book Legal Defense Fund. https://cbldf.org/comics-code-revision-of-1989/.

De Dauw, Esther. 2021. *Hot Pants and Spandex Suits: Gender Representation in American Superhero Comic Books.* Rutgers University Press.

Doty, Alexander. 1993. *Making Things Perfectly Queer: Interpreting Mass Culture.* University of Minnesota Press.

Duggan, Lisa. 2003. *The Twilight of Equality?: Neoliberalism, Cultural Politics, and the Attack on Democracy.* Beacon Press.

Elbein, Asher. 2018. "#Comicsgate: How an Anti-Diversity Harassment Campaign in Comics Got Ugly—and Profitable." *The Daily Beast*, April 2. https://www.thedailybeast.com/comicsgate-how-an-anti-diversity-harassment-campaign-in-comics-got-uglyand-profitable.

Friedlander, Keith. 2020. "Parents, Counterpublics, and Sexual Identity." In *Supersex: Sexuality, Fantasy, and the Superhero*, edited by Anna F. Peppard. University of Texas Press.

Grayson, Devin, Nick Robles, Stephanie Williams, et al. 2022. *DC Pride 2022.* Volume 1 #1. DC Comics.

Grunewald, Joe. 2020. "New Allegations against Scott Lobdell Surface After RED HOOD Departure Announcement." *The Beat*, June 30. https://www.comicsbeat.com/scott-lobdell-harassment-allegations/.

Hassan, Chris. 2022. "X-Men Monday #177—Charlie Jane Anders Talks 'New Mutants.'" *AIPT*, October 31. https://aiptcomics.com/2022/10/31/x-men-monday-177-charlie-jane-anders/.

Kustritz, Anne. 2020. "Meet Stephanie Rogers, Captain America: Genderbending the Body Politic in Fan Art, Fiction, and Cosplay." In *Supersex: Sexuality, Fantasy, and the Superhero*, edited by Anna F. Peppard. University of Texas Press.

Lobdell, Scott, and Marc Pacella. 1992. *Alpha Flight* Volume 1 #106. Marvel Comics.

Lovelock, Michael. 2018. "Gay and Happy: (Proto-)homonormativity, Emotion and Popular Culture." *Sexualities*, 22, no. 4: 549–565.

McCloud, Scott. 1994. *Understanding Comics: The Invisible Art.* William Morrow Paperbacks.

McCullough, Kate. 2018. "'The Complexity of Loss Itself': The Comics Form and *Fun Home's* Queer Reparative Temporality." *American Literature*, 90, no. 2: 377–405.

Miller, Nicholas E. 2017. "Asexuality and Its Discontents: Making the 'Invisible Orientation' Visible in Comics." *Inks*, 1, no. 3: 354–376.

Murray, Ross. 2011. "The Feminine Mystique: Feminism, Sexuality, Motherhood." *Journal of Graphic Novels and Comics*, 2, no. 1: 55–66.

Panuska, Sarah M. 2020. "'Super-Gay' *Gay Comix*: Tracing the Underground Origins and Cultural Resonances of LGBTQ Superheroes." In *Supersex: Sexuality, Fantasy, and the Superhero*, edited by Anna F. Peppard. University of Texas Press.

Schott, Gareth. 2010. "From Fan Appropriation to Industry Reappropriation: The Sexual Identity of Comic Superheroes." *Journal of Graphic Novels and Comics*, 1, no. 1: 17–29.

Scott, Darieck, and Ramzi Fawaz. 2018. "Introduction: Queer about Comics." *American Literature*, 90, no. 2: 197–219.

Scott, Suzanne. 2019. *Fake Geek Girls: Fandom, Gender, and the Convergence Culture Industry.* New York University Press.

Sedgwick, Eve Kosovsky. 2003. *Touching, Feeling: Affect, Pedagogy, Performativity.* Duke University Press.

Shooter, James, and John Buscema. *Hulk!* #23. Marvel Comics.

Stein, Daniel. 2018. "Bodies in Translation: Queering the Comic Book Superhero." *Navigationen*, 18, no. 3: 15–38.

Steinbock, Eliza. 2017. "Representing Trans Sexualities." In *The Routledge Companion to Media, Sex and Sexuality*, edited by Clarissa Smith, Feona Attwood, and Brian McNair. Routledge.

Taylor, Aaron. 2007. "'He's Gotta Be Strong, and He's Gotta Be Fast, and He's Gotta Be Larger than Life': Investigating the Engendered Superhero Body." *The Journal of Popular Culture*, 40, no. 2: 344–360.

Tunnell, Zoe. 2021. "Who Is Marvel Proud of in *Marvel Voices: Pride*?" *ComicsXF*, May 24. https://www.comicsxf.com/2021/05/24/who-is-marvel-proud-of-in-marvel-voices-pride/.

Tynion IV, James, Trung Le Nguyen, Sam Johns, et al. 2021. *DC Pride 2021.* Volume 1 #1. DC Comics.

Wegner, Dyllan. 2022. "Do You Believe in Fairies: Northstar and the Early Erasure of AIDS in Marvel." *The Gutter Review*, November 3. https://www.thegutterreview.com/do-you-believe-in-fairies-northstar-and-the-erasure-of-aids-in-the-marvel-universe/.

Johnston, Rich. 2023. "Justice League Queer and DC Pride – The Ball Was Dropped?" *Bleeding Cool*, July 1. https://bleedingcool.com/comics/justice-league-queer-and-dc-pride-a-missed-opportunity/.

8

SUPER POWERS AND SECRET WARS

The Cultural Value of Superhero Action Figures

Jason Bainbridge

Introduction

In 2024, with *Deadpool & Wolverine* (2024) breaking box office records for R-rated films and confirming the Marvel Cinematic Universe to be the highest grossing cinema franchise of all time (Roeloffs 2024), it seems almost redundant to say that the enormous success of the Marvel Cinematic Universe has made the superhero a truly transmedia phenomenon. Superheroes now dominate every aspect of our culture, to the point that most are better known through their adaptations and intertexts than their source material, the comic books themselves.

These webs of intertexts that surround, inform, and extend superhero texts across different media platforms are all examples of *paratextuality*. As Gerard Genette explains

> a text is rarely presented in an unadorned state, unreinforced and unaccompanied by a certain number of verbal or other productions. ... These accompanying productions, which vary in extent and appearance, constitute what I have called elsewhere the work's *paratexts*.

> *(Genette 1997, 1; emphasis added)*

For superheroes, these paratexts include posters, trailers, reviews, interviews, and, most importantly for this chapter, action figures.

The idea that superheroes have action figure paratexts should not be surprising. Superheroes are intrinsically *toyetic*, a term used to describe media properties that are suitable to be merchandised across a range of licensed tie-ins including toys, games, and novelties. While the term toyetic does not appear in any literature before 1977, where it is generally assigned to former president of the Kenner toy company, Bernard Loomis (Loomis n.d.), the concept certainly existed long before being named such. Superheroes are bright, easily recognizable, costumed *figures*, which makes them easy to reproduce as toys and are often economically cost-effective to manufacture as parts can be re-used, or repainted for costume variations, across multiple individual figures. Many superheroes also have "super powers" that lend themselves to play possibilities and *action* features. And while the word "toyetic" suggests a

 DOI: 10.4324/9781003366911-10

reductionist view of merchandising related only to "toys," like Kenner's *Super Powers Collection* action figures, in practice, toyetics can include any merchandise that has some element of "play" value, like food and clothing, such as Ben Cooper's range of superhero plastic masks and vinyl smock costumes for Halloween.

If we can define merchandising as the materiality of licensing, extending virtual screen and graphic texts into physical paratexts, then toyetics is the interactive "make-and-do" aspect of merchandising, encouraging audiences to engage and play with aspects of the text: acting out film storylines or creating new adventures. Dan Fleming refers to this as "textual phenomenology" (Fleming 1996, 11), where he suggests "a great deal [is] going on when a child plays with the toy, for which a TV programme [and by extension film] cannot be held responsible" (Fleming 1996, 15). Here, the materiality of the superhero figure provides this potential for play in a way that the scripted/acted/mediated superhero-on-screen-or-in-print cannot. Whereas the mediated superhero can only be rewatched, reread, or repeated, the material superhero action figure can be redeployed, rewritten, and reimagined. Here, the superhero is an *action* figure not only through its simulation of super power but precisely because it carries within itself the possibility for new stories and situations through imaginative play. In this way, play itself becomes a space for contestation, contradiction, and critical reading, "hegemonic incorporation and moments of resistance" (Jenkins 1998, 28), where items of consumption can become items of production for exploring sexuality (Rand 1995), autonomy (Rotundo 1993), and storytelling (Jenkins 2006, 145).

Playing with action figures therefore means that merchandising also operates at a second *cultural* level. As Fleming (1996) says, toys like action figures simultaneously function as consumer products and playthings and through these acts of play oscillate between the exterior world of capitalist economics and the interior world of child psychology. Erica Rand takes this a step further, arguing that the very "opaqueness of artifacts of consumption" leads to an "impossibility of judging how and what cultural products signify by looking at the artifacts apart from the consumers and the (partial) context that they can provide" (Rand 1995, 146). Indeed, Henry Jenkins explicitly imbues toyetics with the qualities of digital culture when he notes that "action figures provided this generation with some of their earliest avatars, encouraging them to assume the role of a Jedi Knight or an intergalactic bounty hunter, enabling them to physically manipulate the characters to construct their own stories" (Jenkins 2006, 147).

This chapter is an attempt to understand this cultural value of superhero action figures by mapping the enormous impact the toy industry has had on superhero comics and the narrative evolution of those superheroes into transmedia franchises. It follows media theorist Jonathan Gray's argument that "a proper study of paratexts [should] challenge the logic of 'primary' and 'secondary' texts, originals and spinoffs, shows and 'peripherals'" (Gray 2010, 175). Just as Gray contends that paratexts "often play a constitutive role in the production, development, and expansion of a text" (Gray 2010, 175), this chapter will demonstrate how critical the action figure has become to the definition, evolution, and survival of the superhero.

How Toys "defined" Superheroes

Definitions of "toy" move through three distinct developmental stages. The first use of "toy" refers to *children's playthings* and dates from the late 16th century (Kuznets 1994, 10). Prior to this, "toy" had been a word "associated with triviality, delusion and lust" (Jackson 2009,

139). The second use refers to *status* and dates from the late 19th century. The Industrial Revolution (leading to the mass production of affordable toys) coupled with greater income amongst workers and recognition that, rather than being "little adults," children were in fact moving through a distinct developmental stage (hereinafter known as "childhood"), which meant that "[i]n essence, they [the children] won the right to be children and to play, and toys became part of the formula" (Jackson 2009, 139). Toys were therefore markers of childhood, demarcating childhood from adolescence and adulthood. The third use refers to *culture* and dates from the 1950s. During the post-World War II baby boom, with growing suburban affluence and, perhaps even more importantly, the introduction of television, toys are increasingly drawn from pre-existing narratives providing a shared culture that children can discuss and debate with each other (Seiter 1993, 9).

In this way, toys came to reflect the architectural, aspirational, and cultural trends of society. They are not only miniature reproductions of society *at the time*, but also those aspects of society *deemed worthy of preservation*. These include heroes like Robin Hood and Davy Crockett, events like the lunar landing and World War II, and experiences like getting married or going to the prom. As television presenter James May notes:

> the story of toys is the story of everything … if some bearded archeologist (sic) of the year 3000 wants to know what life was all about in the 20th century, all he has to do is dig up a toy box.
>
> *(May and Harrison 2009, 6)*

More broadly, as markers of childhood, toys

> also serve a larger purpose as they exemplify our cultural truths: what skills we hope to develop, what attitudes we want to cultivate, and what possessions we wish to flaunt. Toys reflect the interplay between our society's view of play and its opposite, work.
>
> *(Jackson 2009, 139)*

From Lego to Barbie to GI Joe, toys offer a way of playing at various careers (builder, architect, model, reporter, soldier, adventurer, astronaut). From Star Wars to Monster kits to superhero action figures, toys also offer a way of playing out fantasies (of an imagined future/past, of the unknown, of having super powers) and engaging in a shared understanding of these fantasy worlds (be they Tatooine, Dracula's Castle, or Wakanda). Most importantly, they provide "a model for non-film properties to survive in other mediums" (Irving 2006, 15), and these "non-film properties" very much include comic-book superheroes.

Superheroes largely remain the product of two companies: DC Comics (a division of Warner Brothers) and Marvel Comics (a division of Disney). This is partly because the word "superhero" (along with supervillain and any variation thereof) is jointly claimed by DC and Marvel as a trademark in the United States. While it is widely known that DC and Marvel applied for joint registration of the superheroes mark for comic books in July 1979, (with the mark being registered for use in comic books from November 1981 and remaining active today), less well known is that the trademark claim itself was initiated through a complicated process of competing claims that didn't originate from these comic-book companies at all, but rather from a costume company and a toy company.

It was during the 1960s that Halloween costume-maker Ben Cooper recognized the toyetic potential of superheroes. The company licensed a range of properties from both DC and Marvel for their inexpensive children's costumes (Petty 2010). They named the line "SUPER HERO," applying for registration in April 1966 and being published for opposition in December 1966. Incredibly, neither DC nor Marvel opposed the application and the trademark SUPER HERO was granted to Cooper on March 14 1967 for use on "masquerade costumes" alongside the marks FAMOUS HEROES and GREAT HEROES (U.S. Reg. No 0825835).

In November 1972, the Mego Corporation (following in the footsteps of the Ideal Toy Company's earlier *Captain Action* line) similarly recognized the toyetic potential of superheroes. Like Ben Cooper and Ideal, Mego licensed characters from both DC and Marvel for a line of 8- and 12-inch dolls with soft-cloth costumes. They sought to promote the line under the trademark "World's Greatest Super Heroes" (WGSH). Ben Cooper filed an opposition to that registration in December 1973 and sought to register the plural SUPER HEROES (Opposition No. 55,127, December 6, 1973) but the examiner suspended all further action on the SUPER HEROES registration until the opposition was decided. Rather than continue proceedings, Mego assigned its interests to DC and Marvel jointly in December 1975 (Petty 2010).

With declining newsstand comic-book sales throughout the 1970s (Wright 2001, 259) and direct distribution to specialty comic-book stores still nascent (Rhoades 2008, 264), DC and Marvel found themselves in the unusual position of receiving more revenue through licensing than actual comic-book sales. Or in another sense, as early as 1975, both DC and Marvel were enjoying more success with their superhero paratexts than their source texts. Unsurprisingly, the comic companies' now saw value in the "super hero" trademark. In the face of their united opposition, Ben Cooper withdrew its opposition to the WGSH mark. This decision, along with a series of efforts by DC and Marvel together and individually to trademark superheroes for various products, meant that the two companies soon had joint control of the term "super hero." But, it should be noted this only happened because a toy company (Mego) had pursued the mark for their toyline (U.S. Reg. No. 1080655, December 27, 1977) in the first place. The value of this decision was fully realized decades later in 2009 when Marvel, with ownership rights to over 5,000 superheroes, was purchased by Walt Disney for US$4.3 billion.

In practice, neither DC nor Marvel waits for actual commercial use of "superhero" before raising an objection. They monitor trademark registration applications, request an extension of time to file an opposition (rather than incurring the expense of a formal opposition), and make their displeasure publicly known to start settlement discussions. Such pressure often means that applicants abandon their applications, effectively creating a superhero duopoly (Petty 2010). As for Mego, they closed down in 1984, were homaged by many toymakers over subsequent years and formally returned to toy shelves in 2018 with a new line of soft-clothed figures, a number of DC superheroes being among them.

How Toys Provide Superhero R&D

By 1984, sales were flagging on Kenner's iconic *Star Wars* toyline and since the Mego Corporation was out of the business, Kenner pursued and were awarded master toy licensing rights for DC's superheroes. The *Super Powers Collection* commenced in 1985 with a 12-figure line-up packaged with mini-comics and by the line's end in 1986, 33 figures, several vehicles and a Hall of Justice playset had been produced. These action figures included the trinity of Superman, Batman, and Wonder Woman, members of the Justice League, supervillains,

Jack Kirby's New Gods, and several original creations. The line was further supported by a change in name, focus, and design for Hanna-Barbera's long-running Saturday morning cartoon series *Superfriends*, along with an array of merchandising and fast-food tie-ins (Rossen 2017).

The "action" of these action figures was the feature of the line. Each figure had an action feature "unique" to that superhero's "super power." You could squeeze Flash's arms together to make him run, squeeze Superman's legs together to make him punch, extend Plastic Man's neck, or make Brainiac's kick. But, beyond the integration of super powers into action figures, the *Super Powers* toyline also functions as an early example of where a paratext can be used for research and development: to test ideas that then find their way into other texts as part of this paratextual relay. This occurred diegetically (in the fictional story world of the superheroes) and extradiegetically (in relation to the real-world creators of these superheroes).

By way of example, diegetically the *Super Powers Collection* popularized Darkseid and Jack Kirby's New Gods characters as enemies (and allies) for the Justice League and made *Teen Titan's* Cyborg a member of the Justice League of America. These paratextual ideas were taken up in the DC comic books (most notably in Geoff Johns' "New 52" relaunch of the Justice League) which in turn informed the 2017 Zack Snyder/Joss Whedon *Justice League* film. Both the theatrical and "Snyder cut" versions feature Cyborg as a founding member of the League and Darkseid (and his forces from Apokolips) as the first villains that they face.

Similarly, extradiegetically the *Super Powers Collection* highlighted how licensing could provide alternative revenue streams for comic artists, offering them more visibility and greater renumeration than they ever received for their comics work. These artists included such greats as Jack Kirby (for redesigning his New Gods characters), George Pérez (for his design of Cyborg and redesign of Superman villain Lex Luthor), and Ed Hannigan (for his redesign of Superman villain Brainiac) (Rossen 2017). Indeed, Kirby received some of the only royalties of his career for this *Super Powers* design work.

It is certainly arguable that this greater recognition of the alternative revenue streams available to comic creators through licensing was a contributing factor in several Marvel creators leaving Marvel to form Image Comics in 1992. Almost without exception, these Image creators quickly licensed their creations for cartoons, movies, and toys, with Todd McFarlane being the primary example. Similarly, this pattern of increased mainstream visibility and/or royalties through licensing became important for comic-book creators as their characters were regularly adapted during the resurgence of superhero movies and television series from 2008 on. Again, the primary example here would be Stan Lee who is much better known to mainstream audiences for his series of cameos in Marvel films than he ever was as the co-creator of most of those characters. As for the *Super Powers* line, it proved to be enormously influential with multiple homage and commemorative lines being released by different toy manufacturers over the years, including McFarlane Toys' revival of the line in 2022 (McFarlane toys being owned by Todd McFarlane and having produced DC Superhero action figures since 2019).

How Toys Built a Superhero Shared Universe

Fearing that superheroes may become the next big thing and envious of the success of Kenner's *Super Powers* action figures, rival toy company Mattel partnered with DC's comic-book rival Marvel to produce the *Secret Wars* toyline. The name was chosen when Mattel's market testing revealed kids reacted positively to the words "secret" and "wars" (McLaughlin 2019). Much as Kenner had licensed DC superheroes to support *Star Wars'* flagging toy sales, Mattel licensed Marvel characters in case their *Masters of the Universe* line faltered.

However, outside of Spider-Man and the Hulk (both of whom had television and toy line exposure), Mattel was concerned that recognition of these Marvel superheroes was not as great as DC's Superman, Batman, Wonder Woman, and their assorted supervillains. They therefore asked Marvel to produce a comic to support the toy line (McLaughlin 2019). As Marvels' then Editor-in-Chief Jim Shooter remembers it:

> I offered an idea that was suggested by a dozen or so correspondents – usually younger ones – in the fan mail every day: one big, epic story with all (or many) of the heroes and villains in it. Everyone agreed… To this day, when I go to conventions, I'm asked to sign many, many copies. Lots of people tell me that *Secret Wars* is what first got them into comics. Makes sense. The idea came from the fans.
>
> *(Shooter 2011)*

Written by Shooter, illustrated by Mike Zeck and Bob Layton, and inked by John Beatty, 1984's *Marvel Super Heroes Secret Wars* was a 12-part miniseries, line-wide event that brought a range of Marvel superheroes and supervillains together to fight for the pleasure of a cosmic being known as The Beyonder on a distant planet called Battleworld. Largely structured around a series of fight scenes to sell toys, *Secret Wars* introduced new characters, brought She-Hulk into the Fantastic Four, and gave Spider-Man a sentient black costume that would later become the fan-favorite supervillain Venom.

Unlike *Super Powers*, the *Secret Wars* toyline had a number of design limitations largely born of a manufacturing push by Mattel to reuse molds to save money. As a result, the toyline was relatively unsuccessful; eight figures were released in series one with a few vehicles and one playset, but series two was cut to five releases with the additional three only being released in Europe (Iceman, Electro, and Constrictor, who never actually appeared in the comic series). Still, the line's clean design is well-remembered by collectors, they continue to sell well on secondary markets like eBay and they have similarly been homaged by a number of toy companies over the years, including a small run of oversized reproductions of the original figures by Gentle Giant in 2015.

In contrast, the comic series, and more particularly the ramifications of that series for the wider Marvel Universe, set up a successful storytelling model that persists. In comics, *Secret Wars*-style line-wide "event" crossovers that draw in multiple titles have consistently featured as part of Marvel (and DC's) release slate ever since. One of these "event" titles (*The Infinity Gauntlet*) even set the narrative direction for the interconnected nature of the Marvel Cinematic Universe. The storytelling model operates in this way: multiple franchises (like Thor, Captain America, Iron Man, etc.) interconnect to build up to an "event" film (like *Avengers: Infinity War* and *Avengers: Endgame*). The model was also reproduced less successfully by the aforementioned DC Extended Universe's *Justice League*.

The fact that *Secret Wars* is so influential is reinforced by the fact that the Marvel Cinematic Universe's present storytelling model is building up to the release of an Avengers film on May 7, 2027, entitled *Avengers: Secret Wars*. But what is sometimes forgotten is that this is a storytelling model originated in the toy industry's desire for an "event" title to promote their accompanying toyline.

How Toys Saved Superheroes

In 1989, millionaire businessman Ron Perelman purchased Marvel for $82.5 million from Marvel's then-owners New World Pictures. By 1991, Marvel was listed on the stock market and making acquisitions that cost Marvel a reported $700 million, including a 46% share in a toy company called Toy Biz. In exchange for this share, the deal gave Toy Biz "exclusive, perpetual, royalty-free licenses" for Marvel characters (Lambie 2018), leading to an extensive line of Marvel action figures, vehicles, and other assorted toys.

During the early 1990s, Marvel enjoyed enormous growth, particularly off the back of titles like *Spider-Man*, *X-Men*, and *X-Force*, so much so that it was valued in excess of (a likely overinflated) billion dollars on the market. This was largely down to the 1990s speculator boom, where collectors purchased multiple copies of individual issues as investment pieces. But, from 1993 on, that speculator bubble burst. Comic book and trading card revenue declined by as much as 70% and Marvel's stock value collapsed from $35.75 per share in 1993 to $2.375 in 1996 (Lambie 2018).

Perelman confronted the collapsing bottom line by extending Marvel into new areas, setting up a film venture (Marvel Studios), and he planned to buy the remaining shares in Toy Biz and merge it with Marvel so that Marvel would effectively become a comic, toy, and trading card company (Norris 1997). Just as it had in the 1970s, Marvel was relying on its licensing and paratexts to save it. Marvel's shareholders resisted and Perelman filed for bankruptcy in an effort to reorganize Marvel without the shareholders' consent, leading to a protracted two-year struggle between various board members vying for control. Following a lengthy court case, the merger with Toy Biz did go ahead, but in a very different way to what Perelman had envisaged. Perelman was ousted out by two Toy Biz executives who'd been Marvel board members since 1993: Isaac "Ike" Perlmutter and Toy Biz's CEO Avi Arad (Rosenberg 2000, 295). Toy Biz, the toymaker primarily known for their Marvel action figures, had raised the money to purchase Marvel Comics, the comic-book company, forming Marvel Entertainment, Inc., and brought the company out of bankruptcy. Part of this restructure involved the formation of various holding companies for various parts of the company, one of which was Marvel Characters, Inc., the licensing wing of Marvel Comics, which contains all of the intellectual property rights of their characters. Unsurprisingly, Toy Biz was keen to protect their "exclusive, perpetual, royalty-free licenses" and saw that the best way of doing this was to take control of the company (Williams 2018).

Arad's original portfolio had been overseeing the production of Marvel action figures at Toy Biz. He gained a 10% share as part of Marvel's 46% acquisition of Toy Biz in 1993 and replaced Stan Lee as head of Marvel Films. Arad served as executive producer on 20th Century Fox's *X-Men: The Animated Series* (1992–1997) and he brokered a deal with Fox to make an *X-Men* movie in 2000 that spawned its own long-running franchise (Raviv 2002). Subsequent funding from the Merrill Lynch bank in 2005 ($525 million over seven years with Marvel's superheroes held as collateral) provided Marvel with the cash reservoir to buy back the rights to many of their characters and launch the Marvel Cinematic Universe. This paved the way for Disney's purchase of Marvel for $4.3 billion in 2009 and their subsequent purchase of 20th Century Fox for $71.3 billion 10 years later in 2019, reuniting the majority of Marvel's superheroes under one studio (Lambie 2018). As for Toy Biz, following their merger with Marvel, the company persisted as Marvel's main toy subsidiary and later 'Marvel Toys' until 2007, where the master toy license for Marvel Entertainment characters was then awarded to Hasbro, having been purchased in 2006 for $205 million (for five years), and where it remains to this day.

How Toys Moved Superheroes into the Mainstream

Back in the 1980s, Marvel developed a three-pronged transmedia marketing strategy for toymaker Hasbro and their *G.I. Joe* and *Transformers* brands. This involved synchronized releases of Marvel comics, Sunbow (a Marvel company) cartoons, and Hasbro toys, where each text and paratext would serve to promote and, in some cases, enrich and deepen the others. It's worth noting that Arad had himself adopted a similar strategy, less successfully, for *Transformers'* transforming robot rivals the *Gobots* in the 1980s, but under Arad's leadership, this transmedia marketing strategy was replicated by Marvel in the 1990s.

Here, the synchronized releases were once again a three-pronged release, with Marvel comics, Fox Cartoon television series, and Hasbro action figures. To a large extent, the latter Marvel Cinematic Universe, commencing with *Iron Man* in 2008, was bound by the series of licensing decisions that Marvel and Arad made in the mid-1990s, including their licensing of the X-Men and Fantastic Four characters (and supporting characters) to Fox, and Spider-Man (and his supporting characters) to Sony in 1999. This meant that when Marvel Studios moved from character licensing to self-financing their own films, commencing under David Maisel in 2004, they had a greatly reduced slate of characters with which to work, mostly comprised of character rights that had reverted back to them because of non-production. These were largely *Avengers*-related (as with Iron Man, Captain America, and Thor) or characters deep in their back catalogue who had never been optioned before (as with the Guardians of the Galaxy).

Given some of their most successful and recognizable characters were now excluded from the Marvel Cinematic Universe, Marvel Studios once again relied on this three-pronged transmedia marketing strategy in the 2000s to build recognition for their characters, with Marvel comics, associated cartoons and Toy Biz (and later Hasbro) toylines. In this way when the relatively obscure Guardians of the Galaxy were being made into a movie, a new Marvel comic-book series written by Brian Michael Bendis and drawn by Steve McNiven and a boxed set of Hasbro action figures were released in the lead-up to the film, with the characters guest-starring on the cartoon series *Avengers Assemble* (2013–2019). This means that while Guardians' character Rocket Raccoon first appeared in 1976 (referencing the Beatles' 1968 song "Rocky Raccoon"), this three-pronged strategy allowed audiences to engage with Rocket as if for the first time through his increased presence in comics, in toys, in the 2014 film, or via his cartoon appearances. As a result, Rocket becomes deliberately multi-origin, textually ambiguous and at home across multiple media platforms. Most importantly for Marvel, he becomes *known*.

To describe these complex textual relationships, I have previously referred to the notion of "toyesis" (Bainbridge 2017), a kind of reverse toyetics where paratextual relays erase a text's origins to the point that they become truly multi-origin and thereby capable of more easily flowing across media platforms, to generate the production of more and more paratexts around them. The word is modeled on the relationship between kinetic (relating to or resulting from motion) and kinesis (motion itself). Whereas toyetic implies a one-way adaptation from screen/literary text to physical paratext (through merchandising), toyesis implies movement both ways across platforms to the point that the distinction between different texts becomes obscured and therefore less important. The exposure of and familiarity with a character like Rocket Raccoon is a demonstration of toyesis at work; paratextual relays frequently obscure the textual origins of superheroes, making them seem truly multiplatform, multi-origin, transmedia characters that flow from screen text to paratext and back again, capturing audiences as they move across each platform.

Conclusion

The cultural importance of toys to superheroes (legally, as R&D, in world-building, in preserving them and in mainstreaming them) remains relatively under-represented in superhero studies. Gray views toys as important paratexts because they "represented to many that media worlds could and should be somewhat *inhabitable*" (Gray 2010, 187). However, as Jackson notes, both children and adults increasingly seek out another type of play experience; physical toy sales are "decreasing" in part because of changes in the marketplace and "the fact that consumers are more likely to bypass the toy store for the computer store. Digital devices have become the mainstay of modern play" and "In computer and video game scenarios, the element of control that was so essential to early play patterns is taken away" (Jackson 2009, 144). Jackson therefore sees the distinction in play in the following way: "classic toys – which developed in the Industrial Age – taught *control and creation*, electronic toys –emblematic of the Information Age – teach *adaptation*" (Jackson 2009, 144, emphasis added). These two different types of play also create different understandings of life: "In traditional play, children could be masters of their own fates, learning to control their roles in life," whereas "digital play creates a sensation of the randomness of life" (Jackson 2009, 144).

Action figures literally pre*figured* the superheroes' embrace of convergence culture and transmedia storytelling engendered by advances in digital technology. Digital technology has similarly prolonged the life of action figures through digital special effects, digital technologies, and digital recording, from the "live-action" *Transformers* (2007) and *Barbie* (2023) films (where toys are the source texts and the films the paratexts), to stop-motion advertisements, reels, and memes created and shared on social media of action figures being posed and in play, where play itself becomes a form of mediated production.

The licensing decisions of the toy industry have in many ways shaped audiences' understanding of superheroes as much if not more so than the comic-book industry ever has. It is these action figure and toy paratexts that have helped define the superhero as a recognizable brand, allowed for research and development around superheroes, provided greater creator recognition and renumeration, built new and successful storytelling models, and reinvested back into the comic-book industry to aid in their transition across multiple media platforms. In this way, I would argue that the real cultural value of superhero action figures, and superhero toys more generally, has been in building a mainstream public awareness, recognition, and engagement with superheroes.

References

Bainbridge, Jason. 2017. "From *Toyetic to Toyesis*: The Cultural Value of Merchandising." In *Entertainment Values: How do we Assess Entertainment and Why does it Matter?* edited by Stephen Harrington and Christy Collis. Palgrave.

Fleming, Dan. 1996. *Powerplay: Toys as Popular Culture*. Manchester University Press.

Genette, Gerard. 1997. *Paratexts: The Thresholds of Interpretation.* Translated by Jane E. Lewin. Cambridge University Press.

Gray, Jonathan. 2010. *Show Sold Separately: Promos, Spoilers and Other Media Paratexts.* New York University Press.

Irving, Christopher. 2006. "The Swivel-Arm Battle-Grip Revolution: How G.I.Joe Recruited a New Generation of Comic-Book Readers." *Back Issue: The Ultimate Comics Experience.* June 16.

Jackson, Kathy Merlock. 2009. "From Control to Adaptation: America's Toy Story." *Journal of American and Comparative Cultures*, September 10, 28, no. 1–2: 139–145.

Jenkins, Henry. 1998. "Introduction: Childhood Innocence and Other Modern Myths." In *The Children's Culture Reader,* edited by Henry Jenkins. New York University Press.

Jenkins, Henry. 2006. *Convergence Culture.* New York University Press.

Kuznets, Loise Rostow. 1994. *When Toys Come Alive: Narratives of Animation, Metamorphosis and Development.* Yale University Press.

Lambie, Ryan. 2018. "How Marvel Went From Bankruptcy to Billions." *Den of Geek*, April 17. https://www.denofgeek.com/movies/how-marvel-went-from-bankruptcy-to-billions/.

Loomis, Bernard. n.d. "Interview." *Rebelscum.com.* Accessed July 5, 2024. https://www.rebelscum.com/loomis.asp.

May, James, and Ian Harrison. 2009. *James May's Toy Stories.* Five Mile Press.

McLaughlin, Jermaine. 2019. "An Oral History of Marvel's *Secret Wars*, The Iconic Crossover That Started It All." *Syfy Wire*, March 4. *https://www.syfy.com/syfywire/marvel-secret-wars-oral-history.*

Norris, Floyd. 1997. "Marvel Proposes a Merger With Toy Biz." *New York Times*, April 29.

Petty, Ross D. 2010. "The 'Amazing Adventures' of Super Hero." *The Trademark Reporter: The Law Journal of the International Trademark Association*, 100:3, May–June 2010: 729–755.

Rand, Erica. 1995. *Barbie's Queer Accessories.* Duke University Press.

Raviv, Dan. 2002. *Comic Wars: How Two Tycoons Battled Over the Marvel Comics Empire – and Both Lost.* Broadway Books.

Rhoades, Shirrel. 2008. *A Complete History of American Comic Books.* Peter Lang Publishing.

Roeloffs, Mary Whitfill. 2024. "'Deadpool & Wolverine' Sets Box Office Records – And Pushes Marvel To $30 Billion Global Gross." *Forbes*, July 28. https://www.forbes.com/sites/maryroeloffs/2024/07/28/deadpool--wolverine-sets-box-office-records-and-pushes-marvel-to-30-billion-global-gross/.

Rosenberg, Hilary. 2000. *The Vulture Investors.* John Wiley and Sons.

Rossen, Jake. 2017. "Breaking the Mold: Kenner's *Super Powers Collection.*" *mentalfloss.com.* February 9. https://www.mentalfloss.com/article/92022/breaking-mold-kenners-super-powers-collection.

Rotundo, E. Anthony. 1993. "Boy Culture." In *The Children's Culture Reader,* edited by Henry Jenkins. New York University Press.

Seiter, Ellen. 1993. *Sold Separately: Children and Parents in Consumer Culture.* Rutgers University Press.

Shooter, Jim. 2011. "Secrets of the *Secret Wars.*" JimShooter.com, April 4. https://jimshooter.com/2011/04/secrets-of-secret-wars.html/.

Williams, Trey. 2018. "How Marvel Bounced Back From Bankruptcy to Become Hollywood's Biggest Brand." *The Wrap*, April 29. https://www.thewrap.com/how-marvel-went-from-bankruptcy-to-hollywoods-most-successful-franchise/.

Wright, Bradford W. 2001. *Comic Book Nation: The Transformation of Youth Culture in America.* Johns Hopkins University Press.

9

FROM ZERO TO THE HERO'S JOURNEY

The Masters of the Universe Franchise across Audiovisual Transmedia

Fernando Gabriel Pagnoni Berns,
Eduardo Veteri and Jorge Traversa

Transmedial storyworlds that are deployed across multiple media platforms result in new media landscapes more complex than those proposed by the classic concept of adaptation. Adaptation was based on the (somewhat simplistic and contested) unidirectional shift from one medium to another and the "fidelity imperative" as quality criteria (Ritterbusch 2020, 60). Transmedia, on the other hand, means that either a narrative or a media is expanded in new directions (Gambarato et al. 2020, 1). Yet, "boundaries between adaptations and franchise expansions are blurry and bound to become artificial or even counterintuitive and counterproductive in cases in which different instantiations of a fictional franchise draw on the same storyworld" (Fehrle 2019, 13). In this sense, some franchises offer recurrent reboots and gaps that make media archeology especially rich for study.

An interesting case of transmedia storytelling is the *Masters of the Universe* franchise. This particular story did not start with the 1983 television cartoon but in 1982 with Mattel's release of the original *Masters of the Universe* 5.5-inch action-figure toy line. It has been argued that toys are not part of the transmedia narrative as they are not "texts" or "narratives," yet, as Jonathan Ray Lee argues, "toys embody key aspects of the kind of corporate media culture that theories of adaptation and transmedia storytelling aim to analyze" (2020, 152–3). Many cartoons are inextricably linked to toy culture, merchandising, guides, video games, comics, and books. As toys, He-Man and his friends had little in terms of "narratives" and, as such, those narratives could be created from scratch across the different iterations. Thus, the different transmedia adaptations had to (re)create the heroic ideal of He-Man. But what does the term "heroic ideal" mean? This Western archetype began in Greek philosophy with Plato "as a force that, by projecting the heroic ideal onto local politics, lends a sense of purpose and cohesion to the amorphous political space of archaic Greece" (Kirichenko 2022, 20). This ideal provides a logical basis for morals, truths, and ethics of a certain era. Many adaptations of the *Masters of the Universe* franchise take advantage of the franchise's origin as a null state: a toy without narrative or background. Thus, each iteration of the story needs to begin with the "hero's journey," tracing a line from defeat to illumination and acceptance of his/her fate, thus adapting not just a toy, but the ethos of tragic Greek drama and the archetypical abiding hero.

DOI: 10.4324/9781003366911-11

In *He-Man and She-Ra: The Secret of the Sword* (Friedman et al. 1985), a sorceress sends Prince Adam on a mission to find the owner of a magic sword in a different world, Etheria. Soon he meets Adora, who is the owner of the magic sword but she has been brainwashed to serve the villains. As the story progresses, She-Ra must find her true nature as a heroine. The theatrical film *Masters of the Universe* (Goddard 1987) starts in media res, with He-Man defeated by the evil Skeletor and is forced to travel to Earth. Another iteration, *Masters of the Universe: Revelation* (Conarroe and Stannard 2021–) starts with the defeat of He-Man, who must now begin the hero's journey anew.

Using theories of adaptation, studies on transmedia and the archetypical ideal of the hero as a trope, this essay will trace the many roads taken by the *Masters of the Universe* franchise and how they converge on the path of the hero as a way to fill the gaps produced by the toy lines.

Starting with Nothing: The *Masters of the Universe* Toy Lines

Marsha Kinder analyzes transmedia intertextuality in the context of a phenomenon she calls a "commercial supersystem of mass entertainment" (1991, 40), where such "a supersystem is a network of intertextuality constructed around a figure or group of figures from pop culture who are either fictional or real" (40). This trend started taking shape at the beginning of the 1990s, and, as Kinder continues,

> In order to be a supersystem, the network must cut across several modes of image production; must appeal to diverse generations, classes, and ethnic subcultures, who in turn are targeted with diverse strategies; must foster 'collectability' through a proliferation of related products; and must undergo a sudden increase in commodification, the success of which reflexively becomes a 'media event' that dramatically accelerates the growth curve of the system's commercial success.
>
> *(122–3)*

Kinder emphasizes that this relationship between several texts facilitates the understanding of the source text, in this case, the action figure, creating complex schemes in the stories where it becomes easier to differentiate elements such as plot, characters, and production. This supersystem, arguably, narrativizes He-Man and the *Masters of the Universe*, giving them what they lack as toys: identities as heroes. Unlike other heroes such as Superman or Batman, who were narratively created in comics, He-Man was first created as a toy; this lack of backstory had to be "fixed" in the transmedia shifts to produce meaning.

Masters of the Universe was not the first toy line turned into a television series. Mattel had already ventured into the subject before with one of its flagship creations: the *Hot Wheels* line of collectible cars in 1968. The first experience within the transmedia television universe would come a year later, when in 1969 the first animated series of these little cars was broadcasted on ABC (1969–1971), being the first one based on a toy. Along with the television series, a line of comics was published by DC Comics but in 1971, due to complaints from parents and child protection communities, as well as from the direct competitor in this field, the company Tonka, the Federal Communications Commission (FCC) banned from children's programming any content that could be considered advertising. The reason given was that children were not able to distinguish advertising from entertainment (Hernandez 2003, 1).

Mattel ended up canceling both the *Hot Wheels* television series and comics and would not make other transmedia content based on its own creation again until 1981. It is at this time when the FCC, as recounted in the documentary *Power of Grayskull: The Definitive History of He-Man and the Masters of the Universe* (Lobb and McCallum 2017), lifted its restriction on including series that came from toys, arguing that the 1969 restriction was too severe and that these series could contain educational values. Thus, it was established that the market, not the Federal government, could regulate what children may see.

The documentary film *Power of Greyskull* and episode 3 from *The Toys that Made Us* (Volk-Weiss and Stern 2017–) recount the intricate story of this particular transmedia phenomenon. By 1979, Mattel was leading the market with its best-known brands: *Barbie* and *Hot Wheels*. However, it was reluctant to enter a particular niche: action figures for children. Although it had a line called *Big Jim* in the early 1970s, it was crushed by the coming *Star Wars* figures. Ray Wagner, then-president of Mattel, turned down the offer to license *Star Wars* because he could not produce the toys in time for the Christmas season. In the end, Kenner, which was presided over by a former Mattel employee, Bernie Loomis, took over the rights, gaining an advantage in the sale of action figures. So, to face its new competition, Mattel bought the rights to the *Flash Gordon* (Hodges 1980) and *Clash of the Titans* (Davis 1981) movies. In the first case, sales were low, although, with *Clash of the Titans*, they initially had good sales as they released the toys months before the movie. But, when the movie was released with little success, sales plummeted.

In market research among five-year-old children, Mattel came to the conclusion that a common axis dominates the game-play modality: to have *power* over what is being played. Later, they define the fantasy theme (of the barbaric type as expressed by Frank Frazetta's illustrations) as having the best sales potential. To make action figures, the company bought the rights to the movie *Conan the Barbarian* (Milius 1982), while it was still in development. The movie met the requirements to be a hit, but it received an R rating (only for those over 17 years old). Mattel knew that a movie not suitable for children would have no future and broke the toy production agreement before it was released.

Meanwhile, a Mattel design artist, Roger Sweet, was working on a low-key project; with a doll from the *Big Jim* line, Sweet added putty to increase the figure's muscle mass, gave him a pose and a battle-face expression (as he considered the figures from other collections to be expressionless). The muscular character had a cape and an axe. Sweet named him He-Man. However, while Sweet provided the name and preliminary design for the main figure, Mark Taylor would shape the rest of the universe, and it is in this first stage that the names of Beast-man, Mer-Man, Teela, Man-at-Arms, Stratos, etc., together with the vehicles and Castle Grayskull as accessories, would make up the first run of the collection.

In 1981, Mattel begun to market the *Masters of the Universe* action figures, as the collection would eventually be named. They were bigger and more spectacular than the *Star Wars* figures, which they would surpass in sales; yet, there was something still missing. While their opponent had two movies known to all, *Masters of the Universe* were just figures with no story to back them up. To fix this, they would begin to produce a series of minicomics for all their characters that would be included as a gift with each figure (Baer 2017).

Mattel used minicomics telling, albeit briefly, a basic narrative predicated on a hero on a journey. The first four minicomics, with scripts by Don Glut and illustrated by Alfredo Alcalá, tell the story of a strong warrior, the greatest of his tribe, who lives in Eternia and is called He-Man. He leaves his people to protect the secret and power of the legendary Castle Grayskull from evil forces. On his journey, he would save the life of the sorceress guardian of the endangered fortress. She sees in him the hero who would protect them and gives him the armor and weapons that would help him in his duty. In 1981, DC Comics published a series of comics where the He-Man story would begin to take shape, until, in 1982, after commissioning an animated advertisement from the Filmation studio, Lou Scheimer, the founder of the studio, proposed to Mattel that they create a television series about *Masters of the Universe*.

Henry Jenkins (2010) writes,

> In many ways, *Masters of the Universe* was already a transmedia story, at least as far as the technology of the time allowed. Not only did He-Man appear in the Filmation-produced cartoons, but his story extended to the mini-comics that came with each action figure, on collectible cards, sticker books, coloring books and children's books, each of which gave us the opportunity to learn a little more about Eternia, Castle Gray-skull and the other places where these stories took place.

Masters of the Universe was clearly born as a transmedia phenomenon, with comics filling the huge gaps that the toys left. Yet, the classic television series took little from the comics; it established that He-Man was a superhero but hardly explained how he had reached said status. Thus, different iterations expanded the He-Man's story, but they did so via two complementary tropes: the heroic ideal and the hero's path.

The Heroic Ideal and the Hero's Journey

As argued by Gregory Kendrick, the heroic ideal remains a constant of the human condition since the era of Classical Greece, when this figure first appeared in myth and literature (2010, 1). This endurance may be related to the ethical functions of the hero figure as the "heroic ideal is connected to what some scholars have referred to as the history of the 'civilizing process' in the West" (Kendrick 2010, 5). Furthermore, the world of antiquity carried this out on Homeric terms. Via *Odyssey* and *Iliad* (circa 8th century BC), Homer established the foundational basis for the heroic ideal where characteristics were firmly established, among them the uniqueness of the hero in contrast with mere men or citizens. It is this "manly" quality that coined the term "he-man":

> Humanity, it appears, is a collective word that has no singular, for to be an individual you have to be a great one. He-men are few, and they are identified with heroes. All the he-men are males, but most males are mere human beings along with all women and children.
>
> *(Mansfield 2010, 95)*

Achilles is one such he-man (*aner*) "above and distinct from human beings" (95), which means that he is a human more noble and more generous than any other.

Mattel's superhero, "He-Man," refers to the Greek hero: the valiant and brave man who is different from all the others, who are ordinary citizens. He-Man may have many brave friends, including Teela-Na, Captain of the Royal Guard, yet is he the only one with real superpowers. His battle cry after getting superpowers is "I have the power" where the pronoun "I" emphases the individualism of the heroic ideal. It may be argued that many of He-Man's friends also have superpowers; certainly, characters like Fisto (a strong warrior with a metal right hand) or Man-E-Faces (a warrior with the ability to change his faces from a human face to a monster face to a robot face) are powerful, yet most of their powers come from a transhuman, enhanced corporeality.

Another characteristic of the heroic ideal, as argued by classic Homeric epics, is that only before the Gods do the he-men resign themselves to being mere humans (Benardete 2005, 13). In other words, the Greek heroic ideal refers to a human being that is more than other humans, but they must also accept their own mortality and inferiority (being mere *anthropoid*) due the existence of superior and divine beings beyond the realm of the perceptible. "Whenever the heroes feel the oppressive weight of their mortality, they become, in their own opinion, like other men, who are always human beings" (Benardete 2005, 14). As with most superheroes, this is illustrated through the aspect of duality. He-Man is also being Prince Adam, heir-apparent to the throne of Eternia, son of King Randor and Queen Marlena of Eternia, and it is Adam who is viewed by most citizens as frivolous and lazy. However, this is an act to keep people from suspecting that he is also the super-powered He-Man.

In classic Greek epics, a last characteristic of the heroic virtue (*arête*) that connects heir Prince Adam with aristocracy is via a variety of "excellences":

these are the virtues possessed by the Homeric hero and they are the qualities of an aristocratic world. They are not available to everyone; indeed, they are limited to a small number of those who enjoy certain advantages with which they are endowed by birth and inheritance. Hence the ordinary person has no *arête*. The characteristics of the Homeric hero are those suited to the warrior: skill, cunning, courage, self-reliance, loyalty, love of one's friends and hatred of one's enemies, courtesy, generosity, and hospitality. These values are intensely individualistic and frankly competitive. Distinctions between individuals are emphasized.

(Ferngren and Amundsen 1985, 4)

This aristocratic trope not only refers to the common narrative trope of the superhero with their "ordinary" alter ego, but it also evokes the classic heroic ideal about accepting one's own limitations and mortality. He-man may be super-powered, but Prince Adam, despite being "aristocratic," is not. The latter is the limited (more human) reverse of the former.

From the minicomics, He-Man was structured around the characteristics of the heroic ideal described above and the hero's journey. The Hero's journey is one of the most used motifs in American narratives, where a hero travels many roads searching for self-discovery, and finds many adventures in the meantime. This travel and self-discovering "demonstrate the commonality of the human experience" (Palumbo 2014, 2). According to Joseph Campbell, "one part of the mythological motif of the hero's journey is acquiescence" (Cousineau 1991, 12), with the main character knowing "when to surrender and what to surrender to. The main theme is to yield your position to the dynamic" (12). He-Man starts many of his transmedia iterations having been defeated, which forces him to begin a new journey of heroism. This trope was used to illustrate a missing backstory, as the *Masters of the Universe*'s toy line had none. The hero's journey means rebirth, rediscovery, and re-creation (Palumbo 2014, 3), the latter an important part of transmedia flexibility. Not only does He-Man take this path, but so do other characters, such as his sister She-Ra or his friend Teela. In the following section, we will study how the franchise, in each new audiovisual installment, offers a new hero's journey where the hero evolves to the heights of the heroic ideal.

The Hero's Journey: She-Ra

The hero in contemporary popular culture was reformulated as societal and ethical values shift through the decades (Pagnoni Berns 2021). Yet, some elements were kept intact, especially those at the roots of the "heroic ideal." The superhero is the fitting embodiment of the classic ideals with the "modern spin" of added superpowers, costumes, and/or amazing gadgets (Wood 2020, 1). The modern superhero is a new iteration of the classic epic vision.

Broadcast in two seasons, *He-Man and the Masters of the Universe* (Wetzler 1983–1985) is an American animated television series that was produced by Filmation and based on Mattel's toy line. The series takes place on planet Eternia, a sword and sorcery world. Whenever Prince Adam holds the Sword of Power aloft and proclaims "By the Power of Grayskull! I have the power!" he is endowed with super-powers and transformed into He-Man and uses his powers to defend Eternia from the evil forces of his main foe, Skeletor.

The classic television series discarded any form of "hero's journey," presenting the main characters as prototypical superheroes and supervillains. Most iterations, however, offered nuanced versions of the journey, with the characters finding their heroism while struggling with their identities. After being adapted for television from a toy line, *Masters of the Universe* then underwent its second shift to another medium, with a theatrical release of the animated movie *The Secret of the Sword* (1985), produced by Filmation. The adaptation process is more complex here, however, as it was not the *He-Man and the Masters of the Universe* series adapted to the big screen. Although released before the television series *She-Ra: Princess of Power* (Wetzler 1985–1987) began, *The Secret of the Sword* was a compilation of the first five episodes of this series but with minor edits made. In brief, a spin-off from *Masters of the Universe* was conceived of as a new television series, but was first exhibited as a film.

Leaving aside this complex intermedial flux, *The Secret of the Sword* was the first iteration in this animated storyworld to build on the hero's journey. The reasons for this are clear: She-Ra was a new character, introduced as a spin-off, and viewers should be able to see what made/makes her so heroic. The narrative follows Prince Adam, who is sent to an other-dimensional world of Etheria, which is ruled by the Horde, an intergalactic evil army. Adam eventually stands up to the soldiers, who are guided by Captain Adora, and he defeats them with the help of an archer called Bow. He-Man is eventually captured and interrogated by Adora. She believes the rebels are evil and the Horde are benevolent rulers, despite not knowing much about life outside of their base. After learning the truth, Adora learns she is He-Man's sister as well. Raising her sword, she becomes She-Ra and helps her brother in defeating the evil Horde leader known as Hordak.

Backing the title's credits, the lyrics of the pop song melody refer to heroic virtues as "the honor of love" and about finding the truth. Finding the truth about her identity is, for Adora, akin to *anagorisis* in Greek drama. "Anagnorisis is when a character onstage realise something about someone else, something that the audience has known for some time (for example, that the person is a long-lost relative) – and the discovery changes his or her behavior" (McLeish 2003, 272). Adora behaves differently after learning she is Prince Adam's sister and takes arms against Hordak, aligning herself with the rebellion.

It is interesting to note how Adora's process of *anagnoris* is staged in the film. She has been manipulated magically by Shadow Weaver, one of Hordak's minions. Adora's heart is pure, but she is blind to the truth of Hordak's dictatorship. Reality is revealed to her when she sees with her own eyes how Hordak and his minions mistreat, kidnap, torture (and, presumably, kill) many citizens. She must learn the truth all by herself, without magical aid, following the hardships of the heroic path. Raising the magical sword will give her magical powers and transform her into She-Ra, but it is Adora who must find the truth and learn how to become heroic.

Neither is Adora the only one traveling the hero's journey. Prince Adam is sent to the other-dimensional world of Etheria without a clear purpose by the Sorceress of Castle Greyskull. She only tells him he will eventually finds what he is looking for, leaving him alone to find a new heroic level uniting his powers with those of She-Ra, thus outlining a typical hero's journey: "The hero is called to an adventure, crosses the threshold to an unknown world to endure tests and trials, and usually returns with a boon that benefits his fellows" (Palumbo 2014, 3). He-Man wins the battle not via brutal force, but with persuasion, as he convinces his sister to seek the truth for herself. The purpose of *The Secret of the Sword* is to present She-Ra as a female counterpart of He-Man, and more significantly for Mattel, as a new toy in the line. Filmation, however, chose to depict her as a woman struggling with her identity and enduring a hero's journey to find her moment of *anagnorisis*. The animated film is the first attempt at making the *Masters of the Universe*'s world more fully developed, showing viewers not just how but why He-Man and, especially, She-Ra are heroes.

Since her debut in 1985, She-Ra has been a female icon in popular culture. With the original *She-Ra: Princess of Power* television series (1985–1987), the character established herself as a symbol of empowerment for girls and young women. In 2018, the series was revitalized in *She-Ra and the Princesses of Power* (Stevenson 2018–2020), under the direction of Noelle Stevenson, providing an update not only aesthetically but also thematically, adapting the character and her world to modern sensibilities. This reinterpretation modernizes She-Ra yet it closely follows the logic of the hero's journey as delineated by the theatrical film.

In *She-Ra and the Princesses of Power*, audiences follow the story of Adora, a young soldier raised by the evil Horde on the planet Etheria. Adora believes she is fighting for the righteous cause until one day she finds a magical sword in the Whispering Forest, which transforms her into She-Ra, a powerful legendary warrior. As is easy to see, this new story largely unfolds as a remake of the previous film, again choosing the hero's path, with Adora starting a path of self-discovery. In both series, She-Ra finds the call to heroism, but the new series focuses on Adora's doubts for letting down those who raised and formed her, thus emphasizing the hero's journey and her struggles with identity. New to this narrative, the hero's journey follows how Adora weaves different alliances with other princesses of power in order to help each other fight the Horde and restore peace. More important, however, is her relationship with Catra, her former best friend in the Horde, who feels betrayed by her departure and becomes her main antagonist. Catra has almost the same origin as Adora, orphaned and raised by the Horde, but as Adora leaves the Horde ranks to join the Rebellion, Catra is chosen as Captain with her main mission being to bring Adora back to the Horde or prevent the plans of the princesses. It is important to note that through all these modifications to her journey, the Adora of 2018 undergoes both an internal and external evolution. Her power as She-Ra manifests itself not only through physical strength, but also in her ability to accept and reconcile the different aspects of her identity. *She-Ra and the Princesses of Power* emphasizes that Adora's true power comes from her emotional growth and the realization that her destiny is not predetermined by the sword, but by her own choices.

The Hero's Journey: He-Man (and Some Friends)

The *Masters of the Universe* (1987) movie adapted the multi-episodic, multi-series television show by compressing and narrowing the story and cast to fit the requirements of a feature film, choosing again the hero's journey as the main narrative framework. The film begins with Skeletor (Frank Langella) and Evil-Lyn (Meg Foster) having conquered Greyskull Castle as He-Man (Dolph Lundgren) is fighting a losing battle before being cast away to a strange, foreign world know as Earth. "Earth" is where He-Man must show his heroism, to fight his everlasting battle but in new territory and with people who do not know who he is. The heroic ideal is, then, doubly displayed here: first, with He-Man losing the battle but fighting nonetheless and second, with He-Man fighting on Earth, trying to save not only his native planet but the new one as well. The film offers little information about who He-Man and his friends, Teela (Chelsea Field) and Man-at-Arms (Jon Cypher), are, as the story is focused on the interactions taking place between the heroes and the people from Earth, especially Julie (Courtney Cox). Like Adora before, Julie is depicted searching for her own path in life. The first time she is shown in the film, she is talking with a friend about leaving town to find her own destiny. Yet, her fate is to aid He-Man and his friends against Skeletor. The prom night's theme in her school is "Around the world," an ironic twist as Julie is ready to leave town to search for her identity when she is found by Skeletor's henchmen. Julie is He-Man's Earthling counterpart: she clashes with the police, as she is adamant to help He-Man in going back to his own world, while the hero from Eternia surrenders to Skeletor to protect not his own people, but that of Earth. Even Skeletor is impressed by He-Man's act of generosity, as the hero demonstrates why he is such a virtuous figure. When taken prisoner to Eternia, He-Man parts ways with his friends with the phrase "good fate," this being another callback to the hero's journey and the classic Greek ethos of destiny.

A similar narrative follows Mattel and Netflix's production *Masters of the Universe: Revelation* (2021), with He-Man seemingly killed in the first episode after being defeated by Skeletor. Without He-Man, Eternia has lost any trace of magic and Teela is now a mercenary for hire. The television series revolves around these worn-out heroes struggling with their past of heroism and how to, albeit in reluctant ways, return to it. Like the other iterations, the television series starts without offering much on who He-Man is, or information on his past. He-Man is absent much of the series, with Teela slowly finding a renewed sense of heroism. In episode 2 ("The Poisoned Chalice"), Teela mentions she now understands why heroes have failed before Skeletor: while "adventures…being a hero…swallows you whole" they offer little in return in terms of personal reward. Teela now wants to help people only for money as a way to reject any heroism: she has been defrauded by the heroic ideal many times before. It is the love that Teela feels for Andra, her girlfriend, who pushes her to act on behalf of others. Slowly and reluctantly, Teela starts her own hero's journey of self-discovery. And she is not the only one, as the "revelation" of the title refers to finding oneself. To save the little magic, there is still left in the world, Evil-Lynn must unite forces with Teela and Cringer to help the Supreme Sorceress of Eternia, finding her own goodness along the way.

All the heroes in *Masters of the Universe: Revelation*, including Teela and Man-at-Arms, try to escape from their heroic past, yet they cannot let people suffer before their eyes and, grudgingly, they return once again to their roles as protectors of Eternia. Evil-Lyn tells Teela in episode 3 ("The Most Dangerous Man in Eternia") that the former Captain is not really turning the page to embrace a new future, but only hiding away. In episode 5 ("The Forge at the Forest of Forever"), a rescue crew finds Prince Adam living peacefully in heaven as he tries to leave his past as a hero behind. Even with the whole universe at the brink of disappearing if magic is not restituted to Eternia, Adam is unwilling to return to be a hero. Yet, he returns to life to aid Eternia at the end of the episode, pushed by his love for his friends.

He-Man, the great superhero, however, only shows up in the television series' last episode ("Comes with Everything You See Here"), which is potentially a culturally and commercially baffling decision as is he the most popular character of the franchise. However, it is not the presence of the hero but his path to heroism that interests the creators of *Masters of the Universe: Revelation*, this being another adaptation to feature the hero's journey. The hero may have been exiled or defeated but they will triumph over evil and, most important for the *Masters of the Universe* franchise, they find heroism in their decisions, overcoming their own doubts, to make the world a better place.

Masters of the Universe started as a line of toys, without much personality besides being "Barbie with muscles." As such, those expanding the classic television series from the 1980s started to create an architecture where the heroism of these characters was explained over and over, not so much through telling their origins but in displaying the hero's journey. The hero's journey is a rite of passage. In these transmedia adaptations, said passages are not just those of the heroes finding their forgotten heroism, but also the identities they lacked in their inception as toys. He-Man and She-Ra are constantly portrayed as characters that must reconstruct their lives and, with that, their heroism, demonstrate to consumers why they must invest in them, and why these heroes are valuable.

References

Baer, Brian. 2017. *How He-Man Mastered the Universe: Toy to Television to the Big Screen.* McFarland & Company.

Benardete, Seth. 2005. *Achilles and Hector: The Homeric Hero.* St. Augustine's Press.

Conarroe, Adam, and Patrick Stannard, dirs. 2021. Masters of the Universe: Revelation. *Powerhouse Animation Studios*

Cousineau, Phil. 1991. *The Hero's Journey: The World of Joseph Campbell.* Harper Collins.Davis, Desmond, dir. 1981. *Clash of the Titans.* United Artists.

Fehrle, Johannes. 2019. "Introduction: Adaptation in a Convergence Environment." In *Adaptation in the Age of Media Convergence*, edited by Johannes Fehrle and Werner Schäfke-Zell. Amsterdam University Press.

Ferngren, Gary, and Darrell Amundsen. 1985. "Virtue and Health: Medicine in Pre-Christian Antiquity." In *Virtue and Medicine: Explorations in the Character of Medicine*, edited by Earl Shelp. Reidel Publishing Company.

Friedman, Ed, Lou Kachivas, Marsh Lamore, Bill Reed, and Gwen Wetzler, dirs. He-Man and She-Ra: *The Secret of the Sword.* Filmation.

Gambarato, Renira Rampazzo, Geane Carvalho Alzamora, and Lorena Tárcia. 2020. *Theory, Development, and Strategy in Transmedia Storytelling.* Routledge.

Goddard, Gary, dir. 1987. *Masters of the Universe.* The Cannon Group, Inc.

Hernandez, John Diego. 2003. "Toys and cartoons: The Correlation between Animated Properties and toy Products." *M.A. Thesis. Rowan Digital Works.* https://rdw.rowan.edu/etd/1321.

Hodges, Mike, dir. 1980. *Flash Gordon.* Universal Pictures.

Jenkins, Henry. 2010. "He-Man and the Masters of Transmedia." *Pop Junctions,* May 20. https://henryjenkins.org/blog/2010/05/he-man_and_the_masters_of_tran.html.

Kendrick, Gregory. 2010. *The Heroic Ideal: Western Archetypes from the Greeks to the Present.* McFarland & Company.

Kinder, Marsha. 1991. *Playing with Power in Movies, Television, and Video Games: From Muppet Babies to Teenage Mutant Ninja Turtles.* University of California Press.

Kirichenko, Alexander. 2022. *Greek Literature and the Ideal: The Pragmatics of Space from the Archaic to the Hellenistic Age.* Oxford University Press.

Lee, Jonathan Ray. 2020. *Deconstructing LEGO: The Medium and Messages of LEGO Play.* Palgrave Macmillan.

Lobb, Randall, and Robert McCallum, dirs. 2017. Power of Grayskull: The Definitive History of He-Man and the Masters of the Universe. *High Fliers.*

Mansfield, Harvey. 2010. "Manly Assertion." In *Hemingway on Politics and Rebellion*, edited by Lauretta Conklin Frederking. Routledge.

McLeish, Kenneth. 2003. *A Guide to Greek Theatre and Drama.* Routledge.

Pagnoni Berns, Fernando Gabriel 2021. "Adapting American Values: Contextualizing Superman and the Mole Men and Superman VI: The Quest for Peace." In *Adapting Superman: Essays on the Transmedia Man of Steel*, edited by john Darowski. McFarland & Company.

Palumbo, Donald. 2014. *The Monomyth in American Science Fiction Films: 28 Visions of the Hero's Journey.* McFarland & Company.

Ritterbusch, Rachel. 2020. "From the Page to the Screen: The Process of Film Adaptation." In *Practical Approaches to Teaching Film*, edited by Rachel S. Ritterbusch. Cambridge Scholars Publishing.

Stevenson, N.D, showrunner. 2018–2020. *She-Ra and the Princesses of Power.* DreamWorks Animation Television.

Volk-Weiss, Brian, and Tom Stern, dirs. 2017. *The Toys That Made Us.* The Nacelle Company.

Wetzler, Gwen, dir. 1985–1987. *She-Ra: Princess of Power.* Filmation Associates.

Wetzler, Gwen, prod. 1983–1985. *He-Man and the Masters of the Universe.* Filmation Associates.

Wood, Christopher. 2020. *Heroes Masked and Mythic: Echoes of Ancient Archetypes in Comic Book Characters.* McFarland & Company.

10

HOW EXTERNALLY LICENSED INTELLECTUAL PROPERTY DICTATED CHANGES IN MARVEL UK'S PUBLISHING OUTPUT OF THE 1970S–1990S

Rob McLaughlin

Introduction

Created in 1972, Marvel UK was launched to introduce Marvel Comics to the wider British comic readership. It was intended to entice comic book readers, whose weekly adventures may well have consisted of long-running British strips such as Dennis the Menace in *The Beano* (1938–), Desperate Dan in *The Dandy* (1937–), and Sids Snake in *Whizzer and Chips* (1969–1990), to pick up and purchase comics themed around American superheroes.

Initially reprinting prior Marvel adventures from its American parent company, Marvel UK's initial works consisted of reproductions of stories involving characters that included Spider-Man, Captain America, etc., all through British printers. They were printed in black and white (with occasional color spots) on bigger formatted paper and, in comparison to their American counterparts, with thicker newsprint paper used in the production process. This was not only a cost-effective way to reprint prior American published stories, but also this sized format and esthetic better resembled other British comics published and on the shelves at the time.

This new line from the publisher initially started with just one title, *The Mighty World of Marvel* (1972–1983), in October 1972, with the release intended to test the British comic readers' appetite for all things superheroes. Due to the title's popularity (and profitability), by 1973, Marvel began publishing other titles, again in this reprint format focusing specifically on their best-known characters such as *Spider-Man* which came via the *Spider-Man Weekly* book (1973–1985) and *The Avengers* (1973–1976), which provided readers with a taste of the World's Mightiest Heroes but also the spectacular adventures of everyone's favorite friendly neighborhood web-slinger.

By 1978, the UK arm of Marvel Comics was granted editorial autonomy by their US counterparts, which allowed the publisher to produce unique creative content based on Marvel's Intellectual Property. Under the guidance of new editor Dez Skinn who, having a wealth of experience in the British comic industry, was brought on board to Marvel UK in August 1978 to develop the publishers' presence in the UK to an even greater extent. In

DOI: 10.4324/9781003366911-12

bringing in Skinn, Marvel went through what has been described as the "Marvel Revolution" (Dakin 1979, 14). This creative freedom allowed for the growth and development of Marvel UK's line. They expanded on the publisher's formative years, which had been reliant on reprinted material, to become revitalized and to flourish with new books and even new characters.

Skinn's tenure at Marvel UK was transformative. His approach of creating new content to supplement the reprinted US comic stories allowed up-and-coming creative talents such as Alan Moore, Dave Gibbons, and Steve Dillon to write and illustrate works based on some of Marvel's flagship characters, as well as introducing some completely new characters. Titles such as *The Hulk* (1979–1980), for example, featured unique material for a UK audience from Dave Gibbons and Steve Dillon, which mirrored the episodic, nomadic wandering of the Hulk represented in the 1970s television series (Vaughan 2017, 85–102). The *Hulk* Comic was also synonymous with a book that highlighted an obscure fan-favorite character: the pulp hero *Night Raven*, a noir-like vigilante created by Skinn himself. As such, by the end of the 1970s, there was a broad range of Marvel superhero books and books based on genre Intellectual Property jostling for shelf space alongside copies of *2000AD* (1977–), *Battle* (1975–1988), *Action* (1976–1977), and BBC's Doctor Who, via *Doctor Who Weekly* (1979–), as well as the recently relaunched *Eagle* comic in (1982–1994; Chapman 2011, 174–175).

These already established books, which contained this new material, were pushed even further with titles being given the go-ahead based solely on new Marvel UK characters. These new books included *Captain Britain Weekly* (1976–1977), which presented the adventures of Brian Braddock the mystically empowered guardian of the British Isles. Created by Americans Chris Claremont and Herb Trimpe in 1976, Captain Britain was a homage to Captain America but with a British twist that tried to fuse American superheroics with British sensibilities (Chapman 2011, 174–175). Battling against antagonists such as The Fury and Slaymaster, the captain eventually became bigger than his initial comic and publishers and was eventually folded into the wider Marvel Comics continuity appearing in his eponymous title as well as the X-Men-related title *Excalibur*. Some of these initially UK-only published stories of *Captain Britain* were written by the likes of Alan Moore and rivaled the quality of writing and art of their American counterpart superhero titles (Murray 2010, 34). This title provided not only a new character but also expanded the British side of the Marvel Universe and featured original comic stories by the likes of Pat Mills, Dave Gibbons, and John Wagner. *Captain Britain* and other contemporary titles which included *The Titans* (1975–1976) and *The Daredevils* (1983) were still reliant on American backup strips to supplement the comics' page count but felt new and innovative in their design and front cover aesthetic. These books reprinted prior stories of the *Fantastic Four* and *Nick Fury* as backup strips for the book (Dittmer 2011, 71–87), but titles such as *The Titans* also saw material contributed to its pages by Alan Moore, Grant Morrison, Alan Davies, and Neil Gaiman, who went onto form the "British Invasion" of American comics in the mid-1980s, where a significant amount of Marvel UK creatives moved to the US to write for DC and Marvel on their mainstream titles.

Skinn in overseeing this popular format of both reprints and unique material did not just restrict Marvel UKs output to just its pantheon of superheroes, but they expanded the Marvel line to embrace the publisher's licensing agreements. Skinn also inherited comic books based on other popular licensed properties from the time such as *Planet of the Apes* (1974–1977) and one of the biggest tie-in comics via *Star Wars Weekly* (1977–1986), based on George Lucas's epic space opera. In looking at which Intellectual Property partnerships the publisher already had agreements in place for, Skinn expanded the line significantly, to embrace the growth of comics and publications based on other properties that came from film and television.

The weekly title based on the *Star Wars* franchise appeared in April 1977 and, while initially being reprints of the American comic book adaptation of the film, also eventually went on to produce new unique stories that took the popular space opera into a wider "extended" universe. As with most of the titles produced at this time by Marvel UK, *Star Wars Weekly* was another anthology book. Its weekly schedule split the main story into smaller installments, usually taking four weeks to complete a story arc to allow for the differing American monthly issue release schedule. As with its superhero line, this differing publishing schedule proved to be beneficial to Marvel UK creatively; as the weekly comics eventually ran out of American material to reprint, it allowed more scope for original content. As such, the transition from American material to uniquely British content was not as jarring for readers, and these new stories involving Luke, Han, Leia, etc., written by the likes of Steve Parkhouse and Alan Moore became the driving force of the publication. In May 1980, the title changed its name, becoming *The Empire Strikes Back Weekly* to reflect the release of the new *Star Wars* film release in the UK. This change of title happened again in June 1983 when the title became *Return of the Jedi*, a name that remained on the comic title until its demise in 1986. Within *Star Wars Weekly* (and its subsequent change in names), a supporting strip was included from reprints of *Micronauts*, a late 1970s comic written by Bill Mantlo. *Micronauts* used an existing Japanese Mego toy line to produce a *Star Wars*-like strip that showed the adventures of a rebellious set of heroes of the sub-atomic micro-verse against the dictatorial Baron Karza. This publishing of a comic book narrative based on a toy line provided something of a precursor for the shape of things to come for Marvel UK toward the middle and late 1980s. While the Micronauts toy line was not as popular as other properties at the time, overshadowed by the likes of Kenner and Palitoys' *Star Wars* or *GI Joe/Action Man* lines, the idea of taking Japanese toy lines and adapting them for a European market led to a swathe of transforming robot lines such as *Voltron*, *Go-Bots/Robo Machines*, and of course *Transformers*, a licensed property that eventually changed how Marvel UK publishing would sustain itself into the next decade (Bainbridge 2010, 829–842).

A Steady Decline

For all its success in the late 1970s, by 1982, Marvel UK had almost completely stopped publishing weekly titles based on superheroes. Some new weeklies were still launched as testers of the market for reprinted material. This included new volumes of books based around The Incredible Hulk *(1982)*; Thor *(1983)* and X-Men *(1983)*, with both of these titles eventually merging; and Fantastic Four *(1982–1983)*, with the popular star of the *Fantastic Four*, Ben Grimm, also featuring in The Thing is Big Ben *(1984)*. Some new weeklies were still launched as testers of the market for reprinted material, which included new titles of second volumes of books based around The Incredible Hulk (1982); Thor (1983) and X-Men (1983), with both of these titles eventually merging; Fantastic Four (1982–1983), and the popular rocky orange star of the Fantastic Four, Ben Grimm, in the pun-laden Th*e Thing is Big Ben* (1984). These titles were, once again, reprints of prior American strips and provided little to no original content. While some Marvel titles still found a market, such as the continuing *Star Wars* titles, and some new Marvel UK original content appeared within books such as *The Daredevils* (1983), which now became a monthly rather than weekly publishing schedule, many of these reprint-only titles did not last long before being combined into one title or were canceled altogether due to poor sales.

By the early 1980s, the lull of Marvel UK's originally produced works was evident. The advent of the home computer (and, of course, computer games), new television channels, the growing availability of American-based toy lines, and the propagation of the obligatory Saturday morning cartoon tie-ins and merchandise meant that the readership of comics (and not just Marvel) began to dwindle (Burke and Burke 1998, 71). As such, comics that did not have instantly recognizable characters from other media, or that were not aligned specifically with new toy lines, did not sell in the numbers required to continue publication. With the appetite for comics dropping significantly (due to so many other things for young readers to potentially spend pocket money on) and issues with erratic distribution, Marvel UK's flagship and biggest-selling title ran their course and, after 400 issues of *Marvel Superheroes* (1979–1983), the title was eventually canceled in the summer of 1983 with Issue #397. *Spider-Man Weekly* (1973–1985), which lasted a couple of years longer, eventually finished its publication run with the final #666 issue being published in December 1985.

With this downturn, Marvel focused specifically on producing titles that tied directly to the cross-platform Intellectual Property the company had in place. While comics of the hugely successful *Masters of the Universe* line of toys had appeared via DC, Marvel, having missed the opportunity to license the property in comic form, instead developed comics based around the *Transformers* line of toys from Hasbro. Based on various transforming *Diaclone* and *Micro Change* toy lines from the Japanese toymakers Takara, the *Transformers* toys appeared both in the US and UK, in 1984, alongside the obligatory cartoon show produced by Marvel and animation studio Sunbow/Toei (Wolski 2022, 131–147). The initial comic adaptation of the "Robots in Disguise" appeared in America in May 1984, with Marvel UK reprinting these stories within the newly launched *Transformers* comic appearing on the shelves of British newsagents later, in September of the same year.

The first few issues of the UK reprinted comics ran the original stories seen in the American limited series. Initially, this was via a fortnightly printing schedule reformatted once again on the larger "magazine" scale British comic format rather than the original smaller American books, to replicate the continuing trend of replicating comic titles on the shelves of British newsagents. The comic changed to a weekly format from #27, a schedule that would stay with the title until #308, only reverting to fortnightly again from #309 to its concluding final issue #332. Consisting of 24 pages of a mix of black and white and color, the *Transformers* comic was printed on a higher paper quality than both its American counterpart and other prior Marvel UK books. The thicker newsprint-style paper which had been seen in prior Marvel books and was prevalent in British comics such as *The Beano* and *Whizzer and Chips* (Stringer 2008) was replaced with thinner glossier paper stock." This increase in paper quality also moved across to the publisher's *Star Wars* comic and became commonplace in the rest of the subsequent titles released by the publisher during the 1980s.

The new *Transformers* comics format again copied prior Marvel UK reprint books with usually half the comic dedicated to the "main" story of the comic while the remaining pages were filled up with backup strips. *Transformers* backup strips included *Machine Man* and *Iron Man 2099*, comedy one-page strips such as *Combat Colin* and *Robo-Capers*, as well as a letters page. The *Transformers* letters page was a hugely popular element of the comic with letters from the title's readership encouraged by the editorial team and responded to by the editor of the book via the personalities of the characters who starred in the comics. These letters page "hosts" included Soundwave via his "Soundwaves" (issues #22–74), Grimlock's "Grim Grams" (issues #75–183), and Dreadwind's "Dread Tidings" (issues #184–299). This encouragement of fans to interact with the comic via letters, pictures, and drawings provided the fanbase with a sense of ownership and media interaction well before the age of the internet or social media.

The first edition of the issues of *Transformers* in the UK was more like a magazine than a comic book, which provided facts and figures about the franchise characters as well as the comic strip itself. The book also had a cameo appearance by *Spider-Man* (in his black costume) in issue #6 giving the fledgling title a boost with another recognizable character on the cover. With the issues eventually running out of the US comic material, to continue the story, new material had to be developed specifically for a UK audience, which eventually blended both American-written stories and ones developed by the team at Marvel UK. This was not something that Marvel UK had done for a few years, with only the publisher's *Star Wars* title still running with original content. However, the popularity of the Transformers via the animated series (shown daily through the British school's summer holiday via ITV's *Wakaday* children's television show) and the toy line made the comic a huge success, selling more than 180,000 copies a week at the height of its popularity. The popularity of the title allowed Marvel UK the leeway to hire creative teams to develop unique content for *Transformers*. New strips and cover art were created by a range of talented artists and writers, including Simon Furman, Geoff Senior, Jeff Anderson, Tim Perkins, Dan Reed, Ian Rimmer, and Will Simpson (Wheeler 2014).

While the creative teams were allowed to create unique and new stories within the pages of the UK Transformers continuity, an editorial caveat was in place, which stated that the comics needed to acknowledge other *Transformers* media. As the cartoon and toy lines evolved and new characters and scenarios were introduced, this would need to be reflected in the comics. Comparable with Marvel UK's *Star Wars* comic, the new material had to work within the pre-set narrative. Therefore, when the wider Transformers media context shifted, such as with the release of *Transformers the Movie* (Shin 1986), or a new wave of characters was produced by Hasbro, the comic needed to reflect these new scenarios and to bring in new characters or situations (McEniry et al. 2016, 55–60).

The comic played out some aspects of this cartoon continuity, but stories such as "Target 2006" (Issues #78–88) brought new characters such as Galvatron and Ultra Magnus into comic continuity in a different manner. This would also be reflected in one of the most recognized *Transformers* stories within the comics, which saw the appearance of Unicron, the World-Eating, planet-sized Transformer. While he had appeared in the *Transformers* cartoon continuity via the aforementioned animated movies, his appearance in the comic books shifted into a different context and allowed the UK comic continuity to do things slightly differently than the cartoon, such as having Unicron arrive at Cybertron in the year 2006 rather than 2005, as in the animated film. This also led to the comics developing stories of the aftermath of the events of the movie where Unicron is still conscious, and his head, after floating through space after his alleged destruction, eventually crashes on the planet of the Junk-themed Transformers (seen in the film), which leads to whole new stories and a new continuity for the Marvel UK comics. This alternative comic continuity introduced specifically UK comics-based characters to the narrative, such as Death's Head. Appearing in issue #113 in 1987 to assist the Autobot leader Rodimus Prime in defeating Unicron, Death's Head is a robotic bounty hunter with a characteristic habit of adding "yes?" to the end of his sentences; he became a fan favorite and a character that the next generation of Marvel UK used in developing their new line of titles.

While the editorial precepts for the creation of new material were framed by the dictate that any new comic strip narratives had to be based on a toy line or Marvel partner IP, the creation of a new "alternative" diegesis for these characters meant that within the mid-1980s, Marvel UK became the innovators of cartoon and toy-centric comic books, creating legacies for fandom and providing a lot of the world-building of the current *Transformers* continuity and canon. The success of the *Transformers* comic, which eventually ran for 332 issues (compared to the American series lasting 80), was hugely important in regard to both the diegesis of the *Transformers* and as a licensed property. For example, main UK writer Simon Furman eventually took over the Marvel US version of the title and became the "guru" of *Transformers* lore and continuity, continuing to work on the franchise at the time of writing, though it is no longer published by either branch of Marvel Comics. *Transformers* also established a new "house style" for Marvel UK that would be used on their subsequent toy-and-cartoon licensed properties.

Secret Wars

With the success of *Transformers* as a title that tied directly to a toy franchise, on April 27, 1985, Marvel UK produced a title based on the 12-issue series *Secret Wars* which had appeared on American shelves in 1984. Retitled *Marvel Super Heroes Secret Wars*, the book coincided with the release of the first wave of Secret Wars toys within the UK. The timing of the release of the book was not coincidental as the entire American mini-series of *Secret Wars* was created as a marketing ploy with the intent to sell toys.

In 1984, DC had already produced a line of toys called *The Superpowers Collection*. Licensing out their repertoire of characters, such as Superman, Batman, and Wonder Woman, to Kenner, who had produced the hugely successful action figure range based on the *Star Wars* franchise, these toys in turn propagated other media such as new comics; merchandise tie-ins; and even a cartoon series entitled *Super Friends: The Legendary Super Powers Show*, which was broadcast on the popular ABC network in America. As such, Marvel intended to counter this popular range from their "Distinguished Competition" with their range of toys based on their IP. Marvel agreed on a deal with Mattel (the makers of *He-Man*) to develop a rival to the popular range of Kenner toys based on the DC characters. An idea to bring together all the major Marvel characters and to do a cross-platform launch into the comic, toy, game, and licensing market was proposed with the original working title of the series being the "Cosmic Champions," based on a prior successful three-issue crossover story, *Contest of Champions* from 1982.

First announced in *Marvel Age* #11 the book title was changed based on market research from Mattel, which discovered that words like "secret" and "wars" did well with their intended child-focused audience. Marvel based the entire range on the simple premise of a story where, as Marvel editor-in-chief notes, "All the good guys and all the bad guys fight." Written by Jim Shooter himself, and featuring artwork by Mike Zeck and Bob Layton, the relatively simple storyline involved a cosmic entity known as The Beyonder, who transports a group of superheroes and villains to a distant planet called Battleworld to fight each other for the prize based on their desire. *Secret Wars* was a great success both in the US and the UK; it spawned a sequel unsurprisingly called *Secret Wars 2*, which once again featured The Beyonder coming to Earth. As Marvel UK had done with its other titles, "Secret Wars" had secondary stories that allowed for the differing publication schedule of the American and British books to work. Published on a fortnightly and then weekly schedule, Secret Wars in the UK broke up the story with a variety of backup titles which included the Canadian-based super-team *Alpha Flight, Iceman*, and another backup strip based on a toy line of robotic dinosaurs called *Zoids*.

The Marvel Super Heroes Secret Wars title also featured one of the most peculiar crossover overs in comic history with a one-off backup strip in issue #25 featuring the UK Saturday morning television show *Wide Awake Club* (1984–1989). The story, entitled "Web-Slinger Against Changeling," had Peter Parker in his role as a photojournalist coming to the UK and meeting presenter Tommy Boyd and the rest of the team of the ITV-produced children's television show, only to find a shape-changing Skrull has infiltrated the production crew and is working for the show. Battling and defeating the alien as Spider-Man, this comic obscurity was one of the first appearances of the Black Suit for readers in the UK.

Zoids and Spider-Man

With Marvel UK's *Marvel Super Heroes Secret Wars* being a publishing success, the issue with the lack of original content produced by Marvel UK became apparent. The title did produce some unique content with a light-hearted two-page strip entitled *The Secret Artist* set in the Marvel UK offices, which had a mysterious Secret Artist producing caricatures of the main cast of heroes and villains of the Secret Wars story. The popularity of the strip eventually evolved to become a competition in which readers had to draw what they thought the Secret Artist looked like, with Simon Wyatt, the illustrator of the later graphic novel series *Unbelievable: The Man Who Ate Daffodils* (2011) being the eventual winner (Freeman 2015).

With the title concentrating on reprinting prior published American material, the only original material that the publication ran, apart from the *Secret Artist* strip, was a pilot series of a strip entitled *Zoids*, which ran from issues #20–26 as an incentive for readers to buy a new comic book in which these characters featured. Zoids was based on the mechanical model kits produced by TOMY, which were based on the Japanese robotic dinosaur model line, "Mechabonica," which came from Takara in 1982. The Zoids toy line featured giant clockwork or battery-operated build-it-yourself robots which resembled animals, insects, and dinosaurs. These combinations of model kits and action figures hit the shelves of the UK in 1984, distributed by Tomy. Up until this point, no other merchandise for the Zoids toy line had been developed, and, unlike successful toy counterparts such as *He-Man* and *Transformers* which both had cartoon lines to assist in toy sales, very little ancillary merchandise in the forms of books, cassettes, and soft furnishings was developed for the Zoids Line of toys. The comic book was one of the only licensing agreements that Tomy used to promote the line.

The blue "guardian" and red "mutant" warring factions of Zoids were paired with Marvel's most iconic character, Spider-Man, for a new publication, *Spider-Man and Zoids*, which launched on March 8, 1986. The *Spider-Man* strip within this new title once again featured reprints of prior American stories notably featuring Peter Davids, Puma, Sin-Eater, and Hobgoblin storylines as well as Spider-Man's return to Earth in his alien black costume (which would eventually go on to become the anti-hero, Venom). The Zoids strip within the comic however was unique material coming from the Marvel UK creative team. Written by Grant Morrison (who went on to achieve acclaim with strips for both Marvel and DC with titles such as *Batman, The Invisibles, Animal Man, Doom Patrol,* and so on) and with art by Steve Yeowell (Singer 2012, 26), the narrative for Zoids was not based on any prior stories, lores, or contexts. As such Morrison and Yeowell created a weekly ongoing strip that drew from a lot of science fiction tropes, genre television, and popular culture. Within the book, the initial story follows the crew of the crash-landed spaceship Celeste, as they try to survive the waring mechanical monstrosities of Zoidstar. The initial justification for the strip's existence was that it was quite simply designed to sell the Zoids' robot toys, however, Morrison, on taking inspiration from *The Thing* (1982), *Back to the Future* (1985), *Aliens* (1986), and *Doctor Who* (1963–present), took the strip beyond its relatively basic toy-influenced roots and created a wider world in which the battling robot Zoids existed.

Producing an origin for the robotic creations, which lived in an eternal struggle of war, Morrison set them as remnants of an ancient race of Zoidaryans who had created the Zoids using the robotic vehicles for "fun" gladiatorial combat in the era of "Heroic Combat." This contextualization, as well as other stories featuring the manipulative Pterodactyl Zoid Krark and Namer, the last surviving member of the Zoidaryan race, evolved the strip into a thought-provoking and intelligent narrative with the Black Zoid story being an especially well-regarded adventure.

The series was canceled with issue #51, which occurred during the finale of the Black Zoid storyline. This meant that none of the unfinished plot lines set within the comic diegesis by Morrison (such as the Zoids making it to Earth and the eventual fate of the malevolent robotic pilot of the Black Zoid, the corporate spy Silverman) were ever followed up or completed. A proposed monthly continuation of the story, again written by Morrison, was unfortunately shelved before publication, with only partial scripts and concepts for this series existing.

Widening the Line Once More

By 1988, with the success of *Transformers* and other titles published via Marvel UK, Marvel UK letterer/designer Richard Starkings suggested that the publisher design, develop, and publish its own uniquely created titles to be presented via a US format. Beginning with *Dragon's Claws* (originally *Dragons Teeth*), a title based around a team of futuristic freedom fighters, a series of releases were planned that mirrored the smaller American-format comic style rather than the larger format the publisher had been using in the UK. These would contain one story of completely new content designed and developed by British creative teams. Following *Dragon's Claws* came *The Sleeze Brothers* (1989), an homage of *The Blues Brothers* by John Carnell and Andy Lanning, then *Knights of Pendragon* (1990–1991). This title, written by Dan Abnett and John Tomlinson with art by Gary Erskine, was a mix of superheroes and Arthurian myth. The final title to be released in this publication window was *Death's Head*, a book based around the eponymous robotic bounty hunter.

The self-styled "Freelance Peacekeeping Agent" Death's Head had already made an appearance via *Transformers* #113 (published on May 16, 1987) and had become part of the Marvel UK Transformers diegesis. Written by Simon Furman and drawn by Geoff Senior Death's Head swiftly became a popular character with readers from his first appearance and had returned for two further stories, printed in *Transformers* #133–134 (with the former featuring a cover rendered by Dave Gibbons) and again for a story in #146–151. The latter story (February 6, 1988) saw the character propelled through a "time portal." The character emerged from the portal in a backup story in the pages of *Doctor Who Magazine* #135, (April 1988), meeting the seventh incarnation of the Doctor. Death's Head had been created to interact with the Transformers, who were vast robots, so here the Doctor uses the "Tissue Compression Eliminator" (which had been used on numerous occasions within *Doctor Who* to shrink people to doll-like proportions) to reduce the building-sized robot to the same rough height as a human, which allowed for more interaction with other Marvel characters. This set Death's Head up for his next appearance within Marvel UK continuity in the new *Dragon's Claws* book in issue #5 (November 1988) where he fought the team and was dismantled. This subsequently allowed for a redesign of the character to make his appearance more superhero-like, sporting a blue and gold costume. This new look gave the character a cape and brighter colors rather than the gritty padded brown and green attire worn by the character in *Transformers*, which was more reminiscent of other British comic characters, such as the robotic ABC Warriors seen with the pages of *2000AD*.

As *Transformers* was a licensed book, any characters created for the title became the property of the franchise's overall owner, Hasbro. To avoid this happening, Furman and Bryan Hitch (best known for his highly detailed, widescreen comic work on DCs *Authority* and Marvels *Ultimates* titles) hastily produced an untitled one-page strip featuring the character, often referred to as "High Noon Tex," to ensure the publisher retained the copyright of Death's Head. The short comic strip was subsequently published in the back of *Transformers* #167 and several Marvel UK titles in May 1988, nearly a year after the character's original appearance on the May 16, 1987, via *Transformers* #113. How the rights to Death's Head still exist and remain at Marvel are unclear; however, the publisher collaboration with Hasbro has seen various iterations of Death's Head appear in action figure form with even a new collector's edition version of the character released in 2024 at San Diego Comic-Con through the Hasbro Marvel Legends line.

Subsequent issues saw Death's Head cross paths with the Fantastic Four and Iron Man 2020 as a character familiar to Marvel UK readers, having first appeared as a backup strip of *Transformers*. Hitch meanwhile had struggled to keep to the monthly schedule, leading to a variety of artists working on the series. However, sales were poor; *Dragon's Claws* had been canceled after 10 issues in April 1989, and *Death's Head* would stop when it reached the same number. Simon Furman noted that the poor sales of these titles were caused by British retailers, who were not used to the US-size dimensions of the book compared to the magazine size of most other British titles and struggled to promote the books correctly.

A Move into the 1990s

For the remainder of the late 1980s, Marvel UK only produced a handful of other titles, again all based on recognizable characters and licenses from other media. Books based around characters such as ThunderCats and The Real Ghostbusters sold well, running for 193 issues, but no title had hit the near 200,000 copies sold of *The Transformers* book, which Marvel UK had reached at the height of its success. Other anthology titles such as *Wicked* and *Marvel Bumper* that reproduced the original material generated by Marvel UK kept the publishers going, and in 1990 *Death's Head* appeared again via the anthology magazine *Strip!* This was Marvel UK's attempt at a more mature anthology comic title to match *2,000AD*, *Heavy Metal*, and *Deadline* which were designed for a mature audience in mind. *Strip!* lasted for 20 issues (February–November 1990) and featured work by many British comics creators, including Alan Grant, Ian Gibson, Pat Mills, Kevin O'Neill, Si Spencer, and John Wagner. A story featuring Death's Head, "The Body in Question," was serialized via *Strip!* issues #13–20 and told the character's origin while also attempting to tie up other loose ends for fans of the original series. This story took a different style in its presentation featuring fully painted art by Geoff Senior. Following the story's completion in the magazine, it was collected in its entirety into a graphic novel format.

In 1992, the character was substantially revised and revived as Death's Head II by Liam Sharpe, Dan Abnett, and Paul Neary as part of Marvel UK's new line of books that rode the resurgent wave of interest in comics during this period. Alongside *Warheads*,

Motormouth & *Killpower*, and *DigiTek* which were presented with a new set of unique "extreme" titles that were not based on existing Marvel IP and not tied into a toy line, the publisher attempted to appease both American and British audiences with some success. However, these lines, while innovative, visually impressive, and well-written with an intriguing concept, had no pre-existing audience or context in which to contextualize these characters. Even with numerous cameos from popular Marvel characters such as Spider-Man and Wolverine within the first few issues, this wave of Marvel UK books did not sell anywhere near the volume of issues that titles such as *The Transformers* had a few years before this. By the mid-1990s, Marvel UK once again became a publisher that dealt mostly with reprinted American material and had very little unique material developed moving forward.

Conclusions

While framing a significant amount of Marvel UK's output from the 1970s until the 1990s, the development and usage of external Intellectual Property could have provided readers with titles and stories that just replicated those seen in cartoons or other media. Indeed, it would have been very easy for the publisher to have just embraced these properties and dictated to their creative talent to produce empty, hollow replications of works already seen. However, the publisher, in using these properties to frame their publication model, drove for innovation and creative content. They underpinned these recognized intellectual properties with a wider diegesis, compelling characters, and stories, ultimately establishing a fanbase and legacy for these properties that still have a lasting effect today. Artists and writers such as Dan Abnett, Simon Furman, and Geoff Senior, overseen by editors like Dez Skinn, could essentially have just produced thin stories based on these external properties, but instead, they committed creativity and passion to these titles, imbuing them with complex intricate storytelling, world-building, and compelling characters.

While character recognition from television, film, and animation from these properties was an intrinsic factor to the popularity of these titles, it can be debated that the talent at Marvel UK was integral in both the creative success of these books and the widening the appeal of these properties. With comic titles such as Zoids being the main medium for Tomy to promote and market their line of toys, Grant Morrison's work, for example, elevated the property into something far more than just wind-up or battery-operated blue and red robotic dinosaurs battling each other.

As such, Marvel UK, from its small roots of reprinting prior Marvel US stories to breaking into the comics market of Great Britain, became so much more. Without the guidance of the likes of Dez Skinn, so many established names within the comic industry would not have been given their first break within the environment of comic books. With titles such as *Transformers*, this impact can be seen to an even greater extent with writers such as Dan Abnett, Simon Furman, Geoff Senior, and others, developing the transforming robot franchise from multiple sets of Takara toys in Japan in the late 1970s to assist in the development of a complex, detailed, and canonically rich universe and established storytelling, characters, and scenarios which still, nearly four decades later, have provided an impact on the wider multi-billion-pound transmedia property.

While now once again Marvel UK is back in the environment of reprinting existing material (having been taken over by Panini), the legacy of the contribution made by the publisher on the wider Western comic market cannot be overstated.

References

Bainbridge, Jason. "Fully Articulated: The Rise of the Action Figure and the Changing Face of 'Children's' Entertainment." *Continuum* 24, no. 6 (2010): 829–842.

Burke, Timothy, and Kevin Burke. 1998. *Saturday Morning Fever: Growing up with Cartoon Culture.* Macmillan.

Chapman, James. 2011. *British Comics: A Cultural History.* Reaktion Books.

Dakin, John. "'Marvel Revolution' in England." *The Comics Journal* 45 (1979): 14.

Dittmer, Jason. "Captain Britain and the Narration of Nation." *Geographical Review* 101, no. 1(2011): 71–87.

Freeman, John. 2015. "1980s Flashback: Marvel UK's Secret Wars "Secret Artist" Investigated – and the artists revealed!" *downthetubes.net*, May 19. https://downthetubes.net/1980s-flashback-marvel-uks-secret-wars-secret-artist-investigated-and-the-artists-revealed/.

McEniry, Matthew J., Robert Moses Peaslee, and Robert G. Weiner, eds. 2016. *Marvel Comics into Film: Essays on Adaptations Since the 1940s.* McFarland & Company.

Murray, Chris. 2010. "Signals from Airstrip One: The British Invasion of Mainstream American Comics." In *The Rise of the American Comics Artist: Creators and Contexts*, edited by Paul Williams. University Press of Mississippi.

Singer, Marc. 2012. *Grant Morrison: Combining the Worlds of Contemporary Comics.* University Press of Mississippi.

Stringer, Lew. 2008. "The Road to Marvel UK – Part 3." *Blimey! The Blog of British Comics!*, February 1. https://lewstringer.blogspot.com/2008/02/road-to-marvel-uk-part-3.html.

Vaughan, Phillip. "'No Cricket Strips Here!' An Interview with Dez Skinn." *Studies in Comics* 8, no. 1 (2017): 85–102.

Wheeler, Ian. 2014. "Robots in Disguise: A Tribute to Marvel UK's 'Transformers.'" *downthetubes.net*, July 12. https://downthetubes.net/draft-robots-in-disguise-a-tribute-to-marvel-uks-transformers/.

Wolski, Michał. "'Everything Transforms and Nothing Changes': Strategies of Adapting The Transformers Toys into a TV Series." *Journal of Adaptation in Film & Performance* 15, no. 1–2 (2022): 131–147.

PART II

Adapting the Superhero

11

BATMAN AND THE BODY ON SCREEN

John Quinn

Introduction

For many of us, the concept of the Batman is easy to bring to mind. Close your eyes and picture the Caped Crusader. We will probably all see different things when we do so. We might even conjure up multiple images. At the core of these imaginings, there will likely be a commonality: a man in a batsuit. This is because there is a fluidity to the representation of the Batman that revolves around a long-established and instantly recognizable template (Brooker 2013, 33). This fluidity has been evolving ever since 1939, when the Caped Crusader first emerged from the shadows to grace the pages of Detective Comics #27. Indeed, the Batman's "survival as a cultural icon... can be attributed to his ability to adapt and change" (Brooker 2013, 33). Constantly reinventing himself for new contexts and audiences, the Batman has become a ubiquitous figure of our cultural landscape. He is drawn and redrawn and then drawn again, all the while maintaining a clear discourse with his predecessors, forming a "hybrid canon" where the Batman's many incarnations live in a state of flux (Durand 2011a, 81).

The filmic Batman perhaps speaks the loudest to this process of reconfiguration. Over the last 80 years, the power and reach of the screen have freed Bruce Wayne from the anchorage of his source text and allowed him to persistently reinvent himself as an icon of mainstream entertainment. This is not to discount the Batman's reach and influence in the comic book, graphic novel, and video game spheres. His influence there is strong and long-lasting. Nonetheless, it is the live-action film and television incarnations of the Batman that have spread the widest of all his texts (Brooker 1999, 185–198). It is from among and between these texts too, that the constantly shifting socio-cultural modality of DC's Dark Knight has become most prominent.

During the era of World War II, Lewis Wilson's patriotic and unfortunately racist Batman crusaded on behalf of Uncle Sam in the cinematic serial *Batman* (1943). There was more of the same, but with less overt nationalism and racism, when Robert Lowery donned the cowl for *Batman and Robin* (1949). Then, when the "swinging sixties" came around, it was over to Adam West, who camped up *Batman: The Movie* (Martinson 1966) and introduced

    DOI: 10.4324/9781003366911-14

viewers to the (not quite) balletic pleasures of "The Batusi", in the iconic television series *Batman* (Dozier 1966–1968).

After taking a well-deserved break in the 1970s, the Batman returned just as the excess of the 1980s began to give way to the cynicism of the 1990s. Brooding his way out from the shadows, Michael Keaton's Batman arose to (at least temporarily) exorcize the camp in director Tim Burton's *Batman* (1989) and *Batman Returns* (1992), before losing that battle when Joel Schumacher took the helm of the franchise in the second half of the decade. Restabilizing an aesthetic of mild homoeroticism, Val Kilmer's Batman was the first to bring nipples to the batsuit in *Batman Forever* (1995) with George Clooney continuing that trend while adding an extra splash of color in *Batman & Robin* (1997).

It was director Christopher Nolan who course corrected the Batman for the 21st century with his Dark Knight Trilogy. Deploying an overt hypermasculinity as a shield against the uncertainty of post 9/11 America, Christian Bale's Batman grappled with the forces of fear, chaos, and pain, respectively, in *Batman Begins* (2005), *The Dark Knight* (2008), and *The Dark Knight Rises* (2012). After this, the franchise took a decade-long pause as a standalone property, with Batman joining the ensemble of the DC Extended Universe. In this universe, Ben Affleck's Batman found himself (re)negotiating his existence against the spectrum of isolation and collaboration explored in *Batman V Superman: Dawn of Justice* (2016), *Suicide Squad* (2016), *Justice League* (2017), and *Zack Snyder's Justice League* (2021).

In the second decade of the 21st century, amidst a cultural discourse of fracturing identities, the notion of a singular consecutive cinematic Batman was about to be eroded. Relaunching the standalone franchise, Robert Pattinson's Batman provided a battered and broken allegory for the loss of faith in contemporary America in *The Batman* (2022). Yet, Pattinson was not the only bat in the cinematic belfry. In 2023, *The Batman* was followed by one more entry in the DC Extended Universe as Michael Keaton and Ben Affleck reprised their roles in *The Flash* (2023), before Pattinson returns to *The Batman Part II*, which is currently scheduled for a 2027 release.

The above litany of portrayals briefly demonstrates the extent to which the screen has continually reconfigured and recodified the Batman to amplify and respond to the socio-cultural context in which he is (re)produced. What follows is an exploration of that amplification and evolution as written by, and on the body of, the Batman. Via an application of Dennis Cutchins' (2017) interpretation of Bakhtin, intertextuality, and adaptation to three short case studies of Adam West, Michael Keaton, and Christian Bale (along with a brief discussion of Robert Pattinson), the notion of simultaneity and dialogic thought is positioned as a mode of resistance against the formation of an absolute Batman. Instead, the notion of the Batman is situated as a relational dialogue through and between the different "batmen". Furthermore, drawing on Bryan Turner's (2008) work on the body and society, this relationship is presented as a grotesque dialogue stuck in the act of becoming, situating the body of Batman as a text for reading that is continually built and rebuilt in a shape and disposition related to the cultural context of his past, his present, and the immediate needs of his consumer.

Before doing so, however, a brief overview of simultaneity, relational dialogues, the grotesque body, and social constructivism is provided as a conceptual framework for that analysis.

Simultaneity, Relational Dialogues, the Grotesque Body, and Social Constructivism

The character and world of Batman is one that exists in a state of constant adaptation and translation. From comic books to graphic novels, from movies to television, from video games to prose, each new incarnation of Batman shares a "significant number of boundaries and interrelationships with other, previously known, texts" (Cutchins 2017, 12). For Cutchins, these boundaries and interrelationships of adaptation are experienced as a form of simultaneity (Cutchins 2017, 81), where the processes of adaptation facilitate the recognition of multiple iterations of the same thing at the same time (Cutchins 2017, 84). These recognitions are formed by the consumer's memories of previously read texts and their perceptions of subsequent adaptations (Cutchins 2017, 73). Such simultaneity can lead, therefore, to the recognition by the consumer that something can be one thing and another thing at the same time.

Cutchins connects this experience of simultaneity with Mikhail Bakhtin's thought on translation. The process of translation "forces the translator to recognise the relational, rather than absolute, status" of one thing to another in a simultaneity of thought (Cutchins 2017, 72). Stories exist not as absolute truth but as an interrelationship with other stories in the same dialogue. Adapted (translated) works are no longer a seamless whole, but rather separated fragments that seek each other out. In this mode, all texts are in constant dialogue, adjusting themselves to the other texts around them as they are consumed. This opens the texts up to multiple interpretations, with "influences between texts moving in every direction simultaneously" (Cutchins 2017, 74). In making these interpretations, consumers can form close relationships with texts, where the texts we experience can become a "part of us, of who we imagine ourselves to be" (Cutchins 2017, 77). When adapting texts, therefore, the process moves beyond the text alone and evokes the potential to undermine "elements of our personalities, implicitly, criticizing who we have become and treading on the sacred ground of ourselves" (Cutchins 2017, 77).

This is particularly applicable to the character and world of the Batman. Via its long history and diversity of adaption, the multiple incarnations of Batman exist simultaneously, overlapping and intersecting in relation to the individual consumption of the viewer. This disrupts the notion of an absolute or "true" Batman, providing instead a dialogue of the Dark Knight, in which the consumers can situate themselves as they please. This notion of dialogue is not, however, restricted to the level of the character and world. As Cutchins notes, some bodies lend themselves to adaptation, while others close themselves off from adaptation (Cutchins 2017, 82). The body of the bat is very much in the mode of the latter. Turning to Bakhtin, Cutchins describes the grotesque body as one in the act of becoming. The grotesque remains a site of construction, where "[i]t is never finished, never completed; it is continually built, created and builds and creates another body" (Cutchins 2017, 82). This forms a chain of bodily life. The life of a new body emerges from the demise of the old (Cutchins 2017, 83), where that demise is, in and of itself, never fully complete.

Who or what is doing the (re)building? Turner positions social constructivism as "the philosophical idea that things are not discovered but socially produced" (Turner 2008, 11). Such constructionism is coupled with the idea that "social reality is a narrative or text" (Turner 2008, 11). The concept of human incompleteness facilitates the construction of such narratives or texts, where the human body becomes a text to be read and constructed. How we see or read the body is dependent on the cultural framework from which it is observed (Turner 2008, 11). In constructionism, therefore, the body is not a given natural phenomenon; it is a "product of social processes of interpretation and fabrication [where] the shape and dispositions of the body are the products of a cultural context" (Turner 2008, 12).

The case studies that follow explore how the iterative processes of interpretation and construction of the Batman abolishes a definitive or true reading of the Dark Knight. In its place, a relational dialogue is produced through and between the different embodiments of

West, Keaton, and Bale, which, when read together with Pattinson, reveal the shifting and grotesque nature of the narrative of the Gotham Guardian.

Adam West

While Adam West is the starting point for this analysis of the relational dialogue of the bat, he was not the first screen incarnation of Batman. The construction of West's Batman is, therefore, in part derived from his predecessors; Lewis Wilson in *Batman* (1943) and Robert Lowery in *Batman and Robin* (1949). Almost indistinguishable from each other, bar the color of their capes, Wilson and Lowery's Batman would be familiar to even the casual consumer of West's show. Wilson and Lowery can also be read as direct aesthetic analogues for the first appearance of Batman in *Detective Comics #27* (1939). Both are near-identical in attire to their comic book counterpart. As such, the surface aesthetics of West's Batman appear to construct a dialogue of a continuity with Wilson and Lowery (and the early comic book incarnations), differing mainly in the color and sheen of his cape and pants, and protuberance of his ears.

Yet, West was the first Batman to make a notable and lasting impact on popular culture (Brooker 1999, 189). With his television show inducing the 1960s cultural phenomenon of "Batmania", West's embodiment of "the Batman brand… leaked into mainstream culture" (Burke 2013, 32) and is commonly seen as the (problematic) stem from which the other live-action forms of Batman departed. So, what was it about West's relational dialogue that brought about divergence in the interrelations of the bat? It was West's performance of the body. While West himself was ultimately unable to overwhelm the concept of the Batman, West's personhood has been forever attached to the template of the bat, where, according to Alan Moore,

> the image of Batman most permanently fixed in the mind of the general populace is that of Adam West delivering outrageously straight-faced camp dialogue while walking up a wall thanks to stupendous special effects and a camera turned on its side.
>
> *(Brooker 1999, 189)*

West's Batman is a product of 1960s America. Moreover, it is a performance of, and parody for, the culture of 1960s America that is "explicitly campy and humorous, with a sensibility in design, plotting, and cinematography that was pure Pop art" (Mamatas 2008, 47). Whereas Wilson and Lowery's performances of the Batman may look camp to the contemporary viewer, and perhaps were unwittingly so, their performances of the body were broadly in keeping with the action-cinema of the period, at least trying at a relatively serious tone. By contrast, West's performance of Batman, particularly in his fight (and dance-fighting) sequences, was not in keeping with the action-cinema of the period. In fact, it was markedly different. With each "Zap!!!", "Bam!!!", and "Biff!!!", West's performance of the body was a parody of seriousness and a celebration of the absurd.

Medhurst (2013) West's embodiment camped the Batman back to life, deploying a "playful, knowing, self-reflexive theatricality… of camp in an unusually public and heavily signalled way" (244). The humor derived from West's performance poked fun at the cultural codes and contexts of preceding decades (as well as Wilson and Lowery) to form a relational dialogue that reconstructed the bat not as a site of the Dark Knight but as a site of the bright knight (Yockey 2015). West did not need to be hypermasculine in physique. In fact, unlike

Wilson, who problematically battled a Japanese sabotage ring as an agent of the US state, "with his podging waistline and painfully slow reactions, [West] would not have been the most obvious choice against the Viet Cong" (Brooker 2013, 229). West's Batman poked fun at the hypermasculine notions of the hero, with his body providing a safe and non-threatening space for his camp to exist.

That said, there is an inherent irony to West's playful embodiment of the bat, as "West did not intend his performance of Batman to be a parody or a satire" (Brooker 2013, 232) and instead "clearly took Batman extremely seriously, while everyone else saw him as ludicrous" (Brooker 2013, 202). This ludicrous camp component remains a rich seam of the Batman's identity. Relationally, the camp dialogue of West's embodiment endures and reaches out in all directions to destabilize readings of a serious or heteronormative Batman. If "*Batman* the series revealed the man in the cape as a pompous fool, an embodiment of superseded ethics, and a closet queen" (Medhurst 2013, 251), then it is possible to read his subsequent (re) constructions as a continuing and "painstaking reheterosexualization of Batman" (Medhurst 2013, 247).

Michael Keaton

Burton's *Batman* (1989) and *Batman Returns* (1992) sought to portray the darker side of the Batman, revisiting the origin story of the character to explore his "psychological depth and purpose as a superhero" (Burke 2013, 31). Calling up a "multiplicity of gothic incarnations" (Collins 2019, 157), Burton encouraged the body of the bat to intersect with the gloomy architecture of Gotham City. With its once grand buildings now providing a narrative of slow decay and decline, the inner darkness of the Batman's psychological past is written prominently into the cityscape of Gotham City. It is here, where "the brooding, shadowy loner of Michael Keaton" (Bledsoe 2008, 177) reconstructed the "Batman as a menacing figure from 'the darkness'" (Collins 2019, 157). This change in aesthetic represented a sudden intrusion of the gothic into the dialogue of the Batman of the screen, where "Keaton's existential agonizing… is a world away from West's gleeful subversion of truth justice and the American way" (Medhurst 2013, 249).

So powerful was this intention to disrupt the dialogue between West and Keaton that West was forbidden from performing his Batman by DC lawyers (Brooker 2013, 176). Their fear was that in allowing West to coexist with Keaton, the distinction between the irreverent play of West's body and the new brooding cynicism of Keaton's may be blurred. This demonstrated a fragile and futile attempt to construct an absolute Batman, with Keaton's embodiment "purging nearly every trace of Adam West's camp Batman" (Hunting 2019, 302). There was also an attempt to purge any homoerotic overtones or undertones. In their place, the baseline of Keaton's Batman was constructed "as a rich, white, heterosexual, American male" (Brown 2019, 28). Any overt queerness was displaced onto the body of the Joker (Jack Nicholson) in *Batman* (1989) or Catwoman (Michelle Pfeiffer) and the Penguin (Danny DeVito) in *Batman Returns* (1992), then "pathologized as the inverse of Batman's hetero-masculinity" (Hunting 2019, 310).

In a step toward the hypermasculine, Keaton's Batman was longer suited in gray spandex with a loose and flowing satin cape. His body is now encased in a muscle-sculpted suit, as dark and brooding as the Gotham City in which he resides. His face too is more obscured, with paint masking his eye sockets and a much larger cowl leaving the lower third of his face as the only part of his body not sheathed in rubber. Keaton's performance of his body in fight sequences is a further departure from West. Gone are the balletic, overly fluid movements, replaced by suit-restricted actions of high violent intensity. Whereas the form of West's physicality was available for consumption, shielded only by a thin layer of spandex, the body of Keaton's Batman is hidden deep beneath an obstructive outer shell of "physical strength, resiliency, and heterosexual desirability" that resists the reality of his form (Brown 2016, 134).

The simultaneity with West could not be escaped, however. Keaton's embodiment of a dangerous sexual infatuation with Catwoman in *Batman Returns* (1992) mobilizes the threat of heterosexuality explored by West in *Batman: The Movie* (1966) and *Batman* (1966–1968). This hints that the "de-queering" of Batman is fragile, incomplete, and tenuous (Hunting 2019, 309). Indeed, Keaton's dark, "edgy and potentially volatile" disruption to the dialogue of West could not hold beyond Burton's films (Durand 2011b, 42). When Joel Schumacher replaced Burton as the series director, Val Kilmer's Batman in *Batman Forever* (1995) and George Clooney's Batman in *Batman & Robin* (1997) adjusted back toward West, "so freely revelling in camp and allusions to the 1960s that mainstream Batman fans, and many critics, recoiled" (Hunting 2019, 302).

For Will Brooker, Clooney's Batman, in particular, "marks a departure from the depressive naval-gazing of his Keaton and Kilmer incarnations and harks back to Adam West's more self-consciously ditzy TV interpretation" (Brooker 2013, 295). Yet, the relational dialogue with the Batman of Keaton is far from broken, as while "Schumacher couldn't have really made it more camp" the camp spectacle the viewer is treated to is one of "gothic pantomime" (Brooker 2013, 295). Similarly, while increasingly camp in their performance of the body, the bats of Kilmer and Clooney were nonetheless reinforced and contrasted as heteronormative, disambiguating Batman's sexuality via the displacement of queerness to the performance of villainous characters, such as Jim Carrey's Riddler in *Batman Forever* (1995), much like with Keaton in the works of Burton (Terrill 2000).

After the underwhelming performance of *Batman & Robin* (1997) at the box office, and the subsequent departure of Schumacher, it was Christopher Nolan who next attempted to disrupt the relational dialogue with camp.

Christian Bale

In Nolan's Dark Knight Trilogy, Christian Bale (re)constructed a Batman who was "hypermasculine, tortured, vengeful, [and] steeped in militaristic technology and authoritarianism" (Hunting 2019, 302). At the core of Bale's embodiment of the Batman are the three core tenets of fear, chaos, and pain. Reflecting an America traumatized by 9/11, Bale's body of the bat "functions as an allegory for... the ethical dilemmas America faced as a nation" during the War on Terror (McSweeney 2014, 126). To facilitate this narrative of trauma, Bale deployed an interpretative framework of the body to be read in opposition to West, Kilmer, and Clooney, expressing a "conservative, sombre, [and] militaristic Dark Knight" (Hunting, 297). Equally, given that "[t]he inner workings of Christian Bale's version of Bruce Wayne are not dark and mysterious, but methodical" (Bledsoe 2008, 177), the Dark Knight of the Nolan trilogy also disrupts the dialogue constructed by Keaton.

Yet like Keaton, Bale's Batman is a product of the city from which he emerges. Bale is fortified and validated by the "quasi-realistic setting and context [of his] Gotham City" (McSweeney 2014, 117). This credible embodiment of the city disrupts the gothic and cartoonish dialogues of the cities in the Burton and Schumacher films. The Gotham City experienced by Bale's Batman becomes a manifestation of chaos, "the perfectly postmodern city", in which Bale "strives to embody reason and make the rational, and thus the 'right' choice[s]" (Yilmaz and Fundalar 2022, 4), amidst the turmoil around him. Bale's realistically chaotic context further validates the abandoning of his "strict code of ethics that has always distinguished him from the villains he fights" (McSweeney 2014, 122). With Bale, Batman's familiar and comfortable morality is replaced by a predatory hypermasculinity that positions "Batman's transgression of the law as necessary and effective" during times of great need (McSweeney 2014, 120).

The Dark Knight Trilogy not only sets out a new origin story for Batman but establishes a new context for the Batman's performance of violence. Bale's Batman is not immediately skilled in the martial ability of his body. He must first transition through a process of training and transformation to become realistically hypermasculine, drawing upon and mastering externally established and recognized forms of martial arts. Bale's Batman is perhaps the most grotesque of the bodies of the bat. Indeed, the focus of *Batman Begins* (2005) is on Bale's process of becoming the Batman.

Unlike Keaton, Bale's body is exposed and performed in keeping with the context of violence in which he exists. He is formidable with and without the batsuit. As such, when Bale's batsuit enters the narrative, it is not performed as a restriction of the body, like Keaton's, but is performed in a more fluid-like fashion, similar to West's. This fluidity is also, however, a realistic disruption of the ludicrousness of West's fluidity. Bale's batsuit is militaristic in body and movement. His armor places an emphasis on quasi-realistic functionality over style. Furthermore, throughout the trilogy, the evolution of Bale's batsuit moves toward more and more tactical functionality as he encounters the increasing chaos of Gotham City.

Bales' performance of violence encodes the realistic consequences of violence onto his body, and the bodies of those with whom he fights. Bale's combat sequences are presented not as a pastiche of violence, as with West, or as a superficial analogue for violence, as with Keaton's, but as a visceral brutality that reflects the realistic nature of his context. Yet, like Keaton (and all the batmen) before him, Bale's embodiment of the bat could not hold. With Nolan completing his trilogy and Bale stepping away from the role, the Batman transitioned to become a cog in the machine of the DC Extended Universe.

In doing so, Ben Affleck's performance of the Batman in *Batman V Superman: Dawn of Justice* (2016) removed the realistic context of Bale's hypermasculinity, replacing it with a "cyborg-like pinnacle of white masculine technological knowledge and capability" (Cummings 2018, 8). Whereas Bale's performance of the batsuit drew upon the aesthetics of real-world militarism, Affleck presented a fantastical performance of hypermasculine supremacy, donning a technologically unavailable exoskeleton to highlight "the centrality of technology and the cyborg-like qualities of Batman's mech suit to his desirability as a masculine subject" (Cummings 2018, 4). It is from this departure point that the simultaneal possibilities of the Batman may be most marked, as 2023, moved toward Affleck, Keaton, and Pattinson concurrently inhabiting the cinematic incarnation of the bat.

A Brief Word on Robert Pattinson

Pattinson's Batman is one of "dysfunction, dysregulation, and despair" (Olson 2022, 249). Moreover, he is the embodiment of post-traumatic stress disorder. In the relational dialogue with the batmen before and around him, he can be read as a consequence of the flux and tensions of the competing narratives. The body of Pattinson's Batman is overwhelmed. He seems lost amidst an "unrelenting mental darkness" and "seems to have suicidal ideation" (Olson

2022, 248). When not in combat, he "moves and speaks in an especially slow, almost drugged pace… and often looks in a sulky, drugged, and depressive trance" (Olson 2022, 248). By way of contrast, when in combat, his violence is often excessive and uncontrolled.

Pattinson's Batman represents a contemporary take on the hard-boiled detective. He is the Batman incarnate of the Neo Noir genre, representing a dark inverse of the bodies of Wilson and Lowery. He is simultaneously hypermasculine and the embodiment of the "weak male" of the noir domain. The enacting of investigation is core to the establishment, construction, and performance of Pattinson's body, more so than any of his live-action televisual or cinematic counterparts. He is armored in his batsuit like Keaton, Kilmer, and Clooney, but is far from the cyborg of Affleck's mech suit. As with Keaton and Bale before him, he is a product of his context, directly integrated with the neon signs and rain-slicked streets of his Gotham City.

The cityscape of director Matt Reeve's *The Batman* (2022) is a modern moral waste ground. This is a space somewhere in between the quasi-realistic city of the Dark Knight Trilogy and the dark spaces of the horror film. In this space, Pattinson's Batman is a younger incarnation of the "world's greatest detective". He is not a performance of the older and jaded man, rather Pattinson's Batman is a performance of nihilism. In "trying to find some element of hope, in himself, and not just the city", as Pattison explains (Riley 2022), his Batman appears to have an almost reckless disregard for life" (Olson 2022, 249) with the collateral ramifications of his actions suggesting "severe injury or death to the innocent" (Olson 2022, 249). In this regard, Pattinson is perhaps as far from West as it is possible to get. He is a late-stage Batman, a disjointed amalgam who embodies the narrative of human incompleteness.

Conclusion

The performance of the bodies of West, Keaton, Bale, and Pattinson demonstrates the extent to which the screen has continually reconfigured and recodified the Batman to amplify and respond to the socio-cultural context in which he is (re)produced. Central to this process is the notion of simultaneity and dialogic thought that extends through and between the different batmen to resist the establishing of an absolute Batman. What is left is a relational dialogue that situates the Batman as a grotesque body stuck in the act of becoming. The bodies of the bat become texts for reading that are continually built and rebuilt in a shape and disposition related to the cultural context of his past, his present, and the immediate needs of his consumer. West's Batman represents the irreverent playfulness of the swinging 1960s. He is an ironic parody of seriousness and an embodiment of ludicrous camp against which the franchise still (re)negotiates itself. Keaton's Batman is a celebration of the gothic. He is a departure from West, representing a psychological exploration of existential agonizing between the excesses of the 1980s and cynicism of the 1990s, whose aesthetic tendrils delve deep within the fabric of the Batman template. The Batman of Bale is one that battles with the fear, chaos, and pain resulting from the 9/11 attacks of the early 21st century, introducing an ethical ambiguity to the body of the bat that seems to have stuck. Finally, Pattison's Batman is a performance of nihilism. He is a narrative of "dysfunction, dysregulation, and despair" (Olson 2022, 249), lost in the hopeless search for human completeness.

As to the future of the bat, with each new incarnation and reinvention, the Batman yet to come is likely to be more and more diffuse in his relational dialogue, with his inferences and disruptions stretching out in multiple directions at once to form a narrative that "is never finished, never completed; it is continually built, created and builds and creates another body" (Cutchins 2017, 82).

Limitations

The interpretations of Batman are spread wide across the popular entertainment spectrum. Due to limitations of scale, this discussion looked only to a small but notable sample of screen embodiments of Batman that represent marked shifts in the cinematic representation of the Dark Knight. Similarly, in providing a brief overview of the live-action Batman on screen, minor, or alluded appearances in *Joker* (2019), *Gotham* (2014–2019), *Birds of Prey* (2002–2003), and *Batwoman* (2019–2022) have been excluded for brevity.

References

Bledsoe, Alex. 2008. "To the Batpole!" In *Batman Unauthorized*, edited by Dennis O'Neil. BenBella Books.

Brooker, Will. 1999. "Batman: One life, many faces." In *Adaptations: From Text to Screen, Screen to Text*, edited by Deborah Cartmell and Imelda Whelehan. Routledge.

Brooker, Will. 2013. *Batman Unmasked: Analyzing a Cultural Icon.* Bloomsbury.

Brown, Jeffery, A. 2016. "The Superhero Film Parody and Hegemonic Masculinity." *Quarterly Review of Film and Video.* 33 (2): 131–150. https://doi.org/10.1080/10509208.2015.1094361.

Brown, Jeffery, A. 2019. *Batman and the Multiplicity of Identity: The Contemporary Comic Book Superhero as Cultural Nexus.* Routledge.

Burke, Liam. 2013. *Fan Phenomena: Batman.* Intellect.

Burton, Tim. dir. 1989. *Batman.* Warner Bros.

Burton, Tim. dir. 1992. *Batman Returns.* Warner Bros.

Collins, Jim. 2019. "Batman: The Movie Narrative – The Hyperconscious." In *Many More Lives of the Batman*, edited by Roberta Pearson, William Uricchio and Will Brooker. BFI Film Studies.

Cummings, Kelsey. 2018. "Life Savers": Technology and White Masculinities in Twitter-Based Superhero Film Promotion." *Social Media + Society.* 4 (2): 1–10. https://doi.org/10.1177/2056305118782677.

Cutchins, Dennis. 2017. "Bakhtin, Intertextuality and Adaptation." In *The Oxford Handbook of Adaptation Studies*, edited by Thomas Leitch. Oxford University Press.

Dozier, William. prod. 1966–1968. *Batman.* ABC. 20th Century Fox Television.

Durand, Kevin, K. (2011a). "*Batman's* Canon: Hybridity and the Interpretation." In *Riddle Me This, Batman!: Essays on the Universe of the Dark Knight*, edited by Kevin K. Durand and Mary K. Leigh. McFarland & Company.

Durand, Kevin, K. (2011b). "Why Adam West Matters: Camp and Classical Virtue." In *Riddle Me This, Batman!: Essays on the Universe of the Dark Knight*, edited by Kevin K. Durand and Mary K. Leigh. McFarland & Company.

Hunting, Kyra. 2019. "The Man behind the Mask: Camp and Queer Masculinity in LEGO Batman." In *Cultural Studies of Lego: More Than Just Bricks*, edited by Rebecca Hains and Sharon Mazzarella. Palgrave Macmillan.

Mamatas, Nick. 2008. "Holy Signifier, Batman." In *Batman Unauthorized: Vigilantes, Jokers, and Heroes in Gotham City*, edited by Dennis O'Neil and Leah Wilson. BenBella Books Inc.

Martinson, Leslie, M. dir. 1966. *Batman: The Movie.* 20th Century Fox.

McSweeney, Terence. 2014. *The 'War on Terror' And American Film: 9/11 Frames Per Second.* Edinburgh University Press.

Medhurst, Andy. 2013. "Batman, Deviance and Camp." In *The Superhero Reader*, edited by Charles Hatfield, Jeet Heer and Kent Worcester. University of Mississippi Press.

Nolan, Christopher. dir. 2005. *Batman Begins.* Warner Bros.

Nolan, Christopher. dir. 2005. *The Dark Knight.* Warner Bros.

Nolan, Christopher. dir. 2005. *The Dark Knight Rises.* Warner Bros.

Olson, Danel. 2022. *Gothic War on Terror: Killing, Haunting, and PTSD in American Film, Fiction, Comics, and Video Games.* Palgrave MacMillan.

Reeves, Matt. dir. 2022. *The Batman.* Warner Bros.

Riley, Daniel. 2022. "The Metamorphosis of Robert Pattinson." *GQ*, February 8. https://www.gq.com/story/robert-pattinson-march-cover-profile.

Schumacher, Joel. dir. 1995. *Batman Forever.* Warner Bros.

Schumacher, Joel. dir. 1997. *Batman & Robin*. Warner Bros.

Terrill, Robert, E. 2000. "Spectacular Repression: Sanitizing the Batman." *Critical Studies in Media Communication*. 17 (4): 439–509. https://doi.org/10.1080/15295030009388415.

Turner, Bryan. 2008. *The Body & Society: Explorations in Social Theory*. 3rd edition. Sage.

Yilmaz, Göral Erinc, and Serkan Fundalar. 2022. "Constructing and Deconstructing the Modern Hero in *The Dark Knight Trilogy*." *Sage Open*. 12(4): 1–11. https://doi.org/10.1177/21582440221128476.

Yockey, Matt. 2015. "The Bright Knight Returns." *in media res*, February 5. https://mediacommons.org/imr/2015/01/26/bright-knight-returns.

12

THE UMBRELLA ACADEMY

Re-imagining the Subversive Superhero Family, from Panel Scenes to Netflix Screens

Ashleigh Prosser and Lorna Piatti-Farnell

Introduction

Superheroes have long been a staple of popular culture, embodying our collective aspirations, fears, and desires. Yet in the postmodern turn of the post-WWII period, they have been able to transcend their early pulp origins and stay relevant into the contemporary moment as reflections of the complex sociocultural contexts of the times and spaces they now inhabit. Particularly since the tragic terrorist attacks of 9/11, the all-American idea of the superhero has become "a reflective lens for society to process tragedy, inspire hope, and tackle serious socio-political issues" (Harrington and Neimeyer 2021, xviii). In recent years, the idea of the superhero has further undergone a remarkable transformation to embrace diversity, from gender and sexuality to race and ethnicity, as well as the intricacies of the role's ethics and morality in a move toward more humanized superhumans. As Carl Wilson and Lorna Piatti-Farnell (2023, 4) assert, superheroes are "a mirror of the contexts in which they are created and (re)interpreted". Moreover, the stories in which we find our superheroes saving the day continue to evolve and now exist in transmedia storytelling forms that challenge the boundaries of the traditional conventions of the genre. In this chapter, we explore the intricate layers of adaptation and subversion in one such example, *The Umbrella Academy*, the Netflix Original series adaptation of Gerard Way's graphic novels of the same name, and the ways in which both forms capitalize on the inherent malleability of the genre to play with the fine line between superhuman and human, between the ordinary and the extraordinary.

An Eisner-award-winning science-fiction comic-book series published by Dark Horse Books, *The Umbrella Academy* (2007–) is written by Gerard Way, illustrated by Gabriel Bá, and colored by Dave Stewart. The story follows a dysfunctional family of seven inexplicably superpowered children born at noon on October 1, 1983, during 43 spontaneous pregnancies with instantaneous births occurring randomly around the world. Wealthy entrepreneurial scientist (and secret alien) Sir Reginald Hargreeves attempted to adopt as many of these children as possible to form The Umbrella Academy, to train them as superheroes ready to save the world. Having disbanded after the death of one sibling and the disappearance of another when they were teenagers, their father's mysterious death causes them to reunite

 DOI: 10.4324/9781003366911-15

a decade later as adults, as they attempt to save the world (and each other) from various impending apocalypses.

Executive-produced by Way and Bá, Netflix has released three ten-episode and one-fourth final six-episode live-action television series of *The Umbrella Academy* (2019–2024) to widespread popular critical acclaim, with AV Club reviewer Jenna Scherer (2022) calling it "the cultiest of cult favourite superhero shows". The first two series loosely adapt the first two collected graphic novel volumes of the comics, *Apocalypse Suite* and *Dallas*, while the third moved further away from the third volume *Hotel Oblivion* and instead toward the confirmed but as-yet unreleased fourth volume of comics titled *Sparrow Academy*. The fourth and final six-episode series was released in August 2024 wrapping up the adaptation's narrative arc, but despite fans' speculations online there has been to date no further release of a fourth volume of comics by Way. Alongside the Netflix adaptation's initial release, Way, Bá, and Stewart did publish a short prequel series of spin-off comics, *Tales from the Umbrella Academy* (2019–2021). The burgeoning transmedia storytelling of *The Umbrella Academy* further expanded into official merchandise and memorabilia, clothing and accessories, collectibles such as Funko Pops and a tie-in book, *The Making of The Umbrella Academy* (2020), a tabletop card game that lets you play as the siblings fighting villains (and each other) to save the world, and there has even been a Call of Duty: Vanguard and Warzone videogame cross-over "skins" bundle released that will allow you to play as villains Hazel and Cha Cha. The official social media for the Netflix series likewise engages in a form of transmedial play with fandom, as Casta Sligh and Crystal Abidin (2023) have recently explored, through its enactment of a "fannish persona". The series' Instagram account has a "bio" tagline of "Super Dysfunctional Family", and on the day of the release of the final season's finale episode, posted a photo of the cast hugging each other with the words "thank you brellies" above them, and the "fannish-persona" caption; "hold me as i log off brellies. ilysm <3. thank u for letting me be in ur weird family" (August 23, 2024, @umbrellaacad Instagram post).

This chapter will offer an introduction to the weird world of *The Umbrella Academy*. It will explore *The Umbrella Academy*'s textually hybrid transmedial form through an analysis of the re-imagining of the superhero family from its comic-book universe to that of Netflix's digital media world. It will examine how cross-media textual play with the comic-book superheroes and their narrative functions to subversively domesticate the story for adaptation to the home-streaming small screen. For, as Lorna Piatti-Farnell argues, "once superheroes are transported from comic books into another medium, they become autonomous figures, whose representations, actions, and meanings are constructed within the newly established platform that gave them renewed life" (2021, 5). This chapter endeavors to show how the superheroes' transmedial adaptation, and the ways in which Way's narrative moves from comic panel scene to Netflix screen and back again, can be read as particularly "ludogothic" for its playfully dark and subversive embrace of the superhero genre "manifest[s] an implosion of reflexive, reversible yet readerly entanglements of conventions and cultural mores" (Botting 2014, 200).

The Weird World(s) of *The Umbrella Academy*

The big bang for *The Umbrella Academy* universe began in 2007 as an Eisner- and Harvey-award-winning science-fiction comic-book series created and written by Gerard Way (the lead singer of 2000s emo-alternative-punk-rock band My Chemical Romance), illustrated by Gabriel Bá, colored by Dave Stewart, and published by Dark Horse Books. Comic scholar Andy W. Smith (2007, 256) argues that the creation of independent comic publishing houses such as Dark Horse Books, which was founded in 1986, was one of the defining factors in the development of graphic novels as a Gothic art form since the 1980s, and indeed, as this chapter endeavors to convey, *The Umbrella Academy*'s comic-book world is certainly a kind of Gothic art form. The comics are distinctive for their vibrant visuals that combine classic American comic-book superhero combat and costuming with the subversive shift in tone in post-1980s and post-9/11 millennial graphic novels toward the gruesome, gritty, dark, and shadowy worlds of Gothic, Horror, and the New Weird. The relationship between these genre modes represents a convergence of speculative literary traditions and thematic concerns, characterized by their departure from conventional narrative structures toward a blurring of the boundaries between the real and the unreal, challenging the reader with the uncanny and the grotesque in fantastical and surreal ways (see Sederholm 2019). Netflix's decision to adapt the weird world of *The Umbrella Academy* has thus been read as a strategically targeted "reaction to the overabundance of superhero tales that have flooded TV and silver screens in the past decade" to instead offer audiences a "self-reflexive examination of its genre's peculiarities in the post-cinematic age" (Ghilardi 2021, 70–71).

The Umbrella Academy's universe is presented thus as a kind of alternate dystopian version of our own 20th- and 21st-century world and its history. Futurism and nostalgia are comingled as technology, architecture, and costuming from different eras are playfully combined into a Westernized society dominated by American culture, plagued by hyperviolence and bizarre monstrous supervillains such as a zombie-robot Gustav Eiffel, a possessed Abraham Lincoln statue, "Viet Cong" vampires and mummies, and in which sentient chimpanzees are just part of the every day population and workforce (for a discussion of the ape-man trope in the series, see Fuller, 2021). The Academy itself is firmly situated in the Gothic tradition through the imposing Victorian Gothic architecturally styled mansion that the superheroes call home, and which is of course haunted (for further discussion, see Shaughnessy, 2021). Adding to this atmospheric milieu are the elements of the Horror tradition that jump-scare onto screens and panel scenes in hyperviolent blood-soaked fight sequences with monstrous killers and gore galore. In the New Weird tradition, *The Umbrella Academy* immerses readers and viewers in a world where the bizarre and the inexplicable intersect with the mundane and every day, where the characters' idiosyncratic superpowers and superhero status, and the otherworldly occurrences they encounter, challenge the conventional and defy rational comprehension. The interplay between such elements of the Gothic, Horror, and the New Weird thus serve as the foundations for *The Umbrella Academy*'s weird world(s) and, as this chapter argues, can help to shape its analysis when read through the lens of the ludogothic. It is, in the words of Grant Morrison, "an ultraviolet psychedelic sherbet bomb of wit and ideas" that heralds "the superheroes of the 21st century are here at last…" (*Apocalypse Suite* cover copy).

To date, there have been three *The Umbrella Academy* volumes collectively published as graphic novels; *Apocalypse Suite* in 2008, *Dallas* in 2009, *Hotel Oblivion* ten years later in 2019, and Way confirmed in July 2020 that he was actively working on volume four, *Sparrow Academy*. As part of the 2011 annual worldwide "free comic book day" event, Dark Horse published a special 12-page adventure featuring The Umbrella Academy titled *The Murder Magician*. An official prequel series of comics, *Tales from the Umbrella Academy*, began in 2019 with the first short story spin-off, *Hazel and Cha Cha Save Christmas*, and the first collected volume titled *You Look Like Death* (2020–2021), which follows Klaus/The Séance's life in Hollywood during the ten-years preceding the Hargreeves children reuniting at their father's funeral in *Apocalypse Suite*. Way revealed in an interview with *The Hollywood Reporter*

(Debden 2019) that there are plans for eight collected volumes in The Umbrella Academy series, and that he is working closely alongside the showrunner and writers of the Netflix adaption to ensure there will be consistency across the universe. To date, no further volumes of the comics have been released.

The Netflix Original *The Umbrella Academy* adaptation, created by Steve Blackman and Jeremy Slater, consists of four series (released in 2019, 2020, 2022, and 2024) loosely adapting the first volume of the comic *Apocalypse Suite* more closely in series one, and *Dallas* more loosely in series two. The third series introduces The Umbrella Academy to their alternate timeline counterparts, Sparrow Academy, their father's strange Hotel Obsidian as a literal hotel, not an off-world prison for all the supervillains the Academy caught as is its graphic novel counterpart *Hotel Oblivion*. Series three and volume three are where the comics and their adaptation begin to most significantly depart, particularly as a confirmed fourth volume, *Sparrow Academy*, is yet to be released but the Sparrows are the main focus of the third series' storyline. The fourth and final six-episode series was announced through the Netflix series' official Instagram account (@UmbrellaAcad) on October 1, 2023, a date well-known to its 3.2 million "Brellies" (followers) as the birthdate of the superheroes and a favorite for previous PR announcements (see Sligh and Abidin 2023). It was released worldwide on August 8, 2024, with the tagline "The Final Timeline", and a trailer featuring Way's band, My Chemical Romance's famous song "The End" from their 2006 album *The Black Parade*, fulfilling many fans' hopes for a fandom "cross-over". The final series takes the Hargreeves' dysfunctional family dynamics, makes them the core focus of the plot, and resolves them with a somewhat unexpected finality foreshadowed by the lyrics of the song. Set six years after the end of series three, we find the siblings trying to live "normal" lives after the reset of their timeline that caused the loss of their powers and the Academy to have never existed – but of course their powerlessness doesn't last and once again they are reunited on an apocalyptic adventure that this time does actually end in "The End" (of the world, and them too).

To attempt to encapsulate, the complexity of the time-traveling intertwining multiverse plots of *The Umbrella Academy* across its textual and televisual media is challenging, but for this chapter's purpose, the following brief summary endeavors to suffice. The story follows a dysfunctional family of superheroes, seven inexplicably superpowered children instantaneously born at the same time from 43 random spontaneous pregnancies that occurred around the world at noon on October 1, 1989. They were adopted to be trained to form the superhero academy by the wealthy entrepreneur and scientist Sir Reginald Hargreeves (played by Colm Feore), a recluse who we eventually learn is a clandestine extra-terrestrial. Assigned only numbers by Hargreeves in ascending order of usefulness (but secretly in descending order by powerfulness), the children are subjected to secret experimentation while they sleep, traumatic psychological testing and intense physical training by Hargreeves to understand and foster their powers in order to avert the apocalypse. Emotionally neglected, pitted against one another, and constantly manipulated by their aloof and unfeeling Father, the children are raised in the more traditional sense by Hargreeves' assistant who is a kind sentient chimpanzee, Pogo (played by Adam Godley), and a robot Stepfordian housewife, Mom – Grace (played by Jordan Claire Robbins), who is revealed to be an android version of Hargreeves deceased lab partner and lover and is responsible for giving the children their "real" names: Number 1, "The Spaceboy", Luther (played by Tom Hopper); Number 2, "The Kraken", Diego (played by David Castañeda); Number 3, "The Rumor", Allison (played by Emmy Raver-Lampman); Number 4, "The Séance", Klaus (played by Robert Sheehan); Number Five who is known only as Five or "The Boy" (played by Aidan Gallagher); Number 6, "The

Horror", Ben (played by Justin H. Min); and Number 7, "The White Violin", Vanya who transitions into Viktor in series three of the Netflix adaptation (played by Elliot Page).

The domino-masked school-uniformed Umbrella Academy children are famous throughout the world for their superpowered crime-fighting, but by the time they have reached adolescence they have experienced the death of one sibling (Number 6, who has haunted Klaus ever since), the disappearance of another (Number 5, who jumped too far forward in time and has been stuck at the end of the world), and the maiming of their self-appointed team leader (Number 1) resulting in his body being merged with that of a gorilla. Once they reach adulthood, The Umbrella Academy disbands as one by one members leave in search of a "normal" life beyond the oppressive "family home". Diego becomes a vigilante, Allison is a famous Hollywood actress (with a family in the Netflix adaptation), Klaus turns to drugs and alcohol to escape the dead, Vanya becomes a professional violinist (and publishes a tell-all exposé on her childhood in the Netflix adaptation), but loyal Luther remains until Hargreeves eventually sends him to live on the moon on what turns out to be a wild goose chase to monitor for alien attacks. However, their father's mysterious death ten years later causes the estranged siblings to reunite at his funeral which ends with the spontaneous return of Five warning of the end of the world in one week's time, and so they are forced together to reform The Umbrella Academy to prevent the impending apocalypse occurring across multiple alternate timelines which seems to have been caused by one of their own. Number 7, Vanya, the supposedly superpowerless sibling, becomes the villain of the first volume and series, The White Violin, when it is revealed that Hargreeves had inhibited Vanya's powers by secretly drugging and emotionally isolating them since they were actually the most powerful of all the children, thereby inadvertently causing the apocalypse.

Adapting the Academy from Panel Scenes to Netflix Screens

What is unusual about the stories of *The Umbrella Academy* is that the as-yet-unfinished collection of graphic novels and their "live" adaptation by Netflix have become entwined and appear to be informing one another's plotlines, going beyond the realms of fandom into the creation of an official transmedia narrative universe. For example, the second series of *The Umbrella Academy* scatters the siblings through time into tumultuous 1960s America, loosely following the *Dallas* storyline that converges on the team's involvement in the assassination of American President John F. Kennedy on November 22, 1963, but it instead ended on a cliff-hanger that is extremely similar to the ending of *Hotel Oblivion*, the third graphic novel. In the final scene of both, The Umbrella Academy team comes face to face with an uncannily familiar team of superheroes in matching masks and uniforms that feature sparrows instead of umbrellas. Way announced that the still-unreleased fourth graphic novel volume of the series would indeed be titled *Sparrow Academy*, but the third Netflix series then follows this new alternate Academy, exploring their relationship with The Umbrella Academy and how their timelines and universes intersect, suggestively echoing the interrelationship between the adaption and its source text that readers are yet to read. Showrunner Steve Blackman explained how this synergy between the two universes came to be in an interview with EW author Christian Holub (2020):

> It was interesting because I had a similar idea I wanted to do early on in the season, and then Gerard said, 'well, look, I'm going this direction with the graphic novel.' It was perfect, everybody thought, 'great, we want the same thing, so Gerard sort of walked me through what he wanted to do with the characters they call the Sparrow Academy.
>
> *(2020, n.p.)*

Blackman then goes on to explain the series has "some elements of the graphic novel", but crucially elaborates that the show will "go in a bit of a different direction like we do every year, but what's nice is Gerard's already working on the next volume, and he's kind enough to share with me where he's going" (Holub, n.p.). So as Blackman indicates, while the Netflix series all loosely follow the plotlines set out in Way's graphic novels, there are some significant, and less significant, changes that have been made to the story, to the characters and their relationships, and to the world in which they live for their adaptation to the small screen. But likewise, the fact that Way is still creating the comics alongside their adaptation means that he too has opportunity to engage in cross-media textual play, to inform and be informed by his characters and their stories in a new transmedial universe.

This transmedial storytelling presented some interesting parallels throughout the first three series but diverges significantly by the fourth series of the adaptation whereby the Academy's story is brought to a significant resolution and the characters' rather final ends. The final series plotline is a culmination of the character studies that the Netflix adaptation has focused on throughout the previous three series, focusing almost exclusively on the dysfunctional dynamic of the superhero siblings' relationships as the uncanny domesticity of their reset timeline drives the narrative. For example, episode one features Lila and Deigo living the classic all-American life raising three small children and arranging their daughter's birthday party, there are numerous scenes with Klaus and Alison arguing about how best to parent her teen daughter, and there is even a hilarious disastrous family road trip for the siblings set to the soundtrack of the children's classic song "Baby Shark" in episode two. The whole series takes place during the traditional family holiday period of Christmas with its finale seemingly set on Christmas Eve, ending with the climactic fight sequence in which Lila saves her family and Alison's daughter Claire, and all the siblings collectively sacrifice themselves to the apocalyptic world-eating monster that Ben has become, thereby erasing themselves and their superpowered world in order to restore one "normal" timeline in which their children can safely live. The question remains for the fandom of both universes if Way will reflect such a final resolution in the comics, or will this divergence become just another alternate timeline for the Hargreeves' family adventures? A recent interview with *Tudum* hinted at the latter, with Way explaining plans for "some pretty radical things in terms of where to take it after this next volume [*Sparrow Academy*] [...] it's not just the comic version of what you're seeing right now" (Bitran 2024).

While the universe's adaptation for Netflix is certainly done in the spirit of the comics, with similar visual aesthetics, set dressing, and costuming employed, there are numerous small changes that have been made that seem to effectively tone down the inherent weirdness of the original textual world. For example, there are no regular-joe anthropomorphized chimpanzee citizens to be found or increasingly bizarre supervillains terrorizing the team in the Netflix adaptation. Instead, there is a shift in focus toward exploring the characters and their relationships more deeply as they attempt to navigate their lives as individuals, and as part of their dysfunctional superpowered family along with all the apocalypse-averting responsibilities that this entails. This of course has meant larger changes to the plot, to individual characters (their creation, deletion, or just redevelopment), and to their relationships with one another, in order to drive the adaptation's narrative forward in a manner suitable for its new medium and audience. For example, the character of Ben, "The Horror" (played by Justin H. Min), dies as a pre-teen when a mission known as the "Jennifer incident" goes wrong and is rarely featured in the comics and predominately appears only through flashbacks. While the adaptation extends Ben's presence to be an ever-present ghost who is haunting (and occasionally possessing) his psychic brother Klaus (unbeknownst to the other siblings), Ben becomes key to Klaus' narrative and character development. Ben eventually assists Vanya to avert the apocalypse, where he can then pass over in the final episode of series two. It is then revealed in series three that the Sparrow Academy's alternative timeline has their own Ben, whom is their Number 1. This Ben, as the only survivor of the Sparrow Academy, reluctantly becomes one of the core Umbrella Academy family members in the final fourth season, and the true story behind his original's death as a pre-teen in the "Jennifer incident" is one of the series main plotlines.

Further notable examples of such changes in the adaptation are its embrace of diversity, from gender and sexuality to race and ethnicity. The comics originally feature an all-white team, while the adaption changes Allison to a Black woman, Diego to a Latinx man, and Ben to a Korean man. In series two, racial prejudice and its ongoing traumatic impact are explicitly addressed through Allison's story arc in which she is transported to 1961 Dallas and finds herself facing the abhorrent violence and racism of segregation, choosing a life of activism by joining a Civil Rights group, protesting and organizing sit-ins, and falling in love and marrying a fellow activist but again loses those she loves most. In series three episode four, the two living non-white siblings, Diego and Allison, share a deep conversation and connection over their frustrations that their siblings cannot fully understand the unique trauma Allison lived through as a Black woman stuck in 1960s Dallas, and so Diego takes her to a white supremist bar flying a confederate flag to release their rage fighting racists since, he says, "they hate people like us". It is worth noting that the third series also beautifully integrated Number 7 actor Elliot Page's transition into the storyline, with the character of Vanya becoming Viktor by coming out to his superhero siblings as a transgender man in the second episode in a series of sweet scenes that were praised for their positive portrayal (Scherer 2022). Netflix also corrected Page's credits on all previous episodes.

While reviews and opinion pieces on *The Umbrella Academy* are numerous, academic scholarship analysing either the original graphic novels or their recent Netflix adaptation is relatively sparse. A singular example of an in-depth scholarly study can be found in Lisann Anders' (2021) edited collection, *The Force of The Umbrella Academy: Essays on Voices and Violence in the Comics and Netflix Series*, that brings together discussion of the graphic novels and the first Netflix series to have been released by its publication, in essays that explore the relationship between the forces of identity, the forces of violence, and the forces of otherness present in Way's multifaceted world. A handful of journal articles and chapters in other edited collections likewise exist, such as Pradipta Michella Wibrinda's (2021) article, "Rethinking the 'truth' of identity: Dissecting queerness and emo subculture in Netflix's *The Umbrella Academy*", which examines the show's representation of emo subculture as dissent through rejection of absolute identification as demonstrated by the LGBTQ+ superhero characters of Klaus and Vanya. Carmel Cedro and Blair Speakman's exploration of the changes that have been made from the graphic novel to its adaptation in the first series in their chapter "An 'Extra-Ordinary' Adaptation: Exploring Time and Trauma in *The Umbrella Academy*", is illuminating for this chapter's analysis. Cedro and Speakman conclude that the "process of transcoding through adaptation affords the series closer scrutiny into notions of trauma and identity, with the central focus on traumatized individuals who just happen to have 'extra-ordinary' powers" (2021, 194–195).

Building on the foundations laid by previous scholars, this chapter endeavors to further scholarship on *The Umbrella Academy* by bringing it, the graphic novels, and the Netflix series adapting them into discussion. At this nexus, one can find the deliberately domestic refocusing of the subversive comic-book superheroes and their weird world for adaptation to the serialized structure of the streaming small screen, in which the uncanny is made strangely familiar; as the site of trauma, the return of the repressed if you will, is firmly situated in the familial, in the unhomely home, in the truest Freudian sense of the term. To quote Cedro and Speakman (2023, 183), these superheroes are "dealing with custody and divorce problems, sibling rivalry and conflict, addition issues, anxiety and depression, as well as identifiable elements of Post-Traumatic Stress Disorder". The Netflix series does not merely adapt Way's source material but reinterprets it, expanding on its nuances to explore the modern superhero's identity and role in a world of shifting moralities, through the characters' existential struggles with who they are and how they have been shaped by complicated family dynamics and the haunting specter of childhood trauma. As Anders (2021, 3) argues, the Netflix series focal shift to the "brokenness of the individual superheroes and the family as a whole" is in response to the "social and political issues we are facing at the moment" of its adaptation, situating itself as "an active part of the ongoing discussions on race, gender, and sexuality" and bringing audience "awareness to current issues such as the inclusion of female voices".

As Robin Rosenberg and Peter Coogan (2013, 4) have argued in their edited collection, aptly titled *What is a Superhero?*, superheroes exist to "fight evil and protect the innocent; this fight is universal, prosocial and selfless". However, the superheroes of *The Umbrella Academy* are instead predominately driven by their own personal motivations; they often must be convinced to fight evil or protect the innocent, and they are increasingly defined by their character flaws which are frequently negative, antisocial, selfish, and self-destructive behaviors. *The Umbrella Academy* can thus be read as a subversion of the superhero's traditional form, instead presenting an inherently flawed and intimate world where familial dysfunctionality collides with heroic duty, where the relationship between power and responsibility is problematized, and where the struggle with trauma and abuse are integral factors that shape the superheroes' experiences and identities. Here we see the superheroes' function, as argued by Wilson and Piatti-Farnell (2023, 5), to be embodied "sites of meaning" which can "be used to engage with issues concerning refugees, fascism, ecology, families, masculinity and many other aspects that form society and the structures contained within, and by, them".

In the introduction to *The Superhero Multiverse*, Lorna Piatti-Farnell (2021, 4) draws attention to the superhero's "simultaneously iconic and malleable status", one which positions them to be "the ideal mediums for re-adaption and revision and exposes them as vocal vehicles for cultural dialogue across global platforms". The very same can also be said for the Gothic and its own iconic and malleable monsters that continue to be re-animated for the 21st century and are likewise known for transgressing the boundaries of their original literary forms across transmedia in contemporary popular culture. Hence, as comic scholar Julia Round (2014) has asserted, comic books are often dominated by a "superhero archetype" that is "more Gothic than it might seem: a figure of fragmented identity, held together by processes of exclusion" (2018, 162). Both0 11111111. the Gothic and comics can be said to function within "areas of generic hybridity" for they occupy a "shared textual *and* contextual space" (Smith 2007, 251), one which Round refers to as in a specific "state of tension (between high/low culture, repulsion/attraction, and exaggerated/hidden)" (Round 2018, 162). This shared nexus of tension is where we believe the ludogothic comes into play, pardon the pun, between the Gothic, superheroes, comics, and their adaptation, as a lens through which one can view *The Umbrella Academy's* uncanny transmedial universe.

The difficulties of defining the Gothic have been well-established, and so to avoid what Catherine Spooner has called the "gothic shopping list" (2017, 53) we offer a summation of sorts; that the Gothic is concerned with the terror and horror of excess, its tensions and contradictions, and its transgressions and transformations. Chris Baldick's (1992, xix) understanding of the Gothic is pertinent here for he describes it as "a fearful sense of inheritance in time with a claustrophobic sense of enclosure in space". Baldick's turn of phrase is also an apt descriptor for the repetition of apocalyptic scenarios that play out in *The Umbrella Academy*, but it is also perhaps an excellent summation of the dysfunctional familial environment of the Academy itself, and all the pressures that being a part of it places on the characters and their relationships. Moreover, this is certainly a lens through which one can read the distinctly domestic approach to the Gothic that the Netflix adaption has taken in depicting its subversive superheroes as players in an, albeit apocalyptic, family drama.

Here one finds the significance of Fred Botting's (2014, 178–179) conceptualization of the ludogothic as a mode specific to postmodernism's "challenge to the structures, hierarchies, values, and exclusions of modernity", as one that focuses on the juxtaposition of "narrative styles and relationships, [...] texts from different periods, mimicking forms, subverting assignations of aesthetic value between high and low culture". The ludogothic is thus found in the "playful inventiveness and subversion" of such juxtapositions to reveal the ways in which "its self-aware reflection on the constitutive dimension of language in forming texts and realities, discloses how ideas and fantasies about self and the world are inscribed in and between the different narratives composing cultural order" (Botting 2014, 178–179). It is worth acknowledging the significance of the ludic itself for our understanding of the ludogothic, since it is a term that is most often associated in contemporary scholarship with Gothic readings of gameplay, gaming, and videogames in particular. Laurie N. Taylor (2009, 48) in their analysis of the relationship between horror fiction and videogames, first used the term "ludic-Gothic" to describe the transformation of literary tropes into gameplay contexts that are dependent on the thematic boundary crossing inherent to the Gothic. So why then would we be using this term to discuss a collection of subversive superhero comics and their Netflix adaption? Well, to return to the term itself, the ludic is by definition concerned with spontaneous play and playfulness (from the Latin *ludere* "to play"), and this concept of playfulness is a key feature of *The Umbrella Academy's* strange and violent universe.

In both the comics and the series there is an embrace of this idea of spontaneous weirdness, in which moments of playfulness are juxtaposed with often some of the most vividly violent visuals. Such jarring surrealism disrupts conventional narrative expectations and serves as a reminder for readers and viewers alike of this weird world's willingness to subvert genre conventions. The fabric of *The Umbrella Academy's* world is woven with such moments; from tongue-in-cheek references to comic-book tropes and superhero clichés, to a character's self-aware reflection, comedic quip, withering look, or outright fourth-wall break, and even musical theater-style breakout dance routines. They function as postmodern signifiers of ludic subversion, and we are reminded of the longstanding role the ludic has played as a performer in the theater of the Gothic. For, to quote Avril Horner and Sue Zlosnik, "if Gothic demonstrates the horror attaching to such a shifting and unstable world, it also, in its comic and ludic aspects, celebrates the possibilities thereby released" (2012, 327).

Within *The Umbrella Academy's* unique form of ludogothic play, there can also be found a specific pop-cultural musicality to the Netflix series in particular, as its contemporary stylized score of "retro hits" spawns spur-of-the-moment surreal dance sequences alongside graphic gory fight scenes that are similarly coded as just another choreographed eight-count.

These moments are not merely visually interesting or aesthetically pleasing quirks used to set the series stylistically apart, but rather they are modes for integral components of narrative and character development to be interwoven into the show's ludogothic storytelling fabric. The first episode of the first series provides an exemplary use of an ensemble dance number. Following their father's funeral, each of the family members are alone in their old teenage bedrooms in the Academy and appear to physically feel the release of the pressure their father held over their lives by dancing to Tiffany's 1980s hit "I Think We're Alone Now". As the camera pans from one character to another, their dancing loses inhibition and increases in intensity, climaxing as the camera zooms out to a wide-angle shot of the Academy as if it were a cross-section of a child's dollhouse. Through dance, this scene not only introduces the audience to each of the characters' individual personality quirks but also serves to underscore the traumatic effects of their dysfunctional childhood and their father's abuse, and the lingering isolation and longing for connection they share with one another. Looking in on the siblings dancing separately in space but together in time through the perspective of a child's dollhouse is a striking visual metaphor for the fractured nature of the family precisely because of their shared childhood trauma. It serves as a powerful introduction to the dysfunctional dynamics of the Academy by setting the tone for the series' exploration of their complex familial relationships.

Indeed, some of the characters are even musicians themselves. Lila (played by Ritu Arya), a new character created for the Netflix adaption, is Diego's love interest introduced in series two and later revealed to be one of the other superpowered children born on that fateful day. In series three episode seven, she becomes the drummer of a punk rock band in Berlin, 1989, and performs a cathartic rage-filled version of "Let's Be Badder" by Lucern Raze and Cherry Pickles, which Arya actually did since she is the drummer for London indie-pop band KIN. Not only is Vanya a professional violinist, and her villainous alter-ego's name is The White Violin, but her superpower is literally based in music: it is the ability to manipulate sound waves into elemental force, governed by her emotions and the use of an "instrument" – in the comics this is her violin, while in the series it is simply anything that produces sound. Moreover, as revealed in the short story "Anywhere But Here" (collected in the *Dallas* volume), Vanya and Diego were even in a punk-rock band together as teenagers called the Prime-8s, and the events of their last gig are what led to Vanya leaving the Academy. Since Reginald Hargreeves vehemently disapproved and sought to send Vanya to pursue classical violin training in Paris instead, the band decides to play one last gig, with Diego and Vanya making a pact that afterward they will leave the Academy together to dedicate themselves to the Prime-8s and touring their first album "I Don't Wanna Kill the President" (a title hinting at the storyline of *Dallas*). However, Diego breaks his promise and stands Vanya up on the night of the gig by instead opting to fight a mime-artist gang with the Academy. Vanya sees the betrayal live on TV, realizing she truly was an outsider in her family and leaves the Academy behind for good, directing her cabdriver to "anywhere but here" (Way et al., 2009).

Herein one finds that another layer of transmedial storytelling, as Way reveals in a 2019 *Rolling Stone* interview, *The Umbrella Academy's* dysfunctional family of famous superheroes were actually inspired by his 2000s emo-alternative-pop-rock band My Chemical Romance, his own "famous adopted family", and that the stories were often written while he was on, or between, their tours:

> Being in a band is like being in a dysfunctional family and all these personalities are really distinct and really big, [...] so there's little bits of me in all the characters, there's

bits of some of the guys in some of those characters and the different roles that we would play in the band and how those roles would change sometimes. We were in a big pressure cooker of fame and notoriety and the characters experience that in the comic and the show.

(Way quoted in Holmes 2019, n.p.)

Subtle references that fans of Way's band will recognize are hidden throughout the comics and the series. For example, in the first episode of the first series, the camera pans briefly to the back cover of Vanya Hargreeves's autobiography, where there is a review praising the memoir: "An incredible read… a revealing portal into the amazing life of Vanya Hargreeves and the way she has lived… I couldn't put it down! – Gerard Way". Sloane Hargreeves, one of the Sparrow Academy superheroes introduced in series three, who later becomes Luther's wife and whose life hangs in the balance in the series finale, was introduced in the first episode reading a book titled *The Jetset Life*, a reference to the My Chemical Romance song "The Jetset Life is Gonna Kill You" and foreshadows her fate. The trailer for the final series was also the first time a My Chemical Romance song was featured, aptly titled "The End" from the 2006 *Black Parade* album. In an interview with *Tudum,* Way explained

We'd never thought a My Chem song would be in an *Umbrella* thing, but we were all very excited actually, because nobody had ever asked for that song, […] We had actually always felt it would be really good in the trailer.

(Bitran 2024)

This layering of transmedial storytelling through the emotional impact Way's own experiences of "the growing dysfunction and discord of his real-life" in the "famous forced family" of his band had on the creation of *The Umbrella Academy* reveals that this world of "murderous children, talking chimps and world-ending violin solos", is at its core "about the ways family can irrevocably damage each other, and how we move past that pain" (Holmes 2019).

Concluding Remarks

The Umbrella Academy serves as a prime example of how the superhero genre continues to evolve, pushing boundaries and subverting conventions while addressing its stock relevant themes such as the question of the superhero identity, the weight and responsibility of their power, and the impact of trauma and family dynamics. By analysing the threads of transmedial storytelling across the graphic novels and their Netflix adaptation, we have explored the series' potential significance as an exemplar of subversion within the broader context of contemporary superhero narratives, fostering a deeper understanding of the genre's adaptability and continued cultural relevancy. *The Umbrella Academy* presents a multiverse of stories that thrive on blending the conventional and the absurd, the heroic and the dysfunctional, and the ordinary with the extraordinary. *The Umbrella Academy* is certainly a celebration of such ludogothic possibilities, and one can look forward to knowing that despite the finality of the ending of its Netflix adaption, its universe remains ever-expanding, with more comics just over the horizon for this dysfunctional family just waiting to explore.

References

Anders, Lisann, ed. 2021. *The Force of The Umbrella Academy: Essays on Voices and Violence in the Comics and Netflix Series*. United States: McFarland.

Baldick, Chris. 1992. "Introduction". In *The Oxford Book of Gothic Tales*, edited by Chris Baldick. Oxford: Oxford University Press, xi–xxiii.

Bitran, Tara. 2024. "Gerard Way Reacts to the Bittersweet The Umbrella Academy Ending "I'm Really Proud of Everybody's Hard Work and How Much They Cared about the World." *Tudum by Netflix*, August 12. https://www.netflix.com/tudum/articles/gerard-way-umbrella-academy-season-4-interview

Botting, Fred. 2014. *Gothic*. 2nd Edition. New York: Routledge.

Cedro, Carmen, and Speakman, Blair. 2021. "An "Extra-Ordinary" Adaptation: Exploring Time and Trauma in The Umbrella Academy". In *The Superhero Multiverse: Readapting Comic Book Icons in Twenty-First Century Film and Popular Media*, edited by Lorna Piatti-Farnell. Lanham, MD: Lexington, 181–197.

Debden, Emma. 2019. "Umbrella Academy Creator Gerard Way Unwinds the Long, Weird Path Toward Netflix: Umbrella Academy creator Gerard Way and showrunner Steve Blackman Discuss Adapting the Dark Horse Comics Graphic Novel into a Netflix series". *The Hollywood Reporter*, February 15. https://www.hollywoodreporter.com/tv/tv-news/umbrella-academy-gerard-ways-superhero-series-explained-1184748/

Fuller, Jennifer. 2021. "Those Damned, Dirty Apes: Netflix's The Umbrella Academy and the Evolution of the Ape-Man." *Victorians Institute Journal* 48, no. 1: 87–107. https://doi.org/10.5325/victinstj.48.2021.0087

Ghilardi, Morgane A., 2021. "Artifice and the Superheroes of the 21st Century: Post-Cinematic Reflections on Constructedness". In *The Force of The Umbrella Academy: Essays on Voices and Violence in the Comics and Netflix Series*, edited by Lisann Anders, Lisann. United States: McFarland, 70–87.

Harrington, Jill A., and Neimeyer, Robert A., eds. 2021. *Superhero Grief: The Transformative Power of Loss*, edited by Robert A. Neimeyer. New York: Routledge.

Holmes, Charles. 2019. "How the dysfunction of My Chemical Romance inspired 'The Umbrella Academy'". *Rolling Stone*, February 22. https://www.rollingstone.com/tv-movies/tv-movie-features/gerard-way-umbrella-academy-my-chemical-romance-interview-797368/

Holub, Christian. 2020. "How The Umbrella Academy Season 2 Finale Syncs Up with the Comic". *EW: Entertainment Weekly*, August 3. https://ew.com/tv/umbrella-academy-season-2-finale-comic/

Horner, Avril, and Zlosnik, Sue. 2012. "Comic Gothic". In *A New Companion to the Gothic*, edited by David Punter. Malden, MA: Wiley-Blackwell, 321–334.

Piatti-Farnell, Lorna, ed. 2021. *The Superhero Multiverse: Readapting Comic Book Icons in Twenty-First Century Film and Popular Media*. Lanham, MD: Lexington.

Rosenberg, Robin S., and Coogan, Peter. 2013. *What is a Superhero?* Oxford: Oxford University Press.

Round, Julia. 2014. *Gothic in Comics and Graphic Novels*. Jefferson, NC: McFarland.

Round, Julia. 2018. *"Grant Morrison, Dave McKean, and Gaspar Saladino's Arkham Asylum (1989)"*. *The Gothic: A Reader*, edited by Simon Bacon. Oxford: Peter Lang, 161–168.

Scherer, Jenna. 2022. "Elliot Page Takes Centerstage in The Umbrella Academy Season 3: The Cultiest of Cult Favorite Superhero Shows Is Back with Absurdist Humor and Real Pathos". *AV Club*, June 15. https://www.avclub.com/the-umbrella-academy-season-3-tv-review-elliot-page-1849059656

Sederholm, Carl. 2019. "The New Weird". In *Twenty First Century Gothic: An Edinburgh Companion*, edited by Maisha Wester and Xavier Aldana Reyes. Edinburgh: Edinburgh University Press, 161–173.

Shaughnessy, Kathleen. 2021. "Gothic Academy: Horror and Crookedness in a Haunted Household". In *The Force of The Umbrella Academy: Essays on Voices and Violence in the Comics and Netflix Series*, edited by Lisann Anders, Lisann. United States: McFarland, 10–31.

Sligh, Casta, and Abidin, Crystal. 2023. "When Brands Become Stans: Netflix, Originals, and Enacting a Fannish Persona on Instagram". *Television & New Media* 24, no. 6: 616–638. https://doi.org/10.1177/15274764221134778

Smith, Andy W. 2007. "Gothic and the Graphic Novel". In *The Routledge Companion to Gothic*, edited by Catherine Spooner and Emma McEvoy. New York: Routledge, 265–273.

Spooner, Catherine. 2017. *Post-Millennial Gothic: Comedy, Romance and the Rise of Happy Gothic*. London: Bloomsbury.

The Umbrella Academy. 2019-. *Created by Steve Blackman and Jeremy Slater*. United States: Netflix.

Way, Gerard, et al., 2008. *The Umbrella Academy: Apocalypse Suite*. Milwaukie, OR: Dark Horse Comics.

Way, Gerard, et al., 2009. *The Umbrella Academy: Dallas*. Milwaukie, OR: Dark Horse Comics.

Way, Gerard, et al., 2019. *The Umbrella Academy: Hotel Oblivion*. Milwaukie, OR: Dark Horse Comics.

Way, Gerard., et al., 2020. *The Making of the Umbrella Academy*. Milwaukie, OR: Dark Horse Comics.

Way, Gerard, et al., 2021. *Tales from the Umbrella Academy: You Look Like Death* Volume 1. Milwaukie, OR: Dark Horse Comics.

Wibrinda, Pradipta Michella. 2021. "Rethinking the 'Truth' of Identity: Dissecting Queerness and Emo Subculture in Netflix's The Umbrella Academy". *Rubikon: Journal of Transnational American Studies* 8, no. 2: 139–152. https://doi.org/10.22146/rubikon.v8i2.6969

Wilson, Carl, and Piatti-Farnell, Lorna. 2023. "Re-Examining Superhero Politics in Popular Culture". *The Australasian Journal of Popular Culture* 12, no. 1: 3–7. https://doi.org/10 1386/ajpc_00064_2.

13

PRINCESSES VS POWER

The Animated Depictions of Original and Rebooted *She-Ra*

Valerie Estelle Frankel

She-Ra, the beloved 1980s icon, was a gorgeous blonde princess. Created by Mattel as Barbie-style action figures, the identically proportioned Princesses of Power stood out for their brushable hair and gauzy miniskirts, while the cartoon was designed to sell those toys. Mike Madrid, in his exploration of superheroine depiction, considers the ambiguous nature of such figures:

> Any power these women may have is often overshadowed by their overly sexualized images. But at the same time, those very images that objectify these heroines can be seen as a source of power. Recently I took a female friend to see the movie adaptation of the graphic novel *Watchmen*. When she caught sight of the movie's heroine, Silk Spectre, descending a staircase in slow motion, sheathed in a skintight latex costume and thigh-high boots with garters, my friend leaned over and said, 'I want to be her.' My friend is an educated, successful career woman, so it struck me that she would find this very sexualized female image inspiring and powerful. In this way, as outlandish as comic books may seem, they actually are a reflection of the world that we all live in.
>
> *(2009, vi)*

In their realm of Etheria, the heroines had exciting, glamorous lives full of adventure. Likewise, fantasy author Leigh Bardugo writes, "I gave my heart to Jem, She-Ra, Sailor Moon-type all-girl crews. Sure, they showed cleavage, wore heels, had ridiculously expressive hair, but at least they got to wear *skirts* instead of just panties in primary colors" (2016, 155). As she explains, they were relatable in their pretty frivolity: "They went on adventures, made friends, stopped evil, wore glitter at every opportunity, and had chaste romances with cute boys named Rio and harmless rogues like the Sea Hawk. They were female fantasies created for girls" (2016, 155).

DOI: 10.4324/9781003366911-16

All these characters, nonetheless, appeared unclear on how to fight for rights in an era that had ostensibly given them equality, even while casting them as frilly and frivolous role models with perfume power or butterfly wings. Sherrie A. Inness explains in her book *Tough Girls:*

> The programs that featured these early heroines had a dual purpose: they offered women viewers potentially powerful role models, but the shows simultaneously helped to reaffirm that women, while more capable than generally given credit for, were still less competent than men.
>
> *(1999, 32)*

In 2018, ND Stevenson created a new era of storytelling with *She-Ra and the Princesses of Power* (2018–2020). She-Ra was still a superheroine fighting the evil Horde in a dystopian kingdom. This time, however, many updates revealed what was required of a 21st-century children's icon. New She-Ra is depicted much less sexually, from her art style to her wardrobe. Her team is more varied, from dark-skinned Bow's two dads to Asian Glimmer's short stockiness. They also transcend the prior sidekick roles, as indicated by the new show title. Seasons have much stronger arcs and character development, as She-Ra battles with guilt over betraying her nemesis, Catra. The villains in turn have much more complexity as they explore the heartache of being shunned by the gorgeous princesses. With all these changes, *She-Ra and the Princesses of Power* establishes that the popular and marginalized girls can band together and save the world without needing a muscle-bound man.

He-Man

The original 1985 cartoon *She-Ra: Princess of Power* (1985–1987) was a spinoff of *He-Man and the Masters of the Universe* (1983–1985), just as *Xena: Warrior Princess* (1995–2001) spun off of *Hercules: The Legendary Journeys* (1995–1999) and *The Bionic Woman* (1976–1978) worked with *The Six Million Dollar Man* (1973–1978). *Conan the Barbarian* (1982) had a capable thief as his love interest and partner, Valeria, and then launched the *Red Sonja* film (1985). Certainly, some superheroines have more unique origins, but Supergirl, Batgirl, and even Wonder Woman were created in the shadow of Superman and Batman.

However, the 1980s also signaled pushback, now labeled as the post-feminist era. As Princess Leia donned her gold bikini onscreen in *Return of the Jedi* (1983), heroines found themselves in briefer and briefer costumes. In comics, these were particularly ridiculous with a thong or loincloth and armored bustier or breast cups. Metallic bracers, collars, and jewelry only emphasized the harem girl associations. Red Sonja succumbed likewise:

> Red Sonja got her own comic in 1975, but instead of the sexy, confident Amazon in the curve-hugging chainmail shirt who strode the bloody battlefields two years earlier, the cover featured a busty redhead spilling out of a tiny silver metal bikini, with heavy black eyeliner and big pouty lips. Red Sonja might have been billed as 'She-Devil with a sword,' but now she looked more like a stripper.
>
> *(Madrid 2009, 168–169)*

Such imagery echoed across fantasy. Even as the women were sexualized and exaggeratedly gendered in works by artists such as Frank Frazetta, powerful men also erupted in fiction. Adam, prince of the planet Eternia with its blasters-and-medieval aesthetic, used his magical sword to transform into muscular He-Man and battle Skeletor. He-Man famously wore little more than furry briefs and boots, while his female counterparts Teela and Evil-Lyn wore leotards decorated with metal breast cups. They took their look from "Good Girl Art," which Madrid describes as "cheesecake with a little kink thrown in for good measure" and "lots of half-dressed, leggy females in pinup poses to entertain the troops fighting overseas" (2009, 45). On Eternia, these rare women are cast in love interest roles, only excluding the spiritual advisor, the Sorceress. John Erwin voiced He-Man/Adam and many other characters, while all the women were voiced by Linda Gary, giving them a subtle sameness.

The half-hour show was "seen each weekday on 166 television stations in the United States, and in 37 foreign countries" (The New York Times 1984). *He-Man and the Masters of the Universe* at the time was the highest rated children's television program in America.

> Since its premiere in September 1983, the program has gained an audience of nearly 9 million people in this country. It is most popular with boys between the ages of 4 and 8, but 30 percent of the viewers are girls, according to Lou Scheimer, the show's executive producer

with 70 million action figures sold worldwide (The New York Times 1984). Next, Scheimer approached Mattel about a female spinoff. Assisted by his daughter Erika Scheimer, Filmation and Mattel created *She-Ra: Princess of Power*. In it, Prince Adam's twin sister Adora would battle Mattel's latest villain, Hordak, tyrannical ruler of Etheria and Skeletor's mentor. The show went into production just after the second season of *He-Man and the Masters of the Universe* was completed in April 1984. Writer J. Michael Straczynski, who had begun writing for Filmation six months earlier, developed She-Ra, her supporting cast, and the world of Etheria with He-Man story editor Larry DiTillio (Eatock 2016, 34). DiTillio wanted to name her Hera after the goddess, but was told someone else had trademarked it. "Then came a bolt out of Egyptian mythology. Ra, a word meaning God. She-Ra" (Eatock 2016, 35). As such, she emphasized mythic energy and strength.

She-Ra toys appeared alongside the cartoon show. This became essentially the first action figure franchise marketed to girls, with a storyline like He-Man's but with the dressable, brushable toys made by the creators of Barbie. Delicate elastic straps and fragile plastic wings emphasized that these were made for gentler play than He-Man. As was common in the 1980s, both conformed to exaggerated gender stereotypes. Some women of the era were becoming "masculine" action heroes like Ripley (*Alien*, 1979 and Sarah Connor (*The Terminator*, 1984); nonetheless, many others were reacting to the gender politics flare-up of the 1970s by returning to gentle sweetness. Furthermore, the fact that both toy lines were marketed to children only held designers back slightly. Brown observes:

> From casting, to filming techniques, to the association of violence with sexuality, to dominatrix influenced costuming – action heroines are a primary example of how the media continues to fetishize women for predominantly male viewing pleasure. And while such kid-oriented animated shows as *The Powerpuff Girls, Atomic Betty, My Life as a Teenage Robot,* and *Kim Possible* may seem light years away from the image of Pamela Anderson, Jennifer Garner, or Angelina Jolie dressed as dominatrixes in *Barb Wire,*

Alias and Mr. and *Mrs. Smith* respectively, they're really just at the kid-friendly end of the fetishization spectrum.

(2011, 165)

As Brown concludes, "They still sport leather boots, miniskirts, and belly-baring midriffs—and many of the villainesses they encounter appear in full fetish gear" (2011, 165). The Princesses of Power were ready for action, but also quite suggestive. Their high boots, bare legs, lipstick, and cleavage de-emphasized might, while long, wild hair evoked jungle princesses and femme fatales.

She-Ra Arrives

She-Ra was introduced in March 1985 via the theatrical release of *He-Man and She-Ra: The Secret of the Sword*, written by Larry DiTillio and Bob Forward. While Melendy Britt voiced Adora/She-Ra and Catra, Linda Gary carried over from voicing all the *Masters of the Universe* women to voice most of those on *She-Ra: Princess of Power*. Erika Scheimer took on nearly all the rest.

Adam journeys to Etheria seeking the heir to his sword's twin. At the Laughing Swan Inn, the faceless armored soldiers of the Horde menace a musician and Adam steps in. "A man of courage," notes Bow (George DiCenzo) admiringly as he watches with his weaponry hidden under the table (Friedman et al. 1985, 00:07:52). As Adam fights decently without his superstrength, upholding traditional gender roles, Bow joins in to help, throwing aside his cloak to reveal a barely present shirt. The two muscled men beat the Horde, and Bow inducts Adam into the rebellion.

Princess Glimmer is the leader of the rebellion since her mother Queen Angella was captured. When a village is attacked, He-Man arrives to help. There, they battle Catra and Scorpia. Jeffrey A. Brown argues of the bad girl in film and comic books,

On the one hand, she represents a potentially transgressive figure capable of expanding the popular perception of women's roles and abilities; on the other, she runs the risk of reinscribing strict gender binaries and of being nothing more than sexist window-dressing for the predominantly male audience.

(2004, 47)

Catra and Scorpia are indeed glamorous and hissing, standing out more for the sexualized art than for any real rebellion or transgression. Scorpia's black and red leotard with cleavage marks her as a femme fatale, while tail and glove-like claws are only a subtle animalistic afterthought. Continuing this imagery, Scorpia and He-Man spar in gendered terms as she uses her claws and calls him "Muscle Man." He-Man retorts: "That's not very ladylike … of course, you're not much of a lady anyway" (Friedman et al. 1985, 00:18:25). He hurls her into a humiliating watermelon cart. As he continues the battle, He-Man smashes Force Captain Adora's sword and tells her, "The fight is over, Young Lady," using condescending gendered terms once more (Friedman et al. 1985, 00:19:55). However, both are surprised when the sword responds to her. The Horde blast He-Man, knocking him out, and carry him off to Beast Island. There, Adora (Melendy Britt) in her leotard-and-bare-legs uniform finds He-Man chained to a table, and they speak honestly at last. She tells him she feels bonded to the sword and he retorts that his mission is "To give that force to someone who serves the forces of good. But you… you serve the forces of evil" (Friedman et al. 1985, 00:22:12–19). Adora insists Hordak is the rightful ruler, though she's rarely left his complex, and He-Man challenges her to find out. She is so naïve she doesn't realize she's working for the oppressors, while He-Man (appropriately) "mansplains" until she goes out to test his assertion.

In the outside world, the fighting continues. Glimmer has used too much power and swoons. Each time she's shown, she is diminutized and shown as an ineffectual leader. She's all in pink and lavender with a flower power staff, further leaning into sweetness. Adora, meanwhile, finds the Horde enslaving villagers and realizes she's on the wrong side. She returns and confronts her parents: "You lied to me, both of you! The Horde is evil, cruel, unjust. The people hate us and with good cause" (Friedman et al. 1985, 00:35:37). The villainous matriarch Shadow Weaver immediately notes that the spell on Adora has weakened, and her master Hordak tells her to strengthen it. The heroine has been mind-controlled all her life, another story element that saps her agency. The Horde try draining He-Man's indescribable might to power all their weapons. Meanwhile, they've renewed Adora's brainwashing and she orders He-Man enslaved. Still, she struggles: "It is for the good of the Horde. It must be done...yet... why do I feel so unsure?" (Friedman et al. 1985, 00:48:28). Once more, Adora's language suggests fragility, while the manipulation weakens her in a particularly feminine way, depriving her of agency.

The Sorceress, He-Man's mystical inspiratrice on his own show, speaks to Adora and tells her to "throw off the enchantments that made you slave to the Horde's will" and protect the helpless, then adds, "And let your first duty be to this man about to be enslaved by the Horde" (Friedman et al. 1985, 00:48:44). Adora's duty is to care for He-Man, which is again problematic as her rebellion is framed in terms of devoting herself to the hero. The Sorceress then reveals the big twist: Adora is actually Prince Adam's twin. Accordingly, Adora claims the sword, transforms into She-Ra for the first time, and frees him. Her new look has cleavage and bare limbs, but also glowing gold light and winged motifs, for a mighty look. At the same time, the fantastical setting makes her less of a threat to everyday gender norms.

She-Ra and He-Man escape together on the newly transformed flying unicorn Swift Wind (soon available across toy stores). They save Queen Angella and then steal a little time to visit their parents on Eternia. There, Skeletor invades the castle (and, in one more admirably gendered moment, Queen Marlena clobbers him). After capturing Adora, Skeletor gloats, "And now, Princess, I must decide what to do with you" (Friedman et al. 1985, 01:15:20). In response, she pointedly faints. Skeletor makes a crack about how this is "just like a woman" (Friedman et al. 1985, 01:15:29). Adora in fact is pretending, which ties in with how Inness considers cleverness and trickery to be vital superheroine tools:

> Along with her stamina and strength, the tough woman's actions reveal her intelligence. Typically, she does not act without carefully thinking through the results of her actions. While others might want to spring into battle, the tough woman hero or anti-hero often pauses for reflection before acting.
>
> *(1999, 26)*

Skeletor sends Adora to the dungeons in the arms of the leering Grizzlor, who smirks, "You're sure a pretty princess. Stupid we have to lock you up in the dungeon" (Friedman et al. 1985, 01:15:52). Before the scene can grow more repellant, Adora rises from her feigned faint, quips, "Thanks for the compliments, Fangs," and locks him in the cell instead (Friedman et al. 1985, 01:16:00). Inness notes that a cool attitude is also vital:

> No matter how a woman's pecs might bulge or how strongly her clothing might be coded as tough, she will not be considered tough unless she has the right attitude.

Generally, she must display little or no fear, even in the most dangerous circumstances; if she does show fear, it must not stop her from acting …. Along with showing little fear, the tough woman must appear competent and in control, even under the most threatening circumstances, when everyone else falls apart. Often her cool nature will be evident in her relative lack of affect; we know that she is feeling a tremendous amount of emotion, but she does not always show it because such a display would interfere with her performance.

(1999, 25)

All of this, Adora accomplishes. Next, she recaptures her sword and transforms. She confronts Skeletor, proudly introduces herself, and tells him she freed Adora, thoughtfully protecting her secret identity. His goons attack, and she quips, "My, you boys are forward. Alright, one dance and that's it!" (Friedman et al. 1985, 01:17:19). She spins them into a heap. "Now you fellows are using your heads" (Friedman et al. 1985, 01:17:30). Next, she goes after Skeletor, calling him "bone brain" (Friedman et al. 1985, 01:17:45). She bounces her power off a mirror and knocks a decorative skull onto his head. "That's definitely an improvement to your look" (Friedman et al. 1985, 01:17:52). Quipping, too, is a traditional heroine power; one that defined third-wave heroines such as Buffy and Xena. As Brown observes:

The girl action heroine who has become a mainstay in youth-oriented television and literature in the new Millennium encompasses a wide range of character types and appeals to an equally wide range of audiences… what these young heroines have in common are their exceptional abilities at fighting, intelligence, beauty – and this sense of humor. Even in their more serious moments, these girls managed to have some fun while beating up bad guys or blasting alien invaders.

(2011, 142)

The official series guide for *She-Ra: Princess of Power* also acknowledges this power:

From Adora breaking the fourth wall to show the audience she's not unconscious to She-Ra's villain-bashing one-liners, Larry DiTillio's script shows that our heroine is smart and funny and, importantly, that she can prove herself without He-Man's help – before they together bash the Horde tanks and troopers in the battle for Bright Moon, that is.

(Eatock 2016, 362)

In their brief (seven-minute) battle, they free Etheria together and Adora decides to remain and defend the people there. She's proven herself spunky, fun, fearless, and competent, though often with He-Man's help.

Furthermore, even as She-Ra defeats evil, she must largely refrain from fighting. J. Michael Straczynski writes that parents' groups like Peggy Charren's Action for Children's Television had come out vociferously against violence in *He-Man and the Masters of the Universe* (2019, 244). As he adds:

To soften the ire of the pressure groups that were hammering He-Man, Filmation enlisted consultants to ensure our female lead was appropriately maternal, nurturing, and nonthreatening to male authority figures. They also decided that while the male characters on the show could use swords or arrows or punch the bad guys, our female lead was not free to do the same. So even though she owned a massive sword, she wasn't allowed to actually hurt anyone with it. Instead she would spin like a ballerina and – almost by accident – kick someone out of frame and hope the audience would fail to ask why the bad guy didn't just walk back into frame and beat the crap out of her.

(2019, 244–245)

She-Ra continues using acrobatics to turn the villains' strength against them, all while never striking them with her magic sword. As episodes go on, She-Ra discovers abilities to communicate with animals, telepathic empathy, healing, and other traditionally feminine powers. The show is episodic, as she goes around encouraging many peaceful communities to stand up for themselves. These moments are charming, though they also emphasize her small-scale battles rather than epic wars. It's a superheroine show, but one about eschewing violence, always with a pointed moral at the end. This not only models gentler play but also contrasts with the lessons of He-Man.

New She-Ra

ND Stevenson created a new era of storytelling with *She-Ra and the Princesses of Power*. The name itself emphasizes more of a hero team, much like Stevenson's prior *Steven Universe* (2013–2019). Furthermore, Stevenson emphasizes that the new version is substantially different:

This story is not about He-Man; it's much less about Adora's connection to He-Man than the original show was. So while we do get into the mystery of where Adora is from and the lore of the civilization that is the remnants of which are all over Etheria, He-Man himself is not a huge part of this show.

(Trumbore 2018)

This time, Adora finds her destiny on her own, linked to intergalactic explorers who created an interactive AI and the Sword of Protection in order to guide the "She-Ra". This is a title, with a science fiction princess empowered to defend the oppressed. As such, she appears more independent. The toys are in different shapes and sizes, like the characters, and this time the television show places more significance on the narrative story.

Adora and Catra's friendship is also much more developed, as a central part of both characters. In both shows, they work as allies, and then Adora defects. This time, the consequences of the love and betrayal shape both heroines. As the show begins, Force Captain Adora (Aimee Carrero) jokes with Catra (AJ Michalka), establishing deeper character. Both look like teens, not sultry adults. Stevenson notes:

That felt like a story that needed a slightly younger protagonist. It's ambiguous in the original show how old Adora is. She looks a little older, but typically, this assumes she's in her early 20s. Our Adora isn't super young, but she's a little closer to her teen years. It felt like the right age for her, 17 or 18 years old, when you're leaving home for the first time, going out into the world. You're studying the ideologies of the people who raised you, and figuring out what your own ideologies are. Adora goes through that, and all of the other characters are also going through something similar.

(Robinson 2018)

Shadow Weaver (Lorraine Toussaint) raised both young women from orphans, once more developing this into a closer family dynamic in the new show. Sensibly dressed in modest armor, Adora accepts her first mission of venturing out to prey on the evil rebel princesses of Bright Moon. Loyally, Adora argues to bring her team along, but is refused. This puts her allegiance and friendship into conflict: "We're gonna see the world. And conquer it. Adora, I need to blow something up," Catra gushes, until she realizes she isn't coming (Henry 2018, 00:07:48). The pair sneak out, and when their ship crashes, they're stranded in the outside world. There, Adora must confront that she has been on the wrong side, and she discovers her new powers.

In the new version, Glimmer (Karen Fukuhara) faints and swoons, but this is because she has stretched her precious transport powers to exhaustion; she is a hero and commander, determined to fight to her limits. This time, She-Ra too doesn't hold back from fighting directly. She is depicted much less sexually, from her art style to her wardrobe. With a high neck and shorts, her superhero minidress emphasizes height rather than curves. She also fails more, appearing human rather than idealized. Adora struggles in episode three since she doesn't know how to transform, and her clumsiness is endearing. She even creates Swift Wind by accident, panicking him into a rampage. When Swift Wind is threatened, Adora transforms and saves him from Horde soldiers. As such, she emphasizes her calling as protector of her friends.

Seasons have much stronger arcs, allowing deeper storytelling. And rather than a lady with no long-term concerns, now She-Ra is tormented with guilt for betraying her "bad-girl bestie" Catra even while she's irresistibly attracted to her. Her foster parents also provoke a great deal of guilt. The princesses squabble and disagree, even while contributing different skills to the team. The villains too have much more personality, with several able to be redeemed from the Horde.

Villains

"By presenting themselves as hybrid creatures, superheroes are able to be simultaneously more and less than human" (Brownie and Graydon 2015, 92), and Catra's stand-out characteristic (original and rebooted) is her hybrid cat features. As such, she follows the tradition of Black Panther, Catwoman, and many others who wield the savagery of the animal kingdom. All these characters emphasize their connections with nature as they incorporate its tools. In their study, Barbara Brownie and Danny Graydon apply Marla Carlson's essay *Furry Cartography: Performing Species* to superhero costume, observing that

> animal costumes enable the wearer to outwardly manifest an 'inner animal that exists as a kind of primitive substratum.' Just as the mask invites freedom from societal constraints, 'performing an animal identity provides a way out of human norms that have become unduly restrictive'.

Therefore, they conclude, "[a]s part-animal, the superhero is able to act savagely and aggressively, apparently without compromising the humanity of his alter ego" (Brownie and Graydon 2015, 91). Catra, with claws and arm stripes, appears much more catlike and less sexualized this time. Her bestial qualities are emphasized through giant hair, multicolored eyes, and an exaggerated sense of smell. She even curls up, catlike, at the foot of her friend's bed with silly snores. Stevenson adds: "One artist who actually works as a board artist on the show now, Mickey Quinn, drew a version of Catra that was smaller and more slight of frame. And that was something I never considered. It was like, "*She was a femme fatale in the original, of course she'll be a femme fatale now.*" And this version was like, "*Oh, what happens if she's not? What happens if she's just this sort of scrawny scrapper? That changes things, and it's more interesting"* (Robinson 2018).

While 1980s Catra purrs and scratches sexily, like Catwoman, new Catra appears as a bestial outsider and throwback. She is surprised to hear that the physically massive Scorpia (Lauren Ash) is a princess, who likewise feels shut out from the more glamorous set of activities. Critic Samantha Nelson notes that Scorpia is "a sweet, brawny scorpion-woman who doesn't fit in with her conventionally cute and pretty magic-using compatriots" (Nelson 2018). As Scorpia explains, "No one liked my family, even before we joined the Horde. Ah I never really fit with the other Princesses. I made them uncomfortable. They don't like that. They don't like me" (Bennett 2018, 00:03:30). Both are monsters in appearance, so they are shunned by the pretty heroines. Indeed, it's suggested this is why they have joined the Horde: it embraces the rejected outcasts. Catra instantly takes Scorpia's side as she sees their conflicts paralleling: "[The princesses] pretend they're better because you're different! They abandon people because they don't fit in... They take best friends and turn them into giant sword ladies, who run off with people clearly inferior to you!" (Bennett 2018, 00:03:48). Faced with this unkindness, the pair have much in common.

A darker villain comes forward in Adora's foster mother, Shadow Weaver. In the third episode, she hurls Catra down at Hordak's feet and insists, "I gave her charge of a simple mission: to return Force Captain Adora to the Fright Zone. Instead, our forces suffered a humiliating defeat" (Stine 2018, 00:21:33). When Hordak promotes Catra to Force Captain in response, Catra is treated as less desirable than Adora, and yet, she must fill her shoes. She is like Loki, from the Marvel movies, or Zuko, the jealous lesser sibling from *Avatar: The Last Airbender* (2005–2008). Nelson notes that

> Catra – like ... Prince Zuko – pivots from her basic role of chasing the good guys around the world and takes on a far richer arc. Her plot is the best animated antihero story since Zuko's, using the conflicted relationship between Adora and Catra as a lens to question why some women feel they must hide their competitive natures and accept being second best.
>
> *(Nelson 2018)*

Each time Catra and She-Ra face off, their mutual knowledge and hurt at the other's choices make the conflict painfully personal. This central bond forms the core of the story. Stevenson explains:

> I think the show is about relationships in a lot of different ways. I think Adora and Catra's is probably the core relationship of the show, the hero and the villain, the dark and the light, even though you see that they started out not very different ... they were close to each other. I think, overall, that there's a lot of exploration in this show in general of both relying on the people around you but also realizing when to sort of walk away, draw boundaries and protect yourself when a relationship, even as much as you might love the person, is causing you pain and heartache and stopping you from being the person you're trying to be. I don't think it ever is something easy or a clean and simple thing to do. We see it play out in so many different ways; the characters hurt each other without even meaning to, without even knowing that they are ... or they hurt each other intentionally to cover up some hurt of their own.
>
> *(Trumbore 2018)*

In "Princess Prom," Catra accompanies Scorpia to the exclusive dance. Inness observes that in 20th-century tough women films,

> Lesbianism is always a 'ghost in the closet' when women act or appear tough, and a label that society uses to police such behavior; in order not to appear as lesbians, women are expected to shun tough actions that might make them appear too masculine.
>
> *(1999, 23)*

For a different era, the potential lesbianism is overt, and Catra and Scorpia are free to abandon the sensual girlish presentation in favor of overt toughness. Catra even wears a tux. At the prom, Adora and Catra must dance together, which gives them time to air their grievances. With comic effect, as Glimmer watches Bow with crazed jealousy, Adora follows Catra (who leaves her notes in a teasing game), emphasizing that Adora's focus is not on a man but on her female former best friend. Meanwhile, Catra outwits Adora and kidnaps Bow, Glimmer, and the sword. Stevenson notes:

> The villains are almost a dual-protagonist in this series. There are times when you don't want them to win because they're doing terrible things. But there are times when you can forget that and start to root for them without realizing it. So that was something I had a huge interest in doing.
>
> *(Robinson 2018)*

As the pair continue sparring and finally admit their feelings, they give the ongoing conflict much more nuance.

Conclusion: Legacy

The She-Ra reboot quickly became beloved by fans, while also being nominated for a Daytime Emmy Award and winning the GLAAD Media Award for Outstanding Kids and Family Programming. It ushered Asian, dark-skinned, gay, and nonbinary characters into its universe, while exploring the burdens of being neurodivergent or having a nonstandard body. It was inclusive, loving, empowering, and epic.

At the same time, the original show has much staying power, while also standing out as a rarity in its time. She-Ra was an early hero and inspiration for many girls:

> She was beautiful and kind, plus she had a cool headdress and rode a unicorn; she had all the glamour of toys usually marketed towards girls but she had a story too, and she was the all-powerful hero of that story.
>
> *(Walsh 2016)*

Original She-Ra even became something of a gay icon decades after her show went off the air, "probably thanks to her combination of true strength and total campiness" (Walsh 2016). Straczynski likewise notes how much her imagery continued:

> The shows took root in popular culture beyond anything we could have anticipated, spawning thirty years of comic books, conventions, cosplay, toys, a He-Man feature film in 1987, sequel animated series in 1990 and 2002, and, as I write this, a new

version of She-Ra on Netflix. DVDs of the series became bestsellers. and featured interviews with me and Larry, as well as digital copies of our original scripts, notes, and the She-Ra series bible. Young women saw She-Ra as a role model, a female action hero at a time when there were very few of those. Their response validated our struggle to maintain her warrior edge against those who wanted to soften her into a mommy figure.

(2019, 246–247)

New and classic, She-Ra offers a complex blend of superheroism and sweetness that in both eras permanently impacted the culture.

References

Bardugo, Leigh. 2016. "We are not Amazons." In *Last Night, A Superhero Saved My Life,* edited by Lisa Mignogna. Thomas Dunne Books.

Bennett, Jenn, dir. 2018. *She-Ra and the Princesses of Power.* Season 1, episode 8, "Princess Prom." Aired November 13, 2018, on Netflix.

Brown, Jeffrey A. 2004. "Sexuality, and Toughness: The Bad Girls of Action Film and Comic Books." In *Action Chicks: New Images of Tough Women in Popular Culture,* edited by Sherrie A. Inness. Palgrave Macmillan.

Brown, Jeffrey A. 2011. *Dangerous Curves: Action Heroines, Gender, Fetishism, and Popular Culture.* University of Mississippi.

Brownie, Barbara, and Danny Graydon. 2015. *The Superhero Costume (Dress, Body, Culture).* Bloomsbury.

Eatock, James. 2016. *He-Man and She-Ra: A Complete Guide to the Classic Animated Series.* Dark Horse Books.

Friedman, Edward, Lou Kachivas, Marsh Lamore, Bill Reed, and Gwen Wetzler, dir. 1985. *He-Man and She-Ra: The Secret of the Sword.* Fabulous Films Limited, 2022.

Henry, Adam, dir. *She-Ra and the Princesses of Power.* Season 1, episode 1, "The Sword, part 1." Aired November 13, 2018 on Netflix.

Inness, Sherrie A. 1999. *Tough Girls: Women Warriors and Wonder Women in Popular Culture.* University of Pennsylvania Press.

Madrid, Mike. 2009. *The Supergirls: Fashion, Feminism, Fantasy, and the History of Comic Book Heroines.* Exterminating Angel Press.

Nelson, Samantha. 2018. "Netflix's *She-Ra* Reboot Follows Closely in *Steven Universe*'s Footsteps." *The Verge,* November 8. https://www.theverge.com/2018/11/8/18075856/netflix-she-ra-review-princesses-of-power-reboot-steven-universe-noelle-stevenson.

Robinson, Tasha. 2018. "She-Ra's Showrunner on Villains, Heroes, and the Show's Controversial Design." *The Verge,* November 15. https://www.theverge.com/2018/11/15/18097423/she-ra-netflix-interview-reboot-noelle-stevenson-showrunner-nimona-lumberjanes.

Stine, Stephanie, dir. *She-Ra and the Princesses of Power.* Season 1, episode 3, "Razz." Aired November 13, 2018, on Netflix.

Straczynski, J. Michael. 2019. *Becoming Superman.* Harper Voyager.

The New York Times. 1984. "He-Man, A Princely Hero, Conquers the Toy Market." *The New York Times,* December 18. https://www.nytimes.com/1984/12/18/nyregion/he-man-a-princely-hero-conquers-the-toy-market.html.

Trumbore, Dave. 2018. "*She-Ra* Showrunner Noelle Stevenson on Why the Title Hero's Return Is Overdue." *Collider,* November 13. https://collider.com/she-ra-noelle-stevenson-interview/#netflix.

Walsh, Megan. 2016. "Masters of the Universe: 12 Things You Need to Know about She-Ra." *Screenrant,* March 7. https://screenrant.com/masters-of-the-universe-best-she-ra-facts-trivia.

14

THE DIVIDED FOURTH PHASE OF MARVEL-LICENSED VIDEO GAMES (2013–)

Carl Wilson

The Early Phases (1982–2012)

Borrowing terminology from the Marvel Cinematic Universe (MCU), there are currently four distinct "Phases" when examining the history and development of Marvel-licensed video games. Unlike the coordinated movies of the MCU, the Phase changes seen in the history of Marvel video game releases have not come from a consistent corporate mandate, as they are spread over a wider period of time and across multiple corporate shifts. The cultural variances that can be seen within the history of Marvel games are also implicitly tied to a history of the emergent video game industry. Rather than attempting to innovate from the front or dominate this sector, Marvel always prioritizes a leveraging of cross-cultural moments in reactionary bursts across established multi-media formats. This is partially because, outside of Marvel's control, one consumer trend or technical discovery can alter the entire ludic and narrative direction of the medium within a short span of time.

The cultural and industrial underpinnings of Phases One through to Three have been outlined in a prior study on Marvel-licensed video games (see: Wilson 2024, 105–122). In brief, Phase One: Origins (1982–1983) is defined by the release of *Spider-Man* (1982). Here, with cross-promotional Marvel-published magazine articles, adverts, and tie-in comics, Marvel expresses an early interest in directly offering the digital Spider-Man as one of many possible authentic Spider-Man narratives across a range of intertexts. These all then benefited from the coherence of being tethered to a familiar "Spider-Man" commodified form. Phase Two: Competition (1984–2006) "demonstrates a growing global awareness of the value of a comic book licenced game, with a greater competition shown by video game producers for licenses and subsequent market space" (Wilson 2024, 110). During this period, Marvel rescinds close control in favor of outsourcing their licenses to third-party game publishers, and by extension developers from around the world. As the video game industry of the 1990s shifted toward the commercial imperatives of promoting recognizable IP and selling branded tie-in products within a crowded market place, so too did the number of video games with Marvel characters increase. With the emergence, then cultural dominance of the MCU, starting with *Iron Man* (2008), Phase Three: Franchise Tenants (2007–2012) maps over the first Phase of their Cinematic Universe counterparts. However, while spin-off games

DOI: 10.4324/9781003366911-17

continue to be the focus of their release slate in this Phase, these titles are now positioned, both through their development and promotion, as a "sub brand" extension of the cinematic "range brand" (Taylor 2017, 268). This not only reflects Marvel's greater control over their licenses but also shows their initial disinterest in the formation of a separate Marvel Video Game Universe (MVU).

The purpose of this chapter, therefore, will be to move beyond 2012, where Phase Three ends, and to consider the parameters of Phase Four: Divided. I propose that it is called "Divided" precisely because there are two distinct strategies at play during this decade of game development, where Marvel licenses have been leveraged from two distinctly different points of intersection with the medium and audience, which also each differ from the prior Phases. There are the prestigiously produced, single-purchase, single-player, and single-branded experiences as seen with *Marvel's Spider-Man* and *Marvel's Guardians of the Galaxy* (which I have labeled "Phase Four S" for "Single"). There are also the easily adaptable/updatable, multiplayer, multi-purchase, multi-branded, and live-service titles such as *Fortnite* and *Marvel Strike Force* (labeled "Phase Four M" for "Multi"). Where significant overlap can be found in Phase Four, namely with *Marvel's Avengers* (2020), there is a suggestion of the type of games that may follow when the two strands converge, but crucially, due to the commercial and cultural failure of *Marvel's Avengers*, there is no certainty on what the late Phase Four games, or Phase Five itself, will exactly look like. This essay will provide a framework for understanding the context of their emergence once they do arrive.

Phase Four S

It is only with the acquisition of Marvel Entertainment, LLC by The Walt Disney Company in 2009 that Marvel Games, a dedicated video game subsidiary, was created to handle third party license agreements. Jay Ong was hired as Marvel's Vice President of Games in 2014 and immediately noted that "The [Phase Three] games we did with Activision were trending poorly" (Kent 2021, 501). For Marvel, working with a company that generated dozens of tie-in titles in quick succession was no longer enough; for Ong, Marvel's new objective was also cultural: they had to "beat *Arkham*" (Kent 2021, 502). By 2014, the *Arkham* series of video games, which started with *Batman: Arkham Asylum* (2009), was being regularly published by Warner Bros. Interactive Entertainment and developed by Rocksteady Studios (made a subsidiary to Warner in 2010) and WB Games Montréal. The games use DC Comics licenses, also owned by parent company, Warner Media. These titles demonstrated to Ong and Marvel Games that critical acclaim, profitability, and increased cross-brand awareness could all be achieved through an IP that was handled sympathetically. Marvel altered their trajectory, terminated their contract with Activision – formally ending a significant aspect of Phase Three game production – and offered exclusive platform rights for a *Spider-Man* game to Sony Interactive Entertainment on their PlayStation 4 console (Kent 2021, 503).

Sony Pictures have owned the rights to use Spider-Man in film since 1999; Sony, in their capacity also as video game publishers SIE Worldwide Studios, handed the new project and around $90 million to one of their own long-term development partners, Insomniac Games Inc., to make *Marvel's Spider-Man* (2018). Within four years, *Marvel's Spider-Man* had sold over 33 million copies worldwide and received over 100 industry award nominations (Yang 2022). As game director, Ryan Smith states "when you think of Insomniac's strengths, Spider-Man is just a tremendous opportunity for storytelling and for building mechanics that really define the character, like the open-world swinging" (Watts 2018). Sony matched the Marvel IP they had acquired with a studio that understood the cultural and industrial demands of the action-adventure genre on their PlayStation games consoles. Insomniac are the developers of the *Ratchet & Clank* (2000–2021) series, a number of popular, fantasy action-adventure games exclusive to Sony; furthermore, Insomniac were also able to utilize the same video game engine that they had recently deployed in *Sunset Overdrive* (2014), a city-based, open-world game where their non-superheroic protagonist also engages in vertical air-traversal for navigation (Mathew 2017).

While *Marvel's Spider-Man* would appear to signify a completely new Phase in the organizational culture within Marvel (as *Arkham* was for Warner), it is a transitional moment from the endpoint of Phase Three, where tenants have been handed a license to make a negotiated product drawing on their collective experiences. The key point of differentiation is that this title was not designed to subserviently tether itself to the comic, cartoon, film, or prior video game incarnation of the web-crawler, although it does persistently make reference to them as brand signifiers. Rather, it is positioned as a prestigious organizing principle in itself, which in terms of brand treatment makes *Marvel's Spider-Man* comparable to the *Arkham*-verse games. Mirroring how Warner bought Rocksteady once *Arkham Asylum* proved a success, Sony did the same with Insomniac in 2019. Here, the video game medium is recognized by Marvel as having the potential to be more than just a "sub-brand" and become fully transmedial, albeit one with a critical difference in structure to *Arkham*:

> The cameo of the Spider-man from the video game *Marvel's Spider-Man* (2018) in the animated movie *Spider-Man: Across the Spider-Verse* (2023) can be seen as an indication of this closer alignment. However, these games and their networked structures are still being formulated by third parties, external to Marvel.
>
> *(Wilson 2024, 120)*

Marvel has less control over this iteration of Spider-Man.

In 2023, "1.3 million files, 1.67 Terabytes" of Insomniac data was leaked by hackers (Tassi 2023). According to *Kotaku*, among these files, "One internal presentation pegged the final cost [of *Marvel's Spider-Man 2* (2023)] at around $300 million, almost three times the cost of 2018's *Spider-Man* for the PS4" (Gach 2023). In terms of budget, this would place *Marvel's Spider-Man 2* alongside *Avengers: Infinity War* (2018) – the fifth most expensive MCU film produced. The article goes on to say

> Games like *Miles Morale*s, a stop-gap spin-off, offer one possible alternative. The shorter adventure had a budget of only $90 million, according to one 2022 presentation on "mid-sized games." But it went on to sell over 10 million copies, making it incredibly profitable in addition to being beloved by fans. The presentation notes that these mid-sized games generally take two years less to make than tentpole games like *Spider-Man 2*, helping to reduce the time between new games, as well as the risks if something goes wrong in development.
>
> *(Gach 2023)*

The stakes are raised within such a short space of time; *Marvel's Spider-Man: Miles Morales* (2020), which cost the same to develop as *Marvel's Spider-Man* was already being considered a "mid-sized game" during production, when the first title, released two years prior, was considered a Triple-A title within the video game industry (NYFA 2019). By February 2024,

Insomniac announced that the *Marvel's Spider-Man* series had sold over 50 million units (Insomniac Games 2024), but while these platform-exclusive titles are among the best-selling games for Sony on their PlayStation consoles, there were still plans to mitigate expansive risk through diversification. This strategy is not only related to the technological size of the game, and the accordant investment required, but the relative cultural size of the Spider-Man license used. Marvel/Sony/Insomniac leveraged the alternative Spider-Man brand associations and connections of the Afro–Puerto Rican Miles Morales featured in the concurrently released animated movies. While Miles also features in *Spider-Man 2*, the Insomniac leak implies that the studios consider him to be something of a financial firewall should the original Spider-Man, Peter Parker, tethered to the MCU and Sony's film slate, falter in his heroic duty to shift exponentially more units for shareholders.

With diversification, the exclusivity of *Marvel's Spider-Man* also changed. Not coming from Marvel/Marvel Games, but in line with Sony Studios' (formerly SIE Worldwide Studios) new strategy of releasing some of their first-party titles on the Windows PC platform two to three years after their console debut, *Marvel's Spider-Man* released for PCs in 2022. This version was the "remastered" edition, which had been released for the new Sony PlayStation 5 console in 2020. Touting some of the technical advancements first implemented in *Marvel's Spider-Man: Miles Morales*, such as "ray-traced reflections and ambient shadows", in a promotional piece for the remastered title, the official Sony blog pointed out that the game would include "better-looking characters with improved skin, eyes, hair, and facial animation (including our new, next-generation Peter Parker)" (Stevenson 2020a). This last point, which was not just a reference to a higher resolution character model, but a full digitally scanned-in face of a recast actor playing Peter Parker (Stevenson 2020b), was considered to be contentious by fans of the "original" Peter (Chapman 2022). This signals that for some fans when it comes to Phase Four S titles, there are limits to the elasticity of the product. Better visuals and gameplay are welcome enhancements, but not at the cost of the consumer's relationship to their idea of the core brand(s) that comprise their fandom.

Phase Four S titles give the impression that they are fixed entities: created once, promoted once, released once, played once, then onto the next Marvel game. However, while they appear to be following a pattern inherited from prior Phases, in a closer examination of Phase Four operations, this is not the case. Every element is open to negotiated, interrelated budgets and "improvements" affecting their representation, all driven by the concerns of studios external to Marvel. Furthermore, while the post-release adjustments represent a step beyond the earlier Phase releases, they also tie these titles more closely with the "always online" game structures and audience expectations seen in Phase Four M titles. Insomniac Spider-Man is considered a range brand by Marvel/Marvel Games/Sony/Sony Studios/Insomniac, but it is one whose face and identity have an elasticity that can be altered or "upgraded" from one platform or game to the next. The differences in how these studios respond to these changes based on their proximity to the IP or production of the games is worthy of further study as "Phase Four: Divided" progresses; it would continue to reveal more about the reconfigured gap between licensee and licensor, and the new connections and/or frictions between emergent cultural and industrial practices.

The success of *Marvel's Spider-Man* series leads to the question: does it represent the start of a MVU? Earth-1048 is the diegetic universe in which Insomniac's *Spider-Man* games all take place, and in this respect it is again similar to the *Arkham*-verse of games. But unlike the Warner/DC Comics games, the Spider-Man titles are also tied to the Marvel Gamerverse. The Gamerverse is not like the *Arkham*-verse or indeed the Marvel (Comic) Universe and the MCU, which are fictional shared universes with transmedia franchises that can also be separated and contained from any other interests that Marvel is pursuing. A critical distinction is that the Gamerverse is primarily only a fragmented form or extension of the latter. Gamerverse games include a mix of Phase Four S and Phase Four M titles such as *Marvel vs. Capcom: Infinite* (2017), *Marvel's Avengers* (2020), *Marvel's Guardians of the Galaxy* (2021), and *Marvel's Midnight Suns* (2022). The Gamerverse covers tie-in comics published by Marvel Comics; novels published by Titan Books, who have also published dozens of Marvel novels and art books; and action figures and collectibles produced by Hasbro and Funko, who, like Titan, already both have a working partnership with Marvel (Snyder 2017). However, it is notable that while the ancillary products to the listed games tie into the video game universes and heavily feature the unifying Gamerverse branding, the games themselves and their packaging and advertising materials do not share this same feature. Furthermore, not all of Marvel's recent games, such as the LEGO games or mobile games like *MARVEL Future Revolution* (2021) appear to be within the Gamerverse brand, with them sharing their own transmedial networks (Harvey 2015). Unlike the shared cinematic or comic universes, there has been no attempt to integrate versions of the characters between games made by other publishers. The Gamerverse, then, is an industry-led marketing device separate to the creation of the games; it may build on the purchasers' cultural understanding of the Marvel universe structure or branding, but it does so without consideration for narrative consistency or coherency.

Phase Four M

The disparate Gamerverse grouping of predominantly Phase Four S products is a partial reaction to the narrowly focused toys-to-life *Disney Infinity* (2013–2015) project. Made possible by the Disney acquisition of Marvel in 2009, *Disney Infinity* represents an early experiment with Marvel licenses and video game multiverses. The toys-to-life genre of game, in which physical toys could be purchased and then inserted within a digital sandbox world, was a trend explored by publishers Disney Interactive Studios with subsidiary developers Avalanche Software. The original release focused on Disney and Pixar figures; the subsequent release of a "2.0 Edition", *Disney Infinity: Marvel Super Heroes* (2014), features an original story by Marvel writer Brian Michael Bendis, with supplementary purchasable "Play Sets" inspired by the MCU and the Disney XD series *Ultimate Spider-Man* (2012–2017). Within ten months of its launch, "Disney reported global revenue of $550 million for Infinity" and was projected by Disney to be "a long-term game franchise" (Richwine and Nayak 2014). However, as Patrick Klepek reports, by 2015 "It seems like a combination of factors — increased competition, miscalculated inventory, complex corporate interests — contributed to *Disney Infinity*'s demise. The result is that Disney seems to be getting out of making their own console games" (Klepek 2016). Continuing from their prior Phases, and reflecting Disney's growing unease in making their own games, it is during this same period that Marvel also started to explore comparable video game avenues that could in many ways mitigate the risks of surplus physical stock or variable market interests in which a prestige genre game could take longer to produce than the genre trend might be around. Marvel did this through free-to-play, fully digital video games that use a live-service model of game design (as in: constantly updating to be as engaging as possible).

These Phase Four M titles include online multiplayer mobile games such as *Marvel Contest of Champions* (2014) and *Marvel: Future Fight* (2015). Indicating the success of this strategy, the flurry of post-*Disney Infinity* multiplayer mobile games includes *Marvel Strike Force* (2018), *Marvel Battle Lines* (2018), *Marvel Super War* (2019), *Marvel Duel* (2020),

Marvel Realm of Champions (2020), *Marvel Future Revolution*, and *Marvel Snap* (2022). Unlike the relatively textually fixed Phase Four S titles, in reinforcing how these Phase Four M games are authentic, yet responsive, ancillary branded products rather than original transmedia narrative extensions, Jason Bender, the creative director at *Marvel Strike Force* developers FoxNext draws parallels between his game and the toys of *Disney Infinity* offering

> when people walk out of *Captain Marvel* or *Avengers: Endgame* or *Spider-Man: Into the Spiderverse*, there's at least one character in *Strike Force* that you can immediately play and have fun with. That's the core toy. That's where all the animation, the effects, and all the pretty art really matters.
>
> *(Thomas 2019, 12)*

In partially anchoring customer engagement in the "core toy" of *Marvel Strike Force* to another media format, Bender echoes Marvel's original intention behind the MCU where "Marvel's 10-film plan was not about making great movies [....] The original Marvel plan was about making movies in order to sell toys" (Ryan 2020). The "3.0 Edition", *Disney Infinity: Star Wars*, came with an additionally purchasable Play Set called *Marvel Battlegrounds* (2016), which was the only way for customers to play with up to four friends in one game instance; by comparison to the siloed off, predominantly single-player experience, the world of online gaming offers consumers a considerably different, competitive gaming experience. Here, players are encouraged to show off a skill and/or financial mastery of their collected digital "toys", all while submitted to a simultaneous barrage of gameplay and marketing techniques designed to sustain engagement and investment, these being the video game industry costs for free-to-play games, which commercially, is arguably all that "really matters".

Yet, while these mobile games appear to inhabit a position reminiscent of the quick-cash-in Phase Two of Marvel video game adaptations, the reality with some of these titles can be quite the opposite, as Bender explains: "With some video games, the experience is over once you beat it after eight hours of playing", but "We view *Strike Force* like we're running an episodic television show" (Thomas 2019, 13). In being always online and therefore, much easier and quicker to update and adapt to market forces, these games are positioned to mirror episodic modes of television production rather than cinematic film productions in terms of length (longer shelf-life but through shorter bursts of gameplay), quality (cheaper to initially produce but there are expectations for constant development in order to maintain interest), and financial returns (lower initial income but with the potential for a much longer tail). This all also signals a divergence in emphasis from the single-units-sold logic framing the perceived successes of Phase Four S titles.

With a Phase Four M game such as *Marvel Contest of Champions*, according to Marvel Games' Executive Creative Director, Bill Rosemann, this episodic design structure also fed back into comics, with "Art imitating [digital] life, imitating art, imitating [digital] life" (Davies 2018, 8). Originally inspired by the limited comic book series *Marvel Super Hero Contest of Champions* (1982), the game was written by Marvel comic writer Sam Humphries. *Marvel Contest of Champions* was then adapted back into a ten-issue Marvel comic book series in 2015. Despite this success, one of the limitations in making a Phase Four M video game where "all that really matters" is an agile, reactive adherence to another text created in another medium is that there may be less room for side-ways expansion and original iterative expression within the same medium. *Marvel Realm of Champions* was developed as a spinoff to *Marvel Contest of Champions*, drawing from *Secret Wars* (2015) and Battleworld-based comics and storylines with cross-promotional links to the parallel running *Marvel Contest of Champions*. Unlike the linear progression of Phase Four S games, where, for example, a consumer may buy *Marvel's Spider-Man: Miles Morales* after having played *Marvel's Spider-Man*, the Phase Four M user base appears to be less interested in getting their fix of Marvel digital diversification from outside of the one title they have already invested time and money in. *Marvel Realm of Champions* was shut down in 2022, while the older game, *Marvel Contest of Champions*, has persisted.

Marvel Strike Force generated $150 million in revenue in its first year (Shanley 2019), and garnered a further $300 million in just 2020 alone (Sinclair 2021); *Marvel Contest of Champions* has been downloaded over 226 million times in its ten-year lifetime (Kabam n.d.) and has reportedly made more than $1 billion in lifetime sales, which is more revenue than several MCU televisions shows or movies (Pocket Gamer 2023). The longtail profitability of free-to-play titles that have additional, purchasable content finds its greatest expression through Marvel's collaboration with developer/publisher Epic Games and *Fortnite* (2017). *Fortnite*, as with all of these Phase Four M games, offers a series of purchasable cosmetic packs or "skins", to tie in with the release of MCU movies, and like the other titles, it has run free in-game MCU inspired based events where a player can, for example, "Join the battle for the Infinity Stones! Fight as Chitauri and Thanos or wield Avengers items in the Endgame LTM [Limited Time Mode]" (Epic Games 2019). A substantial aspect of *Fortnite*'s appeal and popularity rests in its intertextuality, which then drives customer engagement as they fear missing out on limited time (purchasable) products. This is a video game metaverse where rivals DC Comics also have a presence with all of their superheroes and villains, but to understand why Marvel might wish to collaborate in this bustling, shared space with Epic in such a way, court documents show that *Fortnite* made over $9 billion in its first two years (Smith 2021). Undoubtedly such numbers have an effect, both in terms of clamor and willingness to adapt, on the brands and their businesses that, like the players of their own games, fear of missing out on a potential share of the action.

Marvel Studios President Kevin Feige has noted that "A lot of people learn about our characters for the first time [...] through *Fortnite*" and that "Games have become an extension of our storytelling" (Disney Parks Blog 2024). An asterisk must be affixed to Feige's second claim, as there is a difference of intent from the license holder exalting storytelling as a brand extension and storytelling as a transmedial variation. These lines can easily be blurred and combined across all of the Phases, but there are recognizable signs in Phase Four that show where Marvel draws their lines and connections; for example, a Limited Time Mode event may not currently find itself the subject matter of a new entry in the MCU, but they are found in Marvel's comic book publications. When DC Comics published their crossover tie-in comic, *Batman/Fortnite: Zero Point* (2021), it became the best-selling comic in America (Johnston 2021); Marvel immediately followed with their tie-in comic with *Fortnite x Marvel: Zero War* (2022). As with *Marvel Contest of Champions*, this publication strategy echoes Marvel's earlier multi-Phase strategies of having comics tie-in with a digital product (with, for example, the *Questprobe* series of the 1980s). But it is also a dynamic now considerably different in execution; a far more sizable audience plays the core product (*Fortnite*) outside of the superhero niche. The comic becomes an extension of, or at least an expression of, the storytelling devices found in video games, reflecting in part the new expectations of a readership imported in from another media form. Notably, each first print issue of *Fortnite x Marvel: Zero War* also had a code for exclusive content within *Fortnite*, thereby emulating the DLC format from within the game and drawing sales from video game players who may have had little-to-no interest in the contents of the comics-as-products themselves.

Prior to 2024, *Fortnite* differed from the other free-to-play Marvel titles in that it reduced the production risk for Marvel considerably. They only had to stay culturally relevant, primarily through their MCU movies and television shows, to be included in the game through one of many corporate brand partnerships with Epic. This scenario is an extension of Phase Two video games in that Marvel was again working with multiple developers to make a proliferation of similar games based on popular genres, to increase their chances of success in a number of lucrative and emerging fields. It is also an inversion of Phase Three licensee/licensor dynamics in that *Fortnite* is the dominant cultural and financial force in the sector, with more cultural cache than Marvel. Demonstrably, this has proven effective as "Disney and Epic Games have engaged hundreds of millions of players through Fortnite content integrations, season collaborations, in-game activations, and live events, including the Marvel *Nexus War with Galactus* [2020], which drew more than 15.3 million concurrent players" (Walt Disney Company 2024). In February 2024, The Walt Disney Company and Epic Games announced plans for a much deeper collaboration or "content integration" where "Disney will also invest $1.5 billion to acquire an equity stake in Epic Games alongside the multiyear project" to "further expand the reach of beloved Disney stories and experiences" (Walt Disney Company 2024). FoxNext who made *Marvel Strike Force* was bought by Disney in 2019, after *Marvel Strike Force* was released, but they were then sold off in 2020 (Sinclair 2021). This new twist in Phase Four M continues to be about titles made using Marvel properties and with Disney's immense financial leverage, but instead of the parent company wanting to have total control, as with FoxNext, Disney is content to invest and take a greater share of the profits from Epic than they would have had in a solely licensee/licensor dynamic prior to this arrangement. The deal is also about greater access in a convergent future, with Epic's Unreal Engine already being used across Disney's films and television shows, including those made by Marvel, as the production gap between multimedia products closes. This is one of the areas in which Phase Five games are likely to emerge from in the near future.

Emulating Disney's ethos of working with the best video game industry leaders, Marvel continued to make licensed Phase Four M games with external developers, most notably *Marvel Snap* and *Marvel Rivals*. *Marvel Snap* is a card game developed by Second Dinner, a company run by Ben Brode, formerly the director of the multi-billion-dollar juggernaut *Hearthstone* (2014) for Blizzard Entertainment. *Marvel Rivals* was created by NetEase, the Chinese company behind *Marvel Super War* and *Marvel Duel*, but who were also the Chinese region partners with Blizzard Entertainment on games such as *Overwatch 2* (2023), part of the multi-billion-dollar *Overwatch* franchise, before their working agreement expired. Both *Marvel Snap* and *Marvel Rivals* are very much in the style of *Hearthstone* and *Overwatch* respectively, and have actively captured large sections of the total market share (Shepard 2025). While these projects may indicate a solid base from which to organize brands and optimize profit, there is a cautionary aspect first seen in Phase Two productions: when international publishers and developers are involved, control is less firmly in the grasp of the license holder. For example, as a consequence of the U.S. Supreme Court directing Chinese company ByteDance to divest of their ownership of TikTok due to a perceived national security risk of Chinese government interference, video game publishers Nuverse, who are owned by ByteDance, found that along with TikTok, the game that they publish – *Marvel Snap* – was immediately taken offline in the U.S. in January 2025 with no warning. According to developers Second Dinner, "This outage is a surprise to us and wasn't planned" (Second Dinner 2025). In Phase Four M, Marvel has refined and expanded their approach to working with top-tier partners, especially when compared to Phase Three, but their "toys" are now directly shaped by multi-billion-dollar deals and government interventions. With this escalation of scale in intent and consequence, the Marvel video games of Phase Four are more susceptible to division than ever before.

Phase Five?

Based on the trend-following trajectory of their Phase Four ambitions, one might imagine that Phase Five would synthesize strands S and M more fully to make a hybrid game. *Marvel's Avengers* (2020), made by developers Crystal Dynamics with the assistance of four other studios, already represents such an attempt. *Marvel's Avengers* is also a case study of the pitfalls that may befall a Phase Four title.

Studio head Scot Amos, explains how Crystal Dynamics went about creating their composite title:

> We've had to go hire experts like Shaun Escayg, who is our Creative Director. He told stories for *Uncharted* and *The Last of Us*. We needed him to help tell this story. Dave Fifield was a game director who worked on *Halo* and *Call of Duty*, we needed him to help us with multiplayer. [....] and said let's put this together in a new way for something bigger.
>
> *(GVMERS 2022)*

As with Epic and *Fortnite*, these four series are industry-defining landmarks in their respective video game genres. *Marvel's Avengers* (2020) is a direct culmination of Phase Four S and M trends; there is a quality, linear single-player campaign narrative that at a mid-point in the story pivots to onboard players onto multiplayer mission varieties, which then form the bulk of the live-service end game content. However, the game was beset by issues partly because of this ambitious amalgamation of often competing trends and divergent video game cultures. As reported, *Marvel's Avengers* had a significantly delayed release, the first major patch for the game contained over 1,000 bug-fixes, and the road-map (a list of updates the development team was planning) was quickly dispensed in favor of incremental upgrades, additional purchasable costumes, and an overhauling of further issues as they occurred or were discovered (Notis 2021). Criticism for the game ranges from the visual, with characters looking like poor imitations of the MCU cast (Myers 2019); the ludic, with the upgrade system being tedious and illogical (Wong 2020); the narrative, with multiplayer missions lacking the same variety or attention to detail as the front-loaded game content (Fahey 2020); or the mercenary, with console exclusive characters, narrowly focused downloadable content and microtransactions being seen as the markers of a free-to-play title, when *Marvel's Avengers* was a full-price game on release (Gach 2020). When publishers Square Enix held a briefing for investors in November 2020, *Marvel's Avengers* was said to have cost them "7 billion yen ($67 million)" with Square Enix President Yosuke Matsuda offering "it is true that there were aspects in which we were wanting. We intend to leverage the lessons we learned from this experience in future game development efforts" (Ashcraft 2020). In May 2022, Square Enix announced their decision to sell Crystal Dynamics, with all associated licenses and games, allowing them to move forward "with investments in fields including blockchain, AI, and the cloud" (Square-Enix 2022).

These alternative investments momentarily signaled where the Marvel-branded metaverse could move to, with the company also exploring the fad/field of NFT collectibles (Marvel 2021), but ultimately, they have carried on working with studios like Insomniac for their Phase Four S content, and moved toward Epic to start a heightened version of their earlier Phase M content. Notably, Marvel's competitors, DC Comics, have been less fortunate in the post-*Marvel's Avengers* period, releasing their own hybrid games, the multiplayer *Gotham Knights* (2022) and the live-service *Suicide Squad: Kill the Justice League* (2024), to critical silence or deafening cultural condemnation. Where Phase Four for Marvel was inspired partly by the credo of "beat *Arkham*", now the makers of the *Arkham* series appear to have been left behind by their own failed attempts to move forward. For three Phases, Marvel has also indiscriminately pursued trends or let others chase them in their stead, but in Phase Four Marvel have aligned themselves with industry-leading game designers in two distinct fields as a concerted refinement or rejection of the prior Phases. To enter Phase Five, Marvel video games will need to avoid costly missteps caused by industry issues and misinterpreting audience expectations – potentially a comparable malaise already affecting their counterparts in the MCU. Marvel games will need to lead from the front.

References

Ashcraft, Brian. 2020. "Marvel's Avengers Didn't Sell As Expected, Says Square Enix." *Kotaku*, November 27. https://kotaku.com/marvels-avengers-didnt-sell-as-expected-says-square-en-1845763877.

Chapman, Alex. 2022. "Marvel's Spider-Man's Face-Change Controversy: Who's The Better Peter?" *ScreenRant*, September 10. https://screenrant.com/marvels-spiderman-remastered-peter-parker-face-change-actor/.

Davies, Paul. 2018. *Marvel Contest of Champions: The Art of the Battlerealm*. Titan Books.

Disney Parks Blog. 2024. "Disney & Epic Games Share Fortnite Reveals, Sneak Peeks & Future Vision." August 11. https://disneyparksblog.com/disney-experiences/fortnite-announcements-pixar-marvel-star-wars/.

Epic Games. 2019. "V8.50 Patch Notes." April 25. https://www.epicgames.com/fortnite/en-US/patch-notes/v8-50.

Fahey, Mike. 2020. "Crystal Dynamics Claims Relief In Sight For Bored *Avengers* Players." *Kotaku*, October 8. https://kotaku.com/crystal-dynamics-claims-relief-in-sight-for-bored-aveng-1845317433.

Gach, Ethan. 2020. "Enjoy This Word Salad about Why *Marvel's Avengers*' Spider-Man Is a PlayStation Exclusive." *Kotaku*, August 5. https://kotaku.com/enjoy-this-delicious-word-salad-about-why-marvels-aveng-1844624965.

Gach, Ethan. 2023. "What Hacked Files Tell Us About The Studio Behind *Spider-Man 2*." *Kotaku*, December 20. https://kotaku.com/what-hacked-files-tell-us-about-the-studio-behind-spide-1851115233.

GVMERS. 2022. "How To Kill A Game - The Tragedy of Marvel's Avengers." *YouTube*, June 9. https://www.youtube.com/watch?v=LDNpHIWLfFQ&ab_channel=GVMERS.

Harvey, Colin B. 2015. *Fantastic Transmedia: Narrative, Play and Memory across Science Fiction and Fantasy Storyworlds*. Palgrave Macmillan.

Insomniac Games. 2024. "Today, we're honored to celebrate an amazing milestone: Marvel's #SpiderMan2PS5 has surpassed 10 million units sold, bringing the game series sales to an astounding 50 million units!" X, February 14. https://x.com/insomniacgames/status/1757662718604013868.

Johnston, Rich. 2021. "Batman/Fortnite: Zero Point 1 Tops Bleeding Cool Bestseller List." *Bleeding Cool*, April 25. https://bleedingcool.com/comics/batman-fortnite-zero-point-1-tops-bleeding-cool-bestseller-list/.

Kabam. n.d. "Marvel Contest of Champions." *Accessed* January 27, 2025. https://kabam.com/games/marvel-contest-of-champions/.

Kent, Steven L. 2021. *The Ultimate History of Video Games: Vol. 2*. Crown.

Klepek, Patrick. 2016. "Sources: The Ambitious (Now Cancelled) Plans for Disney Infinity's Future Included Rogue One, Bigger Figures." *Kotaku*, May 12. https://kotaku.com/sources-the-ambitious-now-cancelled-plans-for-disney-1776370484.

Marvel. 2021. "Spider-Man Swings into the World of Digital Collectibles." August 6. https://www.marvel.com/articles/gear/spider-man-veve-digital-collectibles-nft.

Mathew, Adam. 2017. "How Deep Is Insomniac's PS4 Spider-Sensibility?" *Red Bull*, January 11. https://www.redbull.com/au-en/insomniac-developer-interview-spider-man-ps4.

Myers, Maddy. 2019. "Something Feels Off About The *Avengers* Gameplay Demo." *Kotaku*, June 13. https://kotaku.com/something-feels-off-about-the-avengers-gameplay-demo-1835466769.

Notis, Ari. 2021. "*Marvel's Avengers*, Six Months Later." *Kotaku*, March 4. https://kotaku.com/marvels-avengers-six-months-later-1846407671.

NYFA. 2019. "Insomniac's Spider-Man and Why AAA Games Still Matter." *New York Film Academy*, January 11. https://www.nyfa.edu/student-resources/nyfa-spider-man-aaa-games-still-matter/.

Pocket Gamer Staff. 2023. "The Mobile Games that Have Made More than $1 Billion in Lifetime Sales." *PocketGamer.biz*, August 22. https://www.pocketgamer.biz/the-mobile-games-that-have-made-more-than-1-billion-in-lifetime-sales-update/.

Richwine, Lisa, Malthi Nayak. 2014. "Disney Sees Infinity Game's Retail Sales Hitting $1 Billion." *Reuters*, June 13. https://www.reuters.com/article/us-disney-interactive-idUSKBN0EN2NM20140612/.

Ryan, Joal. 2020. "The Incredible, Hidden History of the Marvel Cinematic Universe." *CNET*, March 9. https://www.cnet.com/pictures/the-marvel-cinematic-universe-incredible-hidden-history/.

Second Dinner. 2025. "Unfortunately, MARVEL SNAP Is Temporarily Unavailable in U.S. App Stores and Is Unavailable to Play in the U.S. This Outage Is a Surprise To Us and Wasn't Planned. *MARVEL SNAP Isn't Going Anywhere*." *X*, January 19. https://x.com/seconddinner/status/18808 61537981944300.

Shanley, Patrick. 2019. "'Marvel Strike Force' Generates $150 Million in First Year." *The Hollywood Reporter*, March 7. https://www.hollywoodreporter.com/news/general-news/marvel-strike-force-unlock-captain-marvel-as-playable-character-1193065/.

Shepard, Kenneth. 2025. "As Marvel Rivals Soars, Lapsed *Overwatch* Fans Grieve A Game They May Not Go Back To." *Kotaku*, January 15. https://kotaku.com/marvel-rivals-overwatch-2-fans-player-numbers-stream-1851740183.

Sinclair, Brendan. 2021. "How Scopely's Acquisition of FoxNext Led to Boundless Opportunity." *GamesIndustry.biz*, April 15. https://www.gamesindustry.biz/how-scopelys-acquisition-of-foxnext-led-to-boundless-opportunity.

Smith, Graham. 2021. "Fortnite Made over $9 Billion in Its First Two Years." *Rock Paper Shotgun*, May 24. https://www.rockpapershotgun.com/fortnite-made-over-9-billion-in-its-first-two-years.

Snyder, Justin. 2017. "Marvel Gamerverse Unleashed." *Marvel*, September 14. https://www.marvel.com/articles/games/marvel-gamerverse-unleashed.

Square-Enix. 2022. "Execution of Share Transfer Agreement with Change to Subsidiaries (Divestiture of Select Overseas Studios & IP)." May 2. https://www.hd.square-enix.com/eng/ir/pdf/20220502%20A_Press%20Release_fin.pdf.

Stevenson, James. 2020a. "See the Marvel's Spider-Man: Miles Morales New Gameplay Demo." *PlayStation.Blog*, September 16. https://blog.playstation.com/2020/09/16/see-the-marvels-spider-man-miles-morales-new-gameplay-demo/.

Stevenson, James. 2020b. "Marvel's Spider-Man Remastered detailed." *PlayStation.Blog*, September 30. https://blog.playstation.com/2020/09/30/marvels-spider-man-remastered-detailed/.

Tassi, Paul. 2023. "Insomniac Rocked By Massive Leaks, 'Wolverine,' Future Games, Employee Info." *Forbes*, December 19. https://www.forbes.com/sites/paultassi/2023/12/19/insomniac-rocked-by-massive-leaks-wolverine-future-games-employee-info/.

Taylor, Aaron. 2017. "Playing Peter Parker: Spider-Man and Superhero Film Performance." In *Make Ours Marvel: Media Convergence and a Comics Universe*, edited by Matt Yockey. University of Texas Press.

The Walt Disney Company. 2024. "Disney and Epic Games to Create Expansive and Open Games and Entertainment Universe Connected to Fortnite." February 7. https://thewaltdisneycompany.com/disney-and-epic-games-fortnite/.

Thomas, John Rhett. 2019. *Marvel Strike Force: The Art of the Game*. Marvel Worldwide, Inc. Watts, Steve. 2018. "Marvel's Spider-Man: How Insomniac Spun Its Web." *GameSpot*, December 21. https://www.gamespot.com/articles/marvels-spider-man-how-insomniac-spun-its-web/1100-6464062/.

Wilson, Carl. 2024. "Digital Avengers, Disassembled: Understanding Thirty Years of Changing Superhero Bodies in Marvel Licensed Video Games across Three Distinct Phases (1982–2012)." In *Superheroes and Digital Perspectives: Super Data*, edited by Sarah Young and Freyja McCreery. Lexington Books.

Wong, Kevin. 2020. "*Marvel's Avengers* Is Fantastic Once You're Fully Powered Up." *Kotaku*, 22 October. https://kotaku.com/marvels-avengers-is-fantaSstic-once-youre-fully-powered-1845443870.

Yang, George. 2022. "Insomniac's Spider-Man Games Have Sold over 33 Million Copies." *IGN*, June 3. https://www.ign.com/articles/insomniac-spider-man-33-million-copies.

15

FINANCIAL KRYPTONITE

The Foiled Attempts to Bring Superheroes to the Stage

Jarrod DePrado

In the Marvel Cinematic Universe (MCU) miniseries *Hawkeye* (2021), the eponymous Clint Barton and his family visit New York City (NYC) and see the newest Broadway hit, *Rogers: The Musical* (Thomas 2021). Barton sits stone-faced through a theatrical retelling of the life of Steve Rogers, aka Captain America, including the musical number "Save the City" that recounts plot points from the MCU movie *The Avengers* (2012). Outside, the Lunt-Fontanne Theater's marquees herald rave reviews for the "super-powered sensation," labeling the production "a soaring, smashing, flying, fighting musical triumph" (Thomas 2021). While Barton's ultimate assessment is that the musical is "ridiculous," the show-within-a-show's critics clearly disagree. As the MCU uses the commercialization of superheroes to ground its universe in realism, the largest diversion from reality is in how successful its superhero musical appears to be. *Rogers* is a homage to the real-life Captain America musical of the 1980s which never fully materialized on stage. This is not an uncommon story; while the film industry is saturated with well-regarded comic book movies, musical adaptations of superhero stories have been infrequent and received much less successfully, both critically and commercially. Several superhero musicals offer cautionary tales as unsuccessful attempts to adapt comic book characters for the stage over the past 60 years: "*It's a Bird... It's a Plane... It's Superman*" (hereafter cited as "*It's Superman*," 1966), *Captain America* (1986–1990), *Batman: The Musical* (2002–2004), and *Spider-Man: Turn Off the Dark* (2011). Whether struggling to find enough commercial success to sustain a Broadway run, getting stuck in the development stage, or aspiring to lofty technical ambitions that ran into problems and made the production financially unsustainable, none of the musicals achieved the financial boon that the investors envisioned. Despite recruiting strong talent for these attempted musical adaptations, they were ultimately out of sync with the successes of their big-screen counterparts, highlighting that there have only been notable failed attempts to bring these characters to life on stage.

"Killed by 'Capelash'"

By the mid-1960s, *Superman* was the best-selling comic book hero for DC (Miller n.d.) and already had a television show, *Adventures of Superman* (1952–1958). However, in 1966, the

DOI: 10.4324/9781003366911-18

popularity of Adam West's *Batman* – both the television show (1966–1968) that premiered in January and the film released in July – displaced Superman as the best-selling comic book hero through 1967 (Miller n.d.). With signs that its flagship character was seeing diminishing returns, two simultaneous efforts were made to bolster Superman: *The New Adventures of Superman* (1966–1970), an animated television show that premiered in November, and "*It's Superman*," a musical adaptation for the theater. While the former was a boon for CBS's ratings (Wells 2014, 108), the musical was much less successful. The collection of creative talent should have been promising enough to guarantee financial and critical success: nearly everyone involved produced impressive work immediately following the musical. The songwriting team of Charles Strouse (music) and Lee Adams (lyrics) had made their Broadway debut with the smash-hit *Bye Bye Birdie* (1960) and had just adapted Clifford Odets' play *Golden Boy* into a successful and long-running musical (1964); Strouse would find later success in penning another comic-turned-musical, *Annie* (1977). Robert Benton and David Newman, whose son Charles Strouse credits with coming up with the idea of the musical (2008, 168), wrote the libretto at nearly the same time as their Academy Award-nominated screenplay for *Bonnie & Clyde* (1967). Additionally, Harold Prince, a successful Broadway producer, was breaking into directing and served in both roles for this production; his next directing job was the long-running musical success, *Cabaret* (1966).

"*It's Superman*" brings several comic book elements to the stage: notably scenic pieces resembling comic panels, and the penultimate song "Pow! Bam! Zonk!" conjures up the comic's fight scenes, similar to those used by Adam West's *Batman* on screen. Even the musical's title evokes someone calling out Superman's long-associated phrase, though the formatting of it in print frequently omits the quotation marks and the ellipses. While primarily a comedy, "*It's Superman*" moves away from the overt camp of West's *Batman* series and grounds its characters in a more realistic setting. Instead of using Superman's more colorful or well-known villains, the authors invented the begrudgingly overlooked, multi-Nobel Peace Prize-losing Dr. Abner Sedgwick, who plans to take down Superman (the embodiment of goodness) as payback for years of being slighted. There is also Max Mencken, a Walter Winchell-inspired reporter who views Superman as an obstacle to Lois Lane's affection (Strouse 170). Finally, the Flying Lings, a Chinese Acrobatic group, team up with Sedgwick and Max to help destroy Superman. Just as reports of Superman's heroics keep Max's newspaper stories off the front page, his impressive physical abilities easily overshadow the Flying Lings, causing them to lose audience members and money. Sedgwick's plan preys on the relationship between Superman and the diegetic public, who praise him in songs like "We Need Him" and "It's Super Nice." He looks to first determine Superman's true identity and then destroy him in the eyes of the public.

Instead of the larger extraterrestrial threats of the comics, the danger to Superman is internal. His popularity turns into an opening for Sedgwick's exploitation since the love of the people sustains him and gives his life meaning. When Superman is distracted while accepting an award, Sedgwick covertly blows up City Hall. The people quickly turn on Superman, blaming him for not detecting and stopping the explosion. Sedgwick later psychoanalyzes Superman, tying his desire to be loved to his abandonment by his parents as an infant, and arguing that he is only catching criminals, not stopping crime, because he needs to be a perpetual savior (Strouse et al., 1966, 2–6–27). For a 1960's musical comedy, the themes are more reminiscent of recent interpretations of the character; for example, Superman facing public scrutiny for not sensing the impending explosion of a government building is a plot point in the film *Batman v Superman: Dawn of Justice* (2016). With his cutting analysis, Sedgwick momentarily neutralizes Superman by probing why he would create a Clark Kent persona at all if not to counteract some repressed guilt while also questioning who gave him the authority (and presumed arrogance) to take on the task of saving others for his own adoration.

The musical offers a deep dive into Superman's psyche, including his self-exploration song "The Strongest Man in the World," in which he rhetorically asks why there is no correlation between his limitless physical invulnerability and raw emotional vulnerability. Part of this analysis also speaks to the larger issues of vigilantism: Sedgwick points out that costume-wearing is a means to separate the wearer from the rest of society and asks if the love for superheroes is really for them or their abilities as a "performer." Additionally, there is room for analysis of superheroes as part of the American mythos. When the Flying Lings present Sedgwick with the Mao Tse-Tung Peace Prize on behalf of the People's Republic of China, Max backs out of the plan and labels them "Commie rats" (Strouse et al., 1966, 2–7–34). The Lings believe that a subdued Superman who answers to Sedgwick would make an important artifact of "capitalist corruption" for the workers of China. This is in addition to Lois and Jim's debate over the ultimate futility of humanity's destined self-destruction in "We Don't Matter At All." While these heavier and more adult-oriented themes may have resonated with an older audience, the musical's largest appeal was to children, who quickly made up a large portion of the audience (Scivally 2008, 69). Still, the musical is humorous, moves at a brisk pace, and has a happy ending: Superman saves Lois, defeats the bad guys, and rushes up, up, and away to reaffirm his commitment to his philosophy of "Doing Good."

"It's Superman" was listed in noted theater editor Otis L. Guernsey, Jr.'s *The Best Plays of 1965–1966* (1966), an annual top ten list of new theatrical pieces. It also received a positive review from *The New York Times'* Stanley Kauffman (1966), who labeled it "easily the best musical so far this season," singling out the show's successful balance of neither taking itself too seriously nor performing an outright farce. However, there are hints of problems within Kauffman's review, describing the story as one that "suffices" and Superman as "dull," albeit a choice that he believes is intentional: "[the authors] have made a show about a super-boob from outer space who lives by pasteurized milk and pasteurized standards on whom a whole city depends on for its moral force and ethical practice." Additionally, Bob Holiday's portrayal of Superman was overshadowed by other characters, including Tony Award-winning actor Jack Cassidy in the role of Max, who was given the top billing; as John Wells summarizes, Superman became "a supporting character in his own story" (2014, 109). This is reflected in the three Tony Award nominations the show received for acting: Jack Cassidy (Max), Michael O'Sullivan (Sedgwick), and Patricia Marand (Lois). Finally, "You've Got Possibilities," an optimistic song by Max's assistant about the work-in-progress Clark Kent, was the singular popular song recorded at the time, and not sung by Superman.

Ultimately, the show only ran on Broadway for 129 performances, compared to the 1,165 for Prince's *Cabaret* and the 568 performances for Strouse and Lee's *Golden Boy*, which closed four days before *"It's Superman"* began previews (*Playbill* n.d.). Strouse acknowledged that *"It's Superman"* "failed to find its audience" because the show was both "too early and too late," premiering at the same time as *Batman*'s dominance of television but too early for the success that the film version of Superman would find in the late 1970s (2008, 172–3). The writers unknowingly predicted the dilemma that the show would face when Lois remarks that "People *won't* go to night clubs to see The Flying Lings when they can watch Superman fly for *free*" (Strouse et al., 1996, 1–4–23). Seeing *Batman* on television satisfied the same desire without Broadway prices, despite Prince's best efforts to make the show more affordable for a younger audience (Strouse 2008, 172). Prince later conceded that while the musical was

"conceived in anticipation of the Pop art craze, [because] it took so long to materialize…
it wound up opening after the fad was over" (Klein 1992). The production lost its entire
$400,000 investment (Mandelbaum 1991), although Wells reports it was $600,000 (2004,
109), and Scivally says it was $650,000 (2008, 67), making it the largest Broadway flop ever at
the time. Strouse quotes Newman as saying that they were "killed by 'capelash'" (2008, 173).

By the 1970s, despite competition from Marvel, Superman was still selling comics and
was well-known on television with the launch of the animated *Super Friends* (1973–1985).
In 1975, Romeo Muller adapted the musical into a 90-minute television special for ABC.
Between cutting the Flying Lings and several songs, adding a voiceover and a mobster
subplot, and rewriting much of the book, it bears sporadic resemblance to the stage version. While some of these changes were to make the production more timely for the 1970s,
including the popularity of *The Godfather* films (Scivally 2008, 70), the reception was poor
and it was never re-aired or released, though copies can be found on YouTube. The musical
failed to find an audience even when brought to another medium and updated for relevance;
the stage version would continue to be altered, such as a 1992 stage production at the
Goodspeed Opera House which changed the Flying Lings to a group of "Middle Eastern
Terrorists" (Klein 1992). However, the original writing team was not consulted for the
1975 television version, and therefore it is not surprising that the script leans into the campy
elements that the Broadway production avoided. Though making this version more of a
satire can perhaps excuse the cheap production look of the special, which was an attempt to
emulate drawn comic books (Scivally 2008, 70), the final result was far from "the funniest
superhero story ever," as it was advertised (*The New York Times* 1975, 63).

While librettists Newman and Benton may not have been thrilled to see the version of their
work that made it to television, their disappointment would have been short-lived. Three
years later, the two of them collaborated with *The Godfather* author Mario Puzo, with contributions from Newman's wife Leslie, on the screenplay for the critically and commercially
successful film adaptation, *Superman* (1978). The film was a return to familiar ground for
the comics, pitting Superman against Lex Luthor, armed with Kryptonite and a plan to sink
the Western US. The Newmans, without Benton, would write for the sequels, *Superman II*
(1980) and *Superman III* (1983); instead, Benton would win two Academy Awards for writing and directing the film adaptation of *Kramer vs. Kramer* (1979). While the Superman film
franchise was a success for Warner Brothers, it came too late to assist the musical. Since 1966,
It's Superman has had several smaller revivals, with a revised libretto by playwright Roberto
Aguirre-Sacasa. The 2013 New York City Center Encores! production received rave reviews
as a piece that embodies "the quintessence of the 1960s sensibility called Pop" (Brantley
2013). Ben Brantley (2013) speculates that the show "might have thrived for years in one of
the smaller Off Broadway houses that were starting to attract cult audiences" in the 1960s
and, much like the original production's reviews, argues that the "purposefully disposable
entertainment" at the heart of the show is something to be celebrated, not maligned. With
Superman Returns (2006) several years in the past, the bubbly 2013 Encores! production
may have benefited from being released three months before Zack Snyder's grittier reboot
gave the Man of Steel a darker hue.

"Still Very Much Alive"

While the Superman musical adaptation was ultimately financially disappointing, it was a full
production. Between "*It's Superman*" and *Spider-Man: Turn Off the Dark*, two musicals were

stuck in development and remained unfinished despite press coverage claiming otherwise. Shortly after the Superman musical closed in 1966, Marvel's Captain America became a familiar face on the animated show, *The Marvel Super Heroes* (1966). Additionally, Captain America had two films of his own (albeit made for television) in 1979 when, as Miles Beller (1979) reported, Hollywood was "in hot pursuit of the success of 'Superman'" in bringing comic book characters to the screen. Offering characters that addressed the larger drive for escapist fantasy, studios (like Marvel) that owned licensing rights saw dramatically increased requests, and merchandising opportunities were successful for both *Superman* and *Star Wars* (Beller 1979). This same logic should have extended to adapting superheroes for the Broadway stage, especially with the move toward larger megamusicals by the mid-1980s, such as *Cats* (1981), *Les Miserables* (1985), and *Phantom of the Opera* (1986). Captain America was especially appealing as a distinct patriotic symbol during the last stretch of the Cold War. Tracking the development of the musical in Enid Nemy's Broadway coverage in *The New York Times*, there is a five-year gestation period to bring the superhero to Broadway, which never materialized.

In April 1985, Nemy (1985a) reported that the Captain America musical had a $4 million budget, announced writers Mel Mandal and Norman Sachs, and gave an overview of the plot. Notably, elements of this musical are not dissimilar from "*It's Superman*," focusing on a hero experiencing an existential crisis while trying to balance his personal life. When a middle-aged Captain America's girlfriend runs for President and is kidnapped by terrorists, he is motivated to pull himself together and save the day. But unlike with "*It's Superman*," the writers were relatively new to Broadway, having only written one previous show, *My Old Friends* (1979), that ran for a month. By August, 55-year-old John Cullum was cast as the leading man – with existing photos of him looking every bit his age in costume (Billy Rose Theatre Division), and somewhat out of place for a character that ages very slowly – and a planned opening was announced for March 1986 (Nemy 1985b). A "preview" of the musical was presented at the Hotel Pierre in January 1986 by The Drama League of New York (Nemy 1986a), but by December producer Shari Upbin was still looking for major funding, claiming "the project is still very much alive" (Nemy 1986b). In January 1988, the rights were given to the Pennsylvania Stage Company in Allentown to hopefully start a transfer to Broadway that fall (Nemy 1988a). However, in December 1988, Upbin updated the status to "alive but not immediately active," (Nemy 1988b), and by January 1990 it was reported that the musical wasn't "going to fly. It has been grounded" (Nemy 1990).

Carole Gould (1986) wrote about investing opportunities for the Captain America musical, warning readers that "only about 20% of plays and 25% of musicals return a profit to their investors" since "most shows don't run long enough to return the investor's capital." Even though a recent contract renegotiation would "allow investors to recoup their money faster, chiefly by lowering the playwrights' and composers' royalties in exchange for a larger advance... [and allow] the show to break even more quickly than before," Gould cautions readers, "don't let the lure of the bright lights blind you to the financial risks of investing." The primary issue for this production was financial, as it failed to find backing despite the producers' efforts and creative advertising, such as placing "full-page advertisement in six million comic books calling for a girl between 10 and 14 to play a leading role opposite John Cullum" to "stir up investor interest" (Gould 1986). Today, the musical exists solely as an audio recording of the early performances, and some pages of the script have appeared online. By the late 1980s, Marvel was suffering financially and would ultimately file for bankruptcy by the mid-1990s. Failing to fund the musical, Marvel switched to capitalizing on the film successes of the 1980s and began production on a feature-length film instead. After several delays of its own, *Captain America* was finally released in 1990 to abysmal reviews; Captain America would not find big-screen success until 2011. However, another superhero was dominating the box office and public interest moving into the 1990s.

DC found success with Tim Burton's film adaptation of *Batman* (1989), which not only brought a grittier Gotham City to the big screen but spawned several sequels throughout the decade. In late 1998, despite the poor reception of the latest film installment (*Batman & Robin* [1997]), it was reported that Warner Brothers was interested in following Disney into the theatrical production business with a musical version of *Batman* (Simonson 1998). Jim Steinman, the songwriter for Meat Loaf's successful *Bat Out of Hell* album (1977), was attached to compose the songs (McGrath 1999). He had already collaborated with Andrew Lloyd Webber on *Whistle Down the Wind* (1996) and adapted Roman Polanski's *Dance of the Vampires* into a musical (1997). Playwright David Ives, who also worked on *Vampires*, was attached to write the script (McGrath 1999). By 2000, the musical was still reportedly underway, with two years' worth of work to do, but lacking a "current timeframe or specific schedule for development" (Lefkowitz and McGrath 2000). Two years later, Tim Burton was linked to direct the musical in 2002, with a projected opening on Broadway by 2005 (Simonson 2002). While the show was reportedly in pre-production and, according to Steinman, was going to emulate the two Burton Batman films (Hernandez and Simonson 2002), *Batman: The Musical* also never materialized. Perhaps the desire for a Batman musical dissipated when Warner Brothers canceled the planned sequel to *Batman & Robin* in favor of Christopher Nolan's 2005 reboot, *Batman Begins*. Or the musical could have been lost in a sea of other attempts to emulate the recent success of *The Producers* by bringing a slew of musical adaptations of films to the stage (Kakutani 2002).

Similar to Captain America, no script was ever released for *Batman: The Musical*, nor did it even progress further than the developmental stage. However, Jim Steinman released demo recordings of the songs and plot points on his personal blog in 2006. With only seven songs and minimal plot details, it is difficult to pinpoint everything the creative team envisioned. But unlike with "*It's Superman*," *Batman* utilizes two well-known villains from Burton's films, the Joker and Catwoman. The musical opens with Gothamites singing an operatic hymn, complete with Latin verses, asking for a savior from the impending darkness. This lengthy musical number transitions into the appearance of Batman, who sings "The Graveyard Shift," mourning his parents and reaffirming his commitment to stopping criminality in the city. From the beginning, the religious feel and heightened emotional weight make this musical uniquely ambitious compared to its predecessors. While it is not uncommon for Batman stories to focus on the psychological fallout from witnessing his parents' murders, the musical goes further by also focusing on Selena Kyle, making her a witness to the murder as a child as well. The Joker's murder of the Waynes (a plot point taken directly from Burton's film) allows Batman and Catwoman to develop a codependent romantic relationship built out of shared trauma, where they admit their emotional shortcomings and inability to have a personal connection in "Not Allowed to Love." The final tableau is Batman cradling a mortally wounded Catwoman, singing "We're Still the Children We Once Were," as part of a quartet with the ghosts of their adolescent counterparts. Killing off a major character, and a more prominent staging of the effects of childhood trauma, gave the proposed musical the same dark hues as the Burton films that inspired them. Even though the musical was never staged, other artists, including Meat Loaf, would record several of Steinman's songs from the musical.

In 2000, several years into the project's ill-fated development, the animated series *Batman Beyond* (1999–2001) poked fun at a potential Batman musical in the episode "Out of the Past." As in *Hawkeye*, the elder Bruce Wayne grimaces from the audience as his alter ego is turned into a musical character. However, Bruce is also clearly in the minority, as the opening song receives a standing ovation from the audience. Set in the year 2039, *Batman Beyond*'s musical is a look back at a nostalgic character from the past, unlike the more recent heroes of *Rogers* for the audience in *Hawkeye*. While humorous, it also anticipates a future in which a Batman musical is a popular commodity that took Terry McGinnis "weeks to get tickets for" (Tucker 2000). Both the Captain America and Batman musicals went through years-long pre-production stages that were buoyed by optimistic assurances that the show was coming but never did. They were indirectly memorialized by television shows that reveal that success for a superhero musical is only found in a fictional universe, even while gently mocking the concept of a superhero musical itself. Ironically, while both the Captain America and Batman musicals should have benefited from the superhero film successes of the 1980s and 1990s and the clamor for more comic book adaptations, the reboot of a new Batman film franchise steered studios back to the big screen and away from the calculated risks of a Broadway musical.

"The One Thing We Didn't Have to Worry about Was Money"

Shortly after the successful release of Sam Raimi's first entry in his Spider-Man film trilogy *(Spider-Man,* [2002]), "Marvel was eager to capitalize on their superhero's newfound level of popularity" and began to recruit talent to bring the web-slinger to the stage as a musical (Berger 2013, 11). U2's Bono and the Edge were hired to write the songs; director Julie Taymor, who helmed the still-running Broadway adaptation of Disney's *The Lion King* in 1997, was brought on to guide the development of the project; and playwright Glen Berger was recruited to develop their ideas into a script in 2005 (Berger 2013, 19). As with *Batman: The Musical*, hiring established rock musicians and a successful director should have set the musical up for success. Yet, in his memoir, *Song of Spider-Man*, Berger recounts the tumultuous development of the project: from the disagreements between the studio and the creative team over the tone of the show to the unexpected death of co-producer Tony Adams in 2005 (2013, 25–26). From the beginning, the production was assumed to be too expensive, and, after the release of the less-favorably-reviewed *Spider-Man 3* (2007), the concept of a "darker" Spider-Man musical was not interesting to comic book fans (44–47). Given the scope of the ambitious production plans, from large set pieces to studio encouragement to make the effects as cutting edge as possible (79), few Broadway theaters could accommodate the show's mechanics (and even those would still need further renovation) (76). Unlike with *Captain America* and *Batman: The Musical*, *Spider-Man*'s creative team was initially assured that "there was a waiting list of investors" to back the show (78); as Berger recounted, the mindset early on was "The one thing we didn't have to worry about was money" (103).

Taymor initially connected Spider-Man to a larger mythology by integrating the Greek goddess Arachne as a prominent character and utilizing a "geek chorus" to tell the story. The attempt to blend these elements with the existing mythos of the comics and the audience's familiarity with a recent big-screen iteration became muddled and difficult to follow. Later, as the production was revised for cohesion, Arachne's presence in the musical became less prominent, though she still serves as a source of guidance for Peter after the death of Uncle Ben, reiterating Ben's life advice (and a central thematic song for the musical) to "Rise Above" others and be the better person. During the revision stage, the authors abandoned some of the larger concepts to err on the side of familiarity. Hence, the plot of the musical in its final form echoes the plot of Raimi's *Spider-Man* with elements of *Spider-Man 2* (2004): Peter Parker is bitten by a radioactive spider and struggles to balance his personal life (and relationship with Mary Jane Watson) alongside his superhero responsibilities. When Norman Osborn's experiment goes awry, he turns into the Green Goblin and, in a deviation from the films, uses genetic mutation to create a collection of villains (a version of the Sinister Six from the comics) to threaten NYC. Peter briefly abandons his Spider-Man persona before ultimately defeating the Green Goblin and ends the musical optimistic about being able to balance both sides of his life.

One major change from the films was in trying to make Osborn more nuanced and sympathetic (essentially more like *Spider-Man 2*'s Doc Ock). Osborn is openly and regrettably childless, taking paternal pride in Peter's comprehension and appreciation for his life's work. He fights to resist government application for his scientific discoveries, hoping to instead benefit humanity by allowing for genetic modification to address future existential threats. After losing his wife and lab partner Emily in a laboratory explosion while experimenting on himself, the Green Goblin creates the Sinister Six and labels them his "family," seeking reciprocal revenge on Spider-Man specifically for defeating them. After Peter and the Goblin discern the true identities of each other, the latter tries to convince Peter to join him by appealing to Peter's identity as a spider, citing that their instinct is not to protect but to destroy. Instead, Peter makes a near-successful appeal to the Goblin to stop by reminding him of his deceased wife. Yet his larger plan has traces of Osborn's paternal desires, as the Goblin seeks to turn everyone into mutants, labeling them not just his family but his "children." His drive to find perfection in humanity and eliminate perceived weaknesses ultimately pushes aside the portion of his identity that is Norman Osborn in favor of the dominant Goblin. Ultimately, his desire to destroy non-mutant others is his undoing, as he tosses a piano from the Chrysler building while attached to it, ending his reign of terror.

While developing a story that built off the film adaptations, the projected opening was pushed back several times by the end of the decade due to a burgeoning recession, stalled construction, piling up expenses, and the departure of hired actors. By early 2011, several cast members had been injured on set, Roberto Aguirre-Sacasa (who had recently updated the "*It's Superman*" libretto) was brought in to assist with the script on "Spider-Man 2.0," and Julie Taymor begrudgingly departed the project after reviewers grew tired of the perpetual delays and published early, devastating assessments of the previews in February 2011 (Brantley 2011a). Ben Brantley, in particular, described the musical as "so grievously broken in every respect that it is beyond repair" (2011a). When the show officially opened four months later, despite setting some box office records (Berger 2013, 345), reviews for the final version remained unenthusiastic about the finished product: "this singing comic book is no longer the ungodly, indecipherable mess it was in February. It's just a bore" (Brantley 2011b). The most expensive show in Broadway history was found to be underwhelming with flying effects undermined by visible wires and with a tone more geared toward children, lacking "irony" to accompany the moments of self-aware humor (Brantley 2011b). In his review for the Encores! production of "*It's Superman*," Brantley even quips, "I'd certainly rather spend a couple of hours in ["*It's Superman's*"] amiable company than be trapped in the torturous web that is Spider-Man: Turn Off the Dark" (2013), which was still running at the time.

While *Spider-Man* was nominated for Tony Awards for Costume and Scenic Design and ran for three and a half years, the large operating costs were insurmountable and it failed to recoup the financial investment needed to officially open the show. While the revised story was "clearer, funnier, and shorter," focusing less on mere "style" (Berger 2013, 206), the plot did not diverge too far from the films, making the experience arguably too familiar as much as the spectacle was unimpressive. The most famous line attributed to the Spider-Man mythos is, "With great power comes great responsibility." The line itself makes an appearance in the musical but does not appear to be the sentiment behind the production's handling of finances and the tumultuous relationship between the creators. As John Kenrick recounts, "at a time when a lavish Broadway musical could be produced for $16 million," *Spider-Man* cost $70 million and was subject to an unheard-of six months of previews before opening (2018, 308). The scope and ambition of the project created both audience expectations and financial burdens that could not be satisfied. *Turn Off the Dark*'s enduring legacy is one that is plagued by financial- and production-related troubles (Kenrick 2018, 308), as much as the Raimi film franchise (at least the first two films) remains well-regarded.

Despite this, in April 2023, Marvel announced the development of an actual *Rogers: The Musical*, building off of the popularity of the sequence in *Hawkeye* (Paige 2023). While not a full production, the "one-act 30-minute" story of Steve Rogers was given a limited run (June-August 2023) at Disney California Adventure Park, with a libretto by Tony Award nominee Hunter Bell. The show received positive reviews, with Jenelle Riley (2023) in particular saying, although "it's in a theme park, it truly has a Broadway vibe and only convinces me further that a full-length Marvel musical is not only needed, but inevitable." With no official plans for a Broadway attempt announced, Disney (Marvel's parent company since 2009) can learn from their *Spider-Man* experience the benefits of creating a smaller musical in a controlled environment without the necessity of box office success. While this is a very different version of the Captain America musical from the 1980s, it cracks the code of what it takes to make a successful superhero musical: financial stability from a wealthy parent company; low overhead costs, located far outside of Broadway; and residual popularity from the big-screen MCU projects it is emulating.

Though superheroes remain a prominent part of pop culture today, their presence alone does not guarantee a project's financial success, as more recent film box office disappointments can attest. Apart from Captain America, the other three musicals recruited visionary directors (Prince, Burton, Taymor) and successful songwriters (Strouse and Adams, Steinman, Bono and the Edge) to bring well-established and beloved comic book characters to the stage. Looking at a spectrum of results, from demo recordings to full-fledged productions, there are clear efforts to craft substantial musicals while also navigating a relationship to the release of their big-screen counterparts: either too early (Superman and Captain America), too late (Batman), or too similar (Spider-Man). The unique challenges and costs that come with staging a musical are compounded by the expectation of technical wizardry that matches these stories on film. Additionally, the libretto has to be both enticing for established fans to take the project seriously but also accessible for casual fans (including children) to enjoy. While superhero musicals have historically only served as financial Kryptonite to investors, *Rodgers: The Musical* offers a promising small-scale example of what can happen when all of the pieces assemble.

References

Beller, Miles. 1979. "Hollywood Is Banking On the Comics." *The New York Times*, December 9. https://www. nytimes.com/1979/12/09/archives/hollywood-is-banking-on-the-comics-hollywood-turns-to-the-comics.html.

Berger, Glen. 2013. *Song of Spider-Man: The Inside Story of the Most Controversial Musical in Broadway History*. Simon & Schuster.

Billy Rose Theatre Division, The New York Public Library. 1985. "Actor John Cullum in costume as superhero Captain America in a publicity shot from the aborted Broadway musical 'Captain America.' (New York)." *The New York Public Library Digital Collections.* https://digitalcollections.nypl.org/items/553571e0-aa42-0132-4fb7-58d385a7b928.

Brantley, Ben. 2011a. "Theatre Review: 'Spider-Man: Turn Off the Dark': Good vs. Evil, Hanging by a Thread." *The New York Times*, February 7. https://www.nytimes.com/2011/02/08/theater/reviews/spiderman-review.html.

Brantley, Ben. 2011b. "Theatre Review: 'Spider-Man: Turn Off the Dark': 1 Radioactive Bite, 8 Legs and 183 Previews." *The New York Times*, June 14. https://www.nytimes.com/2011/06/15/theater/reviews/spider-man-turn-off-the-dark-opens-after-changes-review.html.

Brantley, Ben. 2013. "Theatre Review: He's the Man of Steel, As Well As a Man of Song." *The New York Times*, March 21. https://www.nytimes.com/2013/03/22/theater/reviews/its-a-bird-its-a-plane-its-superman-at-city-center.html.

Gould, Carole. "Betting on a Broadway Dream." *The New York Times*, February 16. https://www.nytimes.com/1986/02/16/business/personal-finance-betting-on-a-broadway-dream.html.

Hernandez, Ernio, and Robert Simonson. 2002. "Steinman, Ives and Director Tim Burton in Pre-Production on *Batman*." *Playbill*, September 19. https://playbill.com/article/steinman-ives-and-director-tim-burton-in-pre-production-on-batman-com-108384.

Kakutani, Michiko. "The Year In Review; The Idea Was Not to Have a New One." *The New York Times*, December 29. https://www.nytimes.com/2002/12/29/movies/the-year-in-review-the-idea-was-not-to-have-a-new-one.html.

Kauffman, Stanley. 1966. "Theatre: 'It's a Bird… It's a Plane… It's Superman,' It's a Musical and It's Here." *The New York Times*, March 30. https://www.nytimes.com/1966/03/30/archives/theater-its-a-birdits-a-planeits-superman-its-a-musical-and-its.html.

Kenrick, John. 2018. *Musical Theatre: A History*. Bloomsbury.

Klein, Alvin. 1992. "Theatre: Attention Clark Kent: Look Out for Batman!" *The New York Times*, June 21. https://www.nytimes.com/1992/06/21/nyregion/theater-attention-clark-kent-look-out-for-batman.html.

Lefkowitz, David, and Sean McGrath. 2000. "Ives and Steinman Still Working on Warner Bros.' Bway Batman." *Playbill*, December 26. https://playbill.com/article/ives-and-steinman-still-working-on-warner-bros-bway-batman-com-94044.

Mandelbaum, Ken. 1991. *Not Since Carrie: Forty Years of Broadway Musical Flops*. St. Martin's Press.

McGrath, Sean. 1999. "Report: David Ives to Write Book for Steinman's Bway Batman." *Playbill*, April 22. https://playbill.com/article/report-david-ives-to-write-book-for-steinmans-bway-batman-com-81415.

Miller, John Jackson. n.d. "Comic Book Sales by Year." *Comichron*. Last modified July 5, 2022. https://www.comichron.com/yearlycomicssales.html.

Nemy, Enid. 1985a. "Broadway: 'Captain America' boasts a hero-sized $4 million budget.'" *The New York Times*, April 5. https://www.nytimes.com/1985/04/05/arts/broadway.html

Nemy, Enid. 1985b. "Broadway: It's Not a Fantasy: 'Big Chance' Paid Off for One Dancer." *The New York Times*, August 23. https://www.nytimes.com/1985/08/23/arts/broadway.html.

Nemy, Enid. 1986a. "Broadway: A Fosse Musical, 'Big Deal is Read for April Opening.'" *The New York Times*, January 17. https://www.nytimes.com/1986/01/17/theater/broadway.html.

Nemy, Enid. 1986b. "Broadway: 'The Show Will Go On, Tomorrow,' A Frequent Refrain." *The New York Times*, December 26. https://www.nytimes.com/1986/12/26/theater/broadway.html.

Nemy, Enid. 1988a. "On Stage: Despite Time and Its Vicissitudes, Plans, Hope and Projects for the Theatre Continue to Emerge; The Son of a Famous Father Finds His Name a Mixed Blessing." *The New York Times*, January 1. https://www.nytimes.com/1988/01/01/theater/on-stage.html.

Nemy, Enid. 1988b. "On Stage: Optimist if Part of Life in the Theatre, and It's Evidence in Grand Quantity this Season; Frances Conroy of 'Our Town' is the Picture of Contentment." *The New York Times*, December 23. https://www.nytimes.com/1988/12/23/theater/on-stage.html.

Nemy, Enid. 1990. "On Stage: Shows, Shows, Shows: In the Mind, In Rehearsal, On the Back Burner or on the Way; Why Stewart Granger Has Returned to the Boards." *The New York Times*, Jan. 5. https://www.nytimes.com/1990/01/05/theater/on-stage.html.

Nolan, Christopher, dir. 2005. *Batman Begins*. Warner Bros. Pictures.

Paige, Rachel. 2023. "'Rogers: The Musical' Premieres June 30 at Disney California Adventure Park." Marvel, April 10. https://www.marvel.com/articles/culture-lifestyle/rogers-the-musical-june-30-disney-california-adventure-park.

Playbill. n.d. "*It's a Bird... It's a Plane... It's Superman*." Playbill Inc, accessed February 15, 2025. https://playbill.com/productions/its-a-birdits-a-planeits-superman-alvin-theatre-vault-0000000891.

Riley, Jenelle. 2023. "Bringing Marvel's Fictional Broadway Show 'Rogers: The Musical' to Real Life at Disneyland." *Variety*, July 6. https://variety.com/2023/artisans/news/rogers-the-musical-disneyland-1235663122.

Scivally, Bruce. 2008. *Superman on Film, Television, Radio, and Broadway*. McFarland & Company.

Simonson, Robert. 1998. "'Pow!' Batman May Fly on Broadway as a Musical." *Playbill*, December 9. https://playbill.com/article/pow-batman-may-fly-on-broadway-as-a-musical-com-78894.

Simonson, Robert. 2002. "Report: Tim Burton to Direct Musical of *Batman*." *Playbill*, August 30. https://playbill.com/article/report-tim-burton-to-direct-musical-of-batman-com-107963.

Steinman, Jim. 2006. *Words by Jim Steinman* (blog). https://jimsteinman.blogspot.com/search?q=batman.

Strouse, Charles. 2008. *Put On a Happy Face: A Broadway Memoir*. Union Square Press.

Strouse, Charles, Lee Adams, David Benton, and Robert Benton. 1966. *It's a Bird... It's a Plane... It's Superman*. Tams-Witmark. Digital Libretto. https://www.concordtheatricals.com/s/44638/itsabird-itsaplane-itssuperman.

The New York Times. 1975. "Television." *The New York Times*, February 21. https://timesmachine.nytimes.com/timesmachine/1975/02/21/140218222.html?pageNumber=63.

Thomas, Rhys, dir. *Hawkeye*. Season 1, Episode 1, "Never Meet Your Heroes." *Aired*, November 24, 2021, on Disney+. https://www.disneyplus.com/series/hawkeye/11Zy8m9Dkj5l.

Tucker, James, dir. *Batman Beyond*. Season 3, episode 5, "Out of the Past." *Aired*, October 21, 2000, on Kids' WB. https://play.max.com/video/watch/5cfd5dde-4dd0-4db4-8316-bd80552694a5/dfcf233f-4a78-47d9-a63e-4da319b5d444.

Wells, John. 2014. *American Comic Book Chronicles: 1965–1969*. TwoMorrows Publishing.

16

LIFE AND DEATH IN GOTHAM CITY

Batman: The Audio Adventures' Aural History of the Superhero Genre

Dru Jeffries

In her article analyzing Marvel's *Wolverine: The Dark Night* (2018), the comics publisher's first foray into scripted podcasting, Leslie McMurty makes a brief aside about another superhero, speculating that "the frequently terse Batman, while at ease in darkness on the [comic book] page, presents a challenge in the audio medium" (2019, 18). In 2022, DC Comics' parent company, Warner Bros. Discovery, put McMurty's theory to the test, releasing two scripted serialized podcasts presenting distinct variations on the Caped Crusader: the first was *Batman Unburied* (2022), an audio drama created and written by *The Dark Knight* (2008) screenwriter David S. Goyer; the second was *Batman: The Audio Adventures* (hereafter cited as *B:TAA*; 2021–), a semi-comedic take on the Dynamic Duo scripted and directed by *Saturday Night Live* (*SNL*) writer Dennis McNicholas. The press release for the latter describes it as a heterogeneous homage to the superhero's expansive transmedia history, "[drawing] inspiration from the vintage noir atmosphere of the celebrated 'Batman: The Animated Series,' the spirited fun of the classic 1960s 'Batman' TV series, and the entire 80-plus year history of the BATMAN franchise" (Perine 2021). While accurate, this description only scratches the surface of the podcast's complexity and appeal. As James C. Taylor notes, "Each incarnation of a superhero recycles and reworks elements from other incarnations in its franchise. Elements from other superheroes' franchises, and conventions of the superhero genre more broadly, can also be recycled" (2021, 88). The overwhelming variety and diversity of textual articulations present in the Batman franchise thus

> encourages us to think of adaptation not as a binary with 'source' on one side and 'adaptation' on the other, but instead as an ongoing process through which new adaptations continually (re)develop an ever-growing metatext – an intangible "ideal" text formed by the agglomeration and interrelationship of all the texts which deal with a particular superhero's narrative universe.
>
> *(Zeller-Jacques 2012, 143)*

The boast by the press release, that *B:TAA* attempts to integrate "the entire 80-plus year history of the BATMAN franchise" (Perine 2021), can be understood as an attempt to represent the Batman metatext, which encompasses an array of media, periods, aesthetic

DOI: 10.4324/9781003366911-19

approaches, and intended audiences. Though the podcast is explicitly comedic in tone (in addition to McNicholas at the helm, the cast largely comprises comic actors, many of them current or former *SNL* cast members), its humor derives primarily from its juxtaposition of "gritty" superhero tropes associated with the genre in its contemporary manifestation with an anachronistic mode of delivery. As this chapter will show, *B:TAA*'s deliberately anachronistic blend of retro media with contemporary touches unmoors the listener from any one specific era of the Batman franchise or medium-specific articulation of the superhero genre, blending references associated with a variety of media and eras into an audio-based palimpsest. As such, *B:TAA* might be understood as something of an "aural history" of the Batman franchise, if not the superhero genre more broadly.

This chapter will start by briefly establishing the recent entry of the superhero genre into the scripted podcasting space. From there, the chapter will turn to *B:TAA* more specifically, discussing how its episodes are structured as a combination of Old Time Radio (OTR) aesthetics with an increased emphasis on what Raymond Williams famously conceptualized as flow. While certainly inspired by televisual flow, *B:TAA* narrates its plot and builds out its storyworld in a particularly radiogenic way. It uses a variety of styles and formats associated with audio-only content, including segments produced and performed in the style of scripted "theatre of the mind"-style audio dramas, but also through an array of diegetic advertisements, jingles and musical interludes, news alerts, and phone calls, often separated by the sound of static as an imagined listener explores the radio dial. In doing so, *B:TAA* challenges the association of podcasting with intimacy and "authenticity," opting instead for a retro-yet-hypermediated style that simultaneously recalls OTR scripted audio dramas and contemporary media convergence. This chapter will conclude by situating *B:TAA* within the context of the Batman franchise more generally, to interrogate what it means to present a comedic Batman to contemporary audiences.

Podcasts are a relative newcomer to the popular media ecosystem and are often understood as a remediation, refashioning, or digital updating of analogue broadcast radio (Bonini 2022, 19). As Mia Lindgren and Michele Hilmes explain, "podcasts challenge traditional radio structures, forms, genres, production methods, and listening cultures as much as they also extend and shore up the radio medium" (2016, 3), with the myriad convergences and divergences between the two audio-based media spawning debates over the precise nature of their relationship. While scholars continue to debate what common ground is shared between radio and podcasting, the editors of *Podcasting: New Aural Cultures and Digital Media* offer a useful and uncontroversial summation: "Just as cinematic practice influenced television, radio practices have influenced podcasts, even if the resultant works bear little resemblance to contemporary forms of radio broadcasting" (Llinares et al. 2018, 5). Indeed, podcasting's major breakout hit, the true crime series *Serial* (2014–2022), was a spin-off of the popular public radio series *This American Life* (1995–), which itself has reached broader audiences by republishing its episodes as podcasts.

It's impossible to overstate the impact and influence of *Serial* not only on the podcasts that followed it but also on podcasting as an industry, given that it "stands alone as the first 'mainstream' podcast" and "the most influential force upon podcast fiction since Old Time Radio drama" (Hancock and McMurty 2018, 82). But while breakout shows like *Serial* are certainly important, the mainstreaming of podcasts has also been "partly caused by its adoption as a secondary platform; another avenue for diversifying commercial potential of already existing content" (Llinares 2018, 130). Thus, in addition to the more authentic, intimate, and non-professional shows that many associate listeners with the medium, podcasts have increasingly become "an expected paratext" accompanying major television and film releases (Hancock and McMurty 2018, 99). Indeed, when I re-listened to *B:TAA* while drafting this chapter, each episode was preceded by a brief ad promoting a podcast tie-in for a then-airing HBO series – either *Love & Death* (2023) or *White House Plumbers* (2023) – indicating that a salient feature of the show for its intended listenership may be a desire to extend their engagement with serialized media content via podcast paratexts.

It is in the post-*Serial* context that Marvel and DC entered the podcasting space, launching new adaptations of familiar properties in the serialized digital audio format. As McMurty and Cory Barker both conclude in their analyses of Marvel's *Wolverine* podcast, the narration of the series owes a considerable debt to *Serial*, as it "frames its serialized murder mystery in the vein of one of podcasting's most popular genres – true crime" (Barker 2021, 20). *Wolverine* was also followed by a slate of shows adapting other characters and stories, creating a shared storyworld accessible exclusively on the (now defunct) Stitcher Premium platform that Barker dubs the "Marvel Podcast Universe" (2021, 17). DC, which has generally been less invested in (or perhaps merely less successful at) producing a single overarching continuity compared to Marvel, immediately opted for variation in their initial podcasting efforts, both in terms of distribution partners and the content of the podcasts themselves. In collaboration with the audiobook subscription platform Audible, DC first produced a serialized audio adaptation of Neil Gaiman's *The Sandman* (2021–2022), which helped raise the franchise's mainstream profile in anticipation of its live-action Netflix adaptation. Their next two podcasts were *Batman Unburied*, a Spotify exclusive, and *B:TAA*, which was housed on Warner's HBO Max platform as part of an initiative to expand the streamer beyond video content (Chan 2021). In Canada, where HBO Max is not available, the podcast can be heard on Spotify. Thus, the company's first three scripted podcasts were spread across three separate platforms and three separate storyworlds, with two of those three series presenting variations on Batman.

Multiplicity and difference have long been part of DC's *modus operandi*, as it allows the company to serve audiences with diverse preferences simultaneously. In her influential chapter on merchandising strategies in the Batman franchise, Eileen R. Meehan observed this phenomenon in the context of the "Batmania" that attended the release of Tim Burton's *Batman* (1989). Meehan notes how Warner Bros.' marketing of the film "suggests an attempt to hedge its bets" with a "product mix [that] included merchandise using the film images as well as the old comics images," not to mention the 1960s television series (2015, 79). The same strategy is in full evidence here. Both *Unburied* and *B:TAA* were released mere months after the franchise's latest live-action cinematic reboot, *The Batman* (2022), thereby giving audiences a choice as to how they wanted to extend their engagement with the resurgent franchise: they may either double-down on the brooding seriousness of the recent film with *Unburied* or explore the more playful, colorful aspects of Batman's storyworld with *B:TAA*, or both. In the present-day Batman metatext, *B:TAA* is to *The Batman* as the 1960s television series was to Burton's 1989 film: both present Batman within an explicitly comedic framework, deliberately ride the line between pastiche and parody, and offer a deliberate tonal contrast to the feature film. *B:TAA* thus complements rather than competes against other versions of Batman available in the marketplace, even within the narrow cultural space of podcasting.

While *Serial* undoubtedly helped catapult podcasting into the cultural mainstream, in the context of an expansive transmedia superhero franchise, a podcast is almost certainly going to be considered a niche offering, especially in comparison to feature films (which receive the broadest cultural attention) or even to comics (which retain cultural capital as the "original" articulation, even as actual readership is comparatively low). The narrower podcasting audience, however, comes with decreased expectations of mainstream appeal (and profits), allowing unlikely creatives like McNicholas to offer a version of Gotham City and its outsize inhabitants that Batman's corporate owners would never approve for a blockbuster-scale project. *B:TAA* thus joins a tradition of smaller-scale franchise entries – like the animated series *Batman: The Brave and the Bold* (2008–2011), the comic book series *Batman '66* (2013–2016) and the direct-to-DVD animated films *Batman: Return of the Caped Crusaders* (2016) and *Batman vs. Two-Face* (2017) – that have perpetuated the spirit of the 1960s *Batman* television series. The limited audience for these retro texts restricts them to media like comics, animation, and podcasts, as the mainstream metatext has deliberately disavowed the camp sensibility since the neon-tinged pun-fest *Batman & Robin* (1997) was pilloried by audiences (Brooker 2001, 299).

Marvel's first scripted superhero podcast is an important point of comparison for *B:TAA*, not so much because of their similarities but rather because of their significant differences. While *Wolverine* leans into podcasting's association with true crime docu-series like *Serial*, *B:TAA* is less influenced by prior podcasts than it is by OTR. Where the series itself makes this perfectly clear, we see evidence of this association in the podcast's marketing materials as well. As Hilmes points out, podcasting is properly understood as a "screen medium: we access it through screens both mobile and static, using tactile visual and textual interfaces" (2013, 44). The visual cues provided by paratexts, including those directly attached to the podcast itself (e.g., album art) as well as those that surround it more generally (e.g., advertisements, the comic book tie-in), "[imbue] the listening material with a particular aesthetic ... solidifying an otherwise 'invisible' space or appearance" (Hancock and McMurty 2018, 91). The podcast's investment in retro radio was made immediately clear in the promotional materials released prior to the launch of the debut episode. The poster art for the podcast centers upon a large 1930s-style radio featuring an elaborate Art Deco-inspired bat design for its central speaker grille and an illuminated bat-logo above its tuning and volume dials. This radio imagery was also featured in the YouTube trailer for the series, which consisted entirely of a slow camera move away from the radio's illuminated bat-symbol (HBO Max 2021). In both cases, the relative absence of color – the visuals are effectively monochromatic, with a slightly bronzed quality –and antiquated technology on display situates the podcast as a retro, noir-inspired throwback.

B:TAA belies McMurty's claim that the typically terse Batman wouldn't transfer well to an audio-based medium by scripting the character in a specifically radiogenic manner. According to McMurty, "the term radiogenic has a two-part definition: having origins in radio, and following the conventions and aesthetics of radio" (2019, 13). As a fully-produced audio drama, *B:TAA* contains all of the features distinctive to the form as originally practiced in radio: a narrator, sound effects that establish a sense of place and convey narrative action, scripted dialogue performed by actors, and a musical score that sets the series' tone and smooth transitions between scenes. This approach produces what is often referred to as the "theatre of the mind" (Soltani 2018, 192). The primacy of the spoken word in *B:TAA*'s narration is evidenced throughout the series, but a few examples should help illustrate the point. In an action scene in episode five, "My Medium is Crime," for instance, Batman (Jeffrey Wright) carries on a conversation with Commissioner Gordon (Kenan Thompson) while piloting the Bat-plane, whose voice-activated weapons systems are a radiogenic but diegetically plausible touch, allowing the action to be explicitly narrated without redundancy (McNicholas 2021c, 05:24). In episode

10, "Dark Purple Dawn," the ultimate confrontation between Batman and the Joker (Brent Spiner) is a war of words rather than fists, with Batman pressing his psychological advantage over the villain (McNicholas 2021g, 41:18). Chris Parnell's non-diegetic narration also plays a key role in each episode, setting the mood with magniloquent turns of phrase that help establish setting ("Gotham: a splendid cabinet of grotesqueries for the sophisticated degenerate," from episode six, "The Whale of Damocles" [McNicholas 2021d, 12:54]) or convey characters' physical movements or action, often featuring the kind of alliterative language associated with the 1960s television series' voiceover ("As the sullen vulture of vice retreats to the company of his valet...," also from "The Whale of Damocles," [McNicholas 2021d, 21:38]). In each of these cases, verbal description or dialogue carries the storytelling and produces a comprehensible flow of action without the need for any visual accompaniment.

"Flow" is important in another sense as well. As Derek Kompare explains, Raymond Williams used the word to describe how television and other broadcast media divide their "programming into discrete segments" which, when "delivered in a succession of sounds and images, become more than the sum of their parts" (Kompare 2017, 72). Since Tiziano Bonini identifies the on-demand listening culture of podcasting as fundamentally oppositional to audiovisual flow (2022, 19), this would appear to be a counterintuitive approach to structuring a podcast. Rather than actually having flow, it would be more precise to say that *B:TAA* simulates or remediates this radiogenic or televisual style. Whereas the cereal advertisements inserted into each episode of the Kellogg's-produced *Adventures of Superman* (1940–1951) radio serial contributed to its meaning – speaking to the industrial and cultural contexts of radio, or the target demographic of the show – they didn't exist within the show's storyworld. In *B:TAA*, each episode is premised on the flow between narrative segments (told in the "theatre of the mind" style described above) and other genres of audio content that would be familiar to radio listeners and television viewers, all of which contributes directly to the podcast's storytelling and the elaboration of its storyworld. A breakdown of the first episode's structure is useful here:

0:00–0:11: Title announcement
0:11–4:18: Cold open: Gotham City One news segment
4:18–10:42: Narrative segment #1: Catwoman/King Scimitar
10:42–11:40: Advertisement (Blabbo the Birthday Clown)
11:40–23:53: Narrative segment #2: Batman and Robin/Two-Face
23:53–25:29: Advertisement/musical interlude (Iceberg Lounge)
25:29–32:48: Narrative segment #3: Joker
32:48–35:17: Closing credits

("A Fortune in Sin," McNicholas 2021a)

Each narrative segment is bookended by Parnell's narration, and the transitions into and out of each segment often feature the sounds of static and snippets of songs, sports games, or advertisements as an imagined listener wanders around the radio dial. *B:TAA* thus remediates the aesthetic of live broadcast flow in a pre-recorded, on-demand digital medium, drawing attention to flow not as a natural or inherent feature of audio drama (as it was in the context of broadcast radio) but rather as a deliberate stylistic construct – in other words, hypermediated.

The stylization of each of these segments also contributes to the anachronistic feel of the storyworld, with the synthesizer theme of the Gotham City One news network recalling

1980s television journalism while the Iceberg Lounge's featured performer, Stovetop Sullivan, croons to the backing of a 1930s-style big band. All of *B:TAA*'s bespoke music (written by Doug Bossi) skirts this line, combining the retro-coded instrumentation like muted trumpets (1930s) and a siren-like theremin (1950s) over synth-bass lines (contemporary). This logic extends to the show's scripting as well, a tendency perhaps most efficiently embodied in a single line spoken by Batman in episode eight, "Iceberg Dead Ahead": "Robin! Quickly! Encrypt these files, old chum!" (McNicholas 2021f, 04:55). In seven short words, we can discern a great deal about the podcast's epoch-blending approach. The phrase "old chum" directly evokes Adam West's characterization of the Caped Crusader and his paternalistic attitude toward his youthful ward in the 1960s television series, as well as the kid-friendly Silver Age comics that the television series faithfully interpreted (Brooker 2001, 178). At the same time, the instruction to "encrypt the files" unambiguously situates the series in a contemporary technological context. Distinct eras are freely mixed in this way throughout the series, producing an aesthetic survey of the franchise's history, or "aural history" of the superhero genre.

B:TAA similarly plays with the history of the Batman franchise. In "The Whale of Damocles," for instance, the broadcast of an episode of a television docudrama, *Ghosts of Gotham*, detailing the origin of the Joker – the version most famously articulated in Alan Moore's *Batman: The Killing Joke* (1988) graphic novel – is hijacked by the Joker's crony Charlie Charleyhorse, who ridicules the abysmal performance of the actor portraying the Joker in the show's re-enactments (McNicholas 2021). The actor, described as a "schlubby Polish immigrant," botches familiar lines from both *The Dark Knight* and Burton's *Batman* with line readings that are closer to actor Tommy Wiseau than Heath Ledger: "I now call my*self* the Joker. Why are *you* so serious? Ha ha ho ho. Wait until you are getting a load of *me*" (McNicholas 2021, 27:25). This segment thus references several previous comic book and filmic iterations of the Joker while also explicitly parodying true crime re-enactment shows like *Dateline* (1992–). Significantly, Charleyhorse is voiced by Paul Scheer, who may be known to listeners as the host of a long-running comedy podcast *How Did This Get Made?* (2010–), which celebrates bad movies like Wiseau's *The Room* (2003). Scheer's familiarity to podcast listeners adds another layer of intertextual complexity to the segment.

Advertising is, of course, central to the experience of OTR, much of which was produced by corporations to advertise their products. As such, "Listeners of American radio drama of the 1940s, raised (for the most part) on a diet of commercial sponsorship, understood the conventions of scene-setting and -shifting" (McMurty 2019, 7). In other words, flow was a natural by-product of ad-supported broadcasting. While many podcasts are monetized through advertising in ways directly comparable to OTR, this is not the case with *B:TAA*. Given the podcast's exclusivity to HBO Max, a subscription-based video streaming platform, *B:TAA* is freed from the need to bookend its episodes with sponsored content as *The Adventures of Superman* did on broadcast radio. The presence of advertising in *B:TAA* must then be understood more specifically as a self-conscious remediation of OTR aesthetics.

Of course, the advertisements that appear between narrative segments in *B:TAA* are not legitimate sponsored content, but rather fictional advertisements that exist within the diegetic world of the show. They are an integral part of the show's narration, which does not replicate the experience of listening to a particular radio *show* so much as the experience of listening to *the radio itself*, including the kinds of listener-dictated flow that occur while exploring the dial to navigate between stations in mid-broadcast. In fact, *B:TAA*'s advertisements are crucial to fleshing out the show's storyworld by providing glimpses of the kinds of products and services that would be on offer to consumers in a city like Gotham, hyperbolically riddled with super-criminality as it is. In "The Whale of Damocles," for instance, listeners hear an ad for Heating Oil Doyle's House of Home Heating Oil, whose sales pitch hinges on the imminent release of Mr. Freeze from Arkham Asylum: "Sure, we all know winter's on its way out, but so is Mr. Freeze – of lockup – again! That's right folks, Gotham's own old man winter is scheduled for release from Arkham Asylum on March 1. Do you have enough heating oil to last the summer?" Doyle (Ray Wise) fleshes out his fear-based sales pitch with examples: "Do you remember when Mr. Freeze flash-froze Gotham Harbour? Pretty sure that was in May! Oh, and how about that great Gotham blizzard? That was the blizzard that cancelled the fourth of July fireworks!" Perhaps most significantly, the ad concludes on a note that explicitly identifies why ads like this are funny and salient for contemporary (read: post-COVID, Trump era) listeners: "I know it sounds insane, but don't fight it – this is the new normal!" (McNicholas 2021d, 11:15). Normalization is also at issue in a political attack ad featured as the cold open of episode seven, "Spot the Crook," which uses an incident in which Killer Croc ate the members of a knitting club while on furlough from Arkham Asylum to support the candidacy of Gotham's incumbent mayor, whose opponent endorsed the furlough program in question: "Does Gotham really need a mayor who's soft on cannibalism – *of the elderly?*" (McNicholas 2021e, 01:43). Again, a recognizable form – the fear-mongering political attack ad – is taken to a comic extreme due to the hyperbolic nature of Gotham City's criminality.

In episode three, "Forged Without a Smith," an ad for the Gotham-View Bus tour portrays the city as a comically dangerous urban space. Rather than making a traditional appeal to potential tourists, the ad copy instead draws attention to features of the bus itself: antiballistic windows, amour-plating, and other contingency measures befitting a metropolis brimming with supervillains. Between jaunty, close-harmony jingles reminiscent of 1940s radio advertisements, the enthusiastic sales pitch of the ad boasts that

> In safety tests, Gotham-View Bus could not be rolled over by fewer than *fifteen* able-bodied hostiles! And every Gotham-View Bus in the fleet is stocked with enough water and rations to sustain passengers for three days in case of a siege event!
>
> (*McNicholas 2021b, 22:46*)

The unexpected juxtaposition of such dystopian imagery against the upbeat, nostalgic tone of retro advertising draws attention to the sharp clash between the superhero genre's disparate tones over its evolution: the content here is in keeping with the "grim and gritty" sensibility associated with the modern superhero genre – comics like Frank Miller's *The Dark Knight Returns* (1986) or films like *The Batman* – while the mode of delivery is uncharacteristically light, more in keeping with the kid-friendly camp of Silver Age comics or the 1960s television show. Seemingly incompatible variations on Batman's storyworld thus become audible simultaneously, with the dissonance between them registering as comedic commentary.

The podcast similarly contrasts two of its main supervillains – the Joker and the Riddler (John Leguizamo) – to draw attention to the contrast between the innocent, kid-friendly play of the franchise in the 1960s compared to its darker, more adult-oriented manifestations today. Leguizamo's Riddler, a self-styled "artist of crime" (or "the Julius Caesar of devious teasers," per his own description in "Spot the Crook" [McNicholas 2021e, 12:28]), is depicted as a harmless and outmoded relic while Joker embodies legitimate threat and terror. Much of the humor in scenes featuring the Riddler emerges out of the dynamic between him and his "young executive assistant," Miss Tuesday (Heidi Gardner). Gardner plays Tuesday with apathetic Gen Z energy, constantly dismissing his plots as unnecessarily elaborate and ineffectual, and even calling him a "cringe-fest" in "Spot the Crook" (McNicholas 2021e, 14:25). In episode eight, "Iceberg Dead Ahead," Riddler's confidence is rattled when he discovers that the bat-computer's file on him is only one-fifth the size of the Joker's file – "Well, Joker is A-list," Batman replies (McNicholas 2021f, 06:11). This culminates in "Dark Purple Dawn" when Joker has a *tête-à-tête* with Riddler, making the latter's obsolescence in the context of the contemporary superhero genre explicit: "These are crazy times we're living through. It's tough to hear, but maybe it's time to think about whether your act is still relevant. Does Gotham City really need a Riddler right now?" (McNicholas 2021g, 10:27). Following this conversation, a dejected Riddler surrenders himself to the authorities. The Silver Age conception of supervillains that *B:TAA*'s Riddler represents – essentially crime as performance art, executed with childlike glee rather than any genuine bloodlust – is out of step with the world as reflected in the contemporary superhero genre. Between Leguizamo's heightened, comedic performance, Miss Tuesday as his Gen Z comic foil, and his overly theatrical plots, Riddler embodies a 1960s approach to supervillainy, while the Joker is scripted (and portrayed by Spiner) more as a mirthless pastiche of contemporary Joker actors like Ledger, Jared Leto, and Joaquin Phoenix.

While Batman is strongly associated with the medium of comic books, the character has only occasionally been represented in an explicitly *comic* manner. In an interview promoting *B:TAA*'s second season at New York Comic Con, McNicholas pointed out the strangeness of this:

> we've spent thirty years convincing ourselves that [a billionaire in a bat costume fighting crime is] not silly and we've done a really good job at that – you know, the notion that you would joke about Batman is foreign to people, but really it has always been an absurd and ridiculous premise.
>
> *(CBR Presents 2022)*

The repression of Batman's comic side has everything to do with the legacy of the 1960s television series, whose dual address strategy pitched itself as comedic satire to sophisticated, adult viewers, and straight-faced action to children, leaving the kids in the room wondering why their parents were laughing (Medhurst 2013, 237). As Will Brooker describes it, "The paunchy, portentous Batman played by Adam West … is generally seen by comic fans as a clown whose 'inaccurate' version of the character has unfortunately become the predominant image in the mind of the general, non-comics-reading public" (2001, 171). In West's wake, the franchise set upon a long-term project of remasculinizing, reheterosexualizing, and decamping Batman (Medhurst 2013, 247), with the franchise's latest cinematic iteration, *The Batman*, representing only the latest attempt at taking the character ever more seriously.

The success of recent texts like *B:TAA* and the mainstream animated film *The LEGO Batman Movie* (2017), however, seem to suggest an increased willingness among fans to embrace the lighter side of the Dark Knight, at least around the margins of the franchise. At the very least, texts like *B:TAA* suggest that a significant portion of the fandom may have moved past the wholesale dismissal of the campy *Batman* described by Brooker and others and are increasingly willing to acknowledge its legacy and legitimacy within the overall franchise metatext. Even Jeffrey Wright, who plays Jim Gordon in *The Batman* and voices

Batman in *B:TAA*, describes his relationship to the franchise as having originated with the 1960s television series. This testifies to the enduring success of that show's dual address strategy:

> Even though there is a kind of camp and tongue-in-cheek nature to the Adam West series, as a kid, for me, it was pretty serious business. I didn't really appreciate the irony so much then, I guess, as I do now.
>
> *(Batman Statue Collector 2022)*

Franchises naturally evolve over time, responding to the cultural zeitgeist and audience preferences, and fans' relationship to different texts within franchises evolves similarly.

While broadcast media like OTR and television aimed their content squarely at mainstream mass audiences, podcasting still remains a more niche affair, especially in the context of an established transmedia franchise with more than eight decades of history. In his chapter on animated superhero parodies, Taylor notes that "Animation's elasticity, its ability to perform intertextual negotiations that may not be possible in live-action, and its subordinate status, facilitate the parodic approach" (2021, 87). While I agree with Taylor's argument, the qualities he associates with animation apply even more strongly to a podcast like *B:TAA*, which is undoubtedly a less mainstream cultural product than a theatrical animated film like *The LEGO Batman Movie*. This niche status arguably allows *B:TAA* even greater leeway to explore the comedic side of Batman. Whereas *LEGO Batman* is explicitly parodic, directly poking fun at the hypermasculinity and Vantablack darkness so often associated with the character, *B:TAA* is more of a pastiche, surveying the various tonal registers adopted by the superhero genre across its more than 80-year history and palimpsestuously collapsing those decades onto each other. While the result is extremely funny (though, as with all comedy, your individual mileage may vary), the podcast's humor is most often the result of the anachronistic juxtapositions that result when framing contemporary, "gritty" superhero content through the podcast's antiquated, OTR-inspired aesthetic. Batman himself isn't the butt of the joke, as he often is in *The LEGO Batman Movie*; rather, it is the hyper-seriousness of the contemporary superhero genre and its audiences, who insist that "a billionaire in a bat costume fighting crime" (CBR Presents 2022) be treated as the height of realistic drama, that are targeted for satire. *B:TAA* thus offers something comparable to the 1960s *Batman*'s dual address, at once indulging in gritty superhero action and playful, affectionate satire of the same; unlike the television series, however, the podcast wagers that its listeners are sophisticated enough to appreciate both registers of its dual address simultaneously.

References

Barker, Cory. 2021. "From Cinematic to Podcast Universe: *Wolverine: The Long Night* and the Multiplication of the Marvel Multiverse." In *The Superhero Multiverse: Readapting Comic Book Icons in Twenty-First-Century Film and Popular Media*, edited by Lorna Piatti-Farnell. Lexington Books.

Batman Statue Collector. 2022. "Batman: The Audio Adventures Panel With Jeffrey Wright & Bobby Moynihan @ New York Comic Con 2022!" Filmed October 2022 at New York Comic Con. Uploaded October 18, 2022, on YouTube. https://www.youtube.com/watch?v=m1DXkUWLxsg.

Bonini, Tiziano. 2022. "Podcasting as a Hybrid Cultural Form between Old and New Media." In *The Routledge Companion to Radio and Podcast Studies*, edited by Mia Lindgren and Jason Loviglio. Routledge.

Brooker, Will. 2001. *Batman Unmasked: Analyzing a Cultural Icon*. Bloomsbury.

CBR Presents. 2022. "NYCC: Batman: The Audio Adventures' Cast & Creator Raise the Stakes for Season 2." Filmed October 2022 at New York Comic Con. Uploaded October 7, 2022, on YouTube. https://www.youtube.com/watch?v=HVfVOvlIXvU.

Chan, J. Clara. 2021. "'Batman: The Audio Adventures' to Release Exclusively on HBO Max as Streamer Expands Podcasting Efforts." *The Hollywood Reporter*, August 4. https://www.hollywoodreporter.com/business/digital/hbo-max-podcasts-batman-1234992314/.

Hancock, Danielle, and Leslie McMurty. 2018. "'I Know What a Podcast Is': Post-*Serial* Fiction and Podcast Media Identity." In *Podcasting: New Aural Cultures and Digital Media*, edited by Dario Llinares, Neil Fox, and Richard Berry. Palgrave Macmillan.

HBO Max. 2021. "Batman: The Audio Adventures | Official Trailer | HBO Max." Uploaded September 13, 2021, on YouTube. https://www.youtube.com/watch?v=qzk43SX9vxg.

Hilmes, Michele. 2013. "The New Materiality of Radio: Sound on Screens." In *Radio's New Wave: Global Sound in the Digital Era*, edited by Jason Loviglio and Michele Hilmes. Routledge.

Kompare, Derek. 2017. "Flow." In *Keywords for Media Studies*, edited by Jonathan Gray and Laurie Ouellette. New York University Press.

Lindgren, Mia, and Michele Hilmes. 2016. "Editors' Introduction to *RJ* 14:1 Podcast 2016." *The Radio Journal – International Studies in Broadcast & Audio Media* 14 (1): 3–5.

Llinares, Dario. 2018. "Podcasting as Liminal Praxis: Aural Mediation, Sound Writing and Identity." In *Podcasting: New Aural Cultures and Digital Media*, edited by Dario Llinares, Neil Fox, and Richard Berry. Palgrave Macmillan.

Llinares, Dario, Neil Fox, and Richard Berry. 2018. "Introduction: Podcasting and Podcasts—Parameters of a New Aural Culture." In *Podcasting: New Aural Cultures and Digital Media*, edited by Dario Llinares, Neil Fox, and Richard Berry. Palgrave Macmillan.

McMurty, Leslie. 2019. "Dark Night of the Soul: Applicability of Theory in Comics and Radio Through the Scripted Podcast Drama." *Studies in Comics* 10 (2 November): 235–254.

McNicholas, Dennis. 2021a. *Batman: The Audio Adventures*, Podcast, "S1 E1 – 'A Fortune in Sin.'" Produced by Blue Ribbon Content, September 18. https://open.spotify.com/episode/3KYVGlEy9Uwhb4PkJUZ74K.

McNicholas, Dennis. 2021b. *Batman: The Audio Adventures*, Podcast, "S1 E3 – 'Forged Without a Smith.'" Produced by Blue Ribbon Content, September 18. https://open.spotify.com/episode/4xNq3Wm5rz23Em89MoWKGt.

McNicholas, Dennis. 2021c. *Batman: The Audio Adventures*, Podcast, "S1 E5 – 'My Medium is Crime.'" Produced by Blue Ribbon Content, September 18. https://open.spotify.com/episode/5VWzBimNXbIz6yIZhZX5NS.

McNicholas, Dennis. 2021d. *Batman: The Audio Adventures*, Podcast, "S1 E6 – 'The Whale of Damocles.'" Produced by Blue Ribbon Content, September 18. https://open.spotify.com/episode/0YgTYqBrWS0RRM7yl0XGWW.

McNicholas, Dennis. 2021e. *Batman: The Audio Adventures*, Podcast, "S1 E7 – 'Spot the Crook.'" Produced by Blue Ribbon Content, September 18. https://open.spotify.com/episode/6CdaXnNSOvelRQdZjfbSj8.

McNicholas, Dennis. 2021f. *Batman: The Audio Adventures*, podcast, "S1 E8 – 'Iceberg Dead Ahead.'" Produced by Blue Ribbon Content, September 18. https://open.spotify.com/episode/5ptznEJbLSgZqeWR4xwdSp.

McNicholas, Dennis. 2021g. *Batman: The Audio Adventures*, podcast, "S1 E10 – 'Dark Purple Dawn.'" Produced by Blue Ribbon Content, September 18. https://open.spotify.com/episode/7idq9DyDkLov1u786HQ5yi.

Medhurst, Andy. 2013. "Batman, Deviance and Camp." In *The Superhero Reader*, edited by Charles Hatfield, Jeet Heer, and Kent Worcester. University Press of Mississippi.

Meehan, Eileen R. 2015. "'Holy Commodity Fetish, Batman!' The Political Economy of a Commercial Intertext." In *Many More Lives of the Batman*, edited by Roberta Pearson, William Uricchio, and Will Brooker. Palgrave Macmillan.

Perine, Aaron. 2021. "Batman: The Audio Adventures Now Available on HBO Max." *ComicBook*, September 18. https://comicbook.com/dc/news/batman-the-audio-adventures-hbo-max/.

Soltani, Farokh. 2018. "Inner Ears and Distant Worlds: Podcast Dramaturgy and the *Theatre of the Mind*." In *Podcasting: New Aural Cultures and Digital Media*, edited by Dario Llinares, Neil Fox, and Richard Berry. Palgrave Macmillan.

Spangler, Todd. 2023. "HBO Max to Be Renamed 'Max' with Addition of Discovery+ Content, Launch Date and Pricing Revealed." *Variety*, April 12. https://variety.com/2023/digital/news/hbo-max-renamed-max-pricing-launch-date-1235532179/.

Taylor, James C. 2021. "Postmodern Parody in Animated Superhero Cinema." In *The Superhero Multiverse: Readapting Comic Book Icons in Twenty-First-Century Film and Popular Media*, edited by Lorna Piatti-Farnell. Lexington Books.

Zeller-Jacques, Martin. 2012. "Adapting the X-Men: Comic-Book Narratives in Film Franchises." In *A Companion to Literature, Film, and Adaptation*, edited by Deborah Cartmell. Wiley-Blackwell.

17

REHEARING THE SUPERHERO IN THE 21ST CENTURY

Superman, Wonder Woman, and Music

Steve Halfyard

In 2013, I published an essay that examined how superhero films had moved away from using scores built on easily identifiable musical themes. That same year, *Man of Steel* came out, beginning a new period of film production in the DC Extended Universe that appeared to be heading down the same road as the Marvel Cinematic Universe and the Avengers, with multiple DC Comics superhero characters appearing in solo films and going on to form the Justice League. Creative disagreements over the *Justice League* movie resulted in two versions of it (2017 and 2021) and, at the time of writing, the franchise has largely come to a halt, but what is notable about two of the biggest solo movies in that sequence, namely *Man of Steel* and *Wonder Woman* (2017) is the unequivocal return of film scores driven by strongly melodic, thematic writing.

In this essay, I examine these two films and the way in which their scores continue the project of "decolonising superhero cinema through music" that Dina AlAwadhi and Jason Ditter (2020) identify in *Thor: Ragnarok* (2017). As in that film, both of these scores specifically play against traditional musical tropes as a means of resistance to the conventional, implicitly colonial narrative of a benign external force that will take control and solve the problems of a society. Similarly, they engage with gendered tropes of what a powerful man or woman "sounds" like.

Man of Steel

In the late 1970s, John Williams wrote a pair of themes for two superheroic characters – Luke Skywalker and Superman – that encode in music a specific idea of masculine heroism and, indeed, heroic masculinity: they are energetically buoyant and supremely confident. Williams himself described Luke's theme, heard in the opening credits of *A New Hope* (1977), as "brassy, bold, masculine and noble" (quoted in Lerner 2004, 99). As Lerner observes, "The martial duple rhythms, the trumpet timbres for the melody and the leaping, disjunct quality of the melody's shape … are all ways that many composers have earlier connoted masculinity through music" (Lerner 2004, 99). An almost identical description could be given of the *Superman* theme. Williams's main themes for both films are characterized by similar rhythms, timbres, upwardly leaping gestures (musically leaping buildings in a single bound), and absolute tonal stability, that is, they use no destabilizing notes from outside the home key of the music that might send the music off in another tonal direction.

The heroic construction is reinforced by the orchestration and its emphasis on brass instruments. The melodic line is given to the horns and trumpets, with strings and wood-wind mostly in a supporting and decorative role; timpani and snare drum assist the rhythmic drive. The overall rhythm is that of a march, but within the *Superman* theme, Williams employs a dotted, short-long rhythm in the triplet figures, the rhythm of a galloping horse. These musical features are all part of what music theory would describe as the "military topic" that, as Raymond Monelle observes, reflects "the classical image of the hero; and … has several signifiers, notably the military march and the trumpet fanfare" (Monelle 2006, 6). Superman's theme conforms to what Robert Hatten identifies as the *victorious heroic* mode of the military topic, characterized in music with "marches, fanfare figures and drum riffs" and typically at a fast tempo and in a major key (Hatten 2014, 523). The energetic confidence and complete tonal stability of Superman's music point to a hero that no danger can genuinely threaten.

I have previously discussed Superman's shift away from such certainties to a melancholy and more psychologically complex characterization in Bryan Singer's 2006 *Superman Returns* (Halfyard 2013, 180–84). In the process, the film turns him into a messianic figure, willing to sacrifice himself for humanity. Despite the efforts to make Superman seem less sure of himself, more vulnerable, the film ultimately does nothing to make him any less God-like. The music turns to a spiritual, religious topic, with wordless voices singing an ethereal chorale as the principal new musical idea alongside Williams's original 1970s themes. Even though the melody is often stripped out, Williams's heroic march reaffirms Superman's heroic identity as he brings a crashing aircraft safely down in a baseball stadium early in the film. The galloping rhythms and trumpet fanfare reinforce the construction of Superman as victorious hero at the start of *Superman Returns*, a position confirmed by the end, despite the sacrifice and near-failure he experiences in the interim.

Whether he acts more as a vigilante crime-fighter or a messiah, Superman tends to fall into the role of colonial authority figure, no matter how benevolently he is presented. Superheroes are always at some level an outsider and are always set apart from the mainstream by their differences (alien from Krypton; god; eccentric billionaire; science experiment, intentional or accidental), and their self-appointed role as defender and enforcer of whatever they deem to be just for both individuals and wider populations reveals the colonialist narrative underpinning superhero fantasies. Chris Gavaler, for example, asserts that "since its earliest manifestations, the superhero genre has been a production of imperial culture" and although much of his argument focuses on 19th-century narratives, he illustrates this using Superman: "a mild-mannered citizen of Metropolis reveals himself to be an exotic alien with unparalleled powers fighting to safeguard his adoptive culture, a transformation that mirrors empire's claim as a rightfully dominating global power" (2014, 108).

Nonetheless, *Man of Steel* strives valiantly toward a more decolonized version of Superman, and music is part of the process. The usual music of superheroes in cinema encodes the tropes of colonialism through the use of the military topic, based as it is on the mechanisms of conquest and subjugation, the marching of soldiers and the signaling calls of the battlefield. Those regular march tempos, the affirmatory, ascendant fanfares, the use of horns and trumpets singing out over the body of the orchestra, and the "simplicity" of themes that avoid the intrusion of chromatic notes foreign to the theme's key, all serve to construct a symbolic figure of authority and moral certainty who stands above the masses as a heroic leader. However, in *Man of Steel*, the military topic is now largely the territory of General Zod and his minions: they are explicitly presented as colonizers, coming to Earth with their world engine to terraform it, create themselves a colony, and eliminate the indigenous population in the process. Superman's music conversely avoids many of the obvious militaristic tropes; and he is presented as fighting with the people of Earth against the Kryptonians, one of us more than one of them. He is aware of his problematic position as an alien, reassuring the military authorities that he is on their side, and presenting himself as an ally and an asset rather than someone who might wish to take control. Equally, he resists being controlled and used as a weapon according to anyone else's agenda. With the rare exception of some imaginative vandalism in retaliation to an uncouth bar customer, the examples we are shown of him using his abilities involve saving people from life-threatening situations rather than becoming a vigilante.

Superman's music, as well as avoiding the military topic, also does not belong exclusively to Clark Kent/Kal-El. With one exception, his group of themes is first used in association with Jor-El and Lara, his biological parents, before becoming associated with him; the exception is the gentle piano theme that is used for his relationship with Martha and Jonathan, his adoptive parents. In previous films, Superman's themes were exclusively his own, marking and celebrating his exceptionalism and his difference from mere Earthlings. In this film, the music works to show his connection to others, but there are also several occasions later in the film where other characters appropriate his themes.

Superheroes usually have just one theme representing their superheroism. This Superman has a group of themes that often interact with each other as melody and countermelody. Using my own labels, there is a "Mother" theme, initially associated with Lara, and later with Clark when he is hurt or vulnerable; the "Family" theme for his human relationships; "Hope," named for being heard at the point that Jor-El explains what the S actually means; and finally, a theme I am calling "Flight," heard very clearly when Superman masters the art of flying, which has the most in common with the military topic at the same time as involving ideas of striving and yearning.

The latter three themes all start with upward intervals of either a fourth or a fifth, both intervals that, as Lerner notes, are typically associated with a masculine-heroic idea in music and found in the opening of both the *Superman* and *Star Wars* heroic themes. Here, however, most of the important affective features of the military topic have been removed, often taking with them both the energy and confidence that were key to the heroic construction of Richard Donner's Superman, and which were still very much in play with Bryan Singer's. The "Family" theme, heard on piano, is quiet and profoundly gentle: it is hard to imagine a musical cue with less rhythmic drive (this theme can be heard on the full soundtrack at the end of the cue entitled "Young Clark Freaks"; the secondary theme intertwining with this is a theme representing Krypton). Pauses on the second and final note of each phrase feel like hesitations, undermining the music from even having a clear sense of pulse. After the initial upward ascending note, the melodic line in each phrase mostly descends, further undercutting any potential sense of heroic agency that upward leaps might create. Where film scores use a secondary theme for a male hero, super, or otherwise, it is usually a love theme and usually presents a woman as the object of a male gaze, the gaze made audible as it were. The "Family" theme plays a similar role here, allowing us to see Superman's loving side, but by making the subject of the theme the strong familial bond between Clark, Jonathan, and Martha, it sidesteps the issue of an eroticized male gaze and presents us instead with Superman as a loving son, with the gentleness of the love between him and his parents and, at times, with his uncertainty about his role in the wider world, away from the safety of his family. Families can be quite disposable in superhero narratives, but *Man of Steel* maintains Martha as an important character throughout the film, reinforcing the importance of her stabilizing influence on Clark and continuing to include Jonathan in this through the use of the theme in flashbacks that continue into the final moments of the film.

"Hope" also works against the unassailable certainty that was a key part of the agency of previous Supermen (the fullest version of the theme is heard in the first half of the cue "First Flight"). First, although it turns out to be in C major, it does not firmly establish this key until its third phrase, quite unlike Williams's harmonically unambiguous themes. Zimmer's theme then ascends, but with a sense of the effort involved. Each musical step upward feels hard-won, not like Williams's exuberant bounce but more of a slow and determined striving. Each step up is interrupted with a fall back down to the starting note, musically highlighting the process of pushing upward toward the goal of the full octave. When that goal is finally reached, rather than confirming the key, Zimmer audibly shifts the harmony into A flat major (in technical terms, the flattened submediant, but a genuinely chromatic move away from C major), followed by a second shift before bringing the theme back to C again. These unexpected tonal shifts seem to reinforce the sense of the journey and the effort involved in achieving the goal; and they also evoke the sense of transformation as the octave leap is reiterated with different harmonizations – the transformative power of hope – when that goal is achieved.

The heroic "Flight" theme gets one of its clearest outings when Clark learns to fly and is finally getting the hang of things (and is the theme heard in the second half of "First Flight"). This is the most conventionally heroic theme and the closest to the military topic with its use of a horn melody and drums. The music is still based around ascending leaps upward, now mostly fifths and sixths, but the unusual aspect here is the way the upward leaping phrases keep going – an upward leap, a fall back down, another, higher leap, another fall, and so on. In the flying scene, there are a dozen of these leap-fall phrases in succession. This emphasizes the sense of yearning in the theme that echoes the upward striving of "Hope." Williams's themes communicated the confidence and certainty of the superhero with regular, balanced musical phrases that quickly provided a sense of closure. Zimmer's heroic theme is much more mobile, more the theme of a superhero looking for answers than one who knows them all already.

Perhaps, the greatest confirmation of the way the score avoids constructing Superman in conventional terms is found in the battle sequences. In the first of these, as Superman fights two of Zod's followers in Smallville, his own themes are absent, and the fight is scored with the loud, fast, minor key, drum-driven music of the invading Kryptonians, plus a tritone theme that is used for perilous situations rather than being tied to a specific character. This Peril theme, heard in the latter half of the cue "We Have a Plan/ Terraforming," is widely used in the major conflict in which Superman battles the world engine on one side of the planet while Lois and the military prepare to send Zod and his ship back to the Phantom Zone on the other. It is only quite late in the scene, as it looks as if all is lost for Lois's Daily Planet colleagues on the streets of Metropolis, that we finally hear "Hope" as Superman gathers his strength and flies up into the heart of the world engine. However, what is notable in this scene as a whole is the way it demonstrates that Clark does not have exclusive use of these themes. As the computer-generated imprint of Jor-El tries to persuade Zod not to destroy Earth, he is accompanied by "Hope"; as Lois and the military line up for their run on Zod's ship, they too acquire "Hope" as part of their musical arsenal; and as Zod, in his final confrontation with Superman, accuses him of having destroyed Krypton, Zod himself is accompanied by "Hope," indicating the extent to which he regards himself as the last (if now lost) hope of Krypton.

Superman's battle with Zod also avoids using either the Hope or Flight themes, introducing a new and very obviously tragic theme to frame their fight, up to and including the point that Superman is forced to kill Zod. The main musical idea, therefore, avoids any triumphalist use of heroic music for Zod's defeat and replaces it with a theme that represents tragedy for both characters, Zod's loss of his hopes for a new Krypton and Kal-El's loss as he is forced to kill the only other Kryptonian left alive.

What then might we understand this music to be telling us about the Man of Steel and the kind of hero he is? The most iconic of superheroes is scored against type and instead of the easy confidence and unassailable power of the 1970s Superman, the powerful and nobly self-sacrificing version of the early 2000s, or even the dark determination of the various cinematic Batmen, the Man of Steel steps away from the military topic and from the tropes of triumphalism and conquest. Instead, his music constructs him as someone who is fundamentally gentle and who must struggle and strive rather than achieve victory effortlessly; and for whom victory itself is overshadowed by tragedy.

Wonder Woman

If Superman broke with convention by using multiple themes for the superhero, *Wonder Woman* was, to some extent, forced into a position of using more than one theme because of the musical material established for her in *Batman v Superman: Dawn of Justice* (2016). In this film, which introduced Gal Gadot in the role, Wonder Woman's theme, composed by Hans Zimmer and Junkie XL (the Dutch film composer, Tom Holkenborg) is openly described by Zimmer as emulating a banshee – that is, a shrieking and unwelcome harbinger of death – because he wanted the music to be less masculine. Zimmer says:

> One thing that has bugged me forever is that our superhero movies are so masculine and male generated. I wanted Wonder Woman to be … I wanted the music to be full of more female … but you know, I wanted a banshee wail, like you've never heard before.
> *(Zimmer in Eisenberg 2016)*

It might have been possible to build an entire score on this theme although it could have resulted in some cognitive dissonance between the idea of Diana as a compassionate warrior princess and the potential messages of the music. The Banshee theme has both precedents and parallels in scoring powerful women and reflects the particular challenge that there is no established musical model for scoring the female-heroic in the way there is for male superheroes; but the theme is not unproblematic, all of which makes it worth examining in more depth.

The Banshee theme has little common ground with the military topic. It may have a very audible drum beat, but the tempo is much too fast for a march and the meter is an asymmetric 7/8 (2+2+3 beats in each bar) rather than regular, duple (left-right marching) rhythms. The fanfare-style motifs of horn and trumpet battle calls are replaced with a chromatic motif on electric cello that is both constantly loud and distorted; and rather than emphasizing the open fifth of a fanfare, the most compelling interval here is the tritone, a dissonant interval often reserved in film music for monsters, supernatural evil, criminals, and aliens, and used as a key interval in the Peril theme in *Man of Steel*. The theme is, in short, unusually aggressive in comparison to conventional superhero themes, and the irregular meter, distortion, and dissonant intervals open it up to negative readings.

The main precedents for scoring a female superhero in this manner come not from film but television, and three important examples are found in the theme music of *Xena: Warrior Princess* (1995–2001); *Buffy the Vampire Slayer* (1997–2003), and *Alias* (2001–2006). A summary of the characteristics of these themes is shown in Table 17.1.

The theme of *Xena* is the only one that makes obvious reference to the military topic in its use of horns doubling the voices (appropriate, perhaps, given that Xena is a former military general). The other themes avoid the military topic and focus on modern, popular music idioms and instrumental sounds rather than the classical sound of the orchestra. An important part of leaving the classical orchestra behind is the focus on drum kit and guitars (*Wonder Woman*'s electric cello is almost indistinguishable from the sound of an electric guitar in Zimmer's cue). All four themes contain an idea of distortion, heard not only in the electric guitar and electric cello sounds of *Buffy*, *Alias*, and *Wonder Woman*, but also in the use of minor seconds in *Xena*, the clash of the voices producing an equivalent sense of distortion in the way vocal harmonics interact with each other when singing such close intervals. *Wonder Woman*'s theme has a fast, quasi-fanfare opening motif that then falls onto the dissonant tritone (Figure 17.1); *Alias*'s main melodic idea is a repeating four-note motif that describes a tritone (Figure 17.2). All four themes are notably fast: in terms of musical conventions, *allegro* (fast) starts at 120 beats per minute (bpm) and turns into *presto* (very fast) at 168 bpm. *Xena* and *Buffy* both fall into that latter category; *Alias* and *Wonder Woman* are merely fast but are still notably quicker than Williams's *Superman* main title, which is just on the edge of *allegro* at 120 bpm. While *Buffy* and *Alias* keep to a regular 4/4 meter, *Xena* and *Wonder Woman* both use the irregular 7/8 meter.

I have previously discussed (Halfyard 2010) how Buffy's theme tune corresponds to the male-gendered characteristics identified in a study by Philip Tagg with Bob Clarida and Anahid Kassabian (Tagg 1989; see Table 17.2). All four themes, including the allegedly less "masculine" *Wonder Woman* theme, have more in common with the male side of Tagg's analysis than the female. However, what Tagg identifies as male-coded music does not describe the type of music associated with the agency of male superheroes and is instead what one might hear for a car chase or a fight scene: fast, strumming, repetitive music that provides pace and energy. Such music does not, however, communicate the ideas of "noble" heroism typically

Table 17.1 Comparison of musical characteristics in four female-heroic themes

Musical characteristic	Xena: Warrior Princess	Buffy the Vampire Slayer	Alias	Wonder Woman
Idiom	Balkan folk song	Surfer punk	Techno	Rock
Tempo	190 bpm	190 bpm	140 bpm	144 bpm
Meter	7/8	4/4	4/4	7/8
Key intervals	Minor seconds	–	Tritone	Tritone
Tonality	Minor	Minor	Minor	Minor
Melodic instruments	Voices and horns	Electric guitar	Synth piano	Electric cello
Accompaniment instruments	Drums	Bass guitar, drum kit	Electronica, bass guitar, synth strings	Drums

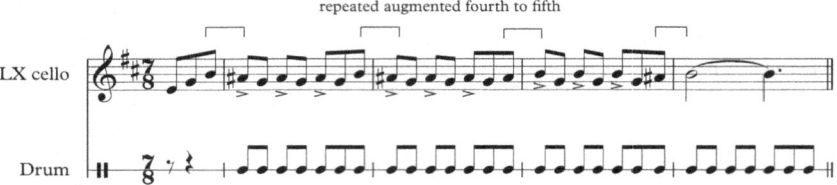

Figure 17.1   Wonder Woman

Figure 17.2   Alias

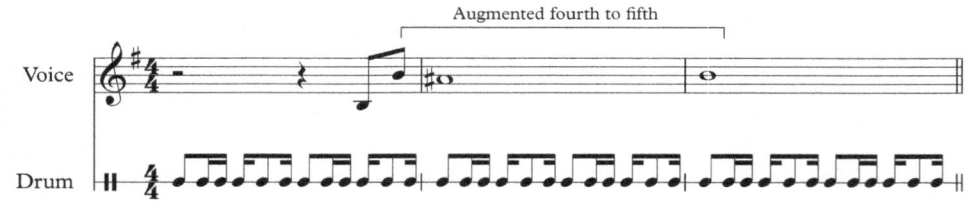

Figure 17.3   Thor Ragnarock "Immigrant Theme"

Table 17.2 Tagg's taxonomy of gendered musical characteristics

Musical parameter	Male characteristic	Female characteristic
Tempo	Faster	Slower
Note values	Shorter (therefore appearing faster)	longer (therefore appearing slower)
Rhythm	More rhythmic irregularities (e.g. syncopations, repeated notes)	More regular: normal dottings and divisions of note groups.
Phrasing	Staccato, quick repeating notes	Legato, smooth and flowing
Dynamics	Same volume throughout	Phrases get louder, then softer
Instruments (melody)	Electric guitar, synthesizer, trumpet, percussion	Strings (e.g. violin and cello), flute, piano
Instruments (accompaniment)	Strumming guitars, brass, synths, percussion (drums)	Strings, piano, woodwind

found in scores using the military topic to describe the nature of the hero, and which is often found in a film's main title to establish this idea of the heroic in advance of the narrative. For all four women, their themes perform this same function. Three are title themes, and Wonder Woman's is first used in *Dawn of Justice*, a film in which she is a fairly minor character, to present her to the audience at the point that her superheroic nature is revealed.

Given that they avoid the military topic, and calling them "masculine" seems of limited value for a type of music used for female superheroes since the mid-1990s (and one which Zimmer specifically considers to be "feminine"), what then is the topic of these themes? While this music stands up well against Tagg's masculine category, it also actually stands up quite well to Clive McClelland's description of another musical topic, Tempesta, which he pairs with the Ombra topic; so, storm and shadow, specifically a musical version of the 18th-century *Sturm und Drang* movement. Tempesta is the storm aspect, characterized by (among other things) an agitated or declamatory affect, fast tempo, minor keys, repeated notes, relentless motion, and irregular rhythms (McClelland 2014, 282).

The characteristics of the music used for these women represent what might be thought of as a danger topic. In representing strong, powerful, superheroic women, music constructs the idea of a powerful woman as a dangerous one in a way that their heroic male counterparts (with the exception of Batman) are not unusually constructed. Why female-led heroic narratives seem to use this danger topic rather than the military one could be argued as straightforwardly misogynistic, the musical equivalent of calling a man strong and a woman strident, but equally, it might be argued as a form of resistance to the underpinning colonialist ideologies of mainstream superhero narratives.

If the superhero is usually scored with the military topic's marching, brass-led themes, the superhero's enemies are likely to be scored in an opposing manner, using chromaticism, tritones, alternative scales, or atonality; syncopation, waltz rhythms (that is, triple rather than duple), irrational rhythms; strange and unfamiliar timbres; unusual juxtapositions of very high and very low pitch, or of very fast and very slow rhythms. These techniques serve to Other the superhero's opponents, the music positioning them as deviant and dysfunctional in contrast to the "self-evident" well-formedness of the superhero's sound. Almost all of the techniques above are used in the array of music accompanying the Joker in Danny Elfman's *Batman* score (1989) in combination with the non-orchestral sound of Prince's songs; Zimmer's music for the Joker in *The Dark Knight* (2008) is an exercise in distortion and sliding or otherwise manipulated pitches, with a fast, rhythmically steady ostinato interrupted by erratic bursts of rhythmically unpredictable noise. Williams's 1978 Lex Luthor theme is a fun-house mirror of Superman's march, with a chromatically quirky melody played in unlikely unison by a very low tuba and high flute, and with rhythmical irregularities upsetting the march rhythm. Zimmer's Lex Luthor (*Dawn of Justice*) also explores extremes, with ultralow, manipulated piano sounds, on the one hand, and a high, virtuosic violin, on the other, accompanied by baroquely chromatic chords. The music of villains is unpredictable, quirky, and unusual, in comparison to the "simple" and "natural" authority of the superhero's themes.

The four female-heroic themes discussed above evidently have more in common with villain themes than conventionally heroic ones. The major distinction is that of predictability. Where the villain themes all tend to introduce elements such as tempo shifts and sudden interpolations of unexpected musical ideas, the women's themes are all constructed from regular phrases that reiterate the same idea several times with minor, non-disruptive transformations (e.g. repeating a melodic shape but starting on a different note; repeating the same material using a different instrument). The themes are, therefore, musically coherent, avoid the conventions of the military topic, and possess a remarkable honesty about the nature of power, not concealing the raw aggression of the hero in action in the way that most heroic themes tend to do. It is for these reasons that accusations of potential misogyny in writing this kind of music for female superheroes needs to be balanced with a critique of the colonialism embedded in conventional superhero music.

This idea is further supported by examining an additional parallel to Wonder Woman's theme, which lies in the use of Led Zepplin's "Immigrant Song" (1972) in both *Thor: Ragnarok* (2017) and *The Girl with the Dragon Tattoo* (2011). The Banshee theme's main motif has a pronounced similarity to the distinctive sung phrase that opens the song, with the shared melodic shape that begins with a (heroic) rising fifth that then slips down to settle on the much more disruptive tritone (see Figures 17.1 and 17.3).

AlAwadhi and Ditter's discussion of the use of "Immigrant Song" in *Thor: Ragnarok* positions both the song and the superhero genre as "colonial fantasies" (2020, 89):

> Guitarist Jimmy Page has ... often referred to the band's musical influence from other cultures as the 'C-I-A Influence': Celtic, Indian, and Arabic music ... [influences that] were once under the control of the British Empire. As an English band, Led Zeppelin comes to function as an enforcer of empire, appropriating this music while invoking landscapes of overthrowing and subjugating the villainous Other.

As AlAwadhi and Ditter note, this is explicit in the lyrics of the song (e.g. "We are your overlords") and implicit in the history of superhero narratives. *Thor: Ragnarok* directly engages with the idea of the Asgardians as colonial enslavers and then reduces the Asgardians themselves to refugees after they lose their battle with Odin's long-imprisoned daughter, Hela. The film's two uses of the song mark Thor's journey in understanding the history of his people. At the start of the film, we hear it when he is still thoroughly subsumed within the colonial fantasy, indiscriminately slaughtering his opponents, actions which the song invites us to regard as both justified and heroic. The second time we hear it, he has learned the truth of how Asgard gained its wealth and power; and it now accompanies his fight against Hela, who is revealed as the original architect of Asgard's empire (see AlAwadhi and Ditter, 90–91). Thor "becomes the marginalized Other. The song's narrator becomes Hela, with her earlier declaration that 'Our destiny is to rule over all others' reinforcing *Immigrant Song's* imperial tone and revealing the darker meaning of the song" (91).

They further note that both Led Zepplin and Taika Waititi, the film's director, regarded the song as funny (90). Using it in the film was a key part of its agenda to present *Thor: Ragnarok* as much more comedic than the previous films in Thor's franchise and as a "radical superhero text," subverting the usual course of such texts "by bringing the audience's attention to the colonial and imperial past of the Asgardian empire" (90). What is striking is that the cover version of same song used in the opening credits of *The Girl with the Dragon Tattoo* has no hint whatsoever of humor. It allies itself even more strongly with the group of themes used for heroic women in its use of a faster tempo and more distortion than is heard in the original, both on the instruments and the female voice singing the lyrics; the words are often indecipherable due to these distorting effects. Lisbeth, the eponymous Girl, is a highly problematic figure: while, on the one hand, she is a central female character who does not conform to conventional ideas of feminine beauty, she is also shown as socially and emotionally dysfunctional; and her response to being violently abused is to take equally violent revenge, without ever seeming less of a victim. The film (like the novel) persists in presenting her as "broken" (see Schorn 2013). The song that opens the film, then, with its pounding rhythms, noisy distortions, and inaudible lyrics sung by a female voice not only constructs the violence and danger of Lisbeth's world, but also symbolically renders her incoherent and unheard.

Ragnarok offers the superhero narrative as "reflective nostalgia," challenging the overly coherent narrative of the traditional "restorative" narrative (Zornado and Reilly 2021, 192–93) and using well-known music that is nonetheless quite unlike the usual music of the male superhero to help make its point. Although *Xena* and *Buffy*, in particular, have the time and space to reflect on and question the nature of their central characters' power at various points in their extended television narratives, it is ultimately difficult to argue *Wonder Woman* as a reflective rather than restorative text. *Wonder Woman* fails, ultimately, to challenge the superhero's underpinning colonial narrative. Gavaler's description at the start of this essay of how Superman stands as a symbol of a globally dominating power adapts to this version of Wonder Woman with little difficulty, and throughout the film, she repeatedly takes the same kind of unilateral action that male superheroes are prone to. The music in her 2017 film supports this: the Banshee theme is used only twice, becoming representative of her power when she unleashes her divine wrath. The rest of the film uses a theme based around the same kind of upward-leaping brass fanfares found in male superhero military-topic themes, binding her firmly into the colonialist myth of the noble hero who comes to bring order to a troubled world.

Ultimately, the issue here is the one this essay started with: *Wonder Woman* does not start out from the same position as *Man of Steel* in being able to subvert and reject the established narratives and established sounds of the superhero, as those narratives and sounds have not belonged to women to begin with. The *Wonder Woman* score creates an orchestral superheroic theme unlike anything else written for a woman in the current era of superhero films, balancing this with the Banshee theme that connects her to superheroic women on television; and other films since 2017 have continued to explore the musical construction of the female superhero. *Captain Marvel* (2019) follows the same two-pronged approach as *Wonder Woman*, combining another upward-leaping brass fanfare theme with the use of a sassy pop track ("Just a Girl," in its original 1995 version by the band No Doubt) for Carol Danvers' final battle with the Kree as she comes fully into her powers; *Black Widow* (2021) has a pair of connected themes (a melancholy melodic theme and a short, chromatic fanfare motif) both of which, as in *Man of Steel*, are used not just for Natasha Romanov but for all the members of her dysfunctional pseudo-family. Nonetheless, the project of discovering what a superheroic woman sounds like is ongoing.

Superhero soundtracks have continued to engage with complex musical themes as a mechanism for constructing the identity of the superhero, and as such, the composers have had to consider what, specifically, the music needs to do in presenting the superhero both as a sympathetic individual, but also as a figure of astonishing power in an era where power has been thoroughly problematized through critical engagement with the West's colonial history. In the context of a contemporary narrative, this results in *Man of Steel* engaging directly with the issues of colonialism that have always underpinned Superman's narratives. *Wonder Woman* and other recent female-led superhero films are in the process of negotiating how one writes music for a powerful woman without simply falling back on to the established, male-coded, colonialist tropes of the military topic. The films discussed here strive to construct superheroes for the 21st century, and music plays an active role in allowing their central characters to play against gender tropes, genre expectations, and assumptions around the nature of power, while remaining audibly superheroic.

References

AlAwadhi, Dina, and Dittmer, Jason. 2020. "'We Come from the Land of the Ice and Snow': De-Colonising Superhero Cinema through Music." *Politik* 23 (1): 88–93.

Eisenberg, Eric. 2016. "One Change Wonder Woman Should Make From Batman V Superman, According To Hans Zimmer." *Cinemablend*, March 30. https://www.cinemablend.com/new/One-Change-Wonder-Woman-Should-Make-From-Batman-v-Superman-According-Hans-Zimmer-121617.html.

Gavaler, Chris. 2014. "The Imperial Superhero." *PS: Political Science & Politics* 47 (1): 108–111.

Halfyard, Janet K. 2010. "Love, Death, Curses, and Reverses (in E minor): Music, Gender, and Identity in *Buffy the Vampire Slayer* and *Angel*." In *Music, Sound, and Silence in Buffy the Vampire Slayer*, edited by Paul Attinello, Janet K Halfyard, and Vanessa Knights. Ashgate Publishing.

Halfyard, Janet K. 2013. "Cue the Big Theme? The Sound of the Superhero." In *The Oxford Handbook of New Audiovisual Aesthetics*, edited by John Richardson, Claudia Gorbman, and Carol Vernallis. Oxford University Press.

Hatten, Robert. 2014. "The Troping of Topics in Mozart's Instrumental Works." In *The Oxford Handbook of Topic Theory*, edited by Danuta Mirka. Oxford University Press.

Lerner, Neil. 2004. "Nostalgia, Masculinist Discourse and Authoritarianism." In *Off The Planet: Music, Sound, and Science Fiction Cinema*, edited by Philip Hayward. John Libbey.

McClelland, Clive. 2014. "*Ombra* and *Tempesta*." In *The Oxford Handbook of Topic Theory*, edited by Danuta Mirka. Oxford University Press. https://doi.org/10.1093/oxfordhb/9780199841578.013.0011.

Monelle, Raymond. 2006. *The Musical Topic: Hunt, Military and Pastoral*. Indiana University Press.

Schorn, Johanna. 2013. "Empowerment through Violence: Feminism and the Rape-Revenge Narrative in *The Girl with the Dragon Tattoo*." *Gender Forum: An Internet Journal for Gender Studies* 41: 8–17.

Tagg, Philip. 1989. "An Anthropology of Stereotypes in TV music?" *Swedish Musicological Journal* 71: 19–42.

Zimmer, Hans. 2013. *Man of Steel: Original Motion Picture Soundtrack*. Water Tower Music WTM39424, compact disc.

Zornado, Joseph, and Reilly, Sara. 2021. *The Superhero with a Thousand Faces*. Palgrave Macmillan. https://doi.org/10.1007/978-3-030-85458-4.

18

COSPLAY CAPERS

The Twinned Genealogies, Cultural Imaginaries, and Affects of Superhero Cosplay

Paul Mountfort

Costume Play

Who does not remember, as a child, donning more or less makeshift costumes based on some superhero, villain, or other figure from popular media, regarding themselves in the mirror, and engaging in a form of fantasy role-play? Growing up in the 1970s, I vividly recall squeezing into a Spider-Man costume, tights and all, casting a critical eye on myself through the mesh eye slits, and scissoring up the passage wall as best I could with my slippery soles. "Look out! Here comes the Spider-Man!" Typically, adulthood involves putting away such "childish things" but not for cosplayers, calling into question this deep cultural bias against play itself. This chapter explores the twinned genealogies of cosplay and the superhero genres of comics media. I argue that the two are intimately connected from birth, as it were, and that they share overlapping yet distinct cultural imaginaries. Imaginaries can act as bridges to the affective planes of the Imaginary and beyond. Correspondingly, this study will speculatively sketch a psychoanalytic model of superhero cosplay and, where that reaches its outer limits, a schizoanalytic one.

Affinities between the superhero genre and cosplay at the foundational level are fairly self-evident. The superheroes of early comics media had dual identities and sought to hide or disguise behind their everyday personas their extraordinary heroic selves. They were clothed as Clark Kent, Diana Prince, and Bruce Wayne in the everyday world; Superman, Wonder Woman, and Batman when suping it up. Similarly, a committed cosplayer who is a student, receptionist, or tattooist "by day" becomes, in the extraordinary world of the cosplay convention, a "caped crusader" of one kind or another, whether hero, villain, or somewhere in between, drawn from the fictional worlds of popular culture. While the superhero subgenre is only one subset of the panoply of publicly available media texts cosplayers utilize, one could say that the subgenre and the tropes associated with such figures are in many ways metonymic of cosplay itself.

Cosplay scholar Ellen Kirkpatrick first explicitly theorized this metonymy in a 2015 article correspondingly titled "Toward New Horizons: Cosplay (Re)Imagined through the Superhero Genre, Authenticity, and Transformation." Kirkpatrick set out to "identify and explore connections between cosplay and costuming practices characterizing the superhero genre," with

 DOI: 10.4324/9781003366911-21

cosplay positioned as "a simultaneous performance – as source character and as member of the cosplaying community" (Kirkpatrick 2015, [0.1]). On the first count, she argues the practice is "readable as an embodied reception of the unstable modes of identity worked within the superhero genre" ([0.1]). However, she frames her discussion within "concepts of authenticity, context, and transformation" ([0.1]), which are rather different from my interests here.

Kirkpatrick discusses well-known "alter/hero" pairings in the source media, with the proviso that "Popular and easy considerations of the alter/hero pairing [which] imagine it in terms of simple duality" are ultimately limiting ([1.3]). The duality of such figures resides in how, with two distinct identities inhabiting one character, when one is present, the other is by definition absent. For Kirkpatrick, the "alter" ego is the everyday one (e.g., Bruce Banner and Peter Parker) which becomes overrun by the super aspect, such as the Hulk, and Spider-Man. While she also discusses other figures such as Superman and Wonder Woman, where the originating identity is the super aspect disguised by the everyday Clark Kent or Diana Prince, she does not separate these out as opposing types. The important thing for Kirkpatrick is that "both aspects hold authenticity; within specific contexts, both are accepted and considered as real and true" ([1.3]). This accords with her concern, after Derrida, with the inadequacy of binary identity as "inherently unequal, marked by violent hierarchy," and the concomitant danger of "the normalizing or naturalizing of the superior as the general, the normal, or the benchmark" ([1.4]).

Superhero studies more generally demarcate between characters who are born supes versus those "everydays" who transform. Regarding the latter, Richard Reynolds notes that "These heroes experience a profound alteration of their identity, often marked by trauma or accident, highlighting the idea that heroism is thrust upon them rather than chosen" (1992, 34). By contrast, characters like Superman and Wonder Woman are the a priori forms, their civilian identities serving merely as a disguise or performance. Superman's Clark Kent persona, for instance, is often described as a way to only "pass" as human. Peter Coogan contends that "Superman's civilian identity, Clark Kent, is less a true identity and more a mask, reflecting his alien nature and the distance he maintains from humanity" (2006, 46). At first glance, you might assume that the transformation trope associated with the former is more appropriate as a governing metonym for cosplay. Real humans are mundane and terrestrial by birth, after all. However, one could conversely argue that cosplay provides a pretext to express a priori or emergent elements of otherness within ourselves, that is, through superhero personas to flirt with alternate selves and associated affects not easily available outside cosplay.

Here, I wish to pursue an avenue of speculation which is twofold. On the one hand, if we accept the basic metonymy between the superhero genre and cosplay as residing in the masking and unmasking of alternate identities, how is this elucidated by the genealogies of each, and the cultural imaginaries from which they arose? On the other, if we accept that through cosplay the psyche becomes affectively nested in cultural texts themselves rooted in broader imaginaries, what can we say about cosplay in relation to emergent senses of self within a broadly psycho-analytical framework? Lacan's orders of the Imaginary, Symbolic, and Real are helpful here, though at a certain point, psychoanalysis gives way to a provocation for schizoanalysis with its cognizance of the "desiring-machines" of late capital in the Deleuzo-Guattarian sense.

Superhero Cosplay's Twinned Imaginaries

Cultural imaginaries are narrative and fictive skeins that bind together to act as powerful determinants in social life. As conceptualized by Charles Taylor, they involve "the ways people imagine their social existence, how they fit together with others, how things go on between them and their fellows" (Taylor 2004, 23). These imaginaries are not just theoretical constructs but lived embodiments in various cultural practices, including, of course, through popular cultural pursuits such as cosplaying or consuming comics media. Here, I want to sketch a brief genealogy in the Foucauldian sense of the imaginaries underpinning cosplay and superhero figures from comics media as suggestive of their points of intersection and divergence.

From Costuming to Cosplay

Thèresa Winge has dated early or proto-cosplay to the late 19th century, with Jules Verne's hosting of a "masked ball" in 1877 where guests dressed as characters from his novels (Winge 2018, 17). There are also antecedents in commercial promotions involving the titular lead from one of the earliest science fiction strip cartoons, A. D. Condo's *Mr. Skygack, from Mars* (1907–1917) (Mountfort et al. 2018, 48). However, it is widely agreed that cosplay's immediate precursor, costuming, debuted at the inaugural World Science Fiction Convention (Worldcon) on the fringes of the 1939 New York World's Fair. There, dynamic duo Forrest J. Ackerman and Myrtle R. (Morojo) Douglas comported themselves attired in "futuristic costumes" that riffed off the pulp magazine artwork of Frank R. Paul and Orson Welles' screen adaptation of H. G. Wells' *Things to Come* (1936). Though Superman (*Action Comics* #1, June 1938) narrowly predates the inception of costuming at Worldcon, Ackerman, and Douglas did not model the superhero genre, but a science fictional one.

The couple (they never married) were instrumental in the formation of fan cultures as we know them today. The influential Welles adaptation, which envisioned a technologically advanced, utopian society risen out of the ashes of a global war, provided inspiration for Morojo's space-age costume designs and use of state-of-the-art Celanese rayon. Thus, she may be credited as the progenitor of fannish costume construction and provides an archetype both for female fan labor and for the now niche practice of creative cosplay; that is, when a cosplayer models their own fictional character. As co-editors of one of the first fanzines, *Voice of the Imagi-Nation* (VOM), which ran 1939–1949, and more widely as publishers, she and Ackerman championed sci-fi when it was despised as lowbrow and fanfiction when it was almost unknown.

The context in which Worldcon took place, adjacent to the World's Fair, helps us to recognize the wider imaginary surrounding these developments. On the one hand, the Fair was saturated with the spirit of techno-optimism (Clute 1995; Roberts 2016), with its dominant imagery of futuristic spires, domes, and space-age transportation. Willy Ley's fabled talks on rocketry, blending science fact with fiction, channeled a broader cultural belief that further technological triumphs were within humanity's grasp (Roberts 2016). The event was also infused with themes of the Golden Age of Science Fiction (Clute 1995). Exhibits immersed attendees in visions of space exploration, robots, and futuristic cities. This optimism extended to utopian ideas of societal progress, where technological advancements would bring fixes to global issues like disease, poverty, and war. On the other hand, the Fair opened the same month that Germany invaded Czechoslovakia, a year after its annexation of Austria. As several of Wells' novels aver, science fiction is just as capable of envisioning dystopian futures of failure and subjugation as future utopias. It may be too early to talk about a counter-imaginary as such but attendees of Worldcon were already out on a literal and metaphorical rim from the main proceedings. Modern fan cultures have typically arisen from such margins, far removed from today's ubiquity of nerd, geek, and otaku cultures, and the costuming displayed at Worldcon was more or less a sideshow to the wider proceedings.

Within a short year, however, the craze was on, and by the 1940 Chicago Worldcon, the tradition of an annual Masquerade of costumed participants was established, originally as a kind of fancy dress ball (Resnick 2006, 106). While precise dating of these events from scattered accounts and archival photographs is difficult, it does not appear that superheroes loomed large in the Cons of the 1940s, 1950s, or even 1960s. This is less surprising when we recall that these were sci-fi Cons, not yet the megacons nor more dedicated niche events, such as anime expos, of today. In this formative phase, elaborate costumes featuring stock SF figures, such as mad scientists and characters inspired by pulp fiction covers, were common. Instead, it seems the meteoric rise of comics-inspired superheroes only really took off in the wake of later small-screen adaptations, especially campy TV series such as *Batman* (1966–1968) and *Wonder Woman* (1975–1979).

With the birth of Comic-Con in 1970, the strands of costuming and comics media truly began to fuse into the sorts of fandoms we are familiar with. The San Diego–based convention and its spin-offs were originally relatively niche affairs with considerable representation by independent comics artists, though attendees frequently donned costumes from big-ticket comics franchises such as DC and Marvel. Japan's equivalent, Comiket, was inaugurated in 1975, and by 1979, if not earlier, manga and anime characters were evidenced in Comic-Con Masquerades. Though this chapter is largely concerned with Western cosplay and superhero representations, it is worth mentioning that the neologism "cosplay" as a replacement term for costuming was imported from Japan in the 1980s, though ironically deriving from a Japanese appropriation of costume-play (*kosuchuumu purei*), which was contracted to *kosu-pure* (cosplay) (Ashcraft and Plunkett 2014, 17). Between the poles of cultural production constituted by the world's two largest cultural producers, by the 1980s and 1990s, cosplay and its supes were poised to take on the world.

The Golden Age of Comics

While comics media took some time to occupy center stage in the US convention scene, their originating cultural moment was intimately twinned with costuming's. Superman landed a year before the first Worldcon in *Action Comics* #1, against the same backdrop of rising conflict in Europe and Asia-Pacific. Batman followed shortly after (*Detective Comics* #27, May 1939), then Captain America (*Timely Comics* #1, March 1941) and Wonder Woman (*All-Star Comics* #8, October 1941) in the year the US joined the war. The heroism of these figures blended more-or-less superhuman powers with utopian ideals of the common good, or at least, the Western imperium which they would soon be tasked to uphold.

All but Batman literally wore the regalia of the Stars and Stripes. Superman in his blue leotard with red accoutrements; Captain America's white-starred blue bodysuit with a red-and-white striped lower torso; and Wonder Woman's red bustier festooned with a golden eagle above a star-spangled skirt. All three would be rapidly mobilized to project idealized American power on the world stage, acting as a foil to contemporary geopolitical anxieties (Wright 2001, 13). Indeed, comics were quickly requisitioned as propaganda tools, with supes, like soldiers, defending civilization against malevolent forces (Wright 2001, 49). Captain America was the patriotic hero who fought against fascism, mirroring the US cultural imaginary of a just and powerful nation standing against tyranny (Fingeroth 2004, 29). Wonder Woman would symbolize women's potential to contribute to the war effort while lassoing some conventional gender norms (Madrid 2009, 49; see Hanley 2014, 54; Lepore 2014, 175). As secretary of the Justice Society of America, she also led the first and decidedly jingoistic superhero team in the genealogy of comic books (Wright 2001, 62; Hanley 2014, 49). By and large, these figures' super powers stood for projections of Western technological prowess, mixed with fantasy tropes. They would emerge from the war perfectly suited for redeployment in the Atomic Age.

The Silver to Iron Ages of Comics

The dark and brooding Batman was a harbinger of the Silver Age of comics of the mid-1950s to early 1970s, with its more complex, flawed ensemble of characters, coincident with the Cold War, Space Race, and growing anxiety about nuclear technology. The world could burn at the push of a button, and superheroes were cultural mediators between the age's promises and the perils of scientific and technological progress. Marvel's Spider-Man (*Amazing Fantasy* #15, August 1962) is further emblematic of this turn. Like Batman, his costume is not just a disguise but a utility suit, a technological carapace extending human prowess into super powers gained from a radioactive spider. As Reynolds notes, "Spider-Man is a hero for an age in which power comes with responsibility and consequence, reflecting the fears of unchecked technological progress" (1992, 56). Unlike Superman or Captain America, Peter Parker is a teenager with relatable problems: school, work, and girls. He goofs and suffers personal losses, resonating with a cultural moment of doubt and ennui.

Marvel Comics soon introduced a new kind of superhero team, embodied in the Fantastic Four (1961), the Avengers, and X-Men (1963), who were notably alienated from the mainstream. The latter, coinciding with Kennedy's assassination and the fall of the Camelot-imaginary, took the stage in an age of anxiety that also saw the unprecedented rise of the counterculture. As Johnson writes, "The X-Men represent a form of social critique, offering a symbolic commentary on marginalization and the anxieties surrounding human difference in a world increasingly shaped by science and technology" (2013, 91). Here, we might genuinely talk about the emergence of a counter-imaginary – allied to Cornelius Castoriadis' (1987) "radical imaginary," referring to the ability of a society to imagine radical breaches from established norms – in opposition to the largely positivist one preceding it.

Superheroes, then, served as a mirror for the collective desires and anxieties of changing times. As Karin Kukkonen observes, "The superhero genre's enduring appeal lies in its ability to mediate between the fantastical and the real, offering a space where cultural desires and fears can be played out and resolved" (2013, 212). Thus, by the rebellious 1970s, the scene was set for complex identity play around such characters in the increasingly bustling convention scene. They were not mere action figures but conflicted characters with complex inner lives who often lived on the cultural margins, like many of their fans. Some scholars have identified a Bronze Age of comics when "superhero comics took on darker and more socially relevant themes, reflecting the turbulent times of the 1970s and 1980s" (Wright 2001, 221). *Watchmen* (1986) from Alan Moore et al. springs to mind. Arguably, we now inhabit the following Iron or "Dark Age" of comics media marked by morally ambiguous characters, violent storytelling, and the deconstruction of the traditional superhero archetype (Duncan and Smith 2009, 156), appropriate perhaps in an era of ecological overshoot and superhero overload. In toto, these contested cultural imaginaries would provide superhero cosplayers with an arena for both engagement with and escape from the cultural dominants of their era.

Psychoanalytic Speculations

What does it mean to take on such personas within the cosplaying context, where storied figures nested in richly layered cultural imaginaries are made flesh, as it were, in the costumed body? What type of play is this? What are its affects? There have been a number of published fanthropologies, exploring the cosplay experience from direct accounts by cosplayers, including embedded testimonies by cosplayer-researchers. It is not my intention here to reprise fanthropological approaches so much as to speculate on the underlying psychoanalytics at play in the practice of superhero cosplay, though my understanding is grounded in such accounts, and supplemented by my own Con attendance over many years and critical practice as a cosphotographer (see Mountfort et al. 2018, 45–102; 2019, 91–110).

Lacan's tripartite of the Imaginary, Symbolic, and Real might seem too obvious a choice, but there has been surprisingly little engagement of Lacanian psychoanalytic theory in cosplay scholarship, including the major monographs. My co-authors and I address the subject only glancingly in *Planet Cosplay: Costume Play, Identity and Global Fandom* (2018), as does Frenchy Lunning in *Cosplay: The Fictional Mode of Existence* (2022), while Lacan does not figure at all in Therèsa Winge's ethnographically oriented *Costuming Cosplay: Dressing the Imagination* (2018). However, Lacan's developmental orders seem ideal for mediating between cultural imaginaries and the embodied selves of cosplaying subjects.

Conflating imaginaries and the Imaginary might sound like a bad pun. Lacan's Imaginary is not, of course, to be confused with cultural imaginaries as such and centers on the formation of the ego and the subject's relation to idealized images, particularly through the *mirror stage*, where we construct a coherent but illusory sense of self (Lacan 2006). By contrast, cultural imaginaries, as described by theorists like Cornelius Castoriadis and Charles Taylor, refer to the shared, socially constructed symbols and values that shape how a society imagines itself (Strauss 2006), more akin to Lacan's Symbolic order. However, while Lacan's Imaginary is distinct from these essentially Symbolic values, cultural imaginaries function on a collective level to influence the formation of group identities and societal norms. As Lacan points out, the Imaginary order functions at the level of fictive unity (Lacan 2006), and the individual fictive is reflective of the shared narratives of identity and power societies collectively build (Steger 2008). These dual structuring forces can be seen as coinciding in the embodied citation of cultural texts that occurs in cosplaying moments. These concerns lead us beyond the Imaginary in the Lacanian schema to the Symbolic and the Real to further tease out the terrain.

The Imaginary

In Lacan's schema, the Imaginary is the realm of images, identifications, and the ego. This is most famously articulated in the mirror stage, a critical moment in the development of subjectivity. This is the catalyzing event, an infant's recognition of their own image in a mirror, giving rise to the sense, or illusion, of self as unified and whole. Lacan explains that the self is constituted through this misrecognition, or *méconnaissance*, as the infant's sense of self becomes tied to an external representation (Lacan 2006, 75–76). The child identifies with the image, or *imago*, of their body, yet this image is exterior to them. We never entirely escape the mirror phase. As Lacan avers, "The mirror stage is far from a mere phenomenon that occurs in the development of the child: it illustrates the conflictual nature of the dual relationship" (Lacan 2006, 76). Cosplay can be understood as an extension of this process of identification with external images, both in the sense that it extends the self-regarding gaze into a panoply of material costumes and accoutrements but also in that it extends the Imaginary temporally as a site of ongoing negotiation. Of course, the mirror is always the site of repeated returns (and of the return of the repressed, as the specter of physical aging "in the looking glass" reveals). In a sense, all the images of ourselves, we see projected back to us in the mirror world are masks. But as the name suggests, in cos*play*, the duality of this reflection functions within a conscious strategy of play. Cosplayers adopt the accoutrements of a fictional character, aligning their sense of self, at least fleetingly, with an idealized, often heroic or otherworldly figure. However, while the identification of the child with their imago is naive, the cosplayer's identification with the costume and character is knowing, a mediated form of "as if." The costume becomes a vehicle for the cosplayer to perform an idealized version of themselves, a suped-up one, albeit rooted in broader cultural imaginaries and counter-imaginaries.

This process of identification is not purely superficial and should not be taken to mean – as the hostile, touristic gaze of outsiders often assumes – that cosplayers have merely refused to grow up and embrace adulthood. As Dylan Evans notes, the Imaginary is "the register of identification" (Evans 1996, 82), meaning that it underpins the construction of the ego and personal identity. For the cosplayer, this identification or identity play is a pleasurable immersion (*plaisir*) in the fantasy of being someone else – somebody with special powers, and with a double identity. However, this identification is always incomplete, as the cosplayer is still aware of the gap between their real self and the fictional personas they embody. This echoes the Lacanian view that the self is never fully realized but is constantly mediated by external images and the gaze of the Other. Furthermore, for Lacan (1992, 184), plaisir is a regulated, moderated form of enjoyment governed by the pleasure principle and may thus act as a brake on attaining a deeper *jouissance* – a more complex, often paradoxical affect that exceeds regulated pleasure (plaisir).

The Symbolic

We have seen that cosplayers not only identify, however vicariously, with superhero characters on an Imaginary level but also engage with them within the Symbolic matrix of cultural representation. The Symbolic order in Lacan's theory is also the domain of language, social laws, and cultural codes. As Žižek has it, "the Symbolic order functions as a web of intersubjective relations, maintained by the subject's entry into the system of signs and language" (Žižek 2009, 97). It is through entry into the Symbolic order that the subject becomes a speaking being, capable of relating to others within the phallogocentric regime. Under Lacan's construction of the Freudian mommy-daddy-me triad, transition into the Symbolic is marked by the introduction of the *Name-of-the-Father*, the figure that enforces the prohibition of incest, steering the subject away from the Imaginary dyad with the mother (Lacan 2006, 214–215). Whatever the problematics of these Freudian framings, it is hard to argue with the basic mechanism of repression within the social order; the more-or-less eternal frustration of the ego's covert desires, leading to sublimation and conflict. This is also the realm in which we navigate meaning and subjectivity through cultural codes and shared narratives. For cosplay as a social practice, the Symbolic order is evident most concretely in the shared conventions, narratives, and roles that define its boundaries and parameters. It operates within a highly structured form of play (the ludic) and within broader fan cultures where participants adopt roles, follow conventions (such as how to accurately represent characters), and engage with a shared realm of pop-cultural mythology.

At the same time, the characters cosplayers model from comics, films, and video games are also part of this Symbolic order, representing archetypes, values, and meanings that are collectively recognized by the community and are expressions of wider cultural imaginaries. However, within fandoms, as with the wider culture, counter-imaginaries also operate. Thus, a cosplayer dressing as a superhero might not identify with the character's culturally dominant Symbolic function (such as upholding the American imperium) at all, but rather with the counter values that the character putatively embodies, such as justice, strength, and resistance. Cosplay's affinity groups provide space for disrupting and subverting the symbolic system of meaning that extends beyond personal identification into contesting broader cultural narratives. When Coogan talks about Superman as merely "passing" as Clark Kent, we are reminded of the capacity for queering the Symbolic order. Crossplayers swap out genders and races, both fantasy and real world. In East Asia where cosplayers frequently disguise their activities from peers, family, and the workplace, identity play holds particular horrors, as the prohibitions against drag (crossplay, in the cosplaying context) suggest (see Mountfort 2023). The act of cosplaying can be seen as subversive, a re-negotiation of the subject's identity in the co-opting of other identities from these media, reflecting Lacan's notion of the Symbolic as the space in which subjectivity is defined in relation to the Other. As Lacan emphasizes, the gaze of the Other plays a crucial role in the constitution of the subject (1978, 72). Cosplayers perform their roles in front of an audience, whose gaze validates their performance, though at times it may also be agonistic. The cosplayer also becomes Other, or multiple others, to themselves. In this sense, cosplay is not merely an individual fantasy but a social act that is mediated by the play of intersecting selves and others within the Symbolic order.

The Real

The Real, in Lacan's framework, is the most elusive of the three registers. Outside of language and representation, it cannot be fully symbolized or imagined. The Real represents the limits of human understanding, being the kernel of existence that resists assimilation into the Imaginary or Symbolic realms. It is associated with trauma, the unnamable, and the disruption of meaning. For cosplayers, the Real might manifest in moments where the constructed fantasy breaks down, as moments of disillusionment when a cosplayer's idealized vision of a character does not match the realities of their experience in costume. As Joan Copjec argues, the Real represents the "point of impasse" in human subjectivity, where the limits of identification and representation are encountered (1994, 204). The outfit is too tight, security won't allow my sword on the premises, hentai leeches are circling for a panty shot, *you are too old to be here, aren't you ashamed of yourself*? In my photo-essays from cosplay conventions, I linger on the spectacle of cosplayers in outlandish costumes juxtaposed with the more mundane settings of hallways and cafeterias, where the light is often too bright or too dim, the magical girl from an anime stuffs her mouth with a hotdog or the Arrow-boy sits exhausted on the sidelines. In such moments, the Real disrupts the Imaginary harmony of identification and the Symbolic network of recognition. Or are such moments mere realism rather than the Real? Despite the immersive nature of cosplay, there is always an aspect that remains inaccessible, beyond capture. The cosplayer feels alienated from the character they portray, and/ or the symbolic recognition from others does not align with their internal sense of identity.

Desire is eternally frustrated because its achievement is the primal sin, yet not to achieve it is to be left always wanting. This is not to say that the Lacanian Real is to be conflated solely with disappointment or the repressions of the Symbolic order. That which escapes symbolization and resists being integrated into language opens the door to radical possibilities, unscripted by its social structures and strictures. Julia Kristeva's (1984) "poetic language" resides not in meter or verse but the ruptures and gaps from which the unconscious erupts and directly speaks. I believe myself, over many years as a cosphotographer clicking away at such conventions, to have witnessed and perhaps captured such moments of reverie, even jouissance in the faces of participants, masked or unmasked. A kind of psychological transportation, as Joel Gn names it in his appositely titled article "Queer Simulation" (2011, 588), appears to be taking place. Lack becomes a portal to other spaces, beyond representation. Imbricated in the traumatic are moments of ecstasy or transcendence, intense satisfaction or fulfillment beyond the constraints of normal pleasure. At this point, however, a schizoanalytic framework may be of more help in gesturing to these outer limits than a psychoanalytic one.

Conclusion: The Call of the Schizoanalytic

Associating cosplay practice with the schizoid might seem like another bad pun: this time on the discredited popular cultural linking of schizophrenia to multiple personality disorder. Some superheroes may be somewhat schizoid in this unreconstructed sense of the term but in a Deleuzo-Guattarian analysis, this may not be a bad thing. David Burrows and Simon O'Sullivan describe schizoanalysis as a project of

> experiments that dissemble and dissolve the self and other configurations and modes of organisation, but that also propose that an individual is composed of a diversity of different individuations, of other durations, both organic and inorganic […] it is schizoanalysis that reveals that a sense of self can be made and unmade.
>
> *(2019, 59–60)*

Schizoanalysis was Gilles Deleuze and Félix Guattari's rebellious retort to Freudian and Lacanian psychoanalysis. In *Anti-Oedipus: Capitalism and Schizophrenia* (1983), they set out to explode the Oedipal myth (pun intended), which positions the incestuous drive as *the* primal desire at the frustrated root of all desires. Close, but no cigar. Instead, they argue that this myth is a con, a ruse staged to convince us that our desires are always doomed either to frustration, or utter dissolution in their fulfillment. By contrast, they argue that incest has been set up as the primal taboo that justifies all taboos and the policing of them. If we can be frightened into disavowing our desires because of the filthy fount of their origin, we can be controlled by the Father and the Law. If, however, the taboo-of-all-taboos is against something we have never actually wanted (it is ridiculous, as Deleuze and Guattari avow, that we all covertly dream of screwing our parents), then we can free ourselves from the primal guilt that clouds the infinite play and panoplies of the desiring self.

For Deleuze and Guattari, the body is a network of desiring machines, nested in the family as desiring-machine, nested in society and institutions as desiring machines, nested in technology and media as desiring-machines, and nested in the world system of capitalism as a desiring-machine. Within this schema, we can also locate the cosplaying body in its friction with and queering of identities assigned by family and society, even if these determinants are paradoxically subverted through playing characters derived from media franchises and associated tech platforms driven by and through the culture flows of global capitalism and its imaginaries. However, the cosplayer is not and does not fundamentally pretend to become a supe by donning a costume. Rather, they may enjoy moments of transportation in which, in the words of cosplayers interviewed for *Planet Cosplay*, they feel "Like a Death-god!" (Grell from *Black Butler* [*Kuroshitsuji*]) or "Like a Pokémon" [Umbreon from Pokémon] (Mountfort et al. 2018, 37). The same goes for playing Superman, Wonder Woman, Batman, Ultraman, Sailor Moon or Deku, and the like, as if one were stepping out of the everyday personas of Clark Kent, Diana Prince, Bruce Wayne, Shin Hayata, Usagi Tsukino, or Izuku Midoriya, and so forth, and into a new skin. Or perhaps, this doxa can be flipped, and we can understand the adoption of the supe identity as a stripping away, an elliptical return to a realm prior to the repressed, of a self or selves imbued with super powers. These circuit breakers, cosplay's capers, are schizoanalytic in the Deleuzo-Guattarian sense because they short the apparent taxonomies of these nested parts (embodied self, family, society, tech, capital, etc.), busting up these crude blocks. Out of the rubble we assemble new configurations, unpredictable arcs, and trajectories of becoming lines of flight.

References

Ashcraft, Brian, and Luke Plunkett. 2014. *Cosplay World*. Prestel.

Burrows, David, and Simon O'Sullivan. 2019. *Fictioning: The Myth-Functions of Contemporary Art and Philosophy*. Edinburgh University Press.

Castoriadis, Cornelius. 1987. *The Imaginary Institution of Society*. Translated by Kathleen Blamey. MIT Press.

Clute, John. 1995. *Science Fiction: The Illustrated Encyclopedia*. Dorling Kindersley.

Coogan, Peter. 2006. *Superhero: The Secret Origin of a Genre*. MonkeyBrain Books.

Copjec, Joan. 1994. *Read My Desire: Lacan against the Historicists*. MIT Press.

Deleuze, Gilles, and Félix Guattari. 1983. *Anti-Oedipus: Capitalism and Schizophrenia*. Translated by Robert Hurley, Mark Seem, and Helen R. Lane. University of Minnesota Press.

Duncan, Randy, and Matthew J. Smith. 2009. *The Power of Comics: History, Form and Culture*. Continuum.

Evans, Dylan. 1996. *An Introductory Dictionary of Lacanian Psychoanalysis*. Routledge.

Fingeroth, Danny. 2004. *Superman on the Couch: What Superheroes Really Tell Us about Ourselves and Our Society*. Continuum.

Gn, Joel. 2011. 'Queer Simulation: The Practice, Performance and Pleasure of Cosplay.' *Continuum: Journal of Media and Cultural Studies* 25 (4): 583–593.

Hanley, Tim. 2014. *Wonder Woman Unbound: The Curious History of the World's Most Famous Heroine*. Chicago Review Press.

Johnson, Derek. 2013. *Media Franchising: Creative License and Collaboration in the Culture Industries*. NYU Press.

Kirkpatrick, Ellen. 2015. 'Toward New Horizons: Cosplay (Re)Imagined through the Superhero Genre, Authenticity, and Transformation.' *Transformative Works and Cultures* 18. https://doi.org/10.3983/twc.2015.0613.

Kristeva, Julia. 1984. *Revolution in Poetic Language*. Translated by Margaret Waller. Columbia University Press.

Kukkonen, Karin. 2013. *Studying Comics and Graphic Novels*. Wiley-Blackwell.

Lacan, Jacques. 1978. *The Four Fundamental Concepts of Psychoanalysis: The Seminar of Jacques Lacan, Book XI*, edited by Jacques-Alain Miller. Translated by Alan Sheridan. W. W. Norton & Company.

Lacan, Jacques. 1992. *The Ethics of Psychoanalysis: The Seminar of Jacques Lacan, Book VII*, edited by Jacques-Alain Miller. Translated by Dennis Porter. W. W. Norton & Company.

Lacan, Jacques. 2006. *Écrits: The First Complete Edition in English*. Translated by Bruce Fink. W. W. Norton & Company.

Lepore, Jill. 2014. *The Secret History of Wonder Woman*. Knopf.

Lunning, Frenchy. 2022. *Cosplay: The Fictional Mode of Existence*. University of Minnesota Press.

Madrid, Mike. 2009. *The Supergirls: Fashion, Feminism, Fantasy, and the History of Comic Book Heroines*. Exterminating Angel Press.

Mountfort, Paul. 2023. 'Becoming-Animal: Cosplay as Sorcery through Deleuze and Guattari's Tenth Plateau.' *Journal of Asia-Pacific Pop Culture* 8 (1): 22–51. https://doi.org/10.5325/jasiapacipopcult.8.1.0022.

Mountfort, Paul, Anne Peirson-Smith, and Adam Geczy. 2018. *Planet Cosplay: Costume Play, Identity and Global Fandom*. Intellect.

Mountfort, Paul, Anne Peirson-Smith, and Adam Geczy. 2019. 'Cosplay at Armageddon Expo.' *Journal of Geek Studies* 6 (2): 91–110. https://doi.org/10.5281/zenodo.8351919.

Resnick, Mike. 2006. 'Introduction.' In *Worldcon Guest of Honor Speeches*, edited by Mike Resnick and Joe Siclari. ISFiC Press.

Reynolds, Richard. 1992. *Super Heroes: A Modern Mythology*. B. T. Batsford. Roberts. 2016. *The History of Science Fiction*. 2nd ed. Palgrave Macmillan.

Steger, Manfred B. 2008. *The Rise of the Global Imaginary: Political Ideologies from the French Revolution to the Global War on Terror*. Oxford University Press.

Strauss, Claudia. 2006. 'The Imaginary.' In *A Companion to Psychological Anthropology: Modernity and Psychocultural Change*, edited by Conerly Casey and Robert B. Edgerton. Blackwell Publishing.

Taylor, Charles. 2004. *Modern Social Imaginaries*. Duke University Press.

Winge, Thèresa M. 2018. *Costuming Cosplay: Dressing the Imagination*. London: Bloomsbury Academic.

Wright, Bradford W. 2001. *Comic Book Nation: The Transformation of Youth Culture in America*. Johns Hopkins University Press.

Žižek, Slavoj. 2009. *The Plague of Fantasies*. London: Verso.

19

RENEGOTIATING CANONICITY

Fanboy, Parody, and Mark Garvey's *Union Jack* (2019)

Cathrine Avery

When Mark Garvey decided to make his own version of a Marvel superhero film, he did it in the spirit of most fan work, with no expectation that his work would be acknowledged by anyone beyond the fan community. Fan or participatory culture is often defined in opposition to dominant cultural aesthetics, negatively structured through a binary of what constitutes the legitimate or the illegitimate text, and Garvey's fan work does not have legitimacy (Jenkins 2012; Morimoto 2019). Marvel comic books, along with Disney's Marvel Cinematic Universe films (MCU) function as the canonical and legitimate texts; so, while there are questions about whether fan work such as Garvey's violates accepted cultural hierarchies or contributes a valuable addition to ever-widening forms of adaptation, the work is largely dismissed as secondary. However, this chapter argues that the work of self-acclaimed fanboy Garvey constitutes a renegotiation of canonicity by blurring the boundaries between producers and consumers and challenging the singular authority of commercially produced work.

Garvey's 10, 30-minute films are a parodic revision of Roger Stern and John Byrne's canonical depiction of British superhero, Union Jack from *Captain America Vol. 1* #254 (1981). The use of parody operates as an interrogative lens through which to examine the genre and the masculinity of the superhero. Garvey's *Union Jack* (2019) incorporates both an intentionally homemade stylization (that arguably exemplifies the accusation of derivative fan creation) and sophisticated production techniques; humor is derived from overblown acting and idiomatic references to the everyday. An opening statement, revealed through faded capital letters, establishes the films as part of the gift economy: "made by fans for fans and is not for profit" (Garvey 2019a, 00:00:07). The revisioning of the original comic sees Union Jack as a largely incompetent hero relying on his girlfriend Romany Wisdom to "save the day". In this way, Garvey challenges the idealistic American masculinity of MCU heroes and although Garvey does not have proprietorial ownership of the legitimate text, his appropriation and transformation of Union Jack is nonetheless a challenge to the perceived superhero canon.

The canon of superhero literature is conceptually significant; it validates the existence of superheroes as part of academic discourse and functions as a gatekeeper, to quantify what texts can be constituted as canonical. In many ways, the superhero canon works like other literary canons: it outlines its textual boundaries and the logic and ownership of these

DOI: 10.4324/9781003366911-22

boundaries. Albert S. Fu defines the superhero canon as "the official or popularly recognized history of a fictional universe" although he acknowledges that this definition is an oversimplification and that the canon is inherently complicated (2015, 272). Alex Romagnoli and Gian Pagnucci note that "the canon of superhero literature is subject to evolution, change, addition, and subtraction" in that it encompasses ever-changing and expanding forms of storytelling (2013, 190). They use the phrase "multiple continuities" to indicate the fluidity of this canon, suggesting that "every type of media that presents superhero narratives is vital to the overall understanding of superheroes in culture and society, and us" (Romagnoli and Pagnucci 2013, 189). Kevin K. Durand also perceives the canon as unstable and uses the phrase "canon in flux" to identify its ever-shifting additions (2011, 81). The breadth and expanding variation of the superhero canon should in theory be receptive to the inclusion of fan work; while a single author may be responsible for the creation of a superhero, her or his ongoing story never remains the sole responsibility of the originator. Romagnoli and Pagnucci use the example of Batman and outline how the story of this particular superhero has developed significantly since he was first introduced by the writer Bob Kane. They point out that "Batman may 'legally' belong to DC, Warner Brothers, and the Kane estate, but many people have added to the character over a long span of time, thereby establishing Batman as a multifaceted creation" (2013, 190–191). However, there is a tension between those who own the official superhero canon (in all its temporal changes) and fans who tinker with its authenticated specificity, with an assumption that ownership trumps most if not all, forms of fan engagement. Ellen Kirkpatrick identifies the complications that arise when comic book fans challenge the status of the authorized version: "[it] destabilizes official meaning-making processes" and while she argues that this can give rise to "oppositional practices", which "helps blur the official/unofficial division that separates authorial positions and knowledge productions", this does not legalize fan work or give it entry to the authorized canon of superhero literature (2023, 53).

Questions about ownership, the superhero literary canon, and fan communities are an ongoing focus within fan studies, which developed in the 1990s through a growing academic engagement with popular culture consumption. A definition of a fan (superhero, comic, or otherwise) is not simple; it is bound by their uncertain relationship with the legitimate text and endlessly complicated by their personal preferences and terms of engagement. The form of their desired text; their point of entry into the originary text; and how they participate with or through the text and their sense of ownership are all categorizing factors. The variety of these changeable attributes makes the study of fandom and fan communities one of complexity, a study of shifting, multifaceted interactions. Henry Jenkins notes the negativity directed at fan communities. He comments that among those who would wish to maintain a division between high culture and popular culture there is a perception that fan "preferences are seen as abnormal" (2012, 17). The fact that many fans are often "highly educated, articulate people", who cannot be dismissed as unintelligent, adds to this notion of their supposed abnormality (Jenkins 2012, 19). Other academics have pointed to the level of a fan's involvement and commitment to their fanship, reading it as a mark of their respect for the agreed canon or legitimate text. For example, Bart Beaty differentiates between the hardcore fan and the casual audience in relation to the superhero canon:

> the hardcore superhero fan base (which is comprised of only a few hundred thousand members worldwide) is the one with a deep and abiding interest in superhero comic books (and, by extension, films), while the casual audience (which numbers in the tens

of millions) is frequently assumed to be solely interested in superhero films, television, and licensed products

and as such do not have a regard for the originatory text (2016, 318). Fu considers the impact of questioning the irrevocability of the canon; he examines the backlash to a proposed black Spider-Man observing that "A major critique against the casting of Glover and a black Peter Parker largely rested upon 'canon', or what is 'official' in the Marvel comic-book universe" (2015, 273). Antagonism toward those who wish to change the canon is part of Kirkpatrick's work on the experiences and practices of excluded and marginalized superhero fans:

> Challenging canon on any front is a perilous strategy, as many non-progressive superhero fans couch their bigotry and prejudice as concerns for 'canonical accuracy.' Attempts to recover canon routinely expose racebending cosplayers to vitriolic backlashes and barrages of in-person and online abuse from privileged sections of superhero fandom.
>
> *(2023, 148–149)*

Thus, superhero fans are perceived within an intricate framework of inclusion and exclusion, one that often rests on the perceived status of the canon.

Issues with defining fans and their varied consumption of the superhero literary canon extend to debates about whether fan work can be considered to "violate" the authority of the canon or contribute valuable additions to transmedia adaptation (Kirkpatrick 2023, 274). The division between the amateur and the professional is perceived as an ongoing point of conflict because fans do not possess legal and financial legitimacy. Since participatory culture is often defined in opposition to legitimacy, fan work is branded as "a refusal of authorial authority and a violation of intellectual property" (Jenkins 2012, 18). Part of the issue lies with how involving fans and "their textual desires and practices" has become an important part of current industry promotional processes (Scott 2013, 44). Jeffery A. Brown points out the potential contradictions when studios encourage fan engagement: "In creating an interrelated and multi-platform universe, Marvel has constructed a form of 'converged' media that encourages active rather than passive audience consumption" with consumption, rather than creation, as the unifying factor (Brown 2017, 24). Even though there is a consensus that the fan is an important cog within the creative industries, their work is simultaneously dismissed as derivative or guilty of unacceptable infidelities. There is some (grudging) affirmation of fan output and its value, with Jenkins claiming that "fans possess not simply borrowed remnants snatched from mass culture, but their own culture built from the semiotic raw materials the media provides" (2012, 49). Equally, Mafalda Stasi describes fan work as "a non-hierarchical, rich layering of genres" that complements the original text (2006, 35). However, these positive responses always tend to be set against ongoing questions about whether fans can be genuine producers and what value their work has within a canon that centers on the authentic text.

So, how does Garvey's work fit into this complex, hierarchical community? It is perhaps easier to start by establishing what his work is not: it is not a fanvid or as Turk clarifies a "short video integrating repurposed media images with repurposed music" which "interprets, celebrates, or critiques the original source" (2011, 84–85). Nor is it hyperbolic rhetoric, in that it is a proficient filmic engagement with the comics and not, as some fan work is critically described, "written in the spirit of... religious devotion" (Jewett and Lawrence 1977, 26).

Garvey's *Union Jack* is a perceptively crafted set of short films that pay homage to the comic book writing of Stern and Byrne and the ever-expanding Marvel Universe. The films are also contradictory; they play with key ideas and concepts and like much fan work, quietly question some of the values enshrined in the legitimate text. Garvey's work is an explicit commentary on the canon; it engages with the source material at a fundamental level, replicating panels from the comic and then reworking its characterization and narrative. In this way, it conforms to Abbott's definition of a "palimpsest" text and Later's explanation of intertextual layering in that it "constructs meaning from multilayered processes of adaptation and generic mixing" (Abbott 2018, 1; Later 2018, 538). *Union Jack*, like most Marvel comics, lends itself to this kind of adaptive approach because it is a "multifaceted, multilayered universe where one character's actions could affect other characters" (Romagnoli and Pagnucci 2013, 42). This multidimensional world, created by Stan Lee as a way of maximizing readership, offers filmmakers such as Garvey, a set of pre-existing intertwining narratives that can be accessed at differing points (Romagnoli and Pagnucci 2013, 41). On his website, Garvey outlines how his work fits in with the MCU, which both establishes a narrative timeline and reinforces the perception of authenticity:

> [*Union Jack*] exists in the continuity of the Marvel Cinematic Universe, and makes reference to it. Our timeline starts in 2017 with the later episodes taking place in 2018, around the time of the events in *Ant-Man and the Wasp* (2018), and we wrap up our story just before Thanos's snap in *Avengers: Infinity War* (2018).
>
> *(Garvey n.d.)*

Thus, Garvey's work complies with the modular approach of Marvel. His films reference other superheroes and suggest that these characters are simultaneously completing tasks as part of the complex narrative threads that MCU has taken from the original comic format. He also maintains the stylistic palette of the original comics, so that visually the spaces where the action happens replicates the artwork of Frank Robbins, Vince Colletta, and Frank Springer, something he illustrates on his website with stills from the films set against the comic panel they are reproducing (Garvey n.d.).

The Union Jack storylines that Garvey has adapted are from the hero's third iteration in comics. The original version was introduced in *Invaders* #7 (1976) by Roy Thomas and Frank Robbins, a second Union Jack appeared in *Invaders* #21 (1977), and the third incarnation in *Captain America Vol. 1* #254 (1981). This third Union Jack is different from the preceding two; unlike the former characterizations, he is not part of the British aristocracy. The first two are Lord James Montgomery Falsworth and his son, Brian. The third is Joey Chapman, described as the working-class son of a shipbuilder and a friend of the Falsworths. This difference is made clear through the comics and is an element that Garvey draws on to establish a man who is categorized as ordinary. None of the Union Jack iterations have superhuman skills and this is also an aspect that Garvey uses to reinforce Chapman's difference from other superheroes. At the center of the narrative is Union Jack's ongoing battle with a vampire cult and its current leader Baroness Blood; he is also active in the male-dominated, UK espionage community, as a member of MI5. Garvey's commitment to the source material is made evident on his webpage where he outlines the editions and authors which he has made use of:

> [T]he series feature episodes inspired by/based on specific Marvel comics, including: *Union Jack* Volume 1 by Ben Raab and John Cassaday; *Union Jack* Volume 2 by

Christos N. Gage and Mike Perkins; *Invaders Now!* #1–5 by Christos N. Gage, Alex Ross and Caio Reiss; *The New Invaders* Volume 1 #4–5 by Allan Jacobsen, C.P. Smith and Chris Walker, and "The Daredevils" Volume 1 #3 by Alan Moore and Alan Davis.

(Garvey n.d.)

This level of specificity is not just about acknowledging the authors and avoiding any conflict that might arise from a failure to cite their work, it is a measure of Garvey's devotion to the comic superhero canon. It is also about his determination to create an adaptation that incorporates the nuances of the original, including key and secondary characters and importantly, the villains.

In addition to remaining true to the narrative complexity of Marvel, Garvey also develops the humor that many of the Marvel comics and films incorporate as an aside to the action. Garvey discusses this aim on his website: "We have tried to produce a show that is in keeping with the tone of the Marvel Cinematic Universe, especially their more absurd and humorous outings, such as *Thor: Ragnarok* (2017)" (Garvey n.d.). The comedic element of Garvey's *Union Jack* parodies the genre through a form of cartoonish slapstick and casts an interrogative lens on the status of the superhero. The use of parody in superhero films is not new and has been productively discussed by Brown, where he notes that most "Superhero films are always dangerously close to self-parody" and importantly, that "Modern superhero parodies are well aware of the political underpinnings of the genre and often seek to expose or ridicule certain themes" and that "even when the goal of parody is a revealing deconstruction, it also typically carries with it a great deal of homage" (2016, 137; 139). Anupam Chander and Madhavi Sunder agree with this binary, commenting that: "The act of copying can be simultaneously homage and subversion" (2007, 626). They reason that "parodic social commentary gathers its unique power because of its use of cultural icons" and that the popularity of the Marvel comics and the MCU, with its elaborate narratives, and identifiable characters, contributes to the desire of fans to parody it (Chander and Sunder 2007, 618). "Superhero parodies mock some of the most foundational beliefs perpetuated by the genre, such as American moral superiority, rugged individualism, and heroic selflessness" making it a rich source for fans to adapt their own versions (Brown 2016, 138). And, as Jenkins asserts: "fan culture responds to actual historical and social contexts" (2012, 36). Garvey's work is both homage and subversion; he uses comedy as a means to deconstruct some of the "foundational beliefs" that the genre perpetuates and creates a series of films that could not exist without consistent reference to the source material.

Underpinning both the original comic and Garvey's work is a depiction of the social and cultural landscape of Britain. This is a significant contrast to most of the Marvel comics and films, which have at their center the representation of America. For Garvey, it was important to incorporate sensibilities relevant to Britain in 2019 and while a sense of place is visually embedded within the films, using iconic images such as London Bridge and The O2, there is also a thread of political commentary. On his website, Garvey comments that he wanted to create a superhero series that was not simply a replication of existing Marvel offerings which according to him, "lacked British characters as the lead" (Garvey n.d.). He also wanted to address a collective unease about British politics: "with the Brexit fiasco and other awkward embarrassments" (Garvey n.d.). This political representation is in keeping with Jerrod MacFarlane's perception of the American superhero genre which he argues has been identified as one that offers "significant indicators of trends and changes, particularly in times of national crisis or distress" (MacFarlane 2014, 446). Garvey's depiction of Britishness is largely understated; evident in everyday idioms, including an excess of expletives, rather than flamboyantly portrayed power struggles that can be aligned to Britain and its enemies. In "Episode 8: 'Right'", Union Jack and Wisdom are called to a meeting to discuss the problems resulting from people being accidentally infected with a virus. The gathered agents are representative of different nationalities and religions and their arguments about the morality of the mission quickly deteriorates into name-calling based on appearance and gender, with the words "Sinbad", "racist", "terrorist", and "whore" said in quick succession (Garvey 2019c, 00:08:08). The pace of the exchange has both comic timing and provides a political point about the judgments people make based on limited information, thereby highlighting negative cultural assumptions, which Robert Saunders connects directly to the uncertainties and discomforts created by Brexit. Romagnoli and Pagnucci see the genre as "responsible for producing definitions of heroism that evolve with audiences and that reaffirm what is important to the collective, cultural consciousness" (2013, 185), but this exchange, which is presented with a critical lens about tolerance and acceptance, is started by Union Jack and works in opposition to the moral certainty that the hero is expected to embrace.

It is perhaps not surprising that the greatest focus of Garvey's comedic attention is directed at the titular Union Jack. The role of the superhero has been extensively examined, with the gender representation of the male superhero in comics and films at the center of much scholarly writing over the last decade (Weltzien 2005; Lebel 2009; Purse 2011; Brown 2016; Kvaran 2017). The consensus of these authors suggests that a superhero is a man of idealized strength and one who fulfills fantasies about desirable American masculinity: his "body is a physically empowered one, strong, agile and resilient, asserting itself in the field of action and risk, and thus acts out fantasies of empowerment that are inherently literalised and physicalised, rather than abstracted" (Purse 2011, 3). Kara Kvaran defines these men as possessing a form of "hypermasculinity" that lesser men aspire to (2017, 226). Sabine Lebel goes further and regards these portrayals as retrograde: "What becomes obvious in watching these films, is that they are … positively regressive in terms of their portrayal of male and female bodies, and gender relations" (2009, 56). Interestingly, Scott Bukatman sees that the superhero "as visually, kinetically, and even verbally performative" (2008, 114). The performance of this idealized but regressive masculinity might usefully be connected to Judith Butler's understanding of the formation of gender through acts of repetition: "Gender is the repeated stylisation of the body, a set of repeated acts within a highly rigid regulatory frame that congeal over time" (1999, 33). The "repeated stylisation" of the superhero's masculine body began in 1938 when Superman first appeared as "an extreme heroic fantasy who could leap tall buildings, bend steel bars, see though walls, and was faster than a speeding bullet", and this masculine imagery has been maintained (Brown 2017, 132). In films, such as Garvey's, that have parody as part of the gendering, the comedic form draws attention more acutely to the structures that socially regulate normative gender. Brown argues that parodies "function to ultimately reinforce the dominant messages of the mainstream superhero films and to validate the very model of masculinity that it superficially condemns" (2016, 132). Garvey's work conforms to this contradictory representation. His revisioning of the original comic sees Union Jack as a largely incompetent hero dependent on his girlfriend to come to his rescue. This ineptitude is designed to be the source of much of the humor. His poor sense of direction, his questionable time management, and his uncertain fighting skills all impact on his efficacy as a classic superhero. Importantly, this is also a man who is farcical; in comparison with the extraordinary capabilities of his contemporaries such as Captain America, he consistently falls short of expectation.

Bukatman considers the visually performative element of the superhero as significant since the "iconography of superheroes depends upon costumes and masks" (2008, 114). For the comic book Union Jack, this iconography is an important melding of nationalism and the traditional tropes of the superhero. His costume is a vibrant red and blue with the colors set in such a way that they replicate the Union Jack flag. Garvey's Union Jack is dressed in black and looks more like a hackneyed villain from a TV drama than a superhero. His Union Jack coding is reduced to a small credit card-sized, removable patch on his chest. An early scene watches him "suit up" and the quick cuts from gun holsters to bulletproof vest to mask give precedence to the physicality of the character, suggestive of other superheroes donning their disguise and establishing their readiness for battle. The shot choices, quick editing, and upbeat music all conform to a visual expectation that Joey Chapman has a vital mission and is changing into the hero Union Jack. His mask, in particular, connotes his superhero status because of the nature of the superhero disguise; this is despite the fact that it is a balaclava and traditionally connected to villains. Weltzien regards this transformation as complete, it involves "the whole personality and is connected with specific abilities; the new person has a different name, different friends and enemies, different jobs to do, a completely different mode of behavior" (2005, 233). For Garvey's Joey Chapman, the change is simply visual; superhero qualities are not acquired when he dons his costume. Having made himself battle-ready he stands facing the camera. He is just about to exit the scene when he announces "I really need to do a poo" (Garvey 2019b, 00:17:39). Initially, the transformation into Union Jack appears bounded in realism as there are no overtly colorful tights and slashes of red and blue to scream out his status. This then is a man who is arguably more subtle than his counterparts. The fact that he needs to go to the bathroom before he heads off and the use of the juvenile word "poo" not only diminishes the carefully edited transformation but infantilizes him. The performance of Union Jack's uncertain heroic characterization is further drawn out on several occasions when he stops the action, quite often mid-fight, and announces that he is Union Jack and he will win. If he does not manage this declaration in a tone of voice that he is happy with he will repeat it, lowering the timbre so that it approximates a more assertive, stereotypical, heroic, male intonation. Bukatman argues that "The mask of the superhero shields his face and makes his expressiveness a bodily function rather than a facial one – this means that the canonical hero uses his body as a method of portraying emotion" (2008, 114). Garvey's Union Jack does not rely on bodily expressiveness or a "gestural body" to perform what cannot be said, his comically childish responses are the trope of his heroic flaws (Bukatman 2008, 115).

The performance of Union Jack's failed, and comic masculinity is set against the comprehensive competence of his girlfriend, aptly named Wisdom. The portrayal of Wisdom is central to Garvey's narrative; she is vital to the successes of Union Jack but she is also a woman molded against the grain. She is not the stereotypical romantic interest (they are already a couple), and she fits closer to the technical expert or forensic analyst role in current police procedurals television programs whose "stories privilege the female expert, celebrate the pursuit of scientific knowledge and justice" (Steenberg 2012, 174). But she is more than this; she is both every-woman, in opposition to the singularity of the superhero, and the real holder of power. In Episode 8, Wisdom is the voice of reason in a debate about the sacrifice of the few to save the many. Her questioning of what makes a monster and justifies killing another human is set against the political "spin" of "localised damage" (Garvey 2019c, 00:06:35). Her argument persuades Union Jack to follow her lead and leave the meeting. Brown argues that superhero parodies "function hegemonically to support ideal masculinity by maintaining the fantasy that even without a magical transformation all men can become heroic"; however, the role of Wisdom challenges this fantasy (2017, 140). Her intelligence, physical capabilities, and dominant voice further diminish Union Jack's super-hero status and add to an understanding of gender relations that is counter to the idealistic, regressive masculinity of the genre. Raewyn Connell and James Messerschmidt's discussion on hegemonic masculinity is relevant here; they argue that this form of dominant masculinity is "distinguished from other masculinities, especially subordinated masculinities" and that it "embodied the currently most honored way of being a man" (2005, 858). This, they suggest, "required all other men to position themselves in relation to it, and it ideologically legitimated the global subordination of women to men" (Connell and Messerschmidt 2005, 858). This structuring is critiqued in Garvey's *Union Jack*. Even though Garvey's work infers this hierarchy, with Union Jack situated as a "subordinated" man in comparison to Captain America, the women in Garvey's series are not subordinate, as evidenced through the character of Wisdom. This restructuring positions *Union Jack* as "violative fan work" in Kirkpatrick terms because Garvey refuses "to maintain or respect dominant laws, traditions, or privileges" of the canon (2023, 274).

If Garvey's *Union Jack* is a homage to Marvel comics and films, but at the same time parodically questioning the status of the superhero and repositioning Union Jack as subordinate (not just to a notion of hypermasculinity but also women), then this work is renegotiating some of the basic laws of the genre and its canon. In doing so, it reformulates the unquestioned status of the hero. By making Union Jack the lesser of the characters, Garvey questions the strictly singular representation of the superhero. While Union Jack is a man of endless self-belief, he is neither a man of intellect nor finely tuned instincts. His errors prolong the narrative in much the same way that comedic characters in sitcoms make a catalogue of mistakes that others have to correct. So, he is not disruptive in the way a black Superman might be or a trans gender Thor but Garvey's Union Jack nonetheless disturbs the assumed representation of heroic masculinity and thus disturbs the canon. Garvey may not have proprietorial ownership of the legitimate text, but his appropriation and transformation are such that his work is a contribution beyond that of simple (and dismissible) fan work. His output, his seriousness as a filmmaker, and his attention to detail, both in relation to the source material and as a practitioner, make his work valuable. Morimoto, in discussing fanboy auteurs such as Bryan Fuller, comments that their work "often confound[s] original/copy binary distinctions in textually innovative ways" (2019, 261). Garvey's independent, outsider status means he cannot claim auteur status nor have it bestowed on him; however, his work encapsulates Morimoto's delineation of the complicated relationship between fans and the legitimate text such that he is more than just an amateur fanboy. His parodic work offers an alternative approach to the superhero genre, one that renegotiates canonicity through palimpsestic storytelling and a refusal to reinforce the gender and genre tropes that are arguably no longer relevant. The infantilization of Union Jack comes full circle at the close of the final episode when the Director of MI5 says to him: "Ten minutes of adult conversation can achieve more than an entire year of your self-proclaimed superhero antics" and suggests a nice cup of tea instead of violence (Garvey 2020, 00:22:14).

References

Abbott, Stacy. 2018. "Not Just Another Serial Killer Show: Hannibal, Complexity, and the Televisual Palimpsest." *Quarterly Review of Film and Video* 35 (6): 552–567. https://doi.org/10.1080/105 09208.2018.1499348.

Beaty, Bart. 2016. "Superhero Fan Service: Audience Strategies in the Contemporary Interlinked Hollywood Blockbuster." *The Information Society* 32 (5): 318–325. https://doi.org/10.1080/01972243.2016.1212616.

Brown, Jeffrey A. 2016. "The Superhero Film Parody and Hegemonic Masculinity." *Quarterly Review of Film and Video* 33 (2): 131–150. https://doi.org/10.1080/10509208.2015.1094361.

Brown, Jeffery A. 2017. *The Modern Superhero in Film and Television: Popular Genre and American Culture*. Routledge.

Bukatman, Scott. 2008. "Secret Identity Politics." In *The Contemporary Comic Book Superhero*, edited by Angela Ndalianis. Taylor and Fransis group. ProQuest Ebook Central.

Butler, Judith. 1999. *Gender Trouble: Feminism and the Subversion of Identity*. Routledge.

Chander, Anupam, and Madhavi Sunder. 2007. "Everyone's a Superhero: A Cultural Theory of 'Mary Sue' Fan Fiction as Fair Use." *California Law Review* 95 (2 April): 597–626. https://www.jstor.org/stable/20439103.

Connell, Raewyn W., and Messerschmidt, James W. 2005. "Hegemonic Masculinity: Rethinking the Concept." *Gender & Society* 19 (6): 829–859. https://www.jstor.org/stable/27640853.

Durand, Kevin K. 2011. "Batman's Canon: Hybridity and the Interpretation of the Superhero." In *Riddle Me This, Batman! Essays on the Universe of the Dark Knight*, edited by Kevin K. Durand and Mary K. Leigh. McFarland & Company.

Fu, Albert S. 2015. "Fear of a Black Spider-Man: Racebending and the Colour-Line in Superhero (Re)Casting." *Journal of Graphic Novels and Comics* 6 (3): 269–283, https://doi.org/10.1080/21504857.2014.994647.

Garvey, Mark, dir. 2019a. *"Union Jack" (Marvel Fan Series)*. Episode 01, "Tradition." Uploaded October 31, 2019a, on YouTube. https://youtu.be/mxc0sVMtf5E?si=zn--CKsH453pApqO.

Garvey, Mark, dir. 2019b. *"Union Jack" (Marvel Fan Series)*. Episode 02, "Faith." Uploaded November 6, 2019b, on YouTube. https://youtu.be/P_bCGFHGVQ4?si=L52YJVejAqEnnshD.

Garvey, Mark, dir. 2019c. *"Union Jack" (Marvel Fan Series)*. Episode 08, "Right." Uploaded December 19, 2019c, on YouTube. https://youtu.be/Fs9J22ji1aY?si=Vf8jcEce1ZgME90j.

Garvey, Mark, dir. 2020. *"Union Jack" (Marvel Fan Series)*. Episode 10, "Family." Uploaded January 2, 2020, on YouTube. https://youtu.be/8xXfH5LMmtI?si=6aDzE2lpwLJDQpkL.

Garvey, Mark. n.d. "Union Jack (2019–20)." Accessed February 4, 2025. http://www.markgarvey.co.uk/mark-garvey-union-jack.html.

Jenkins, Henry. 2012. *Textual Poachers: Television Fans and Participatory Culture*. Taylor & Francis Group.

Jewett, Robert, and John S. Lawrence. 1977. The American Monomyth. Anchor Press.

Kirkpatrick, Ellen. 2023. *Recovering the Radical Promise of Superheroes Book: Un/Making Worlds*. Punctum Books.

Kvaran, Kara M. 2017. "Super Daddy Issues: Parental Figures, Masculinity, and Superhero Films." *The Journal of Popular Culture* 50 (2): 218–238. https://doi.org/10.1111/jpcu.12531.

Later, Naja. 2018. "Quality Television (TV) Eats Itself: The TV-Auteur and the Promoted Fanboy." *Quarterly Review of Film and Video* 35 (6): 531–551. https://doi.org/10.1080/10509208.2018.1499349.

Lebel, Sabine. 2009. "Tone Down the Boobs, Please! Reading the Special Effect Body in Superhero Movies." *CineAction* #77 (Summer): 56–67.

MacFarlane, Jerrod S. 2014. "Desperate Times and Desperate Measures: False Representation and Distortion of Terrorism in Post-9/11 Superhero Films." *Critical Studies on Terrorism* 7 (3): 446–455. https://doi.org/10.1080/17539153.2014.956460.

Morimoto, Lori. 2019. "Hannibal: Adaptation and Authorship in the Age of Fan Production." In *Becoming: Genre, Queerness, and Transformation in NBC's Hannibal*, edited by Kavita Mudan Finn and EJ Nielsen. Syracuse University Press. ProQuest Ebook Central.

Purse, Lisa. 2011. Contemporary Action Cinema. Edinburgh University Press.

Romagnoli, Alex S., and Gian S. Pagnucci. 2013. *Enter the Superheroes: American Values, Culture, and the Canon of Superhero Literature*. Scarecrow Press. ProQuest Ebook Central.

Saunders, Robert. 2020. "Brexit and Empire: 'Global Britain' and the Myth of Imperial Nostalgia." *Journal of Imperial and Commonwealth History* 48 (6): 1–48. https://qmro.qmul.ac.uk/xmlui/handle/123456789/68608.

Scott, Suzanne. 2013. "Who's Steering the Mothership? The Role of the Fanboy Auteur in Transmedia Storytelling." In *The Participatory Cultures Handbook*, edited by Aaron Alan Delwiche and Jennifer Jacobs Henderson. Routledge.

Stasi, Mafalda. 2006. "The Toy Soldiers from Leeds: The Slash Palimpsest." In *Fan Fiction and Fan Communities in the Age of the Internet*, edited by Karen Hellekson and Kristina Busse. McFarland & Company.

Steenberg, Lindsay. 2012. *Forensic Science in Contemporary American Popular Culture: Gender, Crime, and Science*. Taylor & Francis Group. ProQuest Ebook Central.

Turk, Tisha. 2011. "Metalepsis in Fan Vids and Fan Fiction." In *Metalepsis in Popular Culture*, edited by Karin Kukkonen and Sonja Klimek. De Gruyter. ProQuest Ebook Central.

Weltzien, Friedrich. 2005. "Masque-Ulinities: Changing Dress as a Display of Masculinity in the Super-hero Genre." *Fashion Theory* 9 (2): 229–250. https://doi.org/10.2752/136270405778051374.

20

WINTER SOLDIERS

National Identity and Responsibility in *Captain America* Fanfiction

Sarah Regier

Who'll rise or fall/give his all/for America?

(Johnston 2011, 00:49:25)

Since his first appearance in 1941, Steve Rogers as Captain America (often simply called "Cap") has embodied the American national identity. This observation is nothing new; many scholars have discussed Rogers' representation of Americanism from the first propaganda comics, through the turmoil of the 20th-century and post-9/11 politics, and into the now long-running Marvel Cinematic Universe (MCU). Aside from the patriotic name and imagery, Rogers' identity as the "man out of time" further allows him to comment on what it means to represent America in its political complexity. The "man out of time" narrative stems from the *The Avengers #4* (1964) storyline wherein Rogers is found frozen in the Arctic, where he has been since World War II, and awakened again. Since 1964, "it has been customary to frame Cap stories as if he had been revived for about ten years, no matter how much time actually passes in the real world" (Stevens 2015, 8). In the MCU, the time gap is from 1945 to 2012. This allows writers to position the character as both America's favorite and truest son, as well as a figure on the outside of American politics looking in, with all the defamiliarizing power that entails. In such a way, Rogers and his perceptions of his country are a constant commentary on American values and identity.

Jason Dittmer catalogues the ways in which Rogers bridges the nation and the individual, defining what it means to be American: Rogers' weapon is a shield, and so he "embodies defense rather than offense" (2005, 630), and, though his strength and vitality are due to the super-soldier serum, "the success of Captain America in crime fighting is clearly attributed... to his hard work" (2005, 629–630). Dittmer also notes that "Captain America's willingness to die for his country illustrates the essential centrality of the nation to him and, by extension, to every American reading the comic book" (2005, 630). In short, Captain America, and therefore the ideal American, pulls himself up by his bootstraps and supports his country's politics unrelentingly. Those politics, also embodied by the hero, prioritize the defense of others.

DOI: 10.4324/9781003366911-23

Dittmer's analysis focuses on Rogers as a strictly positive symbol of Americanism, but others examine him as a tool for wrestling with the inconsistencies of American identity and policy. Neal Curtis notes that

> there is a gap between the *idea* of what [Cap] stands for and the *actuality* or state of the nation from which he takes his name. This lack of correspondence… destabilizes any claim over what he is or even represents, giving rise to political questions time and again.
>
> *(2020, 3)*

In *Captain America* comics, the figure of Cap disappears and returns frequently, and he often returns changed or out of place. Curtis therefore examines the hero as a spectre, arguing that "[in] this constant revisiting and retelling, the revenant that is Captain America is able to do unsettling and disturbing political work by reintroducing the ghosts that America continually tries to exorcise in its projection of the preferred moral image" (2020, 15).

Through Captain America's deaths or disappearances, whether via plot convention or a canceled comics run, creators leave ample space for the character to change. In the 1950s, for example, there was a short and largely unsuccessful "Commie-smasher" run. In a 1972 storyline, when McCarthyism was less popular, it is revealed that the Commie-smasher of the 1950s was not Steve Rogers at all, but an imposter, and the "true" Captain America is given the opportunity to denounce the racism and hyper-vigilance of his counterpart. In his comprehensive overview of the *Captain America* canon, J. Richard Stevens examines how the figure of Captain America has changed over the course of 70 years, discussing the politics of the comic and the character in conjunction with the political issues of the day (2015, 290). Stevens asserts that

> [though] Cap's outlook and values have changed from era to era, his moral code is consistently strong. He believes fiercely in whatever he considers to be right. His devotion to American ideals is absolute: even when he comes into conflict with America's politicians or its laws, his faith in the corrective system of democracy prevents him from complaining.
>
> *(2015, 290)*

Stevens focuses on Rogers' moral idealism as an unchanging characteristic, quoting Marvel writer Steve Englehart as saying "I could see [Cap] pretty clearly as a guy who exemplified the best that America had to offer, not what it was offering" (quoted in Stevens 2015, 105) and noting that "[Cap] in effect becomes the standard by which other heroes' morality will be judged" (2015, 151). Stevens also discusses fan reactions to Rogers' values, quoting one who wrote to Marvel to say that "[Cap's] monologues about freedom and the American Way always make me feel proud to be a part of this country" (quoted in Stevens 2015, 132).

It is not only scholars who have observed how Rogers represents the American ideal. *Captain America* media habitually comments metatextually on how the figure of Captain America reflects and creates the boundaries of American identity. In August 1974, at the end of the Secret Empire storyline in *Captain America and the Falcon* #176, Peggy Carter tells Steve,

> You're a *symbol*—a symbol of the country that's given *everything it has* to light the torch of *liberty* throughout the world!… This is *bigger* than *you* or any *other* individual, Cap!

It's bigger than *all* of us! But you *symbolize* all of it in your own way—and you're the *only one* who *does!*

(Englehart 1974, 13–14)

Rogers, however, feeling his ideals betrayed by his president who was secretly a villain, decides that he no longer wants to represent America. A few issues later, in March 1975, he demonstrates the commitment to idealism Stevens discusses when he realizes,

the people who had *custody* of the American Dream had *abused* both *it* and *us!*... there has to be *somebody* who'll fight for the *dream*, against *any* foe... somebody who'll do the job I started—*right!* And God knows I can't let *anybody else* run the risks that job entails *for* me!

(Englehart 1975, 16–17)

In the comics, Rogers is constantly handed the responsibility of protecting America and upholding its values singlehandedly; despite his many teammates and friends, the American identity is Rogers' burden alone.

This trend continues into the MCU movies. In *Captain America: The First Avenger* (2011), Rogers spends time on the war bond circuit. The song "Star Spangled Man", sung by bond-circuit chorus girls, plays over the montage footage of his tour. The song asks, "Who's strong and brave/here to save/the American way?... Who'll rise or fall/give his all/for America?" and to each question it answers "The Star Spangled man with a plan!" (Johnston 2011, 00:48:23-00:50:45). Within the narrative, Rogers becomes a public figure with the responsibility to represent the fighting heart of America to its people, at the same time, the real-world audience (as always) watches Rogers be the pinnacle of American ideals.

In many ways, *Captain America* fanfiction continues to turn to Rogers to represent the American standard and to make metatextual commentary on that representation. Fan studies are particularly suited to *Captain America* media because, as J. Richard Stevens discusses, *Captain America* comics have been fan productions since Roy Thomas began working on *The Avengers* in 1969: "[Thomas] represented the beginning of the first wave of fan-creators, individuals who had grown up as fans of the properties they were to eventually work on" (Stevens 2015, 119). In short, to analyze most *Captain America* media is to analyze fan-works. Online fanfiction is simply a newer medium; however, the treatment of fanfiction in this chapter requires some brief context. Bronwen Thomas asserts, in her survey of fan studies, that the history of fan studies is a history of studying the power dynamics and systems within which fans produce fanworks: "trying to impose terms and values on [fans'] activities" (2011, 5). I concur with Thomas' assertions that "it is important to start by looking at what fans are *doing*" instead of making value judgments (Thomas 2011, 5). This chapter will examine how some themes of *Captain America* media carry through multiple fan texts, taking the three installments of the *Not Easily Conquered* series by dropdeaddream and WhatAreFears as a case study in order to carry out a more in-depth analysis.

Despite the long proliferation of comics, most *Captain America* fanfiction produced recently is about the MCU movies. Most recent scholarship, my own included, focuses on stories found on the website Archive of Our Own (AO3). On AO3, a vast majority of fanfiction focusing on Captain America characterizes him as a queer man: nearly 70,000 stories pair him with Bucky Barnes, and nearly 50,000 pair him with Tony Stark, which is distinctly higher than the nearly 7500 stories matching him with Peggy Carter, the top straight pairing for the character.

It will be relevant to know that in MCU canon, Bucky Barnes is Rogers' childhood best friend, who supposedly died during World War II, but was instead captured by the fascist super-villain organization Hydra and brainwashed to become a superpowered assassin, the Winter Soldier. Peggy Carter is Rogers' love interest in *Captain America: The First Avenger*. After Rogers is frozen in the Arctic Ocean, she works as a spy and helps to found SHIELD, an intelligence organization kept secret even from the American people. *Captain America: The First Avenger* follows Rogers as he becomes Captain America and fights Hydra in World War II, culminating with his waking up in 2012. The sequel, *Captain America: The Winter Soldier* (2014) reveals Barnes' capture and transformation. It also reveals that Hydra had been growing within SHIELD since its founding as a result of Operation Paperclip. A great deal of fanfiction speculates about how Rogers would save and deprogram Barnes in the aftermath of those revelations.

Prior scholarship on *Captain America* fanfiction approaches the genre by examining the power dynamic of fanfiction production that Thomas discusses. Carlos Rodriguez Rosa suggests that "by writing slashfic about superheroes, then, queer writers carve themselves into a genre in ways that challenge the very structure that casts them aside" (2021, 5). Within the context of fanfiction and scholarship about it, queerness is political and inherently anti-normative, which creates tension between Cap's queerness and his position as the (centrist) American ideal. Rodriguez Rosa suggests that queer Cap narratives can integrate the marginal position of queerness with the central American identity, that "in [fanfiction] Steve Rogers' Captain America is given permission to be motivated by his love… and to let that love become a source of strength as he goes on to fulfill his duty as Captain America more authentically" (2021, 43).

Similarly, Sarah E. Beyvers and Florian Zitzelsberger examine coming-out narratives in *Captain America* fanfiction as "[prompting] cultural/social movement and [contributing] to a renegotiation of American identity which is, after all, based on the very idea of mobility" (2020, 9). In short, though queering Captain America modifies the American identity by "[re-situating] queerness as genuinely American", fanfiction also presents coming out as "the epitome of self-reliance", emphasizing how queer narratives can coincide with pre-existing American values of individualism (Beyvers and Zitzelsberger 2020, 15). Studying how *Captain America* fanfiction explores and modifies the American ideal fits in with Stevens' perception that *Captain America* stories are "open texts" which are "a reflection of the political conditions in which they were produced" (Beyvers and Zitzelsberger 2020, 13). In this formulation, the (perceived) explosion of queer identities and queer politics in the 2010s allows Captain America to represent, at least in marginal storytelling spaces, a quintessential queer American identity.

Fanfiction texts uphold the pattern of commenting metatextually on Rogers' embodiment of American values. In "Steve Rogers at 100: Celebrating Captain America on Film", collaborative authors invent a false history chronicling films which might have been made about Captain America in the MCU. The first segment is an academic article: "Steve Rogers: A Hauntology: A History of Captain America on Screen, 1946–2011" (eleveninches et al. 2014), written before Rogers is retrieved from the Arctic. The fictional academic writes,

> Steve Rogers is a ghost haunting the American people – or, rather, haunting the twentieth century, for the question we should be asking ourselves is not who he is but rather what he means to us… wouldn't we like to imagine ourselves as purely good as he seemed to have been?
>
> *(eleveninches et al. 2014)*

217

Fanfiction in which Rogers is queer is also metatextually aware of how it is modifying the American ideal. In "Brooklyn", by togina, after Steve comes out to the public by revealing that he had been in love with Barnes before the war but had never told him, he becomes a queer icon. He is interviewed by queer reporters, which he is conflicted about:

> they eyed him with sympathy and asked too many questions about his best friend. But first they would tell their own stories, of schoolyard bullying or a family's rejection and being so grateful to have a childhood icon stand up and announce he was *proud* to be gay. It would have been the coward's way out to offer them nothing back.
>
> *(togina 2014)*

Here, the theme from the comic of March 1975 returns: despite the pressures, moral or personal, that the role of Captain America places on him, Rogers feels a responsibility to embody what Americans need. In "Brooklyn", however, that need is focused on queerness and authenticity instead of the patriotism and good government found in Englehart's Secret Empire storyline. Later on in the story, a film is made about Rogers' and Barnes' love story. It is called "*Brooklyn*, as though Steve represented all of America and his untold love story represented an entire borough" (togina 2014). In short, fanfiction is very conscientious about how Rogers represents Americanism and how queering the character reshapes the American identity.

Besides making Cap a queer man, fanfiction deviates from other *Captain America* media by interrogating the right which the American people have to Rogers' body, image, and life. This is done in two primary ways: first, by taking a critical tone towards the fictional media which sensationalizes Rogers' life, and second, by displacing the responsibility of representing and living up to the American Dream onto other characters and the general public. Though other *Captain America* media occasionally considers Steve Rogers the individual, any choices Rogers makes to step away from the role of Captain America are temporary and framed as selfish. In *Captain America* #176, as discussed above, Rogers reflects that *I'm no legend! I'm a man!!* (Englehart 1974, 2), as he decides whether or not to give up the shield. However, a few issues later, Rogers is reflecting on how only he can bear the responsibility of the American Dream (Englehart 1975, 16–17).

This pattern, too, continues into the MCU. In *Captain America: Civil War* (2016), when Rogers drops his shield and therefore the persona of Captain America, it is out of disillusionment with the politics of his situation and because he is choosing to save Barnes over being a superhero. Later, in *Avengers: Infinity War* (2018), he returns to the role as soon as the alien threat manifests. Unlike Tony Stark, who frequently considers giving up his superhero persona in the MCU, Rogers has only one protest against being a symbol, when he draws himself, critically, as a dancing monkey while he is on the bond circuit instead of fighting with the troops (Johnston 2011, 00:52.00).

Fanfiction, however, seriously questions Rogers' role as a public figure. "United States v. Barnes, 617 F. Supp. 2d 143 (D.D.C. 2015)" by fallingvoices and radialarch, chronicles the public trial of the Winter Soldier following the events of *Captain America: The Winter Soldier*. The story is told through news stories, court transcripts, and social media posts. This multimedia format emphasizes how the trial makes the details of the worst days of many people's lives public property; not only do the torture and brainwashing of the Winter Soldier become public, but so do the impacts left on his victims. When Rogers takes the stand, the prosecution pressures him into admitting that he is in love with Barnes, which throws the whole nation into an uproar: the story presents immediate headlines from the Associated Press and Fox News, and then a trending hashtag speculating on Rogers' sexuality. Characters use social media to critique the spectacle: one tweet reads "Cap didn't 'lie' to any of us. He doesn't owe us shit. Think on that" (fallingvoices and radialarch 2014). By emphasizing the horror of having personal secrets made the subject of public sensation and by having characters themselves critique the media, the story draws into question how media and audiences hold characters up on a pedestal to represent the totality of a fractured nation.

Besides looking at media response, the other way that fanfiction challenges Rogers' role as the embodiment of American values is by displacing responsibility onto others. copperbadge's "A Partial Dictionary of the 21st Century By Captain Steve Rogers, US Army" revisits the song "Star Spangled Man" from the first movie. Rogers hears it performed by a young woman at a bar and reflects that far from the peppy anthem of the bond circuit, her performance is

> slow, and sad, and not all the lyrics are the same... the song was always just a lot of questions about who will fight for America or save America... And she's left the answer out. So it's not an anthem to raise money for a war or get enlistment numbers up. It's a cry out for help.
>
> *(copperbadge 2012)*

After the show, Rogers meets the singer, Meg Boudoun, and she responds with horror that he heard her cut him out of a song written about him, but he tells her he likes it better without him in it:

> if it's just some Star Spangled man doing it all, ordinary people feel like they don't have to do anything. And I think the point of democracy is that everyone has to do their part. I sure don't want to do it all myself, anyhow.
>
> *(copperbadge 2012)*

The sentiment of the song rewrite appears to resonate with the community, as there are three links at the bottom of the story to people singing "Meg Boudoun" covers of the song.

One fanfiction which combines all of these tactics (changing the definition of Americanism, critiquing the public ownership of Rogers' life, and displacing the responsibility for the American identity) is the case study for this chapter: the *Not Easily Conquered* series by dropdeaddream and WhatAreFears. The series begins with "A Long Winter", which chronicles an alternate 20th century wherein Rogers, instead of being frozen in the arctic, swims to shore and marries Peggy Carter. In 1966, love letters written from Barnes to Rogers are leaked to the press, which causes a rupture in Rogers' marriage and sends him into a journey of self-discovery. "The Thirteen Letters", the middle installment, looks back in time to the war and the circumstances of Barnes' letter writing. The third story in the series, "Not Easily Conquered", chronicles how Rogers uncovers the Hydra infiltration of SHIELD and seeks out Barnes as the Winter Soldier, culminating in the whole conspiracy being revealed to the public. This fanwork was chosen for the immense fan response it received: over 3,000 comments on AO3, a Twitter bot, which only tweets quotes from the series, and a still-thriving tag on the social media site Tumblr, which contains multiple accounts of people getting tattoos based on the work. The popularity of *Not Easily Conquered* suggests that its themes resonate strongly with the fan community.

The series title comes from Thomas Paine's *The American Crisis*, which reads at the opening,

> These are the times that try men's souls. The summer soldier and the sunshine patriot will, in this crisis, shrink from the service of their country; but he that stands by it now, deserves the love and thanks of man and woman. Tyranny, like hell, is not easily conquered.
>
> *(Paine 1776)*

This quote also serves as a primary motif by which the narrative displaces responsibility for the American identity. Over the course of the narrative, it identifies "winter soldiers", those who are able to stand by their country in crisis, as the truest representation of America. At the same time, it shows how the nation's concerns constantly infringe on Rogers' (and others') private lives and metatextually criticizes the American people and even the reader for their perverse attention to Rogers and those around him. In the author's note on "Bone of my Bones", a fanwork for the series, thegeminisage writes, "[part] of the point of NEC is that [Steve and Bucky's] personal lives aren't any of our goddamn business" (thegeminisage 2015).

The first appearance of the "winter soldiers" is in "A Long Winter", when Rogers is visiting Jim Morita, a member of Rogers' squad from the war. Morita makes Rogers aware of the Winter Soldier Investigation, the (real) historical event wherein Vietnam veterans gathered to testify about the war crimes they saw and participated in. Morita explains the name by quoting Thomas Paine, and Rogers puts the pieces together:

> 'So if the summer soldier shrinks away from the truth…'
> 'The winter soldier accepts accountability,' Jim agrees.
> 'I'm proud of them, then,' Steve decides.
> *(dropdeaddream and WhatAreFears 2014a)*

Here, Rogers' endorsement begins the process of displacing the American identity. While these veterans have chosen a name to bear their responsibility from *The American Crisis*, Rogers realizes that he barely remembers who Paine is and wonders if somebody who knows so little of American history can even be Captain America.

As the reader knows, even when Rogers does not, the Winter Soldier at the center of the story is Barnes, and like the veterans, Barnes takes on much of the weight of representing American identity. Even before his letters are leaked to the public, Rogers reflects that he is a national hero, someone kids write about in school: "Sergeant Barnes, James Buchanan: as much as Captain America, he's larger than life, a legend that refuses to die" (dropdeaddream and WhatAreFears 2014a). With the release of his letters, he attains icon status. In 1972, Rogers comes across a demonstration supporting two police officers arrested for sodomy. At the protest, there is a woman with a poster of Barnes' photograph and the words "SHOW SOME RESPECT". "The Thirteen Letters" contains an excerpt from a TED Talk about Barnes' letters and their cultural impact, and the speaker says, "[The letters] belong to all of us. As a country they identify us and as a people they move us" (dropdeaddream and WhatAreFears 2014b). Barnes becomes a figurehead whose image and writing are used to stand in for American values and identity, and as he does so, said identity is queered by virtue of Barnes being queer, the letters being a queer-love narrative.

Centering Barnes in the American narrative also strips away the glorious war story that America tells itself in Rogers. Anecdotes about the war in other sources come primarily from "A Boy From Brooklyn: The Authorized Biography of Captain America" (dropdeaddream and WhatAreFears 2014b), which the narrative of "The Thirteen Letters" shows to be a glossed-over narrative focusing on Rogers' heroism. By contrast, Barnes' letters reveal to the public the horrors of war. More than that, they reveal that Rogers' idealism is the thing which holds Barnes back from his worst self, as he writes, "[if] you leave me alone in this world I'll turn into something terrible. I'll turn into the nasty creature that's growing inside me. This war, it'll swallow me whole" (dropdeaddream and WhatAreFears 2014b). Like America, Barnes relies on Rogers to embody a goodness that does not truly exist. However, as Barnes overtakes Rogers as the symbol of America, telling the ugly truth becomes the truer American virtue.

By contrast, Rogers is demonstrated to be unable to shoulder the ugly truth of America in two ways. First, his position as Captain America prevents him from speaking the truth. At the White House Correspondents' Dinner in 1962, he argues with Vice President Johnson about the effectiveness of duck and cover drills against nuclear attacks, and Howard Stark (inventor, co-founder of SHIELD, and father to Tony Stark) immediately pulls him aside to say "You're a national icon, pal [...]. You can't just go around *saying* shit like that" (dropdeaddream and WhatAreFears 2014a). The message is clear: if Cap is unable to speak the truths Americans need to know, he is also unable to represent them or protect them.

Second, *Not Easily Conquered* shows Rogers to be weak at the moment of crisis. At the end of "A Long Winter", Carter reveals to Rogers that she has known for years that Barnes, one of the loves of Rogers' life, was the Winter Soldier and has never told him. She explains,

> The balance was too delicate; we were facing a nuclear war. If you had known, Steve.... You would tear the world apart to find him, and you wouldn't give a damn about anything else.... You would have tipped the nation into a world war.
>
> *(dropdeaddream and WhatAreFears 2014a)*

Rogers acknowledges, even as he prepares to go out seeking Barnes, that Carter is right. The winter soldier bears the needs of America, and Rogers cannot.

Despite this weakness inherently tied to Rogers' inability to set aside the private in favor of the nation, the story not only respects Rogers' private life but defends it. Repeatedly, the narrative condemns the attention paid to Rogers' every move and the way the nation invades his privacy. The level-headed and staunchly moral Morita tells Rogers that he has not read Barnes' letters: "I figured it was private. Between you and him and no one else, even if nobody agreed with me" (dropdeaddream and WhatAreFears 2014a). "Not Easily Conquered" features an article about a film written about the leak of Barnes' letters. In this article, the director speaks about how his film metatextually condemns its audience:

> At the end of the day the private became public, and it upended a man's life. You get caught up in this whole fantastic drama, how big it is, how it's going to impact the country... The last shot: this is what matters. One man. And he's ruined... Shame on you for watching.
>
> *(dropdeaddream and WhatAreFears 2015)*

The interview simultaneously addresses the fanfiction reader who has spent the better part of 100,000 words consuming the spectacle of Rogers' life and love: shame on you for watching, for making him stand in for the reality of your world.

The strongest condemnation of how Rogers has been made to stand in for the nation, however, is the trial at the culmination of the story. Following the revelation that Hydra has infiltrated SHIELD, America is thrown into crisis, and nobody knows who to blame. An FBI team shows up at Rogers' door and tells him the "law isn't satisfied and neither are its citizens… Unless a public figure rises up and takes the blame this nation's going to fall into chaos" (dropdeaddream and WhatAreFears 2015). When Rogers resists taking the fall, the agent threatens to arrest all of his loved ones instead, weaponizing his private life to push him to satisfy the public's thirst for justice. He accepts the blame out of love for his family, not for his country, and the country becomes not something which deserves respect or protection but a predatory force against which Rogers must defend himself.

In the trial, the narrative returns a final time to the figure of the winter soldier, this time in Peggy Carter, the final witness. The public discovers that she has been hiding the Winter Soldier from the public for over 40 years, and she explains the same calculation she had once told Rogers. She reveals the extent to which, though it nearly destroyed her marriage, she has given everything to America:

> I knew secrets, one secret, that could bring this nation to its knees. More than Howard Stark or President Kennedy or Director Hoover, I held a single responsibility… none of these men could have done their jobs if they weren't standing on my back and my shoulders while I held the USSR at bay.
>
> *(dropdeaddream and WhatAreFears 2015)*

At Rogers' own trial, Carter, not Rogers, is revealed to hold America's ugly truths. Even as she steps into the role of symbol, of winter soldier, Carter condemns the eyes of the nation on her: "learn this… attempts to sensationalize us and our hardships will not do" (dropdeaddream and WhatAreFears 2015). Instead, she returns to *The American Crisis* to call upon the nation to rise up against tyranny, just as Barnes walks into the courtroom with proof of the Hydra conspiracy. Carter and Barnes, the two representations of America's dirty, but true, work, throw the responsibility for the future at the feet of the nation.

After the trial, the reader reaches the resolution of Rogers' personal arcs, and, near the end, is confronted with an epilogue from a semi-autobiographical novel written by Barnes in the aftermath. Barnes, whose love letters made him the symbol of the nation, sends the reader away: "Why would I tell you, when I've already spread myself at your feet, butterflied? Don't read what comes next, I dare you. It's only for him" (dropdeaddream and WhatAreFears 2015). The excerpt stands alone without context, and the effect is startling and personal: after the many in-narrative intrusions into Rogers' and Barnes' lives, the fanfiction reader themself stands accused of their proprietary voyeurism.

The original *Captain America* comic was created to build support for a war that America had not yet entered, and it encouraged every child to do their part in protecting the country. After the war, however, when overt propaganda became either less necessary or less popular, Steve Rogers stopped calling readers to action. Over time, instead, he became an unachievable ideal, the symbol of a virtuous America that was out of reach for anyone except him. In fanfiction, *Captain America* media condemns the idea of putting the responsibility of the nation onto one man and instead turns back to that original question: in this, in any, time of crisis, what will *you* do? Stop simply watching.

> So if the summer soldier shrinks away from the truth…
> the winter soldier accepts accountability.
> *(dropdeaddream and WhatAreFears 2014a)*

References

Beyvers, Sarah E., and Florian Zitzelsberger. 2020. "American Queeroes: Coming Out Narratives in the *Captain America* Fandom." *Comparative American Studies An International Journal* 17, no. 1: 6–22. https://doi.org/10.1080/14775700.2020.1720405.

copperbadge. 2012. "A Partial Dictionary of the 21st Century by Captain Steve Rogers, US Army." *Archive of Our Own*, April 22. https://archiveofourown.org/works/551094.

Curtis, Neal. 2020. "The Specters of Captain America: Time and the Haunting of American Politics." *Inks: The Journal of the Comics Studies Society* 4, no. 1 (Spring): 1–21. https://doi.org/10.1353/ink.2020.0005.

Dittmer, Jason. 2005. "Captain America's Empire: Reflections on Identity, Popular Culture, and Post-9/11 Geopolitics." *Annals of the Association of American Geographers* 95, no. 3 (September): 626–643. https://www.jstor.org/stable/3693960.

dropdeaddream and WhatAreFears. 2014a. "A Long Winter." *Archive of Our Own*, June 17. https://archiveofourown.org/works/1799623.

dropdeaddream and WhatAreFears. 2014b. "The Thirteen Letters." *Archive of Our Own*, November 30. https://archiveofourown.org/works/2689091.

dropdeaddream and WhatAreFears. 2015. "Not Easily Conquered." *Archive of Our Own*, July 7. https://archiveofourown.org/works/4289208.

eleveninches, hellotailor, M_Leigh, neenya, saintsideways, and tigrrmilk. 2014. "Steve Rogers at 100: Celebrating Captain America on Film." *Archive of Our Own*, May 11. https://archiveofourown.org/works/1599293.

Englehart, Steve. 1974. "Captain America Must Die!" *Captain America and the Falcon* #176. Marvel Comics Group.

Englehart, Steve. 1975. "Nomad: No More!" *Captain America and the Falcon* #183. Marvel Comics Group.

fallingvoices and radialarch. 2014. "United States v. Barnes, 617 F. Supp. 2d 143 (D.D.C. 2015)." *Archive of Our Own*, September 27. https://archiveofourown.org/works/2304905.

Johnston, Joe, dir. 2011. *Captain America: The First Avenger*. Marvel Studios. DVD.

Paine, Thomas. 1776. *The Writings of Thomas Paine—Volume 1 (1774–1779): The American Crisis*, edited by Moncure Daniel Conway. Project Gutenberg. https://www.gutenberg.org/cache/epub/3741/pg3741-images.html.

Rodriguez Rosa, Carlos. 2021. "'We Can (All) Be Heroes' The American Monomyth and the Problem with a Queer Captain America." MA thesis. Nova Southeastern University.

Stevens, J. Richard. 2015. *Captain America, Masculinity, and Violence: The Evolution of a National Icon*. Syracuse University Press. ProQuest Ebook Central.

thegeminisage. 2015. "Bone of My Bones." *Archive of Our Own*, October 5. https://archiveofourown.org/works/4941823.

Thomas, Bronwen. 2011. "What Is Fanfiction and Why Are People Saying Such Nice Things about It??" *Storyworlds: A Journal of Narrative Studies* 3: 1–24. https://doi.org/10.5250/storyworlds.3.2011.0001.

togina. 2014. "Brooklyn." *Archive of Our Own*, May 21. https://archiveofourown.org/works/1669439.

PART III

National Superheroes and Translations

21

FLYING BRITISH SUPERHEROES OF WORLD WAR II AND BEYOND

The Historical Turn in Britain's Aviation War in Popular Culture

Lisa J. Hackett, Jo Coghlan,
Huw Nolan and Chris Comerford

Introduction

In this chapter, the rich history of British superheroes is considered. In reflecting on British superheroes, it becomes evident that British political and social history, specifically the events of World War II, including the Battle of Britain and the blitz bombings of London, shaped the development and advancement of British superheroes in terms of narratives and ideology. Also shaping the British superhero was British colonialism, or more precisely the decline of British hegemony in the colonies and the rising up of formerly subjugated nations. Consciously or otherwise, in these spaces, British superheroes played a role in embodying and representing ideas of British heroism (especially that of British war pilots) and British imperialism. American superheroes, with only a couple of exceptions, were not tied to the logics of nation, war, and colonization in the same way as their British counterparts. Adding a further layer of embodiment was the role and place of class in British superhero narratives, again frames not evidenced specifically in American superheroes. Furthermore, the use of satire and parody is also evident in British superheroes, but not so much in American superheroes. While the field of British superheroes is rich, this chapter begins with Biggles as a starting point to consider the narrative and ideological aspects of British superheroes, moving through to examinations of British superheroes Dan Dare, Marvelman, and the Steel Claw. It also includes a discussion of Dr Who and the character's place in British superhero traditions. This chapter concludes with a comparison of British and American superheroes.

War and Its Impact on British Superheroes

Superheroes, according to Richard Reynolds, are by their development and performance a "highly potent cultural myth" (1992, 82), who embody myths and discourses of national identity (Murray 2017, 3). The superhero story is generally a "morality tale" which functions as a "parable about power and identity" as old as the myths of Hercules or Robin Hood

 DOI: 10.4324/9781003366911-25

(Murray 2017, 9). As such, they represent many things to audiences and fans, as well as to nations and states. Lorna Piatti-Farnell argues that superheroes are more than their "fighting abilities" or their "superhuman powers," and to frame them as simply having these markers is "reductive" (2022, 3). Piatti-Farnell explains that superheroes understood as "overarchingly motivated by a desire for justice, while also embodying all that is 'good' and 'right'... fails to fulfill the specific characteristics of the multifaceted iconic figure" (2022, 3). While American superheroes are largely framed within discourses of "truth, justice, and the American way," British superheroes are informed by their national histories, namely, those of empire and war. In the case of British superheroes, perhaps more so than their American counterparts, they embody actual historical events that directly inform their development (Geraghty 2015, 89). Piatti-Farnell's observation that the 21st century has provided a "fertile areas for superheroes to mutate and readapt" while also "mirror[ing] and challeng[ing] the zeitgeist of the changing landscape with which they are placed" (2022, 1) can also apply to early British superheroes.

World War I and World War II directly shaped the development of British superheroes. The large-scale air war of World War II in particular saw the figure of the Royal Air Force (RAF) pilot loom large in the national imagination (See Francis 2013). Winston Churchill's House of Commons speech in August 1940, "Never, in the field of human conflict, was so much owed by so many to so few," paid tribute to the RAF pilots who defended the United Kingdom against the German Luftwaffe during the Battle of Britain. As a result, representations of both fictional and real pilots are evident in British popular culture, notably the 1956 film *Reach for the Sky* (Dir. Lewis Gilbert) which tells the story of RAF pilot Douglas Bader, who despite losing both his legs in a plane crash, became a World War II ace pilot. The film is based on the 1954 book of the same name written by Australian author and pilot Paul Brickhill who also wrote the World War II novels *The Dam Busters* (1950) and *The Great Escape* (1951), both adapted into successful films in 1954 and 1963, respectively. Also notable is the 1969 cinematic rendition of the *Battle of Britain* (Dir. Guy Hamilton) with its all-star cast and spectacular flying sequences. As James Chapman (2011) notes in his research of British comic characters, the British pilots of World War II came to represent how the nation understood heroism and superheroes. Chapman quotes British journalist Harry Pearson who observed that

> American kids had Spiderman, Daredevil, Batman and Thor. British kids had the second World War. Burma and the Western Desert were our Gotham City and Megalopolis [*sic*]. The men who saved our world didn't have extraordinary powers, fancy gadgets or bizarre costumes. Our superheroes were our dads, uncles and grandfathers.
>
> *(2011, 97)*

In early British superheroes specifically, and British comics generally, the British superhero is largely male, white, and heterosexual. On the issue of gender in relation to British superheroes and comic protagonists, Mel Gibson's work is particularly insightful (2000, 2003a,b, 2008, 2015) as is that of Angela McRobbie (1991). However, it is James Chapman's 2011 text *British Comics, A Cultural History* and Christopher Murray's 2017 work *The British Superhero* that well examines the social-political context of the British superhero especially in the context of World War II and "his" role in terms of nationalism and propaganda, which is the focus of this chapter.

Murray's work begins with how the "idea of a British superhero is often considered a contradiction in terms" because "superheroes belong to America" (2017, 3). Murray contextualizes the development of early 20th-century British superheroes against the decline of the British Empire. This sits against the rise of American superheroes occurring as America is becoming a global superpower and hegemon. Weary from war and with the empire in decline, along with the tyranny of distance from American superhero and comic production houses, British superheroes did not closely follow American superhero conventions. Instead, they adopted a style and content more domestic in flavor. Early American superheroes were more conservative than British superheroes, functioning as a "near-perfect metaphor for America's view of itself." positioned as an "icon of national identity" steeped in "patriotism and manifest destiny" (Murray 2017, 12–13) with "strong moral codes" (DiPaolo 2011, 5). The British superhero tended to subvert, counter, satirize, and even parody the British state and its class system and did not adopt the "full-on American model" of superhero (Dittmer 2012). This left the British superhero looking "slightly odd." Early British superheroes instead mix the heroic (the British war pilot), with narratives of humor, resulting in a "discursive construct for the purposes of political commentary challenging the commonly understood politics of the [American] superhero" (Murray 2017, 4). How the British superhero is culturally and ideologically framed in early post-war popular culture is evidenced in the following discussion.

Early British Superheroes

Prior to the romanticization of the World War II superhero pilot, Biggles (1932–1999), who began his career in World War I, is perhaps the most recognizable figure. His character combines that of the quintessential British gentleman with the noble patriot fighting for King and country. Biggles was created by British author and serving veteran of the Royal Flying Corps (later the RAF) William Earl John in 1932 when he was editor of the magazine *Popular Flying*. Major James "Biggles" Bigglesworth appeared in over 90 books marketed for boys published between 1932 and 1970. Over the series, Biggles grows from being a World War I pioneer fighter pilot to a post-World War II international air detective. Biggles is a divisive hero in British culture. He is a fictional representation of British colonialism at a time when the British Empire was crumbling. Yet Biggles, via his national and international popularity, provided a way for Britain to continue its imagining of its glorious empire, in an emerging post-colonial world (Goodrum 2019, 19). Biggles represented the ideal types of Britishness and British masculinity, but his upper-class white Britishness posited his heroism as an "imaginary assemblage" of British colonial ideology. This assemblage was "written into the very fabric of his character" (Goodrum 2019, 21).

Biggles functioned within "nationalist discourses" in which soldiers and pilots were "both underpinned by, and powerfully reproduce[d], conceptions of gender and national as unchanging essences" (Dawson 1994, 243). Given this inscribed ideology, and Althusser's (2001) warning that ideology has a historical context, by the 1970s, postcolonial perspectives challenged Biggles imperialist heroism and he faded from popularity. While perhaps not a superhero, Biggles does in many ways provide some of the foundations for the direction of British superheroes in the 1940s and beyond. Like the author of Biggles, Roald Dahl was himself an RAF pilot. Dahl wrote the children's book *The Gremlins* (1943) featuring Air Force pilot Gus and the mischievous creatures of RAF folklore who had a predilection for destroying airplanes. The character of Fifinella from *The Gremlins* was used by the American Women Air Service Pilots as their mascot during World War II.

One of the mainstays of superhero origin stories is the catalyst for the development of superhuman powers; Peter Parker is bitten by a radioactive spider; scientist Bruce Banner is exposed to high doses of radiation and transforms into the Hulk; and Dr Pamela Isely is injected with a combination of plant poisons and toxins, becoming Poison Ivy. Here too are parallels with British pilots. During World War II, the British government, keen to conceal their new radar technology which allowed for the RAF to "target German airplanes with astonishing accuracy" (Byun and Spaide 2021, 895), created a propaganda campaign featuring Flight Lieutenant John Cunningham. With his nickname "Cats Eyes," he revealed how the consumption of carrots was behind his seemingly super-human night vision. While carrots seem removed from superhero origin stories, the mechanics are the same; ordinary human becomes extraordinary through exposure to an outside element. It possibly also served as the inspiration for the parody superhero *Bananaman* (1980), as the opening monologue to his animated adventures always informs the viewer: "For when Eric eats a banana, an amazing transformation occurs. Eric is Bananaman, ever alert for the call to action!"

Considering the British use of parody and satire in the development of British superheroes as opposed to the superhero origin story of superhuman powers, the character Phantom Eagle (1942–1948) is insightful. Phantom Eagle is American teenage boy Mickey Malone based in an American base in England, who wants to fly in the war, making his own airplane and dressed in a costume, akin to an aviator suit. He is joined by teenagers from occupied countries to fight the Axis powers. After the war, Malone/the Phantom Eagle searches for the mysterious and elusive "Formulae for Peace," a nod perhaps to the doctrines of the League of Nations, later the United Nations. The more well-known of the early British war superheroes is, however, The Amazing Mr X, commonly thought to be the first British superhero, who appeared in *The Dandy* (1944). Mr X is thought to have been developed in response to the successful *Superman*. Like Clark Kent, Les Manners/Mr X was a spectacle-wearing everyday man whose secret non-bespectacled hero persona is endowed with super-human strength. While Mr X may tear off the tail off planes, his narrative is about his efforts spent during the war fighting petty criminals in his hometown rather than using his skills to destroy Luftwaffe planes (Albion British Comics Database n.d.). Later, he would find out that his superhero flying powers were Nazi technology, which he then disowned.

British Superheroes of the 1950s and 1960s

Colonel Daniel McGregor Dare, known as Dan Dare, made his debut in the British comic series *Eagle* in 1950 with the tagline, "Dan Dare, Pilot of the Future" (Murray 2010, 33). *Eagle* began its life as a religious publication, and Dare was initially scripted as a chaplain. The Dan Dare comic series ran from 1950 to 1967 and continued in reprints. The comic was dramatized daily by Radio Luxembourg from 1951 to 1956. Dare returned in 1977 and was part of the *Eagle* relaunch in the 1980s. In 2003, Dare is reimagined in the comic series "Spaceship Away" and Titan Comics published a Dare mini-series in 2017. Perhaps, more science-fiction hero than superhero, Dare is a patriotic fighter pilot for the Interplanet Space Fleet, a futuristic organization. The stories were originally set in 1990 (his fictional biography has him born in Manchester in the 1960s). Dare is a skilled martial artist and an inventive strategist who is notable for his commitment to truth, preferring death to dishonor or dishonesty. David Barnett (2017) describes Dan Dare as

> Born in the white heat of the Cold War and the impending Space Race, Dan Dare was the square-jawed, morally upstanding and thoroughly British hero who thrilled a post-war generation of children who could finally look up at the sky in wonder as to what lay among the stars, not with fear at the prospect of bombs raining from above.

In the case of Dan Dare, the memory of the Blitzkrieg bombing of England by the German air force during 1940 and 1941 is embodied in his superhero's narrative. Different from American superheroes of the era in historical context and costume, Dare is a more like Biggles than his American contemporaries, Buck Rogers and Flash Gordon. While set it the 1990s, the dialogue, plot, and characterizations are more akin to the British war films being made in the 1950s. He looks more like a British actor of the era rather than a superhero and his uniform more resembles that worn by the British Army. Colored stripes and circles on his uniform's shoulders look more like military rank than anything futuristic, though his cap has a vertical retro-looking rocket ship motif captured in a circle with a five-pointed star on either side. Where Dare's characterization lacks in superhero traits, the comic did focus on scientific possibilities, with Arthur C. Clake acting as a science and plot advisor in early editions. By the mid-1950s, Dare had taken Britain into space, piloting a successful flight to Venus and includes stories of habited planets, advanced civilizations in space, and encounters with aliens, not unlike the futurism of H.G Wells or Jules Verne.

The focus on science and technology in Dan Dare narratives has to do with advancements that occurred during World War II, particularly in jet rocket technology followed by the breaking of the sound barrier and the achievement of supersonic flight in 1947, as well as the successful launching of Sputnik 1 in 1957. British scientists were also at the height of their success in the 1950s, winning the Nobel Prize for Physics for their work on splitting the atom. As such, Dan Dare is contextualized within the emerging possibilities of science and technology and its benefits of futuristic cities, flying cars, and the advancement of civilization. There is a utopian optimism in Dare; however, there is also caution about the threats posed by technology when left to the "emotionless" scientists who may subjugate the earth (Chapman 2008, 62). More problematic for the comic series is its use of racial stereotypes and advancement of white superiority, with patronizing discourses and framing the Other as suspicious and untrustworthy. These discourses sit in tension alongside Dare's Britishness and his platitudes of tolerance, fair play, and decency (Chapman 2008, 62–65). This tension leaves James Chapman to argue the reasoning for Dan Dare as a "chief ideological import," providing

> reassurance at a time of political and cultural anxiety for Britain. It was part of a tendency in post-war Britain popular culture including, variously, the war films of the 1950s and the James Bond novels of Ian Flaming – to protect Britain as a major world power at a time when her global authority was in decline.
>
> *(2008, 64)*

Introduced in the 1950s was Marvelman (later renamed Miracleman), devised in 1953 by British writer Mick Anglo as a British counterpart to American superheroes Superman and Captain Marvel (later renamed Shazam). Published at a time when imported American comic books were on the decline in Britain (Khoury 2001), Marvelman's origin story bore a striking resemblance to that of Captain Marvel. Both characters were children, with the former's powers imbued by a scientist using atomic energy while the latter was magically empowered by a wizard, and both were transformed into superpowered adults, respectively "Kimota" and "Shazam." Marvelman's popularity was such that for a time it exceeded its American contemporaries. However, once American imports again flowed to Britain, Marvelman fell out of popularity and was canceled in 1963. A revival of the character, and a rename to Miracleman, occurred in the 1980s which led to a renowned story arc by Alan Moore and

Alan Davis that was far more morally complex and graphically violent than the comparatively more straightforward superhero fare of Anglo's run. The title then passed in the mid-1990s to Neil Gaiman and Mark Buckingham to continue the story shortly before a convoluted, decades-long legal battle over the ownership of the Miracleman character ensued, which ended in 2009, allowing the story to continue (Melrose 2009).

In the sense of being a more conventional and less moralistic superhero, one of Britain's most popular superheroes of the 1960s was the Steel Claw who appeared in British weekly *Adventure Comics* from 1962 to 1970, and in *The Return of the Claw* from 1970 to 1973 (Treasury of British Comics 2023; DC Database n.d.). The superhero was revived by DC Comics in 2005. In the revived DC Comics book series plotted by iconic British author Alan Moore (See Murray 2010), the Steel Claw finds himself in Tony Blair's Britain where he is hunted down by the government because he and other British superheroes are embarrassing to the government. Blair wants all superheroes arrested and imprisoned in Scotland. Blending the political history of IRA attacks with science-fiction, including robots and time travel, along with origin stories of orphaning, body injury, and disfigurement, the Steel Claw infiltrates 10 Downing Street and confronts Tony and Cherie Blair over their role in the taking of superhero possessions. The Steel Claw more closely resembles aspects of American superhero narratives. His fictional biography is that of Louis Crandall/Lewis Randall (depending on the edition) who is a laboratory assistant that lost his right hand in a laboratory accident. His missing hand is replaced by a metal prosthetic. A later laboratory accident sees him receive a high-voltage electric shock making him invisible except for his metal hand. However, his "kryptonite" is that the length of his invisibility is unpredictable and it leaves him depleted and vulnerable (Treasury of British Comics 2023).

Crandall/the Steel Claw uses his powers initially to steal before joining the British secret service and an espionage agency, the Shadow Squad. His metal hand is now a steel claw, equipped with weapons and tools in each finger, which he uses to fight criminals, aliens, and the villainous organization F.E.A.R (the Federation for Extortion, Assassination, and Rebellion). During his crime-fighting, the Steel Claw wears a metal mesh outfit, and his claw increasingly becomes more technologically advanced, including the ability to fire missiles. After his retirement (not a narrative commonly evidenced in American superhero stories), Crandall becomes a detective and bounty hunter which leads him to living in South America where he continues to fight crime. In other reimaginations, he is also narrated as a burnt-out government assassin. The Steel Claw enjoyed widespread international fandom especially as part of the Shadow Squad franchise which was especially popular in Europe throughout the 1970s and achieved cult status in India where the character spawned several Indian spinoff superheroes who could, for example, make themselves invisible via a wristwatch.

Doctor Who provides a unique British superhero archetype even though the Doctor does not possess superhero strength, and the Doctor's superhero outfit is of everyday attire, all be it, a little eccentric. First aired on 23 November 1963 (the day after the assassination of J. F. Kennedy), running until 1989 and revived in 2005, the series was initially aimed at families to educate them about science, space travel, and famous moments in history. Despite the science-fiction elements of Doctor Who, the character does embrace superhero narratives as the Doctor confronts moral dilemmas, uses his intelligence to overcome evil, and is in the possession of extraordinary technology, including a time travel machine (the TARDIS). The Doctor can also regenerate, which allows the Doctor to receive a new body and personality. Like other British superheroes, national and cultural identities are embodied in the character. These elements collectively position Dr Who as a unique blend of science fiction protagonist and superhero archetype. Considered one of the "central heroes of British popular culture" (Hardt 2022, 12), and a "window into the British cultural imagination" (Sandbrook 2015, 402), the Doctor has traits of heroism that when combined with his time travel and regenerative abilities, posit him as a superhero. The Doctor is extraordinary, autonomous, moral, and has agency (Hardt 2022, 13). More so, his narrative posits superhero traits, particularly his liminality. Not unlike Superman, Doctor Who is "drawn to and emerges from… liminal spaces where they are forced to overcome boundaries and venture into the realms of the unknown, unimaginable and impossible" (Hardt 2020, 121). Doctor Who also retains characteristics of Britishness. Jones (2010, 86) cites Rusell T. Davis, writer and producer of Doctor Who from 2005 to 2009, attesting to his "desire to make the series essentially British." Evidencing this is the 2007 episode "The Family of Blood" which recalls scenes of British wartime bombing "steeped in the familiar iconography of the British experience of war" (Jones 2010, 85), albeit in fact an episode about an alien invasion. However, as with aspects of liminality so central to Doctor Who, it is a "temporal jigsaw" and a "patchwork simulacra of the British war experience" (Jones 2010, 86). The episode also brings to the fore the Doctor's own alienness and how this sits with the character's Britishness (comparable to the many stories of Superman and his dual alien/American identities). Earlier episodes also engage with British experience and history, particularly that of postcolonial Britain. The 1979 episode "City of Death" shows Britain becoming subjugated by the European parliament framed as the "evil alien from the continent" (Jones 2010, 92). During the period of Tom Baker's Doctor Who (1974–1981), we see Doctor Who framed largely as an "isolated wanderer," a metaphor for the decline of British global influence (Jones 2010, 90). In this discussion, Doctor Who, like previous British superheroes, embodies the "flying" heroes of Britian's past, as well as signifying the decline of British hegemony.

Discussion

Not surprisingly the British superhero is defined by their Britishness, be it British histories of heroism (as in the case of RAF pilots), the British class system and the hero's aspirational social status, Britain's military and scientific past, or lingering ideas of the British Empire (Ecke and Gill 2015, 134). Thinking about Doctor Who as a superhero posits how Britishness, class, as well as satire are evident in British comic representations (Geraghty 2015, 89). Such framing, positionality, and performance mean that British superheroes do not sit comfortably with other national superhero tropes, especially those of American superheroes (Ecke and Gill 2015, 134).

By contrast, American superheroes more directly inhabit the realms of sociopolitical discourse regarding nationhood, warfare, and culture clash. Thematically and narratively, this constructs the American superhero as a stand-in for issues of patriotism and the American Spirit (Dittmer 2012). Representations can range from the explicit – heroes such as Captain America, Stargirl, and the Iron Patriot wearing the stars and stripes on their costumes, quite literally tackling political problems head-on – to the more subtle – as one example, the vigilante Batman being interpreted as commentary on exceptional justice and the War on Terror in the 2000s and 2010s (see DiPaolo 2011; Brooker 2012; Höglund 2014). With rare exception are American superheroes fashioned out of real-world events; the most well-known of these exceptions are Superman, created in 1938 as a remedy for Americans coming out of the Great Depression (Morrison 2011, 4), and Captain America, whose first issue was published in 1940 as a direct response to World War II prior to the US joining the conflict

(Wright 2003). Otherwise, the characters already exist and are mostly enabled to *respond* to real-world events that can then be incorporated into their character development, such as the Avengers' in-universe response to 9/11 in *The Amazing Spider-Man #36* (2001).

Rare also is the American superhero's parodic take, especially at the so-called "Big Two" publishers of DC and Marvel Comics. Outside of parody examples such as Marvel's fourth-wall-breaking wise cracker Deadpool or DC's campy 1960s Batman TV series, starring Adam West as the Caped Crusader, the Big Two more often turn toward satire and alternate reality tales that reframe characters into outlandish or comedic settings, such as the "Marvel Zombies" comic series where existing Marvel characters are a ravening undead horde. When American superheroes have their own Cats Eyes or Bananaman-esque elements they are usually retroactively excised or reframed as something more substantial; as one example, in the 1960s, Green Lantern had an infamous weakness to anything involving the color yellow, which later became a plot point in the 2000s when the evil Sinestro Corps drew upon the emotional power of fear – colored yellow in the "emotional spectrum" of the comic book – as an opposite to the Green Lanterns' use of green willpower. American superhero satire is far more widespread, especially in critiquing the superhero as a national institution and a figure of exceptional justice, first with the seminal *Watchmen* (Moore and Gibbons 1988) and later seen in series such as *Black Summer* (Ellis and Ryp 2007–2008), *The Boys* (Ennis and Robertson 2006–2012), and *Transhuman* (Hickman and Ringuet 2009).

British and American superheroes approach readers via different discourses and *modus operandi*, and with largely separate approaches to how "realistically" these characters can be embodied, one could train to become an RAF pilot like Biggles, but not a super serum-enhanced soldier like Captain America. However, both fulfill similar social, cultural, and political functions. Both can challenge structures of modernity and realism by presenting suitably postmodern, surreal, and *irrational* states of being, framed by Jason Bainbridge as "a process of estrangement by which to highlight the inadequacies in the present system in the same way a test case might highlight the inadequacies in the law" (2007, 462). Both are useful conduits that embody (Gavaler 2014) and critique structures of imperialism and hegemony even if unintentionally, as in the cases of Biggles and the Steel Claw, and more contemporary renditions of both countries' characters put moral and ethical dilemmas narratively front and center; compare for example the exceptional vigilante justice of America's Batman and the fascistic violence of Britain's Judge Dredd, both of whom have been articulated as stand-ins for critiquing US drone strikes in the Middle East in the early 2010s (Comerford 2015; Lloyd 2015). Most crucially, both countries rely on the superhero being a figure of wish fulfillment and addressing inequity and injustice in a world where the structures of the law cannot fully deliver (Phillips 2010; Sharp 2012). Will Brooker articulates this as "imagining a better world and creating an alternate version of yourself… to patrol and protect it" (2013, 11). The British wartime superheroes discussed in this chapter ultimately represent, however fanciful or flawed, characters empowered to defend the British in the same way many American superheroes defend their citizenry.

References

Albion British Comics Database. 2020. "The Amazing Mr X." Fandom. Accessed September 4, 2024. https://britishcomics.fandom.com/wiki/The_Amazing_Mr._X.

Althusser, Louis. 2001. *Ideology and the Ideological State Apparatus*. Monthly Review.

Bainbridge, Jason. 2007. "'This is The Authority. This Planet is Under Our Protection', An Exegesis of Superheroes' Interrogation of Law." *Law, Culture and the Humanities1*, 3, pp. 455–476.

Barnett, David. 2017. "Dan Dare, How the British Superhero Survived to Make the Digital Age." *The Independent*, September 1. https://www.independent.co.uk/news/long_reads/how-the-british-superhero-survived-to-make-the-digital-age-a7924386.html.

Brooker, Will. 2012. *Hunting the Dark Knight: Twenty-First Century Batman*. I.B. Tauris.

Brooker, Will. 2013. "We Could be Heroes." In *What Is a Superhero?* edited by Robin S. Rosenberg and Peter Coogan. Oxford University Press.

Byun, Stephanie S., and Richard F. Spaide. 2021. "Carrots, Blueberries, and Spinach-Vision Superfoods." *National Library of Medicine*, May 1. 41, 5, pp. 895–897. doi: 10.1097/IAE.0000000000003089. https://pubmed.ncbi.nlm.nih.gov/33394962/.

Chapman, James. 2008. "Onwards Christian Spaceman, Dan Dare – Pilot of the Future as British Cultural History." *Visual Culture in Britain*, 9,1, pp. 55–79.

Chapman, James. 2011. *British Comics, A Cultural History*. Reaktion Books.

Comerford, Chris. 2015. "The Hero We Need, Not the One We Deserve, Vigilantism and the State of Exception in *Batman Incorporated*." In *Graphic Justice, Intersections of Comics and Law*, edited by Thomas Giddens. Routledge.

Dawson, Graham. 1994. *Soldier Heroes, British Adventure, Empire, and the Imagining of Masculinities*. Routledge.

DC Database. n.d. "Loise Crandall (Albion)." Fandom. Accessed September 4, 2024. https://dc.fandom.com/wiki/Louis_Crandell_(Albion).

DiPaolo, Marc. 2011. *War, Politics and Superheroes, Ethics and Propaganda in Comics and Film*. McFarland & Company.

Dittmer, Jason. 2012. *Captain America and the Nationalist Superhero, Metaphors, Narratives and Geopolitics*. Temple University Press.

Ecke, Jochen, and Patrick Gill. 2015. "Alterity in the Genisis of the Contemporary British TV Superhero." In *Superheroes on World Screen*, edited by Rayna Denison and Rachel Mizsei-Ward. University Press of Mississippi.

Ellis, Warren, and Juan Jose Ryp. 2008. *Black Summer*. Avatar Press.

Ennis, Garth, and Darick Robertson. 2006–2012. *The Boys*. Dynamite Entertainment.

Francis, Martin. 2013. *The Flyer, British Culture and the Royal Air Force, 1939–1945*. Oxford University Press.

Gavaler, Chris. 2014. "The Imperial Superhero." *Political Science and Politics* 47,1, pp. 108–111.

Geraghty, Lincoln. 2015. "Heros of Hall H, Global Media Franchise, Dr Who and the San Diego Comic-Con as Space for the Transnational Superhero." In *Superheroes on World Screen*, edited by Rayna Denison and Rachel Mizsei-Ward. University Press of Mississippi.

Goodrum, Michael. 2019. "Like a Cinema When the Last of the Audience has Gone Home and Only the Staff Remain, Biggles and (Post-) Imperial Heroism." In *Heroism as a Global Phenomenon in Contemporary Culture*, edited by Barbara Korte, Simon Wendt, and Nicole Falkenhayner. Routledge.

Gibson, Mel. 2000. "On British Comics for Girls and Their Readers." In *Consuming for Pleasure*, edited by Julia Hallam and Nickianne Moody. University of Liverpool John Moores Press.

Gibson, Mel. 2003a. "'What Became of Bunty?' The Emergence, Evolution and Disappearance of the Girls' Comic in Post-war Britain." In *Art, Narrative & Childhood*, edited by Morag Styles and Eve Bearne. Trentham Books.

Gibson, Mel. 2003b. "'You Can't Read Them, They're for Boys!' British Girls, American Superhero Comics and Identity." *International Journal of Comic Art*, 5,1, pp. 305–324.

Gibson, Mel. 2008. "What You Read and Where You Read It, How You Get It, How You Keep It, Children, Comics and Historical Cultural Practice." *Popular Narrative Media*, 1,2, pp. 151–167.

Gibson, Mel. 2015. *Memory, Comics and Post-war Constructions of British Girlhood*. Leuven University Press.

Hardt, Maria-Xenia. 2020. "Discovering New Dimensions, Affect and the Heroic in Doctor Who." *European Journal of Popular Culture*, 11,2, pp. 191–130.

Hardt, Maria-Xenia. 2022. *Heroism in Doctor Who, 1963–2020*. Ergon Verlag.

Hickman, Jonathan, and J.M. Ringuet. 2009. *Transhuman*. Image Comics.

Höglund, Johan. 2014. *The American Imperial Gothic, Popular Culture, Empire, Violence*. Ashgate.

Jones, Matthew. 2010. "Aliens of London, (Re)Reading National Identity in Doctor Who." In *Ruminations, Peregrinations, and Regenerations, A Critical Approach to Doctor Who*, edited by Chris Hansen. Cambridge Scholars Publishing.

Khoury, George. 2001. *Kimota! The Miracleman Companion*. Tomorrows Publishing.

Lloyd, Chris. 2015. "Judge, Jury and Executioner, *Judge Dredd*, Jacques Derrida, drones." In *Graphic Justice, Intersections of Comics and Law*, edited by Thomas Giddens. Routledge.

McRobbie, Angela. 1991. *Feminism and Youth Culture, From Jackie to Just Seventeen*. Macmillan.

Melrose, Kevin. 2009. "McFarlane Responds to Marvelman News." *Comic Book Resources*, August 6. https://www.cbr.com/mcfarlane-responds-to-marvelman-news/.

Moore, Alan, and Dave Gibbons. 1988. *Watchmen*. DC Comics.

Morrison, Grant. 2011. *Supergods, Our World in the Age of the Superhero*. Jonathan Cape.

Murray, Christopher. 2010. "Signals from Airstrip One, The British Invasion of Mainstream American Comics." In *The Rise of the American Comics Artist, Creators and Contexts*, edited by Paul Williams and James Lyons. University of Mississippi Press.

Murray, Christopher. 2017. *The British Superhero*. University Press of Mississippi.

Phillips, Nickie. 2010. "*The Dark Knight*, Constructing Images of Good vs. Evil in an Age of Anxiety." In *Popular Culture, Crime and Social Control (Sociology of Crime, Law and Deviance, Vol. 14)*, edited by Mathieu Deflem. Emerald Group Publishing.

Piatti-Farnell, Lorna. 2022. "Introduction." In *The Superhero Multiverse, Reading Comic Book Icons in Twenty-First Century Film and Popular Media*, edited by Lorna Piatti-Farnell. Lexington Books.

Reynolds, Ryan. 1992. *Super Heroes, A Modern Mythology*. University Press of Mississippi.

Sandbrook, Dominic. 2015. *The Great British Dream Factory, The Strange History of Our National Imagination*. Allen Lane.

Sharp, Cassandra. 2012. "'Riddle Me This...?' Would the World Need Superheroes If the Law Could Actually Deliver 'Justice'?" *Law Text Culture*, 16,1, pp. 353–378.

Treasury of British Comics. 2023. "Thrilling! Incredible! Weird! Who Is The Steel Claw?" *Treasury of British Comics*. Accessed 4 September 2024. https://treasuryofbritishcomics.com/news/thrilling-incredible-weird-who-is-the-steel-claw/.

Wright, Bradford W. 2003. *Comic Book Nation, The Transformation of Youth Culture in America*. Johns Hopkins University Press.

22

CANADIAN SUPERHEROES AND THE STRUGGLE FOR NATIONAL REPRESENTATION

Anthony Enns

In the early days of comic books, critics often equated the superheroes' use of extra-legal force with fascist ideology, and American publishers sought to address this problem by introducing overtly patriotic superheroes, whose violence was justified because they were acting as state functionaries. Even if they were not officially employed by the government, their function as symbols of the nation allowed them to serve as national representatives within the political sphere, who "engage in battle from time to time as proxies of U.S. foreign policy" (Reynolds 1994, 18). One of the most famous examples is the image of Captain America punching Nazi leader Adolf Hitler on the cover of *Captain America Comics #1* (1941) which was explicitly designed to promote American intervention in World War II (WWII). The political function of such superheroes not only explains why they "enjoy their greatest popularity during times of transition and uncertainty" (Bainbridge 2015, 746), when patriotic feelings are at their peak, but it also shows how they are connected to the history of political cartooning, which similarly employs national personifications to represent geopolitical relations.

The political function of national superheroes was particularly evident during WWII, which began soon after superheroes were first introduced. As Jason Bainbridge points out, their "involvement in foreign policy meant that superheroes were increasingly caught up in the propaganda machine around World War II and over time were actually absorbed into that machinery" (Bainbridge 2015, 755). One of the clearest examples of this "absorption" was the transformation of Superman from a progressive reformer to a symbol of American military strength, who often appeared on bombers and was used to sell war bonds. The idea that Superman fights for "the American way" was first articulated in "The Wolfe," a 1942 Nazi storyline on the radio series *The Adventures of Superman* (1940–1951), and it was later incorporated into the opening credits of the television series *Adventures of Superman* (1952–1958), which further reinforced the character's status as a national icon.

These superheroes not only promoted the idea of American exceptionalism, but they also helped to establish the dominance of American popular culture through their international circulation, which effectively equated the strength of American superheroes with the strength of the American comic book industry. This situation posed a unique problem for English Canada, which initially served as a secondary market for American comics due to its close proximity and shared language. As John Bell explains, comics were often seen as an "American

 DOI: 10.4324/9781003366911-26

medium" because the "heroes were American," and they thus conveyed the "implicit message" that "Canada was a backwater bereft of heroes" (Bell 1992, 19). While Bell argues that this situation created a sense of Canadian cultural inferiority, some readers have attempted to address this problem by reimagining Superman as Canadian. This reading was bolstered by the fact that Joe Shuster, one of Superman's creators, was originally from Toronto, which was the inspiration for the city of Metropolis, and he even credited the *Toronto Daily Star*, where he worked as a newsboy, as the inspiration for the original name of Clark Kent's workplace, the *Daily Star*. Mordecai Richler also described Superman as "a perfect expression of the Canadian psyche" because "he is a hero who does not take any credit for his own heroism" (Richler 1978, 123). Historica Canada reaffirmed the country's claim to Superman in a 1991 "Heritage Minute," which featured Shuster discussing Superman with his friend "Lois," and the accompanying book also featured a special section devoted to Superman's Canadian origins (Boulton 1994, 171–173). In 1995, Canada Post also released a collection of commemorative Canadian superhero stamps, which included Superman, and in 2013 the Royal Canadian Mint released seven commemorative Superman coins. There has thus been a sustained effort for many years to claim Superman as part of Canada's cultural heritage, which reflects a desire on the part of many Canadians "to have a national comics history" (Gray 2017, 645). Lee Easton and Kelly Hewson also argue that this superhero has been particularly appealing because "Superman offered a powerful masculine image," which "reassur[ed] Canadians that they are not a feminized nation" (Easton and Hewson 2018, 128).

Another way of satisfying this demand was to create Canadian versions of American superheroes, a practice that also dates back to WWII, when the importation of "non-essential" items from the US was temporarily suspended, including the importation of American comic books. This period has been described as the "Golden Age" of Canadian comics (Bell 1986, 22), as publishers in English Canada were able to produce their own comic books for the first time; however, some publishers merely reprinted material that had already been published in the US. For example, F. E. Howard's *Super Comics* (1943–1944) included partly redrawn versions of stories that originally appeared in M. L. J. Magazines' *Pep Comics* (1940–1956), including stories featuring The Shield, one of the first national superheroes with a costume based on the American flag (predating Captain America by over a year). While he was originally introduced as an FBI agent fighting to protect the US from Nazi spies, Howard's redrawn version replaced the stars and stripes on his shield with the Union Jack, which effectively transformed him into a symbol of British national identity for the Canadian market. Just as some Canadian readers sought to reclaim Superman as a national symbol of Canada, therefore, *Super Comics* can be seen as an effort to Canadianize an already extant American national superhero.

Some Canadian publishers also created new superheroes for the Canadian market, like Johnny Canuck, whose stories appeared in nearly every issue of Bell Features' *Dime Comics* (1942–1949). However, most of these companies went out of business after the restrictions on American imports were lifted, and many Canadian artists were subsequently forced to move to the US. For example, Leo Bachle, the creator of Johnny Canuck, briefly worked for Croydon Publishing before finally abandoning comics and becoming a nightclub performer. It wasn't until the 1970s and 1980s that Canadian publishers began to introduce new Canadian national superheroes, like Captain Canuck and Northguard, in a period that became known as the "Silver Age" of Canadian comics. Many of these publishers also found it difficult to compete with American publishers, yet the enduring popularity of these characters shows that there is still a desire on the part of many readers to consume narratives featuring

Canadian superheroes, and these narratives often frame Canadian identity in opposition or relation to American identity due to the economic dominance of American publishers and the close connection between the superhero genre and American popular culture. The history of Canadian superheroes thus reflects an ongoing struggle to imagine an appropriate symbol of Canadian identity, which has proven to be extremely difficult within a marketplace that is dominated by American companies and saturated with American characters.

This chapter will examine some of the most prominent examples of national superheroes in Canadian comics, and it will particularly focus on how these characters are used to represent the nation itself. While these comics are often celebrated for disrupting the hegemony of American popular culture, which makes any representation of Canada seem inherently progressive, it is important to note that the differences between Canadian and American national superheroes are often limited to cultural references (like the iconography of costumes and the depiction of familiar landmarks), as the style and conventions of superhero narratives are largely defined by American comic books, which tend to emphasize universal virtues (like truth, justice, courage) that transcend geographical boundaries. In this sense, Canadian superhero comics are often seen as exceptional merely because they are produced in Canada, which shows that Canadian publishers are able to compete with their American counterparts, yet their success often depends on their resemblance to American superhero comics, as they must also appeal to a secondary market of American readers. When framed within a Canadian context, however, many of these fantasies of national empowerment can be seen as inherently conservative, as they often fail to reflect the diversity of the nation and its problematic history.

Johnny Canuck

The character of Johnny Canuck clearly illustrates the close connection between national superheroes and the history of political cartooning, as he was directly inspired by 19th-century political cartoons, in which he was often used to personify Canada itself. He was initially represented as the son of "Papa" John Bull, a popular figure commonly used to represent Great Britain, and in many early cartoons, his father refuses to protect him from "Uncle Sam," the personification of the US, or "Brother Jonathan," the personification of New England (see Anonymous 1862, 432; Anonymous 1871, 64). These cartoons thus conveyed the idea of Canada as a young nation that was incapable of defending itself or acting independently in geopolitical affairs. By the end of the century, "Canuck" had also become slang for a Canadian soldier, and the character was often described as fighting for the British in songs like "Johnny Canuck's the Lad" (Godfrey 1900a) and "When Johnny Canuck Comes Home" (Godfrey 1900b), which celebrate Canadian participation in the Second Boer War.

The transformation of Johnny Canuck into a superhero was directly inspired by WWII, which was the first time that Canada declared war on another nation as an independent state rather than as part of the British Empire. As such, the war marked a turning point in Canadian independence, and Johnny was used to represent this newfound independence by working as "an independent operative" (Kocmarek 2016, 154). He was also introduced at the beginning of each story as "Canada's answer to Nazi oppression," and he was shown fighting the Axis powers all over the world, including Africa, Europe, Asia, and the South Pacific. While Bart Beaty argues that "the exploits of Johnny Canuck... tended to overemphasize Canada's importance in the war" (Beaty 2006, 430), Bachle was clearly attempting to represent Canada as a modern world power that was capable of providing a major contribution to the war effort, which was designed to inspire patriotism and promote military recruitment. These comics were also created in response to WWII-era comic books imported from the US, as Bachle explained: "We used to look in the American books and see all the heroes," but "we never had a hero here, and I felt that Johnny Canuck typified the Canadian character" (quoted in Hirsh and Loubert 1971, 25). He even drew not one but two scenes in which Johnny Canuck punches Hitler in the face, in *Dime Comics #2* (1942, 29) and *Dime Comics #5* (1942, 43), which implied that Canada was even more aggressive in its fight against the Nazis than America, whose national representative only punched Hitler once. In addition to representing a Canadian national superhero who was comparable to American national superheroes, these comics also served to represent Canada itself as a major producer of superhero comics that could compete with the American comic book industry.

This project was somewhat at odds with the origin of the character, however, as the cartoon figure on which Johnny Canuck was based was typically shown as subordinate to his British counterpart. While Johnny Canuck frequently identifies himself as a Canadian, and he even describes his signature punch as a "Canadian Special" in *Dime Comics #3* (1942, 39), he is also repeatedly described by his enemies as British, and he always takes his orders from the War Department in London. In *Dime Comics #1* (1942), for example, he is shot down during a "reconnaissance flight" over the "Libyan jungle" (23), and he discovers a "lost city" that has "secret mineral wealth," with which "the British could build a terrific war machine" (27). He then returns to London, reports the location of the city to his superiors, and is given orders to return and occupy the city on behalf of the British Empire. In other words, he is effectively ordered to assist in the British occupation of Libya, which was already underway at the time. When Germany discovers the location of the city and sends their own troops to occupy it, Johnny Canuck incites a rebellion among the indigenous population, which weakens the German defenses and helps the British to seize control. He is thus represented as a freedom fighter seeking to foment anti-German resistance as well as an imperialist seeking to acquire territories and resources for the British Empire, for which he receives a commendation from Prime Minister Winston Churchill at the end of the story (41).

Johnny Canuck continues to receive orders from the British government and to identify as a British agent throughout the rest of the series. In *Dime Comics #6* (1942), for example, he is assigned to lead resistance fighters in Kharkiv, which is under Nazi control, and in *Dime Comics #11* (1943) he is ordered to transport a Russian fighter plane "to my country for observation" (42), although the reference to "my country" refers to Britain rather than Canada. In *Dime Comics #15* (1944), he is sent back to Africa, where the Nazis are attempting to incite an uprising among the "Bawanias," who "are supposed to be loyal to the British government" (51), and he once again manages to defeat the Nazis and secure British control over a colonial territory. In *Dime Comics #19* (1945), he is ordered to defend Allied supply lines from Japanese attacks and rescue a Chinese general, who tells him that he has helped to "make bond between our people strong" (28), which is yet another reference to Johnny Canuck's nationality as British rather than Canadian. In *Dime Comics #20* (1945), he is also sent to warn Tito, leader of the Yugoslav Partisans, of an impending German attack, as Churchill chose to support the Partisans instead of the official Yugoslavian government, which had relocated to London following the German invasion in 1941. Like the British forces, he turns his attention to the Asian front following the German surrender in May 1945. In *Dime Comics #21* (1945), for example, he is stationed at "an allied base somewhere in the South Pacific," where he is ordered to bomb "the railway hub at Kokato" to force the Japanese to retreat (23). He is subsequently shot down, captured, and tortured, but he does not reveal any information and eventually manages to escape. There is thus a recurring tension throughout these stories between Johnny Canuck's affiliation with Britain and his role as a symbol of Canada, which reflects the difficulty of representing Canada at a time when it was largely seen as nothing more than a dominion of the British Empire. His role in the expansion and maintenance of the British Empire seems particularly problematic in this regard, as these comics repeatedly represent it as a force for good in the world, and they suggest that there is no better evidence of its goodness than the dedication of its loyal colonial subjects, like Johnny Canuck. The wartime context even makes his participation in British imperialism appear noble and heroic, as he often helps to protect indigenous people from the Germans, who were intent on reacquiring African colonies at the time these comics were published.

Captain Canuck

There was a resurgence of interest in Canadian national superheroes in the 1970s, and the most prominent superhero from this period was Captain Canuck, who appeared in a series of self-published comic books produced by Richard Comely. Unlike Johnny Canuck, who wore a generic military-style uniform, Captain Canuck had a more traditional superhero costume adorned with the colors and symbols of the maple leaf flag, which had just been introduced as the National Flag of Canada in 1965. Comely explained that the character was inspired by his own patriotic and religious convictions (Dittmer and Soren Larsen 2007, 742), and Ryan Edwardson similarly argues that his "moralism, natural strength, and self-sacrificing persona reinforced conceptions of Canadians as polite, kind, moral, heroic peacekeepers" (Edwardson 2003, 186). However, it is somewhat unclear how morality, strength, and heroism could be seen as uniquely Canadian qualities, as they could just as easily apply to any number of American superheroes. Instead, it appears that the most unique aspect of the character was that he was explicitly identified as Canadian, and Bell argues that this series "was resurrecting a national pride that Canadians had not experienced since the 1940s" (Bell 1986, 39). *Captain Canuck #1* (1975) also presented a hopeful vision of a future in which Canada has become "the most important country in the world" (5), and this is clearly shown in the opening story, "Arctic Standoff," which depicts an attempted communist invasion of Canada's northern territories. The "Canadian International Security Organization" sends Captain Canuck to defend the nation, and he successfully averts disaster by deactivating the communists' nuclear missiles (16). The ending thus emphasizes "Canada's great responsibility in the efforts to maintain World Peace" (18), which reinforces the idea of Canada as a major global superpower and a key player in the Cold War.

In later issues, it is revealed that this invasion originated not from the Soviet Union but rather from "radicals" in South America, and in *Captain Canuck #4* (1979), he is taken to their hidden base in an "ancient Incan" city (7) in the Andes Mountains, where he meets the villainous Mr. Gold, a criminal mastermind with a gold eye and a gold plate in his head, who is determined to take over Canada by installing a puppet regime. Gold's obsession with accumulating wealth suggests that he is a capitalist rather than a communist, although this is never fully explained. He has also enslaved the indigenous population of the region, who are forced to work in his illegal weapons factory, which has been sacrilegiously "built on top of an ancient Incan temple" (12). When Captain Canuck's mask is removed, readers also learn that he is "part Indian" (2), which appears to explain his sympathy for the indigenous people and his desire to liberate them by destroying Gold's factory. *Captain Canuck #5* (1979) also evokes the WWII-era stories of Johnny Canuck, as Captain Canuck is sent to Germany to stop a Nazi leader using the title "Der Führer," but he eventually discovers that this villain is none other than Gold himself, after which he is recaptured and taken back to Gold's base in South America. In *Captain Canuck #6* (1979), readers are reminded of Gold's oppression of the indigenous people, who are "forced to share their city with white men," whose "souls... are as black as midnight" (1), and their frustration leads to an uprising after one man declares, "no longer will we be the slaves of these evil men!" (16). The uprising begins at the same moment Captain Canuck escapes from Gold's clutches, and his sense of solidarity with the indigenous population is made particularly evident when he thinks to himself: "Those Incans are brave! I've got to do something fast before Gold's men slaughter them!" (16). This storyline clearly illustrates the differences between Captain Canuck and Johnny Canuck, as Captain Canuck repeatedly expresses his support for indigenous sovereignty and even serves as an agent of decolonization, while Johnny Canuck only expresses his support for the British Empire and actively serves as an agent of colonization.

This technique of paralleling concurrent action sequences is used repeatedly throughout the series. In *Captain Canuck #9* (1980), for example, readers learn that aliens are attempting to invade the Earth, and in *Captain Canuck #12* (1980), the alien leader attempts to get Captain Canuck out of the way using a temporal portal that transports him to the year 1040, where he witnesses a Viking attack on a group of "Micmac Indians" (15), a reference to the Mi'kmaq people, who were the original inhabitants of Canada's Atlantic Provinces. The comic thus establishes a connection between two different invasions taking place during two different time periods, which are temporally separated by nearly 1,000 years but are visually juxtaposed in parallel panels on the same pages. The explicit parallels between these two invasions also help to explain why Captain Canuck feels that "his place in the ensuing battle is immediately clear" (16). He instinctively knows that he must support indigenous sovereignty, in other words, because he immediately identifies with the struggles of the indigenous people and perceives the Vikings, like the aliens, as foreign invaders on Canadian soil. He is also concerned that the indigenous warriors will not see him as an ally, as "the costume must make me seem very strange to them, but if they see that I have Indian blood, they may be more receptive" (17). While he is unfamiliar with their language and customs, and he sees himself as generically "Indian" rather than a member of a particular nation, he clearly believes that the color of his skin will allow him to win their support and friendship, which is precisely what happens.

This storyline clearly reflects the contradictions of the character, as he is repeatedly shown to be an agent of the federal government, who is helping to reinforce the power of the settler state, but he also identifies as an indigenous person, who is helping to promote anti-colonial resistance. His indigenous identity also remains hidden for most of the series, which explains why critics like Bart Beaty condemn the comic's representation of a "white, male government employee" as a "symbol for the nation," as it "reduces Canada's multicultural heritage" (Beaty 2006, 434). Jason Dittmer and Soren Larsen similarly argue that Captain Canuck represents an "Anglo-Canadian version" of Canadian national identity, which obscures the diversity and heterogeneity of the nation as a whole (Dittmer and Larsen 2007, 740). It is easy for critics to overlook Captain Canuck's indigeneity because it only appears in isolated moments when he interacts with other indigenous people, and it often functions as a form of cultural appropriation that serves to assimilate indigenous identities into a more normative image of Canadian national identity. In a similar way, this storyline also equates indigenous sovereignty with Canadian national sovereignty by representing the indigenous population of Atlantic Canada as ancestors of the modern Canadian state, who are already helping to protect and defend its borders from foreign threats, which obscures the role that settler colonialism historically played in the formation of the state itself.

While *Captain Canuck* was canceled in the early 1980s, there have been several attempts to reboot the series. For example, there was a four-issue limited series *Captain Canuck: Reborn* (1993–1996), which featured a character named Darren Oak, who is inspired to assume the identity of Captain Canuck in an effort to fight a global conspiracy called the "New World Order," which is attempting to take over Canada. This conspiracy was reportedly inspired by the real-life "Communist-Super-Capitalist Conspiracy," which was based on the idea that western businesses and communist governments were working together to create a global totalitarian regime – a conspiracy theory that was also the focus of Comely's comic book series *Star Rider and the Peace Machine* (1982). While Darren is clearly identified as white, he also has an indigenous partner named Daniel Blackbird, a homeless alcoholic who was rescued by Darren and eventually completed an "Intelligence Gathering and Investigation" course. *Captain Canuck: Unholy War* (2005–2007), produced under the direction of Riel and Drue Langlois with assistance from Comely, also introduced RCMP Constable David Semple, who is similarly inspired by the original series to assume the identity of Captain Canuck. Like the previous series, David also has an indigenous partner, Keith Smoke, and their friendship seems to reflect the contemporary state of settler-indigenous relations, as Dittmer and Larsen point out:

> The very invisibility of Keith Smoke's aboriginality within the storyline, and within the symbolic presence of the Canadian state (the RCMP), makes the claim that the relationship between Canada and its exotic internal others has changed—they are no longer exotic, no longer other at all, but are now living in the suburbs, fully assimilated.
>
> *(Dittmer and Larsen 2010, 64)*

Indigeneity is not erased, in other words, but it is "assimilated within the dominant sociocultural forms of the Canadian South," which reinforces "the conventional form of internal Orientalism in Canadian comics" (Dittmer and Larsen 2010, 66). The same could be said of the earlier comics as well, as they also represent Canada as a transtemporal geographical phenomenon entirely divorced from any political or historical context, as its indigenous and settler populations are shown to be a unified and continuous community that is tied to a particular place yet somehow transcends time.

Northguard

Captain Canuck #2 (1976) introduces his two sidekicks, Redcoat and Kebec, who represent English and French Canada, respectively. Their ability to work together (under the hero's direction) was another part of Comely's hopeful vision of a future in which Canada is no longer culturally divided, as its English and French populations are both loyal to the federal government. Anglophone-Francophone relations are even more central to Mark Shainblum and Gabriel Morrisette's comic book series *New Triumph* (1984–1986), an allusion to Bell Features' WWII-era series *Triumph Adventure Comics*, which introduced another Canadian national superhero named Northguard. John Bell describes this character as "the most sophisticated vision to date of a Canadian superhero," and he also notes that Shainblum and Morrisette challenged "American superhero conventions" by setting the story in a more realistic world and emphasizing the suffering of the hero (Bell 2006, 79). Northguard is introduced as a young student from Montreal named Phillip Wise (an anglicized form of the Jewish name "Weiss"), who is recruited by a company named P.A.C.T. (Progressive Allied Canadian Technologies), developers of the "Uniband," a futuristic weapon that provides heightened abilities to someone with the appropriate "brainwave patterns." This weapon was designed to help operatives perform surveillance on multinational corporations, but its first user uncovered a plot "to overthrow the Canadian government" (8), which resulted in his death. As a fan of Captain Canuck, Wise recognizes that he has a responsibility to use this weapon to defend his country, and he agrees to serve as a P.A.C.T. agent only if they agree to give him a superhero costume adorned with a maple leaf.

In the opening story, Northguard thwarts an assassination attempt against Quebec Premier René Lévesque, the first Québécois leader to hold a referendum on independence (in 1980). Northguard also discovers that this assassination attempt was disguised as an English-Canadian attack on the French-Canadian separatist leader, but it was really orchestrated by a right-wing American organization named ManDes (an abbreviation for "manifest destiny"), which seeks to overthrow the Canadian government and establish a Christian theocratic dictatorship. This storyline was possibly a response to the expansion of Christian nationalism in the US under President Ronald Reagan, who received support from Jerry Falwell's Moral Majority and Pat Robertson's Christian Coalition, and it implied that tensions between English and French Canada were being exploited by Americans in order to weaken Canadian resistance to foreign influence: "Someone's trying to reopen old wounds, someone from outside. Well I won't let them! We've come too far in this province, I'll be damned if I let anyone push us back to hate and paranoia!" (28).

This series also featured a Québécois superhero named Manon Deschamps, who adopts the name Fleur de Lys, which refers to the official emblem of Quebec (not to be confused with the French superhero Fleur de Lis, who appeared in the American series *Infinity, Inc.* in 1987). Deschamps is first introduced as a Tae Kwon Do champion who befriends Phillip and is recruited by P.A.C.T. to train him in martial arts. She later adopts her own superhero persona as a joke to point out the silliness of Phillip's Northguard identity, but it stops being a joke after Phillip is captured, and she is sent to rescue him armed with a taser weapon shaped like a fleur-de-lys. She thus becomes his partner (and love interest), which further reinforces the idea of a harmonious union between Canada's "two solitudes."

Conclusion

Following the end of the "Silver Age," Canadian artists interested in producing superhero comics were once again forced to work in the US, and Canadian national superheroes could only be often found in American comic books like *Alpha Flight* (1983–1994), which featured a Canadian superhero named Guardian whose costume was remarkably similar to that of Captain Canuck. Anna Peppard points out, however, that these Canadian superheroes were primarily intended for American readers, and they reflected "popular perceptions of Canadian identity warped (or mutated) by and through an American lens" (Peppard 2015, 316). Some American publishers attempted to produce superhero comics aimed at the Canadian market by appropriating familiar characters, like Moonstone's *Northern Guard* (2010–2011), which features an assortment of characters taken from WWII-era Canadian comic books (including Johnny Canuck, who is reimagined as a scientist). Canadian publisher Chapterhouse also attempted to resurrect Captain Canuck and Northguard in 2016, but due to problems with American distribution the company was eventually relocated to the US and reestablished as an imprint of Lev Gleason Publications in 2021. While many aspects of these characters remain the same, the need for American distribution resulted in several significant changes. For example, *Captain Canuck: Invasion #0* (2018) introduces the main character as "not simply a Canadian hero" but "a hero for everyone" (1), and *Northguard #1* (2016) shows him working for the CIA instead of defending Canada from American encroachment.

Jason Dittmer argues that national superheroes can be interpreted in many different ways, as they are designed to appeal to a wide range of readers, and

> the multiplicity of national discourses, produced not only by transnational corporations trying to identify the 'pulse' of their target markets but also by those who consume the material culture, confounds any attempt to align the interests of governments and popular-culture producers.
>
> *(Dittmer 2011, 85–86)*

While it is certainly true that the meanings associated with national superheroes are often ambiguous and mutable (particularly when their narratives are produced by foreign companies), this does not necessarily mean that they do not serve political interests. Rather, it shows how political and economic interests are often aligned, as these narratives represent fantasies of national empowerment that are designed to appeal to the patriotism of readers, and national identity is usually represented as uncomplicated and unproblematic, as reader identification helps to facilitate the monetization of patriotic feelings. A closer examination of Canadian national superheroes thus shows how these national symbols function not only as political propaganda, which obscures the problematic history of settler-colonial and Anglophone-Francophone relations, but also as a way of integrating citizens into commodity capitalism. Perhaps, the most hopeful aspect of these comics is that they represented attempts on the part of Canadian companies to compete with US imports, yet this history clearly shows that Canada has not been as successful within the economic sphere as its superheroes have been within the cultural sphere, and economic success would only indicate the convergence of national interests with the interests of multinational capitalism, regardless of the fact that capitalists are often presented as villains within the narratives themselves. An understanding of the political and economic function of national superheroes thus requires an examination of how national identity is constructed as well as the economic interests that fuel these constructions.

References

Anonymous. 1862. Cartoon. *Harper's Weekly* 6, no. 288 (July 5): 432.

Anonymous. 1871. "Johnny Canuck's Idea of It." *Canadian Illustrated News* 4, no. 4 (July 22): 64.

Bainbridge, Jason. 2015. "'The Call to Do Justice': Superheroes, Sovereigns and the State During Wartime." *International Journal for the Semiotics of Law* 28, no. 4 (May): 745–763.

Beaty, Bart. 2006. "The Fighting Civil Servant: Making Sense of the Canadian Superhero." *American Review of Canadian Studies* 36, no. 3 (October): 427–439.

Bell, John. 1986. "A History: English Canadian Comic Books." In *Canuck Comics: A Guide to Comic Books Published in Canada*, edited by John Bell. Matrix Books.

Bell, John. 1992. *Guardians of the North: The National Superhero in Canadian Comic-book Art*. National Archives of Canada.

Bell, John. 2006. *Invaders from the North: How Canada Conquered the Comic Book Universe*. Dundurn Group.

Boulton, Marsha. 1994. *Just a Minute: Glimpses of Our Great Canadian Heritage*. Little, Brown & Co.

Dittmer, Jason. 2011. "Captain Britain and the Narration of Nation." *Geographical Review* 101, no. 1 (January): 71–87.

Dittmer, Jason, and Soren Larsen. 2007. "*Captain Canuck*, Audience Response, and the Project of Canadian Nationalism." *Social & Cultural Geography* 8, no. 5 (October): 735–753.

Dittmer, Jason, and Soren Larsen. 2010. "Aboriginality and the Arctic North in Canadian Nationalist Superhero Comics, 1940–2004." *Historical Geography* 38 (January): 52–69.

Easton, Lee, and Kelly Hewson. 2018. "Heroes, Borders, and Canadian Culture: The Superman Reclamation Project." In *Reading between the Borderlines: Cultural Production and Consumption across the 49th Parallel*, edited by Gillian Roberts. McGill-Queen's University Press.

Edwardson, Ryan. 2003. "The Many Lives of Captain Canuck: Nationalism, Culture, and the Creation of a Canadian Comic Book Superhero." *Journal of Popular Culture* 37, no. 2 (November): 184–201.

Godfrey, Henry Herbert. 1900a. *Johnny Canuck's the Lad*. Gourlay, Winter & Leeming.

Godfrey, Henry Herbert. 1900b. *When Johnny Canuck Comes Home*. Gourlay, Winter & Leeming.

Gray, Brenna Clarke. 2017. "Canadian Comics: A Brief History." In *The Routledge Companion to Comics*, edited by Frank Bramlett, Roy T Cook, and Aaron Meskin. Routledge.

Hirsh, Michael, and Patrick Loubert. 1971. *The Great Canadian Comic Books*. Peter Martin.

Kocmarek, Ivan. 2016. "Truth, Justice, and the Canadian Way: The War-Time Comics of Bell Features Publications." *Canadian Review of Comparative Literature* 43, no. 1 (March): 148–165.

Peppard, Anna F. 2015. "Canada's Mutant Body: Nationalism and (Super)Multiculturalism in Alpha Flight vs. the X-Men." *Journal of the Fantastic in the Arts* 26, no. 2 (Spring): 311–332.

Reynolds, Richard. 1994. *Super Heroes: A Modern Mythology*. University Press of Mississippi.

Richler, Mordecai. 1978. "The Great Comic Book Heroes." In *The Great Comic Book Heroes and Other Essays* edited by Robert Fulford. McClelland & Stewart.

23

MODERN CZECH SUPERHEROES

Miracle and the Spring Man as the Defenders of the Nation

Michaela Weiss

Czech Illustrated Heroes: Insects, Children, and Other Creatures

This chapter discusses the historical rootedness and social significance of two Czech comics superheroes, Dechberoucí Zázrak (the Breathtaking Miracle) and Pérák (the Spring Man).

In the Czech Republic (including former Czechoslovakia), superhero comics do not have a long tradition. Under the communist regime, comics as a genre was considered either as belonging strictly to children and the young adult market, or, as a bourgeois, politically hostile propaganda (Prokůpek n.d.). The majority of artists were either banned or had to focus on mainly humorous or educative stories. One of the first, as well as most famous, Czech illustrated heroes was Ferda the Ant, whose first appearance in 1927 was in Ondřej Sekora's story "Příhody opilého mravence" ("The Tales of a Drunken Ant") for *Pestrý týden* (*Colorful Week*). Sekora drew his inspiration from his stay in Paris in 1923, where he gained experience as a sports correspondent. Besides becoming a rugby lover, he also became the founder of comics in Czechoslovakia. His animated character was originally designed for adults, commenting on the onset of fascism and the Spanish Civil War. Because of his wife's Jewish origin, Sekora was sent to labor camps in Kleistein and Osterode (1944–1945). In the postwar years, his ant tales were turned into children's stories, fused with socialist ideology.

Among other famous serialized heroes was *Čtyřlístek* (*The Cloverleaf*, published since 1969) by Jaroslav Němeček. This Czech "Fantastic Four" includes Myšpulín, the cat inventor; Bobík, the strong and food-loving pig; Fifinka, the brave and caring female dog; and Pinďa, the athletic rabbit. Besides these four, there is occasionally the character of Myška, Myšpulín's assistant, who is usually not involved in the action.

The last series to be mentioned, this time targeted at young adults, were *Rychlé šípy* (*The Rapid Arrows*, 1938–1989; publication was often discontinued because of the Nazi or Communist regimes) by Jaroslav Foglar. The Rapid Arrows follows the adventures of five boys aged 10–15. While the stories were moralistic and didactic, they represented a new era of Czech comics, using text balloons instead of a description below individual panels. Because of Foglar's affinities to the Czech variant of the Scout Movement, Junák, Foglar's books were banned, first by the Nazis and later by the Communists. They started to be republished only after the fall of the Communist regime in 1989. Despite the long period of discontinuity,

DOI: 10.4324/9781003366911-27

the stories inspired many youth clubs and organizations, and the name of one of the boys, Mirek Dušín, entered the Czech lexicon, referring to someone who is an embodiment of morality, self-sacrifice, and honesty. Mirek Dušín was therefore the hero (though not a super-hero) of many generations. All the abovementioned comics heroes are firmly embedded in the national culture and conventions both in terms of their origin and conduct; they do not come from different planets, nor do they have any supernatural powers. On the contrary, they are either children or animal figures who fight for justice, providing both education and entertainment.

The first serious attempt at comics art is to be found in the works of Karel Saudek (1935–2015), who became a major Czech comics artist. Due to the Jewish origin of his father Gustav, Karel, and his twin brother Jan (an internationally acclaimed Czech photographer) were imprisoned in the concentration camp Luža in Poland, while their father was deported to Theresienstadt Ghetto in 1945. All of them reunited after the war. Despite Karel's admiration for Walt Disney, Will Eisner, and the underground comix of Robert Crumb, his illustrations were gaining popularity and were used for the scripts of Jaroslav Foglar or the famous Czech science fiction writer, Ondřej Neff. He drew the comic elements for the cult Czechoslovak movies *Kdo chce zabít Jessie?* (*Who Wants to Kill Jessie?*, 1966), directed by Václav Vorlíček: a science fiction comedy using word balloons and comics imagery. He also authored illustrations for the detective comedy *Čtyři vraždy stačí, drahoušku* (*Four Murders are Enough, Darling*, 1971), directed by Oldřich Lipský, which featured staple comics lettering and sounds such as "Boom" and "Crash." Both movies passed the political censorship as they were presented as popular entertainment parodying the American comics format. However, Saudek's own comics were banned as they were considered politically subversive, and too sexually explicit and violent.

As becomes evident with the example of Karel Saudek and Ondřej Sekora, comics and its creative expressions only flourished in the times of a more relaxed political regime, i.e., in the 1920s, the years preceding the 1968 invasion of Warsaw Pacts troops to Czechoslovakia, and after the fall of the Communist regime in 1989. Since popular genres, including fantasy and science fiction, were under a scrutiny of the political censorship, they only started to develop in the 21st century. As Czech comics historian and artist Tomáš Prokůpek (n.d.) notes, in the 1990s, all restrictions and censorships were dropped. Yet, as it became evident in 1993, television and other media turned out to be more attractive; moreover, there were no established authors, publishers, or distributors of Czech comics.

Consequently, until the beginning of the new millennium, the Czech cultural scene was mainly discovering and absorbing international productions. The Czech scene has been only slowly catching up with the superhero trends. The first Czech serialized superhero comics, *Breathtaking Miracle*, thus emerged as late as in 2015. The authors, Petr Macek and Petr Kopl, did not seek to imitate existing superheroes but drew on the rich tradition of Bohemian legends and folklore, bringing to life supernatural (and superheroic) characters, including the Golem, the White Lady, and the Spring Man. Their Miracle is a young Czech student who absorbs the magical power of the Golem after an explosion at the Museum of Prague. He turns into a superhero who, under the guidance of Edward Kelly (the English alchemist of the Bohemian King and the Holy Roman Emperor, Rudolf II), learns how to use his superstrength to save his homeland.

Macek and Kopl thus designed a new Czech superhero universe which included another, already existing Czech superhero, the Spring Man. Based on the war-time urban legends of Prague, the Spring Man was named after large springs on his boots. This mechanism enabled him to fight the Nazis and their collaborators and turned him into the symbol of Czech resistance during the occupation. Due to the character complexity, his humor, and subsequent reception, they created an independent spin-off, which serves as a prequel to the *Breathtaking Miracle* series.

The Spring Man, Czech History, and (Popular) Culture

The Spring Man figure first appeared in urban legends dating from the first half of the 20th century and his reputation has grown into national popular culture mainly in the World War II era. In the urban legends, the character was not associated with any supernatural powers; he predominantly relied on technological advancements. He became associated with the anti-fascist resistance movement, though as Petr Janeček documents, this association is rather artificial (2022, 61). Yet, as shall be manifested in this chapter, this connection turned out to be crucial for the Spring Man's revival as a superhero.

Despite the amount of attention the character of Spring Man received in popular culture, the first book-length study addressing the Spring Man appeared as late as 2017, when the folklorist and ethnologist Petr Janeček published *Mýtus o Pérákovi* (*The Spring Man Myth*; English version: *Spring Man: A Belief Legend between Folklore and Popular Culture*, 2022) where he devoted one chapter to the "Phantoms of the Industrial Age," addressing the affinities between the Spring Man and other phantoms and ghosts, especially Spring-heeled Jack (2022, 78–118).

The road from a robber and urban phantom, via a patriotic fighter against the Nazis, to a superhero took several decades. In 1946, Jiří Trnka, a Czech puppet-maker, illustrator, and film director directed a short, animated film, *Pérák a SS* (*The Spring Man and SS-Men*; *The Chimney Sweep* in the United States). Featuring a mixture of animation and photography, the black-and-white silent films are reminiscent of propaganda reels. The chimney sweeper, portrayed as a generic character, uses springs from a couch and provokes the SS-Men by using the swastika flag as a handkerchief. He manages to outwit the SS-men and free all objects and animals accused and imprisoned for violating the laws of the protectorate. After his task is done, he takes off the springs and returns to his job.

A more concrete and complex version of the Spring Man was introduced in Petr Stančík's novel *Pérák* (*The Spring Man*, 2008). The young protagonist has a name, Franta Pérák (Francis Springman) and the story reveals his personal life, including a romantic relationship. The book is accompanied by illustrations, period leaflets and advertisements, and drawings of guns. The hero is depicted as graceful, possessing "a manly beauty reminiscent of an exquisitely built ship," with golden hair and blue eyes:

> The face of a man who spoils the dreams and the routines of every Gestapo in the Protectorate. The man that mothers use to scare disobedient children, yet all the boys want to be him, while none want to be Hácha [Czechoslovak president from November 1938 to March 1939, and from March 1939 to June 1945 was a president of the German Protectorate of Bohemia and Moravia, who opted for German occupation of his homeland instead of its bombing and destruction]. The man whose face thousands of women paste on the faces of their husbands and lovers during love making. The face of Franta Pérák! The hero is dressed in a tight-fitting leotard made of first-class brown cowhide leather.... On his chest, he bears his symbol: a yellow, thrice-spun spring.
>
> (*Stančík 2008, 15*)

Stančík's Spring Man even gets married and has a son. Yet, at the end of the book, he is to be deported to Germany, as a native Sudeten German, named Udo von Schlitz. To escape the separation from his family and his fate in postwar Germany, the Spring Man says good-bye to his wife and son and jumps into space, where he suffocates, explodes, and freezes at the same time. (Stančík 2008, 117) His name, appearance, and his romantic relationship form the basis of Macek's and Kopl's new version of the hero.

The Spring Man in Comics and Cartoon: The Superhero Material

The first comics adaptation of the Spring Man's adventures was serialized in *Haló, Nedělní noviny* (*Hello, the Sunday paper*; issues 13–27, 1948,) under the title "Pérákovy další osudy" ("More Stories of the Springman"). Adopting Trnka and Brdečka's animation, Vladimír Dvořák turns the Spring Man into a common man, ardent defender of the new, socialist Czechoslovakia, fighting against all imperialist enemies: "At the beginning of May 1945, the Springman took off his uniform and became an ordinary man – a Czech worker with all the worries and joys of a citizen of a liberated nation" (Dvořák 1948, 16).

The politically engaged Spring Man reappeared in August 1968 in a special issue of *Mladý svět* (*The Young World*) magazine, within the four-panel strip "Pérák a SSSR" ("Spring Man and the USSR") by Ondřej Jelínek. The strip was published in the year of the Warsaw Pact invasion of Czechoslovakia. This openly anti-Soviet comic brings the Spring Man back to life, using him as a subversive national superhero; here, he knots up the barrel of a Russian tank and sprays it with graffiti: "Do not forget to get the hell out of here! The Spring Man" (Jelínek 1968, 2–3).

The subversive power of the hero and his embeddedness in the national consciousness is documented by a 2015 graffiti at a pig farm at Lety, a site of a former labor camp signed by the Spring Man. The drawings were commemorating the deaths of 327 Romani people who died there during World War II. This protest was announced by an email sent by "The Spring Man" to the media, stating: "The pig farm in Lety is a shameful reminder of Czech version of Auschwitz. I am back to make amends." Soon after, a series of posters appeared in Prague: "I still feel sick at the memory of all those slimy Czech fascists, spineless officials, gendarmes and guards who set up their own concentration camp in Lety near Písek" (Kopřiva 2015).

The comic that marked the first attempt to use the Spring Man's potential to become a superhero was Ondřej Neff's *Pérák, český super-hero: Toho dne byla mlha* (*Spring Man, Czech Superhero: There Was Fog That Day*, 1989), which provides an origin story, linking the Spring Man to the Golem legend, as well as the story of Frankenstein's monster, as the hero was created by Professor Karas to serve as a weapon against the Nazis. After the war, the Spring Man was put into cement to harness his power. He then comes back to life to battle the wild "gray zones" of late 1980s Czechoslovakia. In 2001, Neff published a sequel, *Pérák contra Globeman* (*Spring Man vs Globeman*), taking place in the first decade of the democratic Czechoslovakia, showcasing the rise of private businesses, corruption, and non-critical admiration of Western mass culture. The Spring Man fights the Globeman, who turns out to be SS general Stauff in disguise of a McDonald's clown. While Neff's comics feature the Spring Man, it is still more of a social commentary than a full-blooded superhero comic.

The Spring Man as a Super Nazi Fighter

After his appearance in the *Breathtaking Miracle* series, the specific and often politically incorrect humor of the Spring Man was receiving perhaps too much attention and threatened to overshadow the young protagonist. As Macek admits in the epilogue to *The Spring Man: Eye of the Future*, there was no space for such two highly individualized heroes. Together with Kopl, they decided to give the Spring Man his own space and a more natural setting: Prague during World War II, in two book-length stories, *Pérák: Oko budoucnosti* (*Spring Man: The Eye of the Future*, 2019) and its sequel *Pérák: Jantarová komnata* (*Spring Man: The Amber Chamber*, 2021). The Spring Man's central agenda is to fight the Nazis, namely, his arch-enemy, Major Verner, who is searching for magic artifacts for the Third Reich. Besides that, the hero faces other phantoms of urban legends, namely the Razorman, a mass murderer and sadist, who collaborates with the Nazis and is known to have knives in his gloves, and later, a mechanical construction that includes three pairs of wing-size razors.

The Eye of the Future expands Spring Man's "origin story," using the name and depiction from Stančík's novel. František Pérák was tortured in the Theresienstadt Ghetto and the Nazis were running experiments on him. As he discloses: "They skinned me alive and burned some mysterious runes into my flesh to protect me against black magic. Then they sewed the skin back on" (Macek 2019). As a result, the Spring Man is immune to black magic. The plot revolves around the search for the relics of a mythical Bohemian Dutchess Libuše, who founded the city of Prague and in one of her prophetic visions, foresaw its great future. Her skull shall serve as a source of power to secure Hitler's rule over the world and the whole universe. The Spring Man is captured by the Nazis and blackmailed into collaboration, as Major Verner has imprisoned his pregnant partner, Libuška. This is a great triumph for the Germans, as the Spring Man is a symbol of strength, wit, and Czech cunning.

After finding the Dutchess Libuše's skull and defeating the Valkyries who are protecting their Dutchess, the Spring Man watches a Russian spy take the skull and have a vision of Hitler's death, the rise of Stalin, and the election of Václav Havel, the first democratic Czech president. After that, the spy's body explodes into flames and the cave is flooded. Major Verner escapes with the skull, believing the Spring Man to be dead. Little does he know that not only is the Spring Man alive but that he found his lover's name on a list of executed collaborators. As revenge, the Spring Man attacks the train on which Verner is escaping. What he does not know though is that members of the Czech resistance have planned an explosion of the railroad bridge. Heavily wounded, the Spring Man wants to die, as he has lost his family. The only thing that gives him motivation to live is the news that Verner managed to escape.

The Spring Man's weakness is thus his humanity and the love he felt for Libuška. Under his dark humor and cynicism, he is portrayed as a hero capable of emotions, who often acts irrationally and is willing to collaborate with his enemy to save those close to him. And, it will be the Spring Man's emotions that will dramatically affect the hero's actions. In the sequel *Spring Man: Amber Chamber*, Major Verner gets access to an amber chamber, an artifact of endless value, which can bring about an apocalypse. The Spring Man seems to care less for the defeat of the Nazis than for his personal revenge on Verner.

The roots of his blind desire for revenge are uncovered in the flashback in the opening panels, where he remembers his sister whom he failed to protect from their abusive father. His mother could not take her daughter's loss and died soon after. Since then, the Spring Man was determined to protect all women against violence. He also recalls the terrible deeds of the Coalman (another urban legend character), who was torturing women and hiding their mutilated bodies in coal heaps in cellars. To stop the devilish plan, the Spring Man must beat a genetically modified Phosphorman (a Slovak urban legend character). The Phosphorman was a young nationalist who supported the independent, totalitarian Slovak state. When he was diagnosed with cancer, Dr. Mengele used him for experiments. While his cancer was gone, his blood structure was changed, and he can shoot out a mixture of phosphoric and sulfuric acids, and corrosives.

When finally confronting Verner, the Spring Man falls into a similar trap as in the previous story: Verner holds a small resistance boy as a hostage, laughing at Spring Man's morals that always turn him into a weak loser. Using an amber stone, the Spring Man is tele-transported into an alien spaceship, which gives the Nazis access to a portal, which allows them to travel in time, change the past and thus affect the future. In a struggle with Verner, the Spring Man crushes the relic of the Dutchess Libuše, which frees her soul. The only thing he asks of her is freedom for his occupied land. Selfishly, he hopes the ghost will kill Verner but is disappointed, as the Dutchess tells him she can see Verner's future and his bleak end by the hand of Satan himself. She also gives him good advice: to free himself from the hatred and desire for revenge, otherwise he shall never find peace. As her final deed, she shows the aliens the true nature of the Nazis and pleads for female solidarity, as the aliens turn out to all be female archeologists. They follow her lead, break the arrangement with the Nazis, and fly to another galaxy.

The final panels show the combat between the Spring Man and the Phosphorman. Spring Man reveals his chest and shows his opponent that they were both misused. He urges him to choose the right path, admitting that he killed common German soldiers and is not proud of his actions, which were motivated by personal revenge and robbed him of his humanity. He even admits that he does not want to kill Verner, as he wants to watch him suffer. The closing panels foreshadow the next developments, featuring Verner who is planning his submarine trip to Argentine, including a panel with Spring Man's Libuška with oxygen mask and a growing belly.

In these Spring Man tales, Macek and Kopl not only incorporated the Spring Man both into Czech (oslovak) history but also embedded his character into popular culture by drawing on the Protectorate urban legends. Even though he is still a human drawing his strength from special gear, he has one quality that turns him into a mighty opponent: he is immune to black magic. As such, he can face the Nazi manipulation with the occult. Still, he is not a moral emblem, admitting to his bitterness and suppressed frustration, which turns him into a more relatable, flawed character, which is not too far from the conflicted versions of his urban legend origin.

The Breathtaking Miracle and the Mysteries of the Old Prague

The Breathtaking Miracle is a pioneering project of Petr Macek and Petr Kopl who, following the American superhero comics format, started to publish a serialized story of the first Czech superhero, the Breathtaking Miracle. The first issue, "Magický počátek" ("The Magical Beginning", 2015), introduces the superhero, who is accidentally shot when trying to overpower two masked robbers. It is, therefore, clear that Miracle is a vulnerable human who is only learning to harness his magic willpower. His origin story is explicated in issue #2, "Golem ničitel" ("Golem the Destroyer"; 2016), which indicates that the authors will not be relying on the American superheroic scene and will, instead, draw on local, Czech folklore, legends, and myths. Breathtaking Miracle was not born a (super)hero but became endowed with magical powers after an accidental explosion in the National Museum, while his younger brother Jan ended up in a coma. By opting for a Golem as a source of the magic, Macek and Kopl not only draw on the national emblem, connected with Prague, but also use a widely known creature from Jewish folklore. The Golem also has its place in the comics universe (see Marvel's *Strange Tales* [1974] and *The Invaders* [1993]) and is called the predecessor of superheroes in Michael Chabon's novel *The Amazing Adventures of Kavalier & Clay* (2000).

The Golem holds a special position in the Czech popular culture and national mythology. Macek and Kopl not only use the legend of rabbi Judah Loew ben Bezalel who created the Golem to protect the Jews of Prague, they also draw on popular movies, especially the two-part historical fantasy comedy *Císařův Pekař* a *Pekařův císař* (*The Emperor's Baker and The Baker's Emperor,* 1951). Directed by Martin Frič, written by Jan Werich and Jiří Brdečka, with costumes by Jiří Trnka, the two Czechoslovak movies were re-distributed in the United States in 1955 as a single film: *The Emperor and the Golem.* The movies are set at the court of the Roman Emperor, Rudolph II, featuring the renowned occultist and scryer Sir Edward Kelley (presented under the Czech spelling Kelly), and the mystical creature, Golem of Prague.

The humanoid was presented as a lump of clay in a shape of a big man without emotions or thinking, who blindly follows the orders of any person who brings him to life. In the movies, he is activated by a *shem*, in this case a small clay ball, inserted into his forehead (or mouth). After many failed attempts to misuse his power for military purposes, the shem ends up in the hands of the baker Matěj, who uses the humanoid for baking bread for all common people. The movie can thus end on a cheerful, collective note, manifesting to the world that the Czechoslovak atomic energy shall be used for peaceful purposes only. However, in Macek's and Kopl's comics, the Golem is to be awaken by a techno-shem. In line with the mad scientist trope, the Golem's power is to be used for military and political manipulations.

As each hero needs a mighty villain, an arch-enemy of his own, in issue #4, "Zrození zla" ("Birth of Evil"; March 2016), a new superheroic character is born: multimillionaire Oskar Pleksl, the head of an IT company, which employs Miracle's mother. Oskar becomes the embodiment of greed and evil, calling himself the Complex. As it turns out, Oskar is the one who caused the explosion in the museum and who tried to harness the power of the Golem. Facing Miracle, he becomes aware that they both share the Golem's power. Complex is a variation on the traditional mad scientist trope, a genius IT manager who managed to create a "beyondspace," which turns out to be dangerous, especially in combination with the Golem's power. Miracle manages to beat him, yet, as the end of the issue suggests, the victory is far from final, as Complex becomes united with the mind of Dr. Faustus who seeks ways for how to return to life in the beyondspace.

Besides featuring the fantasy elements, a key element of Czech superhero comics is history, mainly World War II. Both Miracle and the Spring Man consider the Nazis their major opponents. In "Smrt z rukou králů" ("Death by Kings' Order"; April 2016), issue #5 of the *Breathtaking Miracle* series, Macek and Kopl blend the Czech legend of St. Wenceslas' crown with the Nazi occupation of Bohemia. The crown was made in 1346 for the coronation of Charles IV, King of Bohemia and Holy Roman Emperor, and was named after the patron of the land, St. Wenceslas. According to a legend, the crown can be worn exclusively by rightful rulers of Bohemian kingdom. If misused, the trespasser shall die a violent death within one year. Macek and Kopl draw both on this legend and the historical events of 1941, when Reinhard Heydrich, the Deputy Protector of Bohemia and Moravia, put the crown on his head in St Vitus Cathedral and was assassinated by Czech resistance less than a year after. In the comics, Heydrich lives for only eight hours, suffering a painful and violent death. To keep the nation subdued, he is replaced by a double. The mastermind behind the cover-up is an ardent Nazi called Verner, the Spring Man's nemesis, who seeks to extract the magic power from the St Wenceslas crown with the help of the Golem's techno-shem.

In the *Breathtaking Miracle* series, Macek and Kopl have not only created the first Czech superhero but that they also have created a whole universe, steeped in local folk tales, fairy tales, urban tales, and national legends. Another character entering the scene is the White Lady, a ghost of a woman who suffered pain and oppression. She is based on the historical character of Perchta of Rozhmberk and her abusive marriage. After refusing to forgive her dying husband for all the suffering she had to endure, he cursed her, which led to her iden- tification with the White Lady legend (Klassen et al., 2001).

Another example of incorporation of popular culture into the narrative is the employment of the black ambulance legend. The car was rumored to drive at night and kidnap children and young people to harvest their organs and sell them to wealthy foreigners (Janeček 2006, 2007). This line is masterfully linked with the announced return of Dr. Faustus, whose ghost is looking for a body that fits his requirements: a young male without a strong will power, somebody who is not dead but not fully alive: in the case of the narrative, Miracle's brother who lies comatose in hospital. To protect him, Miracle takes him away from the hospital, despite the hysterical scene created by their mother.

All these events changed the public attitude toward Miracle, exactly as his opponents expected. The police believe that not only has he kidnapped his brother but also that all the other missing children were abducted by him. Miracle saves his brother's life but does not fully protect his team member Michaela, who suffers severe injuries. What is more, his brother disappears without a trace from the hiding place, and his own mother hates him. At this moment, the second Czech superhero, the Spring Man, enters the scene to teach Miracle a lesson. In issue #9, "Hon na Zázraka" ("Hunting Down the Miracle") of the *Miracle* series, Spring Man is depicted as a retired, cynical man who is skeptical of superheroes:

> Superheroes, the whole world is crazy about them and what good did they bring? Just more harm and suffering. This would never have happened in my younger days… You don't need superpowers to do good… Because if you overdo it, when the heroes fail… they can turn into villains in the eyes of the public… Who remains here to stop them? Only he whose civic duties are not limited by pension.
>
> *(Macek and Kopl 2020)*

This is a curious scene, where two "protectors" of the land stand against each other. The Spring Man confronts Miracle, accusing him of kidnapping and murdering children, and destroying his beloved city of Prague. The Spring Man seems to follow the outfit descrip- tion as depicted by Stančík in his novel *The Spring Man*. He wears the leather suit and gog- gles, only he is much older. He has come to give Miracle a lesson, telling him that even the Nazis stood no chance against him. Here, Miracle recognizes him, yet shows no respect. On the contrary, he tells him that he must be the Spring Man his grandmother was telling him about and dismisses the Spring Man's warnings: "You can't be serious, grandpa. You are old as Methusalem, it's strange that you have not smashed your face on those springs yet. You should get a walker." (Macek and Kopl 2020). The Spring Man and Miracle fight and to his unpleasant surprise, Miracle realizes that the Spring Man is immune to his magic powers and he loses the fight with a bleeding nose.

Yet, the Nazis and the Spring Man are not the only adversaries that Miracle must face: he has to stand against his brother, whose body and mind are controlled by Faustus, as well as his mother who does not know that Miracle is her other son. The family line is not commonly revealed in superhero comics. If superheroes have known human parents, they are usually dead with the most famous exception being perhaps the father-son relationship between Tony Stark and his father Howard. In this sense, Miracle is unique, as he is put in prison by his mother who is not willing to release him, even after he reveals his identity to her. As such, he must rely on his team of "the mightiest Czech heroes" (issue #13, "Nejmocnější hrdinové Česka" / "The Mightiest Czech heroes"; January 2017), which fully formed in the final issue of the first season, consisting of Dr. Kelly in rejuvenated form, the White Lady, the Spring Man, a journalist, and an IT hacker friend. While not all members of the team have supernatural powers, they share an enemy: Dr. Faustus, who wants to open the Hell Gate and flood earth with undead monsters. The season's finale thus ends with a new superhero team and its unresolved plot points suggest that the journey is far from over. This open ending emphasizes the comic's serialized structure and highlights its thematic complexity. Such a conclusion reinforces the dynamic nature of comics as a medium, where each new issue or season continues to build upon a layered, evolving world, comprising superheroes, folklore, history, and humanity.

Conclusion

The Breathtaking Miracle is in many ways a pioneering project that laid the basis of a new, national superhero universe, a feat unprecedented in Czech popular culture. Petr Macek and Petr Kopl not only made their (childhood) dreams of creating a Czech superhero come true, but they also gave a new resonance to the Spring Man, a long-known character from the urban legends. Both Miracle and the Spring Man are human beings, who fall in love, have conflicted relationships with their families, and make mistakes, which makes them more relatable. The flaws of their characters, as well as self-doubts, also strengthen their humanity. In the *Miracle* series, the Spring Man is even depicted as an old, retired man, who is, however, still mentally and physically capable of fighting evil and protecting his beloved city of Prague, as well as the nation. The Czech superheroes thus inhibit the same socio-cultural space and are firmly embedded in national history, politics, and culture. While the Spring Man, with a significant amount of mischief and cunning, has become a symbol of subversive protest against (neo)fascism and other totalitarian ideologies, the Miracle still has a long path ahead.

Acknowledgments

This paper is a result of the project SGS/12/2023, Silesian University in Opava internal grant *Text Interpretation from the Genre Analysis Perspective*. SGS/12/2023.

References

Dvořák, Vladimír. 1948. "Pérákovy další osudy." *Haló nedělní noviny* 4 (13): 16.
Janeček, Petr. 2007. *Černá san itka – druhá žeň. Pérák, ukradená ledvina a jiné pověsti. Lidé města.* Plot.
Janeček, Petr. 2006. *Černá sanitka: Současné pověsti a fámy v České republice.* Plot.
Janeček, Petr. 2022. *Spring Man: A Belief Legend between Folklore and Popular Culture.* Lexington Books.

Jelínek, Ondřej. 1968. "Pérák a SSSR." *Mladý svět* 10 (35): 2–3.

Klassen, John M., Eva Doležalová, and Lynn Szabo. 2001. *The Letters of the Rožmberk Sisters: Noblewomen in Fifteenth-Century Bohemia*. D. S. Brewer.

Kopřiva, Jan. 2015. "Na vepříně v Letech se objevily kresby připomínající oběti války. A podpis Pérák." *iROZHLAS*, January 27. https://www.irozhlas.cz/regiony/na-veprine-v-letech-se-objevily-kresby-pripominajici-obeti-valky-a-podpis-perak_201501271213_vkourimsky.

Macek, Petr, and Petr Kopl. 2019. *Pérák: Oko budoucnosti*. Crew.

Macek, Petr, and Petr Kopl. 2020. *Dechberoucí Zázrak*. Kompletní první sezóna. Czech News Center.

Macek, Petr, and Petr Kopl. 2021. *Pérák: Jantarová komnata*. Crew.

Prokůpek, Tomáš. n.d. "Interviews." *Stripburger*. https://www.stripburger.org/en/tomas-prokupek-2/.

Stančík, Petr. 2008. *Pérák*. Druhé město.

Trnka, Jiří, and Jiří Brdečka. 1946. *Pérák a SS*. 13 mins. https://www.youtube.com/watch?v=7Uws XOv5XXg.

24

LOOK! UP IN THE SKY! IT'S A BIRD! IT'S A PLANE. NO, IT'S SUPER-FRENCH!

Chris Reyns-Chikuma

Introduction

Superman (created in 1938), *Batman* (1939), *Wonder Woman* (1941), *The Fantastic 4* (1961), *Spider-Man* (1962), *X-Men* (1963), *Black Panther* (1966), in short, all superheroes, appear to be made in America. All of them? No, there are some in other countries, including France, both in the form of translations-adaptations of American superheroes and as original French creations. However, who has heard of Fantax, Satanax, and Mister X? Except for a few thousand or, possibly, hundreds of fans, these heroes represent unknown quantities to the vast majority of the planet. The only French superhero famous in France, and a bit beyond, is Asterix, that is to say, a series that could be read as a parody of superheroes.

In this article, I explain why superheroes have never succeeded in acclimatizing themselves in Franco-European comics, exploring the various factors that would elucidate this absence. Starting with a definition of a superhero, among a list of about ten criteria that could define them, only three or four are often necessary and/or sufficient. For example, a superhero usually has one or more superpowers, but Batman does not (he is only superpowered by his wealth and electronic gadgets). Also, most of them have a costume, a mask, and a double identity, but not the Fantastic 4. For this article, the definition should also be limited historically and semiotically: I consider 1938, the birth date of the first superhero, as the starting point and only within the comics media. Hence, the Count of Monte Cristo (from the eponymous 1844 novel) is not a superhero, not so much because he has no superpowers (nor does Batman) but because he belongs to an era and a way of thinking and "writing," a way of communicating, different enough to exclude him from the world of Superheroes as we commonly talk about it today.

Similarly, Francophone academic criticism has shown little interest in superheroes in general and even less in the few French ones, except through English and American studies programs (Gabilliet 2004). Equally, in the few collections of essays published to date on superheroes, only one chapter is devoted to French superheroes (by Désirée Lorenz in Marc Atallat and Alain Boillat's book, *Les Comics vus par l'Europe* [2016]; Lorenz has written another article on the adaptation of the US superhero to France [2019]). Neither the second academic book, by Boucher et al. (*Mythologies du super-héros* [2014]) nor the third one,

 DOI: 10.4324/9781003366911-28

edited by Laurent de Sutter (*Vies et morts des super-héros* [2016]) deals with French super-heroes. Finally, Thierry Groensteen and Harry Morgan, in their article on the superhero in Groensteen's *Le Bouquin de la bande dessinée* (2020, 754–763), dedicates only a couple of sentences to French superheroes and the rest to US superheroes.

Then there are also some brief allusions in non-academic books written by university graduates such as those by Thierry Rogel (2012), Jean-Philippe Zanco (2012), Vincent Bruner (2017), and Simon Merle (2023). I should also mention a superhero study that one would tend not to give too much credit to because of the series title "… for dummies." In his interesting synthesis, Eric Delbecque does not mention any French-speaking superhero, but he does include a note on Japanese ones: "we do not spontaneously think of manga heroes when we speak of superheroes… as for our criteria for defining superheroes, they don't really fit the heroes of Japanese comics" (2016, 100). There is also Jean-Marc Lainé and Jean-Marc Lofficier's *Le dico des super-héros* (2013) which includes about ten entries related to French superheroes, which on the one hand is a lot, considering that there was almost nothing before, but on the other hand, the attention spent is too little, considering that there are several hundred entries for American superheroes. In their *Critical Survey of Graphic Novels: Heroes and Superheroes* (2012), Bart Beaty and Stephen Weiner cite one French superhero out of several hundred entries total, including several Canadians and various other nationalities (e.g., Japanese).

This absence of French references confirms both the slowness of French cultural studies, popular studies, and cultural history to develop in French universities, and the difficulty to integrate objects that had been academically de-legitimized for so long, such as comics (e.g., Ory 2008) and even more so, the French superhero. Both issues explain their absence from the physical maps (books) and mental maps (memories) that have been mostly formatted by an Americanized horizon of expectation.

An Emblematic Example

In 2013, Delcourt, one of the big French comic book publishers, published a superhero story entitled *Mikros et Photonik: L'Ombre et la Lumière* (Mikros and Photonik: Shadow and Light). The book is an intermediary between the publication format of "comic books" and the so-called *album* of the Franco-Belgian *bande dessinée*. Format has long been in the comics world an essential element for the success of a story. Hence, the 48CC *album* format ("48CC" being 48 pages in color with a *cartonné*-hardcover) played a primary role in the failure of *Tintin* and *Asterix* in the United States (Gabilliet 2013). However, in 2013 the format is no longer a rigid model even in the Franco-European world, which among other things is due to the cultural influence by different and popular formats of manga and graphic novels. If these book-album-comics are an accepted hybrid product, these are also more visibly American by their chaptering, equivalent to the periodical publication of comic books and, even more especially, by its subject.

Mikros et Photonik tells the story of the meeting of two teams of three superheroes to save the world from a villain. On the back cover, there is the following text:

Before becoming Mikros, the microcosmic superhero alongside Saltarella and Big Crabb, Mike Ross was an entomologist at Harvard and an Olympic-level athlete. Tad-deus Tenterhook was a hunchbacked young man surviving in New York City. After an accident, he was transformed into Photonik, the luminescent hero flanked by the

brilliant Professor Siegel and the bouncy Tom Thumb. While our two teams of superheroes live happily ever after, they must unite against an enemy that is beyond imagination, and threatens all of humanity.

(Mitton and Navarro [Naughton] 2013)

One can see that in these adventures, created in the French language by French people, everything is American: the six characters are all Americans, and almost the whole story takes
place in the United States. Moreover, while the book contains a chapter that takes place in
France, the fact that this shows the second team of three superheroes taking their vacations
there reinforces the idea that they do not work in France. All of this helps to support the idea
that the saviors of humanity and the protectors of France and Europe are necessarily American. In the same way, the characters accumulate all the characteristics of American symbolic
power: Harvard, New York, and the Olympic Games (where the Americans are most often
the first in terms of the number of medals and disciplines perceived as central, like swimming), which taps into the Manichean vision of Good (the United States and its allies) and
Evil (those who are against the United States) regularly repeated in comics but also more
broadly by politicians, especially American Conservative Christians.

Finally, these superheroes and what they might connote are not taken seriously by the
French editorial team of this album, since, in the text on the back cover, a somewhat
ironic phrase, "without having aged," was inserted, which creates ironic distance (Mitton
and Navarro [Naughton] 2013). This type of humor can be found as a fundamental trait
in the French superhero genre and is deployed several times in *Mikros et Photonik*. The
writer, Jean-Yves Mitton, plays a lot with the codes of comics of the time. For example, he
stages himself in the adventures of his characters, and, as the narrator, regularly calls out to
the reader: "Reader! While you fill the tank […] of your scooter with refined gasoline…"
(2013, 57). The fourth wall is sometimes crossed also in comics and the superhero genre
but it is the systematic use in Mitton's works, and those of other French-speaking comic
artists, which makes adherence to the ideals carried by superheroes difficult or even impossible to believe in, reinforcing this ironic, parodic, French attitude that we find with the
few famous superheroes like Astérix.

While the author of these later adventures, Jean-Yves Mitton, signs with a French name, this
has not always been the case. These stories are a sort of remake of adventures that appeared
in the 1980s. In 1980, *The adventures of Mikros* by John Milton and Malcolm Naughton
and *Photonik* by Cyrus Tota and Malcolm Naughton were published almost simultaneously
but separately in the magazines *Mustang* and *Titan* by the Lyon-based publisher LUG. This
tendency to Americanize pseudonyms was common in the Franco-Belgian comics world
of the 1950s and 1960s (e.g., Morris for Maurice de Bevere, author of *Lucky Luke*), but it
was almost systematic until today in the small world of French superheroes. Thus Thierry
Mornet, author of the superhero *Republican Guard*, a patriotic hero whose stories take place
in various epochs but all based in France, has taken the pen name of Terry Stillborn in the
2010s (Mornet pronounced mort-né, which translates as "dead-born" or stillborn).

All these elements (Americanness of the characters, the symbolism of American power,
location of the action, American pseudonyms, etc.,), including a lack of "faith" in the subject
(created by the humor), reinforced by certain amateurism (e.g., the stylistic clumsiness of
the back cover), are proof that since at least the 1980s the superhero genre is dominated by
the United States which, in turn, influences the other cultures that try to produce a modern
superhero.

Brief History of the French Superhero

To create compelling work, at least the majority of those involved in the production and reception of that work must be more or less in agreement. Yet, what we see is a repeated series of disagreements and disorganizations. What characterizes the production of French superheroes is the constant disruptions, first between the producers (creators, publishers, distributors, and booksellers) and then with the receivers (the critics and the public). Thus, Xavier Fournier notes about *L'Homme d'acier* (1940), a modified version of Superman strips by René Brantonne and his anonymous writer, that "the script and the drawing serve two different logics" (2014, 110).

All of this takes place in the context of the continuing rise of the United States as a world power, including in cultural terms, which is illustrated, among other things, by the invasion of comic books in the 1930s. This provoked an anti-American reaction that can be seen through the ambiguous anti-Americanism of Hergé, whose *Tintin in America* (1932) is parallel to the anti-Sovietism of *Tintin in the Land of the Soviets* (1929), but which also reveals an influence (partly acknowledged) of US comics. This invasion culminated in *The Journal de Mickey* (1934–1944) created by Paul Winkler, in which Mickey Mouse sold ten times more copies than all the French magazines combined in those same pre-war and post-war years. From March 1939, nine months after its publication in the United States (May–June), Superman appeared in *Spirou* magazine (created in April 1938), under the name of Marc, as the title indicates: "Marc, modern Hercules." On the one hand, this avoids the reference to Superman, and on the other hand, it makes him French while creating two interesting connotations: one of mythology and the other to the circus. Superman is then published in *Aventures* and his name is changed to Yordi. The two publications result in a series of inconsistencies, such as him being called Yordi despite retaining the Superman 'S' on his chest, or spellings are changed (Karl for Kal-El, thus eliminating a possible allusion to Jewish culture). Then came the war, its disorder, and its curtailments, including paper restrictions and censorship, which would finally, and ironically, be favorable to the autonomous development of the Franco-Belgian comic strip, since, for four years, it would not have to face the American competition, among others of *The Journal de Mickey*.

During the war, a few attempts appeared: *François l'imbattable* in *Hurrah!* in the autumn of 1940; *L'homme d'acier* in the magazine *Les grandes aventures* in October 1940; then *Fantômas*, the anti-superhero, in the weekly *Gavroche*, censored after a few issues by the Germans in 1941; and *L'Eclair* by René Brantonne and an anonymous writer the same year. However, both the French and the German occupiers had other things to worry about during this period, and the adventures of superheroes almost completely disappeared, while *Les Aventures de Tintin* and a few other heroes continued. As soon as the war was over, two superheroes appeared; at the end of 1944, *Homo le robot* by Remy Bourles (only one issue), and *Fulguros* by Brantonne in 1946 in *Pic et Nic*. But, even if it also failed to anchor itself in the popular francophone memory, it is *Fantax* that is important for the sad history of the genre. The authors of *Fantax* are going to live a series of misadventures because of the Law of July 1949.

The July 1949 Law

The July 1949 Law played a primordial role across France both in "disciplining" French and Franco-Belgian comics, and to exclude non-French comics (especially American ones, and therefore, a lot of superheroes at the time). The setbacks of the creator-artist of *Fantax*, Pierre Mouchot [Chott], illustrate the negative impact of this law. Mouchot, given his tenacity (or his stubbornness according to other interpretations), was indeed the only one to be sentenced to prison for his publications in the comic world (Crépin and Groensteen 1999). He tried everything, including "translating" his *Fantax* comic book into a novel to avoid censorship, which was limited to the most obvious publications for young people, such as the "illustrés" (illustrated youth books). However,

> [h]arrassed by censorship, he eventually closed the business in the early 1960s. Culturally, by bullying one of the only French publishers capable of producing a counterpart to Batman and the other supermen from across the Atlantic, the supervisory commission created a vacuum in local production, leaving the field open to Americans.
>
> *(Fournier 2014, 108)*

But to blame this law for all the ills that comics, and in particular the superhero genre, has experienced, would be to simplify the reality. Authors have sought and sometimes found all sorts of alternative solutions to try and publish their work. Thus, given the mistrust about fantasy elements in the story and art, presented as dangerous for children in the 1949 Law, some would try to recreate equivalents of superheroes. Some would fly thanks to technology rather than their superpowers. For example, Super-Boy uses a kind of "jetpack" to fly, and correlatively, the adventures of this boy would "be the record holder for longevity among French superheroes" (Fournier 2014, 147). It should be noted, however, that this success is to be put into perspective since, first of all, he is a boy and not a man like the majority of superheroes, and, above all, the French collective memory has retained nothing of him today. Similarly, to escape the censorship of this same law, some stories were published in the mainstream press instead of in comics (Fournier 2015, 181), but this had little effect on the collective memory in France or Belgium, except on a few thousand fans through a magazine like *Strange* (Maigret 1999).

Finally, the considerable success of the Franco-Belgian bande dessinée schools, with their semi-realistic style, also contributed to the failure of many attempts to create and sell superhero stories. Because the Franco-Belgian formula worked so well, they attracted artists and audiences, but that success was also, to some extent, to the detriment of other possible comic blueprints, including that of the superhero genre and even the most artistically successful attempts, such as *Atomas* in 1948 by cartoonist René Pellos (Fournier 2014, 140).

Horizon of Expectation

However, these few factors alone cannot explain the high number of attempts followed by failures after only a few issues. After all, the Franco-Belgian comic strip flourished despite the censorship. Everything suggests that a "zeitgeist" was missing, or that the "horizon of expectation" was too unstable, as much on the side of the production as their reception. Thus, Fournier writes "[René] Brantonne will propose a total overhaul of Fulguros, a complete reboot" in 1954 (2015, 98); *Atomas* was canceled in 1948 because "For Charroux, it seems to have been a food job. Pellos had already gone back to other comics" (117). Similarly, for *L'Homme d'airain* of 1974, Fournier writes: "his origins and motivations will vary over the issues. In a few episodes, the scriptwriter C-J. Legrand and the draftsman Bernasconi regularly change their tunes" (192). And one could go on like this until the year 2000, the decade in which things stabilized for French superheroes influenced by the mostly revisionist superhero genre (Klock 2002). To understand these issues over at least 50 years, one must add other factors such as the negative associations surrounding the superhero (as Nazi misuse of the *Ubermensch*), the decreasing presence-prestige of France (due to objective conditions, such as a relative decline of its economic power, but also to subjective conditions, such as the strong elitist tendency of its cultural policies), and the absence of creators of Jewish origin in the Belgian-French world of comics.

In the United States, the creation of superheroes is often attributed at least partially to the Jewishness of many comic book artists from Shuster and Siegel, fathers of Superman, to Stan Lee (Lieber), father of Spiderman, to Bob Kane (Kahn), father of Batman, and Jack Kirby (Jacob Kurtzberg) to name but a few. Moreover, many other agents of the "Comic World" had ties to Jewish culture (e.g., editors like Moe Goodman, founder of Timely Comics, later Marvel) (Kaplan 2008). For reasons yet to be explained, and in contrast to other cultural domains, in France (or in Belgium), the world of comics includes very few creators of Jewish origin. The author of Asterix, René Goscinny, was of Jewish origin, but his stories were transposed to a French "resistancialist narrative" and in the well-known comical mode. A compensatory and/or revanchist interpretation that was possible for American superheroes (i.e., Superman as a response to *Ubermensch*) is therefore unlikely for Franco-Belgian comics.

Soft power, Geopolitics, and Cultural Policy

The 1949 censorship law is not usually included in discussions of French cultural policy, yet it does represent a repressive side of those promotional policies. French cultural policy only allowed the official recognition of comics as one of the popular arts after the 1980s; before that, French cultural policy was traditionally elitist (including through Malraux's "democratization of culture"). The various French governments thus projected French Culture into the world through images of elitist culture, such as Literature and Fine Arts (e.g., painting), and since the 1960s, cinema. In this field, as Serge Guilbaut has shown in the case of post-war-years painting, the battle for symbolic power, especially with the United States, is hard (2006). When comics are exhibited in a museum for the first time, as is famously the case at the Musée des Arts Décoratifs (Paris, in 1967), it is in a rather ambivalent way to enhance painting and attract a new audience to this academic art rather than to promote comics (Beaty 2012).

More fundamentally, despite the Gaullist policies (continued by Pompidou, and again by subsequent French Presidents Giscard, Mitterrand, and Chirac), because France had lost the majority of its colonies and was caught between the two Great Powers, few French people still believe that France is a Superpower. Each decade since 1940, France has been losing ground, literally and symbolically, to maintain only an increasingly elitist presence. Thus, France has lost its position as a popular culture in the world, but also since the 1960s, the French youth have become increasingly attracted by American and Anglo-Saxon productions, even if the government (especially through the education system), intellectuals, and fans will allow a more than honorable resistance put forth by some "French" artistic productions (of which Asterix can be read as an example).

After the repeated failures of the elitist French cultural policies of Malraux's democratization of culture, it would take another ten years to see a policy of cultural democratization (Poirrier 2006). Jack Lang's cultural policies were well anchored in defense against what was perceived as American imperialism; reasons given at the time were both ideological (among others anti-Americanism) and economic, however, its hierarchies also included the world of the comics, where there were good comics (alternative and auteurist) and commercial genres (e.g., Fantasy), with the superhero genre at the bottom.

Through all its cultural industries of soft power, the United States has created many products to convince the world of its "American Way of Life" (Nye 2005). Since the beginning of the 20th century, this has been especially true, starting with Hollywood and continuing with its American superheroes that can be seen as symbolic projections of the American superpower. Their cultural supremacy reveals the prevalence of the American model. This type of symbolic influence has been examined in cultural studies, specifically in cultural geopolitics studies (Douzet and Kaplan 2012, 246). Similarly, Delbecque writes: "[comics] automatically contributes to American soft power, i.e., to the seduction exercised by this country, and to the capacity for influence that this power of attraction gives it" (2016, 156). What seems to be missing in this world of Franco-Belgian comics, and beyond that in Franco-Europe, is this zeitgeist of the "American dream" that could feed a mythology of the superhero.

Parodies

France seems to have chosen to laugh rather than cry about their status in the world, as seen across several Franco-Belgian products and productions, which range from Tintin to Spirou, Titeuf, and other popular comic characters, and especially for what concerns us here, Asterix.

The two key dates in this parodic life of French superheroes would be 1959, the date of publication of the first episode of *Asterix* in *Pilote,* and 1972, the date of the first episode of *Superdupont* in the new version of *Pilote*. One cannot help but draw a parallel between these publication dates and the date of de Gaulle's entry into office in January 1959, and his exit from political power in May 1969, followed by his death in November 1970. The gradual replacement of Gaullism, including cultural Malrauxism, by more neo-liberal policies, led to Giscard in 1974, and to France being more open to popular culture. This in turn led to a socialist government headed by Mitterrand in 1981 and to the recognition of comics as one of the popular arts.

Asterix is both inextricably a satire and a parody. It is a satire of French society, of some of its shortcomings, and is a comic parody of both the ideas or stereotypes of France that French people and foreigners have. It is also a comic parody of the superhero genre, which itself presents an idea of what the United States is like. Just as the homologies between politics and culture are never perfect, there is no homology between the characters of Asterix and de Gaulle or the Gaullist movements. However, even though it has been disputed many times, the parallels are hard to avoid. Asterix and his resistance perfectly illustrate the explicit agenda of de Gaulle's administration: resistance against the Romans, of course, reaffirms the unifying Gallic ideology of the 3rd Republic. This not too subtly refers to the anti-Nazi resistance, re-promoting unity after the division of France between Vichy and Resistance fighters, according to a Resistentialist ideology. Finally, it is about the resistance against the new American hegemony. Asterix is indeed a superhero that the French of the 1960s were waiting for, like De Gaulle, but in a comical way.

But of course, Asterix is both a satirical and parodic superhero. Satirical in the sense that, unlike the American superheroes of the war years and even of the 1960s, Asterix makes fun of his government and the French stereotypes, first of all in a carnivalesque way by turning the big into the small; the contrast between the diminutive size of Asterix and the legendary size of de Gaulle's character is just the beginning of the comparison. In the same way, parody is the reversal of certain foundations of the genre. Thus, the traditional superhero duo is reversed: Asterix, the superhero, is small, and his companion, who is usually smaller than the protagonist, is huge, heavy, and clumsy. Similarly, instead of being oriented toward the future as science-fiction, as most superhero stories are, Asterix is oriented toward the past.

The creators of *Asterix* (Goscinny and artist Albert Uderzo) have both challenged the political interpretations of their creations. However, this type of ideological interpretation goes far beyond the intention or psychology of the authors. The fact that they deny it is hardly relevant as the parallel is too obvious, which does not mean that other interpretations are not possible at the same time, on the contrary, some of them are entirely non-political (Rouvière 2008). Faced with the resounding success of Asterix, the French government quickly understood that this series was a powerful symbol in France and abroad. It therefore named the first French satellite after Asterix in 1966. This Asterixian resistance continues in *Le Ciel lui tombe sur la tête* (*The Sky Falls on His Head*, 2005) where it is a question of resisting the invasion of the new superheroes, not only American but also especially the Japanese, with the "Nagmas" being an anagram of "Mangas."

A Mini-Renaissance Since about the Year 2000

The French parodic superhero genre continued after 2000, with, for example, the ingenious album *Imbattable* (2015) of Pascal Jousselin, or, by the cover of *Parodies: la bande dessinée au second degré* (2010), by one of the greatest specialists of comics, Thierry Groensteen, where we see Superman pied in the face. But none of these new representations reached the quantitative and/or qualitative presence of earlier parodies. Meanwhile, a new type of French superhero appeared. In a surprising way, the parody since 2000 is exceeded by a genre movement toward serious stories made in good faith. The French superhero is coming back in force and is supported by an ideology that is both nostalgic and trying to re-conquer the lost decades with a tone that is sometimes even almost revengeful (Lorenz 2016). This movement is led by Serge Lehman, and supported by learned fans like Fournier and Lofficier. Scriptwriter and refined critic, Lehman began his successful career as an SF novelist. Later, in his first bande dessinée series, *Les Brigades chimériques* (2009–2010), he tries to explain in a rather successful way how the French superheroes disappeared during World War I. In the second series, *Masked* (2012–2013), he gives birth to new French superheroes in a fictional near future. These series were followed by others, such as *Métropolis* (2014–2017). With Lehman and others, the genre is undergoing a mini-renaissance with a serious tone. This movement is amplified by several other productions of superhero stories in various media, including novels such as Lehman's *F.A.U.S.T.* (1996–1997) and Xabi Molia's *Les Premiers* (2017), and movies, including "How I became a Superhero" (2021).

Conclusions

One can see that it is the combination of many factors, both national and international, economic and cultural, diplomatic and political (e.g., cultural diplomacy), material (e.g., format), and legal (e.g., censorship), that explain the quasi-absence of "real" superheroes in France. Much research still remains to be done to further investigate the role and confluence of these many factors by decade and the detailed history of certain superheroes created in France (Fournier 2015). But unknown, unrecognized, or forgotten, one thing is certain: there are no credible superheroes in France.

Alexandre Dumas' *The Count of Monte Cristo* (1844) may be a "super man" in the sense of a man out of the ordinary, but he is not a superhero because he has neither superpowers nor a civilizing mission, and above all the medium of representation used (the novel), precedes the science-fiction genre and multimodal era of comic books (Thoveron 2008). Asterix is not a "superhero" because he is a parody created in an era that, despite its heroic fictional resistance, no longer believes in France as a superpower. Since the 1960s, Asterix has tried to resist and reconquer prestige and soft power, in France and abroad, and the plan partly succeeded, but in a different way, communicating its good-naturedness through laughter and good food, i.e., an ideal French way of life. The Mikros and Photonik of the 2010s, like their 1980s versions, and most other attempts of the previous years, are superheroes, but they are all foreigners, most often American; they only work in the United States and are in France to have a good time, partly confirming the Asterix's new ideal. Finally, when French heroes are produced and meet a certain success, they are created by non-French people, like the Nightrunner (*Parkoureur des banlieues*) who belongs to the DC universe, was scripted by the British David Hine, and drawn by the American Tom Lyle.

If there has been a mini-revival of the French superhero since about the year 2000, especially with the "texts" of Serge Lehman, it is through a refined and subtle but somewhat partly nostalgic reconstruction of a glorious past of French literature, science, and culture. Understanding how this reconstruction works would be the subject of another article.

References

Beaty, Bart. 2012. *Comics vs Art*. University of Toronto Press.

Beaty, Bart, and Stephen Weiner. 2012. *Critical Survey of Graphic Novels: Heroes and Superheroes*. Salem Press.

Boucher, François-Emmanuël, Sylvain David, and Maxime Prévost, eds. 2014. *Mythologies du super-héros*. Presses Universitaires de Liège.

Brunner, Vincent. 2017. *Les Super-héros, un panthéon modern*. Laffont.

Crépin, Thierry, and Thierry Groensteen. 1999. *"On tue à chaque page!" La Loi de 1949 sur les publications destinées à la Jeunesse*. Editions du Temps.

Delbecque, Eric. 2016. *Les super-héros pour les Nuls*. First editions. Pour les nuls.

de Sutter, Laurent, ed. 2016. *Vies et morts des superhéros*. PUF.

Douzet, Frédéric, and David Kaplan. 2012. "Géopolitics : La géographie dans le monde angloaméricain." *La Découverte-Hérodote* 3, 146–147.

Fournier, Xavier. 2014. *Super-héros: une histoire française*. Huginn-Munnin.

Fournier, Xavier. 2015. *Super-héros francais, une anthologie*. Huginn-Muninn.

Gabilliet, Jean-Paul. 2004. *Des comics et des hommes: histoire culturelle des comic books aux États-Unis*. Editions du temps.

Gabilliet, Jean-Paul. 2013. "A Disappointing Crossing: The North American Reception of Asterix and Tintin." In *Transnational Perspectives on Graphic Narratives Comics at the Crossroads*, edited by Shane Denson, Christina Meyer, and Daniel Stein. Bloomsbury.

Groensteen, Thierry, and Harry Morgan. 2020. "Superhéros." In *Le Bouquin de la bande dessinée*, edited by Thierry Groensteen. Bouquins.

Guilbaut, Serge. 2006. *Comment New York vola l'idée d'art modern*. Hachette.

Kaplan, Arie. 2008. *From Krakow to Krypton: Jews and Comic Books*. Jewish Publication Society.

Klock, Geoff. 2002. *How to Read Superhero Comics and Why?* Continuum.

Lainé, Jean-Marc, and Jean-Marc Lofficier. 2013. *Le Dico des super-héros*. Moutons électriques.

Lorenz, Désirée. 2016. "Modalités et enjeux de la réappropriation culturelle de la figure du super-héros dans La Brigade chimérique et Masqué de Serge Lehman », dans Marc Atallah et Alain Boillat (dir.)." In *Les Comics vus par l'Europe*, edited by Marc Atallat and Alain Boillat. Folio.

Lorenz, Désirée. 2019. "Ce que l'exposition fait aux comics de super-héros: domestication ou résurgence d'une culture populaire?" In *La Bande dessinée à la croisée des medias*, edited by Désirée Lorenz and Elsa Caboche. Presses universitaires de Rennes.

Maigret, Eric. 1999. "Strange Grew Up with Me: Sentimentality and Masculinity in Readers of Superhero Comics?" *Réseaux The French Journal of Communication* 7, 5–27.

Merle, Simon. 2023. *Super-héros et philo*. Breal.

Mitton, Jean-Yves (John Mitton), and Marcel Navarro (Malcolm Naughton). 2013. *Mikros et photonik: L'Ombre et La Lumière*. Delcourt.

Nye, Joseph. 2005. *Soft Power. The Means to Success in World Politics*. Public Affairs.

Ory, Pascal. 2008. *La Culture comme aventure*. Ed. Complexes.

Poirrier, Philippe. 2006. *La Politique culturelle en débat*. La Documentation française.

Rogel, Thierry. 2012. *Sociologie des super-héros*. Hermann.

Rouvière, Nicolas. 2008. *Astérix ou la parodie des identités*. Flammarion.

Thoveron, Gabriel. 2008. *Deux siècles de paralittératures*, 2 vol. Ed. Céfal.

Zanco, Jean-Philippe. 2012. *La Société des super-héros*. Ellipses.

25

RAT-MAN

An Italian Superhero Parody

Marco Favaro

Created by Leonardo "Leo" Ortolani in 1989 as a Batman parody, Rat-Man became, in less than 30 years, probably the most famous and loved (anti)superhero in Italy. Rat-Man is a superhero parody, but he is also much more. Leo Ortolani's character was soon inserted into each corner of popular culture, from Manga to Blockbusters Movies, and from Horror to Fantasy. Rat-Man explores the far, far away galaxy of Star Wars and climbs Mount Doom to destroy the Ring; he fights against the Walking Dead's zombies or Matrix's Agent Smith. Rat-Man challenges the superhero genre in many different ways. Like Deadpool or She-Hulk, he is "aware" of being just a comic book character; the narrative is often divided between Rat-Man the "superhero," and Rat-Man the "actor" who plays a fictional character. Ortolani chose to end the series in 2017 with issues #122 and #123, thus challenging one of the pillars of the superheroic narrative: the endless seriality, which Marvel called "the illusion of change" (Elving 2022). For these superhero stories, characters are able to act without developing themselves; Rat-Man, on the contrary, grows and changes until his story is concluded.

The purpose of this chapter is twofold: (1) to investigate how the superhero figure is deconstructed through parody and caricature; (2) to analyze how the American pop-cultural universe, and especially the superhero genre, are reinterpreted and reworked in Italian comics, considering Rat-Man as a case study.

Who Is Rat-Man?

Leo Ortolani created Rat-Man in 1989 with an initial six-page short story. It is a clear parody of DC's Batman, from his tragic origins to his enemies and allies. Orphaned after losing both his parents during a mall sale, "per una curiosa e alquanto oscura associazione di idee, decise di vendicare la scomparsa dei suoi genitori combattendo la criminalità!" ("by a curious and rather obscure association of ideas, he decided to avenge his parents' disappearance by fighting crime!"; Ortolani 2002). It is not the entry of a bat that inspires him, but the arrival of the postman, who hands him *Topolino*, the Italian Disney magazine about Mickey Mouse. "Ed ecco che lo vide... inconfondibile, nei suoi calzoncini rossi con i bottoni gialli..." ("And there he saw him... unmistakable, in his red shorts with yellow buttons..."; Ortolani 2002). The first

DOI: 10.4324/9781003366911-29

confrontation is with Il Buffone (the Buffoon), a clear reference to the Joker, who kidnaps an orphan who will later briefly become Topin (a reference to Batman's sidekick, Robin). After this first appearance others followed, but it was only eight years later, in 1997, that Marvel Italia became interested in the character and began publishing the bimonthly *Rat-Man Collection,* which by 2007 sold more than 30,000 copies each issue (Giampaoli 2007). The series continued until issue #122 *Quando tutto finisce* and special issue #123 *La Porta,* when Leo decided to end it, although he continued to use the character in his other works.

Especially at the beginning of the series, many of the Rat's adventures are stand-alone stories with events that place the character in different contexts, usually based on famous works of popular culture. Over time, however, Ortolani develops several interconnected sagas that recount and deepen the life of the character. The story, full of pop-cultural references particularly related to the Marvel and DC universes, begins as a simple parody of the origins of the Dark Knight, and expands to make the character more complex and multifaceted.

The story within the diegesis of the comic begins in 1927 with the Prima Squadra Segreta (First Secret Squad), inspired by the superheroes of the Golden Age. This is led by Il Pipistrello (the Bat), who later becomes Rat-Man's master. The first team is killed in 1966 by the government. Deboroh La Roccia (the real identity of Rat-Man) is born on October 4, 1967. His six-page origin story is expanded, recounting not only his loss in the mall but also his orphanage years. This is where Deboroh's passion for comic books and superheroes was born, in particular for the Squadra Segreta. The ruthless Janus Walker, a member of the evil shadow organization who killed the original Secret Squad, believes that Deboroh is his son. For this reason, he takes him out of the orphanage and puts him in the Seconda Squadra Segreta, created and controlled by his evil organization, and commanded by Lupo (Wolf), an original member of the first squad and government accomplice in the murder of his old comrades. Here Deboroh becomes Rat-Boy for the first time, but after realizing the corruption of Lupo, Deboroh leaves the team. Walker, who in the meantime has discovered that he is not Rat-Boy's father (although he has now bonded with Deboroh), decides to erase his memory before letting him go. After leaving the team, Deboroh finally arrives at the Città Senza Nome (City Without a Name), where he assumes the identity of Marvelmouse, is trained by Il Pipistrello, and, after the death of his master, finally assumes the identity of Rat-Man. This is followed by various sagas recounting his exploits, up to the final one, which recounts Rat-Man's final confrontation with L'Ombra (the Shadow), his true nemesis.

One of the most striking things about Rat-Man is how the author has constantly sought new challenges. Not content with using it as comic relief but creating a real "Rat-Man Universe," Ortolani not only delves into the history and psyche of the character, but also Rat-Man's sidekicks, for example, with the graphic novel *Cinzia* (2018a). Leo Ortolani states in this regard:

> Rat-Man could very well live on short stories alone, but his life wouldn't change one iota and that's not what I have in mind for him! I would like to make him grow, characterize him more and more accurately and bring him to a natural and convincing conclusion to his adventures... We will thus have a Rat-Man who is not only comic, but at times dramatic, at times tender, at times hateful and unbearable....
>
> *(Ortolani 1998, 60–64)*

Hence, who is Rat-Man? He is a parody, but also a complex character. He is undoubtedly a superhero, but inept, mean, unfortunate. Furthermore, he is short, weak, and petty; women find him repulsive; his enemies defeat him without any difficulty; and his friends and allies are as dumb as he is. He resembles in this sense the archetype of the inept antihero who would like to be a superhero, but is utterly unable to do so. The challenge Rat-Man poses to the concept of the hero is not in the values that he carries, but in his ability to act and be effective. Andrea Bernardelli defines this type of character as "I would like to, but I cannot," being an antihero who "seems to have the heroic model in front of him, but is unattainable due to his limited physical, mental or moral capacities" (Bernardelli 2012, p. 84.) Yet, against all odds, and against all logic, Rat-Man continues to fight.

Parody and Laughter, Seriousness and Status Quo

From his first story, Rat-Man is a parody, a caricature, a comic relief. The character acquires depth and complexity over the years, but this core remains. He is a parodistic antihero who questions the concept of the (super)hero by following the inept antihero archetype. But also, like the metatextuality of Deadpool or She-Hulk, Rat-Man is aware of his being fictitious. Therefore, it is not only the concept of the hero that is being questioned, but also the very structure and rules of comics, of the superhero genre, or of the many different narratives and pop media in which the character is inserted from time to time (see Favaro 2022, 217–222). However, on a broader level, the Rat-Man stories question our "seriousness," this being the societal rules and values we consider stable or "holy."

The irony, the joking, the ridicule, and the laugh should not be underestimated. They reveal a disruptive force often linked to the antihero. The eternally sneering mask of V in *V for Vendetta* (Moore and Lloyd 1982–1985), which becomes a symbol of the struggle against the serious totalitarian power of the Norsefire government, is an emblematic example. The idol-destroying philosopher Friedrich Nietzsche was aware of the destructive power of the joke. In *On Truth and Lies in a Nonmoral Sense* he states that happiness requires "a playing with what is seriousness," (1990 [1873], 91), while in *The Gay Science* he writes that to play "with everything that was hitherto called holy" is what characterizes the "great health" (2008 [1882], 246–7). Nietzsche refers to the fool, writing that "precisely because we are at bottom grave and serious human beings and more weights than human beings, nothing does us as much good as the *fool*'s cap: we need it against ourselves" (2008 [1882], 104). Even the Übermensch (Overman) is characterized by the laughing: he is "a transfigured being, a light-surrounded being, that laughed! Never on earth laughed a man as he laughed!" (2006 [1883–1885], 127). The fool and the Übermensch mock the "serious man," the *esprit de sérieux*, as Sartre called it. The serious spirit "considers values as transcendent givens independent of human subjectivity" (Sartre 1993 [1943], 626), and "It thinks of values as having an absolute existence independent of human-reality" (Sartre 1993 [1943], 633). The laugh has the power to unmask this illusion.

Laughter destroys the power that seriousness attributes to the things of the world; it makes them ridiculous. Comedy undermines the meaning canonically attributed to the world when we experience it "seriously." It shows its aporias and reveals its absurdities; it makes the world slip into non-sense. The consequence of this destruction of meaning is a loss of univocal power. Emblematic examples are the great monotheistic religions or the absolute totalitarian political systems: much of their power resides in affirming a meaning (a code of values, a morality, a truth) that is unique and unquestionable. Contemporary Italian philosopher Umberto Galimberti states that

we do not laugh at the proliferation of meaning, but at its reversibility, at its return to itself, which unleashes that non-sense that is laughed at, a moment of liberation … The non-sense that is produced is not a counter-sense, but it is the refusal that things, all things, have a single meaning.

(2018, 474–76)

It follows that "laughing overturns social laws, undermines the power of institutions, builds nothing … but simply reaffirms the movement of life where it was meant to be stopped" (Galimberti 2018, 489). The object, or rather the victim, of the joke becomes entangled in the nonsense or double meaning. It is in the nonsense that accompanies the laugh that the antiheroic force of characters like Rat-Man is fully revealed.

In the superhero parody, this characteristic of the joke is even more pronounced as it desecrates a figure that is, by nature, serious. Although it deals with men and women in tights fighting mad scientist aliens, the superhero genre in fact proposes a worldview with defined values and meanings. Superheroes stand for a well-defined and unambiguous idea, as the symbols on their chests usually show. Superheroes are defenders of the status quo, and they embody the values of the society they are protecting (usually the Western and particularly the American one). The core idea that characterizes the genre is that good and evil are clear and separated. Today, with the proliferation of antiheroes and the increasing complexity of characters, the "pure" superhero has disappeared, and the values and truths that superheroes represent have become more ambiguous. Nevertheless, this "seriousness" remains in the superhero concept.

A parodistic antihero like Rat-Man, however, questions the serious and unambiguous meaning of things that the superhero defends. The consequence is that il Ratto does not reassure, make us feel protected, or instill fear. Playing a role similar to that of the Nietzschean fool, Rat-Man mocks the (super)serious man. For example, in *Legami di Sangue!* Rat-Man briefly obtains the powers of Spider-Man thanks to a blood transfusion, but to really become a great hero like the Webslinger, something is still missing... too bad that Rat-Man's uncle is not willing to get killed! (Ortolani 1997) In *Vendetta!* we see him asking the Punisher if "va tutto bene in famiglia," ("Is everything all right with your family?") and then commenting that the giant skull on Frank's chest is really kitsch. "Poi noto il teschione disegnato sul petto: che pacchianata!" ("Then I notice the skull drawn on his chest: how trashy!"; Ortolani 1996).

Rat-Man can parody every popular culture corner, and he does. His being a superhero is a key element directly linked to this serious-unserious dichotomy. Parody operates on numerous and diverse aspects of the superhero, dismantling specific stories or contexts as well as the genre as a whole. One of the primary targets of parody is the very essence of what defines a superhero. Superheroes, for instance, are often closely associated with their iconic cities, whether it be New York, Metropolis, or Gotham City. In contrast, Rat-Man operates within a relatively small and nameless city, so anonymous that it is aptly called "Senza Nome" ("Without Name"). Another key element of the genre, which further underscores its "seriousness" in the conventional sense, is the symbol. The symbol is an essential component of the superhero genre as it represents what the superhero stands for. For example, Superman's symbol conveys hope; the iconic "S" also signifies "Savior" and resembles a shield, symbolizing protection. Batman's decision to adopt the persona of a bat stems from a theatrical scene where a bat, intruding through his window, assumes a totemic and symbolic significance, representing his father's will. In Rat-Man's case, the choice of symbol is derived from a comedic gag and draws inspiration from the world of "non-seriousness" and childlike wonder, particularly the realm of Disney comics. Additionally, Rat-Man's relationship with heroism, as mentioned earlier, deviates from the traditional archetype. While superheroes are typically portrayed as strong, courageous, and selfless, Rat-Man is portrayed in directly oppositional terms.

The destruction of unambiguous meaning is even more evident in the meta-textual elements that anti heroes such as Rat-Man deploy. Aware of being fictional characters, they have no problems breaking the rules of the media itself, tearing up the pages of the very comic strip they are in, jumping between the cartoons, and finding themselves in dialogue with their authors. Breaking the fourth wall changes the rules of the game, and their actions acquire a completely different meaning than the one they would have if the illusion of reality were preserved. If we are reminded that we are immersed in an imaginary reality, a character like Deadpool can go on an anti-heroic spree, killing all of the Marvel Universe or iconic characters from literature like Don Quixote, Captain Ahab, or Pinocchio without being seen as an evil monster (Bunn and Talajić 2012; Bunn and Lolli 2013). It is not real, after all.

Being a Comic: Awareness and Multimedia

In *Rat-Man*, the narrative operates on two different levels; on the one hand, there are the adventures of the superhero Rat-Man, and on the other hand, there are those of the comic book character Rat-Man. Breaking the fourth wall deconstructs the rules of the genre and of comics, but it also has the further advantage of facilitating the integration of the character in virtually every fictional work without denaturing him.

Just as Deadpool can travel freely across and between literary classics (Bunn and Lolli 2013), Leo Ortolani can insert Rat-Man into any pop universe. Playing with the possibilities of a comic book, Rat-Man becomes the protagonist of a Manga (Ortolani 2009b) and of a book of crossword puzzles (Ortolani 2009a); he experiences the world of James Cameron's *Avatar* (2009) shown through a three-dimensional comic, complete with special 3D glasses for the reader (Ortolani 2010), and even imitates *Playboy* magazine with *Ratboy: La rivista per uomini soli* (*The lonely man's magazine*), complete with centerfold (Ortolani 2018b). True to his catchphrase, Rat-Man "flette i muscoli e si getta nel vuoto" ("flexes his muscles and jump into the void"), landing each time in a different world and media, adapted to another genre, imitating formats, styles of comic books, magazines, or even films.

Rat-Man is not only an inept (anti)superhero, but his anti-heroism extends to different genres and narrative dimensions. Leo Ortolani inserts his character into numerous popular culture classics and franchises of all genres, from science fiction with *Star Wars* (Ortolani 2011d) and *The Matrix* (Ortolani 2004b); fantasy with *The Lord of the Rings* (Ortolani 2004a), *Harry Potter* (Ortolani 2011a–2011c), and *300* (Ortolani 2007a, 2007b); or horror, quoting and parodying *The Walking Dead* (Ortolani 2015a–2015c), *The Ring* (Ortolani 2003), and *Friday the 13th* (Ortolani 2007c). Using his character, Ortolani desecrates and deconstructs every pop cultural production, focusing in particular on the American output that sees the superhero genre as one of its favorite sons. This aspect not only distinguishes Rat-Man, but it also identifies him as a perfect example of an Italian superhero, allowing a comparison with the American characters he parodies. If superheroes can only function in the seriousness of the United States, the Italian superhero can only be a parodistic antihero.

Dolce vita or American Dream?

Rat-Man's self-awareness serves as a platform for satirical critique and social commentary, enabling him to engage with American popular culture from a distinct perspective. Through his satirical lens, Rat-Man deconstructs and challenges the seriousness and larger-than-life portrayals commonly associated with American superheroes. He offers a counter-narrative that not only parodies the conventions of superheroes and, in general, of the American popular culture, but Rat-Man's irreverent approach serves as a commentary on the influence and dominance of American popular culture while offering a distinctly Italian perspective on the superhero genre.

If we wish to delve into why Rat-Man is the most successful Italian superhero, we can turn to a song by Giorgio Gaber for some insight. In one of his renowned songs, titled "Io Non Mi Sento Italiano" ("I Don't Feel Italian", 2003), G.G. sings:

> Rispetto agli stranieri
> Noi ci crediamo meno
> Ma forse abbiam capito
> Che il mondo è un teatrino

> "In comparison to other countries,
> We have less belief,
> But perhaps we have grasped
> That the world is a mere stage"

Here, the phrase "We have less belief" directly correlates to the previously discussed "lack of seriousness." Having less faith in idols, truths, and ideologies allows us to perceive that "the world is a mere stage," in essence, that there is an underlying absurdity of things. Within these words, we may find the profound significance of a character like Rat-Man and, on a broader scale, the nature of the relationship between the strong influence of American pop culture and the intrinsic "lack of seriousness" often found in Italy. After all, what truly encapsulates the renowned "dolce vita" if not a form of hakuna matata, a way of life *sans souci*, evading the seriousness that characterizes the American Dream? The American Dream not only involves hard work for individual prosperity and success but invariably relies on an unquestionable system of certainties and values – a system that American superheroes defend and embody. A system that enforces a seriousness based on unshakable certainties, which is absent in Italy, a country where, as historian Alessandro Barbero (2017) puts it, "even tragedy is always on the verge of becoming farce." If Giorgio Gaber is correct in asserting that what unites Italians is, at its core, the conviction that "il mondo è un teatrino," implying that idols are merely fragile constructs and ultimately ridiculous or prone to ridicule, then we can perceive the *Rat-Man* comic, beyond its comedic elements, as a nuanced form of social commentary. It serves as a contrast to the American mindset upheld by superheroes, which *Rat-Man*, while drawing inspiration from it, irreverently dismantles and mocks.

Rat-Man's comparison with the idols in tights highlights this aspect. Where in the United States the superhero embodies American values and is their ultimate defender, in Italy, the only possible superhero is a parody. This comparison can become, in some cases, even dramatic. In one of the latest sagas, for instance, Deboroh partially returns to his origins, once again confronting the superhero myth. Having apparently defeated l'Ombra, Rat-Man becomes useless to the city and leaves, destination: New York, the city of superheroes. Here he will be confronted with reinterpretations of the most famous Marvel characters. Ortolani ridicules them, but behind the apparent lightness of the parody lies a much deeper criticism of the "certainties" defended by superheroes. While the blond god Zoth (a parody of Thor) is ridiculous in his pseudo-courtly speech and his lack of understanding of the modern world, the Lo spettacolare Arrampicamuri (Spectacular Climber, a parody of Spider-Man) is already a sadder and more dramatic character. However, Capitan Battaglia (Captain Battle, inspired by Captain America) and Ironcrash (a parody of Iron Man) reveal the fundamental violence that characterizes superheroes, who ultimately impose their truth through physical dominance. In particular, the latter characters ultimately emerge as the true villains of the story: heroes who firmly believe they are in the right, blinded by their ideals and willing to do anything to achieve them. In the end, superheroes prove to be nothing more than villains. Rat-Man, however, precisely because he is inept, flawed, and non-serious, is saved. By renouncing the idol that he has pursued all his life, the myth of the American superhero, Rat-Man becomes the hero of the story.

Rat-Man is the embodiment of the Italian cultural response to the dominance of American popular culture. He stands as a prime example of how Italian comics reinterpret and rework the American pop-cultural universe, particularly the superhero genre. Through parody and satire, Leo Ortolani not only offers a refreshing and entertaining alternative to the traditional superhero narratives but also challenges the fundamental "seriousness" of American society and culture.

References

Barbero, Alessandro. *Le reti clandestine. Una rete di terroristi: le BR e il rapimento Moro.* Conference Festival della mente, XIV edition. Video uploaded September 22, 2017. on YouTube. https://www.festivaldellamente.it/it/evento-n-41-8/.

Bernardelli, Andrea. 2012. "Il personaggio narrativo." In *Il Trionfo dell'Antieroe nelle Serie Televisive*, edited by Andrea Bernardelli. Morlacchi.

Bunn, Cullen, and Dalibor Talajić. 2012. *Deadpool Kills the Marvel Universe.* Marvel Comics.

Bunn, Cullen, and Matteo Lolli. 2013. *Deadpool Killustrated.* Marvel Comics.

Elving, Jack. 2022. "Re-Examining Spider-Man 06 – Illusions Behind the 'Illusion of Change.'" *Elving's Musings*, blog, January 9. https://elvingsmusings.wordpress.com/2022/01/09/re-examining-spider-man-06-illusions-behind-the-illusion-of-change/.

Favaro, Marco. 2022. *La maschera dell'antieroe: Mitologia e filosofia del supereroe dalla dark age a oggi.* Mimesis Edizioni.

Gaber, Giorgio. 2003. "Io non mi sento Italiano." *CGD East West*, 4:51.

Galimberti, Umberto. 2018. *Il Corpo.* Translated by author. Feltrinelli.

Giampaoli, Emanuela. 2007. "Con il mio antieroe Rat-Man al festival dei divi del fumetto." *La Repubblica*, February 27. https://ricerca.repubblica.it/repubblica/archivio/repubblica/2007/02/27/con-il-mio-antieroe-rat-man-al-festival.html?ref=search.

Moore, Alan, and David Lloyd. 1982–1985. *V for Vendetta.* Warrior/DC Comics.

Nietzsche, Friedrich. 1990 [1873]. "On truth and lies in a nonmoral sense," Translated by Daniel Breazeale. In *Philosophy and truth. Selections from Nietzsche's notebooks of the early 1870s*, edited by Daniel Breazeale. Humanities Press.

Nietzsche, Friedrich. 2006 [1883–1885]. *Thus Spoke Zarathustra.* Translated by Adrian Del Caro. Cambridge University Press.

Nietzsche, Friedrich. 2008 [1882]. *The Gay Science.* Translated by J. Nauckhoff. Cambridge University Press.

Ortolani, Leonardo. 1996. "Vendetta! Rat-Man Contro Il Punitore." *WIZ* n.12, October 12. Marvel Italia.

Ortolani, Leonardo. 1997. *Rat-Man Collection #1. Legami di sangue!* Panini Comics.

Ortolani, Leonardo. 1998. "Uomini e topi." In *Rat-Man Collection #9. Cinzia la barbara!* Panini Comics.

Ortolani, Leonardo. 2002. *Le Sconvolgenti Origini Del Rat-Man.* Panini Comics.

Ortolani, Leonardo. 2003. *Rat-Man Collection #39. Sette Giorni!* Panini Comics.

Ortolani, Leonardo. 2004a. *Il Signore dei Ratti*. Panini Comics.

Ortolani, Leonardo. 2004b. *Rat-Man Collection #45. Rat-Max*. Panini Comics.

Ortolani, Leonardo. 2007a. *Rat-Man Collection #62. 299*. Panini Comics.

Ortolani, Leonardo. 2007b. *Rat-Man Collection #63. +1*. Panini Comics.

Ortolani, Leonardo. 2007c. *Venerdì 12 Omnibus*. Panini Comics.

Ortolani, Leonardo. 2009a. *Il Rat-Man Enigmistico*. Panini Comics.

Ortolani, Leonardo. 2009b. *Rat-Man Collection #74. Yellow!* Panini Comics.

Ortolani, Leonardo. 2010. *Avarat*. Panini Comics.

Ortolani, Leonardo. 2011a. *Rat-Man Collection #88. Il Grande Magazzi e il Principe Mezzorospo*. Panini Comics.

Ortolani, Leonardo. 2011b. *Rat-Man Collection #89. La Donna Filosofale*. Panini Comics.

Ortolani, Leonardo. 2011c. *Rat-Man Collection #90. La Camera delle Sorprese*. Panini Comics.

Ortolani, Leonardo. 2011d. *Star Rats*. Panini Comics.

Ortolani, Leonardo. 2015a. *Rat-Man Collection #106. The Walking Rat*. Panini Comics.

Ortolani, Leonardo. 2015b. *Rat-Man Collection #107. La Città dei Morti Viventi*. Panini Comics.

Ortolani, Leonardo. 2015c. *Rat-Man Collection #108. Il Trionfo dei Morti Viventi*. Panini Comics.

Ortolani Leonardo. 2018a. *Cinzia*. BAO Publishing.

Ortolani, Leonardo. 2018b. *Ratboy. La Rivista per Uomini Soli*. Panini Comics.

Sartre, Jean-Paul. 1993 [1943]. *Being and Nothingness*. Translated by Hazel E. Barnes. Washington Square Press.

26

SUPERHERO TOYS, NOSTALGIA, AND THE ASSASSINATION OF ABE SHINZO

Sophia Staite

Introduction

This chapter explores the interlinkages between television, toys, and demographic change in relation to the Japanese superhero television program *Kamen Rider Black Sun* (Shiraishi 2022). Carl Wilson and Lorna Piatti-Farnell (2023, 3) write that through their continuous re-imaginings, superheroes have "maintained their ability to reflect our socio-historical and sociopolitical contexts, telling us much about the world we live in, and our desires and anxieties at given moments in time." This observation is particularly true of one of Japan's longest running superhero franchises, *Kamen Rider*. Because the franchise is made up of barely related stories and characters year upon year, it is remarkably attuned to microtrends within Japanese society. Indeed, social critic Uno Tsunehiro (2015) has written a cultural history of 21st-century Japan based on each year's *Kamen Rider* season.

Kamen Rider Black Sun (hereafter, *Black Sun*) is an adult adaptation of children's program *Kamen Rider Black* (Kobayashi 1987), but despite being R-rated, it is, like every season of *Kamen Rider*, a merchandise-driven program tasked with selling a toy line. It is also a bleak and furious indictment of Japan's fascist history and contemporary politics. *Black Sun* blurs the distinction between fact and fiction by prolifically referencing actual historical events and figures within its fantastical setting. Japan's longest-serving Prime Minister, Abe Shinzo, appears as one of the program's central villains under the character name of Prime Minister Dounami Shinichi. The blurring of the real and the fictional took a peculiar turn when Abe was assassinated in July 2022. In the fictional narrative of *Black Sun,* released in October 2022, Dounami is also assassinated. This coincidence does not appear to have negatively impacted sales of the program's toy line.

The chapter begins with a brief introduction to the broader *Kamen Rider* franchise and its primary tie-in toy, the transformation belt. It then considers the interaction between an aging, shrinking population and the imperative that *Kamen Rider* sells toys. The third section of the chapter focuses on the story of *Black Sun* and the real-world history and politicians the program transposes into its fantastical setting. The final section returns to the issue of low birthrates, considering the complex role of nostalgia in what is both a celebratory

 DOI: 10.4324/9781003366911-30

anniversary season of *Kamen Rider* and a program that unflinchingly draws attention to a number of brutal and difficult historical moments.

The Biggest Superhero You've Never Heard of: *Kamen Rider*

Kamen Rider has a cultural significance in Japan similar to that of *Superman* in the Anglophone world; it is instantly recognizable, even to those who have never specifically consumed it, and it is endlessly referenced, spoofed, and the subject of homage in the broader media landscape. *Kamen Rider* was launched as a media-mix (Steinberg 2012) franchise in 1971, initially comprised of a manga and a live-action television program with associated toy line and branded merchandise, but soon expanding to include feature films, novels, stage plays and musicals, animated programs, and video games. The weekly Sunday morning children's television program remains the heart of the franchise and is geared toward preschool-aged children, but importantly for this chapter, other texts within the franchise are adult-oriented.

The mothership program is coproduced by Tōei studios and toy maker Bandai. It is a *tokusatsu* (practical special effects) martial-arts program comprised of unrelated yearlong seasons. Each season has a unique premise and characters. They exist broadly within a shared multiverse (there are regular crossovers), but there is no particular overarching continuity. Each season does share some basic characteristics, namely that the heroes are called Kamen Riders, that they transform using a belt device sold as a tie-in toy, that they at some point ride a motorcycle, and that they are intimately connected to the monsters they battle (see Staite 2021b).

The franchise has a substantial international profile across Asia, South America, Spain, and Italy, and the television program aired on Japanese language television channels in Hawaii. Despite this international presence, *Kamen Rider* has only recently begun to build a profile in the English-speaking world. In part, this is a side-effect of the popularity of the closely related franchise *Super Sentai*'s transcultural adaptation into *Power Rangers*. I have argued elsewhere that producer Tōei was discouraged from promoting *Kamen Rider* after two commercially disappointing American remakes: *Saban's Masked Rider* in 1995 and *Kamen Rider Dragon Knight* in 2008 (Staite 2021a).

Within *Kamen Rider*'s long history, *Kamen Rider Black* stands out as a particularly beloved iteration. Unusually within the franchise, it received a sequel season featuring the same protagonist, *Kamen Rider Black RX* (1988–89). These two seasons carry a particular weight in the franchise, as they were the last to involve original creator Ishinomori Shōtarō before his death. *Kamen Rider Black* has a melodramatic plot tracing the betrayal of orphan Minami Kotaro by his foster father and subsequent battles against his beloved foster brother Nobuhiko, who has been brainwashed by an apocalyptic cult called Gorgom. Kotaro is a traumatized hero, forced to become a Kamen Rider through a surgical procedure he did not consent to. It is something painful, and something he endures only because he does not want anyone else to suffer the way he has suffered. In the final episode, Kotaro chooses to save the world by killing Nobuhiko, who tells him not to consider it a victory because "you will live in painful regret forever, knowing that you have murdered your best friend." The suffering of the young superhero captured hearts and imaginations around the world.

Kamen Rider is a toyetic (Bainbridge 2017) franchise, and presenting and marketing toys is one of the television program's core purposes. The central tie-in toy is the *henshin,* or "metamorphosis," belt, which is a faithful reproduction of the prop worn by the actors on screen. This belt has a new design and theme every year and is frequently represented among the winners of the Japanese toy awards (for a recent example, see Tsuji 2024). In addition to marketing toys, the *henshin* belts serve an important practical role in the production of the television program. When the Kamen Riders use their belts to *henshin,* they metamorphosize into their superhero forms and replete with masks and gloves that completely cover the wearer. This enables the "face" actors to switch places with stunt professionals for fight scenes, motorcycle stunts, pyrotechnics, and so on. While this is a practical consideration, the *henshin* scene has become an iconic element of the franchise. Each Kamen Rider performs a unique stylized choreography to trigger their belt-facilitated *henshin,* and the transformation scene is often accompanied by a unique musical cue and a higher quality of special effects (as the *henshin* scene is reused across multiple episodes, this is a cost-effective approach). Anne Allison describes the *henshin* scene as the "money shot" of *Kamen Rider,* provocatively using a term associated with pornography (2006, 105).

The *henshin* belt toy associated with *Kamen Rider Black* featured a remarkable piece of technology for its time. The toy was equipped with a light sensor that reacted to a specific sequence of flashes in the *henshin* scene of the television program. When positioned in front of a television playing *Kamen Rider Black*, the toy would be activated by these flashes during the *henshin* scenes and produce its own lights and sounds in synchronous response. Children could wear the belt while watching the program, and join in with the *henshin* choreography as their own belt reproduced the diegetic sounds and effects, eliminating the distance between child and superhero on opposite sides of the screen. As Ruth Barratt-Peacock and I have argued, the visual similarity between the toy and the prop, as well as the toy's reproduction of aural cues, allows the toy to carry the affective loading of the television narrative into the child's everyday life (Barratt-Peacock and Staite 2022). The *Kamen Rider Black* belt takes this further than most by having the television program itself activate the toy.

Superhero Toys and Politics in a Super Aging Society

Since *Kamen Rider Black's* 1987 release, Japan's population pyramid has undergone a radical inversion, and Japan today is one of the world's most rapidly aging and shrinking populations (Ng 2023; Associated Press 2024). These demographic changes have naturally impacted a toyetic franchise like *Kamen Rider* in various ways, but the focus of this chapter is on how both the tie-in-toy and the overall story of *Kamen Rider Black* have changed in *Black Sun,* read as a reflection of demographic and political upheaval. Both *Kamen Rider Black* and *Black Sun* follow the conflict between foster brothers, protagonist Kotaro and antagonist Nobuhiko. Although both characters have been altered between the two programs, this chapter focuses solely on Kotaro, as he is the character who wears both of the *henshin* belt toys analyzed.

In *Kamen Rider Black* (1987–88), the children's program, Kotaro and Nobuhiko are teenagers abducted by a cult called Gorgom, which their father has been working for, and they are both subjected to surgery that will turn them into human, insect, cyborg hybrids. Kotaro is able to escape before the final stage of the surgery: mind control, but Nobuhiko is not. Kotaro suffers terrible pain and loss as he tries to protect others from Gorgom, particularly as he is repeatedly forced to fight a brainwashed brother he loves and does not want to harm. His story is that of a young person betrayed by his father's generation but sustained by the indomitable optimism that a better world is not only possible but almost inevitable. There will be suffering along the way, but good will undoubtedly triumph.

Black Sun, the contemporary adult reimagining, takes place in an alternate timeline in which Kotaro is born in the 1930s, although genetic modification has slowed the aging process, allowing him to be played by Nishijima Hidetoshi, star of Oscar-nominated film *Drive my Car* (2021). In this timeline, Kotaro is a cynical and disengaged middle-aged man, burnt by the failure of the 1960s and 1970s student radical movement to bring about substantive political change, and reliant on black market ketamine to manage his pain. He has withdrawn from social engagement until an encounter with a teenaged civil rights activist forces him once more into the thick of political struggles.

The *henshin* belt toy associated with this program retails at ¥53,780 (approximately US$372). For comparison, the children's toy associated with the most reason season at the time of writing (*Kamen Rider Gavv* 2024) retails for ¥7,920 (approximately US$52). Both the price of the belt and the rating of the television program itself suggest that this toy has been created for adult collectors rather than children; collectors who are probably adults of the generation who stood in front of their televisions wearing the *Kamen Rider Black* belt 30-odd years earlier.

In order to activate the *Black Sun* belt's transformation sequence, the wearer must perform the transformation choreography. Motion sensors in the belt detect the wearer's movements and respond by initiating motion, lights, and sound. The toy does not allow for any adult reticence about engaging in superhero role-play. In order to make the belt work, one must set aside any embarrassment or self-consciousness and strike the requisite poses. Despite the high price of purchase, then, this is not designed as a collector's item to be displayed in a glass case; the toy demands to be played with. The interactivity of the *henshin* belt requires users to stand in Kotaro's position, literally, and roleplay his character. Thus, the changed character may be understood as speaking once again to the same audience who were encouraged to identify with the optimistic Kotaro of 1987.

Kamen Rider Black Sun

Although it may be argued that *Kamen Rider Black* has a political message, like most superhero media, it is allegorical. Teenaged Kotaro battles bizarre-looking rubber-suited monsters called *kaijin* in a fantastical defense of humanity, while in contrast, middle-aged Kotaro's opponent is the Liberal Democratic Party or LDP. The true villains of *Black Sun* are two Prime Ministers, the first from the 1972 flashback storyline and the second, his grandson, who governs in the 2020s. There is no mistaking the identity of these two men as actual former Prime Ministers Kishi Nobusuke and his grandson, former Prime Minister Abe Shinzo.

In the alternate timeline of *Black Sun*, the *kaijin*, human-animal or -plant hybrids, were created during the Second World War under the oversight of character Dounami Michinosuke, who represents the real former Japanese Prime Minister Kishi. The fictionalized experimentation on human subjects to produce *kaijin* evokes the actual history of the infamous biological weapons research facility Unit 731, which was located in the Japanese puppet state Manchukuo. Unit 731 conducted horrific experiments on human subjects (Tsuneishi 2011), and Kishi oversaw Manchukuo as Finance Minister (You 2018, 94). Kishi was initially considered a Class A war criminal, but avoided prosecution when US priorities in the region shifted (You 2018, 104). With the support of the United States, Kishi was instrumental in founding the LDP, which has been in government in Japan for all but four years since 1955. Kishi himself became Prime Minister in 1957.

The initial post-war US investigators of Unit 731 were explicit in seeking access to the research the Unit had produced without seeking to prosecute the war crimes committed to produce that research (Tsuneishi 2011, 192–193). The Japanese government did not formally confirm the existence of Unit 731 until 1982 (Dickinson 2007, 12). Similarly, in *Black Sun,* fictional Prime Minister Dounami Shinichi, the grandson of Dounami Michinosuke (thus representing real former Japanese Prime Minister Abe Shinzo), is shown in the first episode denying any Japanese involvement in the origins of the *kaijin*. By the 2020s, *kaijin* have become a naturally reproducing minority population in Japan, and are subject to discrimination and victimization.

Black Sun opens with human schoolgirl Aoi giving a speech to the UN about human-*kaijin* harmony. After returning to Japan, Aoi joins her childhood friend and classmate Shunsuke, who is a *kaijin*, in a public demonstration for *kaijin* rights. The demonstration is met by alt-right counter-protestors. Their leader, an avatar for Sakurai Makoto (founder of the far-right Japan First Party), provokes a confrontation, and the police respond by shooting one of the *kaijin*. It is through Shunsuke that the everyday suffering of Japan's *kaijin* is made visible to the audience. It is notable that *Black Sun* does not use *kaijin* as an allegorical replacement for real minorities, as is so often the case in superhero texts. Instead, anti-*kaijin* discrimination is shown as intersecting with other social issues, including classism, homophobia, and racism, particularly racism against Zainichi Korean communities. Zainichi Koreans are descendants of Koreans who migrated or were forcibly transported to Japan during the Japanese colonization of Korea (Yoon and Asahina 2021, 378). Despite having resided in Japan for generations, Zainichi Koreans are deemed stateless and face ongoing legal and social discrimination (Kinukawa 2021, 143).

Shunsuke and Aoi live in a slum-like Zainichi neighborhood that is subjected to constant harassment, which reflects actual alt-right harassment campaigns targeting such communities. Citing Ministry of Justice statistics, Sharon Yoon and Yuki Asahina write that there were 1,152 officially recorded hate rallies targeting Zainichi Korean communities between 2013 and 2015 (2021, 364). Shunsuke and Aoi are also harassed at school, reflecting another real-world tactic of the Japanese alt-right (Yoon and Asahina 2021, 385). The aforementioned protest scene in *Black Sun* specifically references the period of protests and counter protests that took place between 2015 and 2016, leading to legislative action to curb hate speech (Kotani 2017, 227–228). The distinctive yellow protest signs of the anti-hate speech activists of that period are recreated for the *kaijin* rights activists in *Black Sun,* but rather than using *kaijin* to allegorize racism against Zainichi Koreans, whose real-life struggles would then be obscured within the text, the program is explicit in linking the exploitation of all colonized peoples' bodies with the origin story of the *kaijin*. *Kaijin* do not stand in for other minoritized groups, but simply add another intersection to existing axes of oppression. This can be seen expressed in Episode 7, where the alt-right group beat Shunsuke to death outside a public toilet on the edge of his Zainichi neighborhood, while higher-class passers-by hurry their steps and look the other way, ignoring Shunsuke's pleas for help.

Through flashbacks to Nobuhiko and Kotaro's involvement in the student radical movement in the 1960s and 1970s, viewers learn that the *kaijin* liberation movement fell apart after a series of schisms, and that the once radical group Gorgom became a political party, followed by a deal with (now Prime Minister) Dounami Michinosuke to become junior coalition partners in his government. Gorgom has kept Nobuhiko imprisoned since 1972 and believe Kotaro to be dead. Upon a first viewing of *Black Sun,* it may be surprising that so many key events take place in 1972, rather than 1971 (the year of *Kamen Rider's* creation, the anniversary of which *Black Sun* was created to commemorate). As the story unfolds, however, the significance of 1972 becomes clearer. It was 1972 that saw the collapse of the Japanese New Left student protest movement in violent internal conflicts (Steinhoff 2013,

129), which *Black Sun* recreates as a kind of foundational trauma that leads to Kotaro and Nobuhiko's divergent character trajectories. In 1972, the United Red Army (*Rengō Sekigun*) occupied a mountain lodge, taking a hostage in the process, and faced off against police who laid siege for over a week (Steinhoff 2013, 153). The final day of the siege, Patricia Steinhoff writes, was watched live by more than 90% of Japan's television viewing audience (2013, 153), rendering it a deeply significant cultural touch-stone moment.

In the aftermath of the siege, authorities discovered that while camping in the mountains, the United Red Army had undertaken a deadly internal purge; 14 bodies were found buried around the campsite (Steinhoff 2013, 154). In the 1972 of *Black Sun's* alternative history, Kotaro and Nobuhiko have joined a splinter group opposing Gorgom's transition into parliamentary politics, and they retreat to the mountains with Prime Minister Dounami Michinosuke's grandson, Dounami Shinichi, as a hostage. Persistent in-fighting sees character Yukari (Kotaro and Nobuhiko's shared first love) murdered by a fellow member of the splinter group before they are discovered by Gorgom and Nobuhiko is imprisoned. This bloody end to their youthful idealism sees Kotaro become completely disengaged from society, while Nobuhiko is propelled into ever more violent extremism.

The timelines come together as Kotaro befriends Aoi after initially accepting a work order to kill her. He holds back after recognizing a stone Aoi wears as a necklace; called a King Stone, it was part of Kotaro's body that he had removed and given to Yukari shortly before her death. After realizing that Gorgom is behind the hit job, Kotaro attempts, fairly unsuccessfully, to protect Aoi. Nobuhiko, meanwhile, escapes from Gorgom and, following Shunsuke's death, decides that *kaijin* liberation should be replaced by *kaijin* supremacy. He takes control of Gorgom with a violent coup. Gorgom can be read as a fictional composite of two real, politically influential religious organizations sometimes considered to be cults in Japan: Nichiren Buddhism and the Unification Church. After the actual former Prime Minister Abe Shinzo's assassination during the 2022 election campaign, police described the attack as being related to a certain religious organization. There was immediate social media speculation that the un-named organization was Soka Gakkai, an LDP coalition partner widely considered to be the political wing of Nichiren Buddhism. The religious organization was later revealed to be the Unification Church, so this dual referencing in *Black Sun,* written before the assassination, is particularly impactful in hindsight.

As those around Aoi are killed one by one and she herself is eventually subjected to *kaijin* surgery by Gorgom, Kotaro is irresistibly drawn back into the ideological conflict, and the fan-expected heartbreaking duel with Nobuhiko. Aoi reveals herself to the UN as an artificially created *kaijin*, proving that *kaijin* are made from humans, and shares evidence about the original creation of the *kaijin* as stemming from Japanese biological warfare research. Despite the ensuing public outcry, the LDP and Gorgom deal with the matter by dissolving parliament, a frequently used LDP strategy, coordinate on the assassination of the Prime Minster and then take a reshuffled line-up to an election that they comfortably win. Frederick Dickinson (2007) points out that the Japanese public was well informed about the history of Unit 731 through multiple documentaries, exhibitions, and works of public-facing scholarship, so there are traces here too of frustration that public knowledge of wrongdoing seems to have little electoral impact. Filming for *Black Sun* had wrapped up before the real-life assassination of Abe, but the program was in post-production, and it is a reasonable assumption that the assassination plot point could have been edited out before the release; the decision to include it in the release is therefore probably a reflection of a conscious decision rather than unfortunate timing. In contrast, an August 2001 trailer for *Spider-Man* (2002) that depicted the Twin Towers was withdrawn within a day of the September 11 terrorist attacks (Leaver 2012, 155).

Black Sun is an explicitly, insistently political program that does not shy away from an explicit critique of individual politicians. The program is extremely clear about who it is depicting, although it does not name names and includes the standard disclaimer about the program being a work of fiction with any resemblance to real people being coincidental. This disclaimer is particularly disingenuous when the program recreates actual scenes from Japanese parliament, including Communist Party member Tamura Tomoko's questioning of Abe over corruption allegations on November 12, 2019 (テレ東BIZ 2019). *Black Sun* recreates the scene meticulously in Episode 3, with one exception: the character who acts in Tamura's role in *Black Sun's* recreation does not look or dress like Tamura. Given the attention to detail in other aspects of the recreation, this difference may draw the viewer's attention. The character questioning Dounami is instead referencing (in casting, hairstyle, and the specific clothing she is wearing) another significant parliamentary scene, this time with Democratic Party leader Renho asking probing questions of Abe. During that altercation, on December 7, 2016, Renho famously retorted to Abe's obfuscations "you lie as easily as you breathe" (yzjps 2016; Adelstein 2022). There are many other examples of *Black Sun* specifically referencing actual political figures and incidents within its narrative. This very literal approach sets *Black Sun* apart from most superhero media, which tend to use allegory or metaphor (albeit sometimes thinly veiled) in their social commentary.

Nostalgia

After this dive into a series of distressing moments in Japanese history, returning to a discussion of toys and play may feel jarring, but this is a juxtaposition that *Black Sun* itself explores through its complex relationship with nostalgia. Colleen Kennedy-Karpat (2020, 285) invites us to consider the questions *whose nostalgia?* and *nostalgia for what?* In attempting to address these questions, let us return briefly to the issue of birthrates and population growth, because these are significant considerations for a superhero franchise that is intimately interconnected with toy sales. In 2022, Japan's population shrunk by the largest decline ever recorded, and the fertility rate was well below replacement at just 1.27 (Nakatani 2023, 257). That is a concerning number for toy manufacturers, and one might assume that an adult remake of a nostalgic 1980s children's television program would be an attempt to compensate for a dwindling child consumer base by leveraging nostalgia amongst adult collectors who would then purchase the toys. In the context of how expensive the *Black Sun henshin* belt is, this is a reasonable answer to the question of *whose* nostalgia. The plot of *Black Sun* complicates this, however, by presenting a *what* that seems at odds with this *who*.

The program itself does not lean into a warm, friendly glow of nostalgia for a dependable childhood superhero. It is a furious and desolate look at the past century of Japanese politics, particularly focusing on unresolved issues of racism and wartime atrocities in Asia, where *Kamen Rider* has a strong presence. As Nayoung Aimee Kwon highlights, "a perceived and real difference in spatial and temporal relationships to that same object of desire renders the nostalgia of the colonizer and that of the colonized untranslatable across the colonial divide" (2014, 118). Therefore, while this argument will expand on nostalgia and the Japanese audience in a moment, it is also worth briefly considering the potential role of other, younger markets. In 2022, the Philippines had a fertility rate of 2.7, Cambodia 2.3, and Indonesia 2.2 (World Bank Group Data n.d.). If one were cynically inclined, one could read *Black*

Sun's engagement with Japan's wartime legacy in Asia as an expression to these new parents that *Kamen Rider* is a good Japanese title that should not be lumped in with other targets of anti-Japanese sentiment. Japanese media have been subject to various boycotts and even banned, as it was in South Korea until 1998 (Sugawa-Shimada 2014, 170), for example, although notably, *Kamen Rider* was distributed in a thriving black market during that time. Further research in this area would be a welcome addition to the current body of knowledge regarding transnational superhero media flows.

Black Sun is careful to cater to a nostalgic audience (both domestic and international), using music from 1987s *Kamen Rider Black* and including scenes and characters that have little meaning for the new narrative but hold a lot of nostalgic affection for fans; the motor-cycles are examples of this, as is an entirely redundant swimming scene with a whale *kaijin*. Episode 10 opens with an almost shot-for-shot remake of *Kamen Rider Black's* opening sequence, replete with the original opening song and a slightly grainy quality to the film-stock. These elements are included as nostalgic fanservice. However, rather than being a homage in the mode of the other major fiftieth anniversary project, *Shin Kamen Rider* (2023), *Black Sun* is an unflinching demand that nostalgia must not eclipse memory. The contrasting between these terms is visible in the way *Black Sun* repeatedly interrupts fans' sites of pleasure before they achieve the moment of climax, to borrow Allison's "money shot" terminology. Instead, it drags the viewer's attention back to the direct line the program is drawing between historical and contemporary racism, public apathy, and violent extremism. *Black Sun* features *Kamen Rider's* signature fight scenes (a combination of thrilling choreography and amusingly camp rubber monster suits), but never allows the spectacle to subsume the reasons behind the violence.

As Barratt-Peacock highlights, the music of *Black Sun* is also particularly notable in its refusal of harmonic and emotional resolution. It is not that the music is minimalist, Barratt-Peacock argues; rather it creates clear and pointed moments of recognizable, melodically accessible pieces only to time their use in such a way that it avoids any climax or catharsis (Barratt-Peacock, forthcoming). This pattern is even noticeable in the official trailer (TOEI TOKUSATSU WORLD OFFICIAL 2022); the music seems to be building to a climax then abruptly cuts or is interrupted repeatedly. The same pattern is also mirrored in the narrative structure. The first *henshin* scene comes halfway through Episode 5 of *Black Sun,* which is only ten episodes long in total. The wait for the money shot is longer than in any other instance of *Kamen Rider.*

A remake or adaptation of a beloved superhero program is an inherently nostalgic exercise, but with its refusal of climax *Black Sun* is tonally more elegiac than celebratory. As Svetlana Boym argues, nostalgia can allow us to look backward to search

> for unrealized possibilities, unpredictable turns and crossroads. Nostalgia is not always about the past; it can be retrospective but also prospective. Fantasies of the past determined by the needs of the present have a direct impact on the realities of the future.
>
> *(2001, xvi)*

Black Sun does, on one level, rewrite the past, creating an alternate but recognizable timeline of Japanese history that includes *kaijin,* but it does so to initiate a conversation about the future. It then invites, or perhaps challenges, its audience to engage with the conversation through the design of the *henshin* belt toy. Like the child audience of the 1980s, standing in front of their televisions and waiting for the *henshin* sequence on screen to activate their belt toys, viewers are invited to stand in Kotaro's position when wearing his belt.

Coda

Black Sun's audiences are not permitted to comfortably assume the viewing position of children who can rely on a Kamen Rider to save everyone. Instead, the viewer is confronted by Aoi who, during her second UN address in Episode 9, stares unflinchingly into the camera (perhaps even breaking the fourth wall) and demands "Hey, you! With your bored looks while you're watching me talk on your screens. Why aren't you furious? You're pretending not to see what's really happening; and laughing it off." The optimism of young Kotaro from the 1987 program is completely denied Aoi, who, unable to effect change through the "proper" channels, begins training a terrorist fighting force of disturbingly young children.

Young Aoi's desperate attempts at correcting the violence and injustice of the world around her is contrasted with the burned-out cynicism and disengagement of Kotaro and the apathy of a wider society who pretend not to notice hate crimes happening in front of them. Low voter turnout is a major factor behind the repeated election of LDP governments on a handful of votes mobilized through reciprocal agreements with organizations like the Unification Church. Although this chapter has focused on the elements of *Black Sun* that are specifically related to Japanese politics, and the potential appeal to the region most impacted by Japanese fascism, there is also a clear broader message in *Black Sun*.

The younger generation are denied political representation around the world, whether by demographics as is the case in Japan, or by generational wealth imbalances and the role of money as speech in places like the United States and Australia. Movements such as The Last Generation, Extinction Rebellion, and so on, represent an increasing desperation and sense that there is nothing left that can be lost. *Black Sun* addresses the probable political disengagement and cynicism of its middle-aged audience through the design of the *henshin* belt toy, as well as through the television narrative.

It is not enough to wait for a Kamen Rider to come and save you, the program repeatedly insists to its audience; you were supposed to grow up and become the heroes! Standing in front of the TV and pretending was fine when you were five, but now you need to move. The television won't make the lights come on for you anymore. This time, the toy won't even switch on unless *you* move. Get outside and do something about this mess. Stop leaving the kids to carry the burden alone. If they have no support and no reason to believe they have a future left to lose, the kids will stop buying toys and start making bombs.

References

Adelstein, Jake. 2022. "Master Liar Shinzo Abe Doesn't Deserve This Lavish Funeral." *The Daily Beast*, September 27. https://www.thedailybeast.com/former-japanese-prime-minister-shinzo-abe-does-not-deserve-this-lavish-state-funeral.

Allison, Anne. 2006. *Millennial Monsters: Japanese Toys and the Global Imagination*. University of California Press.

Associated Press. 2024. "Births in Japan Hit Record Low as Government Warns Crisis at 'Critical State.'" *The Guardian*, February 28. https://www.theguardian.com/world/2024/feb/28/birth-rate-japan-record-low-2023-data-details.

Bainbridge, Jason. 2017. "From Toyetic to Toyesis: The Cultural Value of Merchandising." In *Entertainment Values: How Do We Assess Entertainment and Why Does It Matter?* edited by Stephen Harrington. Palgrave MacMillan.

Barratt-Peacock, Ruth. 2025 (in press). "Look Back in Anger but Speak to the Present: Examining Sound, Climax, and Allegory in Kamen Rider anniversary series *Black Sun*." *East Asian Journal of Popular Culture* 11 (2).

Barratt-Peacock, Ruth, and Sophia Staite. 2022. "Gothic Trajectories of Childhood: Play as a Third Space, Affective Dissonance, and the Melodrama of *Kamen Rider Kiva*." *Aeternum: The Journal of Contemporary Gothic Studies* 9 (1): 1–14.

Boym, Svetlana. 2001. The Future of Nostalgia. Basic Books.

Dickinson, Frederick. 2007. "Biohazard: Unit 731 in Postwar Japanese Politics of National 'Forgetfulness.'" *The Asia-Pacific Journal* 5 (10): 1–19.

Kennedy-Karpat, Colleen. 2020. "Adaptation and Nostalgia." *Adaptation* 13 (3): 283–294. https://doi.org/10.1093/adaptation/apaa025.

Kinukawa, Tomomi. 2021. "'De-national' Coalition against Japan's Gendered Necropolitics: The 'Comfort Women' Justice Movement in San Francisco and Geography of Resistance." *Feminist Formations* 33 (3): 140–174.

Kobayashi, Yoshiaki, dir. 1987. *Kamen Rider Black*. Toei Company and Mainichi Broadcasting System.

Kotani, Junko. 2017. "A Comment on Hate Speech Regulation in Japan after the Enactment of the Hate Speech Elimination Act of 2016." *The Journal of Law and Politics* 21 (3–4): 228–218.

Kwon, Nayoung Aimee. 2014. "Conflicting Nostalgia: Performing 'The Tale of Ch'unhyang' (春香傳) in the Japanese Empire." *The Journal of Asian Studies* 73 (1): 113–141.

Leaver, Tama. 2012. "Artificial Mourning: The Spider-Man Trilogy and September 11th." In *Web-Spinning Heroics: Critical Essays on the History and Meaning of Spider-Man*, edited by Robert Peaslee and Robert Weiner. McFarland and Company.

Nakatani, Hiroki. 2023. "Ageing and Shrinking Population: The Looming Demographic Challenges of Super-Aged and Super-Low Fertility Society Starting from Asia." *Global Health & Medicine* 5 (5): 257–263. https://doi.org/10.35772/ghm.2023.01057.

Ng, Kelly. 2023. "Japan population: One in 10 people now aged 80 or older." *BBC News*, September 19. https://www.bbc.com/news/world-asia-66850943.

Shiraishi, Kazuya, dir. 2022. *Kamen Rider Black Sun*. Toei Company and Ishimori Productions.

Staite, Sophia. 2021a. "*Kamen Rider*, Masked and Unmasked: Tales of Transcultural Transformation." In *The Superhero Multiverse: Readapting Comic Book Icons in Twenty-First-Century Film and Popular Media*, edited by Lorna Piatti-Farnell. Lexington Books.

Staite, Sophia. 2021b. "Kamen Rider: A Monstrous Hero." *M/C Journal* 24 (5): n.p. https://doi.org/10.5204/mcj.2834.

Steinberg, Marc. 2012. *Anime's Media Mix: Franchising Toys and Characters in Japan*. University of Minnesota Press.

Steinhoff, Patricia G. 2013. "Memories of New Left protest." *Contemporary Japan* 25 (2): 127–165. https://doi.org/10.1515/cj-2013-0007.

Sugawa-Shimada, Akiko. 2014. "Japanese Superhero Teams at Home and Abroad: Super-Sentai in Japan and Their Adaptation in South Korean Cinema." *Journal of Japanese and Korean Cinema* 6 (2): 167–183.

TOEI TOKUSATSU WORLD OFFICIAL. "【NEW TRAILER】Kamen Rider BLACK SUN (2022)." Uploaded October 13, 2022, on YouTube. https://youtu.be/lV5ppyigAUg.

Tsuji, Taimu. 2024. "[Kamen Rider] Kamen Rider Gavv's Transformation Belt Wins 'Toy of the Year' in the Character Category – Featuring Candy-Eating Action!" *Oricon News*, August 27. https://us.oricon-group.com/news/1548/.

Tsuneishi, Keiichi. 2011. "Reasons for the Failure to Prosecute Unit 731 and its Significance." In *Beyond Victor's Justice? the Tokyo War Crimes Trial Revisited*, edited by Yuki Tanaka, Timothy L. H. McCormack, and Gerry Simpson. BRILL.

Uno, Tsunehiro. 2015. リトル・ピープルの時代 [The Era of Little People]. Gentosha.

Wilson, Carl, and Lorna Piatti-Farnell. 2023. "Re-Examining Superhero Politics in Popular Culture." *The Australasian Journal of Popular Culture* 12 (1): 3–7. https://doi.org/10.1386/ajpc_00064_2.

World Bank Group Data. n.d. "Fertility rate, total (births per woman)." https://data.worldbank.org/indicator/SP.DYN.TFRT.IN.

Yoon, Sharon, and Yuki Asahina. 2021. "The Rise and Fall of Japan's New Far Right: How Anti-Korean Discourses Went Mainstream." *Politics & Society* 49 (3): 363–402. https://doi.org/10.1177/00323292211033072.

You, Mi. 2018. "Manchukuo, Capitalism and the East Asian Modern: Transhistorical Desire in *Kishi the Vampire*." *Southeast of Now: Directions in Contemporary and Modern Art in Asia* 2 (2): 93–117. https://dx.doi.org/10.1353/sen.2018.0003.

yzjps. "「私は独裁者ではない ！ 」安倍晋三vs蓮舫「息をするようにウソをつく」12/7党首討論" ["I am not a dictator!" Shinzo Abe vs Renho "You lie as easily as you breathe" 12/7 party leader debate]. Uploaded December 7, 2016, on YouTube. https://youtu.be/c7nWeVSLfoo?t=1900.

テレ東 BIZ. "「桜を見る会」共産党が総理批判【ノーカット】" ['Cherry Blossom Viewing Party.' Communist Party criticizes Prime Minister (Uncut)]. Uploaded November 12, 2019, on YouTube. https://youtu.be/lhBau1klxCc?t=533.

27

THE *TOKUSATSU* HEROES AND MAGICAL GIRLS OF *SENKI ZESSHŌ SYMPHOGEAR*

Leo Chu

Introduction: Unjustifiable Justice

A catchphrase widely circulated in Japanese popular culture since the 2000s is "cuteness is justice" (*kawaī wa seigi*), used as a tagline in the manga series *Strawberry Marshmallow* (2001–). Yet, the popularity of the phrase originates less in the portrayal of cuteness by particular works than a cute subculture that began in the 1970s as a women's celebration of a distinct girl (*shōjo*) identity, before turning into an industry exporting cute characters in anime, manga, and games, as well as youthful idols to the international market (Kinsella 1995; Madge 1998). By the start of the 21st century, cuteness has been incorporated into the government's "Cool Japan" soft power strategy to improve Japan's image, while women, once central to the creation of the subculture, are ironically overshadowed by the global expansion of cute media to male audiences (Bardsley 2011; Petit 2022). Especially in the *otaku* fandom, male consumption of beautiful girl (*bishōjo*) characters, usually depicted in an infantilized and sexualized aesthetics of big eyes and slender bodies, has gained extensive attention from Japanese and international scholars. The utterance of "cuteness is justice" can be understood in this context as the desire for fictional things that are normally unjustifiable. As Patrick Galbraith observes in his ethnography of male *otaku*, fans can present their obsession with cute characters as "righteous" (*seigi*) only by rejecting "images that are 'real and dangerous' (*riaru de yabai*)" so as to maintain their "orientation toward the fictional bodies of manga/anime characters" (2021b, 165).

This chapter contributes to the study of superheroes by analyzing the intriguing confluence of the male-dominated cute culture and a genre that upholds justice as its central tenet: *tokusatsu* heroes. A word literally means "special filming," *tokusatsu* includes many subgenres centering on special effects emerging between the 1950s and 1970s: *kaijū* (giant monsters) like *Godzilla* (1954–), gigantic heroes like *Ultraman* (1966–), and masked heroes teaming up against villains as in *Kamen Rider* (1971–) and *Super Sentai* (1975–). Although *tokusatsu* hero shows mostly target boys, since the 1990s, some of their elements have been incorporated into the magical girl (*mahō shōjo*) anime and manga, a genre targeting girls with stories about girls helping others with magic, exemplified in the pioneering *Sally the Witch* (1966–1968). The convergence is achieved largely through the trope of "transformation" (*henshin*) shared by

DOI: 10.4324/9781003366911-31

both genres – an often-repeated sequence showing heroes putting on sci-fi combat suits and magical girls putting on elaborate outfits, during which time seems to stand still as the transformation happens in a transient space separated from reality. One famous example of magical girl work appropriating *tokusatsu* is the manga *Sailor Moon* (1992–1997), which depicts a group of middle school girls transforming into magical warriors defending the world from mysterious enemies. Notably, in the 1980s, cute magical girl characters increasingly attracted male *otaku* fans, and the introduction of combat was well received, leading to a plethora of male-oriented shows featuring magical girls alternating between their carefree everyday life and fantasy battles. As Kumiko Saito suggests, if magical girls were originally intended as role models for preadolescent girls, toward the end of the century, they gave adult men an escape from their social responsibility with the spectacle of girls fighting with superpowers even though women's "entry into the adult world of 'real' power is precluded" (2014, 161).

While agreeing with the salience of the male gaze in the *tokusatsu*-magical girl fusion, I argue that the popularity of this hybrid genre stems not only from the male obsession with girl characters but also from the forms of heroism that magical girls embody. If *tokusatsu* heroes who overcome adversity through individual powers and teamwork reflect "the optimistic and economically affluent period of the early 1970s" (Wallin and Sandlin 2020, 569), the growing appeals of magical girls as heroes speaks to the economic stagnation Japan has experienced following the "bubble economy" of the early-1990s, which commentators link to the disillusionment of traditional masculinity and social aspirations among young men, many of whom eventually find solace in fictional media (Miyadai 2011). In contrast with *tokusatsu* heroes who attain justice by triumphing over the evil, the malice magical girls face and the justice they pursue are far more ambivalent and abstract.

This chapter will study *Senki Zesshō Symphogear* (hereafter cited in text as *Symphogear*), a five-season anime series (2012–2019) that has developed into a successful multimedia franchise including manga spin-offs, a mobile game, and, remarkably, live concerts performed by the characters' voice artists, with the latest concert in 2022 attracting more than 28,000 attendees. These events are possible due to a unique premise: characters in the series must sing to use their powers, and songs recorded for the anime are then performed on the stage. The next section explains how *Symphogear* makes the addition of music and singing to an already bewildering genre mix legible to its audience, and how this expansion of the scope of *tokusatsu* is relevant to the problem of justice.

From Masked Men to Singing Girls

Created by the studio Satelight under the direction of Ito Tatsufumi and Ono Katsumi, *Symphogear* begins with a live concert performed by two idols, Amō Kanade and Kazanari Tsubasa (following the naming convention, Japanese surnames come first in this essay; characters are referred to by their given names). As a horde of monsters storms the stadium, the idols take up magical weapons, and Kanade sacrifices herself to protect a girl, Tachibana Hibiki. Two years later, Hibiki arrives at Tsubasa's school and realizes that she has inherited Kanade's "Symphogear," magical gadgets developed from "relics" (*seibutsu*), powered by singing, and capable of transforming into various weapons and armors. The series then follows the adventure of Hibiki and Tsubasa, with each season showing the rise and fall of distinct villains, former enemies joining as friends, and the secrets behind Symphogear gradually unveiled.

The scenes of girls and young women wearing shining armor, smashing magical weapons against monsters with lethal power but almost campy design, while singing along with the upbeat soundtrack, may appear bizarre at first glance. A closer look suggests that the musical elements fit nicely into the established convention of *tokusatsu* heroes, especially the versatile ways heroes can "combine" (*gattai*) their gadgets into imaginative weapons or *mecha* (giant robots): Symphogears can similarly be combined to deal powerful attacks or generate protective barriers when characters sing in unison, and a lack of mutual trust can lead to literally out-of-tune combat performance. For critics, the significance of such sequences of gadgets disassembling and regrouping into new forms is not only its stunning choreography but also a symbolism of post-Fordist production methods used by Japanese firms, which install "a system with greater flexibility to match the uncertainties of the labor market" (Allison 2006, 101). Scholars have also contrasted these *tokusatsu* series with earlier shows like *Moonlight Mask* (1958–1959), which pioneered the depiction of masked heroes. Unlike later heroes who are first introduced to the audience as ordinary people before putting on masks or helmets to unleash their superpowers, no transformation sequence is shown to pin down Moonlight Mask's identity, and the hero possesses no superpower to distinguish him from his likewise masked foes. Jonathan Abel (2014) links this ambiguity to the struggle of Japan to re-establish a sense of justice and national identity following its defeat in the Pacific War (1941–1945), which was once portrayed as a righteous war to protect Asia from Westerners. If Japan in the 1950s still grappled with the aftermath of the war, the firmer identity of *tokusatsu* heroes in the 1970s, along with their ability to fight alone and in teams, implied a harmony between individuality and collective spirits, as well as the confidence the nation gained from its economic success. Justice, for the post-1970s *tokusatsu* hero shows, thereby denotes the protection of socioeconomic structures enabling Japan's recovery from the identity crisis of the immediate postwar years.

Importantly, in its reinterpretation of *tokusatsu* tropes like transformation and combination, *Symphogear* simultaneously upholds the convention of magical girl anime. One crucial distinction is that characters in the series, despite their *tokusatsu*-inspired design, do not wear masks. Since their powers are influenced by musical performance, closeups of characters' faces appear regularly in combat to capture emotions like anger, frustration, and determination; a technique consistent with the focus on facial and bodily expressions in anime in general (Suan 2021). Meanwhile, the series reinforces the cute, sometimes sexualized, design of characters for a male-dominated genre, and the transformation sequence typically shows a character's naked body – enveloped in bright light so as to avoid direct depiction of nudity – gradually cladded by armor. Scholars of the magical girl anime point out how the juxtaposition of characters' confident demonstration of their powers and the audience's voyeuristic pleasure in transformation scenes creates the "spatial dissection of the female body" and enables "the camera's gaze to explore the depth of the viewer's affection in the disembodied body" (Saito 2014, 155).

A *tokusatsu*-magical girl fusion like *Symphogear* thus differs from the traditional *tokusatsu* superheroes in the way it engages the audience. Teenage viewers of *Kamen Rider* and *Super Sentai*, while serving as potential customers of toys derived from the shows, are expected to mimic the heroes and defend their affluent society in future workplaces. In contrast, the adult male fans of magical girls are not expected to see characters as role models or partake in cross-dressing, and the shows seem to aim solely to motivate their consumption of merchandise such as CDs, live concert tickets, and even affiliated *pachinko* slot machines. In this way, *Symphogear* benefits from the recent trend for voice artists to "debut" by performing their characters on live stage, an event called *kaodashi*, or "face-exposing" (Nozawa 2021). Actually, Mizuki Nana, who voices the main character Tsubasa in the series, was already renowned for her singing and acting performance in *Magical Girl Lyrical Nanoha* (2004–), one of the most popular magical girl anime, while musician Agematsu Noriyasu and game designer Kaneko Akifumi, both veterans of the *Lyrical Nanoha* project, serve as writers of *Symphogear*. Despite the continual popularity of *tokusatsu* heroes, the series embodies a new heroism emerging in the 2000s which drops all pretenses at providing role models for its audience, male and female alike. If justice formally means to defend the society through values conducive to economic productivity, the magical girls as heroes redefine justice as the consumption of their cuteness

The Politics of Occult Technology

The emphasis on consumption rather than (re-)production of heroism in the *tokusatsu*-magical girl fusion echoes the characterization of male *otaku* subculture as a response to the crisis of traditional salarymen and breadwinner masculinity in Japan's economic stagnation since the 1990s (Miyadai 2011). Interestingly, while *Symphogear* offers its viewers an escape from the socioeconomic reality, it alludes to the troublesome political reality of Japan. For instance, Finé, villain of the first season, works with American intelligence to sabotage Japan's relic collection, and the antagonists in the second season are rogue Symphogear users from a US institute. In the third season, pressures from the US forces Japan to reorganize Symphogear users into a United Nations unit, while US military bases and fleets are involved in battles throughout the franchise, though their weapons are barely effective against supernatural monsters. The girls and women protecting the world by fighting and singing are thus caught in the complex politics between Japan, the UN, and the United States.

In fact, the *tokusatsu* genre has a long history reflecting on the political situation of postwar Japan, especially its status as a pacifist nation. Scholars notice how the sufferings of the public under the conventional and atomic bombing in the last days of the Pacific War complicated the memory of Japan's aggression in Asia, while American military presence since the Occupation (1945–1952) and the 1947 Constitution renouncing Japan's right to wage war fueled right-wing critics' equation of the defeat to the "primal catastrophe of castration that has demasculinized the Japanese nation-state" (Ivy 2008, 178). Seen in this light, mutant monsters in early *kaijū* films like *Godzilla* (1954) and *The Mysterians* (1957), through their threat of radiation and their destruction by sci-fi weapons, some powered by nuclear energy, embodied Japan's ambivalent role as an aggressor and a victim (Miyamoto 2016). The *tokusatsu* hero shows in the 1970s, in contrast, assumed a more optimistic tone by making the defense of economic prosperity a just cause for intervention, and the preference for teamwork over the American vigilante heroes suggested that a pacifist Japan can still be collectively "rearmed" with superpowers (Kim 2015a).

In addition to this allusion to Japan's problematic military legacy, *Symphogear* attends to another facet of the politics of superpower: the question of technology. Rather than outright magic, Symphogear and the relics are referred to in the series as "heretical technology" (*itan gijutsu*), and various governments have embarked on efforts to utilize this occult power. The magical quality of technology (and the technological essence of magic) is both a classic feature of *tokusatsu* and a reflection of the deep-rooted belief in the connection between technological advancement and the fate of the nation. Historians have called attention to how, as a latecomer in empire-building, Japan sought rapid growth in industrial and military capacity not only by directly transplanting Western technoscience but by adapting domestic methods to the demands of mass production, and how the defeat in the Pacific War strengthened the government's conviction in the imperative of innovation (Samuels 1996; Morris-Suzuki 1994). The image of Japan as a nation adopting technology to make up for its scarce resources is mirrored by *tokusatsu* heroes who gain superpowers by donning sci-fi suits, and *Symphogear* extends this open embrace of cyborgian fusion to the realm of the occult.

While casting technology in a generally positive light compared to the 1950s *kaijū* films, tokusatsu hero shows still warn about the potentially dangerous ramifications of powers promised by sci-fi gadgets. As Kim (2015b) argues, the original *Kamen Rider* (1971), by making the cyborg bodies of the hero and his enemies a product of neo-Nazi terrorists, turns the battle into a symbol of the hope to redeem Japan's wartime trauma and the anxiety to demarcate the just and evil uses of technology. To delineate how technology serves both peace and domination, *Symphogear* moves a step further and invokes Japan's alliance with Nazi Germany: many European relics like Gungnir, a Norse mythological spear recast as Hibiki's armor, were actually collected by Nazi mystics for a secret weapon project and arrived in Japan before the collapse of the regime. This Axis tie can be more problematic than simply using Nazi occultism as a trope. Critics notice how prewar American comics were full of German and "Oriental" villains to show the moral and racial righteousness of American superheroes (Dittmer 2007).

Although *Symphogear* understandably steers clear from the stereotypes, it rather unconventionally includes a Japanese villain, Kazanari Fudō. Introduced as Tsubasa's grandfather and an ultranationalist who started Japan's relic project under the Imperial Army, Fudō is revealed in the third season to be so obsessed with his bloodline that he actually fathers Tsubasa. This makes her half-siblings with her father Yatsuhiro, a government agent, and her uncle Genjūrō, commander of the Symphogear unit. The links between Symphogear and the dark side of Japan's past become more salient in the fourth season, when a mission to retrieve wartime research data brings the protagonists to the Matsushiro Headquarters, a site notorious for its use of forced Korean labor and recruitment of "comfort women" (Han 2012). Fudō becomes a main antagonist in the fifth season as he brainwashes Tsubasa and attempts to usurp the "Power of God" (*kami no chikara*) sealed in a relic to revive Japan's superpower status. When confronted by his two sons, Fudō (a sword-wielding old man with a long beard, uncannily muscular body, and supernatural strength) overpowers Genjūrō and kills Yatsuhiro, before being defeated by Tsubasa. The entanglement between Tsubasa's family tragedy, nationalism, and occult technology can then be read as the failure of Imperial Japan as a technological and a family state, in which the Emperor was worshiped as the divine leader of State Shinto and the father figure of a racial purity that must be buttressed by eugenic laws (Robertson 2001).

Despite this reference to the lurking risks of ultranationalism in Japan's relationship with real and imaginative superpowers, *Symphogear* is, in general, affirmative to the value of technology, even military technology, to Japan's pacifism. The third season begins with Hibiki and her friends stopping a crashing space shuttle to rescue its crew, and the fourth season starts with an action-packed sequence of Symphogear users launching a UN-led invasion of a fictional South American country that is trying to weaponize supernatural monsters. Such plots are congruent with the roles Japan's Self-Defense Forces began to assume in peacekeeping and humanitarian missions since the 1990s, though the constitution has limited its forces to non-combat positions (Hook and Son 2013). In the meantime, the series highlights the *de facto* American hegemony in the US-Japan alliance. The US government not only intervenes in Japan's relic research in the first two seasons so as to monopolize the occult power, but it targets Japan with nuclear missiles when a mission to defuse the "Power of God" goes sour. Moreover, many relics controlled by the United States are in fact collected in the Iraqi War as the series extends the connection between war and occultism from the Axis powers to the US empire. By dramatizing the real-world politics, *Symphogear* combines the escapist desire in male-oriented magical girl anime since the 1990s with wartime traumas in the *kaijū* films of the 1950s and the cautionary optimism among *tokusatsu* heroes of the 1970s, thus continuing the lineage of *tokusatsu* works alluding to Japan's struggle to rebrand itself as a peaceful power through technology.

Love amid Disasters

Japan in the 2010s undoubtedly faced new questions concerning technology. The triple disaster of earthquake, tsunami, and nuclear meltdown striking Fukushima on March 11, 2011 is widely seen as another blow to the technology-dependent society. Situated in the long line of postwar industrial incidents, most infamously the mercury pollution in Minamata, the Fukushima disaster stands out by reviving the anxiety over radiation and by showing the costs of sustaining the fabric of modern life (with electrical power) and how such costs are unevenly distributed between the rural, poor Northeast region generating electricity and the metropolitan Tokyo that actually uses it (Yoneyama 2019).

What connects *Symphogear* to post-Fukushima Japan is not only the frequent portrayal of disasters and destruction caused by the supernatural battles but, crucially, the association between idol performance and disaster response in the series. While the state's reaction in the aftermath of the disaster have attracted much criticism, especially its callous bureaucracy and suspected cover-up of the extent of the pollution, the prompt mobilization of the Self-Defense Forces and the resilience shown by local communities gave conservative critics opportunities to argue for the rejuvenation and "re-masculinization" of Japan's national spirits (Koikari 2019). In reality, what received a great boost in the 2010s was less Japan's masculine identity than the industry of female idol groups. As a part of male *otaku* subculture emerging in the 1980s, the popularity of cute and amateurish idols reached the climax in the 2000s through groups like AKB48 that emphasized performers' intimate interaction with fans and dependency on their support (Galbraith 2021a). While not all idol groups pursue the strategy of intimacy and dependency as AKB48, which has been under critical scrutiny after several harassment incidents, the prominence of female idols in post-Fukushima Japan does increase through their support for community recovery and tourism (Tajima 2018; Katayama 2021).

The ambition of *Symphogear* does not stop at reflecting the growing significance of idols in post-Fukushima Japan but seeks to turn musical performance into a philosophical commentary on human relationships with technology and one another. This commentary is based on the origin myth of the series: in the first season, Finé, the villain, reveals herself as an ancient priestess whose desire for God was punished with the "Curse of Balal," a reference to the story of the Tower of Babel and God's decision to confuse (*balal*) humanity. The confusion of tongues, Finé contends, is the source of human conflicts and sufferings, and her plan is to reunify the world by destroying the moon, which is the device used to spread the curse. In response, Hibiki insists that humans can understand each other despite their incomplete language and, above all, Symphogear users know how to communicate beyond the limits of words: namely, through singing. Throughout the series, Hibiki embodies the faith in mutual understanding by fighting with fists rather than weapons, and extending her hands whenever an enemy is brought to reason. This presentation of heroes as those befriending everyone mirrors later installations in the *Kamen Rider* franchise, where the demarcation of "just" versus "evil" uses of technology gives way to an idea of friendship that dismantles the division between self and other (Kim 2015b).

What is this power in songs that promises to tear down the barrier between self and other? The series has a seemingly cliché answer: love. What is remarkable about love in *Symphogear* is its entanglement with technology. Since only very few people can naturally equip the relics, both Japanese and American governments carry out secret human experiments, often using orphans as their subjects, and a drug called "Linker" is invented to boost the performance of these subjects. For Symphogear users relying on Linker, an excessive or insufficient dose can trigger side-effects like internal bleeding or an electrical shock, and they face higher risks when singing the *zesshō* (not only "superb song" but also "last song"), which boosts the power of Symphogear tremendously but can kill a user in the process, a fact testified by Kanade's death in the first season. Later, it is unveiled that a key ingredient of the drug is oxytocin, the so-called "love hormone" involving in human bonding, and the strong tie between the characters, through their singing in unison and will to protect each other, ultimately makes Linker-dependent and "natural" users equally capable of unleashing the full power of Symphogear. Indeed, the focus on the bonding between Symphogear users caters to male fans' desire to enjoy a fantasy of magical girl anime "devoid of romance, sex, and even male figures that can be a threat to *shōjo*'s pre-pubertal utopia" (Saito 2014, 159). The implicit reduction of love to a molecule associated with gestation and lactation can also deepen the essentialist representation of nurturing and caring as biological feminine qualities. After all, only girls and young women can ever become Symphogear users.

The limitation notwithstanding, by showing how emotion, music, biochemistry, and magic intertwine, *Symphogear* expands the inquiry into cyborg transformation in *tokusatsu* hero shows with the technological nature of love. The love that brings the self to the other aims not to negate the self or fuse with the other, which is a message the final season amplifies. As the Symphogear unit lands on the moon to investigate the device maintaining the "Curse of Balal," they find a message left by Enki, one of a group of Mesopotamian deities called Anunnaki. Enki confessed that he was the "God" Finé once admired, but his intention to confuse humanity was not to punish them but free them from the domination of Shem Ha, another Anunnaki whose soul Enki trapped inside a relic before he perished. Nevertheless, Kazanari Fudō's attempt to take over the Power of God awakes Shem Ha, who then begins to invade, connect, and control every life on the Earth.

In contrast with this forceful unification of multifaceted living forms into one organism, Hibiki and her friends envision to bring people together, not despite, but because of, their differences. The end of the second season already includes a scene where people around the world join the chorus to help protagonists stop the moon from crashing into the Earth. In the fifth season, as national leaders realize how Shem Ha's power functions like a giant computer, they swiftly mobilize all computing devices in the world to counter the influences. Convinced by Hibiki's perseverance, the ancient Anunnaki eventually consents to let humanity decide their fate under the curse, but also the blessing, of a life that is inseparable from either technology or other people.

Conclusion: Living as Heroic Consumers

This chapter examines how *Symphogear* creatively combines and reinterprets genre conventions in live-action *tokusatsu* hero shows, male-oriented magical girl anime, and the culture of popular idols. While the emphasis on cute female characters singing and fighting for male viewers reduces the function of *tokusatsu* heroes as models of justice, such media creates another form of heroism and justice through its consumption. Not only does the purchase of merchandise make the *tokusatsu*-magical girl fusion a profitable venture, but the allusion to viewers' latent anxiety and desire over changing geopolitical contexts weaves the series into the long history of the *tokusatsu* genre, which searches for the identity of a postwar Japan, wary of the technological foundation of its prosperity.

Amid Japan's persistent economic struggle, by the time of the Fukushima disaster, attending idol concerts and joining online fan communities have become an experience spreading well beyond the *otaku* subculture, even tantamount to a "social infrastructure or life support system" that is also "entangled with economic interests" (Galbraith 2021a, 82). The characters in *Symphogear*, singing to save the world, and their voice artists, performing in live events, seem to signal the convergence of such "life support systems" in fiction and reality. The idol performer, in this sense, becomes the hero who can bring even those seeking to escape from social reality back to that reality, thus defending the society through encouraging consumption. However, by treating popular groups like AKB48 as "national idols" (*kokumin-teki aidoru*), mainstream media generates new imagined communities through the problematic representation of Japanese women as infantilized and sexualized, while their men are presented as pathological and perverted (Galbraith 2017). The anxiety over the apparent weakness of a nation sustained by idols and technology-mediated entertainment is translated into *Symphogear* as the ultranationalist zeal of Fudō conspires to rejuvenate an ailing Japan with occult technologies. Certainly, whether male *otaku* fans are more receptive to right-wing, militarist rhetoric is a subject under fierce debate among Japanese academics since the 2000s (Lamarre 2014).

Beyond the cautionary tale about the potential of technology to revive ultranationalism, the occult references (mythological or sci-fi) in *Symphogear* offer insightful comments on human relations in general and *otaku* fans in particular. A subculture considered technology-savvy, *otaku* raises wider questions on the social and political ramifications of human interaction in the age of technological mediation (Azuma 2009). The series appears to be optimistic about the diverse ways humans and technology can co-exist. Rather than establishing a hierarchy where love constitutes the essence of singing, which in turn serves as a purer language prior to the "confusion" of tongues, *Symphogear* argues that affects, songs, and words not only entangle with, but essentially *are*, forms of technology that mediates human relations with each other and with themselves. The motif of idol performance as a technology to bring people together without diminishing their differences, without the desire to enforce a unity in the name of a nation or people, becomes the most powerful message that the series delivers.

References

Abel, Jonathan E. 2014. "Masked Justice: Allegories of the Superhero in Cold War Japan." *Japan Forum* 26 (2): 187–208.

Allison, Anne. 2006. *Millennial Monsters: Japanese Toys and the Global Imagination*. University of California Press.

Azuma, Hiroki. 2009. *Otaku: Japan's Database Animals*. Translated by Jonathan Abel and Shion Kono. University of Minnesota Press.

Bardsley, Janice. 2011. "Taking Girls Seriously in 'Cool Japan' Ideology." *Japan Studies Review* 15: 97–106.

Dittmer, Jason. 2007. "'America Is Safe While Its Boys and Girls Believe in Its Creeds!': Captain America and American Identity Prior to World War 2." *Environment and Planning D: Society and Space* 25 (3): 401–23.

Galbraith, Patrick W. 2017. "'National Idols': The Case of AKB48 in Japan." In *Routledge Handbook of Japanese Media*, edited by Fabienne Darling-Wolf. Routledge.

Galbraith, Patrick W. 2021a. "Idol Economics: Television, Affective and Virtual Models in Japan." In *Idology in Transcultural Perspective: Anthropological Investigations of Popular Idolatry*, edited by Hiroshi Aoyagi, Patrick W. Galbraith, and Mateja Kovacic. Palgrave Macmillan.

Galbraith, Patrick W. 2021b. *The Ethics of Affect: Lines and Life in a Tokyo Neighborhood*. Stockholm University Press.

Han, Jung-Sun N. 2012. "Conserving the Heritage of Shame: War Remembrance and War-Related Sites in Contemporary Japan." *Journal of Contemporary Asia* 42 (3): 493–513.

Hook, Glenn D., and Key-Young Son. 2013. "Transposition in Japanese State Identities: Overseas Troop Dispatches and the Emergence of a Humanitarian Power?" *Australian Journal of International Affairs* 67 (1): 35–54.

Ivy, Marilyn. 2008. "Trauma's Two Times: Japanese Wars and Postwars." *Positions: Asia Critique* 16 (1): 165–88.

Katayama, Rio. 2021. "Idols, Celebrities, and Fans at the Time of Post-Catastrophe." *Celebrity Studies* 12 (2): 267–81.

Kim, Se Young. 2015a. "Children of the Atom: Postwar Anxiety and Children's Play in Super Sentai." *Asian Communication Research* 12 (2): 54–72.

Kim, Se Young. 2015b. "Human/Cyborg/Alien/Friend: Postwar Ressentiment in Japanese Science Fiction and Posthuman Ethics in Kamen Rider Fourze." *Cinema: Journal of Philosophy and the Moving Image* (7) (December): 48–66.

Kinsella, Sharon. 1995. "Cuties in Japan." In *Women, Media and Consumption in Japan*, edited by Brian Moeran, and Lise Skov. Routledge.

Koikari, Mire. 2019. "Re-Masculinizing the Nation: Gender, Disaster, and the Politics of National Resilience in Post-3.11 Japan." *Japan Forum* 31 (2): 143–64.

Lamarre, Thomas. 2014. "Cool, Creepy, Moé: Otaku Fictions, Discourses, and Policies." *Diversité Urbaine* 13 (1): 131–52.

Madge, Leila. 1998. "Capitalizing on 'Cuteness': The Aesthetics of Social Relations in a New Postwar Japanese Order." *Japanstudien* 9 (1): 155–74.

Miyadai, Shinji. 2011. "Transformation of Semantics in the History of Japanese Subcultures since 1992." Translated by Shion Kono and Thomas Lamarre. *Mechademia* 6 (1): 231–58.

Miyamoto, Yuki. 2016. "Gendered Bodies in Tokusatsu: Monsters and Aliens as the Atomic Bomb Victims." *The Journal of Popular Culture* 49 (5): 1086–1106.

Morris-Suzuki, Tessa. 1994. *The Technological Transformation of Japan: From the Seventeenth to the Twenty-First Century*. Cambridge University Press.

Nozawa, Shunsuke. 2021. "Idolatry and Mediumship: Topologies of Affect in Japanese Media Culture." In *Idology in Transcultural Perspective*, edited by Hiroshi Aoyagi, Patrick W. Galbraith, and Mateja Kovacic. Palgrave Macmillan.

Petit, Aurélie. 2022. "'Do Female Anime Fans Exist?' The Impact of Women-Exclusionary Discourses on Rec.Arts.Anime." *Internet Histories* 6 (4): 352–68.

Robertson, Jennifer. 2001. "Japan's First Cyborg? Miss Nippon, Eugenics and Wartime Technologies of Beauty, Body and Blood." *Body & Society* 7 (1): 1–34.

Saito, Kumiko. 2014. "Magic, *Shōjo*, and Metamorphosis: Magical Girl Anime and the Challenges of Changing Gender Identities in Japanese Society." *The Journal of Asian Studies* 73 (1): 143–64.

Samuels, Richard J. 1996. *"Rich Nation, Strong Army": National Security and the Technological Transformation of Japan*. Cornell University Press.

Suan, Stevie. 2021. *Anime's Identity: Performativity and Form beyond Japan*. University of Minnesota Press.

Tajima, Yuki. 2018. "Japanese Idol Culture for 'Contents Tourism' and Regional Revitalization: A Case Study of Regional Idols." In *Global Leisure and the Struggle for a Better World*, edited by Anju Beniwal, Rashmi Jain, and Karl Spracklen. Springer International Publishing.

Wallin, Jason J., and Jennifer A. Sandlin. 2020. "Plastic Fantasies: Globalization and the Japanese Cultural Imaginary." *Cultural Studies ↔ Critical Methodologies* 20 (6): 524–34.

Yoneyama, Shoko, ed. 2019. *Animism in Contemporary Japan: Voices for the Anthropocene from Post-Fukushima Japan*. Routledge Contemporary Japan Series. Routledge.

28

CHINESE TRANSLATIONS OF AMERICAN SUPERHERO FILMS AND TELEVISION SERIES

Dingkun Wang

Introduction

The weekend prior to the premiere of the movie *The Flash* (2023) in Hong Kong, we saw its trailer on the mega billboard screen outside the SOGO shopping center in Causeway Bay. My seven-year-old daughter was thrilled by the visuals and said that she could not wait to watch it. Throughout the trailer, a caption in bold typeset and white color appeared at the left corner of the screen, which displayed "少兒不宜" (*shaoer buyi*; inappropriate for children). This did not attract her attention because she had never learned to read traditional Chinese characters until we moved to Hong Kong from Sydney in 2022. Thus, I had to break the "bad news" to her but also promised to not watch the movie either. I further suggested that we should find out what the movie was about and how fans similar to us would respond to it.

This was our first off-screen experience of a superhero film that we could not watch together. First, I helped my daughter better understand the enforced age restriction by reading a blog written by fan writer tanialamb, titled "Is The Flash (2023) Kid Friendly? Parents Guide" (tanialamb 2023). We then searched the film on Wikipedia, listened to a series of Mandarin Chinese and English podcasts, and watched several fan reviews on YouTube. Meanwhile, I tried my best to narrate a child-friendly version of the comic book story *Flashpoint* (2011) as part of her bedtime story. Furthermore, I found a video on YouTube shared via the CineCapsules channel on June 16, 2023. In "You can't change the fate | The Flash 2023 'movie recap'" (CineCapsules 2023), the video-maker (vidder) paired a 23-minute plot summary with visual sequences recorded from *The Flash*. While the question of how and where the vidder accessed such a resource for creating the "recap" may be investigated by the platform management and other stakeholders, the YouTube video had again instantiated how a media work may be spread across multiple platforms and venues of exhibition.

The experience I shared with my daughter in Hong Kong led me to reevaluate my plans for writing this chapter. Initially, I sought to present the variety of translational practices that facilitated the reception of American superhero films in Chinese-speaking societies. The indirect engagement with *The Flash* led me through a sense-making process. I could not access the translated version of the film in my local context and was obliged to select and filter the relevant media resources to piece together an age-friendly experience of the movie for my

 DOI: 10.4324/9781003366911-32

daughter. In doing so, I also shared the complex synergy of translation with her, although we did not merely rely on the translation to comprehend the film's story that was narrated in English. Translation specific to our experience is part of the process of adapting ourselves to the linguacultural and media environments of Hong Kong and searching for tangible ways to maintain our audienceship in superhero films and television. My daughter was not aware of the age restriction imposed on her when she was watching the movie trailer on a public screen owing to her lack of proficiency in reading Chinese. I took the opportunity to lead her through a variety of media works to discover not only what the film was about but also how it was related to the DC multiverse. We eventually gained more than what a cinema-going experience could have offered.

Although our experience of *The Flash* is not unique in the present convergent mediascape, it helps us understand not only the superhero film but also how it is being translated across languages, the recipient contexts, and media platforms for a variety of purposes. Translation fulfills the instrumental role of linguistic transfer (e.g., from English into Chinese) in addition to a wide range of intermediary and interpretive functions to bring a specific film and the associated story universes, franchises, value systems, and fandoms into contact with the audience in a particular recipient culture. The breadth and diversity of translational work were first identified by Roman Jakobson (1956), who categorized the types of translation as follows: intralingual, interlingual (the translation per se), and intersemiotic. Intralingual translation renders meaning within the same language, while interlingual translation (translation proper) facilitates communication between languages. Intersemiotic translation involves complex meaning-making processes that traverse diverse languages and expressive sign systems.

Rather than remain stringently separated, the three types of translation tend to overlap and converge in everyday communication and professional practices. In 2018, to engage young readers in mainland China, Marvel Comics published a picture book series called 漫威超级英雄双语故事 (*manwei chaoji yingxiong shangyu gushi*; Bilingual Stories of Marvel Superheroes) in collaboration with the Eastern China University of Technology Press. Each book contains stories about the original Marvel characters in English and Chinese and displays colorful and black-and-white drawings adapted from various Marvel comic books. The production involved a complex procedure of remediation, at least between English and Chinese; the comic book medium and that of children's literature; as well as the American context of comic book readers and the Chinese context, where Marvel comics were largely unknown until the inception of the Marvel Cinematic Universe (MCU). Thus, translation operates in a variety of relational, processual, and nonlinear forms that intersect and extrapolate beyond the Jakobsonian tripartite.

Building on Peircean semiotics, Kobus Marais (2018) proposed that translation builds new relations and opens new pathways for comprehending, sharing, and interpreting articulated meanings and distributed signs within, across, and beyond designated systems of social practice. In the abstract sense, non-material domains of communication and translation occur across the media, social domains, and semiotic spaces to harmonize different worldviews and cater to diverse needs for social interaction maintained by participants in specific communicative events (Bayham and Lee 2019). In the material domains, translation is made available to individuals in social interactions while converting physical objects and phenomena into generative entities of representation. Specifically, as the transformation of media modalities, translation builds "relations between several interpretations evolving from at least two different signification processes emanating from several media that are understood to be interrelated" (Elleström 2023, 390). As transmediality, translation connects the multitude of different media products and types in a specific "succession of interconnected representations, intrinsically interwoven with interpretants" (Elleström 2023, 397). This chapter takes initial steps to explore such a semiotic construct and the process of translation in the Chinese recipient contexts of superhero films and television series.

The following sections will first discuss how the transversal practices of translation facilitate the reception and remediation of American superhero films and television series in three Chinese-speaking contexts: mainland China, Hong Kong, and Taiwan. With reference to the promotion of the first two *Deadpool* (2016, 2018) films in these three market locales, it will further explore off-screen translations distributed in public spaces and other domains beyond the main screen. In summary, this study seeks to demonstrate how the latest theoretical breakthroughs in translation studies may enrich cross-cultural superhero studies.

Audiovisual Translation of Superhero Films and Television Series

Audiovisual translation (AVT) linguistically and culturally mediates specific meanings generated by the interaction between language and moving images. Foreign language audiovisual content is translated into different Chinese-language versions through the mediation of subtitling and/or dubbing for audiences in mainland China, Hong Kong, and Taiwan. In China, simplified Chinese subtitled versions of movies are released with the dubbed versions in Putonghua (a standardized variety of Mandarin that is also prescribed as the national lingua franca of China). For audiences in Hong Kong and Taiwan, subtitling in traditional Chinese characters is a method of linguistic and cultural mediation while dubbing is used to translate films, such as *Big Hero 6* (2014) and *Spider-Man: Across the Spider-Verse* (2023), for the consumption of children and teen audiences. Moreover, the traditional Chinese subtitles displayed in Hong Kong contain idiomatic expressions in Cantonese, which are not applicable to the Mandarin-based subtitles shown in China and Taiwan. In addition to the ideographic differences between simplified and traditional Chinese scripts, more nuanced variations exist between the two Mandarin-based subtitling systems in terms of usage and creativity.

Translators create in accordance with the expressed meaning articulated in a given source work. They adopt a certain aesthetic attitude to enable the source work to fulfill the demands, needs, or desires of a particular recipient context or audience group. The translated work brings shared or individualized interests into the source work and, therefore, aligns it with the target audience. In terms of language translation, the creativity lies in the generation of "a [new] language object that resembles another [i.e., the source text] without being distorted by the need for that resemblance" (Malmkjær 2020, 38). Essentially, the translator strives for originality based on their interpretation of a given source work. They seek to combine that source work with the language they are translating into and integrate them in an unprecedented and often creative manner. In doing so, they introduce a new work that gets incorporated into the repertoire of the linguaculture.

Audiovisual translators encounter complex tasks. They must render linguistic information in combination with visual–graphic and acoustic convergence from which meaning is generated. To reach a sound solution, they also need to overcome technical constraints in the audiovisual medium through creative thinking. Subtitling translates speech into writing and simultaneously visualizes the sound effects and remaining multimodal ensemble on the screen. These often include music, spoken but inaudible words, intonation, and extra- and paralinguistic effects (Jordà Mathiasen 2018). It is increasingly standardized and compulsory for the contemporary industry, particularly transnational streaming platforms, such as Netflix and Disney+, to provide comprehensible and holistic verbal descriptions of audible cues via subtitles to amplify the accessibility of content for viewers with hearing loss (Díaz-Cintas and Remael 2020). Hence, subtitlers must exercise translational and descriptive creativity in their professional conduct. In comparison, dubbing requires more complex, expensive, and time-consuming processes of co-creation during the stages of script writing, casting for dubbing directors and voice talents, rehearsing, performing, recording, and post-production (Miggiani 2019). The end product must synchronize the voice performance in a new language with the visual and audio cues on the screen.

The following excerpts are cited from the first episode of *Wanda Vision* (Shakman 2021; see Table 28.1). The series was streamed on Disney+ from January 15 to March 5, 2021 as the first television series in the MCU. Disney+ provides Putonghua dubbing (PD), Mandarin-based simplified and traditional Chinese subtitles (MSCS, MTCS), and Cantonese-based traditional Chinese subtitles (CTCS). The platform provides the ideal infrastructure to compare the translated versions, as one can focus on the selected scene and view it with different versions of subtitles while listening to the dialogues in English and various dubbed versions.

Wanda Vision narrates the adventures of Wanda Maximoff and her lover, Vision, after the stories depicted in *Avengers: Infinity War* (2018) and *Avengers: Endgame* (2019). Wanda reanimates Vision with her power and lives a surrealistic life with him in Westview, New Jersey, where their idyllic life undergoes mythic changes, showing the tropes of television sitcoms of different eras. The following scene is reminiscent of a classic American fantasy sitcom. Wanda uses her telepathic powers to make a plate fly back onto a kitchen shelf when Vision walks in. The plate shatters when it crashes on his head. The couple immediately slap and tickle each other. The PD track renders the meaning of the English dialogues and precisely matches the actors' lip movements. The version also demonstrates a rhyming effect at the end of each line with the even tones of 飞 (*fei*; fly) and 摧 (*cui*; destruct), thereby recreating a humorous effect that is appealing to Putonghua and potentially other Chinese-speaking viewers. The same rhyming effect was achieved in the MSCS version, which also presented the most concise translation. In contrast, the MTCS version is a word-for-word translation

Table 28.1 Wanda Vision: Season 1, Episode 1, "Filmed Before a Live Studio Audience" (Your Daily Dose Of Internet 2021)

Original dialogue (OD)	Putonghua-dubbing (PD)	Mandarin-based simplified Chinese subtitles (MSCS)	Mandarin-based traditional Chinese subtitles (MTCS)	Cantonese-based traditional Chinese subtitles (CTCS)
Vision: My wife and her flying saucers.	我的老婆能让盘子在天上飞 (My wife can make plates fly.)	我妻子的盘子会飞 (My wife's plate can fly.)	我老婆和她的飛盤 (My wife and her flying saucers.)	我太太，她令盤子飛起 (My wife, she can make plates fly.)
Wanda: My husband and his indestructible head.	我的老公的脑袋硬的坚不可摧 (My husband's head is so hard that it's indestructible.)	我丈夫的脑袋坚不可摧 (My husband's head is indestructible.)	我老公和他坚不可摧的頭 (My husband and his indestructible head.)	我丈夫，他的頭撞不爛 (My husband, his head can't be crashed into pieces.)

that may not succeed in replicating the intended humor. The Cantonese subtitles resonate with the scenes in everyday life and, therefore, the target audience. Overall, these translated versions retain the form of a couplet composed for the English dialogues, although they cope with the visual and audio cues at play differently in terms of the viewing experiences of target audiences. The area of audience research can be further explored in future collaborations between superhero studies and experimental research in AVT (see also Kruger and Liao 2022).

Major streaming platforms are heavily investing in the quality control of their multilingual translation services by cooperating with a globalized network of language service providers specializing in AVT. They maintain rigorous quality control, develop indoor and outsourced training programs with various partnerships at designated market locales, and innovate translation technologies to improve Cloud-based workflows and AI-generated translations (Díaz-Cintas and Remael 2020. Concerning Chinese, the existing services are only available for audiences in Hong Kong, Taiwan, and other Chinese-speaking communities outside mainland China, which remain closed to leading streaming services, such as Netflix, Disney+, Amazon Prime Video, and Apple TV+. Their content is made available to mainland Chinese viewers through the non-official distribution of Chinese fansubbing networks that have provided abundant media content, both old and new, translated from a wide variety of languages (Li 2017). Due to ethical and legal controversies regarding their informal and unregulated media practices, fansubbing networks in China are constantly facing repercussions due to domestic authorities, overseas production companies, and distributors. The most widely noticed case was the prosecution against the former largest fansubbing community, *Renren Yingshi* (YYeTs), in February, 2021 (Minster 2021). YYeTs generated significant use value and cultural meaning for contemporary media life in mainland China by synchronizing the audience with the expanding platform ecosystem and multilingual translation and content production that it globally instigates. Their existence and the persistent culture of fan translation have proven to create a considerable audience demand for international media entertainment. Despite this, informal media economies, such as fansubbing, prevent global streaming service providers from conducting meaningful negotiations with distributors and policymakers in China.

The downfall of the YYeTs caused other fansubbing communities to exercise greater caution and operate more strategically. Many gave up sharing subtitled video content and circulated their translations in sub-rip text files via their community websites, fansubbing archive SubHD, and peer-to-peer closed groups on the Chinese platform WeChat. Viewers in China must download a specific subfile and synchronize it with the corresponding video resources found on other online sites. Therefore, the fansubbing culture evolved into a new stage where part of the work was given to target viewers who formed new DIY communities with fansubbers to share tips for video hunting and troubleshooting. Meanwhile, a new trend in fan-ripping is emerging. The participants use diverse technologies to transfer ready-made Chinese-language versions from host platforms to local-facing, rogue streaming, and file-sharing sites in China. Although fan-rippers may no longer translate the ripped content or revise the existing translations, they still need to curate and converge the resources found for archiving and further sharing in the Chinese context. They also provide explanatory information about the synopses, main casts, production companies, and directors in Chinese. Whether these outputs of human translation will be subject to future inquiries remains to be seen, as the latest survey on Chinese fan translation communities revealed the tendency to use generative AI to enhance productivity (Xiao 2023).

How, then, does the current situation of fan translation relate to the reception of American superhero films and television series in China? These practices continue to pave the way for Chinese audiences and superhero fans to access their beloved audiovisual worlds. In particular, through their ground-level operations, blockbusters, such as *Zack Snyder's Justice League* (2021), *Shang-Chi and the Legendary Ten Rings* and *Black Adam* (2022), reached audiences in China despite stringent lockdowns and cultural blockages during the coronavirus disease 2019 pandemic. In parallel with fan-driven distribution, creators of podcasts and review videos played critical roles in helping the Chinese audience cope with the rapidly changing superhero franchises. Together, they have cultivated a robust convergence culture of superhero fandom by strategically creating and distributing their works through audio and video platforms, such as the China-based podcast streaming site Himalaya and video-sharing platform Bilibili as well as global platforms, such as YouTube, Spotify, and Apple Podcast. Their consistent cross-platform engagement with the superhero genre spreads the pleasure of media texts through content analysis and speculation on future plots. They also take the opportunity to share gossip and anecdotes about the local superhero fandom.

The hosts of "黑水公园" (*Heishui Gongyuan*; Blackwater Park; *Blackwater Park* 2021), an award-winning podcast program on popular culture, discussed a screening event that was held in Suzhou by a local DC fan club shortly after *Zack Snyder's Justice League* premiered on HBO Max. The event organizers exhibited their homemade IMAX copy of the film with fan-made, simplified Chinese subtitles. They took a picture during the screening and tweeted it by hashtagging Zack Snyder, despite the official ban on Twitter in China. According to the podcast hosts, the director replied to the Chinese fans with *hao*, which is the Romanized transliteration of the Chinese character "好" (good). Although no record of this correspondence is retrievable, the narrated anecdote reveals the following facts: (1) the unsolicited use of international social media platforms, such as Twitter (now X), is widespread among young Chinese Internet users and particularly, the fans of global entertainment media; (2) the film director acknowledged the affection conveyed by the Chinese fans, as many of them were deeply involved in the "Release the Snyder Cut" movement; (3) fans are constantly seeking to sustain their alternative media life in parallel to the dominant apparatus of infrastructure in the Chinese media context. Podcasters quickly changed the subject after sharing the story by urging their audiences to comply with copyright protection. However, they had discussed a film that was not officially released in China, which they had watched through illegal channels of distribution. They shared an anecdote that was widely noticed among their audiences and superhero fans in China. Their actions can be interpreted as an essential strategy for fan creators to survive in the robust but heavily censored Chinese digital economy. To successfully engage their audiences, promote their beloved content, and profit from their content creation, fan creators must be resilient to further negotiate the status quo on the terms and conditions under which their fandom can be sustained. Despite being transgressive, they do not seek to turn the system upside down.

Off-Screen Translation from the Screen to Social Spaces

This section explores off-screen content production, which extends the functionality of translation beyond translated screen stories. The paratext illustrated in this section may not provide meaningful entryways for films or television programs. Nevertheless, they help translate the hype and synergy that influences the understanding of, and engagement with, various storyworlds in different market locales. With reference to the abundant and omnipresent media

Table 28.2 Promotional message distributed in Hong Kong

Source text	Translation into English
最醒	The coolest
最玩嘢	The wildest
最寸寸貢	The cockiest
最反傳統嘅	The unruliest
超級漫畫英雄	Super comicbook hero

paratexts, such as trailers, video games, podcasts, posters, interviews, promotional texts, and toys, Jonathan Gray suggested that they "do more than just ask us to believe them or not; rather, they establish frames and filters through which we look at, listen to, and interpret the texts that they hype" (2010, 3). He called for additional studies to explore the wealth of media entities that create textuality and facilitate social interactions beyond the consumption of mainstream stories and corporate-driven monetization. The following examples show translations that contribute to commercial distribution and audience-based remediation.

In an interview with Digital Spy, a UK-based online entertainment media owned by Hearst Communications, Inc., Ryan Reynolds was asked if he could respond to the Chinese censorship of *Deadpool* (2016) in the exact manner of his foul-mouthed screen persona. Reynolds improvised as if he was in a film trailer made specially for the Chinese market (Digital Spy 2016). He said, "In a world divided by fear, one man must stand alone. *Deadpool.* Rated 'fuck you, you'll never see this!'" However, he further commented as himself that, "No, honestly, it's easy for me to wear that as a badge of honor, like 'we got banned in China!' I hate that. I love China, and I'd love the people of China to see *Deadpool.*" His costar in the film, T. J. Miller, supported him and said, "So we encourage everybody to make their way over to America and check it out, starting in February!" Miller's comment coincided with the already existing cinema tourism of Chinese viewers, as the film was shown in many international cities where Chinese tourists travelled during the Lunar New Year.

In addition to America, mainland Chinese audiences watched *Deadpool* (among other films banned in China) in Hong Kong and Taiwan, where it was promoted and subtitled in Chinese. In these two locations, the film was promoted as a holiday season blockbuster in sensational styles that foregrounded the charm and vibe of R-rated characters. In Hong Kong, the film title was translated as 死侍：不死現身 (Deadpool: The Undying Show-Up; see also Table 28.2; 20th Century Fox 2016). The translated title highlights the genetic transformation of the main character, Wade Wilson, from that of a dying cancer patient into the immortal Deadpool. The promotional messages, used on *Deadpool* posters and other promotional imagery, provide further contextual information about the antihero through colloquial Cantonese.

In comparison, the film posters distributed in Taiwan introduced the title as 惡棍英雄：死侍 (The Villainous Hero: Deadpool). This translation adopted the official Chinese name of the main character, that is, 死侍 (*sishi*; servant of Death) and portrayed him as a paradoxical phrase 惡棍英雄 (*egun yingxiong*; villainous hero). It portrayed Deadpool as a nontraditional character in the broader superhero genre, who is both heroic and condemnable. An additional message was inserted in the poster to address the Taiwanese audience from the perspective of Deadpool, who considers himself "the cutest" superhero. The slang expression 啾咪 (*qiumi*; cute) was used to enable the character to gain proximity to the local audiences (see Table 28.3).

Table 28.3 Promotional message 1 distributed in Taiwan

Source text	Translation into English
超級英雄	Among all the superheroes
我最啾咪	I'm the cutest

Table 28.4 Promotion message 2 distributed in Taiwan

Source text	Translation into English
全台票房 衝破4億	Grossed more than 400 New Taiwan Dollars
惡棍英雄	(TWD) in Taiwan
死侍	The Villainous Hero
持久熱硬中	Deadpool
	Hot and Hard in cinemas

Another poster was released after the film grossed more than 400 million New Taiwan Dollars (see Table 28.4; 20th Century Studios 2016). The promotional message aligned with Deadpool's speech style, which is loaded with sex-oriented puns and outrageous swearing. This was realized through the pun 持久熱硬中 (Hot and Hard in cinemas), which emphasizes the homophonous resemblance between 硬 (ying; hard) and 映 (ying; showing). Thus, the line celebrates the commercial success of the film by imitating Deadpool's graphic language.

The above-mentioned promotional messages were circulated in public spaces, including bus stops, roadside billboards, and metro stations. Language styles corresponded to Deadpool's body gestures and facial angles depicted in the posters to generate persuasive messages. The image–text ensembles enabled the antihero to speak to the intended audience in a language that was not his native language. In contrast to mainland China, Hong Kong and Taiwan are more tolerant of foul language, sexual allusions, irony, humor, and excessive violence depicted in *Deadpool* due to their well-established rating systems and advanced media literacy and intercultural capacity maintained by the general public. Hence, local distributors can exercise their creativity in displaying these elements in local public spaces to facilitate off-screen interactions with the audience. This does not lead to the conclusion that *Deadpool* and its sequel (released in 2018) had no audience in mainland China.

To enter the mainland Chinese market, the production company 20th Century Fox released a "clean" and "family friendly" edited version of Deadpool 2. The sequel was rebranded as 死侍2：我爱我家 (*sishi 2: woai wojia*; Deadpool 2: I Love My Family) for authorized exhibition from January 25, 2019. This title stimulated a sense of nostalgia among the audiences by referring to a classic and the first sitcom made in China, 我爱我家 (*woai wojia*; I Love My Family 1994), although the series is unrelated to the Deadpool universe. Hence, the new title was a marketing essential and, to a great degree, conveyed the filmmaker's intention to resolve issues under the Chinese censorship regime for greater commercial benefits. The Central Chinese Television also promoted the film on the program 今日影评 (*jinri yingping*; M TALK; Central Chinese Television 2019). The two hosts of the program deliberately discussed the film's "family" theme. They explained that this movie was about Deadpool and his X-Force family.

Posters were designed for use in various public places. Local distributors managed to tone down the mature elements of the film (see 20th Century Studios 2016). However, the promotional messages continued to reflect some of the original characteristics. For example, they promoted Deadpool as 漫威最贱英雄 (manwei zuijian yingxiong; the cheapest Marvel hero) but added another layer to the message by striking off the character 贱 (*jian*; cheap) with red ink and inserting the character "红" (*hong*; popular; famous) in red font color, which literally means "red." Conversely, readers also received the message as 漫威最红英雄 (*manwei zuihong yingxiong*; the hottest hero of Marvel), which is, at least in the rebranded Chinese version, in contrast to the other message conveyed with *jian* (cheap). On the one hand, this palimpsest addressed Marvel's Chinese fans by applying their interpretation of Deadpool as cheap and outrageous but simultaneously famous and adorable. On the other hand, the message visually enacted a self-correcting performance on the wording to demonstrate the distributor's compliance with censorship. Nevertheless, the character "贱" is a derogatory term, which is unacceptable in public communication. Hence, the creatives at play not only promoted the film in China but also repackaged it into a new story that appealed to the fans, audience, and, most importantly, Chinese authorities.

Concluding Remarks

This chapter explores the Chinese-language translation of superhero films and television on and beyond the main screen. Media resources are distributed in the discussed market locales rather unevenly, owing to various economic and political restrictions. Although mainland Chinese audiences have greater international mobility, traveling overseas remains a luxury for most Chinese audiences and media fans. They must still rely on unsolicited resources shared online. The Chinese fansubs of *Deadpool* and other banned superhero films, such as *Watchmen* (2009) and *Dr. Strange: In the Multiverse of Madness* (2022), are well-preserved in the fansubbing archive SubHD and other online sites (see SubHD 2023). In addition to translation and circulation, fansubbing communities in China have created nonofficial posters and other media paratexts for their audiences. Scholars might retrieve and collect fan-made paratexts distributed as part of the Chinese superhero fandom in the future.

Future research on the AVT of superhero storyworlds can also explore the work of intersystemic translation from the visual storytelling of comic books into audiovisual media. Superhero films and television realize what Drew Morton theorized as "stylistic remediation," which foregrounds "the representation of formal or stylistic characteristics commonly attributed to one medium with another" (2017, 8). This is different from adaptation because the remediated work is not subject to any specific source but rather evolves either linearly or dialogically from a cluster of media works that may or may not be attached to a particular transmedia intellectual property. Those works on adaptation seek to appropriate or quote from a particular source and its associated medium, while stylistic remediation transgresses medial boundaries without relying on "another art form for material to translate" (Morton 2017, 23). Future research might explore the strategies and creativity in transferring meaning from static frames and panels into audiovisual performances: the atmospheric stylization shown on screen and its effect on the depicted characters, actions, and emotions; the ways in which the audiovisual medium enriches the narrative arc(s) built on specific character(s); and the changing audienceship of stylistic remediation. The potential findings may provide critical feedback on translational work, such as subtitling and dubbing.

Further understanding of the process and products of stylistic remediation can help improve the practice of media accessibility and, therefore, bring the audiovisual arts of the superhero genre to audiences who have special needs. In particular, audio description (AD) renders a nonverbal visual performance on the screen as a verbal narration for audiences with sight loss. A deeper understanding of stylistic remediation can help those who are involved in the AD production process (e.g., translators, AD script writers, and readers) interpret the intersystemic translation from the visual–graphic medium into live-action representation, search for more verbally economic and comprehensible solutions to describe the increasingly sophisticated visual and choreographic techniques, and, therefore, stimulate cognitive and emotional responses from the target audiences of AD as much as other AVT varieties can achieve for the hearing and seeing audiences. At present, the volume of AD production is consistently increasing in cinematic, televisual, and streaming distributions in Europe, the UK, North America, and some Asia Pacific markets. In comparison, AD in China remains scarce, particularly for global entertainment franchises, such as superhero films and television series. Since the consumption of American superhero media franchises continues to rise across Chinese-speaking societies, it is essential that filmmakers, production companies, and local distributors increase their efforts to not only expand the amount and avenues of consumption but also make them more inclusive and accessible. This will be a further area of future research endeavors where the industrial development further aligns with academic interests in superheroes.

References

20th Century Fox. 2016. [Deadpool Poster]. WMOOV, January. Accessed on June 29, 2023. https://wmoov.com/assets/movie/photo/201601/Deadpool_cmpC_HKposter_13_releasedate changetoFeb09_1454160208.jpg.

20th Century Studios. 2016. "超! 好! 笑! 梗! 超! 多! 認同請分享~[Super! Good! Laughing! Meme! Super! So Many! Please Share If You Agree~👍]" Posted March 3, 2016, on Facebook. Accessed on June 29, 2023. https://m.facebook.com/20thCenturyStudios.tw/photos/a.152473376484/10153421010711485/?type=3&eid=ARApaX8i0SwRrbh7Kl6wPpqSHPrFZ0q_vwQm0u-t3Hgueu8QVK1slarQxWw_1JAfg_wnIZyOOOJ&locale=zh_HK.

Baynham, Mike, and Tong-King Lee. 2019. *Translation and Translanguaging*. Routledge.

Blackwater Park, podcast, Episode 204, "扎克施耐德的《正义联盟》及《黑暗正义联盟》[Zack Snyder's Justice League and Justice League Dark]." *Released* March 26, 2021. Apple Podcasts. https://podcasts.apple.com/hk/podcast/%E6%89%8E%E5%85%8B%E6%96%BD%E8%80%90%E5%BE%B7%E7%9A%84-%E6%AD%A3%E4%B9%89%E8%81%94%E7%9B%9F-%E5%8F%8A-%E9%BB%91%E6%9A%97%E6%AD%A3%E4%B9%89%E8%81%94%E7%9B%9F/id1078007055?i=1000665260047.

Central Chinese Television. *M Talk*. "《死侍2 ：我爱我家》为春节档暖场 "话痨"英雄魅力何在 ？ 【今日影评 | Movie Talk】["Deadpool 2: I Love My Family" Is a Warm-Up for the Spring Festival. What Is the Charm of the "Talkative" Hero? 【Today's Movie Review | Movie Talk】]" Uploaded February 6, 2019, on YouTube. Accessed on June 29, 2023. Video no longer available on February 22, 2025. https://www.youtube.com/watch?v=GAbSz98saHE.

CineCapsules. "You Can't Change the Fate | The Flash 2023 'Movie Recap.'" Uploaded June 16, 2023, on YouTube. https://www.youtube.com/watch?v=UunwgwOGZhQ.

Díaz-Cintas, Jorge, and Aline Remael. 2020. *Subtitling: Concepts and Practices*. Routledge.

Digital Spy. 2016. "Ryan Reynolds on Deadpool 2, X-Men Crossover and China Ban." Uploaded February 4, 2016, on YouTube. https://www.youtube.com/watch?v=tzYfcLi8mLk.

Elleström, Lars. 2023. "Intermedia Approaches." In *The Routledge Handbook of Translation Theory and Concepts*, edited by Reine Meylaerts and Kobus Marais. Routledge.

Gray, Jonathan. 2010. *Show Sold Separately: Promos, Spoilers, and Other Media Paratexts*. New York University Press.

Jakobson, Roman. 1956. "On Linguistic Aspects of Translation." In *Fundamentals of language*, edited by Roman Jakobson and Morris Halle. Mouton & Co.

Jordà Mathiasen, Eivor. 2018. "Deconstruction Subtitled – Subtitling Deconstructed." *Babel (Frankfurt)* 64, no. 5–6: 777–791.

Kruger, Jan-Louis, and Sixin Liao. 2022. "Establishing a Theoretical Framework for AVT Research: The Importance of Cognitive Models." *Translation Spaces* 11, no. 1: 12–37.

Li, Luzhou Nina. 2017. "Rethinking the Chinese Internet: Social History, Cultural Forms, and Industrial Formation." *Television & New Media* 18, no. 5: 393–409.

Malmkjær, Kirsten. 2020. *Translation and Creativity*. Routledge.

Marais, Kobus. 2018. *A (Bio)Semiotic Theory of Translation: the Emergence of Social-Cultural Reality*. Routledge.

Miggiani, Giselle Spiteri. 2019. *Dialogue Writing for Dubbing: An Insider's Perspective*. Palgrave Macmillan.

Minster, Adam. 2021. "China's 'Fansub' Crackdown Spells Trouble for Hollywood." *Bloomberg*, December 6. https://www.bloomberg.com/opinion/articles/2021-12-06/china-s-fansub-crackdown-spells-trouble-for-hollywood#xj4y7vzkg.

Morton, Drew. 2017. *Panel to the Screen: Style, American Film, and Comic Books During the Blockbuster Era*. University Press of Mississippi.

Shakman, Matt, dir. *WandaVision*. Season 1, Episode 1, "Filmed Before a Live Studio Audience." *Aired*, January 15, 2021, on Disney+.

Sub HD. "死侍 ['Deadpool' search results]." Accessed June 29, 2023. https://subhd.tv/search/%E6%AD%BB%E4%BE%8D.

tanialamb. 2023. "Is The Flash (2023) Kid Friendly? Parents Guide." *Lola Lambchops*, June 21. https://lolalambchops.com/the-flash-2023-kid-friendly-parents-guide/.

Xiao, Weiqing. "How Non-Professional Subtitlers Embrace Technologies: A Survey Study on Fansub Groups in China." Keynote at *The International Symposium on Linguistics, Language Applications and Translation Studies in the Big Data Era*. City University of Hong Kong, China, June 6–8, 2023.

Your Daily Dose Of Internet. "'My Husband And His Indestructable Head' Scene | WandaVision (2021)." Uploaded February 7, 2021, on YouTube. https://www.youtube.com/watch?v=tJ-D_Aq6wJk.

PART IV

Superhero Bodies and Identities

29

WITH GREAT POWER, COMES AN ARMORED CORSET

Clothing as Empowerment for Female Superheroes

Yael Rachel Novich

Introduction

The subject of female garment design and its representation as indicators of strong female characters is actively debated in contemporary media discussions. In a scene from the superhero series *The Boys* (2019), episode 3, "Get Some," the superheroine Starlight is asked to rebrand her image by Big Corporation. They ask her to ditch the outfit of her own personal design: a star-patterned skirt and a robe with gold and white colors, in favor of a tighter fitting corset, a panty cut, and a collar that exposes the chest. The design team tries to convince her that this is a "feminist," empowering garment. She strongly claims it does not represent her at all. The character wants her outfit to equally represent her as a strong woman and as an individual (Sgriccia 2019).

The scene, as does this research, revolves around the question of "How does a garment or accessory portray strength in female characters?" This chapter will discuss the representation of powerful female characters through clothing and props in "Fantastic Cinema": science fiction, fantasy, and superhero genre films. As this will be our main focus, we will not compare designs across the different genders; note that the portrayal of strength in male characters is well-researched (Berger 1977; Darowski 2014; Brown 1999; Nevins 2017; Attebery 2002). A lot of resources are invested in costume design, certainly by big corporations such as Disney and Warner Bros. There is no doubt that the considerations for choosing one garment or another are not arbitrary. The tools used for the portrayal of strong female characters influence our cultural language. Our shared visual culture plays an important role in conveying messages and shaping worldviews, such as those related to gender and power relations.

This study will conduct quantitative research of over ~260 costumes from various fantastic films. Key insights on the connections between the portrayal of strength and garment design are extracted via statistical analysis. I apply the newly gained statistical insights to an analysis of the costume design from a scene in the Marvel superhero movie *Avengers: Endgame* (Russo and Russo 2019). The film was the climactic ending of the highest grossing box office movie series of its time, concluding a run of 23 films. The scene features most of the notable female heroines of the Marvel Cinematic Universe (MCU) up to that year. I analyze how these women's clothing empowers them, in design and meaning.

DOI: 10.4324/9781003366911-34

Background

Women, Clothing, and Cinema

While focusing on feminist theories in cinema, this study is anchored in three research fields: material culture, semiotics, and visual culture.

Material culture studies the relationship between people and objects, specifically how people shape and use objects, as well as how objects shape people and their identities (Thomas 2006). Within this field, clothing is seen as a means to express and glorify their personalities through its spiritual and aesthetic qualities. These objects often embed the names, biographies, memories, and histories of previous owners, adding depth and meaning to them (Schnieder 2006).

The field of semiotics is the study of how objects are represented, interpreted, and become symbols themselves (Palmer 1993). In the context of clothing, semiotics can involve analyzing the symbolism of gender, social culture, power relations, and color (Barthes 1983; Halliday 1994; O'Toole 1994; Owyong 2009). It is believed that the interpretation of color is a social construct that is influenced by the culture and period in which it is experienced, and that the meanings of colors are learned through the objects, form, and matter they are associated with (Young 2006; Gombrich 1960; Bousfield 1979; Coote 1992)

Visual culture deals with how meaning is conveyed through visible media and how it influences aesthetic values and stereotypes within a culture (Mirzoeff 2002). Popular culture, including films and movies, is often studied within visual culture as a way of understanding modern society (Zeisler 2008). Feminist film theory can be used to understand the portrayal of strong women in visual media, including the contrast between weak and strong female characters and the common portrayal of female side characters as lovers, helpers, and victims (Tasker 1993; Brown 1996).

Fantastic Genre and "Avengers: Endgame"

The "Fantastic" film genre portrays the supernatural or has a story that could not exist in reality or the present day. It contains sub-genres such as fantasy, where elements such as mythical creatures/places and magic exist; it conveys a sense of adventure and contains moral messages and usually establishes gender roles (Tiffin 2008; Fry 2009; Fowkes 2010; Haase 2008). Science fiction revolves around a futuristic setting and envisions a future where every phenomenon can be explained by advanced technology and science; it offers easy-to-recognize iconography and often uses female empowerment narratives, unlike fantasy (Balic 2009; Stankow-Mercer 2009; Telotte 2001; Brown 2011). The Fantastic includes superhero movies, which are generally based around a protagonist who usually is heroic, with supernatural abilities, an iconic costume, and a villainous character that serves as an equal opponent (Ina et al. 2018; Coogan 2013). All of these genres contain certain archetypes within visual design and writing conventions. Within those genres, the female characters are (re)contextualized across various aspects such as femininity, race (or different species), and power dynamics, where they are presented not only through how the character is written but by their clothing (Lee 2008; Snyder 2004; Jarvis 2008; Cornea 2007; Ashliman 2008).

Data Collection

To perform the quantitative study, ~220 female characters featured in ~215 fantasy films between the years 1939–2020 were documented. Images of scenes with their various apparels were collected, totaling over 260 outfits. Characters could be used more than once, as long as their clothing was substantially different.

The characters were dichotomously labeled as projecting strength or weakness while wearing the outfit. The labeling was assigned based on relevant literature: Marcy Kennedy's study on writing about the female character, as she establishes that strong female characters often have three attributes: smarts, the ability to act, and standing loyal to their beliefs (Kennedy 2013). Edward Schiappa's examination on weak female characters and the "Damsel in Distress" compared to their male counterparts (Schiappa 2008). Jeffrey Brown's application on the contrast between the two types of female characters in movies (Brown 1996). Yvonne Tasker's work on female side characters as lovers, helpers, and victims, among others (Tasker 1993). Susan Jeffords's analysis on Sarah Connor's character and her evolution from weak to strong between films (Jeffords 1993).

The visual features of the outfits were recorded: colors, articles of clothing, hair, textiles, and accessories. Additionally, the narrative features of the characters were recorded by character archetype and narrative importance. I extracted quantitative features from the detailed descriptions by a series of dichotomous (yes/no) questions. Every question used was verified to manifest both positive and negative answers at least ten times over the outfit list. In all, 78 visual features and eight narrative features were documented. The data is publicly available (Novich 2021a).

1   *Visual features:* Note that each of the options in questions with multiple endings is asked separately. For example, outfits could be characterized by multiple colors, and the existence of each individual color is a separate dichotomous query.

- Is the outfit characterized by one of the following colors: black/white/blue/red/green/gold/silver/grey/brown/bright/dark?
- Is the hair color white/brown/blonde/black/red/ginger/other?
- Is the skin color white (visually – not necessarily ethnically)?
- Is the hairstyle long/medium/short/tied/partially tied?
- Is the top article of clothing a tight suit/dress/shirt/best?
- Is the sleeve long/short/sleeveless/puffy?
- Are there any arm accessories, such as bracelets/ribbons/bandages/rings, etc.?
- Is the bottom article of clothing long pants/short pants/skirt/tights?
- Is there a belt?
- Is there a cape?
- Is there hand apparel that is protective (gloves)/aesthetic (rings)?
- Is the type of shoe with heels/flat/boots/leather/long, or tall?
- Is there a head ornament of some kind?
- Is the head ornament a hat/protective (like a helmet)/aesthetic (like a ribbon)/tiara/crown?
- Are there face ornaments such as heavy makeup/tattoos/sunglass, etc.?
- Are there ear ornaments such as earrings, etc.?
- Is there a neck ornament such as a necklace/collar?
- Is there an additional article that especially stands out, anything from an ornamental pin to a tail?
- Is there a means of attack of some sort?

- Is there a type of means of attack such as magic/cold weapons/guns/bow and arrows/ martial arts?
- Is the primary textile fake leather/cashmere/silk/cotton/iron/chiffon/gabardine/Lycra?
- Is the design noticeably asymmetrical?

2 *Narrative features*

- Is the character a hero/helper/love interest/villain?
- Is the character in a lead/supporting/side role?

Analysis of Association between Garment and Strength

We wanted to discover if there is a clear connection between a character's strength and her outfit. A "chi-squared" test (specifically Fisher's test) was performed to examine the correlation between each visual feature and the strength label (Pearson 1894; Fisher 1922). A positive correlation means they are associated with strength. A negative correlation suggests an association with weakness. The test result includes the correlation value and its significance. Significance scores were corrected for multiple testing using Holm-Bonferroni (Holm 1979). The top features are listed by order of significance in Table 29.1.

The presence of weapons of any kind (and guns and magic) has a high, significant positive correlation. The articles of clothing with positive correlation were boots, protective hand apparel, arm accessories, and body suits. Those with a negative correlation were dresses, flat shoes, and puffy sleeves. Among colors, bright and white colors had a negative correlation, while black had a positive correlation. Among textiles, leather and fake leather had a positive correlation.

Table 29.1 Top features with association to strength

Feature	Correlation (Log-odds-ratio)	Significance (p-value)
Weapon exists	4.805	<2.22e-16
Boots	1.899	4.72e-08
Dress	−1.812	1.59e-07
Protective hand apparel	2.343	2.01e-07
Magical weapon	3.403	1.86e-06
Bright outfit colors	−2.364	6.94e-06
Tight suit	Inf	1.33e-05
Leather	2.622	7.03e-05
Black outfit color	1.516	0.000132
Fake leather	3.014	0.000346
Cold weaponry (blade)	Inf	0.000579
White outfit color	−1.323	0.00073
Hot weaponry (gun)	Inf	0.00335
Arm accessory	1.996	0.00472
Flat shoes	−1.565	0.0101
Puffy sleeves	−2.571	0.0226
White skin color	−2.562	0.0311

All displayed features surpassed the 5% significance threshold. Features are sorted in a decreasing significance scale – the first feature ("Weapon exists") is the most significant.

Weapons were expected to have high correlation ratings with projecting strength because the role of the action heroine often involves the use of these traditional signs of masculinity. Holding a weapon and being physically strong are seen as heroic traits. Brown notes that the association between weapons and muscles suggests a lack of "soft" or feminine features and that there are fetishistic sexual implications of women holding weapons as phallic symbols (Brown 2011; Lentz 1993). The study also expected protective hand apparel and arm accessories to signify strength because items related to protection and offense are associated with strong characters.

Two visual features that were found to have a high correlation with strength were leather and fake leather textiles. These textiles are associated with sadomasochism, specifically the "dominating woman," and have been used in superheroine genres in the 2000s, such as Catwoman and Elektra (Brown 2011; Bowman 2005; Pitof 2004). In the present day, the association with sadomasochism is less emphasized. Leather and fake leather clothing are associated with a "tough" and "active" woman in contrast to the airy and silky clothes of "damsels in distress" (Brown 2011).

The color black also shows a strong association with strength. Indeed, black may generally remind us of death and an evil presence. Specifically, usurper characters are of a generally dark nature (Vaz da Silva 2008). According to Luthi, darker colors are associated with death, shock, and the seizing of power (Luthi 1982). It should be noted that movies sometimes deliberately choose a dark palette for a realistic look. Furthermore, bold colors for superheroes were at times considered "tacky."

Dresses, bright colors, and puffy sleeves were all found to have a negative correlation, meaning that they are associated with weakness. These features are not suitable for quick movement or protection. The bright colors represent purity and innocence in stories where the weak women's existence was not meant to provide a solution to the story or the hero, beyond them advancing the hero. Additionally, it seems that white skin is associated with weakness. White skin symbolizes purity and virginity in fantasy films (Vaz da Silva 2008). Alternatively, it can be stated that any skin color that is not white (aliens can be green or blue) has a strong positive correlation with strength, although it is unclear what the theoretical justification for that is.

Interestingly, neither the use of pants nor their length was identified as having an association with strength, which contradicts conventional wisdom (Owyong 2009). It is possible that pants do not differentiate between masculine or feminine features, or between strength or weakness, but rather between the day-to-day and the heroic. However, tight full-body suits, which include a form of pants, did show a significant association with strength. Full-body suits can be considered tights commonly worn by heroes from comic books and are believed to have originated in the representation of male strength. The origins of the tights lie in the representation of male strength, and the modern designs of superheroes show a trend of increasingly muscular and buff bodies (Brown 1996). The change in the semiotics of superheroes is believed to have influenced the semiotics of their outfits, resulting in a constant search for new materials that accentuate muscular bodies (Owyong 2009). The phenomenon of showcasing more muscular characters is believed to be a result of the increasing obsession of modern society with maintaining and nurturing the appearance of the human body. This trend also affected superheroines in films (Brown 1996).

In footwear, flat shoes were found to have a correlation to weak characters. It makes sense, as they are rather neutral or even banal. Surprisingly, high heels (commonly associated with sexist and fetishist stereotypes and also restricting one's movement) were not found to have any association with strength or lack of. Additionally, boots (which often had heels incorporated with them) were found to have the second highest correlation to strong characters.

Beyond being identified as having military, and maybe fetishist, connotations, there are no cultural associations with boots. On a visual level, boots give a dominant design to the lower part of the body, as they can sprawl across a more substantial part of the leg. As such, they have the option to stand out more in their design than any other type of shoe.

Analysis of Association between Garment and Narrative Features

In this section, an analysis of the outfits given their narrative role is conducted. In order to examine the features that were specifically associated with a role, a chi-squared test was performed on the distribution chart of features over the roles (Pearson 1894). The test was done on all visual features. Significance was corrected for multiple testing using Holm-Bonferroni (Holm 1979). The foremost features (with a significance of at least 5%) associated with the narrative role of the character wearing the outfit were dresses, boots, silk textiles, having a weapon, and physical martial arts as a weapon.

Dresses and silks are more common amongst love interests and villains. It is possible that the reason for this is that silk is the fabric of nobles, mostly seen in fantasy, and that it accentuates the character's narrative, be it as a princess, queen, witch, fairy, etc. The silk dress of a villain in fantasy films is mostly presented with dark colors, with the addition of strength-associated elements, such as magical powers and leather-like accessories. The fantasy genre has traditionally accepted gender conventions, and as such, dresses are a part of this world (Nikolajeva 2008).

Boots are common amongst support characters and less so amongst love interests. Such heavy footwear is functional to characters that need to fight, an action that love interests do not usually do (Owyong 2009). Weapons are generally less common amongst love interests. They are not written with the need to fight; rather, people fight for them. Finally, designing characters around martial arts is more common amongst villains and heroines. As close combat scenes invite camera attention and screen time, it makes sense that the protagonists and antagonists have this association.

Additional Comments Regarding Lack of Significance

While color brightness was found to be associated with strength, no correlation was found between the hue of color to the narrative role or the strength of the character. Following this, color group features based on comic book literature (Leong 2006 [1983]) were tested, including the existence of primary colors (red, blue, and yellow/gold) in the outfit, and the same for complementing colors (purple, green, and orange). For these as well, no significant correlation was found.

The feature of hair showed no significance either. It is possible that hair is something that is more related to the narrative. For example, if the character undergoes an ordeal or a journey, a hair change could be used as an expression of that transition. Today, hairstyle variety is crossing genders. Characters are presented with varying hairstyles and colors. It seems that hair style is more related to artistic expression than to any association with strength or weakness.

Expressions of Strength and Weakness through Clothing in the Movie

Avengers: Endgame

We now turn to analyze some of the characters from the action scene starting at 02:26:47 to 02:27:22, lasting about 1:20 minutes. The outfits which we will analyze here were not included in the quantitative analysis. Therefore, we can use the insights we have gained so far to categorize them while avoiding circular reasoning. All of the following characters in this scene are strong, super-heroic females, as is evident by their active participation in combat. They are smart, self-assured, active characters. For a full analysis of all the characters in the scene, please see my thesis publication (Novich 2021b).

Captain Marvel

The character wears a tight full-body suit that accentuates the breast area, the hips, the arms, and the quadriceps. There are body parts that are accentuated while the body itself is wrapped entirely in tightly stretched fake leather, so that the curves remain visible without actually revealing skin. This feature matches Owyong's research, in which she emphasizes how much the full body outfit defines superheroes. She claims that the reason for comic book heroes wearing tights is to emphasize their physical powers (muscles) without exposing human skin (Owyong 2009). On Captain Marvel's hands can be seen gloves and protective hand gear, a feature that appears in the research as something relating to strength. Another noticeable feature is her boots, which appear to be a part of the whole outfit. Captain Marvel's colors are primary, which relates to heroes in comic books, but the lightness (except for the hold) is darker than that in the original comic book, and there are even parts of the outfit that are black, such as underneath the armpit, the neck, and under the shoulder (Leong 2006 [1983]).

Shuri

Shuri's outfit is based on African clothing, with many geometrical shapes. There are intense bold colors over a tight leather black base. She uses a laser gun, which covers her hands and doubles as gloves, both features associated with strength. Her outfit is also full body, with light-colored cloth around the waist, which brightens it, although she does not have sleeves. Shuri is a scientist princess of African descent, and it is interesting to compare this current outfit to scenes in which her princess status is heavily emphasized (Coogler 2018). In those scenes, the white dress, with textile that looks as smooth as silk, with no shapes or other features, presents her as innocent and pure. These are all features associated with weak characters in the research. It stands in stark contrast to her combat outfit, which is dark and possessing of hard shapes and a colorful presence.

Scarlet Witch

While her outfit changed between each one, in previous MCU movies, the colors that define the Scarlet Witch are always dark red and black (Russo and Russo 2014, 2016, 2018; Whedon 2015). The dark colors define her not only as a strong character but also as a witch. By the color coding in fantasy, red and black represent darkness, death, and blood (Vaz da Silva 2008). Her coat and pants are made of leather, and she wears gloves on her hands, which are a classic article of clothing signaling strength. Scarlet wears high black leather boots with a heel, which, while boots represent strength through ease of movement, should be limiting due to said heel. Her clothes radiate sexuality due to the shape of her corset, with cleavage. The fact that she functioned as a love interest in previous movies could explain this. Her fighting style consists of supernatural powers that work from afar. This fighting style fits supporting characters and less heroic characters, and she is indeed in a supporting character role. In 2021, the television show named *WandaVision*, starring her as the main character, was aired. In that show, her final outfit, where she has awoken to her new powers, matches the analysis in all regards: texture, color brightness, accessories, footwear, and so on (Shakman 2021).

Mantis

Mantis is an interesting character, as her powers are used to control and interpret the feelings of others. They can cause mental harm but otherwise do not cause physical damage. The character, in regards to how she is written, is neither strong nor weak. Despite that, based on the research, her outfit is very much characterized by elements of strength: The outfit contains dark and black colors, the textiles being made of fake leather, and she wears long gloves that cover her arms all the way above the elbow. Mantis fights through a martial art that involves touching the head of her enemies in order to control their feelings. This kind of outfit and fighting style describes both villain and hero characters, which actually fits Mantis, as in her previous movie, *Guardians of the Galaxy Vol. 2*, she was on the side of the bad guys then switched loyalties partway through (Gunn 2017). Despite not being written in the normal ways that a strong character would be, the visual features strengthen her character. It can be claimed that, often, a character with no clear narrative features of strength could pass as strong or be labeled as strong through proper outfit design. In this way, despite Mantis being physically/intellectually/magically weaker than the other heroines, she can join them and fit among them as equals.

We will conclude with several general notes. First, note that the modern heroines shown in the scene are not required to present physical muscles and to be "manly women," like the heroines of the 1980s and 1990s, such as Sarah Connor and Ellen Ripley (Cameron 1991; Scott 1979). Rather, the clothes do the work by highlighting the muscles with lines and in being tight. The characters use all the features that were found to have a positive correlation with strength among women: dark colors, protective hand gear, the existence of arm accessories, leather and fake leather textiles, body suits, and boots. In that regard, it seems as though their designs are a lot of variations on the same outfit, and the variety of clothing features associated with strength is generally narrow. For example, no character was wearing a dress or had puffy sleeves; yet, these are fantastic stories involving magic and futuristic tech, and there is no theoretical reason why they would refrain from such an outfit design. At first glance, it appears as though the outfits are different and varied, as each character is from a different world and genre: fantasy, science fiction, and comic books. However, in the end, they all use the same features associated with strength.

Discussion

This study shows that it is possible to quantitatively identify associations of strength in women through clothing and accessories in Fantastic Cinema. The results are that the choice of dark colors, leather and fake leather fabric, protective hand appeal or accessory, boots, weapons, and tight clothing are design patterns associated with strong female characters. On the other hand, bright colors, puffy sleeves, dresses, and flat shoes are patterns associated with designing weak female characters. We could not establish an association between hues (red/blue/green/etc.) to narrative roles or strengths. However, the brightness of the color was deemed a significant factor. Moreover, some typically stereotyped articles of clothing, such as pants and high heels, were not found as significant as other clothing, such as a tight bodysuit.

A qualitative evaluation of heroic characters in the superhero movie *Avengers Endgame* shows that the statistically significant features associated with strength were present among the characters in the movie, while those associated with weakness were not found in their design.

In 2010, Stuller wrote that the lines of sexual gender will begin to fade only when the myths of "superhero" and "superheroines" integrate the characteristics of both genders together. According to her, until the experiences of women will be integrated into the superhero myth, it will always be lacking and inaccurate (Stuller 2010). More than a decade has passed since then, and the experience of women as superheroes (as perceived, among other things, and perhaps mainly, through their visual design in pop culture fantastic films) has developed and exhibits novel changes. It will be interesting to see if it continues and where it leads us.

Acknowledgments

My research has been supported by Shenkar Engineering, Design, and Art College. I want to give thanks to Dr. Utin Pablo, my mentor and guide through the whole process of my thesis and research.

References

Ashliman, Dee L. 2008. "Princess." In *The Greenwood Encyclopedia of Folktales and Fairy Tales Vol.2*, edited by Donald Haase. Greenwood Press.

Attebery, Brian. 2002. *Decoding Gender in Science Fiction*. Routledge.

Balic, Iva. 2009. "Utopia." In *Women in Science Fiction and Fantasy*. 2nd edition, edited by Robin Anne Reid. Greenwood Press.

Barthes, Roland. 1983. *The Fashion System*. Hill and Wang.

Berger, John. 1977. *Ways of Seeing*. Penguin.

Bousfield, John. 1979. "World Seen as a Colour Chart." In *Classifications in Their Social Context*, edited by Roy F. Ellen and David Reason. Academic Press.

Bowman, Rob, dir. 2005. *Elektra*. 20th Century Fox.

Brown, Jeffrey A. 1996. "Gender and the Action Heroine: Hardbodies and the 'Point of No Return.'" *Cinema Journal* 35 (3): 52–71. https://doi.org/10.2307/1225765.

Brown, Jeffrey A. 1999. "Comic Book Masculinity and the New Black Superhero." *African American Review* 33 (1): 25–42. https://doi.org/10.2307/2901299.

Brown, Jeffrey A. 2011. *Dangerous Curves: Action Heroines, Gender, Fetishism and Popular Culture*. The University Press of Mississippi.

Cameron, James, dir. 1991. *Terminator 2: Judgment Day*. Tri-Star Pictures.

Coogan, Peter. 2013. "The Hero Defines the Genre, the Genre Defines the Hero." In *What Is a Superhero?*, edited by Peter Coogan and Robin S. Rosenberg. Oxford University Press.

Coogler, Ryan, dir. 2018. *Black Panther*. Walt Disney Studios Motion Pictures.

Coote, Jeremy. 1992. "Aesthetics and the Cattle-Keeping Nilotes." In *Marvels of Everyday Vision*, edited by Jeremy Coote and Anthony Shelton. Clarendon Press.

Cornea, Christine. 2007. *Science Fiction Cinema: Between Fantasy and Reality*. Edinburgh University Press.

Darowski, Joseph J. 2014. *X-Men and the Mutant Metaphor: Race and Gender in the Comic Books*. Rowman & Littlefield.

Fisher, Ronald A. 1922. "On the Interpretation of χ^2 from Contingency Tables, and the Calculation of P." *Journal of the Royal Statistical Society* 85 (1): 87–94.

Fowkes, Katherine A. 2010. *The Fantasy Film*. Wiley-Blackwell.

Fry, Michele. 2009. "Quest Fantasy." In *Women in Science Fiction and Fantasy*. 2nd edition, edited by Robin Anne Reid. Greenwood Press.

Gombrich, Ernst H. 1960. *Art and Illusion: A Study in the Psychology of Pictorial Representation*. Phaidon Press.

Gunn, James, dir. 2017. *Guardians of the Galaxy Vol. 2*. Walt Disney Studios Motion Pictures.

Haase, Donald. 2008. "Fairy Tale." In *The Greenwood Encyclopedia of Folktales and Fairy Tales Vol.1*, edited by Donald Haase. Greenwood Press.

Halliday, Michael A.K. 1994. *An Introduction to Functional Grammar*. Edward Arnold.

Holm, Sture. 1979. "A Simple Sequentially Rejective Multiple Test Procedure." *Scandinavian Journal of Statistics* 6 (2):65–70.

Ina, Batzke, Eric C. Erbaclher, Lindca M. Heß, and Corinna Lenhardt. 2018. *Exploring the Fantastic: Genre, Ideology, and Popular Culture*, edited by Batzke Ina, Eric C. Erbaclher, Lindca M. Heß, and Corinna Lenhardt. transcript Verlag.

Jarvis, Shawn C. 2008. "Sorcerer, Soreceress." In *The Greenwood Encyclopedia of Folktales and Fairy Tales Vol.3*, edited by Donald Haase. Greenwood Press.

Jeffords, Susan. 1993. "Can Masculinity Be Terminated?" In *Screening the Male: Exploring Masculinities in Hollywood Cinema*, edited by Steven Cohan and Inna Rea Hark. Routledge.

Kennedy, Marcy. 2013. *Strong Female Characters (Busy Writer's Guides Book 1)*. Tongue Untied Communications. Kindle.

Lee, Linda J. 2008. "Witch." In *The Greenwood Encyclopedia of Folktales and Fairy Tales Vol.3*, edited by Donald Haase. Greenwood Press.

Lentz, Kirsten Marthe. 1993. "The Popular Pleasures of Female Revenge (or Rage Burst- Ing in a Blaze of Gunfire)." *Cultural Studies* 7 (3): 374.

Leong, Tim. 2006 [1983]. "Super Graphics." *IEEE Computer Graphics and Applications* 3 (2): 10–10. https://doi.org/10.1109/mcg.1983.262981.

Luthi, Max. 1982. *The European Folktale: Form and Nature*, edited by John D. Niles. Institute for the Study of Human Issues.

Mirzoeff, Nicholas. 2002. "The Subject of Visual Culture." In *The Visual Culture Reader*. 2nd edition, edited by Nicholas Mirzoeff. Routledge.

Nevins, Jess. 2017. *The Evolution of the Costumed Avenger: The 4,000-Year History of the Superhero*. Praeger.

Nikolajeva, Maria. 2008. "Fantasy." In *The Greenwood Encyclopedia of Folktales and Fairy Tales Vol.1*, edited by Donald Haase. Greenwood Press.

Novich, Yael Rachel. 2021a. "List of Heroines and Damsels in Distress – Accessories and Clothing: Fantastic Women in Cinema." Google Sheets, https://cutt.ly/KhfXXpD.

Novich, Yael Rachel. 2021b. "With Great Power, Comes an Armored Corset: Clothing as Empowerment in Female Characters in Fantasy Films, Science Fiction and Superheroes." Thesis, Shenkar College of Engineering, Design, and Art.

O'Toole, Michael. 1994. *The Language of Displayed Art*. Leicester University Press.

Owyong, Yuet See Monica. 2009. "Clothing Semiotics and the Social Construction of Power Relations." *Social Semiotics* 19 (2): 191–211. https://doi.org/10.1080/10350330902816434.

Palmer, Frank R. 1993. *Semantics*. Cambridge University Press.

Pearson, Karl. 1894. "Contributions to the Mathematical Theory of Evolution." *Philosophical Transactions of the Royal Society of London*, 285: 71–110.

Pitof, dir. 2004. *Catwoman*. Village Roadshow Pictures.

Russo, Anthony, and Joe Russo, dirs. 2014. *Captain America: The Winter Soldier*. Walt Disney Studios Motion Pictures.

Russo, Anthony, and Joe Russo, dirs. 2016. *Captain America: Civil War*. Walt Disney Studios Motion Pictures.

Russo, Anthony, and Joe Russo, dirs. 2018. *Avengers: Infinity War*. Walt Disney Studios Motion Pictures.

Russo, Anthony, and Joe Russo, dirs. 2019. *Avengers: Endgame*. Walt Disney Studios Motion Pictures.

Schiappa, Edward. 2008. *Beyond Representational Correctness: Rethinking Criticism of Popular Media*. State University of New York Press.

Schnieder, Jane. 2006. "Cloth and Clothing." In *Handbook of Material Culture*, edited by Chris Tilley, Webb Keane, Susan Kuechler, Mike Rowlands, and Patricia Spyer. Sage Publications.

Scott, Ridley, dir. 1979. *Alien*. 20th Century Fox.

Sgriccia, Phillip, dir. 2019. *The Boys*. Season 1, episode 3, "Get Some." Amazon Prime.

Shakman, Matt, dir. 2021. *WandaVision*. Disney+.

Snyder, Lucy A. 2004. "The Portrayal of Scientists in Science Fiction." *Strange Horizons*, May 24. http://strangehorizons.com/wordpress/non-fiction/articles/the-portrayal-of-scientists-in-science-fiction/

Stankow-Mercer, Naomi. 2009. "Dystopia." In *Women in Science Fiction and Fantasy*. 2nd edition, edited by Robin Anne Reid. Greenwood Press.

Stuller, Jennifer K. 2010. *Ink-Stained Amazons and Cinematic Warriors: Superwomen in Modern Mythology*. I.B.Tauris & Co Ltd.

Tasker, Yvonne. 1993. *Spectacular Bodies: Gender, Genre and the Action Cinema*. Routledge.

Telotte, Jay P. 2001. *Science Fiction Film*. Cambridge University Press.

Thomas, Julian. 2006. "Phenomenology and Material Culture." In *Handbook of Material Culture*, edited by Chris Tilley, Webb Keane, Susan Kuechler, Mike Rowlands, and Patricia Spyer. Sage Publications.

Tiffin, Jessica. 2008. "Film and Video." In *The Greenwood Encyclopedia of Folktales and Fairy Tales Vol.1*, edited by Donald Haase. Greenwood Press.

Vaz da Silva, Francisco. 2008. "Colors." In *The Greenwood Encyclopedia of Folktales and Fairy Tales Vol.1*, edited by Donald Haase. Greenwood Press.

Whedon, Joss, dir. 2015. *Avengers: Age of Ultron*. Walt Disney Studios Motion Pictures.

Young, Diana. 2006. "The Colors of Things." In *Handbook of Material Culture*, edited by Chris Tilley, Webb Keane, Susan Kuechler, Mike Rowlands, and Patricia Spyer. SAGE Publications.

Zeisler, Andi. 2008. *Feminism and Pop Culture*. Seal Press.

30

WHAT IT MEANS TO BE FREE

Disability, Neurodivergence, and the Super "Freak"

Gwyneth Peaty

This chapter examines how contemporary superhero narratives are associating real neurolo
gical conditions, such as mental illnesses and autism, with the possession of superpowers.
It builds on the observation that, within popular discourse, disability is increasingly linked
with being supernaturally "gifted" or having superhuman potential. In 2019, climate activist
Greta Thunberg famously tweeted that her autism is a "superpower." Media by and about
people with disabilities often emphasizes a similar refrain: "my disability is my superpower"
(Douglas 2021; Lee 2021; SunGod 2022; Ranjana 2023). This chapter explores how recent
superhero narratives lean into such characterizations and the contradictions that can emerge
as a result. While the formative role of Marvel and DC superheroes is acknowledged, the
analysis is also concerned with media produced beyond these universes, including the German film *Freaks: You're One of Us* (Binder 2020). Within this text, the very concept of the
superhero is explicitly reimagined through the lens of disability and mental illness. Protagonists wrestle with traits that mark them as categorically different from the norm, while
medicalized discourses surrounding the treatment, medication, and institutionalization of
disabled people are reimagined in the context of regulating superpowers. The classic visual
markers of a superhero – the cape, costume, and impressive physique – are missing in action
as these characters shuffle through their lives looking relatively average. Yet the audience
is left in no doubt that they are not regular people; something powerful hums below the
surface.

The degree to which superhero narratives disrupt and/or reinforce ableist cultural stereotypes is critical to explore. Disability advocates have argued that "the way superhero movies
handle a character's disability can have a heinous impact on how people perceive real-life disabilities" (Jackson 2018). Media representation directly shapes public opinion, attitudes, and
beliefs about disability (Ellis 2016). Indeed, to be disabled is to exist within a nexus of cultural assumptions: "the reality of people with disability is overlaid with the suppositions and
implicit social attitudes of a nondisabled world, making their 'reality' as much a product of
excessive interpretation as of mundane fact" (Quayson 2007, 14). Socio-political discourses
and policy decisions about disability are informed by the stories circulating within mainstream popular culture, and what may seem "empowering" on first glance can in fact work
against inclusivity and acceptance. As Luterman (2019) notes, "it's important to remember

DOI: 10.4324/9781003366911-35

that superhuman and subhuman are both something other than human." Embracing an allegorical relationship between superheroes and disabled or neurodivergent people involves accepting their shared status as something beyond the boundaries of normal. The evolving complexities of this maneuver are important to track within popular storytelling, as they not only reflect but work to produce how people with disabilities are viewed by society.

Popular narratives can also impact how people with disabilities view themselves. Richard Chapman argues that contemporary storytelling tends to divide disabled people into two categories: the tragic character to be pitied or the "superhuman" who overcomes their disability (2019, 204). Neither are useful points of reference for people with disabilities, because "victim and superhuman characters are both insufficient models upon which to develop understandings of self or others" (204). Being an object of pity, and seeing yourself represented as such, is hardly conducive to a joyful and empowered self-image. Conversely, the goal to go above and beyond one's disability, to "overcome" what may be a permanent state of being, is impossible for many. In fact, such pressure "invalidates the lived experience of the majority of disabled people because they cannot meet such expectations" (Overboe 1999, 19). This figure is often described as the "supercrip" stereotype in disability scholarship (Grue 2015).

A different dynamic emerges when disability itself is seen as a source of power, rather than a flaw or weakness to be overcome. A shift away from deficit-based models of disability has increased the popularity of this perspective. As Robert Rozema points out, "When Thunberg uses *superpower* to describe her autism, she is voicing a key tenet of the neurodiversity movement—namely, that neurological differences should be viewed as assets, not liabilities" (original emphasis; 2020, 10). Increasingly, forms of neurodivergence (autism in particular) are being reframed as strengths that can offer a "competitive advantage" in life (Austin and Pisano 2017). In addition to revisiting the relationship between superheroes and disability, the following chapter begins to explore how this perspective is filtering into contemporary superhero narratives.

This analysis uses person-first language (people with disability) and identity-first language (disabled people) interchangeably at times, as both are acceptable within Australia and Australian disability scholarship (People with Disability Australia n.d.). Different individuals have their own preferences and may prefer one over the other (Best et al. 2022). Importantly, "both proponents of person-first and identity-first language are aligned in their quest to maximise respect and inclusivity of people with disabilities and health conditions" (Grech et al. 2023). As a neurodivergent Australian scholar, the author of this article is comfortable with both forms of description.

Disability and Superheroes

A significant overlap exists between representations of superheroes and representations of disability within popular media and culture. Basic everyday tasks are frequently depicted as heroic or even superhuman when undertaken by people who experience physical or cognitive impairment (Silva and Howe 2012). While this might appear flattering on the surface, the representation of people with disabilities as innately heroic and inspirational has been heavily critiqued by disability studies scholars (Young 2014). Describing people with disabilities as brave for simply living their lives is often seen as patronizing and damaging (Manley 2024). In fact, it can betray how low societies' expectations are when it comes to disability. As writer and advocate Greg Burkholder (2022) points out, "the dangerous subtext that lurks under cries of 'bravery!' and 'heroism!' is that they can't believe I am still alive." In turn, the representation of superheroes has been shaped by their connection with disability and narratives of difference (Alaniz 2014; Grue 2021). The divergence of superhuman characters from "normal" humanity and the alienation this generates has made the contemporary superhero a powerful device through which to explore segregation, marginalization, and prejudice in the real world (Miller 2003; Darowski 2014). But this was not always the case, especially in the 20th century.

In their introduction to *Uncanny Bodies: Superhero Comics and Disability*, Scott T. Smith and José Alaniz explain that the superhero genre has exploited representations of disability since the very beginning. The first comics supervillain, appearing in 1939, was a wheelchair user; a "paralyzed cripple" whose eyes "burn with terrible hatred and sinister intelligence" (original caption; cited in Smith and Alaniz 2019, 3). As such, they argue, "disability as a facet of human corporeal/cognitive existence entered the genre as a blatant and simplistic marker of evil" (2). In fact, early superhero narratives perpetuated a long-standing mode of representation described by Ato Quayson as "disability as moral deficit/evil" (2007, 42). Linking one's moral status with physical appearance, this damaging ideology frames immorality and evil as synonymous with disfigurement and impairment. It exemplifies a physiognomic approach to framing disability that has deep historical roots, observed in the works of Aristotle and even earlier (Mitchell and Snyder 2001, 57–60). During the "Golden Age" of comics, this simplistic model served a key purpose. Along with the bright colors, exciting storylines, and impossible feats of strength, disabled villainy was an important, if not pivotal, element in the formula that made superhero comics successful.

Superheroes, by their very nature, have capabilities beyond the limits of regular, able-bodied human beings. They offer a hyper realized vision of cultural ideals that are much longed for, but impossible to achieve in reality (Eco 1972). In *Superman on the Couch: What Superheroes Really Tell Us about Ourselves and Our Society*, Danny Fingeroth argues that villains help define the hero by providing a crucial counterpoint (2004, 15). Antagonists bring a story to life by providing the challenge that protagonists must overcome. As writer and director Kevin Smith summarizes: "you can't have good guys without the bad guys" (2014, 4). The use of disability to embody moral deficit/evil when representing supervillains has helped to define an equally simplistic vision of super able-bodied heroism. The moral superiority of superheroes is linked to their idealized anatomies, while deformed supervillains are presented "as a contrast to nonpareil superheroic physiques" (Smith and Alaniz 2019, 3). The contours of these characters are determined by culture and thus have evolved over time. In the early days of the superhero, "readers took it as basic 'common sense' that good guys were handsome and bad guys ugly, disabled, maimed, insane, or otherwise defective" (Smith and Alaniz 2019, 4). As society has changed, representations of disability have become much more nuanced within superhero comics and the superhero genre at large. So too have representations of heroism, as superheroes themselves are repeatedly reimagined by different creators in different contexts (Piatti-Farnell 2021).

The rise of disabled heroes has played an important part in the evolution of superheroes, although it has not come without complexity. For example, Marvel's Daredevil character is blind and, in many ways, "proved a landmark for the depiction of disability in a notoriously ableist genre" (Alaniz 2014, 69). At the same time, Matt Murdoch (Daredevil's "normal" alter ego) played into stereotypes and clichés about vision impairment and disability in order to conceal his superhero identity. What resulted was a character that "both affirmed and undermined a positive vision of disability" (Alaniz 2014, 71). Jessica Benham observes a similar duality in Marvel's depictions of Professor X, whose partially paralyzed character arguably fits the "supercrip" image and "simultaneously challenges and reinforces existing stereotypes about disabled individuals" (2016, 171). Simply having a disability does not automatically make a superhero a progressive or positive representation beneficial to people with disabilities.

It is possible to observe less direct, more subtly coded references to disability in superhero narratives. Superheroes often have a special "weakness" that offsets their super powers, adds tension to the stories, and makes them more relatable to the audience. If a superhero is all-powerful and has no vulnerabilities, they can never lose; their adventures are low stakes. Indeed, Jan Grue argues that "Superhero stories are often also disability stories, either explicitly or implicitly" (2021, 1). Both superheroes and people with disabilities grapple with social acceptance, prejudice, and stigma. José Alaniz's *Death, Disability, and the Superhero: The Silver Age and Beyond* (2014) is an excellent text for those looking to learn more about this. Collections such as *Disability in Comic Books and Graphic Narratives* (edited by Foss et al. 2016), *Uncanny Bodies: Superhero Comics and Disability* (edited by Scott T. Smith and José Alaniz 2019), and *Disability and the Superhero: Essays on Ableism and Representation in Comic Media* (edited by Amber E. George 2023) are also important resources.

While a body of scholarly work has been undertaken exploring physical disability in the context of superhero narratives, less is available when it comes to focusing on the role of neurological conditions, such as mental illnesses and autism. This is because disability scholarship is closely related to studies of the body and cultural spectacle (Alaniz 2014, 26). In particular, the "enfreakment" of physical differences via strategies of cultural framing has been extensively studied in connection with disability representation (Hevey 1992). This process, by which disabled people have been reduced to (and produced as) visual spectacle, is an important historical precedent for today's media and culture (Garland-Thomson 1997). Studies of "invisible" disabilities do not map as readily onto this legacy and perhaps present more theoretical challenges as a result. That is not to say there has been no research on neurological diversity in superhero narratives. Specific characters, for example, DC supervillain the Joker, have been singled out as important for their depiction of psychological illness or "madness" (Preston and Rath-Paillé 2023; Wheeler 2024). Mapping the trajectory of such characters over time can provide a guide to changing attitudes towards cognitive disability. In this vein, Elizabeth Wheeler (2024) argues that "*Batman's* maniacal supervillain reflects shifting social constructions of mental difference in the US across eight decades." There is room for more research in this area, as new superhero films, comics, television series, games, and novels are released each year that incorporate mental illness and cognitive disability in one way or another. The remainder of this chapter will focus on one such example.

The Medicated Hero

On first appearance, Wendy Schulze (Cornelia Gröschel) in *Freaks: You're One of Us* is the antithesis of a stereotypical superhero. A quiet fry cook working at a fast-food restaurant, Wendy struggles to lift boxes and meekly accepts being ignored, harassed, and disrespected by others. She lives a meager life with her security guard husband Lars (Frederic Linkemann) and their young son Karl (Finnlay Berger). Wendy is also medicated for an unspecified mental health condition, shown taking pills each morning as soon as she wakes up. According to her therapist, Dr. Stern (Nina Kunzendorf), these pills are what enable Wendy to possess the most important markers of a normal life; "your family, your job, your home." The doctor praises her for these achievements, affirming that she should be "proud" of these things given her (as yet unspecified) illness. At the same time, the film emphasizes the unpleasantness of

Wendy's daily routine as she struggles to carry large bags of trash, gets dirty cleaning other people's messes, and narrowly avoids leering men. A letter reveals her family cannot afford their rent and is about to be evicted. These are not easy times, and the film is direct in its framing of Wendy as the opposite of a hero. "She's such a wimp, that woman," comments a young neighborhood bully. "Where is your assertiveness?" exclaims Wendy's boss, grabbing her arm roughly, "You've got no power!" If we revisit Chapman's assertion that contemporary storytelling divides disabled people into the tragic character to be pitied or the "superhuman" to be admired, it seems clear that Wendy falls into the former category.

This initial framing of Wendy's life is significant when contextualized in relation to disability studies frameworks. Dr. Stern can be seen to articulate a medicalized point of view, also referred to by disability scholars as the "medical model" of disability (Ellis and Goggin 2017, 21–24). The medical model frames disability as a pathological problem centered within an individual who is identified as abnormal or faulty in some way. It privileges the opinions of medical professionals over the individual, the patient, who is expected to follow the instructions of these experts in order to be treated or, ideally, cured (Clogston 1994, 47). In the context of medical discourse, the purpose of expert intervention is to bring each person closer to the realm of "normal" as it is socially and medically defined. According to Dr. Stern, Wendy is doing the correct thing by undertaking treatment, hiding her mysterious condition, and trying to live normally. Yet these opening scenes simultaneously undermine the concept of "normal" as a desirable state.

The character of Marek (Wotan Wilke Möhring) hints at an escape from the banal suffering of Wendy's medicated life. A seemingly homeless man, first shown looking for food near the bins, Marek appears to have private knowledge of Wendy's life. As she walks home from work, he approaches her. "The pills," he says, "how long have you been taking them?" She shakes her head in surprised denial (although the audience has already seen her take them). He continues:

> Those little blue ones we're supposed to take so that we are like everyone else. Without all that fear, sadness. Without the anger. Those pills suppress so much more… our true selves! […] Throw them away. Don't take those pills anymore. Then you'll see who you really are. Then it will show itself… your superpower.

Marek himself has a power, invincibility, which he cheerfully demonstrates by throwing himself off a bridge and being run over by a truck. "You're One of us," he smiles before going over, "you just don't know it yet." The next day, he is back looking for food at the bins. Intrigued, Wendy begins flushing her pills down the toilet. As the effects of her medication wear off, she quickly develops a more assertive personality, combined with powerful physical strength and agility reminiscent of the most famous superhero of all: Superman.

Pathology and Power

"Disability is multi-factorial," disability scholar Tom Shakespeare argues; "In other words, it results from the interplay of many different factors" (2018, 19). Establishing this has played an important part in advancing disability studies in the late 20th and early 21st century. One of the most pivotal theoretical shifts has involved moving away from the medical model of pathology towards more complex understandings of how experiences of physical and cognitive variation are shaped by external factors. Both the "social model" and "cultural model" are examples of this shift, each emphasizing the importance of society and environment in disabling the individual (Ellis 2016, 2–4). *Freaks: You're One of Us* invites viewers to consider the physical, economic, and social landscape in which Wendy lives. In doing so, the film can be seen to undermine Dr. Stern's medical perspective on her as a patient undergoing treatment. Wendy may appear to be living a "normal" life, but it is relentlessly challenging and unpleasant. Despite her unremarkable appearance, she is unique. Suppressing this uniqueness just makes things more difficult, and only benefits the people around her who don't want to acknowledge or accommodate it. Worse, it makes her vulnerable to predators, like the sleazy group of men who attack her walking home.

Freaks: You're One of Us consistently links disability with superpowers through the use of language, imagery, and narrative. Dialogue in the film uses terms commonly associated with disability and neurodivergence in reference to super abilities. "Suddenly I'm able to throw people through the air. That's not normal!" Wendy exclaims to Marek. "That's who you are," he replies, "It's your true self, this superpower. You're special." Wendy wonders how many "psychos" might be out in the world, unknowingly taking the blue pills to suppress their powers. "They're not psychos," Marek corrects her, "just different. Like us." Terms like "different" and "special" have been used in reference to disability for some time, although they are now often viewed as condescending euphemisms designed to avoid addressing disability directly (United Nations n.d.). The term "psycho" represents more overtly stigmatizing language, still being used "to insult people with mental health conditions, to frame them as irrational, violent, and less than human" (Feder 2021). Wendy grapples with her own internalized ableism as she struggles to accept herself. "Why am I such a freak?" she asks Dr. Stern. "You're not a freak," she replies calmly, "you're just… ill." The word "freak" is perhaps the most loaded term used within the film, and its place in the title is significant. Of all the settings in which disabled people have been exploited and displayed for profit, the historical "freak show" is the most famous (Fiedler 1993; Garland-Thomson 1997).

While Wendy's "illness" is framed as a psychosocial disability within the narrative, the film also makes overt links with autism. When overwhelmed, Wendy puts on headphones to calm herself and block out the world. She carries the headphones and an old portable Walkman everywhere she goes. The use of noise-cancelling ear covers or headphones is a well-known strategy allowing autistic people to manage sensory input and prevent overstimulation, which can cause distressing meltdowns (Foley 2024; The Autlaw 2024). In a flashback, the audience is shown that having her headphones confiscated is what triggers Wendy's first big eruption of power, as she smashes the principal's desk (and the principal) through the wall at school. The difficulties she experiences as an adult are similar to an autistic person who hides or "masks" their autism in order to appear neurotypical. This masking process is largely undertaken for the benefit of others and causes significant stress and exhaustion for the person with autism (Evans et al. 2024). Running parallel to the classical superhero, who hides their true identity beneath a mask and costume, the autistic likewise hides their authentic traits beneath a performative mask in order to pass as "normal."

In this film, social control is disguised as treatment by medical professionals who pathologize and fear neurological divergence. As Merek explains,

> These people out there keep telling us we're sick. They claim they want to help us, but the truth is, they sedate us and make us compliant […] They're hiding us from the rest of the world because they're scared of us.

It is not being neurodivergent that is disabling Wendy here (quite the opposite), but the world and its treatment of her. By fusing the concept of cognitive disability with the possession of superpowers, the film draws attention to how institutionalized medical power presses down upon the individual. To access her true potential, Wendy must work to free herself from oppressive medical and social power structures. Read as an allegory for the experience and treatment of mental health disorders or autism, it critiques the idea that normalcy must be achieved by suppressing neurodiversity. "Show them what it means to be free," says a dying Merek after they break out from Dr. Stern's clinic/prison. The film ends with Wendy dedicating herself to locating others like herself and helping them become their true selves, free of repressive medical control. Her quest for individual freedom has become a social movement.

Born Different: The Super "Freak"

Superheroes with powers that stem from innate genetic mutations, rather than outside forces, have become increasingly popular since the emergence of the *X-Men* comics in the early 1960s. Such characters are not bitten by radioactive spiders or sent from an alien planet, but born different. As a result of their genetic divergence, these heroes are often rejected, feared, and segregated from regular people. The "mutant metaphor" has since become an apt vehicle for exploring struggles experienced by oppressed minorities and outsiders within human societies of the late 20th and early 21st centuries (Darowski 2014; Grimsted et al. 2024). While much has been written about the mutant metaphor in relation to race, gender, and sexuality, neurominorities offer another important, if under-explored, reference point. Historically, neurodivergent people have experienced significant social exclusion, abuse, and marginalization as a result of their variance from the norm. Prejudice and discrimination continue to be an ongoing concern for this community. In his conclusion to *Death, Disability and the Superhero*, Alaniz points out that cognitive difference is often linked to stories about perpetrators of real violence in the media. All too often, schizophrenia, autism, and other forms of neurodiversity are cited "as a catalyst for their demonization, the pointed-to 'reason' for evil, violent acts" (2014, 293). Autism in particular has been associated with "mystification, metaphor, and moral panic" due to the wide variety of symptoms and traits associated with it (294). It is, therefore, especially important that representations of people with cognitive disabilities do not play into ableist stereotypes or villainous fear-mongering, as it may increase their vulnerability to social exclusion or even physical harm from a fearful society.

As mentioned in the introduction, the neurodiversity movement is working to change public dialogue by reframing neurological divergence as an asset, rather than something dangerous to be feared or avoided. When Greta Thunberg described her autism as a "superpower" she was tapping into this precise shift in rhetoric. It can be argued that *Freaks: You're One of Us* also draws on the movement towards inclusion and acceptance. Links with autism are implicit in the character of Wendy, the quiet woman masking a secret identity, who is prone to social frustration, sensory sensitivity, and emotional overload. Her condition is not named as such, but as Robert Rozema (2020) points out in "Waiting for Autistic Superman: On Autistic Representation in Superhero Comics," characters do not need to be explicitly labeled in order to be recognized as autistic-coded.

At the same time, *Freaks: You're One of Us* also taps into cultural legacies that are less than empowering in the context of disability. The film's title contains a dual reference to another well-known disability-themed film: Tom Browning's *Freaks* (1932). In this narrative, beautiful able-bodied trapeze artist Cleopatra (Olga Baclanova) joins a travelling circus group full of disabled sideshow entertainers. Although readings of its message vary, *Freaks* is renowned for its unexpectedly in-depth focus on diverse characters played by real people with disabilities. Merek's statement, "You're one of us," is relevant because it echoes a famous chant taken up by the circus performers in *Freaks* as they welcome Cleopatra into their group; "We accept her, one of us. We accept her, one of us. Gooble-gobble, gooble-gobble." While there is not room here to expand further on the relationship between these two films, it is worth noting that Cleopatra is transformed into a sideshow "freak" herself by the end of the film, having deceived and betrayed her new disability community. In the case of *Freaks: You're One of Us*, the film's denouement is full of mixed messages and contradictory impulses. No opportunity is offered for Wendy to resolve her situation and return home to her family. Instead, to avoid being caught by Dr. Stern, Wendy must go on the run. Rather than experience inclusion within regular society, she becomes part of a new outcast community consisting of fellow super "freaks." Although her difference is cognitive rather than physical, like Cleopatra, she cannot return to the "normal" world. The "freaks" are the only community that will accept her.

Conclusion

When considering the future of disability representation within the superhero genre, we might advocate for greater involvement from disabled writers. Shoshana Magnet and Amanda Watson argue that graphic texts created by people with disabilities have the potential to offer "a helpful corrective to mainstream and commercial representations" (2017, 251). Prioritizing the voices of disabled people themselves in the creation of popular culture at least allows space for the expansion of disability representation beyond reductive stereotypes like the "supercrip." This expansion does not mean the superhero as we know it will perish. As Beth Haller (2023) points out in "Disability as Superpower: Comics, Graphic Novels, and Music," the figure of the superhero is often used by people with disabilities as part of their own writing to represent empowering and diverse images of self. This shift is important because the superhero genre presents plenty of opportunities to critique the treatment of minorities within society, including people with disabilities. However, in mainstream quarters, disability is still being offered as a counterpoint to what the superhero represents.

Cognitive and physical disabilities continue to be used as an easy shorthand for villainy – a point of contrast against which the "hyper-normative" superhero reflects a glowing ideal (Kane 2023). One recent example from Marvel is *Ant Man and The Wasp* (2018), which features a villain whose crimes are motivated by the experience of chronic pain. DC's *Wonder Woman* (2017) was a resounding box office success and critical hit; however, the main villain, Isabel Maru or "Dr. Poison," has a facial disfigurement that contrasts dramatically with Diana's symmetrical super-beauty. Whether texts such as *Freaks: You're One of Us* reflect a growing willingness to engage with cognitive disabilities, autism, and mental illness via the figure of the superhero remains to be seen.

References

Alaniz, José. 2014. *Death, Disability, and the Superhero: The Silver Age and Beyond*. University Press of Mississippi.

Austin, Robert D., and Gary Pisano. 2017. "Neurodiversity as a Competitive Advantage." *Harvard Business Review*, May-June 2017, 95(3), 96–103.

Autlaw, The. 2024. "Why You Should Never Take Headphones from an Autistic." *Medium*, June 24. https://medium.com/@theautlaw/why-you-should-never-take-headphones-from-an-autistic-d703e2e184cf.

Benham, Jessica. 2016. "Reframing Disabled Masculinity: Xavier as Marvel's Supercrip." In *The X-Men Films: A Cultural Analysis*, edited by Bucciferro C. Rowman & Littlefield.

Best, Krista L., W. Ben Mortenson., Zach Lauzière-Fitzgerald, and Emma M. Smith. 2022. "Language Matters! The Long-Standing Debate Between Identity-First Language and Person First Language." *Assistive Technology*, 34(2), 127–128.

Binder, Felix, dir. 2020. *Freaks: You're One of Us (Freaks – Du bist eine von uns)*. Netflix.

Browning, Todd, dir. 1932. *Freaks*. Metro-Goldwyn-Mayer.

Burkholder, Greg. 2022. "I'm Not 'Brave' for having a Disability." *The Mighty*, July 26. https://themighty.com/topic/treacher-collins-syndrome-tcs/im-not-brave-for-having-a-disability/.

Chapman, Richard A. 2019. "Neither Victim nor Superhero: Reflections on Disability and Mental Health Counseling." In *New Narratives of Disability: Constructions, Clashes, and Controversies*, edited by Sara E. Green and Donileen R. Loseke. Emerald Publishing.

Clogston, John S. 1994. "Disability Coverage in American Newspapers." In *The Disabled, the Media, and the Information Age*, edited by Jack A. Nelson. Greenwood Press.

Darowski, Joseph J. 2014. *X-Men and the Mutant Metaphor: Race and Gender in the Comic Books*. Rowman & Littlefield.

Douglas, Emily. 2021. "Wall Street VP: 'My Disability Is My Superpower.'" *HRD Australia*, April 16. https://www.hcamag.com/au/specialisation/diversity-inclusion/wall-street-vp-my-disability-is-my-superpower/252519.

Eco, Umberto. 1972. "The Myth of Superman." Translated by Natalie Chilton. *Diacritics*, 2(1), 14–22. https://doi.org/10.2307/464920.

Ellis, Katie. 2016. *Disability and Popular Culture: Focusing Passion, Creating Community and Expressing Defiance*. Routledge.

Ellis, Katie, and Goggin, Gerard. 2017. *Disability and the Media*. Bloomsbury.

Evans, Joshua A., Elizabeth J. Krumrei-Mancuso, and Steven V. Rouse. 2024. "What You Are Hiding Could Be Hurting You: Autistic Masking in Relation to Mental Health, Interpersonal Trauma, Authenticity, and Self-Esteem." *Autism in Adulthood*, 6(2), 229–240. https://www.liebertpub.com/doi/10.1089/aut.2022.0115.

Feder, Jill. 2021. "Disability Language: Stop Using These Words Now." *Accessibility.com*, September 8. https://www.accessibility.com/blog/disability-language-stop-using-these-words-now.

Fiedler, Leslie A. 1993. *Freaks: Myths and Images of the Secret Self*. Anchor Books.

Fingeroth, Danny. 2014. *Superman on the Couch: What Superheroes Really tell us About Ourselves and our Society*. Bloomsbury.

Foley, Kitty-Rose. 2024. "Noise-cancelling headphones, earplugs and earmuffs – do they really help neurodivergent people?" *The Conversation*, May 27. https://theconversation.com/noise-cancelling-headphones-earplugs-and-earmuffs-do-they-really-help-neurodivergent-people-230113.

Foss, Chris, Jonathan W. Gray, and Zach Whalen, eds. 2016. *Disability in Comic Books and Graphic Narratives*. Springer.

Garland-Thomson, Rosemarie. 1997. *Extraordinary Bodies: Figuring Physical Disability in American Culture and Literature*. Columbia University Press.

George, Amber E. 2023. *Disability and the Superhero: Essays on Ableism and Representation in Comic Media*. McFarland & Company.

Grech, Lisa B., Donna Koller, and Amanda Olley. 2023. "Furthering the Person-First Versus Identity-First Language Debate." *Australian Psychologist*, 58(4), 223–232.

Grimsted, Sonora. R., Katerina G. Krizner., Cynthia D. Porter, and Jay Clayton. 2024. "Genetics in the X-Men Film Franchise: Mutants as Allegories of Difference." *Frontiers in Genetics*, 14, 1331905.

Grue, Jan. 2015. "The Problem of the Supercrip: Representation and Misrepresentation of Disability." In *Disability Research Today: International Perspectives*, edited by Tom Shakespeare. Routledge.

Grue, Jan. 2021. "Ablenationalists Assemble: On Disability in the Marvel Cinematic Universe." *Journal of Literary & Cultural Disability Studies*, 15(1), 1–17.

Haller, Beth A. 2023. "Disability as Superpower: Comics, Graphic Novels, and Music." In *Disabled People Transforming Media Culture for a More Inclusive World*, edited by Beth A Haller. Routledge.

Hevey, David. 1992. *The Creatures Time Forgot: Photography and Disability Imagery*. Routledge.

Jackson, Chelsea. 2018. "Superhero Movies Should Stop Using Disabilities as Problematic Plot Devices." *The Mary Sue*, August 27. https://www.themarysue.com/superhero-movies-and-disability/.

Kane, Kelly. 2023. "Hyper-Normative Heroes, Othered Villains: Differential Disability Narratives in the Marvel Cinematic Universe." In *Disability and the Superhero: Essays on Ableism and Representation in Comic Media*, edited by Amber E. George. McFarland & Company.

Lee, Deborah Jian. 2021. "My Disability Is My Superpower. If Only Employers Could See It That Way." *Elle Magazine*, June 24. https://www.elle.com/life-love/a36688889/my-disability-is-my-superpower-if-only-employers-could-see-it-that-way/.

Luterman, Sara. 2019. "Don't Call Greta Thunberg 'Superhuman.'" *Slate*, October 11. https://slate.com/human-interest/2019/10/greta-thunberg-autism-superpower-debunk.html.

Magnet, Shoshana, and Amanda Watson. 2017. "How to Get through the Day with Pain and Sadness: Temporality and Disability in Graphic Novels." In *Disability Media Studies*, edited by Elizabeth Ellcessor and Bill Kirkpatrick. New York University Press.

Manley, Michael. 2024. "I Am Mighty. I Am Mundane. I Am Not Your Hero." *The Mighty*, June 4. https://themighty.com/topic/cerebral-palsy/disability-not-your-hero/.

Miller, P. Andrew. 2003. "Mutants, Metaphor, and Marginalism: What X-actly Do the X-Men Stand For?" *Journal of the Fantastic in the Arts*, 13(3 (51)), 282–290.

Mitchell, David T., and Sharon L. Snyder. 2001. *Narrative Prosthesis: Disability and the Dependencies of Discourse*. University of Michigan Press.

Overboe, James. 1999. "'Difference in Itself': Validating Disabled People's Lived Experience." *Body & Society*, 5(4), 17–29.

People with Disability Australia. n.d. *PWDA Language Guide: A Guide to Language about Disability*. People with Disability Australia. Accessed February 25, 2025. https://pwd.org.au/resources/language-guide/.

Piatti-Farnell, Lorna. 2021. "Introduction." In *The Superhero Multiverse: Readapting Comic Book Icons in Twenty-First-Century Film and Popular Media*, edited by Lorna Piatti-Farnell. Lexington.

Preston, Jeff, and Lindsay Rath-Paillé. 2023. "How He Got His Scars: Exploring Madness and Mental Health in Filmic Representations of the Joker." *Societies*, 13(2), 48.

Quayson, Ato. 2007. *Aesthetic Nervousness: Disability and the Crisis of Representation*. Columbia University Press.

Ranjana, Vaishnavi. 2023. "Stuttering Is My Superpower." *International Stuttering Awareness Day Online Conference*. https://isad.live/isad-2023/papers-presented-by/stories-and-experiences-with-stuttering-by-pws/stuttering-is-my-superpower-vaishnavi-ranjana/.

Rozema, Robert. 2020. "Waiting for Autistic Superman: On Autistic Representation in Superhero Comics." *Ought: The Journal of Autistic Culture*, 1(2), 10–41. https://scholarworks.gvsu.edu/ought/vol1/iss2/5.

Shakespeare, Tom. 2018. *Disability: The Basics*. Routledge.

Silva, Carla Filomena, and P. David Howe. 2012. "The (In)validity of Supercrip Representation of Paralympian Athletes." *Journal of Sport and Social Issues*, 36(2), 174–194. https://doi.org/10.1177/0193723511433865.

Smith, Kevin. 2014. "Foreword." In *Super-Villains – The Complete Visual History* by Daniel Wallace edited by Chris Prince. Insight Comics.

Smith, Scott T, and José Alaniz. 2019. "Introduction." In *Uncanny Bodies: Superhero Comics and Disability*, edited by Scott T. Smith and José Alaniz. Pennsylvania State University Press.

SunGod. 2022. "'My disability is my superpower': Meet triathlete Sam Holness." *SunGod*, November 4. https://www.sungod.co/en-us/explore/athlete-stories/meet-neurodivergent-triathlete-sam-holness.

Thunberg, Greta (@GretaThunberg). "When haters go after your looks and differences, it means they have nowhere left to go. And then you know you're winning! I have Aspergers and that means I'm sometimes a bit different from the norm. And - given the right circumstances- being different is a superpower. #aspiepower." *Twitter (now X)*, September 1, 2019, 5:4⁻ AM. https://x.com/GretaThunberg/status/1167916177927991296

United Nations. n.d. "Disability Inclusive Language Guidelines." *United Nations*. Accessed February 25, 2025. https://www.ungeneva.org/en/about/accessibility/disability-inclusive-language.

Wheeler, Elizabeth A. 2024. "The Joker's Shifting Face: Eighty Years of Mad History in *Batman* and American Culture." *Journal of Literary & Cultural Disability Studies*, 18(3, 369–385.

Young, Stella. 2014. "I'm not your inspiration, thank you very much | Stella Young." *TED Talk*. Uploaded June 9, to YouTube. https://www.youtube.com/watch?v=8K9Gg164Bsw.

31
THE LEGAL ASPECTS OF THE OWNERSHIP OF A SUPERHERO IDENTITY

Liam Sunner

Introduction

The question often asked within the complex superhero narrative is "who is the person under the mask?", and given the narrative implications, it remains a valid question (if not a dated plot point). However, the question then arises of who actually owns the mask, or rather the overall super heroic identity. In a multiverse of Spider-Man and Batman expanding his reach through Batman Inc., the question of how intellectual property (IP) law applies to these vigilantes/pillars of justice must be addressed. At the same time, this mirrors real-world implications of ownership through licensed use, such as Conan and the Savage Avengers, or derivative use, such as homages, parodies, or pastiches of existing heroes. How does the real-world legal landscape provide regulation on such issues? And can this be adapted within the continuity of superheroes?

This chapter seeks to examine and outline how the legal aspects of the ownership of a superhero identity can be protected through IP law within the continuity of a publisher, and how this process can operate to maintain the secret identity of the hero. In this connection, this chapter examines the narrative implications of such an approach to IP. At the same time, this chapter will examine the issue of how the use and protection of the superhero identity can shape the internal narrative of the publishing and real-world context, as well as broader questions of likeness rights relating to the hero through licensing and other merchandizing agreements.

The scope of this chapter is limited to Western-focused publications of the superhero genre in comics. While the majority of the focus will center on "The Big Two" of Marvel and DC Comics, this is reflective of their impact on the genre and the medium as a whole. The discussion will be supported with references to wider media adaptions and to various creator-owned/independent properties where appropriate.

From a methodological approach, where appropriate, this chapter refers to Marvel and DC Comics while acknowledging their existence under a varied and often changing corporate structure. To reflect the legal developments in the real world and the application of this law to the published narrative elements, this chapter refers to this development as "within continuity."

DOI: 10.4324/9781003366911-36

What Is Intellectual Property in the Context of Superheroes?

This chapter takes a broad view of what IP encompasses, taking into account that "[n]one of the traditional or even emerging realisation for intellectual property rights fully or satisfactory account for all intellectual property regimes" (Menell 2000, 163; see also Oguamanam 2009). This is reflective of the broader international consensus and builds on the elements as defined under the Agreement on Trade-Related Aspects of Intellectual Property Rights (TRIPS Agreement). The TRIPS Agreement is the international standard of IP law that governs and standardizes IP terms for international trade. In essence, the TRIPS Agreement provides a common floor for the development and operation of IP. While certain countries develop it further and in relation to specific elements of IP, it nonetheless facilitates the international mutual development of IP.

Thus, the question, or more accurately the scope of application, is how IP rights can be attributed to the internal continuity within superhero publications. Martin Husovec has noted that

> intellectual property rights are legal constructs which govern the use of information. They mostly come in the form of exclusive rights which are expected to be traded on the market in exchange for licensing revenue. Exclusivity and remuneration are thus two defining features of IP rights.
>
> *(Husovec 2019, 841)*

The international consensus would suggest that the broader and overarching goals of the current understanding of IP rights relate to the protection and the facilitation of "innovation." However, the precise scope, purpose, and limitations of such "innovations" remains heavily contested at the overall conceptual level of what "innovation" is, but even more so at the individual level for each element of IP. In this connection, it is important to define and illustrate how each element of IP applies within the continuity of superhero comics, as well as how lessons from the real world influence this operation.

At the international level, patents are intended to protect the innovations and inventions of their creators under State protection. The rationale for this protection is that such protection would encourage future research and development costs in exchange for 20 years of protection. Patents offer protection for innovations that could be reverse-engineered if disclosed, and they give their owner the right to prevent others from making, using, or selling the invention without permission by controlling distribution channels. The precise degree of protection and mechanism will vary country to country, but at the broad level, and following the underlying basis of Article 28 of the TRIPS Agreement:

1 A patent shall confer on its owner the following exclusive rights:

   a where the subject matter of a patent is a product, to prevent third parties not having the owner's consent from the acts of: making, using, offering for sale, selling, or importing for these purposes that product;
   b where the subject matter of a patent is a process, to prevent third parties not having the owner's consent from the act of using the process, and from the acts of: using, offering for sale, selling, or importing for these purposes at least the product obtained directly by that process.

   (WTO, n.d.-b)

The protections afforded under trademark law extend to encapsulate protection granted to signs of graphic representation by the trademark holder in an economic manner to distinguish themselves from similar, yet competing, products. The precise requirements of the scope and operation of trademarks will vary at the technical level, but will be built on the rights agreed upon under Article 16 of TRIPS:

1   The owner of a registered trademark shall have the exclusive right to prevent all third parties not having the owner's consent from using in the course of trade identical or similar signs for goods or services which are identical or similar to those in respect of which the trademark is registered where such use would result in a likelihood of confusion. In case of the use of an identical sign for identical goods or services, a likelihood of confusion shall be presumed. The rights described above shall not prejudice any existing prior rights, nor shall they affect the possibility of Members making rights available on the basis of use.

(WTO, n.d.-a)

Copyright is intended to protect literary and artistic works against copying and to reward ability and skill, which will enhance the cultural life of the community. Due to the broad nature of literary and artistic works, the international basis from which copyright operates can be seen as the codification of the previous Berne Convention and subsequent revisions. However, the important aspect to note is Article 9(2) of the TRIPS Agreement that "Copyright protection shall extend to expressions and not to ideas, procedures, methods of operation or mathematical concepts as such" (WTO, n.d.-a).

What Can Superheroes Teach Us about the Law?

This chapter seeks to contribute to the ongoing engagement of literature as a tool to explore questions of law.

[l]iterature, it is said, sheds light on law's gap, rhetoric, and moral stances. It elucidates law's limits and highlights law's exclusion. Interpretation methods conventionally applied to fictional texts can be applied productively to legal texts, and narrative techniques that draw readers into novels and plays can be employed in the service of legal arguments.

(Baron 1999, 1060)

Comics, in particular superhero comics, have a history as a tool to examine areas such as politics, sociology, philosophy, ethics, and of course law (Peterson and Gertain 2005; Dittmer 2005; Sunner 2023). While the overall engagement and intersection levels may vary, Thomas Giddens notes the success of the disciplines which "have all positively engaged at some level with the medium" (Giddens 2012, 87). At the same time, the broader socio-legal discussion is a dynamic and "dazzlingly complex array of social, cultural, linguistic, and normative practices" (Halley 1998, 391).

From the publishing or real-world perspective, the explosive birth heralded by *Action Comics* #1 (1938) brought about the start of the genre and the subsequent level of popularity. While there were ebbs and flows as a result of economic changes, moral outcry, rebirth, and shifts to new media, the concept of superheroes has been ingrained in society since this issue.

During this period, Marvel operated on the principle of being the "world outside your window" and using real-world developments as a backdrop to continuity, with some allowance for "Marvel time" compression (Johnson 2023). DC Comics, on the other hand, operates a little more loosely in this regard with significant focus relating to fictional locations such as Gotham City, Metropolis City, Kahndaq, or any number of cities and nations that don't exist in the real world. On this front, the mass proliferation of superheroes as a concept has resulted in real-world developments of how specific elements of law operate.

Enforcement and Engagement of Intellectual Property in Superhero Continuity

Patent law presents an interesting application of the law where time travel, inter-planetary trade, and Reed Richards exist. However, such considerations must be done with care. Our current legislation basis is essentially planetarily locked, with some exceptions to the International Space Station. But to simply apply "Earth law" to the broader universe in relation to the control of innovation is difficult, if not impossible, in part not only due to the practicality but also the requirements for a patent requiring a novel or new application. When factoring in the more advanced technological aliens present in superhero comics, relatively few of the innovations originating on Earth would satisfy the novel or innovative step required as such technology and process would already exist. Additionally, the various legal jurisdictions require the disclosure of the innovation under patent law with the relevant authorities. This disclosure requirement was in part why the Iron Man technology was never patented by Tony Stark, due to fear of the innovation being disclosed or revealed to the public following the patent period expiring. This lack of patent protection was an underlying issue during the Armor War (1987–1988) storyline, the premise being that technology based on the Iron Man suit was used by third parties, which led him to attack and destroy potential uses, as legal methods were not available.

On the flip side of the patent disclosure issue, Reed Richards presents an interesting case study. Due to the exploits of the Fantastic Four, Reed Richards has traveled across space, time, and dimensions. As such, he has experienced many new technologies or avenues for discovery, many of which would satisfy the new or novel requirements. However, such exploration requires a strong moral application for knowledge and discovery, and Richards actively works to make such discoveries for the sake of knowledge rather than merely to patent it under his control. At the same time, Reed Richards is repeatedly noted as a leading scientist and innovator in many fields, responsible for many discoveries or innovations through his research. Such discoveries would satisfy the conditions of the patented as seen in Case 15–74 *Centrafarm v. Sterling Drug*, where the CJEU set out a definition of the "subject matter" of a patent, and stated that it is:

> the guarantee that the patentee, to reward the creative effort of the inventor, has the exclusive right to use an invention with a view to manufacturing industrial products and putting them into circulation for the first time either directly or by the grant of licences to third parties, as well as the right to oppose infringements.
>
> *(EUR-Lex 1974)*

From a copyright perspective, there are several additional elements to consider concerning the superhero identity. The main component is that limit in which the character exists in continuity, for example: to what degree does Peter Parker perform as the character

Spider-Man? In that, to what degree Spider-Man is a separate public character or professional persona from Peter Parker – a rough comparison may be the personal identity of Óscar Gutiérrez Rubio and his public persona as wrestler Rey Mysterio as opposed to individuals who publicly have combined their private and public personas, such as the musician Lady Gaga. Additionally, the privacy of the personal identity, or secret identity to give it its correct term, is a factor that must be considered in the context of security requirements that may not translate to real-world example, i.e., Lady Gaga and Rey Mysterio may have over-eager fans stalking their private life, but their family would not be targeted by the Green Goblin. There are also a number of outliers where the identity of the superhero is created and maintained by a commercial entity. This will have a significant degree of crossover with the operation of trademark protections, but where the commercial entity holds rights, they can prevent the use of others, even the individual under the mask. This is significant in relation to Spider-Man, owning his original appearance at a wrestling event in costume and working under the name. Often such companies would retain the ownership of the character and iconography even if they were independently developed. As such, the wrestling company could claim the copyright on the identity of Spider-Man. Such use was recently addressed in the comic book *Amazing Spider-Man: Beyond* arc in 2022, which allowed the company to make commercial use of the costume and assign their own candidate as the official Spider-Man. And this follows the legal developments in the real world. For example, the recording artists MF Doom and Deadmau5 are known for performing behind masks. While they hold the copyright for their artistic expression under these names and masks, they can permit others to perform in their place under the mask. Although this may be contrary to the performance contract, it is perfectly permissible from a copyright perspective. DC Comics has also touched upon this in issue #5 of the WildC.A.T.S (2023) comic series where an official and public-facing team were revealed to be under the control of the Halo Corporation. Based on the language and with some degree of comparison to real-world industries such as the ownership of characters within Worldwide Wrestling Entertainment, the Halo Corporation would hold the copyrights to such costumes and identities.

In this connection, we can draw on the enforcement and protection of identities within the professional Clown communities, having both a strong public connection and social taboos against the infringement of identity, something superheroes have repeatedly touched upon. However, in protecting their clown identity, this is primarily through non-legal methods. This lack of legal enforcement may be attributed to the resources required to process the matter through courts for what could be a marginal benefit; the high degree of difficulty in which it would be required to prove ownership of the identity, as "all but the most famous clowns would find it difficult to prove that consumers regard a particular makeup design or costume as an indication of the source of the performance"; but also, for the collegiality of the creative industry (Fagundes and Perzanowski 2019, 1329). Again, this approach of non-legal recognition and what can be attributed to as professional courtesy or an "honor system" is a common occurrence discussed in many creative industries and their respective outputs (Darling and Perzanowski 2017). The non-legal enforcement of the clown identities is "admittedly an unorthodox topic for legal scholarship, but upon closer examination, it reaffirms that insights about law and regulation may lie in the least likely places" (Fagundes and Perzanowski 2019, 1379). Thus, we can draw on the norms of one community or industry and apply them to the legal and non-legal enforcement of the superhero person and identity with some degree of success and appropriateness.

In most instances, the copyright of costumes/broader identity is not so legally enforced. Rather, it operates on a system of good faith and non-legal enforcement. From this, we can draw on real-world instances of similar non-legal enforcement in creative works and performing industries. The development of this non-legal preference mirrors many other creative industries (Fauchart and von Hippell 2008; Sarid 2014; Iljadica 2016; Fagundes 2012; Oliar and Sprigman 2008; Perzanowski 2013). Despite the creation and expression of a character or persona for a performance, studies "have found very little evidence that clowns have relied on copyright protection for their makeup, costumes, or acts" (Fagundes and Perzanowski 2019, 1327). By comparison, in the comic book limited series *Fallen Son: The Death of Captain America* #3 (2007), the character Clint Barton refuses to wear the Captain America suit, despite it being legally owned by the US government, due to the social and moral connotations of representing himself as Captain America. Thus, this reflects a two-fold engagement with norms and non-legal enforcement. First, it illustrates the acceptance of modifying behavior through social obligation rather than external (state) input (McAdams 1997, 350–352; see also Cooter 1996). Second, we can see this expanded in practice and how community members often engage and internalize such norms, such that the violation runs contrary to their morality (McAdams 1997, 376–378); in this instance, the refusal by Clint Barton to mispresent what the role/identity of Captain America means, both as a figure and the legacy of Steve Rogers as a person. While the example of Captain America would be considered a heightened example due to narrative elements and broader continuity-related propaganda, the core lesson can be seen throughout the history of superhero continuity.

An additional element to consider in relation to Captain America is the protection of his costume from a trademark perspective. First, his costume (and overall public persona, title, and rank) was created by the US government as a propaganda tool for the war efforts. As part of the propaganda efforts, this would have been trademarked to prevent unlawful, or rather unlicensed, use by commercial entities. Second, the costume incorporates the US flag to a significant degree. Across most jurisdictions and calling back to the origins of IP law as a means of state control and authority, trademark legislation contains provisions that restrict the use of the flag or other state seals and associated iconography to prevent misuse and misappropriation. As such, the US government would be able to prevent commercial use by third parties. This would include the sale of branded material which often appears in the form of clothing or toys of popular superheroes. A key example of this in relation to the issues of ownership and its subsequent commercial exploitation was in *Ultimate Spider-Man* #110 (2007), where, as a result of the appearance of Spider-Man as part of a wrestling program, the media company behind the wrestling promoters and organizers held the trademark. Through corporate mergers and acquisitions, Kingpin came to own the likeness of Spider-Man. This allowed him, through his legitimate corporate interests, to license and mass market Spider-Man paraphernalia and flood New York with merchandise. While not physically damaging, it is shown to harm the mental health of Peter Parker.

More recently, in the television series *She-Hulk: Attorney at Law* (2022) on Disney+, a plot point of episode 5 was the registration, and opposition of the trademark of the name, "She-Hulk" by a villain in an attempt to commercially exploit the name as part of a fashion line. The trademark was ultimately canceled in court by way of showing a prior use, which nullified the original application. Broadly, this is related to the underlying economic nature of trademark law and the objective to protect the public from confusion surrounding the source and linkages of the trademark (Anderson 1991, 180). Additionally, trademark law seeks to protect the secondary meaning of a sign or icon that creates "an association in the minds of the buying public between the name of the product and the product itself or its source" (Anderson 1991, 182). In this instance, the source is a Hulk-derived superhero. In *She-Hulk*, the argument commented on how Dr. Strange was both an actual name and a superhero identity. While the episode highlighted the confusion between using a protected title and name as a superhero identity, as framed as a joke, it nonetheless touches upon the exception to trademark law concerning the use of names. Under EU (with a similar restriction existing under UK law following Brexit) and US legislation, the in-continuity trademark use of the "Dr. Strange" would not be permitted by another as it is merely a reflection of his name and title. However, a trademark on "Doctor Doom" would be permitted, as Victor Von Doom does not hold a doctorate and lacks the "Von" element of the surname, in essence, Doctor Doom is a performative role rather than a personal identifier. Despite the number of legal-themed superheroes, there is little within the continuity of comics or adaption in other media to address the legislation or case law. As such, by shifting to the real-world context, we draw on similar use of the names, both ring and legal, of US wrestlers and Luchadores. We can draw on similarities due to the nature of trademarks relating to masks or uniforms but also the instances where the public persona is blended into the identity. At the same time, drawing on the Luchador tradition, we retain the trademark protection with the masked individual and their somewhat secret identity (Harrington 2016), something that has been a salient feature in comic book identities. The US has not arrived at a consistent or

> universally accepted criteria to determine if wrestlers' names (whether they are based on real names or not) should require the consent of the wrestler or if the wrestling promoter registering the wrestler's name as a mark is distinguishable as the source of the product or service.
>
> *(Harrington 2016, 294)*

As such, on the assumption that the superhero has applied for the trademark on their superhero name, it would likely follow the instances of wrestlers, where this may be held by the individual or another. But as with wrestlers, this is not absolute and will vary depending on the facts of the cases to come. However, it is important to acknowledge the privacy element and disclosure requirements of such applications, but this would fall within issues of privacy and security law, and thereby would be outside the scope of this chapter.

Finally, within the continuity of many superhero publications and wider media that draws heavily from superhero comics, there is the question of who owns the actual costume design. This exists separate from the copyright of the character/persona and the trademark of what the costume represents or links to. At the international level, the design rights are vested in the original designers. Within continuity, the question of ownership of the precise design presents an interesting application as many superheroes begin their careers in homemade outfits, often assembled from their own clothes or basic fabrics before acquiring an upgrade or redesign from a professional stylist or tailor, the most famous of which would be Edna from the animated movies *The Incredibles* (2004) and *Incredibles 2* (2018). She designed the costumes and had significant control over the superhero fashion industry, so we can infer a strict contract would be in place, but she also had some informal working relationship with the Incredible family and drew on their previous work, suggesting a collaborative effort. Other times, such as within *Invincible* (2003) or *Final Crisis: Rogues Revenge* (2009), where the aspiring hero (or villains at times) would present rough sketches or homemade costume where motifs or styles are then carried over, this would imply some degree of collaboration in effect and place them as a co-creator of the design, as well as the copyright of the work assigned to the personality. The commissioned work and the rights of design rest with the designer, but the finished product transfers to the commissioner on completion and transfer of stated payment. Unfortunately, likely as a result of the limited page count and wider reader interest, the precise legal relationship between the parties tends not to be directly addressed within the comics themselves.

Enforcement and Engagement of Intellectual Property by the Publishers

Across their history, the real world legal analysis of has often impact superheroes comics in unusual manners, such as the tax classification of X-Men figures (*Toy Biz, Inc. v. United States 2001*), preventing the dilution of superhero names in merchandise (*DC Comics, Inc. v. Unlimited Monkey Business, Inc 1984*), or the joint ownership of the publication use of the phrase "superhero" as jointly held by Marvel and DC comics (O'Connell 2020). However, while the above examples have impacted the real-world publisher as economic entities, the purpose of this section is to discuss how the real-world IP-related issues of the publishers have impacted the narrative and internal continuity of superhero comics. This section will examine how questions of publisher or creator ownership have shaped characters. It will look at how the lapse of a trademark led to moniker shifts, and how the appropriation of ongoing iconography by hate groups impacts on the use of certain characters and their continuity.

Unfortunately, for nearly as long as comics have existed as an industry, it has been rife with instances of exploitation of work, mistreatment of creators, and flat-out theft of work and authorship. But if IP rights were correctly assigned and attributed during these early days, many of the lengthy court battles over the rights to Superman or the degree of contributions by Jack Kirby or Steve Ditko would have been brief notes in history and legal texts (Chien 2016). However, this is not the case. On the flip side, if such rights were correctly attributed, it would be unlikely that such vast shared and developed universes would exist. Following the US Copyright Act of 1976, which broadly introduced revisions to the US definitions of work for hire or created work, in the across the late 1970s Marvel asked all creators to sign a page-long agreement that noted that "all work, writing, art work material or services … was and is expressly agreed to be considered a work made for hire" (casetext 2013). This would have removed claims of ownership after the characters were created and published. If these agreements had not been signed and their work acknowledged as work-for-hire, many of the early and foundational creators would be able to claim part ownership of the character. This, is turn, would require permission to use and publish them going forward. This would create several issues: Marvel would be creatively limited in what they could do if permission was required by the original authors, Marvel would be financially restricted in how to commercially monetize such characters, and Marvel may be unable to reprint the material if the permission is withdrawn. In practice, this led many creators to withhold certain ideas or new characters as they would not retain the IP on their work, and we have witnessed the rising economic value of such properties compared to the negative financial circumstances and treatment of their creators.

DC Comics had similar legal issues that impacted both their continuity as well as that of their competitors, Fawcett Comics. This dispute centered on the similarities between Superman and Captain Marvel, with DC Comics contending that Captain Marvel was a derivative work of Superman, thereby infringing the copyright of DC Comics. While such a claim would not have the same weight today – due in part to the evolution of the Superman archetype, wider literary critique, and volume of newer creations with similar superpowers – at the time it was enough to compel Fawcett Comics to settle in damages and reduce the publication of Captain Marvel. DC Comics would later buy Fawcett Comics and incorporate their characters into the DC Comics continuity, but because of the earlier lawsuit would not be able to publish Captain Marvel comics as the trademark had lapsed and was later acquired through use by Marvel for their character Captain Marvel, a Kree soldier. Marvel would subsequently publish the title or some mini-series when required to keep the trademark in use, with the adoption of the title by Carol Danvers in 2012. Since then, Marvel has continued to make use of the title Captain Marvel featuring Carol Danvers, with the use of the title being reflected in continuity.

This issue is not restricted to Marvel or DC Comics as the "Big Two." Following a creator-lead departure and the foundation of Image Comics, Todd McFarland found himself in a legal and creative dispute with Neil Gaiman regarding the ownership of characters created and introduced in *Spawn* #9 (1993), as well as subsequent related series and reprints. The dispute was ultimately found in favor of Neil Gaiman, and the Courts attributed the author's rights for the characters of Angela to him, as well as some commercial and royalty-based rights (*Gaiman v. McFarlane 360 F.3d 644 [7th Cir. 2004]*). However, Gaiman, following a subsequent settlement of outstanding issues concerning the complex and contested ownership of Miracleman, sold the character of Angela to Marvel, marking a rare occasion where Marvel bought a previously created character and introduced them into their continuity. Once again, this shows the impact of real-world legal developments on the continuity of superhero comics.

Finally, the contested or misappropriated use of trademarks by bad-faith actors has presented an interesting development in continuity. In this instance, the trademarked skull logo of *The Punisher* has been co-opted and utilized by the Three Percenters and other far-right hate groups. This presents an issue to Marvel both as a company concerning the requirement of a trademark to be in use for it to be a protected mark, but the continued use of them may imply a connection with such groups. Marvel has recently made a variation to the skull logo to reflect the new continuity narrative at play and also reframed *The Punisher*'s position in Marvel following recent story arcs. However, this as with all superhero conflicts, is an ongoing issue and may only be a stopgap as a character embodies "more than a physical description and a name; it is a creature with a past, that reacts and has reacted in certain ways to the events surrounding it" (Kurtz 1986, 431). This is even more true when applied to trademarks on such characters and if the publishers wish to retain them going forward.

Conclusion

While this chapter has touched on some IP-related issues, there are many others with more complex and crosscutting legal issues beyond IP-related questions. The above examples serve to show how IP and superheroes have an interesting history on and off the page. The exploration of IP law through superheroes is a growing element of discussion, from questions of moral justification and legal regulation of Batman and the Bat-logo, to challenges of the association of the Batman logo in the Courts of Justice of the European Union (*Case T-735/21 Aprile and Commerciale Italiana v EUIPO – DC Comics*); to ongoing questions of branding, association, and licensing of icons. While the current position of IP law functions on and off the pages, it is an area that will develop over the next decade where foundational elements of superhero mythos enter the public domain. As such, in a manner fitting of the ongoing narrative of the superheroes as a whole, such developments can only be described as "to be continued."

References

Anderson, Robert E. 1991. "Alternatives to Copyright Law Protection of Graphic Characters: The Lanham Act and Antidilution Statutes." *Hasting Communications and Entertainment Law Journal* 13, no 2: 181–197.

Baron, Jane B. 1999. "Law, Literature, and the Problems of Interdisciplinarity." *Yale Law Journal* 108, no 5: 1059–1085.

Chien, Colleen. 2016. "Beyond Eureka: What Creators Want (Freedom, Credit, and Audiences) and How Intellectual Property Can Better Give It to Them (by Supporting, Sharing, Licensing, and Attribution)." *Michigan Law Review* 114, no 6: 1081–1107.

Cooter, Robert D. 1996. "Decentralized Law for a Complex Economy: The Structural Approach to Adjudicating the New Law Merchant." *University of Pennsylvania Law Review* 144, no 5: 1643–1696.

Darling, Kate, and Aaron Perzanowski, eds. 2017. *Creativity without Law: Challenging the Assumptions of Intellectual Property*. NYU Press. https://www.jstor.org/stable/j.ctt1bj4rrg.

Dittmer, Jason. 2005. "Captain America's Empire: Reflections on Identity, Popular Culture, and Post-9/11 Geopolitics." *Annals of the Association of American Geographers* 95, no 3: 626–643.

EUR- Lex. 1974. "Judgment of the Court of 31 October 1974. - Centrafarm BV et Adriaan de Peijper v Sterling Drug Inc. - Reference for a preliminary ruling: Hoge Raad - Netherlands. - Parallel patents. - Case 15–74." European Union Law, October 31. https://eur-lex.europa.eu/legal-content/EN/TXT/HTML/?uri=CELEX:61974CJ0015.

Fagundes, David. 2012. "Talk Derby to Me: Intellectual Property Norms Governing Roller Derby Pseudonyms." *Texas Law Review* 90: 1093–1152.

Fagundes, David, and Aaron Perzanowski. 2019. "Clown Eggs." *Notre Dame Law Review* 94, no 3: 1313–1380.

Fauchart, Emmanuelle, and Eric von Hippel. 2008. "Norms-Based Intellectual Property Systems: The Case of French Chefs." *Organization Science* 19, no 2: 187–201.

Giddens, Thomas. 2012. "Comics, Law, and Aesthetics: Towards the Use of Graphic Fiction in Legal Studies." *Law and Humanities* 6, no 1: 85–109.

Halley, Janet E. 1998. "'Notes from the Editorial Advisory Board,' Introductory Essay on the Tenth Anniversary of the Yale Journal of Law & the Humanities." *Yale Journal of Law & the Humanities* 10, no 2: 389–391.

Harrington, Alissa M. 2016. "What's in a Name, Brother—Profit or Publicity: An Analysis of Trademarking Ring Names in Professional Wrestling." *Cybaris* 7, no 2: 227–312.

Husovec, Martin. 2019. "The Essence of Intellectual Property Rights Under Article 17(2) of the EU Charter." *German Law Journal* 20, no 6: 840–63. https://doi.org/10.1017/glj.2019.65.

Iljadica, Marta. 2016. *Copyright Beyond Law: Regulating Creativity in the Graffiti Subculture*. Bloomsbury.

Johnson, Zach. 2023. "Behind the Scenes of Stan Lee with Director David Gelb." *D23*, June 16. https://d23.com/behind-the-scenes-of-stan-lee-with-director-david-gelb/.

Justia 2013, "From Casetext: Smarter Legal Research. Gary Friedrich Enterprises, LLC v. Marvel Characters, Inc. " 716 F.3d 302 (2d Cir. 2013). https://law.justia.com/cases/federal/appellate-courts/ca2/12-893/12-893-2013-06-11.html

Kurtz, Leslie A. 1986. "The Independent Legal Lives of Fictional Characters." *Wisconsin Law Review* no. 3: 429–525.

McAdams, Richard H. 1997. "The Origin, Development, and Regulation of Norms." *Michigan Law Review* 96, no 2: 338–433.

Menell, Peter S. 2000. "Intellectual Property: General Theories." In *Encyclopaedia of Law and Economics, Volume II. Civil Law and Economics*, edited by Boudewijn Bouckaert and Gerrit De Geest. Edward Elgar Publishing.

O'Connell, Aislinn. 2020. "Generic Super Heroes: Can They Exist?" *The Comics Grid: Journal of Comics Scholarship* 10, no 1: 1–23.

Oguamanam, Chidi. 2009. "Beyond Theories: Intellectual Property Dynamics in the Global Knowledge Economy." *Wake Forest Intellectual Property Law Journal* 9, no 2: 106–154.

Oliar, Dotan, and Christopher Sprigman. 2008. "There's No Free Laugh (Anymore): The Emergence of Intellectual Property Norms and the Transformation of Stand-Up Comedy." *Virginia Law Review* 94, no 8: 1789–1867.

Perzanowski, Aaron. 2013. "Tattoos & IP Norms." *Minnesota Law Review* 98: 512–591.

Peterson, Bill E, and Emily D. Gerstein. 2005. "Fighting and Flying: Archival Analysis of Threat, Authoritarianism, and the North American Comic Book." *Political Psychology* 26, no 6: 887–904.

Sarid, Eden. 2014. "Don't Be a Drag, Just Be a Queen—How Drag Queens Protect Their Intellectual Property Without Law." *Florida International University Law Review* 10, no 1: 133–179.

Sunner, Liam. 2023. "To Me My X-Men: An Analysis of the European Union's Engagement with International Intellectual Property Law through the Prism of a trade agreement with the mutant nation of Krakoa." *Liverpool Law Rev* 44: 385–401 (2023). https://doi.org/10.1007/s10991-023-09345-7.

WTO. n.d.-a. "Part II — Standards Concerning the Availability, Scope and Use of Intellectual Property Rights. Section 1: Copyright and Related Rights." *World Trade Organization*. Accessed March 3, 2025. https://www.wto.org/english/docs_e/legal_e/27-trips_04_e.htm#1.

WTO. n.d.-b. "Part II — Standards Concerning the Availability, Scope and Use of Intellectual Property Rights. Section 5: Patents." *World Trade Organization*. Accessed March 3, 2025. https://www.wto.org/english/docs_e/legal_e/27-trips_04c_e.htm.

32

COMPANIONS, APPRENTICES, ENEMIES

The Many Roles of the Sidekick

Philippe Rioux

What would happen to Batman and Captain America if they could not depend on the acolytes who accompany them on their quest for justice? Often understood as simple personifications of young readers, the sidekicks play an important part in superhero narratives by forging superheroic models that deviate from the main archetype. Contrary to solitary heroes, who seem omnipotent, the sidekicks and their superheroic partners share (super) powers and responsibilities. This often leads to the sidekicks' subordination to their mentors, a situation that may reveal certain ideologies and norms. Indeed, the roles assigned to sidekicks cannot be dissociated from the comics' social, demographic, ethnic, political, and cultural context.

This chapter studies the distribution of superheroic roles and how it leads to hierarchical relationships in Canadian and American superheroic narratives. Building on the work of Lauren R. O'Connor (2021), I postulate that the mentor/sidekick dynamics are particularly meaningful when they involve characters differentiated according to national identities, race, or age. Hence, the analysis will focus on three emblematic duos who convene these identity markers: Northguard and Fleur de Lys; Doctor Strange and Wong; and, of course, Batman and Robin.

Through these characters, we will understand how the sidekicks' superpowers, personalities, identities, and visual characteristics impact their relationship with titular superheroes. More precisely, I will ask if these characters are the result of an effort made by creators toward greater diversity or, on the contrary, if they perpetuate a set vision of society. In other words, what is their purpose, from an ideological, editorial, and cultural perspective?

The scope of this essay is quite broad, and given the immense number of superhero comics published since the late 1930s, I had to set limits to circumscribe a practical corpus. I thus chose to specifically address each of the aforementioned characters' origin stories. Indeed, these particular narratives are crucial because, as Marc Atallah explains,

> superheroes are the result of a transformation that is, most of the time, caused by an accident (in Aristotle's sense) …Reinvesting, for the most part, the narrative modalities that had proved their worth in science-fiction novels, and though each one more implausible than the last, these 'justificatory sequences' are frequently part of what

DOI: 10.4324/9781003366911-37

readers or viewers eagerly watch for - which is easy to understand, since they constitute the intimate heart of the story, its center of gravity, its raison d'être.

(2014, 87; translated by the author)

Studying characters through their origin stories is therefore a fruitful act because it is within these defining moments that the enduring parameters of superhero narratives are articulated, including the fundamental attributes of the characters and the dynamics of the relationships they maintain. This doesn't mean that the superhero/sidekick relationship is immutable – quite the opposite, in fact – but origin stories, which are continually reinterpreted at the whim of editorial collections, retcons, and reboots, establish an effective interpretive framework, offering targeted leads for investigation.

In that sense, the research incorporates several comic book issues published after the 2000s, precisely because they reinterpret the sidekicks' original narratives from a revisionist perspective, as theorized by Geoff Klock (2002) and Terrence R. Wandtke (2012). This treatment, which stems from editors and "creators willing to experiment with the sacred stories and looks of superhero comics" (Wandtke 2012, 7), proposes to shed a new light on the crucial moment when the superhero recruits his sidekick and, therefore, when the parameters of their relationship are defined. It should come as no surprise, therefore, that several of the adventures studied here unfold in "Elseworlds," that is, within albums or short comic book series detached from Marvel's or DC's main narrative continuity. Indeed, these parallel universes allow authors to reboot plots and rethink characters within a more flexible framework.

Raising Robin

No character so spontaneously evokes the figure of the sidekick as Robin, the orphan taken in by Batman in 1940 and ever since attached to the Dark Knight. Yet, as O' Connor (2021) notes, comics studies have paid relatively little attention to this prototypical incarnation of the sidekick, other than to recall the perplexing and accusatory discourse directed at him by Frederic Wertham and other comics opponents during the 1950s. Criticism of the series' homoerotic and pedo-erotic subtext, among others, obscured the important role Robin played in the making of American adolescence, as O'Connor brilliantly demonstrates in her monograph devoted to the various characters who wore the iconic red, green, and yellow costume. As the anchor that draws the reader into the story through a process of identification, Robin is given the delicate task of defining the social norms toward which American teenagers must strive. We can guess how intransigent this program is toward racial, sexual, and gendered identities that deviate from the dominant model constantly reiterated by adult superheroic models:

> Creators of Robin(s) indelibly link maturation and heterosexual development, bluntly illustrate the double marginalization of adolescent femininity, and struggle to center on Black adolescence in a society generally unwelcoming of Black teens; these images of Robin all reinforce the dominant cultural notions of adolescence and maturation.
>
> *(O'Connor 2021, 15)*

Yet the inherent conservatism of the prototypical sidekick allows for variations that suggest his possible evolution. Indeed,

> as an adolescent, Robin is a vision of the future: future hero, future leader, future citizen. The change to Robin's identities and personalities, playing off the comparatively

stoic and static Bruce Wayne/Batman, do in fact indicate flexibility in who can inhabit and symbolize American adolescence.

(O'Connor 2021, 16)

Furthermore, it is clear that the expectations placed on teenagers and the attitudes of authority representatives toward them change more or less rapidly, depending on the series and the era in which Robin appears. Without revisiting the titles studied by O'Connor in her essay, this chapter is going to discuss a series recently published and, therefore, not included in her corpus. Titled *Robin & Batman* (Lemire and Nguyen 2021), which already evokes an interesting perspective on the power struggle between the sidekick and his mentor, the three-issue miniseries is significant because it offers a rereading of Dick Grayson's origins, focused on the notions of adolescence, responsibility, and parenthood. In other words, Jeff Lemire and Dustin Nguyen's story reflects on what it means to be Batman's teenage ward and sidekick.

The scenario written by Lemire is relatively conventional: Robin and Batman investigate robberies orchestrated by Killer Croc, depicted here as a circus freak once mistreated by Dick Grayson's parents and their fellow showmen. During his investigation, Robin learns of Croc's involvement in his parents' murder, prompting him to track down the villain and disobey Batman in the process. The originality of the story, however, lies elsewhere. For example, the identity of the main characters always appears as a diptych, which is hardly surprising in a genre based on the stereotypical duality of superheroic characters. Here, however, it's less a question of pitting the civilian against his costumed avatar than of questioning the troubled relationships that arise from such ambiguous identities. Can Robin afford a normal adolescence if he aspires to become a superhero? Should Batman prioritize the education of a son or the training of a soldier? Should Alfred, both a grandfather and a surrogate mother figure, support or confront Bruce Wayne – who is his son as well as his employer – about his parenting methods? These are just some of the dilemmas that arise when questioning the family framework within which the teenage sidekick flourishes, and even more so the adopted sidekick, who suffers from a trauma that alters his worldview (Thurman 2022).

These questions appear to be the miniseries' driving force, if only because they are debated in dialogue scenes as numerous as the action sequences. One episode in particular stands out: after being severely reprimanded by Batman for his overly daring behavior in combat, Robin meets the Teen Titans and is babysat alongside them by Hawkman in the Justice League Satellite while the adult superheroes are on a mission. Robin quickly befriends his fellow sidekicks, with whom he can act as normally as possible for a superhero sidekick: he banters, he laughs, and he mocks his parent. Once the party is over, however, the mask falls off. Back in the Batcave, it is revealed that the meeting between Robin and the other sidekicks was planned by Batman so that his protégé could study the weaknesses of the other up-and-coming superheroes, in case he ever has to fight them. When Batman demands a "mission debrief" (Lemire and Nguyen 2021, 78), Robin, who was ecstatic just a few frames earlier, becomes stoic. He then proceeds to detail the contingency plans he's already had time to draw up. Once his report is complete, Batman congratulates him with a "Good Boy" (80). The expression, which borders on condescension, serves to remind the teenager of his function. Robin is at best a soldier, as Batman stipulates, at worst, a service dog. In either case, he is violently reminded of what is expected of him: he must obey his superior and devote himself completely to his mission; he is denied his right to parental friendship and benevolence. Offended by the scene he has just witnessed, Alfred scolds his master: "They are **children**.

343

Children **like him**. Why can't you just let him have that?" To which Batman replies: "I never did. Why should he?" (80).

Batman's initial stance is eventually softened when he realizes the possible excesses it can lead to. Indeed, in the final act of the series, Robin fully embraces Batman's principles. He rejects the potential friendship of his classmates, loses interest in normal life, and becomes passionate only about his superheroic mission. Freed of all fear, because he has no future beyond what Batman has planned for him, he fights crime with a new confidence, competence, and violence. This eventually enables him to rescue Batman from the clutches of Killer Croc, a pivotal moment that forces Batman to recognize Robin's autonomy, as well as the problematic role reversal that has just occurred. Batman (the adult), in fact, should have been the one to protect Robin (the teenager), not the other way around. Thus, Robin graduates in several ways: on the civilian level, Dick Grayson is finally perceived as a son by Bruce Wayne, while on the superheroic level, Robin becomes Batman's teammate (both characters start using the term "partner"). From that point, Robin's identity will no longer be defined through Batman's vision of superheroism and adolescence, as suggested by the very last page of the series, where the teenager is seen in the company of the sidekicks he formerly met, now his friends and fellow crime fighters.

The end of the story allows readers to envisage superhero adolescence as a period of transition from a state determined by the adult world to one that is partially self-determined. Robin goes beyond emulation to assert himself as a superhero, thereby authorizing another conception of superheroism in the story, one based on the balance between darkness and light. The hero now splits his time between night and day, between fighting and playing with friends, between mourning his parents and appreciating his adopted family, between violence and innocence. In a way, it is a gentle rebellion that is welcomed and protected against the paternal and patronizing figure of the superhero, whose bronze statue oxidizes in an atmosphere of doubt. In Lemire and Nguyen's work, the superhero's mission is less about devotion than obsession, and the training of the next generation proves to be the manifestation of a certain selfishness coupled with grief and envy. In short, by shifting the focus onto Robin, Lemire and Nguyen's work comments on superheroic and parental archetypes, revealing the unhealthy nature of the ones embodied by Batman.

From Servant to Sidekick: the Ascension of Wong

Appearing at the same time as Doctor Strange in *Strange Tales* # 110 (Lee and Ditko 1963), Wong, who is of Chinese or Tibetan descent, depending on the source material, doesn't immediately appear as a typical sidekick. In fact, his role in 1960s comics was often that of a doorman, and a bad one too, seeing as anyone could enter Strange's house without warning or permission. Drawn with a hunched back and a shifty gaze, Wong is presented as being practically enslaved to Doctor Stephen Strange. From the age of four, he has been raised, after all, to serve the next Sorcerer Supreme. His sole purpose is to execute the domestic tasks that Strange neglects due to his superheroic mission. As such, a bleak light shines on the superhero and his apprentice, who deems himself unworthy of his "master" (*Strange Tales* # 119; Lee and Ditko 1964, 3). The situation gets better by the 1970s, when Wong becomes a potent protector of Strange's mansion, the Sanctum Sanctorum. That said, the loyal servant is not yet interested in getting into the action to assist Doctor Strange in his supernatural adventures. As he expresses in *Doctor Strange* #176 (October 1974), after noticing that his "master" is not home in the middle of the night: "…it is not for Wong to question in such matters! I must merely do my duty… as silently as hangs the portrait on yon wall" (Friedrich and DeZuniga, 12). It appears that the relationship between Strange and Wong in the early 1970s still relies on a master/servant dynamic. It is, after all, the exact words used by the narrator and the characters to describe both characters' positions toward each other.

It's not hard to imagine that this representation, already problematic in the second part of the 20th century, has been overhauled in the comics of the new millennium. In the series *Doctor Strange: Beginnings and Endings*, published under the Marvel Knights label in 2004–2005, Wong first takes on the features of an orphaned child cared for in a Tibetan village by Strange, as the latter completes his medical training there. Traumatized by the massacre of his family, which he witnessed at the age of four, young Wong is mute. In Strange's care, however, he surprisingly regains his voice, which forges a special bond between them. At the end of his stay in Tibet, Strange promises Wong that he will return one day to take him back to America. But the self-centered Strange doesn't honor his promise until he loses the use of his hands, six years later, which pushes him to undertake an act of self-examination and try to reunite with Wong. When he does find his former patient, it turns out that the Tibetan, inspired by Strange, has himself become a doctor, although the medicine he practices is described as alternative, and has settled in New York. The premise is interesting because it integrates Wong's origin story into a familiar and recurring pattern, that of the orphan who is taken in and trained by a superhero, modifying it enough to endow the sidekick with his own autonomy and competence. Stephen Strange, in fact, is not yet a superhero when Wong crosses his path. Too preoccupied with vain things (fame, money, superficial romance), he neglects his promise to Wong, betraying his trust instead of offering him the resources he needs to flourish. Therefore, it is through determination and talent that Wong develops his powers, even before Strange does. This makes him at least Strange's equal, if not his superior. The fact that Wong chooses "Stephen" as his own forename, when he moves to New York (Straczynski et al., 2005, 47), supports this sense of a renewed, if not reversed, hierarchy.

The *Doctor Strange: Season One* graphic novel, released in 2012, opts for a similar depiction of Wong. In this further reinterpretation of Doctor Strange's origins, the meeting between the titular superhero and his sidekick, which is based on a misunderstanding, is primarily confrontational: Wong mistakes Strange for Mordo, the story's villain, and immediately sees him as an antagonist. Their brief skirmish, quickly interrupted by an astral projection from their spiritual master, the Ancient One, serves well to warn Strange, and the reader, of Wong's power. Indeed, Wong is perfectly capable of returning the American stranger's every blow. Moreso, it is revealed that Wong is a student of the Ancient One in the same capacity as Doctor Strange, which puts them on an equal footing. In fact, the Ancient One is quick to point out that his two disciples possess opposing, and therefore complementary, qualities and flaws. Wong is brave, loyal, and fair, but lacks discipline. Strange is studious, gifted, and ambitious, but motivated by selfishness. While remaining true to the personality traits that have defined them for decades, each character embodies a fundamental aspect of the superheroic identity, as defined by Peter Coogan (2006): superhuman power (Strange) and dedication to a pro-social cause (Wong). Recognizing this, the Ancient One forces them to continue their magic lessons in tandem, hoping "[t]hat [they] may learn which virtues to embrace… and which vices to avoid." (Pak and Rios 2012, 21–22). After a period of fierce rivalry, in which pride, and a considerable dose of toxic masculinity, drives them to compete for every mark of recognition (a woman's admiration, a rival's jealousy, their master's congratulations), osmosis finally takes hold.

Excessive rivalry, which leads the two wizards to physically harm each other on multiple occasions, thus levels the highly hierarchical relationship between Wong and Strange. But this tension antagonizes the characters, preventing them from reaching their full superheroic status. So, they join forces, in a familiar pattern, to fight a common enemy: the sorcerer Mordo, servant of the devil Dormammu. It's at the end of the final battle, when Wong and Strange's magical prowess is confirmed, that the two heroes abandon their previous feud and seal their friendship. These examples show that, in order to attenuate the racial stereotypes at the heart of the initial relationship between Dr. Strange and his sidekick, and to offer Wong a more interesting role than that of the good servant, the latter had to reach the rank of superhero. In a context such as this, which is already based on a strongly stereotyped orientalism, the sidekick's function simply seems too connoted to be maintained. The last page of the story seals Wong's new status. The physical jousting that constantly pitted him against Strange has given way to verbal teasing. Wong, for example, makes fun of a hand injury Strange sustained during their fight against Dormammu. While these jibes testify to a friendly turn in their relationship, they also serve as a reminder that Wong can stand up to the Doctor, since he is, in every respect, his equal. The last words spoken in the story by the Ancient One and Strange's friend, Dr. Di Cosimo, can be interpreted in this sense

[The Ancient One]: …But they're just sorcerers, not saints.
[Dr. Di Cosimo]: Yeah, well… Give 'em time.

From apprentice wizards to sorcerers, and from sorcerers to saints, Wong and Strange seem to ascend to their superhuman state simultaneously. Once the racial stereotypes have been toned down, there are few arguments left to relegate Wong to the role of second fiddle.

Canada, Québec, and the Nationalist Sidekick

Introduced in 1975, Captain Canuck is the first Canadian superhero to make a real and lasting contribution to the tradition of nationalist superhero narratives, proudly represented in comics since the Second World War. Although the original eponymous series is short (15 issues of 19 pages) and its political dimension secondary, it lays the foundations for Canadian superheroic nationalism. In the story's universe, Canada is a country that never seems to have experienced the internal political tensions of the Province of Quebec independence movement, despite its strong presence in the media at the time of the series' launch. Difficult relations with the First Nations are also glossed over. Instead, Canada is presented as a united country made up of federated cultures. Indeed, in the second episode of the series, we learn that Captain Canuck is not the only superheroic agent looking out for his homeland (Comely 1976). The government also relies on the services of Redcoat (a reference to the military clothing worn by British soldiers), charged with protecting Western Canada; Kébec, defender of the province of the same name and its French-speaking inhabitants; and Stardance, representative of the First Nations. Each of these characters represents a distinct nation whose particularities (linguistic, cultural) tend to be erased in times of crisis, in the name of national unity. All of them, moreover, report without protest to a central power: the Canadian government and its flag bearer, Captain Canuck. By granting his acolytes a certain freedom of action, while ensuring that they work in accordance with the country's interests, Captain Canuck thus exerts an inclusive pan-Canadian nationalism and superheroism.

Inspired by Captain Canuck, *New Triumph featuring Northguard* (hereafter cited as *Northguard*), imagined by Montreal authors Mark Shainblum and Gabriel Morrissette, distinguishes itself by using the political conflicts between federalists and independentists as a central element of its storytelling. For instance, the script for the first issue of *Northguard* echoes a tragedy that occurred in real life, Denis Lortie's 1984 political attack on Quebec City's Hôtel du Parlement. Dressed in a military uniform, Lortie killed three people and wounded 13 others in an attempt to assassinate René Lévesque, Premier of Quebec, and his deputies, members of the pro-independence "Parti québecois" party (Noakes 2022). In the fictional world of *Northguard*, a similar attack is to be carried out by an American terrorist group at a Parti Québécois rally (Shainblum and Morrissette 1984). Intervening at just the right moment, Philip Wise/Northguard manages to foil the plot and narrowly avert catastrophe, despite being a superhero-in-training who has just been recruited by the private security agency P.A.C.T. After the event, Northguard discovers that the attack, masterminded by the American organization ManDes (Manifest Destiny: the divine expansionist mission), was intended to reignite political tensions between English-speaking and French-speaking Canadians. Worse still, it was intended to trigger a civil war that would have led to the annexation of Canada to the United States. As a worthy protector of his homeland, Northguard took offence at this attack on national unity, and henceforth asserted himself as the proud representative of tolerance and openness to others.

Northguard's intentions are good, but he doesn't fully master his new superheroic duties. Above all, as an English-speaking man based in the French-speaking province of Quebec, he feels that he alone cannot represent all his fellow citizens. To compensate for his weaknesses and to act according to the values he advocates, he enlists the services of Manon Deschamps, a French-speaking athlete he met by chance in a dance hall. Deschamps, a martial arts expert, quickly convinces P.A.C.T. to hire her. A fervent independentist, she adopts the sobriquet Fleur de Lys and the Fleurdelysé (flag) costume, both symbols of the Francophonie and the Quebec nation. The unlikely duo she forms with Northguard proves formidable. Fleur de Lys's superior athleticism and Northguard's sense of duty complement each other perfectly. Even their opposing political convictions can't weaken their relationship, which is founded on respect and empathy.

It's clear from this partnership what message the characters, and the series in general, are supporting. On one hand, reconciliation and even cooperation between Anglophones and Francophones are possible and desirable. On the other hand, English Canada and Quebec can compete against (often hostile) foreign powers only by forging a strong union. The sexual tension that develops between Northguard and Fleur de Lys symbolically accentuates this fantasy. What if the two dominant nations of Canada could learn not only to tolerate, but to love each other? Northguard, in particular, is attracted to Fleur de Lys (the opposite is less obvious), which gives rise to new impulses within him. Manon Deschamps is an elusive woman because her language, culture, and political positions are hard to understand from the protagonist's point of view, which makes her exotic and seductive. But she's also romantically elusive because she's already in a romantic relationship. This information, which Northguard learns with surprise, makes him react violently: during a training session with Deschamps, he wounds her with his laser beam, after ignoring warnings about the faulty equipment he is using. As the reader and the characters are left to wonder if the attack was intentional, the implication is striking: what Canada can't get from Quebec the easy way, it pushes back with force.

The accident, which occurs in issue 5 of 8, marks a significant turning point. Fleur de Lys, who forgives Northguard for his action, becomes the series' central superheroine in the following issue. It should be noted that three years elapsed between the publication of issues 5 (June 1986) and 6 (September 1989). During this long hiatus, *Northguard's* publisher, Montréal-based Matrix Comics, published its last comics in 1987 and transferred its intellectual properties to the American publisher Caliber Press. Just before its demise, Matrix was planning to publish a series dedicated to Fleur de Lys, as evidenced by the company's archives, deposited at Library and Archives Canada. The increased prominence of Fleur de Lys in the publisher's catalog, as well as in its superheroic pantheon, may explain the shift in focus that occurs in *Northguard* from the sixth issue onwards. In any case, when the series was relaunched in 1989, Northguard is promptly kidnapped by ManDes and held prisoner in a dungeon, unbeknownst to his employers (Shainblum and Morrissette 1989–1990). Fleur de Lys, meanwhile, continues her training: she is constantly shown honing her fighting skills, at all hours of the day and night. In fact, she proves that she deserves the superheroic status that will temporarily be hers in the seventh episode, when, like Northguard, she finally gets the gadgets she needs to fight any threat. Armed with her newly acquired lily-shaped tasers, Fleur de Lys defends the premises and employees of P.A.C.T. during an attack led by ManDes. At least, that's what she does until the arrival of Northguard, who has managed to escape his prison after miraculously acquiring quasi-divine powers. The return of the protagonist marks a change in Fleur-de Lys's superheroic effectiveness. As soon as the titular superhero appears, she suddenly becomes ineffectual: she gets lost in the building's ventilation ducts on her way to get help, leaving Northguard alone to face their foes and to end the assault.

This outcome is surprising and particularly revealing, as it re-establishes the hierarchy between the superhero and his sidekick that the series had previously striven to deconstruct. For one thing, this step backwards places Fleur de Lys in the line of other female superheroes who "are typically limited to the supporting roles of love interests, temptresses, and sidekicks," with their personalities and meaning constructed "in relation to the male superhero" (Stuller 2013, 20). This ending also imposes an equally connotative reading of the nationalist allegory that served as the series' backdrop: Quebec as embodied by Fleur de Lys can flourish and exert assets that make it the equal of Canada as personified by Northguard, particularly in times of conflict between the two character-nations. But the inevitable return to the status quo, a phenomenon typical of serial and nationalist narratives, will always end up restoring the political hierarchy that exists between them in and out of fiction. The discourse conveyed by the nationalist superhero and his acolytes thus makes it possible to acknowledge the existence of ethnic or cultural minorities while integrating them into an idealistic national project embodied by a superhero who is attentive, yet ultimately authoritative through his omnipotence.

Conclusion

The relationship between superhero and sidekick, as it appears in the duos presented in this chapter, necessarily involves an implicit or explicit power play, whether between adult and adolescent, between a master and his servant, or between the state and its constituent nations. These inequalities are necessary in comic book series centered on traditional superhero archetypes, since they generate contrasting effects that show the ideals and values carried by the protagonists as unshakeable elements.

That said, these conclusions need to be further nuanced by a careful examination of the evolving relationships between sidekicks and titular superheroes as depicted within other titles and over longer periods. A study of sidekicks who entered the editorial landscape in recent years is necessary; for instance, as these characters don't seem to require the support of a titular superhero for more than a few months. Indeed, after a short training and probationary period, the new teenage heroes quickly acquire their autonomy, which results, among other things, in their obtaining an eponymous series in which they act as protagonists. Kate Bishop, Miles Morales, Ghost Spider, Miss Marvel, and Iron Heart, to name but a few, do well without the assistance of their (former) mentors. Among the titles examined, many foreshadowed this reconfiguration of the sidekick archetype, now a trainee aiming to become a full-fledged superhero. It seems that their superheroic emancipation lies in the fact that they now operate within a collaborative group that levels out the effects of hierarchization (Glinoer 2014). Perhaps this reveals that today's superhero fans are less in need of characters to set ideological and moral guidelines for them than of new heroes who more aptly represent their concerns and social reality. The disappearance of the traditional sidekick, eternally subordinate to the actions and authority of their mentor, could then be understood as a disavowal of the canonical superhero, whose quest for justice fails to be adequately reflected in their relationships with their immediate companions. Indeed, the moral values of a superhero are harder to take seriously when these avatars of justice entertain unhealthy, not to say abusive, relationships with sidekicks who are vulnerable (in the case of children and teenagers) or come from marginalized groups. This explains the trend observed in this chapter toward a leveling of hierarchies in contemporary origin stories in comic books. Through Robin, who breaks free from Batman to join the Teen Titans, Wong, who enjoys a power equal to Strange's, and Fleur de Lys, who goes to Northguard's rescue, tiered relationships appear temporary and escapable. The sidekicks are now expected to graduate and assume a full superheroic function, because the latter is now accessible, with and without permission from their mentors, to a wider variety of profiles.

References

Atallah, Marc. 2014. "Pour une sémiotique de la transformation: Quelques superhéros face à leurs origines." In *Mythologies du superhéros. Histoire, physiologie, géographie, intermédialités*, edited by François-Emmanuël Boucher, David, Sylvain, and Maxime Prévost. Presses de l'Université de Liège.

Comely, Richard. 1976. *Captain Canuck*, no. 2 (May). Comely Comix.

Coogan, Peter. 2006. *Superhero: The Secret Origin of a Genre*. Monkeybrain Books.

Friedrich, Mike, and Tony DeZuniga. 1974. *Strange Tales* #176 (October). Marvel Comics.

Glinoer, Anthony. 2014. "La dynamique d'un groupe superhéroïque: Les Uncanny X-Men." In *Mythologies du superhéros. Histoire, physiologie, géographie, intermédialités*, edited by François-Emmanuël Boucher, David, Sylvain, and Maxime Prévost. Presses de l'Université de Liège.

Klock, Geoff. 2002. *How to Read Superhero Comics and Why*. Continuum.

Lee, Stan, and Steve Ditko. 1963. "Dr. Strange, Master of Black Magic." In *Strange Tales* #110 (July). Marvel.

Lee, Stan, and Steve Ditko. 1964. "Dr. Strange Dare to Go… Beyond the Purple Evil!" In *Strange Tales* #119 (January). Marvel.

Lemire, Jeff, and Dustin Nguyen. 2021. *Robin & Batman*. DC Comics.

Noakes, Taylor. 2022. "1984 National Assembly Shooting." *The Canadian Encyclopedia*. Historica Canada. Accessed July 02, 2025, https://www.thecanadianencyclopedia.ca/en/article/1984-national-assembly-shooting

O'Connor, Lauren R. 2021. *Robin and the Making of American Adolescence*. Rutgers University Press.

Pak, Greg, and Emma Rios. 2012. *Doctor Strange: Season One*. Marvel Comics.

Shainblum, Mark, and Gabriel Morrissette. 1984–1987. *New Triumph Featuring Northguard*, #1–5 Matrix Graphic Series.

Shainblum, Mark, and Gabriel Morrissette. 1989–1990. *Northguard: The ManDes Conclusion*, #1–3. Caliber Press.

Straczynski, J. Michael, Samm Barnes, and Brandon Peterson. 2005. *Doctor Strange: Beginnings and Endings*. Marvel Comics.

Stuller, Jennifer K. 2013. "What Is a Female Superhero?" In *What Is a Superhero?*, edited by Robin S. Rosenberg and Peter Coogan. Oxford University Press.

Thurman, Joel. "Roy 'Speedy' Harper, the Archer's Sidekick: Origins that Reflect the American Child Welfare System," Paper Presented at the *Popular Culture Association/American Culture Association National Conference*, April, 2022. Seattle.

Wandtke, Terrence R. 2012. *The Meaning of Superhero Comic Books*. McFarland and Company.

33

MORALITY AND FAMILIAL RELATIONSHIPS IN THE MARVEL CINEMATIC UNIVERSE

Angelique Nairn

Often emphasized in the superhero genre is the triumph of good over evil, with superheroes embodying essential moral dimensions such as care, fairness, authority, loyalty, and purity in their behaviors (Banerjee and Schaff 2022; Jenkins 2015; Yogerst 2017). As moral agents, imbued with virtues like courage, justice, and selflessness, superheroes construct aspirational yet relatable ways of being, rooted in the complexities of the human condition (Koh 2022). Many of the moral narratives within the superhero genre, then, are intricately intertwined with familial dynamics. Families, which act as primary socializing agents, play a pivotal role in individuals' moral development (Berghahn 2013). Hence, it is unsurprising that the moral actions of superheroes are often rooted in fulfilling familial obligations (Jenkins 2015). For instance, the superhero origin story frequently revolves around the loss of parental figures, serving as a catalyst for superheroes' commitment to fighting crime and defending the vulnerable (Reynolds 1992).

Yet, despite the undeniable significance of family in superhero narratives, its role remains largely underexplored (Jenkins 2015), with more attention needed around the influence of family on the moral development of superheroes. Therefore, the primary objective of this chapter is to delve into the relationship between family dynamics and morality within Marvel Cinematic Universe (MCU) films over the past two decades. Specifically, it will scrutinize elements such as the superhero's origin story, the influence of parental figures, the formation of makeshift families, and sibling rivalries. Such an inquiry aims to elucidate the portrayal of families and the conception of morality within superhero narratives, given the potent and far-reaching impact of the genre on societal consciousness (Brown 2016).

Trauma, Origins + Moral Trajectories

Among the myriad lenses through which we can discern the moral motivations of superheroes, the exploration of their origin stories stands as particularly illuminating. As noted by Richard Reynolds (1992), these narratives often highlight the profound influence of family, particularly parental figures, in shaping the trajectory of a superhero's moral compass. Loss, trauma, suffering, and pain are recurrent themes, frequently accounting for the adoption of a particular moral ethos by the superhero (Duggan 2016; Jenkins 2015). Take, for example,

 DOI: 10.4324/9781003366911-38

the case of Spider-Man, whose anguish over the loss of his uncle and later his aunt fuels a deep-seated sense of guilt. Unable to save his family, Spider-Man assumes the responsibility of protecting his neighborhood by dedicating himself to combating crime. His desire to help and, therefore, uphold moral principles of care (Haidt and Graham 2007) ultimately compels him to channel his negative emotions into vigilantism, perhaps in a subconscious attempt to rectify past failures (Duggan 2016). Jennifer Duggan observes that the heroes' relentless pursuit of justice, fueled by the memory of their deceased loved ones, paradoxically impedes their ability to move forward, as their missions perpetually resurrect feelings of loss and guilt.

Such trauma, encompassing emotions ranging from anxiety to sympathy (Earle 2017), disrupts an individual's sense of identity and prompts a critical reassessment of society and one's place within it (Helvie 2012; McSweeney 2018). Yet, the impact of familial loss on self and morality is not confined solely to the superhero origin story. Thor, for instance, grappling with the loss of his mother, father, and brother, succumbs to overwhelming despair, all but relinquishing his role as leader of the Asgardian people. It is not until he encounters his mother after traveling back in time, that he loses his ambivalence toward the Avenger's mission to stop Thanos and is reoriented toward fighting for justice again. Similarly, Tony Stark (Iron Man) initially rebuffs the Avengers' mission in *Avengers: Endgame* (2019) until he is confronted with images of his lost "surrogate son," Peter Parker (Spiderman), compelling him to reevaluate his duty and moral purpose (Hanley 2023). The superheroes' unwavering commitment to justice, then, is inexorably entwined with the adversities they have endured and the sacrifices they have made in service to others (Bergstrand and Jasper 2018; McSweeney 2018; Yogerst 2017).

However, it is worth recognizing that familial trauma and loss can also catalyze a darker descent. Erik Killmonger, the antagonist in *Black Panther* (2018), is molded by poverty and crime following the loss of his father and seeks vengeance against his cousin T'Challa. Killmonger is driven by a desire for reparation rather than "cooperation and compromise" (Yogerst 2017, 22), establishing him as the antithesis of the superhero. Although his moral ambiguity blurs the lines between heroism and villainy (he is motivated in part by the subordination of his African American community), his actions underline the profound impact of environment and parental loss on virtue and moral character (Yogerst 2017). Similarly, Wanda Maximoff, or the Scarlet Witch, is haunted by the loss of her loved ones in *Dr Strange: The Multiverse of Madness* (2022). She ultimately succumbs to selfish motivations (a desire to resurrect her lost children at the cost of others' lives), thereby exhibiting characteristics deemed as villainous such as threatening the lives of others, despite her motivations being born from personal tragedy (Benton 2020; Bergstrand and Jasper 2018). Michelle Balaev (2008) observes that trauma leaves an indelible mark on an individual's psyche, shaping their conception and enactment of self. In the cases of Killmonger and Scarlet Witch, familial loss reframes their moral trajectories, emphasizing the potent role families play in shaping the moral choices of superhero characters.

Undoubtedly, the loss of family members profoundly shapes not only the moral compass of superheroes but also deeply impacts their interpersonal dynamics. Children often look to parental figures as templates for constructing relationships, and the absence or deficiency of such guidance can significantly impede a superhero's early development (Reynolds 1992). Consequently, instead of following principles of reciprocity, loyalty, and communal welfare (Haidt 2007; Yogerst 2017), the absence of familial bonds can initially lead superheroes to adhere to an ethics of autonomy, prioritizing their individual rights and personal preferences over the needs of the communities to which they belong (Haidt and Graham 2007).

Consider the characters of Peter Quill (Star-Lord) and Gamora in the *Guardians of the Galaxy* (2014) film. Both are initially portrayed as loners grappling with their own traumas. Their interactions are marked by competition and guardedness, reflecting the wounds left by their respective familial losses. It is only when circumstances compel them to collaborate and unite against a common adversary that their motivations begin to evolve, and their relationship dynamic transforms (Earle 2017). Through shared trials and challenges, they gradually form bonds of camaraderie and trust, eventually culminating in the formation of what is often termed a "found family" (Yogerst 2017). Thus, the absence of guidance and nurturing or the modeling of inappropriate behaviors by parental figures during their formative years, presents a significant obstacle to their emotional and moral growth (Earle 2017; Reynolds 1992). Consequently, their journey toward forging new familial connections becomes not only a path to healing but also a crucial avenue for personal change and redemption.

Daddy Issues and Missing Mothers

Proposed above is the notion that numerous superheroes grapple with psychological trauma stemming from the loss or betrayal of their parents. Figures like Tony Stark, T'Challa, and Peter Quill, are compelled to endure the aftermath of their parents' murders or abandonment, resulting in profound psychological wounds that shape their behavior and character progression (Earle 2017; Reynolds 1992). However, beyond merely underscoring this trauma and familial discord, superhero cinematic narratives notably emphasize the exploration of father-son relationships, often to craft redemptive arcs for fathers or to accentuate the ascendancy of the son (McSweeney 2018). As indicated by Claire Jenkins, "it is predominantly father-son relationships that are being restored within the 'unconventional families' of family adventure movies" (2015, 76). For instance, throughout the Iron Man trilogy, audiences are exposed to the strained dynamic between Tony and Howard Stark. Tony rebels against what he perceives as his father's shortcomings, and following Howard's death, he grapples with assuming his father's legacy, engaging in extensive introspection regarding Howard's decisions. Essentially, Tony endeavors to uphold and surpass his father's legacy by embodying his values; Howard sought global peace, and so does Tony (Allison and Goethals 2011). Despite potential differences in their approaches, Tony's moral compass evolves through contemplation of his father's methods, identifying the significant role parents play in their son's moral development (Jenkins 2015).

In many respects, despite Howard's absence, Tony strives to conduct himself in a manner that would earn posthumous approval and pride from his father. The exploration of their relationship inevitably mirrors the Oedipal narrative (Jenkins 2015), wherein Tony's yearning for his father's commendation, even in death, becomes his overarching motivation. This desire, as posited by Sigmund Freud, stems from the belief that "the father is a figure of power and authority, and also, in Freudian terms, a rival" (Jenkins 2015, 17). Consequently, despite their tumultuous relationship during Howard's lifetime, which impelled Tony to surpass his father, as their narrative unfolds, Tony's aspiration to honor his father ultimately redeems Howard and solidifies his position as Tony's revered figure. As Jenkins (2015) asserts, due to feeling guilt and loss, the father is restored as a totemic figure who is once again idolized by the son, becoming more potent than the living father ever was. Essentially, the recurrent themes of paternal melodrama, moral evolution, and the paternal influence on sons in superhero narratives reflect a heightened emphasis on reinforcing parental authority (Banerjee and Schaff 2022).

Much akin to Tony Stark, T'Challa undergoes a significant moral evolution in *Black Pan ther*, catalyzed by his relationship with his father (Bucciferro 2021; Phillips 2021). Striving to uphold his father's esteemed legacy and initially adhering to the belief that Wakanda's conceal ment is imperative to safeguard its secrets, T'Challa perceives his actions as serving the best interests of his forebears, his people, and above all, his recently departed father. However, the revelation of his father's morally questionable deeds – namely, the fratricide of his brother and the abandonment of his nephew – in the name of protecting Wakanda, presents T'Challa with an ethical quandary that prompts his moral maturation. As articulated by Claudia Bucciferro (2021), reclaiming his ancestral heritage necessitates a critical re-evaluation of his father's legacy and a process of individuation, while also endeavoring to redefine Wakanda's role on the global stage. This introspection not only prompts scrutiny of his father's fallibility but also empha sizes the significance of the moral imperative to ensure the welfare and avoidance of harm to all individuals (Haidt and Graham 2007). Parallel to Tony Stark's journey, T'Challa's moral growth is facilitated by personal development and a desire to transcend his father's limitations, thereby enabling him to reassess and fortify his ethical principles in his pursuit of maintaining his superheroic stature. Furthermore, T'Challa's narrative trajectory reinforces Jenkins' posi tion that family dysfunction is often caused by parental figures and, therefore, "reconciliation of the family comes about by repairing the problems of, or caused by, the parents" (2015, 78). In other words, the superhero narrative, like other media offerings, explores the residual impacts of generational guilt.

The depictions of father-son relationships in the MCU are not all positive and this is perhaps an attempt to critique the authoritarian role fathers have historically played in child rearing (Tapia et al., 2018). For example, the authoritarian treatment of Shang-Chi by his father Xu Wenwu in *Shang-Chi and the Legend of the Ten Rings* (2021) distresses Shang-Chi, and upon being forced to assassinate the leader of the Iron Gang to appease and impress his father, Shang-Chi is left traumatized and opts to run away for his own well-being. The authoritarian parenting style advocated by Wenwu has long been considered an inappropriate approach to child-rearing because it negatively impacts a child's self-esteem, social compe tence, and happiness (Joseph and John 2008). Therefore, the film can act as a critique of parenting styles signaling the "right way" to parent and capitalizes on the changing parent ing dynamics apparent in society.

Popular culture, such as the superhero genre, emphasizes the shifting attitudes in society to absent and permissive fathers (Fogel 2012; McSweeney 2018). For instance, in *Guardians of the Galaxy Vol. 2* (2017), it is unveiled that Peter Quill's long-absent father, the celestial entity Ego, is alive, but his sole interest lies in enlisting Quill to aid in "galactic genocide," regard less of Quill's sentiments on the matter. Upon discovering Ego's culpability in his mother's demise, Quill battles Ego, symbolizing the son overcoming the malevolent father (Phillips 2021, 92). Consequently, the superhero narrative not only redefines the moral dimension of respecting authority, emphasizing respect rather than sheer power is key (Haidt 2007), but also aligns with society's inclination to interrogate patriarchal dominance (Phillips 2021). Moreover, the confrontation between father and son reinforces fundamental moral distinc tions between right and wrong, good and evil, while providing insight into the notion of ideal fatherhood. The defeat of Ego stresses the value of Yondu, Quill's surrogate father. Unlike Ego, Yondu sought to safeguard Quill, was "soft" on him, and ultimately displayed a willingness to sacrifice himself for the Guardians (Brammer 2020; Koh 2022). As Kendall R. Phillips (2021) contends, Yondu stands in stark contrast to Ego, embodying the archetype of a good father.

Mark T. Morman and Kory Floyd assert that narratives concerning fathers have shifted from solely depicting "authoritarian, emotionally detached fathers... towards the involved, nurturing father" (2002, 39). The portrayal of the involved, nurturing father assumes particular significance when examining the dynamics between fathers and their daughters. Traditionally, films focusing on the father-daughter relationship call attention to the "father's investment in his daughter's life," positioning him as both "confidante and protector" (Jenkins 2015, 18). Typically, the father adopts an overprotective stance, often to the daughter's consternation (McSweeney 2018). Within the MCU, such a paternal approach is exemplified in the conduct of Scott Lang in *Ant-Man: Quantumania* (2023). Having missed five formative years of his daughter Cassie's life due to the snap of *Avengers: Infinity War* (2018), Scott grapples with striking a balance between acknowledging Cassie's newfound independence and his inclination to exert influence over her choices. His tendency toward overbearing behavior becomes an enduring source of conflict, necessitating a negotiation of roles within their relationship to prevent Cassie from feeling infantilized. In grappling with the terms of their relationship, Cassie is able to develop into a strong, independent woman, which is an expectation of female characters in superhero offerings (Nairn 2022) and can indicate how a 'good' father should act toward his daughter.

A comparable scenario unfolds in the original *Ant-Man* (2015) film concerning the relationship between Hope and her father, Hank Pym. Here, Hope harbors resentment toward her father, attributing to him the loss of her mother causing a strained dynamic between them (McSweeney 2018). Despite possessing attributes typically associated with male superheroes – intelligence, determination, strength (Jenkins 2015; Yogerst 2017) – Hope finds herself relegated to a subordinate role until she assumes the mantle of the Wasp. Hank's decision to enlist Lang to follow in his footsteps as the next Ant-Man is motivated by a desire to ensure Hope's safety and well-being. However, this narrative inadvertently perpetuates the notion that females, regardless of their capabilities, exist as auxiliaries to their male counterparts rather than able to take on active roles in their own right (Brown 2020; McSweeney 2018). The depiction of Hope and her father emphasizes the broader societal belief that the stories of fathers and their daughters are less about continuing their fathers' legacies and more about their struggle to define their place, particularly within a genre traditionally oriented toward male audiences (Brown 2016, 2020; McSweeney 2018).

Female characters are often sidelined or excluded in superhero narratives, with male characters and their experiences often given priority. Such focus reflects the broader gender biases of the genre (Brown 2020; McSweeney 2018) and is typified in the treatment of mothers across the MCU. Mothers in superhero narratives are often portrayed as repressed figures tied to the family, with less agency and narrative presence compared to fathers (Hodo 2015; Jenkins 2015). For example, across the MCU, the mother figures of Frigga, Maria Stark, Ying Li, Meredith Quill, Ramonda, Wanda Maximoff, and Aunt May all die. More often than not, their deaths function as motivations for their superhero children's actions (Brown 2020), and as Brandi Hodo argues, such treatment "reinforces the idea that heroism is masculine in nature" (2015, 126) and whether intentionally or not, implies, according to Jenkins, that mothers are then presented "as considerably less interesting characters than their husbands" (2015, 83). In fact, even when mothers are present, they embody stereotypically feminine traits such as being caring, nurturing, and diplomatic and are less inclined to act as mentors to their superhero offspring (Brown 2020; Hodo 2015). For example, in the *Hawkeye* (2021) series, it is Clint Barton who takes Kate Bishop under his wing and works with her to develop her talents and skills with a bow rather than her mother, who we later find out is a criminal. Although much has been written on the treatment of women in superhero offerings (see Nairn 2022), what is clear in the absence and deaths of mother figures is that the MCU prescribes to what Terence McSweeney describes as "the exclusion of females from popular narratives" (2018, 110).

Moving toward the Found Family

Media depictions of families have long advocated for the traditional, "nuclear family of two opposite sex parents and their children" (Fogel 2012, 3). By valorizing what was deemed the "right" kind of family, the media has contributed to shaping understandings of ideal families, essentially instructing audiences on what constitutes the natural and normalized family at the expense of alternatives (Berghahn 2013; Fogel 2012; Koh 2022; Hanley 2023). In the MCU, this "right" family is seen in the portrayal of Clint Barton's family dynamic or Wanda Maximoff's faux family in *Wandavision* (2021), but for the most part, the MCU challenges representations of families, offering new and more realistic depictions of what is observable in contemporary society (Beail 2023; Brammer 2020; Hanley 2023). For example, in *Ms Marvel* (2022), audiences are introduced to a Muslim family, in *The Eternals* (2021), a gay couple is seen raising their children, and in *Black Widow* (2021) the audience sees how a politically forged group of spies and assassins can develop "affection, attachment and love" (Killian 2022, 111) mimicking the family institution. Accordingly, the MCU "supports the possibility of diverse and chosen families" (Beail 2023, 204), which are important for audiences to be exposed to because such depictions "can affect expectations and beliefs regarding the perception of real-life families" (Fogel 2012, 8).

Perhaps, the most obvious challenge to the nuclear family offered in the MCU is in the depictions of both the Avengers and Guardians of the Galaxy. In both groups, the found family emerges where disparate people come together, forge connections, and establish a sense of belonging. That is, even though they might have other kinship ties, these superheroes, by working together, develop "the reciprocal sense of commitment, sharing, cooperation, and intimacy" (Fogel 2012, 10–11) commonly seen in traditional families. Although Wilson Koh contends that the Avengers are not a family, but more akin to "friends from work" (2022, 41), the reality is that this assemblage of superheroes is "a fully-fledged family. They have disputes, they love one another, they come together even as they have been thrust apart due to situational conflicts. They use the language of familial relationships" (Hanley 2023, 283). Therefore, the key to the Avengers is what Jennifer Fogel considers "emotional and psychological security and fellowship that a family can and should provide" (2012, 12). They function as a group of people who have developed strong ties and a commitment to caring for one another.

In essence, the chosen family that is exhibited by the members of the Avengers highlights the moral dimensions of in-group loyalty where trust and cooperation are preferred, and individuals are willing to sacrifice for their in-group (Haidt and Graham 2007). For example, when Natasha Romanoff (Black Widow) sacrifices her life to retrieve the soul stone in *Avengers Endgame*, she does so out of love and protection of her fellow Avengers, her chosen family. Her act, and the sorrow felt by the remaining team members, speaks of a deep relationship between this group of people that has built and intensified over time, and as Hanley (2023) contends, such superhero narratives as that posed across the Avengers films, typify why more emphasis needs to be placed on family assemblages in popular culture to circumvent outdated familial ideologies.

Equally, much like traditional families can influence the moral development of individuals through socialization, so can their found families shape the attitudes and behaviors of super-heroes (Berghahn 2013). Through socialization, individuals learn right and wrong, good and bad and these commonalities become shared by the members of the family helping to forge collective beliefs while cementing relationships (Yogerst 2017). Yet, as Jonathan Haidt and Jesse Graham (2007) suggest, adhering to the authority and the needs of the family can and does constrain individuals with condemnation experienced by those who diverge from familial expectations. For example, Tony Stark and Steve Rogers (Captain America) disagree on the signing of the Sokovia Accords in *Captain America: Civil War* (2016) because of their opposing views on the moral dimension of authority. Thir contrary views lead to con-flict and tension within the Avengers family. As McManus et al. (2021) attest, privileging personal needs or the needs of others at the expense of one's family is perceived to be trans-gressive and less moral, accounting for why Rogers is forced onto the run after disagreeing with Stark, which suggests that even though the MCU challenges familial makeup, it does still project adherence to privileging the moral obligations of family.

Much like the Avengers, the Guardians of the Galaxy serve as both a reflection of and a challenge to societal norms surrounding the concept of family, particularly by acknowledging the inclusion of non-human entities within familial dynamics (Hanley 2023). At the heart of the Guardians' familial unit are Rocket, a genetically modified raccoon, and Groot, a sentient tree, who assume integral roles within the group. The dynamic of the group mirrors what can be expected of families. The "siblings," Rocket and Peter Quill often engage in banter and squabbles. Moreover, Quill takes on a parental role, guiding and nurturing Groot as the latter progresses from infancy to adolescence. Additionally, Gamora's presence within the group extends beyond being Quill's love interest; she also assumes a maternal role, offering guidance and support to her fellow Guardians (Brammer 2020; McSweeney 2018). Moreo-ver, the Guardians' constant traversal of the galactic road and their reliance on one another for support and companionship align with the migratory drives and non-traditional family structures prevalent among millennial audiences (Koh 2022). Through their shared experi-ences and the challenges that they face together, the Guardians embody the millennial ethos of adaptability, resilience, and choice-driven kinship. This narrative resonance with millennial lifestyle choices, coupled with the Guardians' can-do attitude and rejection of conventional norms, contributes to their enduring popularity among contemporary audiences, making them a compelling and aspirational template for familial bonds in the modern era (Koh 2022). They also reinforce that "overall, Marvel Cinema embraces a strikingly pluralistic approach to the concept of family" (Hanley 2023, 279), and that there is no "right" type of family in the 21st century but rather amalgamations of "working mothers, single parenthood, blended and adoptive families, even revised articulations of the married couple" (Fogel 2012, 51).

Sibling Rivalries

Widespread across various film genres is the exploration of sibling relationships (Barnett 2022). Reflecting the intricacies of societal dynamics, popular culture inevitably delves into the complex and multifaceted bonds among siblings, influenced by factors such as birth order, parental dynamics, and individual personalities, which give rise to narratives of both support and conflict (Barnett 2022; Salmon and Hehman 2014; White and Hughes 2017). As noted by Laurie Kramer and Lew Bank, "the sibling realm offers a pivotal perspective for comprehending how children's interactions with their brothers and sisters may forecast variations in individual well-being and adaptation spanning childhood, adolescence, and well into adulthood" (2005, 43). Therefore, it is hardly surprising that the MCU features numerous sibling relationships, some characterized by mutual support and appreciation, while others are marked by recurrent attempts at fratricide.

Irrespective of whether sibling relationships are harmonious or contentious, what remains evident is the prevalence of conflict and rivalry within them, particularly in response to parental attention and resource allocation (Barnett 2022; Salmon and Hehman 2014; White and Hughes 2017). Siblings are acutely attuned to discerning disparities in parental treatment, often leading to complex emotions of envy, jealousy, comparison, and competitiveness (White and Hughes 2017). A poignant example of such competition for parental favoritism is in the dynamic between Nebula and Gamora. Their adoptive father, Thanos, habitually instigates rivalry between his two daughters, favoring Gamora to the chagrin of Nebula. This manipulation engenders a toxic sibling dynamic, wherein both siblings are willing to resort to lethal measures against each other. It is only when they confront each other in *Guardians of the Galaxy Vol. 2* that they realize their shared adversary is, in fact, their father, leading to a reconciliation where they recognize their common bond as sisters without animosity (Brammer 2020). Their experience shows the significant role that siblings play in shaping moral and personal identity formation (Barnett 2022). According to Katie Barnett, sibling influence can positively contribute to "socioemotional development" (2022, 846), as sibling rivalry, while initially disruptive, may prompt the development of coping mechanisms and, in certain cases, foster a "constructive sense of self" (Chen and Wang 2021, 127). However, it is imperative to acknowledge that not all sibling rivalries lead to positive outcomes, and through the portrayal of diverse sibling dynamics on screen, audiences are allowed to discern between those that are beneficial and those that are detrimental.

The sibling dynamics portrayed in the MCU also serve as vehicles for exploring moral concepts and values. Through the depiction of two siblings diametrically opposed in character, the superhero narrative can present a commentary on the dichotomy between goodness and malevolence. Siblings, often raised in similar domestic environments, can offer contrasting responses to their upbringing, providing insight into what defines morality and immorality. In the case of Thor and Loki, despite both growing up together in Asgaard, their paths diverge significantly (Brammer 2020). While Thor evolves into a virtuous defender of his people, embodying traits of a traditional superhero characterized by strength, altruism, and conformity to societal norms (Godfrey 2020; Yogerst 2017), Loki (for much of his time in the MCU) adopts a villainous persona, prioritizing his own desires over the welfare of others. Unlike Thor, whose actions align with super heroic ideals such as protection, selflessness, and generosity (Borgstrand and Jasper 2018; Yogerst 2017), Loki exhibits behaviors associated with villainy, including bullying, domination, and exploitation of the vulnerable (Benton 2020; Bergstrand and Jasper 2018). His lack of empathy and propensity for manipulation (at least in his early role in the MCU) highlights his immoral disposition, contrasting sharply with Thor's morally upright stance. Thus, the contrasting behaviors of Thor and Loki exemplify how sibling relationships can communicate divergent ideals surrounding morality and immorality within the MCU narrative.

Contrasted with the fraught and unhealthy dynamics of relationships such as that between Gamora and Nebula, and Thor and Loki, are the portrayals of sibling bonds between characters like T'Challa and his sister Shuri (*Black Panther*), Kamala and her brother Aamir (*Ms Marvel*), Wanda and Pietro (*Avengers: Age of* Ultron [2015]), and even Natasha and Yelena (*Black Widow*). These sibling pairs, while also experiencing typical sibling banter and rivalry, present alternative perspectives on sibling relationships. For instance, in *Ms Marvel*, Kamala and Aamir exhibit genuine love and mutual respect, collaborating to confront threats to their community, thereby bolstering each other's confidence. Such supportive sibling connections have been shown to correlate with reduced anxiety and enhanced maturity (Chen and Wang 2021; Godfrey 2020). Similarly, although not bound by biological ties, the relationship between Natasha and Yelena exemplifies a sisterly bond founded on loyalty, self-sacrifice, and eventually, mutual esteem. This portrayal underscores the notion that the MCU not only provides a diverse array of family dynamics but also offers nuanced representations of sibling relationships, showcasing their multifaceted nature.

Conclusion

In summary, the superhero genre stands as a fertile ground for the examination of themes surrounding family dynamics and moral constructs. Traditionally, superhero narratives have revolved around the obligation of protagonists to confront malevolent forces that disrupt societal harmony, which often draws upon the protagonists' familial backgrounds as integral elements in their character development (Jenkins 2015). Additionally, superheroes are depicted as emblematic representations of various human virtues and characteristics, evolving in tandem with the genre's evolution. Thus, the realism within the fantastical realm of superheroes shows the genre's capacity to resonate with real-life experiences and ethical quandaries (Koh 2022). Coupled with the fact that the popularity of the superhero genre leads to global impact and reach, the messages of morality and familial relationships could influence audience attitudes and behaviors as they seek to emulate the aspirational identities of their superhero role-models (Brown 2016).

The portrayal of family within superhero narratives is notably nuanced, challenging conventional paradigms while showcasing the dynamic evolution of familial relationships. The MCU's embrace of a pluralistic approach to family representation reflects the diverse array of familial structures and dynamics prevalent in contemporary society (Hanley 2023). The concept of family assemblage, epitomized by the likes of the Avengers, accentuates the notion that familial bonds transcend biological lineage, encompassing chosen relationships forged through shared experiences and mutual support. This inclusive portrayal of family configurations serves to normalize the diverse tapestry of familial connections, shedding light on the intricate interplay within intrafamily relationships. Admittedly, it was outside the scope of this chapter to explore the romantic relationships that are also considered key to family dynamics. However, key to this chapter is that the MCU is considered to proffer varied family formations and as the genre evolves, so too will the messages associated with family dynamics.

In essence, the superhero genre provides an immersive platform for the exploration of the intricate interplay between familial dynamics and moral imperatives. Through the depiction of varied familial relationships and the navigation of complex moral dilemmas, superhero narratives can prompt audiences to contemplate the essence of morality, the significance of familial bonds, and the enduring allure of protagonists who, despite their flaws, embody virtuous ideals.

References

Allison, Scott T., and George R. Goethals. 2011. *Heroes: What They Do & Why We Need Them*. Oxford.

Balaev, Michelle. 2008. "Trends in Literary Trauma Theory." *Mosaic: An Interdisciplinary Critical Journal* 41, no. 2: 149–166.

Banerjee, Koel, and Rachel Schaff. 2022. "Nothing Else Besides a Father: Logan and the Paternal Melodrama." *Screen* 63, no. 3: 367–385.

Barnett, Katie. 2022. "'If Ever There Was Someone to Keep Me at Home': Theorizing Screen Representations of Siblinghood Through a Case Study of Into the Wild (2007)." *Quarterly Review of Film and Video* 39, no. 4: 842–866.

Beail, Linda. 2023. "Wrestling with Power and Pleasure: Black Widow and the Warrior Women of the Marvel Cinematic Universe." In *The Politics of the Marvel Cinematic Universe*, edited by Nicholas Carnes and Lilly J. Goren. University Press of Kansas.

Benton, Darius. 2020. "Hero or Villain? Character and Content Analysis of Erik Killmonger in Black Panther." *Florida Communication Journal* 48, no. 2: 183–207.

Berghahn, Daniela. 2013. *Far-Flung Families in Film: The Diasporic Family in Contemporary European Cinema*. Edinburgh University Press.

Bergstrand, Kelly, and James M. Jasper. 2018. "Villains, Victims, and Heroes in Character Theory and Affect Control Theory." *Social Psychology Quarterly* 81, no. 3: 228–247.

Brammer, Rebekah. 2020. "Family Values: Forging Bonds in the Guardians of the Galaxy Films." *Screen Education* 96: 56–65.

Brown, Jeffrey A. 2016. *The Modern Superhero in Film and Television: Popular Genre and American Culture*. Routledge.

Brown, Jeffrey A. 2020. "Marriage, Domesticity and Superheroes (for Better or Worse)." In *The Routledge Companion to Gender and Sexuality in Comic Book Studies*, edited by Fredrick Luis Aldama. Routledge.

Bucciferro, Claudia. 2021. "Representations of Gender and Race in Ryan Coogler's Film Black Panther: Disrupting Hollywood Tropes." *Critical Studies in Media Communication* 38, no. 2: 169–182.

Chen, Pei-Hua, and Ya-Huei Wang. 2021. "The Transition to Siblinghood: Psycho-Social Perspectives on Tom McGrath's The Boss Baby." *Humanities, Arts and Social Sciences* 21, no. 1: 121–130.

Duggan, Jennifer. 2016. "Traumatic Origins: Orphanhood and the Superhero." In *Good Grief! Children and Comics*, edited by Michelle Ann Abate and Joe Sutliff Sanders. The Ohio State University.

Earle, Harriet E.H. 2017. *Comics, Trauma, and the New Art of War*. University Press of Mississippi.

Fogel, Jennifer M. 2012. "A Modern Family: The Performance of 'Family' and Familialism in Contemporary Television Series." PhD dissertation. University of Michigan.

Godfrey, Rayna Vaught. 2020. "Sibling Grief and Complex Relationships: Thor and the Death of Loki." In *Superhero Grief*, edited by Jill A. Harrington and Robert A Neimeyer. Routledge.

Haidt, Jonathan. 2007. "The New Synthesis in Moral Psychology." *Science* 316, no. 5827: 998–1002.

Haidt, Jonathan, and Jesse Graham. 2007. "When Morality Opposes Justice: Conservatives Have Moral Intuitions That Liberals May Not Recognize." *Social Justice Research* 20, no. 1: 98–116.

Hanley, Danielle. 2023. "Avengers Assemblage." In *The Politics of the Marvel Cinematic Universe*, edited by Nicholas Carnes and Lilly J. Goren. University Press of Kansas.

Helvie, Forrest C. 2012. "The Loss of the Father: Trauma Theory and the Birth of Spider-Man." In *Web-Spinning Heroics: Critical Essays on the History and Meaning of Spider-Man*, edited by Robert Moses Peaslee and Robert G. Weiner. McFarland & Company.

Hodo, Brandi. 2015. "Battles of Family, Freedom and Femininity: Portrayals of Gender in Marvel's Civil War." In *Marvel Comics' Civil War and the Age of Terror*, edited by Kevin Michael Scott. McFarland & Company.

Jenkins, Claire. 2015. *Home Movies: The American Family in Contemporary Hollywood Cinema*. I.B. Tauris.

Joseph, Mary Venus, and Jilly John. 2008. "Impact of Parenting Styles on Child Development." *Global Academic Society Journal": Social Science Insight* 1, no. 5: 16–25.

Killian, Kyle D. 2022. "An Analysis of Black Widow (2021): Marvel's Most Feminist Film Features Powerful Sisters and an Attenuated Male Gaze." *Journal of Feminist Family Therapy* 35, no. 1: 106–113.

Koh, Wilson. 2022. "More Than Friends from Work: The Guardians of the Galaxy, Families, and Resilient Placemaking for Millennials." *The Journal of Popular Culture* 55, no. 1: 36–55.

Kramer, Laurie, and Lew Bank. 2005. "Sibling Relationship Contributions to Individual and Family Well-being: Introduction to the Special Issue." *Journal of Family Psychology* 19, no. 4: 483–485.

McManus, Ryan M., Jordyn E. Mason, and Liane Young. 2021. "Re-examining the Role of Family Relationships in Structuring Perceived Helping Obligations, and their Impact on Moral Evaluation." *Journal of Experimental Social Psychology* 96: 1041842.

McSweeney, Terence. 2018. *Avengers Assemble: Critical Perspectives on the Marvel Cinematic Universe*. Wallflower Press.

Morman, Mark T., and Kory Floyd. 2002. "A 'Changing Culture of Fatherhood': Effects on Affectionate Communication, Closeness, and Satisfaction in Men's Relationships with their Fathers and their Sons." *Western Journal of Communication* 66, no. 4: 395–411.

Nairn, Angelique. 2022. "Super-heroine Objectification: The Sexualization of Black Widow Across Comic and Film Adaptations." In *The Superhero Multiverse: Readapting Comic Books Icons in Twenty-First-Century Film and Popular Culture*, edited by Lorna Piatti-Farnell. Lexington.

Phillips, Kendall R. 2021. *A Cinema of Hopelessness: The Rhetoric of Rage in 21st Century Popular Culture*. Palgrave Macmillan.

Reynolds, Richard. 1992. *Superheroes: A Modern Mythology*. University Press of Mississippi.

Salmon Catherine, A., and Jessica A. Hehman. 2014. "The Evolutionary Psychology of Sibling Conflict and Siblicide." In *The Evolution of Violence*, edited by Todd K. Shackelford and Ranald D. Hansen. Springer.

Tapia, Mike, Leanne Fiftal Alarid, and Courtney Clare. 2018. "Parenting Styles and Juvenile Delinquency: Exploring Gendered Relationships." *Juvenile and Family Court Journal* 69, no. 2: 21–36.

White, Naomi, and Claire Hughes. 2017. *Why Siblings Matter: The Role of Brother and Sister Relationships in Development and Well-Being*. Routledge.

Yogerst, Chris. 2017. "Superhero Films: A Fascist National Complex or Exemplars of Moral Virtue?" *Journal of Religion & Film* 21, no. 1: 1–34.

34

WHEN THE GODS WALK AMONG US

Superheroes as Dangerous Divinities

Matthew Brake

Superheroes are often described as gods. In Zack Snyder's films, for instance, Superman is spoken of as a god by Lex Luthor in *Batman v. Superman: Dawn of Justice* (2016). Luthor argues that g/God cannot be both all-good and all-powerful. In Amazon Prime's *The Boys* (2019–), the character Homelander refers to superheroes as "wrathful gods" (Stein 2024). They are the superhuman figures in stories about heroic journeys, trials, and battles between good and evil. These stories serve to entertain and inspire their audiences. Fans are drawn to these stories of extraordinary figures, who live among normal humans. But having the gods walk among humanity doesn't always lead to heaven on Earth. If superheroes are the gods, then they may be dangerous for the denizens of their storyworlds. In fact, many superhero stories illustrate this very danger.

In this essay, I will consider the ways in which superhero narratives reveal the dangerous aspect of divinity and the sacred. I will do so by examining Alan Moore's run on *Miracleman* (1982–), his limited series *Watchmen* (1986–1987), Mark Waid's four-issue mini-series *Kingdom Come* (1996), and Mark Millar's crossover event *Civil War* (2006–2007). If superheroes are gods, then these stories show readers and viewers the dangers that can be unleashed when the gods get too close to humanity.

I will explicate this point by putting these stories into dialogue with three different thinkers who explore the meaning of the sacred. The first of these is Rudolf Otto, who explores the meaning of the sacred in his *The Idea of the Holy* (1917). Next in my analysis, I will examine the phenomenon of 'shamanism' with the assistance of Thomas DuBois. Finally, I will rely on the work of René Girard whose theories about religion, violence, and scapegoating are explored in works such as *Violence and the Sacred* (1977).

Rudolf Otto and the Numinous Superhero

Otto, like many scholars who helped shape the modern field of religious studies in the late 19th and early 20th centuries, sought to boil religion down to its fundamental essence. What is the "thing" about religion that makes it "religion"; and not, let's say, "economics," or "sociology," or "political science." As J.Z. Smith (1998) has pointed out, ideas about what religion "is" can change from one scholar to another. For every 50 scholars of religion, one

DOI: 10.4324/9781003366911-39

could find 50 definitions trying to define exactly what religion "is," and each definition may indeed contain some analytical value for analyzing the human phenomenon called "religion" (Smith 1998, 281–282). For Otto, the fundamental seed of religion is something he calls "the holy." To speak of the holy is not to speak in moral terms, but in terms of a religious experience, so to avoid confusion, he chooses instead to use the term "the numinous." The "deeply-felt religious experience" of the numinous is "the real innermost core" of religion as a whole (Otto 1958, 5–8). For Otto, all religions find their origin in this felt experience.

Otto uses the phrase "mysterium tremendum" or "aweful mystery" to describe the experience of the numinous feeling. It is fascinating and dreadful, stupefying and horrifying, gentle and wrathful (Otto 1958, 12–13, 18, 26, 31). Otto uses all of these dichotomous descriptions as analogies to attempt to put the ambiguous nature of the numinous feeling into words. This overpowering feeling, which is "felt as objective and outside the self," is accompanied by a second feeling on the part of human being, which Otto calls "creature-feeling" (10). This is the "feeling-response" to the numinous where the human being experiences "submergence into nothingness before an overpowering, absolute might of some kind …. The presence of that which is a *mystery* inexpressible above all creatures" (13). Merold Westphal says that these feelings "are based on a sense of the presence of something that is more real than I myself and the world of my immediate experience" (Westphal 1984, 27). In superhero stories, superheroes have a numinous presence. Non-superpowered characters within superhero stories often experience this numinous presence first-hand.

In Alan Moore's *Watchmen* (1986–1987), Dr. Manhattan is spoken about in divine terms. In the backmatter of issue #4 (1986), Professor Milton Glass discusses the impact of Dr. Manhattan's impact on the world. Glass notes that the media had previously misquoted him as saying, "The superman exists and he's American," when in fact what he said was, "*God* exists and he's American" (Moore and Gibbons 1986b, 31). He isn't the only one to describe Manhattan in divine terms. Janey Slater, Manhattan's ex-girlfriend, feels uneasy around him, saying, "They say you're like a god now" (11). And Manhattan is experienced as a god, not just because of his incredible powers, but because of how people encounter him.

In the first panel of issue #4 (1986) when Manhattan appears, the expressions on the faces of his friends and colleagues are a mixture of terror and awe at this being walking among them. The expressions on the faces of his colleagues oscillate between "stupor," which "signifies blank wonder, an astonishment that strikes us dumb, amazement absolute," and the "grisly horror and shuddering" of religion's "peculiar dread" (Otto 1958, 26, 13). In issue #3 (1986) of *Watchmen*, Hollis Mason discusses Dr. Manhattan and the "unease" that his presence has evoked along with "elation… as if Santa Claus had suddenly turned out to be real after all" (Moore and Gibbons 1986a, 31). However, this elation is combined with "a terrible and uneven sense of fear and uncertainly" (31). Here we read about both the "excitement" and the "fear" involved in the experience of the numinous divinity (Otto 1958, 12–13). There is a pleasant element to the experience, along with an otherworldly shuddering. One can imagine that this fits the description of the Vietcong's surrender to Dr. Manhattan during the Vietnam War, described in issue #4 (1986) wherein Manhattan says that "their terror" is "balanced by an almost religious awe" (20). There is a word to simplify this experience of mysterious awe and terror: the numinous.

The fear people have is not without warrant. It is dangerous to get too close to the numinous. While the numinous can be experienced as pleasant and gentle, like Manhattan's kisses and caresses to Janey and Silk Spectre, the numinous can also be experienced as "wrath." Otto wants to be clear, though, that this wrath is not experienced because of moral transgression. In fact, the experience of wrath is only attributed to moral failing after the fact. Rather, Otto says, it is "'like a hidden force of nature', like stored-up electricity, discharging itself upon anyone who comes too near" in an almost "arbitrary" way (Otto 1958, 18). Manhattan's moral aloofness, a product of his growing more and more distant from humanity, puts him well in line with Otto's understanding of the numinous. Manhattan is less of a moral judge and more of a force of nature; he is just as indifferent as the forces of nature he admires. But getting close to a force of nature can be dangerous, like the electricity that Otto mentions. The Bible itself mentions a man named Uzzah in 2 Sam. 6:1–11. He is one of the people helping to bring the holy Ark of the Covenant into Jerusalem on a cart. At one point, the Ark begins to slip; Uzzah reaches out to steady it and he drops dead. This wasn't because of any moral failing but because being around the numinous can be dangerous. Likewise, when Dr. Manhattan is being interviewed on television in issue #3 (1986), he is ambushed by accusations of causing cancer to his friends and colleagues. As he tries to leave, he is swamped by the press, who crowd him until he acts out, teleporting them all away (a process that has been shown to negatively affect some people's hearts in issue #4). Manhattan does this not with any intentionality; he is just a force of nature acting out, and the press, like Uzzah, forgot that they were dealing with live electricity.

The numinous nature of superheroes can be seen even more clearly in Alan Moore's earlier work, *Miracleman* (1982–). In Moore's run (1982–1989), the titular character is often experienced by others in numinous terms. When Miracleman reveals to his wife Liz that he is a superhero, the text says that she is filled with both fear and wonder (Moore and Leach 2014, 29). Later, the two of them make love, and when Liz wakes up, Moore describes the experience, saying that "her skin remembers a touch that crackled like bare wires" (again one sees the electricity imagery of the numinous) and "her eyes remember his eerie, phosphorescent gaze" (30). As she gets up from the bed, she attempts to re-ground herself in the ordinary world: "She walks from the bedroom to the lounge, drifting, small feet silent on thick carpet... pausing, she touches things... Touching, she re-establishes contact with the world, slowly retrieving her sense of... reality (30)." This scene is not dissimilar from Otto's description of what it is like to "come down" from a numinous experience:

> The feeling of it may at times come sweeping like a gentle tide, pervading the mind with a tranquil mood of deepest worship. It may come to pass over into a more set and lasting attitude of the soul, continuing, as it were, thrillingly vibrant and resonant, until at last it dies away and the soul resumes its 'profane', non-religious mood of everyday experience.
>
> *(Otto 1958, 12)*

In an encounter with the numinous, one may need to re-ground themselves in ordinary life, especially after experiencing a presence that makes them feel like they have encountered something from another world.

Encountering a numinous presence from out of this world can be dangerous. In the world of Miracleman, it can be as gentle as Miracleman's "tinkerbell effect" as his wife calls it (Moore and Leach 2014, 52), but it can also be experienced as something horrifying and dangerous. When Mike Moran first transforms into Miracleman while being held at gunpoint, the sudden transformation burns and blinds the nearby gunman. There is no intent here on the part of Miracleman to harm the gunman (at least, not directly through his transformation), but it is simply the sudden outburst of the power itself. A person who viewed

Miracleman as a god could certainly look back at this moment and interpret this display of power and the resultant injury as a form of this god's "wrath" against the assailant. But this particular injury is not a result of any moral judgment. It is a seemingly arbitrary injury caused by the wild power of the numinous. This injury could have happened to anyone, even Miracleman's wife if she had been standing there. Like Uzzah in the Bible, being too close to the numinous presence can be dangerous simply because of its nature. A person might just be in the wrong place at the wrong time.

Between Two Worlds: Mediating Superhuman Powers

Humans are fragile creatures. As Otto points out, an encounter with the numinous leaves human beings feeling "submerged," as if they are nothing by comparison (Otto 1958, 10). The numinous, like the superhero, can easily overwhelm and harm the world of ordinary human beings. Bringing them into close proximity can be dangerous (for humans). Another biblical passage highlighting this danger is found in Exod. 19:16–19, 21–22 (NRSV), which describes the "thunder, lightning, and … thick cloud on [Mount Sinai]" as the Lord descends to meet with Israel. The text describes the terror of the people as the lightning flashes, as smoke rises from the mountain, and God answers in thunder and "a very loud blast of a horn" while the mountain shakes violently. The terror of the divine moment is further enforced when God tells Moses,

> Go down and warn the people not to break through to try to see the Lord, or many of them will fall dead. Even the priests who come near to the Lord must keep themselves holy, or the Lord will break loose against them.

It can be dangerous to blend the sacred and the profane. Some boundaries are needed, but violating those boundaries can cause a breakout of the dangerous power of the divine. Getting too close to the divine is like getting too close to a lightning storm: a person might get hit by both.

One story that illustrates this point is Marvel's *Civil War* (2006–2007) comic event. When superheroes battle supervillains in places that are cordoned off from a major population zone, the danger to everyday civilians is at a minimum. One thinks of *Avengers: Endgame* (2019) and how the battle between the Avengers and Thanos' forces happens in the middle of nowhere, allowing the film audience to savor and enjoy the mythic battle without worrying about whether any civilians are getting hurt. But in the *Civil War* (2006–2007) comic, tragedy unfolds when a group of young superheroes, the New Warriors, seeking fame on a reality show, confront a group of supervillains in Stamford, Connecticut. Due to their recklessness, their confrontation escalates and leads to an explosion causing the deaths of not only most of the New Warriors themselves, but 600 people, many of whom were children at an elementary school. In a battle of numinous beings, nearby civilians often arbitrarily pay the price when the sacred world of the superhuman mingles with the everyday world of ordinary humans.

This is particularly illustrated by Alan Moore's *Miracleman* (1982–) in the superhuman battles between Miracleman and Johnny Bates, aka, Kid Miracleman. In the final battle between the duo, Bates devastates London, leveling a large portion of the city and brutally slaughtering thousands with all sorts of sadistic torture. The reader sees people with limbs torn off, people skinned alive, and people impaled throughout the city, with Bates at one point raining various body parts down upon the horrified inhabitants below. The mingling of the human and the divine and the blurring of the boundaries between them reap otherworldly horrors on the unsuspecting human population, as if the divine represents forces of nature that were never meant to be unleashed upon the human world.

Michael Nichols has argued that superheroes blur the boundaries between the divine world not only because the world of the sacred comes too close to the human world, but because superheroes are themselves liminal beings that embody both the human and the superhuman within themselves, and this makes them dangerous (Nichols 2021, 66, 72–73). In this way, Nichols compares the superhero to the position of a "shaman" in some cultures, especially inasmuch as they represent those who stand between two different worlds, that of the physical world and that of the spirit world, protecting both, as the superhero might stand between the human and the superhuman worlds, guarding both (Nichols 2021, 18, 35–36). This comparison between shamans and superheroes can be considered problematic for a number of reasons. Foremost, the term "shaman," like "religion," is a blanket term that has been used by scholars to group any number of distinct practices together from different and unrelated parts of the world, which can lead to misunderstanding (DuBois 2009, 3–11; Sidky 2017, 1–19). Nichols himself recognizes that shamanism "as a cross-cultural category may be too amorphous to do anything other than conflate unrelated phenomena and elide crucial practical and theoretical differences," while noting that even if that's the case, "substantive and fascinating commonalities do appear to exist" (Nichols 2021, 26). Thus, he finds that the term remains useful.

While this comparison might seem artificial, Thomas DuBois's discussion of the role that the shaman Thai plays, in mediating between the spirit world and the Hmong people, resonates in comparison to superheroes. Thai is described as a "specialist" whose travels between the visible and the unseen worlds are full of dangers for himself as he seeks to cure and rescue members of his community from illness and various spiritual, physical, and social afflictions. He confronts antagonistic "spirit entities" and he "rescues or recovers fugitive souls that have distanced themselves from their bodies and counters the aggressions of foreign souls that have made incursions on his clients' health or wholeness. He is, in traditional views, *a hero*" (DuBois 2009, 3; emphasis added).

In his role of mediating between the spirit world and physical world, DuBois describes the shaman as a hero, having access to, and standing between, otherworldly forces and his community. And if the shaman is a hero (or superhero), can the superhero be understood as playing the mediating role of the shaman? Creators like Grant Morrison think so, who in their book *Supergods* (2011) says that the superhero is "that bridge between man and the divine," offering the example of Billy Batson, aka Captain Marvel or Shazam, as a type of shaman figure (Morrison 2012, 30–31). In Morrison's *Flex Mentallo*, the protagonist, Wally Sage, attempts to find his secret magic word, seen with missing letters in a crossword puzzle: S-H-A-?-A-?. While comics fans might expect the word to be "SHAZAM," in issue #4, it actually turns out to be "SHAMAN" (Morrison and Quitely 1996, 23). Here again, we see Morrison drawing a comparison between Shazam and shamanism. In Mark Waid and Alex Ross's *Kingdom Come* (1996), Billy does play a mediating role between the human world and the dangerous powers of the superhuman. This story overtly uses a lot of Christian imagery from the book of Revelation, but here I use it heuristically to discuss the mediating role of the shaman as well.

Kingdom Come (1996) tells the story of an amoral future generation of superhumans ten years in the future (from the time of publication) who have become reckless with their powers, fighting each other, not so that good will triumph over evil, but simply to fight, often putting civilians in danger. These are the children and grandchildren of the heroes from the

Justice League, who have left their forebears' code of ethics behind. This is a world where the boundaries between the superhuman and the human have become dangerously blurry, often with destructive and deadly results. Superman, who had gone into retirement, returns in order to try and teach the new generation to live by a code that honors the lives of the humans around them and avoids killing one's enemies. As he tries to do so, Lex Luthor works to undermine Superman's efforts, and he is joined by a mind-controlled Captain Marvel, whose presence and raw power make others uneasy. They perceive him as dangerous. Eventually, the conflict between the human world and the superhuman world reaches its climax. As various factions of superhumans fight in Kansas, which had been violated by nuclear contamination earlier in the story, the United Nations fears that the fighting will overflow from that desolate region and destroy the world. In the face of superhuman destruction, the UN decides to launch a nuclear missile and destroy the superhumans lest they themselves be destroyed by the spreading superhuman violence. While Superman would choose to stop the nuke, he is stopped by a mind-controlled Captain Marvel who is able to block his every move. Superman sees the missile and realizes that his decision to stop it is a choice between humanity and superhumanity. As Superman states, he himself is not a man (implying he is a god), but Billy Batson is both. He is a liminal figure; he has lived in both worlds, and so Superman tells him to choose. Billy detonates the bomb, which kills many of the superhumans, but leaves some alive. By doing so, his actions restore equilibrium between the two worlds and create a path for the future that avoids the overflowing destruction of superhuman conflict.

The shaman, as well, is a liminal figure, serving a mediating function between two very different worlds: the world of the human and the world of the spirits. But this liminal status can be dangerous for the community they are a part of. As Nichols notes:

> The community needs and depends on their ability to mediate with otherworldly powers, but when brought too close into the midst of society, their abilities can create the very chaos they seek to dispel. Like an electrical power line, they bring valuable energy, but, if the boundaries or rules are not observed, also harbor the danger of electrocution.
>
> *(Nichols 2021, 84)*

Again, we see this metaphor of electricity being used to describe the sacred powers of the shaman. While the shaman is a helpful figure, he is also a pariah figure "whose presence is both feared and polluting" (DuBois 2009, 63). As DuBois explains:

> The same confidence in supernatural abilities that made the shaman a valued member of a family, village, or locale could also lead to a nagging distrust of the shaman – or other community members – as potential spiritual aggressors. In a world in which the overall quality of luck was regarded as severely limited, and in which disease and misfortune were regarded as the products of unseen aggression, other people could easily become suspected of performing evil – be it to enemies, to family and neighbors, or to seeming allies. In some traditions, shamans actively attempted to do harm for the sake of gain; in others, shamans with negative intent were categorized as separate from those striving to help others.
>
> *(DuBois 2009, 94–95)*

Like many superhero stories, there is a fear that the "hero" will turn on those he promised to protect, as Johnny Bates does in *Miracleman* (1982–) or as the younger generation of heroes do in *Kingdom Come* (1996). A hero or a shaman may misuse their power, but there is also the danger that they won't be able to control it.

When *Kingdom Come* (1996) begins, Kansas is irradiated when the hero Captain Atom has his containment suit torn open by the villain Parasite. Captain Atom is made of atomic energy held together by a special suit. Part of the reason why his suit is ripped is because of the aggressive and careless way the Parasite was being pursued by the violent next-generation superhero, Magog. Where Superman had cautioned against excessive violence and reckless superheroic action, Magog ignores all such warnings, and his carelessness leads not only to the death of Captain Atom, but to the unleashing of Captain Atom's energy, killing millions and irradiating much of the US's prime farmland. Famine and ecological catastrophes are unleashed because great power requires careful mediation, and when those powers are not carefully controlled, disaster strikes. This is true in *Kingdom Come* (1996) as well as *Civil War* (2006–2007). Like DuBois notes,

> The element of fear in the relationship between a shaman and helping spirits can be powerful: the shaman must be careful to maintain the upper hand with the spirits, lest they come to dominate the relationship to the detriment of all.
>
> *(DuBois 2009, 96)*

A lack of ability by the shaman can lead "to the dominance of the spirits [which results] in unbridled aggression toward other community members" (96). Indeed, like the numinous that Otto describes, the spirits, too, can be experienced ambiguously, since they are "capable of doing either good or ill," hence the need for "the shaman to harness their powers for the advantage of the community" (96). The outcome can be beneficial and pleasant, or it can be dangerous and horrifying. Either way, it is probably better to keep one's distance from such unpredictable forces and those who may control them.

Part of the issue that drives some of the fear in shamanism is the blurring of the boundaries between two realms, which are otherwise separate. According to René Girard, the fear of loss of distinctions in the world and in society is indicative of a breakdown in social order. For Girard, many of our religious and theological systems exist as a means of keeping violence in check by maintaining societal distinctions, distinctions that the presence of a god puts in jeopardy.

René Girard, Social Distinctions, and the Dangerous Prize of Divinity

Like Otto, Girard has his own ideas about what the core of religion consists of. In his work, *Violence and the Sacred* (1977), he argues that the quintessential core of religion is found in the practice of ritual sacrifice. Religion, far from being about "another world," serves a practical social function, originating from some original moment of violence that morphs into the practice of sacrifice (Girard 1977, 14, 32). For Girard, violence can be like an overflowing river (10). Tensions build up in a society based on personal slights, jealousies, and other forms of conflict, and without some kind of outlet, violence can erupt, creating a tit-for-tat back-and-forth of violence and vengeful reprisals that destroys a community (14–15). These reprisals will continue unabated until either one side is completely eliminated, or both parties redirect their violence to some sort of scapegoat who everyone can blame for the conflict (7–8, 12–13,

26). Sacrifice is a reenactment of this moment that almost tore society apart, which is then ritualized and reinterpreted so that the original act of violence is forgotten (84, 92, 167). Instead, sacrifice is given a "theological" or mythological interpretation; it is not humans who need an outlet for their violence, but it is the god or gods who demand it. As long as society remains "tricked" by this explanation, sacrifice can serve its purpose to keep violence in check and everyone in their proper place (7, 24, 49).

A sacrificial system can break down, however, if the misinterpretation of sacrificial violence no longer works. Girard refers to this as a "sacrificial crisis," when the community no longer believes in the sacrificial order. The sacrificial rites serve as the bedrock for the social order as a whole. Without it, not only is the distinction between sacred and non-sacred violence eliminated but all other distinctions are eliminated. Girard writes:

> The sacrificial crisis can be defined, therefore, as a crisis of distinctions – that is, a crisis affecting the cultural order. This cultural order is nothing more than a regulated system of distinctions in which the differences among individuals are used to establish their 'identity' and their mutual relationships.
>
> *(Girard 1977, 49)*

As Girard further explains, "Order, peace, and fecundity depend on cultural distinctions; it is not these distinctions but the loss of them that gives birth to fierce rivalries and sets members of the same family or social group at one another's throats" (49). Everyone becomes alike in their violence and the pursuit of their own ends. When people lose their sense of how they relate to each other, they begin to see each other as objects who are merely in the way of getting what they want (51).

This loss of distinctions extends to the differences between the human and the divine, as Girard states: "To think religiously (in the primitive sense) is to see violence as something superhuman, to be kept always at a distance and ultimately renounced" (135). As long as this violent power is revered and seen as the sole domain of the divine, and this reverence is reinforced by ritual sacrifice, then society has a greater chance of remaining stable. However, if "the fearful adoration of this power begins to diminish and all distinctions begin to disappear, the ritual sacrifices lose their force," each member of the community "tries to correct the situation individually, and none succeeds" (135). As such, the social situation breaks down, and with the "withering away of the transcendental influence … there is no longer the slightest difference between a desire to save the city and unbridled ambition, between genuine piety and the desire to claim divine status for oneself" (135).

The divine is dangerous when it is no longer transcendent and mystified, and when the divine becomes immanent and gets too close to the world of humanity, humans will fight for its power. The result is violent competition among those competing for divine power. Returning to *Watchmen* (1986–1987), does this not happen with the appearance of Dr. Manhattan on the world stage? Returning to Professor Glass's commentary in issue #4, "The Gods now walk amongst us, affecting the lives of every man, woman and child on the planet in a direct way rather than through mythology and reassurances of faith" (Moore and Gibbons 1986b, 32). It is the loss of the mythological "shield" that rouses the ambition in the geopolitical forces of the world. In Glass's estimation, Dr. Manhattan has changed the world, "pushing it closer to its eventual destruction" (32). When the divine is de-mystified and the boundaries between it and the human become too thin, humans themselves might forget to give reverence to the power of the divine and the violence it can unleash. Glass criticizes the Nixon administration in his world by noting the following:

> They continually push their unearned advantage until American influence comes uncomfortably close to key areas of Soviet interest. It is as if – with a real live Deity on their side – our leaders have become intoxicated with a heady draught of Omnipotence-by-Association, without realizing just how his very existence has deformed the lives of every living creature on the face of this planet.
>
> *(32)*

Part of the danger of superheroes, particularly when looked upon as gods, is how human beings react to them. When the gods are separate and kept in their proper place of reverence by appropriate boundaries, a sense of equilibrium can be maintained. But if the gods walked among us, it is true that their power would be dangerous and unpredictable, but a potentially worse consequence might be how humans would treat each other as a result of their presence. In the case of *Watchmen* (1986–1987), a rivalry is created between the US and the Soviet Union, the latter of whom longs for the divinity that the US possesses, a striving that leads to the brink of nuclear war. Fortunately for the world, Adrian Veidt creates a fresh lie or "myth" to keep the violence and competition from getting out of hand… at least for a little while, depending on whether Geoff Johns and Gary Frank's *Doomsday Clock* (2017–2019) is canon.

Conclusion

The divine power of gods, spirits, and superhumans can be dangerous and unpredictable. Otto demonstrated that there is an ambiguity to the power of the divine; a power that can be experienced as beautiful and horrifying. One sees this in the stories about Dr. Manhattan and Miracleman. Because of their incredible, overflowing power, both characters create a simultaneous sense of wonder and fear in those who encounter them, even the people that love them. This power of heroes and gods is not to be trifled with or taken lightly. In shamanism, we see that one should not interact lightly with spirit beings, but respect the boundaries and distinctions between the human and spirit worlds. Otherwise, as in the case of *Civil War* (2006–2007), violence could extend past the world of the superhuman, impacting the world of the ordinary human with deadly consequences. When distinctions are not honored, chaos can erupt, as much from human ambition as from the danger of the powers themselves, as one sees in *Watchmen* (1986–1987) between the US and the Soviet Union. The barriers between humans and superhumans are the same way. Superhumans are beautiful and dangerous. Their powers ought not to be taken lightly, because as one sees in *Kingdom Come* (1996), they risk exposing the human world to untold destruction. Perhaps, it is better they are kept at a distance, lest their closeness cause us to not honor such great power, which we know must come with great responsibility.

References

DuBois, Thomas A. 2009. *An Introduction to Shamanism.* Cambridge University Press.
Girard, René. 1977. *Violence and the Sacred.* Translated by Patrick Gregory. The Johns Hopkins University Press.

Mark, Miller, and Steve McNiven. 2006–2007. *Civil War*. Marvel.

Moore, Alan, and Dave Gibbons. 1986a. *Watchmen* #3. DC Comics.

Moore, Alan, and Dave Gibbons. 1986b. *Watchmen* #4. DC Comics.

Moore, Alan, and Garry Leach. 2014. *Miracleman, Book One: A Dream of Flying*. Marvel Comics.

Morrison, Grant. 2012. *Supergods: What Masked Vigilantes, Miraculous Mutants, and a Sun God from Smallville Can Teach Us About Being Human*. Spiegel & Grau.

Morrison, Grant, and Frank Quitely. 1996. *Flex Mentallo* #4. DC Comics.

Nichols, Michael. 2021. *Religion and Myth in the Marvel Cinematic Universe*. McFarland & Company.

Otto, Rudolf. 1958. *The Idea of the Holy*. Translated by John W. Harvey. Oxford University Press.

Sidky, H. 2017. *The Origins of Shamanism, Spirit Beliefs, and Religiosity: A Cognitive Anthropological Perspective*. Lexington Books.

Smith, Johnathan Z. 1998. "Religion, Religions, Religious." In *Critical Terms of Religious Studies*, edited by Mark C. Taylor. The University of Chicago Press.

Stein, Shana, dir. *The Boys*. Season 4, episode 5, "Beware the Jabberwock, My Son." Released on June 27, 2024, on Amazon Prime Video.

Waid, Mark, and Alex Ross. 1996. *Kingdom Come*. DC Comics.

Westphal, Merald. 1984. *God, Guilt, and Death: An Existential Phenomenology of Religion*. Indiana University Press.

35

NOT LIKE THE OTHERS

Catwoman as Transgressive Hero

Cathleen Allyn Conway

Since her debut as "the Cat" in *Batman #1* (1940), Catwoman has been a complex character that troubles ideas of what makes a hero, and to whom. Alternately employed in varying lines of criminalized work such as jewel thief and sex worker, Selina Kyle is an independent, self-sufficient woman with full autonomy and responsibility for her own physical and financial security. As Carolyn Cocca wrote in *Superwomen: Gender, Power, and Representation:*

> The superhero genre in comics, television, and film is among the many areas in our culture that underrepresents women in positions of power, both as real-life creators and as fictional characters. It is a site at which passionate struggles take place over characters and stories in which fans feel enormously invested.
>
> *(Cocca 2016, 1)*

Readers respond to the character of Catwoman in part because she is a complex Other that is deliberately transgressive. In Kristevian terms, she is abject, as she does not respect boundaries, and she maintains a moral ambiguity throughout her appearances (Kristeva 1984), influenced by the cultural mores of the time as well as the creators' intentions and the publishers' editorial brief in response to market feedback. Catwoman continually crosses the line, no matter what the line is.

However, discussing Catwoman in a scholarly context presents a unique challenge in that she has no singular origin story or background: "the lack of a fixed Catwoman identity also makes her subject to the historically situated impulses of those who interpret and desire her" (Wilson 2023, 141). In contrast to Batman in which Bruce Wayne, who watches as his parents are gunned down behind the Monarch movie theater, is raised by his butler in stately Wayne Manor, Catwoman's origin is never set. She is an orphan, she is the daughter of a crime boss, she is the daughter of a Cuban immigrant, she has a sister, she doesn't have a sister; across her various multimodal appearances, Catwoman's life story prior to meeting Batman for the first time is never canonized.

Another issue in dealing with comics is the nature of the medium. The wide scope of comics makes it almost impossible to fully encapsulate a character, especially with the number of continuity shifts and "retcons" ("retroactive continuity," in which previously established

DOI: 10.4324/9781003366911-40

narratives are amended, ignored, or eliminated) that regularly occur. Even their first meeting is unfixed when recounted by Catwoman and Batman themselves. This is evidenced in *Batman Vol. 2: I Am Suicide,* in which Batman and Catwoman argue over how they met (King and Janin 2017, 123). Was it on the boat, as in *Batman #1*? Or did they meet on the street, as in *Batman* #404 (Miller and Mazzucchelli 1987, 13)? As such, there is no one "true" timeline or version of the character.

Additionally, as Catwoman appears across a number of media, it can be argued the comic book version is the "original," but that does not mean it is the most recognizable in the popular imagination, which adds further complexity. Although her history changes as often as her costume, the one consistent characteristic of Catwoman, regardless of the media she appears in, is that she engages audiences. For the purposes of this essay, by necessity, a broad, general view must be taken, as a character as vast as Catwoman's eight decades of multimedia appearances is difficult to scale; however, it offers many opportunities for more in-depth, rigorous investigation into any number of the aspects highlighted herein. The fact there is so much to say about Catwoman, and so much Catwoman to say it about, is in part proof of concept for this thesis.

Missed Representation

The lack of representation of women in comics and their affiliated media means female readers do not have much variety in terms of superheroes to idolize. We as readers are told the default hero, or indeed superhero, "pretty much assumes that the hero in question is male, and white, and heterosexual, and able-bodied" (Cocca 2015); anything else requires qualification. People don't generally feel the need to say "male superheroes" but tend to clarify when they're talking about "female superheroes" or "black superheroes" or "queer superheroes" or "disabled superheroes" (Cocca 2015). As such, identifying Catwoman as a "superhero" becomes an act of transgression in and of itself.

Catwoman is an antihero. She operates according to her own agenda and moral code, which is in conflict with the hero, Batman. And occasionally, Catwoman drifts into her own brand of heroism when protecting Gotham's East End, such as in *Trail of the Catwoman* (2011) or lending assistance to a Birds of Prey mission, such as in *Birds of Prey Vol 1.* (2002), among other activities that serve her purposes. But "although these elements have been characteristic of Catwoman since her first appearance in 1940, the interpretation that the authors and the public have made of them has varied over time" (Rodríguez Moreno 2014, 117). Introduced as a villain, Catwoman has evolved into "a self-sufficient character, intelligent and willing to help the hero in times of need," with "little or nothing to do with the one offered between the early 1940s and the mid 1950s" (Rodríguez Moreno 2014, 117).

The character of Catwoman is interesting in that she operates outside the bounds of what is considered appropriate social behavior, even by Gotham City's villain standards. Despite the parallel universes and reboots of her story, a common theme in *Catwoman* stories is that she steals cat-themed items from institutions and the elite. The theft demographic is small, specialized, and highly insured. Her "lair" is usually a low-key apartment with many cats, as opposed to the Joker's haunted mansion the Ha-Hacienda, or operating nightclubs and/or casinos like the Penguin's Iceberg Lounge. She eschews a gang of inept henchmen for solo work, and her weapon of choice is a bullwhip instead of customized, traceable weaponry. Additionally, she has a romantic relationship with Batman, which is not common among Gotham City's masked villains.

Selina Kyle is someone who has chosen to live outside society. Her ambivalent (at best) attitude toward authority firmly rooted her as a villain during the Golden Age of comics, but it could be argued her choice, and the act of exercising that choice, is in itself what makes her a hero to many readers. As José Joaquín Rodríguez Moreno wrote:

> In a world like that of comics, in which most of the characters who achieve fame are male heroes, the case of Catwoman never ceases to surprise, which has achieved much greater popularity than one would expect in a villain. This public interest is due, to a large extent, to a series of elements such as the independence and ambiguity of the character on the one hand, as well as the sensual game of cat and mouse that she develops with Batman.
>
> *(Rodríguez Moreno 2014, 117)*

Catwoman's ongoing flirtation with Batman is a manifestation of women's sexuality and empowerment, a role-reversal of sexual power dynamics. From her first appearance in *Batman #1*, she has Batman on his knees at her feet, attending a bandaged ankle as she looks on imperiously, while in the penultimate panel, post-escape, Batman swoons over her as Robin sneers. Despite how creators conceived and wrote her, there is always a core element of Catwoman that finds a way to own herself and advocate for herself; her agency always emerges, and this is why audiences connect with her and root for her. This is what makes her a hero.

Origin Story

Catwoman was created as part of the team effort behind *Batman* at Detective Comics, which was expanding as the industry gained popularity and interest. Editor Vince Sullivan solicited ideas for new titles, and the team of writer Bill Finger and artist Bob Kane produced Batman, a concept heavily influenced by noir and pulp with a Gothic sensibility. Batman debuted in *Detective Comics* #27 (1939) and launched his own eponymous title in the spring of 1940.

Branding was key from the beginning. An editorial team art directed the covers and mapped the storylines, always ensuring continuity and tone adhered to a style guide. Moreover, they capitalized on sales trends by developing "graphic and narrative" formulae that responded to what fans wanted (Rodríguez Moreno 2014, 122). Although the comics were being produced by a large team, their tone and message were controlled by a very small group of people, favoring the existence of a unity in the message. (Rodríguez Moreno 2014, 122) In the case of Catwoman, the message was "sexy nemesis." As co-creator Bob Kane said:

> We knew we needed a female nemesis to give the series sex appeal. [Bill Finger] and I decided to create an enemy who would be a bit friendly and commit crimes, but at the same time be a romantic interest in Batman's rather sterile life. She was kind of like a female Batman, except she was a villain and Batman was a hero.
>
> *(Kane and Andrae 1989, 105–106)*

What Finger and Kane failed to realize is that by making Catwoman a "female Batman," they made her equitable. The concepts of "hero' and "villain" rely on perspective: if Batman is always "good," then Catwoman must always be "bad."

However, the foundation of Batman lies in the fact he is a man perpetuating vigilantism, which, in the context of the United States Department of Justice, is engaging "in violence in order to stabilize the range of acceptable behavior" (Sederberg 1978) Batman, at his core, is violating societal limits to defend those limits from attack or subversion *through* attack and subversion. Kane argues that Batman would try to "reform" Catwoman and bring her to the side of "law and order" (Kane and Andrae 1989, 105–106), but how can Batman reform anyone when he is guilty of the same transgressions? This takes on additional weight once Batman and Catwoman consummate their relationship (King and Janin 2017, 118; Winick and March 2012, 27). The result is one of abjection, as the removal of the costumes reflects the "collapse of the border between inside and outside" (Kristeva 1984, 53). The costumes are identities, or a form of skin, and their removal is an exposition of their emotional insides, their real identities, and as such, that "skin, a fragile container, no longer guaranteed the integrity of one's 'own and clean self'" (Kristeva 1984, 53). Both Batman and Catwoman have crossed a line.

Although Kane asserts that he and Finger created Catwoman as Batman's foil, she managed to foil her creators, as well. Kane's attitudes toward women and men are not flattering:

> I felt that women were feline creatures and men were more like dogs. While dogs are faithful and friendly, cats are cool, detached, and unreliable. I felt much warmer with dogs around me, cats are as hard to understand as women are.
>
> *(Kane and Andrae 1989, 107–108)*

But they are apt for the unintended readings of Catwoman and her impact on audiences. Catwoman taking on the cool, unreliable detachment that Kane assigns women offers an alternate model of womanhood for readers. Kane's view of women as abject, in Kristeva's terms, with his "dark revolt" "against a threat" that "cannot be assimilated," beseeching and fascinating a desire that "does not let itself be seduced" (Kristeva and Lechte 1982, 1), adds some understanding to the Bat/Cat dynamic, as they are both attracted to and repelled by one another. Kane's negative views of women result in a Catwoman who refuses to play by the conventional rules set for them.

Catwoman exists in a liminal zone: she is not a fully formed person with a history and consistent past experiences. Her *raison d'être* was literally to service a man's characterization or narrative needs, as evidenced by DC's publication of *Batman and Catwoman: 80 Years of Romance* (2020), which disregards all the other relationships both Batman and Catwoman had during those 80 years, somewhat undercutting the term "romance."

Catwoman's rebellion, as well as her repeated evasion of permanent capture, has functioned as a metaphor for women who desire to lead lives outside societal norms since 1940. "The very presence of female superheroes during these times showed readers at least some sense of an alternative to the romanticization of the married, white, middle-class homemaker and mother" (Cocca 2016) and Catwoman is no different. She lives an unconstrained life, one which she navigates through her own desire. Sometimes those desires include motherhood, home, and husband, but it must be noted those desires emerge at the cusp and in the wake of third-wave feminism, when a woman's choice was paramount. Catwoman's interest in caretaking and partnership came after decades of independence, and as a result, those narrative turns were shocking. Decades of flatly rejecting the roles of "wife" and "homemaker" provided models of what "womanhood," or a woman's life, could look like to the readership.

Identifying a Hero

While not a "superhero" in the common sense, Catwoman nonetheless embodies values that have real-world applications for an often erased or overlooked segment of the comics-buying market. For her first few years in the Batverse, Catwoman is a villain. In *Batman* #1, she is an "unseen menace" (Finger and Kane 2015, 10), in *Batman* #3 (1940), she is flirting "with danger and death" (Finger 2015, 24). In these early issues, she moves "with curious cat-like grace" (25), she has "slim hands, with nails like claws" (25), yet she, like most "dames," talks "too much" (31) when she dares questions men.

According to Kane, the binary gender dynamic between Batman and Catwoman is a "grim contest between a man and a woman" and is entirely intentional (Kane and Andrae 1989), as Catwoman seemingly becomes the avatar for her entire gender:

> Men feel more sure of themselves with a male friend than a woman. You always need to keep women at arm's length. We don't want anyone taking over our souls, and women have a habit of doing that. So there's a love-resentment thing with women. I guess women will feel that I'm being chauvinistic to speak this way.
>
> *(Kane and Andrae 1989)*

Kane articulates a chauvinistic position, but it's one that Catwoman herself embraces and weaponizes. Readers see Catwoman sass and potentially emasculate men: "Well, that's the matter? Haven't you ever seen a pretty girl before?" (Finger and Kane 2015, 21); they see her seduce and manipulate men: "You saved my life! I'd like to thank you for that! Like this!" and embraces Batman in a kiss before shoving him away from her to escape (Finger 2015, 35). Readers also see Catwoman threaten as well as attack men – "Try to double-cross me, will you? …I'll scratch his eyes out!" – all of which firmly embeds her characterization (Finger 2015, 34).

We, as readers, see a Catwoman of specific definition and shape as the title enters the 1950s as her moral ambiguity begins to emerge. In the Bob Kane-authored issue of *Batman* #65 (1951), the cover puts to readers a key question: "Is the Catwoman an ally of the dynamic duo or has she returned to crime? You be the judge and jury" (Finger et al. 2015, 37). In the issue's introductory setup, readers are told that

> Once again from the dark shadows, there springs the svelte form of that fabulous feline… the *Catwoman!* Does she move through the sleeping city on muted paws in the interests of justice, or is she on a mission of plunder?
>
> *(Finger et al. 2015, 38)*

Readers are told Batman does not have the answers, that "this is the baffling question which faces Batman and Robin" (Finger et al. 2015, 38). Catwoman's role is placed before the reader to make the decision, and as a result, her actions and behavior, as someone who plays by her own rules, becomes visible to *all* readers on the pretense that she be judged.

According to Rodríguez Moreno, Catwoman "disappeared for more than a decade from publications from DC Comics," positing that the reason was because "the Comics Code established that criminals could not be shown in a way that allowed the reader to connect with them" (Rodríguez Moreno 2014, 125). The strict regulations of The Comics Code of 1954 undermine the very characteristics designed by Kane and Finger and accepted by DC's editorial boards: "Females shall be drawn realistically without exaggeration of any physical qualities"; "The treatment of love-romance stories shall emphasize the value of the home and the sanctity of marriage"; "Seduction … shall never be shown or suggested" (CBLDF n.d.). The Code suggests that these characters could in fact be considered to have appealing attributes, and that readers, particularly female readers, could possibly relate to them. Catwoman's return to DC came in 1966, the same year Julie Newmar's incarnation of the character purred across the nation's television screens in the ABC *Batman* series.

Comics have had a female readership from the industry's inception: titles such as *Millie the Model* (1947), *Brenda Starr, Reporter* (1948), and *Betty and Veronica* (1950) are examples of titles targeting this demographic, offering something of interest to female readers and fans. DC's implicit recognition or acknowledgment of her influence as a potential role model by removing her after the introduction of the Comics Code and re-introducing her as a "rehabilitated" persona lends support to the idea that what makes Catwoman "Catwoman" is what makes audiences connect with her. "Seeing someone who looks like you can have a positive impact on self-esteem," meaning that "you are more likely to imagine yourself as a hero if you see yourself represented as a hero" (Cocca 2016, 3). Catwoman demonstrates that contrary to "despising hard work," she actually is a motivated self-starter who conducts extensive research on her crimes, effectively project-managing her capers with occasional henchmen recruitment and team leadership. She also manages to keep fit and healthy to ensure her body can emerge unscathed from hand-to-hand combat as well as scale the outside of a skyscraper, jump off its rooftop, and always land on her feet, sometimes while wearing kitten heels. Catwoman works hard and looks good doing it.

In a post-Rosie the Riveter world, where female superheroes "were not at all diverse" (Cocca 2016, 9), and they were markedly "less threatening in their names and powers" (Cocca 2016, 9), "written and drawn as weaker, more emotional, in need of rescue, more geared toward romance with men, more interested in domestic chores like cooking and sewing" (Cocca 2016, 9), the character of Catwoman presents an alternative hero in *an alternative* to "hero." Women struggling to fit into a patriarchal mold could see another path with Catwoman. The Selina Kyle in the Tim Burton film *Batman Returns* (1992) uses "corn dog" as a pejorative, can only speak up for herself in hindsight, and has notes in her workspace to help moderate her behavior: "Obey," "Don't 'get' jokes," and "Save it for your diary" (Waters and Strick 1991). But once she evolves into Catwoman, those workspace notes become "Defy Authority," "Take No Prisoners" and "Expose The Horror" (Waters and Strick 1991). In the case of *Batman Returns,* this Catwoman addresses the gender inequality she is tired of experiencing:

The world tells boys to conquer the world, and girls to wear clean panties. A man dressed as a bat is a he-man, but a woman dressed as a cat is a she-devil. I'm just living down to my expectations. Life's a bitch – now so am I.

(Waters and Strick 1991)

Catwoman, a female Batman, shows us there are other types of heroes. That sometimes, being a mouthy broad who threatens to scratch a man's eyes out is in itself a type of hero, and that if you yourself are a mouthy broad who prefers the company of your cats or would rather go to jail than change for a man – if you are, in fact, "a bitch" – then there is a hero out there for you, too.

Diverse-kitty

Catwoman launched as a monthly solo title in 1993 and was similar to other titles featuring women superheroes, where it appears "as if female superheroes are objects to be looked at rather than subjects to view the story through" (Cocca 2016, 12). However, she has changed with the times, and so have her creators: "Superhero comic creators and producers are slightly more diverse themselves than in the past. They themselves may want change, and they also cannot afford to ignore how much the fan base has changed just over the last several years" (Cocca 2016, 3). As a result, we see a Selina Kyle whose breast size, height, and shape become slightly more realistic, who wears low-heeled boots with grip instead of thigh-high stockings with no soles or arch support. The "brokeback pose," "an anatomically incorrect pose often used in comics to show [a woman's] boobs and butt at the same time" (Mitchell 2012), is named and shamed by fans. We also see a Catwoman played by a woman of color in live-action representations: Eartha Kitt in the 1960s, Halle Berry in *Catwoman* (2004), Camren Bicondova in *Gotham* (2014–2019), and Zoë Kravitz in *The Batman* (2022). The racial fluidity in casting Catwoman expands the field of representation that audiences see of themselves in media.

Fans of comic books and its offshoot media are not passive anymore: "In the 2010s, many more conversations over such representations were enabled by a number of broader demographic and political changes wrought by the gains of various civil rights movements" (Cocca 2016, 13). And as such, acknowledging the comics-buying market as being more than just white men has provided an expansion in media. In 2012, an Asian Catwoman was introduced in the Cartoon Network short-series *Batman of Shanghai;* in 2015, Japanese-American crime family heiress Eiko Hasigawa appears as another Catwoman, canonizing Selina Kyle's bisexuality in *Catwoman #39* (2018). Also in 2018, the animated Japanese-American film *Batman Ninja* saw Catwoman turning up in feudal Japan.

On the 1960s *Batman* television show, Kitt's Catwoman is camp. She is often seen in a lime-green convertible Kitty Car, complete with whiskers and tail, but she delivers her lines with pitch-perfect assurance. "Her casting speaks to long-standing associations between African American performers, especially women, and the sexually exotic Other" (Yockey 2014, 60), which the showrunners intentionally played on, as assistant executive producer Charles Fitzsimons said:

> We felt it was a very provocative idea [to cast Kitt]. She was a cat woman before we ever cast her as Catwoman. She had a cat-like style. Her eyes were cat-like and her singing was like a meow. This came as a wonderful, offbeat idea to do it with a Black woman.
>
> *(Lewis 2022)*

This move to cast a Black woman as Catwoman was transgressive. For a television series aired during the American Civil Rights Movement, which relied on the recurring conceit that Catwoman proposes a romantic relationship with Batman, it was viewed as a move that "becomes both symptomatic of the need for social change, and the change itself" (Yockey 2014, 60). Eartha Kitt as Catwoman disrupted audiences' ideas of what a Catwoman could look like and who a Catwoman could be. In some respects, this refracts the character's abject, liminal nature, and the lack of a fixed origin allows space for this to happen, as there is no canon or creative brief to adhere to.

Later in the prequel series *Gotham* we see an origin story of a pre-Catwoman Selina Kyle as a street kid. The rationale to cast Latina actress Camren Bicondova finds an antecedent in the Catwoman origin from DC's "New Earth" universe, in which her Cuban mother, Maria, is introduced in *Catwoman #81* (2000), and whose alcoholic husband would beat her for speaking Spanish. Bicondova's portrayal of Selina Kyle (which lasted five years, making her the longest-serving Catwoman to date) is unique in that the actress became personally molded by the character during her teenage years. In an interview with *Bust,* Bicondova said: "I've learned to understand from her that you can't really love anybody else if you don't love yourself" (Wang 2023). Bicondova's interpretation of Catwoman stems from what first engaged the character's readers from the 1940s onward: "She taught me if you want something, you have to go get it, and you have to *want* to go get it. A lot of my morals and values now, as 18-year-old Camren, I've learned from Selina" (Wang, 2023). With Bicondova's interpretation of the fundamental aspect of Catwoman's character, the heroic subtext of Selina Kyle becomes the text.

There is an unfortunate downside with regard to actresses of color and the role of Catwoman. Zoë Kravitz, who plays Selina Kyle in *The Batman,* was denied an audition for *The Dark Knight Rises* (2012) because "they weren't 'going urban'"; she said: "It was like, 'What does that have to do with anything?' I have to play the role like, 'Yo, what's up, Batman? What's going on wit chu?'" (Herndon 2015). Another Catwoman actress, Halle Berry, said she was denied opportunities to read for films like *The Silence of the Lambs* (1991) or *Indecent Proposal* (1993) because "a Black woman would change what the movie was all about" (Hamilton 2023). While in some instances, presenting or casting women of color as Catwoman further embeds notions of the character's strength, resilience, and organization, as well as her refusal to conform to a society that does not see her or her value, in other cases, it perpetuates a white supremacy that erases other races from narratives. Cocca writes:

> Marginalized groups have been forced to 'cross-identify' with those different from them while dominant groups have not … women and people of color have had to identify with white male protagonists. But white males have not had to identify with the small number of women and people of color protagonists. This is not only unfair, but can curtail imagination.
>
> *(Cocca 2016, 3)*

This becomes inherent in Nolan's *The Dark Knight Rises,* when the Selina Kyle in the film, played by white actress Anne Hathaway, tells Bruce Wayne: "I take what I need from those who have more than enough. I don't stand on the shoulders of people with less" (Nolan 2012, 00:35:08). As a result, Christopher Nolan's *Dark Knight* trilogy reinforced ideas of white feminism and perpetuated the whiteness of his Gotham, while the Gotham of Matt Reeves's *The Batman* is a more nuanced and real-world representation of urban life, class warfare, and the racist sexism that underpins it all. As Carwoman tells Batman, "All anyone cares about in this place are these white privileged assholes" (Reeves 2022, 01:38:07).

In contrast, Halle Berry received a Razzie Award for her performance as Catwoman, despite previously winning an Oscar for *Monster's Ball* (2001). In her acceptance speech, she called *Catwoman* "a piece of shit god-awful movie" (Razzie Channel 2011). Berry had to negotiate not only Eartha Kitt's performance, but also the retconned Batcanon of the 1980s and Michelle Pfeiffer's performance in *Batman Returns,* whose success eventually gave way for a solo Catwoman film, which was not a success, and the downside of the film's failure only stained its lead actress. Berry said:

> The disheartening part was, I didn't direct it, I didn't produce it, nor did I write it. I was just the actress in it. But for all these years, I have carried the weight of that film.

And whatever success it had or didn't have somehow seemed like it was all my fault. But it really wasn't my fault. But I've been carrying it.

(Jimmy Kimmel Live 2021)

In *Catwoman*, Berry is not Selina Kyle but Patience Phillips: the same kind of mousy office worker people-pleaser we saw in *Batman Returns*, who is killed for capitalist greed and resurrected by cats pawing at her corpse. There are no other connections to the *Catwoman* story in any multiverse. Her city is unnamed, Batman is not present, and her Catwoman transformation, one in a long line of "Catwomen," is based on Egyptian magic: she was chosen by a messenger of the Egyptian goddess Bastet to save (white) women from a toxic skin cream.

In essence, the changing demographics of the creators and the fans mean Catwoman becomes more tangible; she looks like the reality her readers exist in. It would be negligent however to ignore the colorism in Catwoman's live-action casting: Kitt, Berry, Bicondova and Kravitz are multiracial/multiethnic, and as such, have the light-skin privilege that comes from being ethnically ambiguous. There is evidence of progress in casting these actresses as Selina Kyle, but also demonstrably some ways to go, but as Cocca writes: "Diverse representation benefits everyone, because it shows all of us that anyone can be a hero" (Cocca 2016, 3).

Conclusion

Catwoman's incarnations have shown to generations of readers that women can be independent, self-reliant, even sassy, and while this may be portrayed as outside the norm by a villain, it nonetheless can still be interpreted as attractive, even sexy qualities, especially by those who consider themselves the most morally upstanding. As Cocca writes:

> But if, over and over in a variety of media, we see women represented only a fraction as often as men; if we never see a woman portrayed as a leader, a mentor, a professional; if we see women written and drawn and acted only as supportive, interested in their own looks and in romance, in need of rescue, and emotional; and if we never see women as heroes, what happens to our imagination for ourselves and our world? And if we do see female heroes, but those heroes are almost never people of color, people with disabilities, people who identify as gender-fluid or transgender or queer, what happens to our imagination for ourselves and our world?

(Cocca 2016, 3)

The truth is, we need Catwoman. Readers need to see her out there doing her own thing for her own reasons: indulging in her hobbies of stealing cat-themed art; taking care of strays, both cats and children; treating herself to makeovers. Catwoman's self-care regime is enviable in comparison with what real women are expected to endure; after all, Catwoman is never shown applying a serums-and-acids skincare routine when the mask comes off, but we do see her on her couch, cuddled with cats, reading (Finger and Paris 1947, 3). Selina Kyle, unintentionally or no, often presents the concept of "crazy cat lady" as a viable life choice. And in a context in which Donald Trump and JD Vance won the US 2024 Presidential election on campaign of sexism and anti-choice rhetoric, the representation of Catwoman as an independent, autonomous woman becomes even more necessary for the next generation of readers.

Catwoman may appear to be morally ambiguous, which makes her abject and transgressive, regardless of the medium. But no matter what, Catwoman is always, consistently, on one side: hers.

References

CBLDF. n.d. *The Comics Code of 1954*. Comic Book Legal Defense Fund. https://cbldf.org/the-comics-code-of-1954/.

Channel, Razzie. 2011. "Halle Berry accepts her RAZZIE® Award." Uploaded January 13, on YouTube. Available at: https://www.youtube.com/watch?v=U-7s_yeQuDg.

Cocca, Carolyn. 2015. *Comics and human rights: Wonder Woman and the Trickiness of Superheroines*. LSE Human Rights, February 2. https://eprints.lse.ac.uk/80282/.

Cocca, Carolyn. 2016. *Superwomen: Gender, Power, and Representation*. Bloomsbury Academic.

Finger, Bill. 2015. "Batman #3." In *Catwoman, A Celebration of 75 Years*, edited by Robin Wildman. DC Comics.

Finger, Bill, and Bob Kane. 2015. "Batman #1." In *Catwoman, A Celebration of 75 Years*, edited by Robin Wildman. DC Comics.

Finger, Bill, Bob Kane, and Lew Sayre Schwartz. 2015. "Batman #65." In *Catwoman, A Celebration of 75 Years*, edited by Robin Wildman. DC Comics.

Finger, Bill, and Charles Paris. 1947. *Batman* #42. Detective Comics.

Forster, Marc, dir. 2001. *Monsters Ball*. Lion Gate Films.

Hamilton, Sophie. 2023. "Halle Berry – Biography, HELLO!" *Hello!*, August 30. https://www.hellomagazine.com/profiles/20091008925/halle-berry/.

Herndon, Jessica. 2015. "Zoë Kravitz Nylon Is Our August Cover Star." *Nylon*, July 10. https://www.nylon.com/articles/zoe-kravitz-august-2015.

Jimmy Kimmel Live. 2021. "Halle Berry on Martial Arts Training, Calling Cardi B Queen of Hip Hop & Playing Catwoman." Uploaded November 16, on YouTube. https://www.youtube.com/watch?v=_sTGnp7pew8.

Kane, Bob, and Tom Andrae. 1989. *Batman and Me*. Eclipse Books.

King, Tom, and Mikel Janin. 2017. *Batman Vol. 2: I Am Suicide*. DC Comics.

Kristeva, Julia, and John Lechte. 1982. Approaching Abjection. *Oxford Literary Review*, 5(1/2), 125–149. https://www.jstor.org/stable/43973647.

Kristeva, Julia. 1984. *Powers of Horror: An Essay on Abjection*. Columbia University Press.

Lewis, Miles Marshall. 2022. "A Short History of the Black Catwoman." *GQ*, March 7. https://www.gq.com/story/the-batman-zoe-kravitz-black-catwoman-history.

Miller, Frank, and David Mazzucchelli. 1987. "*Batman: Year One – Chapter One: Who I am – How I Came to Be*." In *Batman* #404. DC Comics.

Mitchell, Nigel G. 2012. "The Problem with Broke Back Catwoman #0." *The Geek Twins*, June 23. https://thegeektwins.com/2012/06/problem-with-brokeback-catwoman-0/.

Moreno, Rodríguez, José Joaquín. 2014. "Peligrosamente bella: el mensaje en las aventuras de Catwoman durante la edad de oro del cómic estadounidense (1940–1954)." *Espacio Tiempo y Forma. Serie V, Historia Contemporánea*, 26, pp. 115–134. doi: 10.5944/etfv.26.2014.14515. https://revistas.uned.es/index.php/ETFV/article/view/14515

Nolan, Christopher, dir. 2012. *The Dark Knight Rises*. Warner Home Video. Blu-ray Disc.

Reeves, Matt, dir. 2022 *The Batman*. Warner Bros. Blu-ray Disc.

Sederberg, Peter C. 1978. "Phenomenology of Vigilantism in Contemporary America – An Interpretation." *Office of Justice Programs*. https://www.ojp.gov/ncjrs/virtual-library/abstracts/phenomenology-vigilantism-contemporary-america-interpretation.

Wang, Lydia. 2023. "'Gotham' star Camren Bicondova Is a New Kind of Superhero: *BUST* Interview." *BUST*, April 3. https://bust.com/camren-bicondova-interview/.

Waters, Daniel, and Wesley Strick. 1991. *BATMAN RETURNS*. Shooting Script, August 1. https://www.dailyscript.com/scripts/batman-returns_shooting.html.

Wilson, Carl. 2023. "'My relationship with Batman Has Never Been What I'd Call 'Stable'": Catwoman's Flirtations with Superheroism and Her Evolving Role as the Monstrous Feline Fatale." In *Batman's Villains and Villainesses: Multidisciplinary Perspectives on Arkham's souls*, edited by Marco Favaro and Justin Martin. Lexington Books.

Winick, Judd, and Guillem March. 2012. *Catwoman Vol. 1: The Game*. DC Comics.

Yockey, Matt. 2014. *Batman (TV Milestones Series)*. Wayne State University Press.

36

SUPERVILLAINS ARE THE REAL HEROES

Mark Hibbett

This chapter will demonstrate how superhero stories differ from most other types of Western storytelling by giving a role usually given to heroes – that of the agent of change – to their villains. It will discuss the historical and practical reasons for this and show what happens when the nominal heroes do occasionally attempt to effect change, before explaining how supervillains arose to fulfill the need for change in order to drive stories. Finally, the Marvel Comics character Doctor Doom will be used as an example of how supervillains are employed as story engines, and what their inevitable defeat can tell us about superhero storytelling as a whole.

Most forms of Western storytelling, from ancient legends to modern blockbusters, can be explained in terms of Joseph Campbell's (1949) "universal myth." This is a story framework that involves an inexperienced hero being called away to adventure and enduring trials, resulting in changes both to themselves and the world around them. Campbell's analysis was hugely influential on American screenwriting, with screenwriters using it extensively as a template (Field 1979). Indeed, templates such as *Save the Cat* (Snyder 2005) and *The Hero's Journey* (Vogler 2007) have since been developed that are designed to help generate outlines based on the plot points that Campbell identified. Campbell's influence can perhaps most clearly be seen in the original *Star Wars* (1977), in which Luke Skywalker heads out into the wider galaxy and, across various adventures, eventually becomes a hero, and destroys the Death Star. This influence has continued to the present day, with more recent movies such as *Barbie* (2023), *Avatar: The Way Of The Water* (2022), and *Oppenheimer* (2023) all featuring a hero who answers a call to action, moves into a wider world, and both causes change and is changed themselves.

However, superhero stories, especially those originating in comics, tend not to follow this format (Reynolds 1994). They use instead a format called The American Monomyth, in which an Eden-like place is disrupted by the invasion of evil forces that are then defeated by a lone figure, who arrives from the outside before disappearing back into the wilderness at the conclusion (Lawrence and Jewett 2002). This story has its roots in Western narratives, with the relative calm of a frontier town being disturbed by bandits, and the townsfolk are unable to defend themselves until a mysterious stranger arrives, take bloody revenge on the bandits, and then rides off into the sunset, refusing all offers of thanks. In the superhero

DOI: 10.4324/9781003366911-41

version of this story the bandits are replaced by supervillains, the frontier town is somewhere like Gotham, Manhattan, or the world itself, and the mysterious stranger is the masked superhero who works only for the restoration of justice (Lawrence and Jewett 2002, 47). Or, as the theme to the *Spider-Man* cartoon series (1967–1970) has it, "In the chill of night, at the scene of the crime… he arrives just in time" and then when the action is all over the hero disappears without asking for acclaim because "Wealth and fame he's ignored, action is his reward" (Grantray-Lawrence Animation 1967). Superhero comics inherited this story framework from pulp and movie serials such as *The Shadow* or *Zorro* (Walton 2008). The main reason that the American Monomyth was used for these serials was that it allowed stories to happen in an "oneiric climate" (Eco 1972, 17). This describes a situation where individual episodes of a series exist almost in isolation from each other, with the same characters and settings but only a hazy idea of what has gone before, with the overall storyworld to all intents and purposes being reset at the end of each story.

There are two key benefits to this kind of storytelling. First, it means that little prior knowledge of previous stories is required, so that episodes can be missed or read out of sequence without losing any enjoyment on the part of the audience. This was especially important during the early decades of superhero comics, when distribution could be irregular and there was no guarantee that specific series would be supplied to the same retailers each month (Lopes 2009). Second, The Heroes Journey causes serious problems for serialized storytelling. If every story in every issue of a comic series ended with the lead character being changed then within a few installments they would become entirely unrecognizable. This is especially the case in storyworlds that exist in shared universes, or that are both transtextual and transmedia. In such storyworlds, radical changes to a character in one comics series, for instance, would need to be echoed simultaneously in all other comics from the same publisher, and take into account changes to other characters as well. This becomes even more complex when characters exist across different media. For example, changes to the character Wolverine would need to be made in every single comic, cartoon, or television series that they appeared in on a monthly basis, with changes to other characters that he interacted with also being kept up to date. This would be almost impossible to manage and so, as Stan Lee explains, "once we've invented a hero, that's it. He's pretty much the same, issue after issue" (1976, 7).

The superhero genre is, of course, by no means the only one that tells this sort of story. In certain kinds of cop shows, especially older ones designed for eventual syndication, each episode can exist in its own oneiric climate where the status quo is reset each time. For example, in *Magnum PI* (1980–1988) Thomas is always broke and Higgins wants to get the Ferrari back. Even here, however, change is inevitable as actors grow older and contracts are renegotiated. Comics characters, however, can go on forever without aging, becoming involved in scandals, or making demands for wage increases. However, even with this in mind, Eco's description of superhero storytelling has never been entirely accurate. Even in the early days of superhero comics there would be gradual changes to the hero and their world over time, as, for example, new characters were introduced or costume designs were finessed. This accelerated when the concept of "The Marvel Universe" was introduced in the 1960s, when ongoing continuity and interaction between different series became part of the appeal of the stories (Reynolds 1994).

However, even when major change does happen it can be reversed, and almost always is. Steve Rogers has been replaced as Captain America many times, with US Agent, Bucky Barnes, Sam Wilson, and others taking over, but he has always returned to the role eventually.

Similarly, Ben Reilley and Otto Octavius have taken over as Spider-Man; Dick Grayson, Azrael, Jim Gordon, and Jace Fox have become Batman; and Jim Rhodes and Victor von Doom became Iron Man; but in the end, Peter Parker, Bruce Wayne, and Tony Stark have always returned. Indeed, it is always strange when self-professed "true comics fans" protest about such changes, as anyone familiar with the history of such characters knows that they are only temporary. Even when entire storyworlds come to an end, such as in the conclusion of Alan Moore's ABC universe in *Tom Strong* #36 (Moore and Sprouse 2006) or the destruction of Marvel's Ultimate universe in *Ultimate End* #5 (Bendis and Bagley 2016), the characters and, eventually, the universes containing them will inevitably return (Johnston 2018; Marston 2020). Tom Strong, for example, was introduced into the DC comics universe in *The Terrifics* #1 (Lemire and Reis 2018) while the entire Ultimate universe was revived in the *Ultimate Invasion* mini-series (Hickman and Hitch 2023).

Superhero comics can thus be described as conservative, in that they are averse to change, but they can also be labeled as socially conservative too. For example, in almost all cases, the job of the superhero is to protect society in its current form, whether that be by stopping a bank robbery or preventing the destruction of the universe (Lewis 2013). By presenting the superhero as the central sympathetic character, and their actions defending the status quo as therefore laudable, these stories are conservative because they stress the importance of maintaining the current consensus (Deis 2013; Costello 2009). When stories deviate from this model, with superheroes actively trying to change the world around them rather than preserve it in its current state, there are invariably repercussions. In series such as *Watchmen* (1986–1987), *Squadron Supreme* (1985–1986), and *The Authority* (1999–2000), superheroes take a pro-active role, seeking to change society for the better. In each case, the superheroes find that power is corrupting and are depicted as villainous, whether explicitly in the case of Ozymandias in *Watchmen* or implicitly in the satirical storytelling of *The Authority*, reinforcing the idea that the true path of virtue is to maintain the status quo (Coogan 2006, 59; Verano 2013).

It should be stated that not all aspects of superhero storytelling are necessarily politically conservative. Superman, for example, originally fought corrupt capitalists and Wonder Woman was created to promote alternative ways of living (Curtis 2019). Additionally, in recent years there have been numerous attempts to introduce characters who do not fit the general default straight, male, white archetype, such as Ms Marvel, Squirrel Girl, and Miles Morales (Ahmed 2021; Millanzi 2021). These characters can be seen as modernizing forces within the current superhero storyworlds, showing the possibility of overall societal change; however, they still act conservatively toward their own narratives in much the same way as previous generations of superheroes. This conservatism generates a practical problem for creators, in that stories usually require an active "protagonist" (i.e. one who instigates change) in order for a plot to be generated. As stated, this position is traditionally taken by a story's hero, but with the lead character of superhero stories dedicated to preventing change, it is up to supervillains to become the generators of action (Coogan 2006).

Supervillains first appeared not long after superheroes. The earliest superhero comics featured the heroes fighting the same sort of non-powered villains (bank robbers, muggers, or corrupt industrialists) who had appeared in the pulp fictions that preceded them (Levitz 2013). Not only did these provide the new super-powered heroes with little in the way of a challenge, but they ran the risk of harming their perceived heroism, painting them almost as bullies who beat up those less powerful than themselves (Lee 1976). Thus, similarly super-powered adversaries were required, to carry a real threat of change and thus allow the superhero to remain the protector of the status quo whilst still being involved in the story (Verano 2013).

Once supervillains were introduced creators quickly realized that they could easily be reused to generate further new stories, and therefore should not be killed off at the end of their first appearance (Thomas 2004; Lee 1976). In some ways this made the villains more important than the heroes, as without them there would be no story for the superhero to take part in. As Stan Lee put it:

> Endowed with a group of great heroes… the main appeal of our frisky little fables must lie with the villains we concoct. What new threats can they pose to our unsuspecting protagonists? What new weapons will they soon unleash upon a dazed and defenceless world? What new powers can they bring to bear that will give our good guys a run for their dough?
>
> *(1976, 7)*

Recurring supervillains would often be created as a twisted mirror image of the superheroes, most obviously in the form of their costumes, which would usually be in secondary colors (green, purple, orange) rather than the reds, whites, and blues that traditionally belonged to the heroes (Jennings 2013; Costello 2009). Similarly, the origins and characterizations of supervillains closely resembled those of their adversaries, differing only in the fact that, at the origin's conclusion, villains choose a life of crime rather than crime fighting, so that "the defect that makes the villain villainous is exactly what the hero resists" (Coogan 2013, 98). Where heroes tended to have a traumatic event in their past which taught them to help others, villains suffered from "a wound – typically psychological and emotional but often with a physical component – that shapes their lives and which they are unable to recover from" (Coogan 2006, 70). This wound often manifests itself visibly, as some form of disfigurement (Gavaler 2018). Once again, this serves to demonstrate the heroism of the lead characters, as "the villain's negative qualities highlight the hero's positive one" (Verano 2013, 84).

Doctor Doom

Within these definitions, Doctor Doom is clearly a supervillain. This was made explicit in his very first appearance on the cover of *Fantastic Four* #5 (July 1962), where he threatens to "destroy the Fantastic Four forever" in a story entitled "Meet Doctor Doom!" He was created in opposition to the Fantastic Four, as "the intellectual equal of Reed Richards." (Lee et al. 2015, 119) He was an Eastern European dictator who mixed science with magic and always acted alone, in direct contrast to the all-American family unit of the Fantastic Four, who follow the familial, science-based, leadership of Reed Richards (Lee 1976; Hatfield 2012). Doom was an immediate hit with readers and quickly returned, teaming up with Namor The Sub-Mariner in the following issue, and then again in *Fantastic Four* #10 (Lee and Kirby 1963). According to Stan Lee:

> Within a matter of days the mail came flying in. And it all carried the same message. Bring back Dr. Doom! Well, there we no flies on us. After the first thousand or so letters we suspected we had a hit! So bring him back we did
>
> *(Lee 1976, 13)*

Doom's popularity was such that, as the Marvel Universe started to develop into a single storyworld, he began to appear in other series (Hibbett 2024a). Just over a year after his first appearance he guest-starred in *The Amazing Spider-Man* #5 (Lee and Ditko 1963) and over the course of his first decade also appeared in *Daredevil, The Avengers, Strange Tales, The Silver Surfer, Sub-Mariner, Thor, Captain America, Iron Man, The Incredible Hulk*, and *Not Brand Echh*, as well as a brief run as the second feature in *Astonishing Tales*.

The character's ability to move beyond his source title was in part due to the fact that, unlike many villains, his origin was not explicitly linked to his arch nemesis. Other popular supervillains such as Loki, Lex Luthor, The Joker, and The Green Goblin have origins and motivations that require the presence of Thor, Superman, Batman, and Spider-Man respectively to work, and so although all these characters have appeared in other series, they are overwhelmingly more likely to appear alongside their "heroes." Doom's origin, on the other hand, is mostly independent of The Fantastic Four, despite first being told in *Fantastic Four* #5 and then expanded two years later in *Fantastic Four Annual* #2 (Lee and Kirby 1964). It begins with Victor von Doom being born into a poor gypsy family in the small Eastern European country of Latveria. His mother is murdered for being a witch and so Victor is raised by his father, who is later hounded to death fleeing from the evil local Baron after being unable to save the life of the Baron's wife. Enraged by these injustices young Victor becomes a scientific Robin Hood figure, battling the aristocracy with ingenious inventions that bring him to the attention of the American establishment, who spirit him away to University in the US. There, his isolation and perceived arrogance lead to a devastating accident and horrific facial injuries. Doom journeys to Nepal in search of a cure, where he discovers an order of monks who help him to combine his technological genius with the mystic arts of his mother. He eventually encases himself in armor and declares:

> From this moment on there is no Victor von Doom! He has vanished… along with the handsome face he once possessed! But, in his place, there shall be another… wiser… stronger! More brilliant, more powerful than ever before!! From this moment on I shall be known as… Doctor Doom!
>
> *(Lee and Kirby 1964)*

In many ways, this is like a superhero origin, with a rich back story giving wide scope for future adventures, an exciting visual identity, and complex, sympathetic motivations for even his most evil deeds. The difference that makes it a supervillain origin is, as discussed earlier, that Doom seeks to change the status quo rather than maintain it. To be specific, Doom seeks to change the status quo so that he is the unopposed ruler of the world. He does this in the belief that only he has the intellectual or moral stamina to achieve a future utopia for humanity (Terjesen 2009; Carpenter 2013). It is this self-justifying yet theoretically moral worldview that makes Doom a complex, often sympathetic, character while still remaining, when all things are taken into account, a supervillain (Coogan 2006; Conroy 2004).

As a supervillain, Doom must always be defeated, and, although this is usually the case, there have been several occasions when he has (temporarily, at least) succeeded in his plans. One such victory takes place in the graphic novel *Emperor Doom* (1987). Here, Doom uses the psychic powers of The Purple Man to hypnotize the entire planet, who then unanimously elect him as world leader. Doom immediately sets to work and, within a few days, has ended apartheid, solved the problems of world hunger with radical farming methods and the redistribution of wealth, and destroyed all nuclear weapons, ending the threat of nuclear annihilation. This apparent utopia is only brought to an end when the superhero Wonder Man breaks the hypnotic effect and leads a team of Avengers to end Doom's rule. Amusingly, Doom is not actually defeated by the Avengers themselves but more by his own unwillingness to engage with the administrative duties of leadership. Either way, he is overthrown and the status quo is almost immediately reinstated, with apartheid brought back, children left to starve, and nuclear arms proliferating once more.

As the Avengers fly home Hawkeye questions whether they have done the right thing in ending Doom's rule. Captain America answers, unequivocally, that they have. "The world isn't perfect Hawkeye," he says, "but people are free to make their own choices – and that's the way it should be" (Michelinie et al. 1987, 64). One could argue that the majority population of South Africa did not have a choice in the matter, and nor did the children born into starvation, who are not free from oppression or hunger in any meaningful way. Captain America's view of freedom has thus been labeled "negative freedom" in that it refers to freedom from obstacles put in the way of personal expression by the state. However, unlike so-called "positive freedom," it does not actively help people to overcome imposed difficulties either (Berlin 1969). Doctor Doom puts forward the idea that this version of freedom is more beneficial. For instance, in the newspaper strip *The Amazing Spider-Man*, he suggests that his totalitarian regime brings peace, telling Peter Parker:

> Our judicial system is based on reason! Incarceration is fruitless! We seek simple justice! If you kill, you must die! If you maim, you must be maimed! If you steal, you must labour until your theft is repaid! Suffice it to say, there is no crime in Latveria...You think me a despot – but my streets are safe
>
> *(Lee et al. 2016, 165–166)*

Doom's version of freedom is painted here as tempting but ultimately to be opposed, not least because it goes against the fundamental principles of liberty upon which the US was founded, and thus the principles for which most American superheroes stand. In this way, we can see that most, if not all, superheroes who come from this mold exist in a paradoxical state where on the one hand they claim to protect the principles of personal freedom but on the other act in a highly conservative manner, protecting and reinforcing the status quo at all times to ensure that change cannot happen.

Conclusion

In conclusion, this chapter has shown that the conservatism of superhero storytelling developed from a need to tell ongoing stories in a serialized format that did not radically alter the main characters. By making the heroes battle to maintain the status quo, and painting those who oppose it as villains, this template generated a way to tell stories where meaningful change was always threatened but could not actually happen, and so provided a stable basis for extending those stories across other media.

In recent years, however, this view of superhero storytelling has been challenged by the success of live-action superhero storytelling, particularly in the Marvel Cinematic Universe (MCU). Here the characters are played by actors who do age and do renegotiate contracts, and so change becomes inevitable. Two key examples of this can be found in the film *Avengers: Endgame* (Russo and Russo 2019), in which Iron Man dies and Captain America is allowed to age and retire, with the actors who played them (Robert Downey Jr. and Chris

Evans) retiring from their roles. Both of these developments were respected and reinforced by subsequent movies and television series, while other changes have been integrated into the ongoing storyline. One notable example is of the so-called "blip," where Thanos killed half of the population of the universe at the end of *Avengers: Infinity War* (Russo and Russo 2018) only for everybody to return five years later during *Avengers: Endgame*. This event has been referred to in almost all films and television shows since as a source of trauma for the world and an integral part of further stories.

However, there are signs that this acceptance of change may only be temporary. As the three different *Spider-Man* movie series have shown, once a character has begun to change too much from their original format, or the actor has aged beyond the range shown in the comic series, then they can be rebooted, with all stories reset to the beginning again. *Spider-Man: No Way Home* (Watts 2021) showed a way that this commercial need could actively be drawn into the narrative, with previous versions of the franchise shown to take place in alternate universes that can interact with the current version. This is a way for the studios to have their cake and eat it; accepting and celebrating past output, while reserving the right to tell the same stories again.

Deadpool & Wolverine (Levy 2024) took this further by not only introducing characters from previous franchises into the MCU but also having Chris Evans, the actor who played Steve Rogers, return to play his previous role as the Human Torch from *Fantastic Four* (Story 2005). This was done for humorous effect in *Deadpool & Wolverine*, but if the proposed *Avengers: Secret Wars* movie is even vaguely similar to what online rumors suggest it will not only see all previous versions of Marvel movies entwined within the current continuity but will also allow for reboots, re-starting individual character franchises with new actors where necessary (Prom 2023).

The Human Torch and the rest of the Fantastic Four will be part of this, with the movie *Fantastic Four: First Steps* due to appear in 2025, alongside their old adversary Doctor Doom, who is due to be the lead antagonist in both *Avengers: Doomsday* and *Avengers: Secret Wars*.

Although at time of writing little else is known about the content of these films, it has been confirmed that Victor von Doom will be played by Robert Downey Jr. (Armstrong 2024). How this will work is as yet unknown, although there have been multiple theories suggested (Hibbett 2024b). What is clear however is that, by casting an actor as high profile and highly paid as Downey Jr. in the role, Marvel Studios are intending to make Doctor Doom the focus of "Phase 6" of the MCU. Further evidence of this can be found in the fact that the next two Avengers movies are named after classic comics storylines – "Doomsday" in *Fantastic Four* #59 (Lee and Kirby 1967) and *Secret Wars* (Hickman and Ribić 2015–2016) – which had Doom as the lead character. The *Secret Wars* series saw different worlds from the Marvel comics multiverse brought together by Doctor Doom into a single world, in order to save them from destruction by an alien race of super-beings. This allowed different versions of the multiple characters to interact with each other in a similar way to that done in *Spider-Man: No Way Home* and *Deadpool & Wolverine*, although on a much larger scale. It is rumored that the movie *Avengers: Secret Wars* will follow a similar path, and allow Marvel to not only bring franchises such as The X-Men into the main MCU but also reboot other series with new actors (Marvel Movies Fandom 2024).

While it is tempting to speculate on the nature of these alterations, and what they will mean for the larger MCU moving forward, it would be unwise to do so – except to say that if the future of this ongoing narrative is anything like that detailed in the comics upon which these stories appear to be based, then ironically, Doom may finally have succeeded in bringing about change.

References

Ahmed, Ibtisam. "Aspiring towards the utopian critical mass of spider-man," paper presented at Trans itions 9: New Directions in Comics Studies conference, April 2021.

Armstrong, Kathryn. 2024. "Robert Downey Jr to return to Marvel as Doctor Doom." *BBC News*, July 28. https://www.bbc.co.uk/news/articles/ckrgd7eek09o.

Bendis, Brian, and Mark Bagley. 2016. *Ultimate End* #5. February 1. Marvel Comics.

Berlin, Isaiah. 1969. "Two Concepts of Liberty." In *Four Essays on Liberty*, edited by Isaiah Berlin. Oxford University Press.

Campbell, Jospeh. 1949. *The Hero with A Thousand Faces*. 3rd Edition. New World Library.

Carpenter, Stanford W., 2013. "Superheroes Need Superior Villains." In *What Is a Superhero?* edited by Robin. S. Rosenberg and Peter Coogan. OUP USA.

Conroy, Mike. 2004. *500 Comicbook Villains*. Collins & Brown.

Coogan, Peter. 2006. *Superhero: The Secret Origin of a Genre*. Monkeybrain.

Coogan, Peter. 2013. "The Hero Defines The Genre, the Genre Defines the Hero." In *What Is a Super-hero?* edited by Robin. S. Rosenberg and Peter Coogan. OUP USA.

Costello, Matthew. J., 2009. *Secret Identity Crisis: Comic Books and the Unmasking of Cold War America*. Continnuum.

Curtis, Neal. 2019. "Superheroes and the Mythic Imagination: Order, Agency and Politics." *Journal of Graphic Novels and Comics* 12(5), 360–374. https://doi.org/10.1080/21504857.2019.1690015.

Deis, Chris. 2013. "The Subjective Politics Of The Supervillain." In *What Is a Superhero?* edited by Robin. S. Rosenberg and Peter Coogan. OUP USA.

Eco, Umberto. 1972. "The Myth of Superman." *Diacritics* 2(1), 14–22. https://doi.org/10.2307/464920. https://doi.org/10.2307/464920.

Field, Syd. 1979. *Screenplay: The Foundations of Screenwriting*. Dell Publishing Company.

Gavaler, Chris. 2018. *Superhero Comics*. Bloomsbury.

Grantray-Lawrence Animation, prod. 1967. *Spider-Man*. First aired September 9, 1967, on ABC.

Hatfield, Charles. 2012. *Hand of Fire: The Comics Art of Jack Kirby*. University Press of Mississippi.

Hibbett, Mark. 2024a. *Data and Doctor Doom: An Empirical Approach To Transmedia Characters*. Palgrave Macmillan.

Hibbett, Mark. 2024b. "How Marvel could avoid disaster with Robert Downey Jr's Doctor Doom." *Radio Times*, July 29. https://www.radiotimes.com/movies/scifi/robert-downey-jr-doctor-doom-marvel-disaster-comment/.

Hickman, Jonathan, and Bryan Hitch. 2023. *Ultimate Invasion*. Marvel Comics.

Hickman, Jonathan, and Esad Ribić. 2015–2016. *Secret Wars*. Marvel Comics.

Jennings, John. 2013. "Superheroes by Design." In *What Is a Superhero?* edited by Robin. S. Rosenberg and Peter Coogan. OUP USA.

Johnston, Rich. 2018. "Finally for the Terrifics – Tom Strong [Terrifics 6 Spoilers]". *Bleeding Cool*, July 25. https://bleedingcool.com/comics/tom-strong-alan-moore-terrifics-6-spoilers/.

Lawrence, John Shelton, and Robert Jewett. 2002. *The Myth of the American Superhero*. Wm. B. Eerdmans Publishing.

Lee, Stan. 1976. *Bring on the Bad Guys: Origins of Marvel Villains*. Simon & Schuster.

Lee, Stan, and Jack Kirby. 1963. "The Return of Doctor Doom!" In *Fantastic Four* #10. January 1, Marvel Comics.

Lee, Stan, and Jack Kirby. 1964. *Fantastic Four Annual* #2. September 1. Marvel Comics.

Lee, Stan, and Jack Kirby. 1967. "Doomsday." In *Fantastic Four* #59. February 1. Marvel Comics.

Lee, Stan, Larry Leiber, and Fred Kida. 2016. *The Amazing Spider-Man: the ultimate newspaper comics vollection volume 3, 1981–1982*. IDW Publishing.

Lee, Stan, Peter David, and Colleen Doran. 2015. *Amazing! Fantastic! Incredible!* Gallery 13.

Lee, Stan, and Steve Ditko. 1963. *The Amazing Spider-Man* #5. October 1. Marvel Comics.

Lemire, Jeff, and Ivan Reis. 2018. *The Terrifics* #1. February 28. DC Comics.

Levitz, Paul. 2013. "Why Supervillains?" In *What Is a Superhero?* edited by Robin S. Rosenberg and Peter Coogan. OUP USA.

Levy, Shawn, dir. 2024. *Deadpool & Wolverine*. Marvel Studios.

Lewis, A. David. 2013. "Save the Day." In *What Is a Superhero?* edited by Robin S. Rosenberg and Peter Coogan. OUP USA.

Lopes, Paul. 2009. *Demanding Respect: The Evolution of the American Comic Book*. Temple University Press.

Lucas, George, dir. 1977. *Star Wars*. Twentieth Century Fox.

Marvel Movies Fandom. 2024. "Avengers: Doomsday rumors." *Fandom*, March 5. https://marvel-movies.fandom.com/wiki/Avengers:_Doomsday_rumors

Marston, George. 2020. "Everything we know about the Ultimate Universe returning to Marvel." *GamesRadar*, April 1. https://www.gamesradar.com/ultimate-universe-return-marvel/.

Michelinie, David, Mark Gruenwald, Jim Shooter, and Bob Hall. 1987. *Marvel Graphic Novel: Emperor Doom*. Marvel Comics.

Millanzi, Riziki. "'Because the city that says it's freed itself of emotion... runs on emotion': Willpower, motional Strength and the 'Angry Black Woman' stereotype in DC's 'Far Sector,'" paper presented at Transitions 9: New Directions in Comics Studies conference, April 2021.

Moore, Alan, and Chris Sprouse. 2006. "Tom Strong at the End of the World." In *Tom Strong*. America's Best Comics.

Prom, Bradley. 2023. "The Problems with Marvel Making Doctor Doom MCU's Secret Wars Villain." *ScreenRant*, April 2. https://screenrant.com/mcu-secret-wars-villain-doctor-doom-problems/.

Reynolds, Richard. 1994. *Super Heroes: A Modern Mythology*. University Press of Mississippi.

Russo, Anthony, and Joe Russo, dirs. 2018. *Avengers: Infinity War*. Marvel Studios.

Russo, Anthony, and Joe Russo, dirs. 2019. *Avengers: Endgame*. Marvel Studios.

Snyder, Blake, dir. 2005. *Save The Cat*. Michael Wiese Productions.

Story, Tim, dir. 2005. *Fantastic Four*. 20th Century Fox.

Terjesen, Andrew. 2009. "Why Doctor Doom Is Better Than The Authority." In *Supervillains and Philosophy*, edited by Ben Dyer. Open Court.

Thomas, Roy. 2004. "Foreword." In *500 Comicbook Villains*, edited by Mike Conroy. Collins & Brown.

Verano, Frank. 2013. "Superheroes Need Superior Villains." In *What Is A Superhero?*, edited by Robin S. Rosenberg and Peter Coogan. OUP USA.

Vogler, Christopher. 2007. *The Writer's Journey: Mythic Structure for Storytellers and Screenwriters*. Third edition. McNaughton & Gunn, Inc.

Walton, Saige. 2008. "Baroque Mutants in the 21st Century? Rethinking Genre through the Superhero." In *The Contemporary Comic Book Superhero*, edited by Angela Ndalianis. Routledge.

Watts, Jon, dir. 2021. *Spider-Man: No Way Home*. Columbia Pictures.

37

THE CULT OF MARVEL'S LOKI(S) AND THEIR (QUEER) REDEMPTION

Karl Johnson

Maybe some stories are so **good**… So **powerful**… So **wanted**… That the **universe** believes them. So good they're **magic**. So good they come **alive**.

Loki: Agent of Asgard *#17 (Ewing, Garbett, and Fabela 2015, 8)*

Marvel's Loki is a hero, a villain, a Young Avenger and a Dark Cabal member; a child, an adult, and an alligator; Prince (and Agent) of Asgard and King of Jotunheim; bi/pansexual and genderfluid; an architect of Ragnarök and sacrificial savior of New Asgard; a Sorcerer Supreme and a Presidential candidate known variously as the God of Evil, Lies, Mischief, Outcasts, and Stories. Each iteration of the 60-plus-year-old character is a legitimate and concurrent variant of Stan Lee, Larry Lieber, and Jack Kirby's original creation, occupying canonical positions within the wider transmedial, multiversal and more-or-less linear Marvel narrative (McMillan 2021; Wolk 2021).

Of course, Marvel's Loki is not an entirely original creation, being based upon the trickster deity of Norse mythology (alongside Thor, Odin, and others) to greater or lesser degrees of faithfulness depending on the writer. The *Prose Edda* and *Poetic Edda*, as they are known today, are works of 13th-century medieval literature that collect tales of the gods and monsters, and the cosmic cycle of life, death, and rebirth, that informed Norse and Viking culture (Sturluson [1220] 2005; von Schnurbein 2000). While many gods, for example the siblings Freyr and Freya, inspired followers of the time to offer sacrifices and wear symbols in return for protection, good luck, etc., there appears to be no recorded evidence of anything similar in the case of Loki. Indeed, the Norse God Loki's origins may lie in much older heretical pagan beliefs in an amoral, mercurial force (Bassil-Morozow 2017; von Schnurbein 2000). Loki's heritage within the Norse pantheon is unclear; they were not related to anyone else and their only stated connections were as a blood brother to Odin, and an unfaithful husband to Sigyn. Notably, the only relationship that Loki ever had with Thor in the mythology was one that mainly fluctuated between traveling companion and damned annoyance, before Loki's depiction in the *Eddas* suddenly, almost inexplicably, became more villainous

DOI: 10.4324/9781003366911-42

following the death of beloved god Baldr (Sturluson [1220] 2005; von Schnurbein 2000; Heide 2011).

It is likely due, at least in part, to the underlying influence of 13th-century Christianity on the *Eddas* author/compiler Snorri Sturluson, in his retelling of the mythology, that Loki is forced into the role of a bitter fallen angel seeking vengeance (von Schnurbein 2000; Sturluson [1220] 2005; Heide 2011). This grounds the medieval text in a more simplistic good vs evil narrative tradition; transforming ambiguous folklore into epic opera, particularly evident in Richard Wagner's 19th-century "Ring Cycle," a four-part opera inspired by Germanic and Scandinavian legends. Almost a century later, during the 1960s (a period that has since become known as the Silver Age of American comics), as Marvel introduced now household names like Spider-Man, The Fantastic Four, The X-Men, Iron Man, etc., Lee, Lieber, and Kirby's superheroic reinterpretation of Thor required an equally grand recurring villain.

Loki's first green-and-horned appearance as a figuratively and literally two-dimensional antagonist in 1962s *Journey Into Mystery* #85 established a saga-like template for what was to follow for many years in these comics: melodrama, battles on a cosmic scale, and monologues. It is no coincidence that after several false starts, Thor's 2011 entry into the Marvel Cinematic Universe (MCU) was ultimately helmed by Shakespearean actor and director Kenneth Branagh. Here, the machinations of Tom Hiddleston's Loki see Thor banished and depowered, the throne of Asgard usurped, and Earth threatened with invasion. So far, so much like a rehash of the repeated (and hence, failed) evil schemes of Thor's jealous brother Loki from half a century of comics.

However, in something of a reversal of narrative from the Loki of the 13th-century *Eddas* that they are inspired by, over the last 20 years the MCU Loki and the character as depicted in the main, ongoing line of Marvel comics have both evolved from villain to antihero. The developments in characterization and situation, coupled with their adaptability and omnipresence during this time have seen the multiple variants of Marvel's Loki(s) rise sharply in popularity and profitability (McMillan 2021). Today, readers and viewers have their pick of multiple, increasingly well-written, Loki variants, both as fictional characters themselves and in terms of the medium by which we may consume them. And so, a fandom has emerged around Marvel's Loki(s) that can identify with and celebrate the Loki of their choosing: by age, gender, sexuality, morality, and/or by; comic, book, film, television, cartoon, Lego, Funko Pop, fashion accessory, and more. The idolizing of Loki in the 21st century is not only based on fandom consumption but also in the creative fan labor of unofficial artwork, writing, and cosplay. As an attractive, queer, antihero, Marvel's Loki(s) now has a cult following that could not have existed for their 1960s counterpart, nor indeed, for the figure of Old Norse myth upon which they are based. Loki's rebirth has been their salvation.

Ragnarök and Rebirth

The cycle of life, death, and rebirth is a key component of Norse mythology known as Ragnarök, or the doom/final destiny/twilight of the gods; an unavoidable and indeed necessary cataclysm that ushers in a new world and new era. Its connotations with renewal, redemption, and to borrow an overused term, rebooting, have made it an ideal (yet relatively sparsely used) plot device in Marvel's Thor-associated comic lines for decades. As a spectacle-centered storyline, Ragnarök provides opportunities to transition between creative teams and character status quos, while also theoretically boosting comic sales by marketing the "event" to casual and dedicated fans alike. It helps those who are new to the Asgardians,

Marvel's interpretation of the Norse pantheon, by establishing relatively clear sides of good versus evil, while reaffirming the allegiances to fictional characters held by long-time readers and introducing the prospect of an unexpected twist or two.

In the MCU, Hiddleston's Loki has shifted from fighting his brother and trying to rule the world in *Thor* (2011) and *The Avengers* (2012) to fighting alongside Thor, not strictly for selfless reasons, in *Thor: The Dark World* (2013) and *Thor: Ragnarok* (2017). More recently, via some time/space travel shenanigans, the version of Loki from the Battle of New York in *The Avengers* has been helping to protect the MCU timeline and multiverse in the Disney+ series *Loki* (2021–2023). The redemptive turning point for the MCU Loki comes during the course of *Thor: Ragnarok*, where there are frequent questions around Loki's true function, purpose, and motivations. They clearly delight in being seen as a savior of Asgard while wrestling with their sense of identity and complicated relationship with Thor. In the film's finale, Loki plays a key role in ensuring the survival of Asgard's people at the expense of the place itself, ultimately joining Thor's side before later, apparently, sacrificing themself in a confrontation with Thanos, the villain of Marvel's *Avengers: Infinity War* (2018) and *Avengers: Endgame* (2019). For the audience, and for Hiddleston himself (Hickson 2022), the villainous Loki is redeemed at the end of their narrative before going through a renewal of sorts as a slightly younger version of themselves, returning in the opening episode of *Loki* (2021) as a reluctant hero.

In the pages of Marvel comics, the rehabilitation of Loki was a more gradual process that had already begun before the MCU franchise came into being. The 2004 *Avengers Disassembled* storyline included what seemed like a true end for Asgard when, with few options and a new perspective on cosmic destiny, Thor actually helps to bring about Ragnarök; the destruction of Asgard, and the death of almost everyone connected to it. What it ended up doing was giving the characters a rest for a few years before writer J. Michael Straczynski and artist Oliver Coipel could relaunch the Thor comics with a new Asgard relocating to Oklahoma, and Loki now possessing the body of a woman from time to time, being referred to as Lady Loki.

> I'm Loki, yes. I can **only** be Loki. But as much as they're able, I want people to trust me.
>
> Journey into Mystery #641 (Gillen et al. 2012, 12)

From then on, change became something of a constant for Loki. Their conscience got the better of them at the end of the *Siege* (2010) storyline when they regretted the assault on the Earthbound Asgard that they had engineered, and Loki seemingly died repenting. Loki would later be reincarnated (of sorts) in the body of a young boy, earning the nickname Kid Loki and seeking to forge a new path while atoning for the actions of their previous incarnation(s), including joining the heroic Young Avengers team in 2013. Another couple of renewals and jumps in age, and Loki embraces more positive, albeit always mischievous, new roles as a magical secret Agent of Asgard; a member of a short-lived version of The Defenders; the Sorcerer Supreme (taking over from Dr Strange briefly); and, more recently, the King of Jotunheim (a realm of Frost Giants where Loki originates from). These changes are all much more positive and purposeful, though never without some degree of Loki having a hidden agenda and deploying highly questionable methods.

Little by little, rebirth by rebirth, Marvel Comic's Loki has spent the best part of the last 20 years becoming a more complex and interesting character, for example in the miniseries now referred to as *Thor and Loki: Blood Brothers* (2004) and *The Trials of Loki* (2010). While retaining the standard of Loki as "the bad guy," both are explorations of the thoughts and feelings behind their actions, seeking to make them more of a sympathetic figure. It has become easier and more profitable to do more interesting things with the Trickster, and for the most part, each evolutionary stage in Loki has been welcomed by fans (McMillan 2021; Stitch 2021b; Johnson 2022).

This has been helped by the fact that Loki and their variants have become notably more attractive over the last two decades; on-screen as portrayed by Hiddleston and Sophia Di Martino, and on the page whether as Lady Loki or the more current genderfluid and younger-looking God of Stories who originated in the *Loki: Agent of Asgard* (2014–2015) series. The so-called Halo Effect (Thorndike 1920) of the physical attractiveness of Loki(s) in 21st-century pop culture has allowed both casual and more dedicated fans to overlook Loki's evil deeds. It has become common for the liar, traitor, and murderer Loki to be viewed in sympathetic and affectionate ways as fans have been guided toward engaging with a character increasingly depicted in androgynous, or at least not heteronormatively masculine, ways. These new depictions of Loki are founded in a white, male context – which is itself problematic (Stitch 2021b) – but it appears that moving away from the uglier, older, serpent-like God of Evil and Lies has facilitated a shift in cognitive bias, or a subconscious distortion in our perception (Thorndike 1920; Gibson and Gore 2016). Our 21st-century Loki is vulnerable and trauma-informed, charming and mysterious, and desirable in such a way to overwrite any negative interpretations of their innate personality traits.

This easier-on-the-eye redesign has crept into Marvel animation too, where the sneering and egotistical Loki of the more classic-styled *Avengers: Earth's Mightiest Heroes* (2010–2012) cartoon was abandoned with the cancellation of that series to make way for a blander, buffer, more attractive and masculine Loki in the lackluster MCU-inspired follow-up *Avengers Assemble* (2013–2019). The Agent of Asgard costume redesign in the *Avengers Assemble* cartoon was the only aspect of Ewing's comic run to be picked up and translated onto the small screen, and the distinct characterization from the more comics-accurate *Earth's Mightiest Heroes* show was dispensed with entirely.

A concerted effort has been made across Marvel's different media outputs to kill-off the long-familiar snarling and wizened evil Loki, whose jealousy and boredom had driven decades (or eons, depending on your perspective) of sinister attempts at seizing power. In their place has arisen several recognizably more attractive Loki variants who are more nuanced, morally ambiguous, and openly queer. The Loki(s) of the 21st century is infinitely more appealing and marketable as a young, queer antihero.

Queer Variants in a Transmedial Multiverse

There is an argument to be made that the poems and tales of Loki in Norse mythology as a shapeshifting, genderfluid, interspecies mating and birthing deity, depict them as being what we would recognize as queer (Worthington 2021). Though historically used in a pejorative way, the word "queer" has been widely seen to have been reclaimed by LGBTQ+ people as an empowering self-descriptor and community-building umbrella term, inclusive of a potentially fluid spectrum of gender, sexuality, and emotional/romantic desire (Jagose 1996; Khayatt 2002). In being queer, one is rejecting and/or subverting the strict heteronormative and binary gendered norms; expectations; and frequently, laws that have structured peoples' sense of who they are and how their lives may be experienced predominantly in modern, Western society (Jagose 1996; Khayatt 2002).

While the Norse people are recorded as having in some respects more liberal laws and practices than one might expect for the time (or indeed, might find today), that is not to say that it was a utopia in terms of equalities. The *Eddas* do not provide a tangible statement of inclusivity and instead hint toward the disgust and contempt that some of Loki's peers in the Norse pantheon felt toward the Trickster and their actions and attitudes. This is most notable in the "Lokasenna" aka "Loki's Quarrel," the equivalent of an Old Norse rap battle of the gods (von Schnurbein 2000; Sturluson [1220] 2005). Thus, the medieval literature, or at least Snorri Sturluson's Christian revision, infers that Loki's lifestyle is seen as subversive or even deviant. Stigma, prejudice, and bigotry have held back positive depictions of LGBTQ+ identities and lives but mainstream Western superhero media have begun to push back on this, tentatively, over the last 20 years in a way that might not have been expected of a traditionally heteronormative and often conservative genre (Curtis 2021). Marvel's Loki is now genderfluid and comfortable presenting in either masculine or feminine bodies, though still more often as masculine. The groundwork for this development began with the introduction of Lady Loki (with Loki possessing the body of a woman as part of a larger, long-term strategy) by the creative team of Straczynski and Coipel, before genderfluidity was cemented as part of Loki's identity by Al Ewing (writer) across the titles *Loki: Agent of Asgard, Defenders Beyond* (2022), *Original Sin* #5.5 (2014, co-written with Jason Aaron), and *The Immortal Thor* (2023 –).

> My son [Thor] and my daughter [Angela – a recent addition] and my child who is both [Loki]
>
> *Odin, referring to his children in* Original Sin *#5.5*
> *(Aaron, Ewing and Bianchi 2014, 18)*

A fleeting reference to Loki having the magical ability to "transform himself into a lovely maiden" was made back in 1963s *Journey Into Mystery* #92 (Lee, Bernstein and Sinnott 1963, 3), but it would take another 30 years for Marvel comic book readers to actually see Loki in female form. A brief sequence in *The Mighty Thor Annual* #18 in 1993 shows Loki shapeshifting into various guises in order to tempt a typically 1950s-style comic villain called The Flame into joining forces. One of Loki's transformations is into a hypersexualised Asgardian woman wearing practically nothing, intended to arouse The Flame (and likely the readership, too). It is not until the introduction of Lady Loki in 2007 that the character's outward plurality of self becomes a core aspect of their identity and thus a recurring plot point.

Loki's genderfluidity in Marvel comics, that up until relatively recently had never been a known component of the character as far as readers were concerned, was swiftly retconned as being a long-established and widely recognized fact of who they were. Marvel comics now routinely include Loki in celebrations of LGBTQ+ characters and community, in for example, the *Marvel Voices: Pride* comics. The 2023 Loki comic miniseries by Dan Watters (writer), Germán Peralta (artist), and Mike Spicer (colorist) casually switches between masculine and feminine depictions of the Trickster, without any need to explain, and Watters routinely refers to Loki using They/Them pronouns in Marvel's promotional material and interviews (Batts 2023). Their genderfluidity was also latterly made canon in the MCU, albeit with a blink-and-you'll-miss-it note on a personnel file in Season 1 of the Disney+ streaming series

Loki (2021). Sophia Di Martino's Sylvie character, written as a female variant of Loki from another universe, also functions within the narrative of the *Loki* series to indicate that the Trickster is not constrained by a binary notion of gender.

Another aspect of Loki's queerness across Marvel properties in recent years is their bi- or pansexuality, depending on the creative team on any particular story; although this has not been as visible a feature of the character thus far. Again, the *Loki* streaming series paid only brief attention to this; frustratingly so for many (Chilton 2021), and contributing to accusations of queerbaiting, was the suggestively queer/homoerotic marketing of the media property with little or no actualization within the show itself (Brennan 2018; Barr 2021). It has been a more explicit and repeated fact in the comic book pages, and a nuanced plot point in the 2019 young adult novelization *Loki: Where Mischief Lies* by Mackenzi Lee, where Loki grapples with their feelings for both the young Asgardian goddess Amora and a young man in Victorian London named Theo. The novel as a medium allows for a more detailed and respectfully handled approach to exploring Loki's queerness. It takes time to explore complex emotions and the internal narrative of Loki as a young person (relative to a god), learning how to be themself and how to reconcile their responsibilities with their own needs and aspirations.

In seeking to better explore Loki's queerness, one benefits from engaging in Marvel outputs from across different media to gain a fuller understanding of how they express and experience their gender(s) and sexuality. This has become a more frequently intentional feature of media corporations with profitable, long-running franchises in the 21st century. Transmedia storytelling sees the same key characters used across different mediums to tell narratives that can be consumed and enjoyed separately from one another, or all together in a fuller interconnected cultural product (Jenkins 2006). It has become a strategic feature of major franchises such as Pokémon, Star Wars, Doctor Who, and Marvel, to produce main storylines for widespread consumption via one medium (typically film and/or television); and supplement with additional content via comics, novels, animated features, video games, audio dramas, and so on (Jenkins 2006). Whether an artistic, editorial, or executive decision, Marvel's transmedia storytelling across (mainly) the MCU, comics, and now novelizations has proven to be a sustained commercial and critical success (Harrison, Carlsen and Škerlavaj 2019; Fisher 2024). Marvel's multiversal worldbuilding and immersive, canonical narratives have been a key factor in solidifying the popularity of its reborn, queer, antiheroic Loki(s).

It would be hard to deny that Marvel's Loki was queer-coded, just as the original Norse Loki was. In terms of historical folklore, the trickster figure is typically a mercurial shapeshifter, whose actions and desires are viewed by many as being transgressive from the norm, sometimes to the point of being deviant or dangerous (Bassil-Morozow 2017). Much of the subtext around Marvel's Loki(s) is built upon a challenging and subverting of structural norms, whether on Earth, Asgard, or anywhere else in the cosmic realms. But queer-coding and/or definitively writing a character as queer could be problematic if that character is a two-dimensional villain and mishandled, potentially equating anyone outside of heteronormative and cisgendered identity as being a threat or somehow 'evil' (Easton 2013). As a more fully developed antihero across Marvel's transmedial output, Loki offers accessible, mainstream, popular representation for many queer people (Bonnelly 2018; Stitch 2021b; Worthington 2021). It would be quite unexpected and perhaps ill-advised at this point to have Loki revert to a purely antagonistic role, and indeed writer Ewing agrees that one is unlikely to see "Loki as an out and out baddie" for quite some time yet (McMillan 2021).

The Cult of Loki

It is of course thanks to the enthusiastic reception and massive consumption of the MCU, the comics, the novelizations, the cartoons, the toys and games, the fashion and accessories, etc., that Loki as an antihero has been so swiftly accepted and embedded across Marvel media. This has relied on the emotional and financial dedication of Marvel/superhero/comic book fandom as much as, if not more than, the more casually acquainted consumer of popular culture. The Marvel fan following has grown exponentially in the 21st century, driven largely by the success of the MCU franchise, but concurrently with the social acceptance and ubiquity of pop culture fandom in general, and most visibly across the so-called Western world.

Fandoms, particularly pop culture fandoms, have existed for decades though many were historically stigmatized or underground, with comic fandom having been a prime example of this for much of the 20th century (Lopes 2006). These object and/or text-based collectives offer fans who share cultural interests and practices a sense of solidarity or even extended family, whether in the virtual world of social media, forums, and fansites; or more tangibly in film screenings, reading groups, cosplay events, specialist shops, conventions, etc. Individual and group identities in Marvel fandom are formed in part around the characters they most enjoy and empathize with from across the multiverse, in part around their relationship with (and expertise in) over 60 years of canonical text and other cultural artifacts, and in part through their social interactions with one another (Jenkins 1992; Hills 2002; Gray, Sandvoss and Harrington 2017). In addition, the MCU has incorporated the fandoms established around specific genre actors, writers, directors, etc., now, too.

One might argue that it is disrespectful to liken a fan following to a cult, given the legacy of negative connotations with some cults and their actions, but that is sincerely not the intention here. Rather, it is meant in this instance to compare the lived experience of Marvel fandom (in some but not necessarily all individuals and/or groups) to a form of neo-religion based on canon, idolism, and sacred practice within a culture-specific community (Hills 2002; Elliot 2021). In addition to the consumption of Marvel outputs and products by the fandom, many fans have expanded their devotion to the production of their own unofficial texts, artifacts, etc., in forms such as fan fiction, films, and artwork; faithful and inspired costuming and other crafting; curation and archiving of canon via fan blogs and wiki databases, and zine-making. These endeavors may place a fan creator within a further social circle of fandom, where the attention to detail and production values of fan labor affords a form of social capital or prestige.

Loki's following is a prime example of where the character and their variants have reached fans and offered a heroic idol to align one's sense of self with, and to focus one's own creative output around. For context, at the time of writing, the popularity of Loki on some prominent online platforms catering to fans, crudely quantified by the tagged appearance of "#loki," is as follows:

- Almost 240,000 videos, and 80,000 channels on YouTube
- Over 25 billion views of TikTok videos
- Almost 450,000 followers on Tumblr
- Over 90,000 pieces of fanfiction on Archive of Our Own

Academic theorizing of fandoms in the West has progressed through a few key stages since approximately the late 1980s, focusing largely on the experience of stigma, the associated practices of cultural production and consumption, the social hierarchies within fandoms, and more recently, the intersections of identity and inequalities within fandoms and their relationship with the object(s) of their following in this regard. Fan labor, notably in the forms of fanfiction and fanart, provides an opportunity for fans from marginalized and/or discriminated backgrounds to effectively insert themselves into their own fan "head canon" (Gray, Sandvoss and Harrington 2017; Stitch 2021a). Relatedly, it allows queer fans to expand on what many see as a rather tentative or gentle queering of Marvel's Loki(s) in official canon. Thus, a substantial amount of Loki fanfiction and fanart centers around exploring what Loki's thoughts and feelings might be around their identity, or shipping Loki in romantic and often sexual relationships with characters such as Thor, or Mobius from the *Loki* show on Disney+ in what is surely a response to the apparent queerbaiting of the inferred "Lokius" (Loki and Mobius) attraction. Other fan labors concern Loki's genderfluidity and present Loki as feminine or non-binary.

A 2022 collection *Variant: A Loki Fanzine* (Amitiel et al. 2022) offers several examples, some more plainly apparent than others, including short stories about Loki struggling with being literally broken and having to rebuild themself, or seducing a man on the dancefloor, or practicing shapeshifting from a male-presenting appearance to a female-presenting one. There are also visual artworks depicting Loki in an almost erotic and feminine-coded pose, or in their *Thor: Ragnarok* guise in intimate proximity with both seemingly male and female individuals, or as a variety of genders. A recurring theme across most of the fanfiction and fanart of *Variant: A Loki Fanzine* (Amitiel et al. 2022) is reference to Loki's nurturing and protective relationship with their mother; a common trope in queer representation across popular culture, particularly with regard to homosexual men.

It would be disrespectful, however, to reduce fan labors to being thought of as amateur archetypal or even clichéd creations. The key connecting thread across the fanart and fandom of Loki – the cult of Loki, if you will – is that fans identify with Loki's outsider status and their feelings around being misunderstood and misjudged.

> I am Loki. God of Outcasts. They see themselves in me. And I in them. All of us. Alone together.
>
> Loki #5 *(Kibblesmith, Yildirim and MacDonald 2019, 19)*

Diversity and representation in mainstream superhero pop culture has expanded and improved over the last quarter century, establishing queer heroes such as Wiccan, Hulkling, and America Chavez (Kid Loki's teammates in the *Young Avengers*) at Marvel, and Aqualad, Superboy/man Jon Kent, and Batwoman at DC. More broadly, superhero comics have sought to better engage with intersecting factors of sex and gender, sexuality, race and ethnicity, disability, mental health, and class, with creative teams and editorial directions that are more progressive, respectful, and inclusive (Curtis and Cardo 2018; Stein 2018; Wolk 2021). In its small contribution, better representation – particularly queer representation – in mainstream superheroes has helped to destigmatize and legitimize marginalized/discriminated groups, as well as providing accessible iconography and characters for fans to focus their own creative development on. By no means has this solved all of society's problems, nor has it eradicated hate (in some respects it has focused it), but often for individual fans it has offered hope and assurance (Curtis and Cardo 2018; Stein 2018). One no longer has to merely wait to be saved by their hero; now they can see themselves in their hero.

Marvel's God of Lies and Mischief has been reborn in the 21st century as a God of Outcasts and Stories, meeting a new, enthusiastic, and more diverse audience. The gradual process of abandoning the Silver Age-inspired evil pantomime baddie in favor of a more complex, malleable, and charming queer antihero across Marvel's media output has aided the progression of more representative mainstream pop culture, particularly in comic books. This in turn has created the right environment for a Loki fandom to flourish, as the character offers an accessible and, significantly, acceptable idol for individuals to explore, understand, and express their own queerness and/or experience of outsiderness. This redemption of Loki has not progressed quickly enough for some, and there is apparently some trepidation in film and television production regarding how identifiably queer to make the subversive, shapeshifting Skald of Realms. Far less so in comics, which have proven to be the ideal art form with which to direct the redemption of Loki across Marvel's transmedia canon, though the attractive physical appearance of Tom Hiddleston in the MCU variant has played a key role in changing the perspective of the audience with regard to Loki's villainous nature. A halo now rests upon the horns, though at a somewhat jaunty angle.

References

Aaron, Jason, Al Ewing, and Simone Bianchi. 2014. *Original Sin #5.5*. Marvel Comics. Marvel Unlimited.

Amitiel, Astramaxima, AuroraWest, et al. 2022. *Variant: A Loki FanZine*. Self-published. https://variantzine.carrd.co/.

Barr, Sabrina. 2021. "Loki fans defend Marvel series over 'queerbaiting' claims as director says God of Mischief's bisexuality won't be explored further." *Metro*, July 2. https://metro.co.uk/2021/07/02/lokis-bisexuality-wont-be-explored-further-in-marvel-series-14863473/.

Bassil-Morozow, Helena. 2017. "Loki then and Now: the Trickster against Civilization." *International Journal of Jungian Studies* 9, no.2: 84–96.

Batts, Alex. 2023. "Exclusive: Dan Watters Blends Norse Mythology with the Marvel Universe in Loki." *CBR*, May 4. https://www.cbr.com/loki-dan-watters-interview/.

Bonnelly, Marlene. 2018. "Loki's Sexuality and Gender Fluidity in Comics." *The Mary Sue*, June 21. https://www.themarysue.com/loki-sexuality-gender-fluidity/

Brennan, Joseph. 2018. "Queerbaiting: The 'Playful' Possibilities of Homoeroticism." *International Journal of Cultural Studies* 21, no.2: 189–206.

Chilton, Louis. 2021. "Russel T Davies launches scathing critique of Loki's bisexual representation: 'It's a ridiculous, craven, feeble gesture.'" *The Independent*, August 11. https://www.independent.co.uk/arts-entertainment/tv/news/loki-bisexual-russell-t-davies-marvel-b1900602.html.

Curtis, Neal. 2021. "Superheroes and the Mythic Imagination: Order, Agency and Politics." *Journal of Graphic Novels and Comics* 12, no.5: 360–374.

Curtis, Neal, and Valentina Cardo. 2018. "Superheroes and Third-Wave Feminism." *Feminist Media Studies* 18, no.3: 381–396.

Easton, Lee. 2013. "Saying No to Hetero-Masculinity: The Villain in the Superhero Film." *Cinephile: The University of British Columbia's Film Journal* 9, no.2: 38–44.

Elliott, Michael A. 2021. "Fandom as Religion: A Social-Scientific Assessment." *The Journal of Fandom Studies* 9, no.2: 107–122.

Ewing, Al, Lee Garbett, and Antonio Fabela. 2015. *Loki: Agent of Asgard #17*. Marvel Comics. Marvel Unlimited.

Fisher, Liz. 2024. "Marvel's stratospheric success." *Accounting and Business Magazine*, December. https://abmagazine.accaglobal.com/global/articles/2024/dec/business/marvel-s-stratospheric-success.html.

Harrison, Spencer, Arne Carlsen, and Miha Škerlavaj. 2019. "Marvel's Blockbuster Machine." *Harvard Business Review*, July-August. https://hbr.org/2019/07/marvels-blockbuster-machine.

Heide, Eldar. 2011. "Loki, the 'Vätte', and the Ash Lad: A Study Combining Old Scandinavian and Late Material." *Viking and Medieval Scandinavia* 7: 63–106.

Hickson, Colin. 2022. "Why Tom Hiddleston Agreed to do Loki After Dying in Avengers: Infinity War." *CBR*, April 29. https://www.cbr.com/tom-hiddleston-reason-for-loki-after-avengers-infinity-war-marvel/.

Hills, Matt. 2002. *Fan Cultures*. Routledge.

Gibson, Jeremy L., and Jonathan S. Gore. 2016. "Is He a Hero or a Weirdo? How Norm Violations Influence the Halo Effect." *Gender Issues* 33: 299–310.

Gillen, Kieron, Richard Elson, Ifansyah Noor, and Sotocolor. 2012. *Journey into Mystery* #641. Marvel Comics. Marvel Unlimited.

Gray, Jonathan, Cornel Sandvoss, and C. Lee Harrington, eds. 2017. *Fandom: Identities and Communities in a Mediated World*. 2nd ed. NYU Press.

Jagose, Annamarie. 1996. *Queer Theory: An Introduction*. NYU Press.

Jenkins, Henry. 1992. *Textual Poachers: Television Fans & Participatory Culture*. Routledge.

Jenkins, Henry. 2006. *Convergence Culture: Where Old and New Media Collide*. NYU Press.

Johnson, Karl. 2022. *The Loki Variations: The Man, The Myth, The Mischief*. 404 Ink.

Khayatt, Didi. 2002. "Toward a Queer Identity." *Sexualities* 5, no.4: 487–501.

Kibblesmith, Daniel, Ozgur Yildirim, and Andy MacDonald. 2019. *Loki #5*. Marvel Comics. Marvel Unlimited.

Lee, Stan, Robert Bernstein, and Joe Sinnott. 1963. *Journey Into Mystery* #92. Marvel Comics. Marvel Unlimited.

Lopes, Paul. 2006. "Culture and Stigma: Popular Culture and the Case of Comic Books." *Sociological Forum* 21, no.3: 387–414.

McMillan, Graeme. 2021. "Loki: How Marvel Comics Turned its Most Selfish Villain into a Hero." *Inverse*, May 28. https://www.inverse.com/entertainment/loki-hero-or-villain-comic-book-history.

Stein, Daniel. 2018. "Bodies in Transition. Queering the Comic Book Superhero." *Navigationen* 1, Summer: 15–38.

Stitch. 2021a. "How Do We Define Fandom? Moving Beyond the Transformative vs. Curatorial Binary." *Teen Vogue*, March 16. https://www.teenvogue.com/story/how-do-we-define-fandom-stitch-fan-service.

Stitch. 2021b. "On Loki, Anti-Heroes, and Who Gets to Be a Lovable Villain." *Teen Vogue*, July 21. https://www.teenvogue.com/story/on-loki-anti-heroes-and-who-gets-to-be-a-lovable-villain-fan-service.

Sturluson, Snorri. (1220) 2005. *The Prose Edda*. Penguin Classics.

Thorndike, Edward Lee. 1920. "A Constant Error in Psychological Ratings." *Journal of Applied Psychology* 4, no.1: 25–29.

von Schnurbein, Stefanie. 2000. "The Function of Loki in Snorri Sturluson's 'Edda.'" *History of Religions* 40, no.2: 109–124.

Wolk, Douglas. 2021. *All of the Marvels: An Amazing Voyage into Marvel's Universe and 27,000 Superhero Comics*. Profile Books.

Worthington, Clint. 2021. "From Myth to MCU, Loki Was Always Queer." *The Companion*, June 23. https://www.thecompanion.app/loki-queer-marvel/.

38

THE POWER IN SEEING YOURSELF IN ANOTHER

X-Men, Audiences, and Queer Rights through *X-Men '97*

Patrick Munnelly, Tanya Cook and Kaela Joseph

Introduction

X-Men '97, a continuation of *X-Men: The Animated Series* (1992–1997), debuted on Disney+ in March of 2024 to enthusiastic response. Accommodating an older audience-base, nostalgic of the original series from their youth, *X-Men '97* is a darker iteration that intentionally speaks to a diverse viewership capable of understanding complex storylines in a fractured media and political landscape. It accesses the collective consciousness of these fans who, as a generation (millennial), have seen firsthand the displacement of relative peace in the US and Global North, where the shows originated and were most popular, by war, terrorism, and neo-fascism. Now adults, with the power to shape the sociopolitical conversations that impact today's youth, *X-Men '97* presents a more honest dialogue about the ways in which differences in power and privilege corrupt social discourse to work against the masses. This is especially true for people who hold lesbian, gay, bisexual, transgender, and additional marginalized sexual and gender identities (LGBTQ+).

We argue that although X-Men as a broader franchise has always presented a noteworthy queer allegory (Roman 2022), the reboot of the franchise through *X-Men '97* represents a shift toward more overt queer representation, which further reinforces its legacy as a countercultural, mobilizing space for queer people. More specifically, this chapter brings together research and literature analysis from communication, psychology, sociology, queer studies, and fan studies to explore the following: (1) how the X-Men franchise as a whole supports queer liberation through its allegorical (queer coded) themes, (2) how the addition of *X-Men '97* to the franchise line-up confirmed and added to the notion that X-Men is a queer allegory, and (3) the limits of the queer allegory and the necessities of increased textual representation. In so doing, this chapter seeks to reflect upon the active consumption of superhero media by queer millennial X-Men fans, galvanized to later social action through series themes and fan identity. Despite cross-cultural appeal and adaptability, this chapter will focus primarily on sociopolitical allegory in the US and Global North since this is the lens through which the franchise is primarily written, set, and viewed.

DOI: 10.4324/9781003366911-43

The Queer [Liberation] Allegory

The X-Men franchise centers around diversified, progressive resistance to fascist attempts at the extermination of minoritized people. In parallel to the real world, the lines between hero and villain are blurred as evidenced by the polarized approaches to liberation via Professor X's X-Men and Magneto's Brotherhood of Mutants. Even though genetic differences do not make someone inhuman, mutants, on the other hand, are considered to be qualitatively different from homosapiens, referred to as homosapiens superior. While the symbolism here could be, and has been, applied to many marginalized communities, the queer allegory is particularly rife with examples. As summed up by Christopher Michael Roman,

> [t]he debate over just how queer mutants are is an important one, as many readers identify with the marginalised mutants, utilising the 'mutant metaphor' as a stand-in for resistance to prejudice and bigotry faced by people of colour, those with disabilities, and the LGBTQ+ community.
>
> *(2022, 771)*

Most of the narratives focused on by X-Men television and film properties revolve around this concept of homosapiens and the threat of their gradual extinction to mutants. These fears parallel social fears of the past 60 years around increasing support for LGBTQ+ rights and identities. In X-Men, prominent political figures and military leaders often gather to discuss how to combat the "mutant problem" with projects like the Sentinels (robots who possess mutant "seeking" abilities and can eradicate or neutralize them), or projects like mutant registration acts. Once captured, the mutants are often collared somehow to tamper their abilities down, essentially removing what makes them different and special, returning them to "human."

From this storyline, one can view the "mutant threat" as analogous to the "queer threat" and the weaponized rhetoric previously and currently seen around the "removal" of queerness. The Sentinel Project, for example, is metaphorically similar to attempts at seeking out and removing queer people from public life and positions of influence. The Sentinels could easily be stand-ins for the mass arrest and imprisonment of queer people, especially gay and bisexual men, in Nazi-occupied Germany before and during World War II, a population whose numbers were smaller than Jewish and other prisoners, but who were killed in concentration camps at disproportionately high rates (Lautmann 1981). Collaring mutants to impede their abilities parallels chemical castration used against queer people (Doan 2017). While not necessarily associated with extermination or extreme altering of the body, McCarthyism and the Lavender Scare Eras in the US saw the hunting down of LGBTQ+ people who were seen as threats and potential "weak" targets susceptible to coercion from foreign governments, thereby removing them from positions of influence in the entertainment industry, education, and government (Adkins 2016; Malone 2019).

In the US specifically, recent increases in anti-LGBTQ+ legislation and rhetoric which labels LGBTQ+ people, especially transgender people, as dangerous (threatening the safety of locker rooms or marriages), has been associated with increased acts of violence against these communities (Brightman et al. 2024). Across the world, there are still a number of anti-LGBTQ+ laws either criminalizing or outlawing sex acts, and homosexual acts specifically (Human Rights Watch n.d.). Still, anti-LGBTQ+ rhetoric across cultures remains the same as anti-mutant rhetoric in media about X-Men: exterminate or be exterminated. Even those countries who maintain greater LGBTQ+ rights are now regularly exposed to media examples of politicians calling for the deaths of queer people (Brightman et al. 2024). Since LGBTQ+ people still make up a minority of the global population at approximately 9% of adults (Moreau 2023), they need the "approval" of the majority in power in order to stay safe and not have to hide, pass, or blend.

Queer theory experts largely agree on queerness as an opposition to dominant, heteronormative discourses (Ahmed 2006; Jagose 2009). As such, because the X-Men challenge dominant discourses with their existence, they can be read as queer. Annamarie Jagose (2009) states queer theory isn't one simple thing, but rather a messy amalgamation of ideas and questions that are constantly reorienting themselves. In other words, to borrow from the X-Men, queer theory itself is a mutation. Sara Ahmed states that a "queer subject within straight culture hence deviates and is made socially present as a deviant" (2006, 21). Using Ahmed's *Queer Phenomenology* (2006), a queer phenomenological reading of X-Men observes that these deviants relate to an orientation (good or evil) and the space/direction of their body (visibly mutated or not). These orientations can thus be ported directly over to LGBTQ+ people and sexual orientations (hetero as good, homo as bad; visibly queer or not).

Queer theory in X-Men has been written about to interpret queerness and feminist approaches, along with clearly established connections to the civil rights movements (Fawaz 2011; Grimsted et al. 2024; Lecker 2007). Ramzi Fawaz provides a large overview of the queer allegories for the franchise: "the X-Men tells the story of an international cadre of superpowered beings known as 'mutants,' genetically evolved humans outcast by a bigoted and fearful humanity" (2011, 357), whose mutations are akin to the critiques of identity via gay liberation and women's rights movements. Outside of the Civil Rights discussions of the 1960s, Grimsted et al. (2024) introduce their article with side-by-side quotes from the 2000 movie entry and a 2023 Florida senator quote, drawing real-life connections between the X-Men and other mentions of bans and registration acts.

Various pop culture resources have also alluded to the allegory of X-Men as queer. In 2000, *X-Men* director Bryan Singer, approached out, gay actor Ian McKellen (Magneto) to discuss the similarities between the X-Men's fight for mutant rights and modern-day LGBTQ+ struggles (Vary 2006). Notably, contributors to X-Men II (2003), "Singer, and screenwriters Dan Harris and Michael Dougherty-were all gay" (Vary 2006, 45). Betancourt (2016) notes that Iceman had an allegorical moment created by Singer in *X-Men II* in which his family asked the pivotal question known to queer people: "have you tried not being a mutant?" (Singer 2003, 00:59:38). Iceman subsequently came out in the comics as gay in 2015, becoming a canonical aspect of his character (Gustines 2015). Other LGBTQ+-focused events happened within X-Men too, like the 1984 comics featuring the queer kinship of Kitty Pryde (Shadowcat) and Logan (Wolverine) through their representation of an atypical, or chosen, family (Roman 2022).

Additionally, Anthony Michael D'Agostino reads heavily into Rogue's place in the comics as "a focal point for an examination of how queer embodiment and subjectivity constitute themselves in the form of the superhero and how the superhero comments on and interrogates queer modes of being" (2018, 255). D'Agostino (2018) goes so far as to claim that Rogue is "butch" and possibly a secret or closet lesbian. Rogue, who has the power to drain abilities, or even a life force out of someone by simply touching them, is symbolic of the anxiety or dread of queer people who fear touching one another in public. In public, a queer couple who does not pass for straight may experience apprehension at touching one another, just as Rogue does. Rogue fears her touch will potentially kill someone, but she also struggles with not being able to touch people in a romantic way. Rogue has also been interpreted as a representation of public fears about HIV/AIDS in the 1980s and 1990s, including early misunderstandings of how it was transmitted, as well as broader fears of sexual expression among queer men who were (and still are) diagnosed at disproportionately high rates (Earnest 2007).

Both race and sexuality have been understood as metaphors for mutations depicted in the world of X-Men (Grimsted et al. 2024). The main differences between the issues of race and sexuality are the apparent versus non-apparent identities held, and to some extent whether they are perceived by broader society as ascribed versus achieved identities (Linton 1936). Some mutants do not experience any outwardly apparent mutations, while others do. These contrasts can be seen through narratives like those of Jubilee or Iceman who have to "come out" as mutants, choosing to reveal otherwise non-apparent identities versus continuing "pass" as homosapiens. Notably, as with real-world queer identities, "passing" is not without its own associated stressors as navigation of outness is multifaceted, taking into consideration physical and psychological safety, as well as community connectedness and the impacts of minority stressors like harassment and discrimination (Huang and Chan 2022; Beagan et al. 2022).

Melanie Kohnen (2015) connects the movie *X-Men: First Class* (2011) to queer visibility by writing directly about the topic of "passing" versus "not passing." In the movie, two standout narratives showcase this contrast: Beast, who cannot hide his blue, large, hairy body without medication that tampers his powers, versus Mystique, who cannot hide her blue, scaled body until she chooses to transform and "wear" a new look that is no longer her own. Both are able to navigate "passing," but with differing levels of personal cost and choice. Kohnen (2015) relates this passing, unnoticed, societal blending to the US policy of "Don't Ask, Don't Tell."

Largely seen and depicted across all of the movies, the mutants who can "pass" as normal often choose the side of Xavier and the X-Men fighting for equality, and those mutants who cannot "pass" often choose the side of Magneto and those fighting for the right to exist. The choosing of sides, especially the need to leave one's birth family or original guardians in order to join one of these mutant factions in the first place, is important and can widely be seen as allegorical in and of itself as a model for found or chosen families. For the X-Men, a found family could be that of Xavier's School for Gifted Youngsters, or Magneto's island salvation of Genosha.

The concept of found/chosen families is one not uncommon to LGBTQ people, or to fandoms (Joseph 2019; Duncan 2022). People of historically marginalized backgrounds, including LGBTQ individuals often share the experience of being rejected by their family of origin. In more recent years, the practice of chosen family or found family is still a survival strategy for those at society's margins, especially LGBTQ+ individuals, and serves to provide the private goods (emotional support, financial assistance, sick care) they may expect from members of their families of origin who are unwilling or unavailable (Cherlin 2012). For the X-Men, a found family fulfills these private needs as an agent of socialization, which then socializes the next generation of mutants into having a shared set of values.

The New Old Mutants of *X-Men '97*

Indeed, the mutant allegory as queer allegory has been written about extensively from a few different vantage points, mostly the movies and the comics (D'Agostino 2018; Grimsted et al.

2024; Fawaz 2011, 2016; Scott and Fawaz 2018). The TV shows, particularly *X-Men '97*, haven't had the same attention. Most recently, Attitude Magazine interviewed five LGBTQ+ men who watched both the original *X-Men: The Animated Series*, and the recent reboot, *X-Men '97* (James 2024). One participant stated:

> To me, X-Men represents and reminds me that no matter how different people and their perspectives may be, we should strive to embrace those differences because they always make us more knowledgeable, improve our understanding, and also make us stronger in the end.
>
> *(James 2024)*

X-Men '97 like some of the other recent additions to the Marvel Universe aim to expand the LGBTQ+ representation (James 2023). The creator of *X-Men '97* also identifies as a gay man (Sim 2024), and confirmed in a tweet that Morph confessed their romantic love to Logan in the season finale (DeMayo 2024).

In *X-Men: The Animated Series*, the first episode focuses on a mutant registration program meant to "help those unfortunate people" (Houston 1992, 00:01:31). Viewers follow the introduction of a new mutant named Jubilee, who states "I used to be a normal kid; it's not my fault" (Houston 1992, 00:01:49). These common refrains ("normal", "fault") are spoken widely in the X-Men universe, and are also common refrains known by queer people. Being different (understood to the general public as a threat) was not something asked for, but rather a difference that simply existed in individuals. An individual's mutant status parallels the concept of a socially ascribed rather than achieved status (Linton 1936). When someone's identities are understood primarily through an ascribed status it can feel like a one-dimensional representation for the individual. The desire to be seen as a fully complex individual that exists at the intersections of one's identities is a common one, especially among historically marginalized people. In fact, this introduction to differences and a rejection of one's own identity is mirrored almost identically in *X-Men '97* through Roberto rejecting his own mutant identity and being befriended by Jubilee, now a seasoned member of the X-Men.

X-Men: The Animated Series and *X-Men '97* presents individuals who are multifaceted and multi-layered; however, the mutation(s) an individual experiences and the abilities associated with it are only one part of what shapes their experience. Grimsted et al. summarize this point well by sharing that the narratives one can experience through the X-Men "give[s] us vivid, if fictional, portraits of how people live with an othered identity, and the various ways they react to the challenges of oppression" (2024, 2). While both the original animated series and revival did not openly represent LGBTQ+ characters, many viewers understood the mutant allegory to be representative of LGBTQ+ identities, among many other marginalized identities (Grimsted et al. 2024).

As millennials age into middle adulthood, one can see a reexamination on the generational progress of LGBTQ+ rights. This narrative can be seen through the choices made by the creators of *X-Men '97*; Sunspot follows in the same narrative vein as Jubilee, and Morph, now added to the core team, has received a redrawn aesthetic, with a slimming down of the masculinity seen in the original series for them to become a nonbinary mutant with They/Them pronouns. In an opinion piece reflecting on the two animated series as queer allegory, David Opie (2024) states that the X-Men in both are "strong and defiant beyond the pain that comes with living in a world that's not built for you," but *X-Men 97'* "explore[s] what the future looks like when acceptance feels like it might actually be in reach."

X-Men '97 also can be viewed through another branch of Queer Theory known as Queer Temporality (Halberstam 2005). Queer Temporality is the notion that queer people experience time differently than non-queer people, for example, a biological clock, or coming out later in life due to delayed sexual development. Given that the onset of most powers in the mutant world is around the time of puberty, this same temporal delay is often experienced by mutants. Michael J. Lecker directly connected this concept to queerness by stating, "[t]he onset of both Rogue's and Rusty's powers occur during their teenage years and at times of high sexual emotions, paralleling the realization of difference for queer youths" (2007, 681). In *X-Men '97* one can see this familiar sight appear in episode 4, "Motendo/Lifedeath," after Jubilee and Roberto escape the video game jail: Jubilee excitedly kisses Roberto and her powers activate in the form of sparks and fireworks levitating off her body.

Queer Temporality is also often present in the world of X-Men through time-travel and mind-bending powers, but also in the narratives about the struggles, disruptions, or non-normative practices that the characters experience through their powers. As demonstrated through Rogue, who couldn't kiss or touch after the onset of her powers, or Wolverine who experiences mental loss around the experimentations done on him, the notions of Queer Temporality extend to bodily autonomy regarding who, what, how, and when a mutant can experience humanity.

In *X-Men '97*, this same notion of non-normative experiences of time can be seen through Bishop and Cable traveling into the future to save Cable's life, only for Cable to return as a fully grown adult, shocking his parents. Queer Temporality doesn't need to be an explicit linear path with regards to time either, but anything where the person's time can become out-of-sync with societal expectations. Storm experiences her own temporal disjunction when her powers are taken from her. Depressed and now disconnected from the elements, she leaves her home, no longer feeling like she is a part of this family, almost akin to queer youth fearing they would be kicked out of their home for being "different."

In 2022, Hantsbarger et al. applied the notion of queer temporality to video games by expressing that game mechanics can not only be queered, but queer temporality can be introduced through narrative structures. Jack Halberstam (2017, in Ruberg and Shaw 2017) also introduced the idea that queer coding, hacking, and cheating are a form of queer theory through which video games disrupt normative experiences. In episode 4, "Motendo/Lifedeath," Jubilee and Roberto are transported into a video game world by the villain Mojo. While playing the game, Jubilee and Roberto meet an older character that helps them through cheat codes/glitches. They find out that this is an older version of Jubilee. When meeting her older self, young Jubilee states, "figures my game has cheat codes" (Conley 2024c, 00:14:39). Jubilee, and by proxy Roberto, experience a twofold version of Queer Temporality through Jubilee's meeting of her older self as well as navigating an unwinnable scenario by hacking the code to succeed. Through these various viewpoints of Queer Temporality, a stronger iteration of queerness is embedded into *X-Men '97*, through Cable's rapid aging, Storm's loss, and Jubilee's uncontrolled powers and cheat codes. While this essay asserts that Morph is the only true LGBTQ+ addition to the show, all of these queer themes can still be reflected upon and moderated by viewers.

The Limits of Allegory

In the reflection on time and place by millennial audiences, it is important to note how far the series has come in turning inexplicit allegory into actual representation, while also noting the need for further textual examples in the future. Research suggests that fandom and popular media can play pivotal roles in LGBTQ+ identity development (McInroy and Craig 2018). While several examples of allegorical influence on identity have been noted throughout this chapter, research suggests broader applicability and influence on self-affirmation and resilience among LGBTQ+ people when representation is both direct/canonical and positive (Dajches and Barbati 2024). This is because LGBTQ+ identity development is necessarily a comparative, social process, and icons can provide a supportive framework when direct role models are not immediately available (Cottle et al. 2024). Conversely, negative and negligible representation has been linked to greater psychological distress among LGBTQ+ audiences (Hughto et al. 2021; Nakamura and Logie 2020). Cheng et al. (2023) note that direct representation influences both moral attitudes and the market, as films with LGBTQ+ representation perform better at the box office than those that do not. In the case of *X-Men '97* one can see some of that increased, direct representation in comparison to the original series, but it still maintains a primary focus on canonically straight couples and cisgender characters. As a result, queer characters remain at least somewhat tokenized, as anomalies even in a community of anomalies. In other words, the reboot is a step in the right direction, but it is hopefully one of many more steps still needed in superhero media.

Conclusion

Quoting T.S. Eliot's poem "East Coker," Beast, addressing matters of identity in *X-Men '97* states, "every moment is a new and shocking valuation of all we have ever been" (Conley 2024b, 3:05). This could not be truer of queer allegory in the X-Men franchise, especially the animated series. As we look to past, present, and future we are faced with new and shocking valuations of queer narratives in these moments in time. With a show that raised a generation of queer millennial fans through allegorical themes, the present lineup of characters further confirms these queer readings. Looking toward the future, there is a hope that queerness will become more explicit in superhero media. This chapter argues that millennial fans, through identity appraisal and Queer Temporality, adjacent to their past and present allegorical identification with the characters of X-Men animated series, are encouraged to share the shows' central value system of tolerance, equality, and inclusion through a generational collective identity.

Millennial and subsequent generations are more likely to identify as LGBTQ+ as well as support same-sex marriage and other LGBTQ+ rights (Berger 2018). As children, they were one of the last generations to experience the ubiquitousness of Saturday morning cartoons, one of those being *X-Men: The Animated Series*. If viewed as both queer liberation allegory and a millennial social location touchstone, it stands to reason that millennial LGBTQ+ fans of the series could have internalized messages about outness and pride consistent with the show's themes.

X-Men '97 is the culmination of this generation's coming of age. Updates to the characters Morph and Jubilee, Storm's depressing loss, Magneto's rise to power, Cable's time travel, Gambit's death, and even the mirrored introduction of Roberto represent the darker aftermath that Millennials are used to seeing in the modern day. Though dark, this persistence of audience attention supports the queer liberation allegory seen in X-Men animated shows. The more canonical queer subtext reinforces both the socio-cultural changes millennials have witnessed since the 1990s and the ongoing appetite for more diverse and more complex representation in media. This chapter argues, however, that *X-Men '97* could have gone even further to include more queer representation and storylines instead of the same, tired heterosexual ones (Storm and Forge, Cyclops and Jean, Rogue and Gambit).

As the first natives of the digital age, millennial X-Men fans are also faced with ways that fandom itself shapes identity, especially through online engagement. LGBTQ+ fans across media properties have noted fandom as important to identity development (McInroy and Craig 2018), while interviews by James (2024) highlight the role of *X-Men: The Animated Series* in specifically shaping some queer fans' identities. Identifying as a fan has come to mean different things depending on the subject of fandom and the frequency and intensity of fannish behavior, but it inherently carries moral, emotional, and behavioral expectations (Cook and Joseph 2023). In addition to aiding the process of identity development, it is through fandom that media and social movements can become cultural agents of socialization. As such, the identity of a 'fan' in a specific context both demands and reinforces action from individuals (Cook and Joseph 2023).

As stated, allegorically, by Magneto in *X-Men '97*, queer fans have a shared "dream" that "does not ask you to love or embrace [us] as your own, but merely to accept that this is a shared world with a common future and [our] kind, like yours, have the right to live in it" (Conley 2024a, 00:23:03). As a generation raised with the increased visibility and acceptability of fandom in the digital age, queer millennial fans are thus less likely to be satisfied with half-measures taken toward inclusion and rights, having been raised with critically reflective, animated shows featuring the X-Men.

References

Adkins, Judith. 2016. "'These People Are Frightened to Death:' Congressional Investigations and the Lavender Scare." *Prologue Magazine*, Summer 48 (2): https://www.archives.gov/publications/prologue/2016/summer/lavender.html.

Ahmed, Sara. 2006. *Queer Phenomenology: Orientations, Objects, Others*. Duke University Press.

Beagan, Brenda L., Stephanie R. Bizzeth, Tara M. Pride, and Kaitlin R. Sibbald. 2022. "LGBTQ+ Identity Concealment and Disclosure within the (Heteronormative) Health Professions: 'Do I? Do I Not? And What Are the Potential Consequences?'" *SSM-Qualitative Research in Health* 2: 100114. https://doi.org/10.1016/j.ssmqr.2022.100114.

Berger, Arthur Asa. 2018. *Cultural Perspectives on Millennials*. Palgrave Macmillan.

Betancourt, Manuel. 2016. "The Queer Subtext of X-Men Shines Bright at Flame Con." *Vulture*, August 30. https://www.vulture.com/2016/08/chris-claremont-on-the-x-men-queer-subtext.html.

Brightman, Sara, Emily Lenning, Kristin J. Lurie, and Christina DeJong. 2024. "Anti-Transgender Ideology, Laws, and Homicide: An Analysis of the Trifecta of Violence." *Homicide Studies* 28 (3): 251–269.

Cheng, Yimin, Xiaoyu Zhou, and Kai Yao. 2023. "LGBT-Inclusive Representation in Entertainment Products and its Market Response: Evidence from Field and Lab." *Journal of Business Ethics* 183(4): 1189–1209.

Cherlin, Andrew. 2012. *Public and Private Families: An Introduction*, 7th Edition. McGraw-Hill Education.

Conley, Chase, dir. 2024a. *X-Men '97*. Season 1, episode 2, "Mutant Liberation Begins," Aired March 20, 2024 on Disney+.

Conley, Chase, dir. 2024b. *X-Men '97*. Season 1, episode 3, "Fire Made Flesh." Aired March 27, 2024b, on Disney+.

Conley, Chase, dir. 2024c. *X-Men '97*. Season 1, episode 4, "Motendo/Lifedeath." Aired April 3, 2024c, on Disney+.

Cook, Tanya, and Kaela Joseph. 2023. *Fandom Acts of Kindness: A Heroic Guide to Activism, Advocacy, and Doing Chaotic Good*. BenBella Books.

Cottle, Jason, Anna L. Drozdik, and Katharine A. Rimes. 2024. "The Impact of Role Models and Mentors on the Mental and Physical Wellbeing of Sexual and Gender Minorities." *Behavioral Sciences* 14 (5): 417. https://doi.org/10.3390/bs14050417.

D'Agostino, Anthony Michael. 2018. "'Flesh-to-Flesh Contact': Marvel Comics' Rogue and the Queer Feminist Imagination." *American Literature* 90 (2): 251–81. https://doi.org/10.1215/00 029831-4564298.

Dajches, Leah, and Juliana L. Barbati. 2024. "Queer on TV: Using the Minority Stress Model to Explore the Role of LGBQ+ Television Exposure in LGBQ+ Audiences' Psychological Well-Being and Identity Status." *Psychology of Popular Media*. https://doi.org/10.1037/ppm0000548.

DeMayo, Beau (@BeauDemayo). 2024. "Yes, Morph Was Confessing Romantic Feelings for Logan #xmen97 Https://T.Co/FhgShK5CX9." *Twitter*, May 16. https://x.com/BeauDemayo/status/17 90902190997110787

Doan, Laura. 2017. "Queer History / Queer Memory: The Case of Alan Turing." *GLQ: A Journal of Lesbian and Gay Studies* 23 (1): 113–136.

Duncan, Catherine. 2022. "Fandom, Homes and Families: Home as an Overlooked Site of Fannish Practice." *Journal of Fandom Studies* 10 (1): 3–17. https://doi.org/10.1386/jfs_00047_1.

Earnest, William. 2007. "Making Gay Sense of the *X-Men*." In *Uncovering Hidden Rhetorics: Social Issues in Disguise*, edited by Barry Brummett. SAGE Publications.

Fawaz, Ramzi. 2011. "'Where No X-Man Has Gone Before!' Mutant Superheroes and the Cultural Politics of Popular Fantasy in Postwar America." *American Literature* 83 (2): 355–88. https://doi. org/10.1215/00029831-1266090.

Fawaz, Ramzi. 2016. *The New Mutants: Superheroes and the Radical Imagination of American Comics*. New York University Press.

Grimsted, Sonora R., Katerina G. Krizner, Cynthia D. Porter, and Jay Clayton. 2024. "Genetics in the X-Men Film Franchise: Mutants as Allegories of Difference." *Frontiers in Genetics* 14 (January): 1331905. https://doi.org/10.3389/fgene.2023.1331905.

Gustines, George G. 2015. "Marvel's Iceman Cometh Out." *The New York Times*, November 5.

Halberstam, J. Jack. 2005. *In a Queer Time and Place: Transgender Bodies, Subcultural Lives*. New York University Press.

Hantsbarger, Matthew, Giovanni Maria Troiano, Alexandra To, and Casper Harteveld. 2022. "Alienated Serendipity and Reflective Failure: Exploring Queer Game Mechanics and Queerness in Games via Queer Temporality." *Proceedings of the ACM on Human-Computer Interaction* 6 (CHI PLAY): 221:1–221:27. https://doi.org/10.1145/3549484.

Houston, Larry, dir. 1992. *X-Men: The Animated Series*, Season 1, episode 1, "Night of the Sentinels, Part One." Aired October 31, 1992, on Fox.

Huang, Yu-Te, and Randolph C.H. Chan. 2022. "Effects of Sexual Orientation Concealment On Well-Being Among Sexual Minorities: How and When Does Concealment Hurt?" *Journal of Counseling Psychology* 69 (5): 630. https://doi.org/10.1037/cou0000623.

Hughto, Jaclyn M.W., David Pletta, Lily Gordon, Sean Cahill, Matthew J. Mimiaga, and Sari L. Reisner. 2021. "Negative transgender-related media messages are associated with adverse mental health outcomes in a multistate study of transgender adults." *LGBT Health* 8, (1): 32–41. https://doi.org/10.1089/lgbt.2020.0279.

Human Rights Watch. n.d. "#OUTLAWED: 'The Love That Dare Not Speak Its Name.'" Accessed July 30, 2024. https://features.hrw.org/features/features/lgbt_laws.

Jagose, Annamarie. 2009. "Feminism's Queer Theory." *Feminism & Psychology* 19 (2): 157–74. https://doi.org/10.1177/0959353509102152.

James, Alastair. 2023. "A Timeline of the Marvel Cinematic Universe's LGBTQ+ Representation." *Attitude*, March 9. https://www.attitude.co.uk/culture/a-timeline-of-the-marvel-cinematic-universes-lgbtq-representation-426232/.

James, Alastair. 2024. "X-Men: The Animated Series – Five LGBTQ+ Men Share What the Show Means to Them." *Attitude*, March 22. https://www.attitude.co.uk/culture/x-men-97-feature-462281/.

Joseph, Kaela M. 2019. "We Chose Family: The Role of Fictive Kinships Among Supernatural's LGBTQ Fans in Convention Spaces." In *CONVentional Wisdom: Every Con Has a Story*, edited by April Vian, Melissa Kennedy, and Shani Irvine. Independently Published.

Kohnen, Melanie. 2015. *Queer Representation, Visibility, and Race in American Film and Television: Screening the Closet*. Routledge. https://doi.org/10.4324/9780203152706.

Lautmann, Rüdiger. 1981. "The Pink Triangle: The Persecution of Homosexual Males in Concentration Camps in Nazi Germany." *Journal of Homosexuality* 6 (1–2): 141–60. https://doi.org/10.1300/ J082v06n01_13.

Lecker, Michael J. 2007. "Why Can't I Be Just Like Everyone Else?": A Queer Reading of the X-Men. *International Journal of Comic Art* 9 (1): 679–687.

Linton, Ralph. 1936. *The Study of Man: An Introduction*. Appleton-Century.

Malone, Aubrey. 2019. *Queer Cinema in America: An Encyclopedia of LGBTQ Films, Characters, and Stories*. Bloomsbury Publishing.

McInroy, Lauren B., and Shelley L. Craig. 2018. "Online Fandom, Identity Milestones, and Self-Identi fication of Sexual/Gender Minority Youth." *Journal of LGBT youth* 15 (3): 179–196. https://doi. org/10.1080/19361653.2018.1459220.

Moreau, Julie. 2023. "Global Survey Finds 9% of Adults Identify as LGBTQ." *NBC News*, June 1. https:// www.nbcnews.com/nbc-out/out-news/global-survey-finds-9-adults-identify-lgbtq-rcna87288.

Nakamura, Nadine, and Carmen H. Logie, eds. 2020. *LGBTQ Mental Health: International Perspectives and Experiences*. American Psychological Association.

Opie, David. 2024. "How the '90s X-Men Cartoon Saved a Generation of Queer Kids." *IndieWire*, March 20. https://www.indiewire.com/features/commentary/how-x-men-cartoon-saved-a-generation-queer-kids-97-1234965416/

Roman, Christopher Michael. 2022. "Queer Kinship in Chris Claremont and Allen Milgrom's *Kitty Pryde and Wolverine*." *Journal of Graphic Novels and Comics* 13 (5): 769–82. https://doi.org/10. 1080/21504857.2021.2009891.

Ruberg, Bonnie, and Adrienne Shaw, eds. 2017. *Queer Game Studies*. University of Minnesota Press.

Scott, Darieck, and Ramzi Fawaz. 2018. "Introduction: Queer about Comics." *American Literature* 90 (2): 197–219. https://doi.org/10.1215/00029831-4564274.

Sim, Bernardo. 2024. "'X-Men '97' Creator Beau De Mayo Is a Sexy Beast & The Gays Are FERAL." *OUT*, May 23. https://www.out.com/celebs/beau-demayo-xmen-97-hot-pictures-instagram#rebelltitem1.

Singer, Bryan, dir. 2003. *X-Men II*. 20th Century Fox. Disney+.

Vary, Adam B. 2006. "Mutant Is the New Gay; Even with the Departure of Gay Director Bryan Singer for Superman Returns, the X-Men Series Continues to Flex Its Queer Metaphorical Muscle. – Document – Gale OneFile: News." *The Advocate*, May 23. Gale.

PART V

Evolving Superhero Debates and Concerns

39

SWAMP THING

EcoGothic Monster or Environmental Champion?

Teresa Fitzpatrick

In the story "Swamp Thing" for *House of Secrets* #92 (1971), Len Wein and Bernie Wright-son co-created a male plant-human hybrid monster for DC Comics that emphasized the ambiguity of the fictional superhero/supervillain figures and captured the popular imagi-nation. From its birth as a comic book marsh monster, Swamp Thing has featured as the protagonist in Wes Craven's film, *Swamp Thing* (1982), a sequel directed by Jim Wynorski, *The Return of Swamp Thing* (1989), a short-lived animated series (*Swamp Thing*, Fox Kids 1991), and two television series (*Swamp Thing*, USA Network, 1990–1993; *Swamp Thing* DC Universe, 2019). This clearly speaks to a public fascination with the uncanny and gro-tesque. Reconceptualized by Alan Moore in the early 1980s as a trans-corporeal monster that engaged with environmental, political, and social issues, many of which continue to resonate with readers, Swamp Thing embodies an environmental posthuman. With Swamp Thing's human origins ultimately challenged throughout its various iterations, is this character an ecoGothic monster or an environmental superhero?

In this chapter, a material ecoGothic approach reveals Swamp Thing's plant-human hybridity as not only embodying our irrational fear of nature, but also advocates for an eco-logical change in attitude as we move toward better understanding our place in the world. Through Stacy Alaimo's concept of trans-corporeality, the character's disturbing act of "becoming-plant" exemplifies "the flows, interchanges, and interrelations between human corporeality and the more-than-human world" (2010, 142) within a monstrous posthu-man character that "reconfigure[s] the very boundaries of the human" (2010, 154). As an eco-monster emerging from the murky, polluted marshland, Swamp Thing disrupts pre-conceived ideas of a pleasant (controlled) nature and forces readers and viewers to recognize the impact of the Anthropocene. Yet, despite Swamp Thing's monstrosity, a material ecoGothic situates this character as an environmental posthuman that classifies him as a superhero.

Ecophobic Origins

The original character by Wein and Wrightson is created when a scientist, Alex Olson, "is caught in a lab explosion set by his jealous partner" that transforms him, when the chemi-cals interact with the swamp, into "a humanoid vegetable monster" (Smith 2015, 368).

DOI: 10.4324/9781003366911-45

Responding to contemporary anxieties about the environment, (agro-)science, and the power of large-scale business models, man and swamp are biologically fused as a result of corporate chemical irresponsibility. Swamp Thing as an eco-monster offered an unsettling representation of real-world events, with the man-plant hybrid evoking the environmental destruction and human casualties of the Vietnam War from US military intervention as it was revealed to the public consciousness in the late 1960s to early 1970s. The use of napalm and wide-spread use of "rainbow" chemicals, such as defoliants and herbicides of which Agent Orange is the most well-known, stirred concerns about agro-science, chemical and nuclear disposal, and land reclamation schemes on the environment. As part of the swamp – a liminal zone mostly devoid of human presence and control, that more often than not becomes the site of chemical testing, waste, and pollution – Swamp Thing is an ambiguous creature. They are both Alex and swamp, part human and part plant; "a grotesque hybrid, existing in a liminal space between human and non-human, life and death, nature and culture" (Gray 2013, 44).

Swamp Thing's monstrosity derives from the infiltration of the swamp as it merges with the human body in a hyperbolic demonstration of Alaimo's (2010) eco-materialist concept that by polluting the environment, we are also polluting ourselves. Arguing that the toxins released into the atmosphere/soil/water are absorbed by plants and subsequently ingested by humans, trans-corporeality traces this movement of matter as it travels from one body to another, transforming as it goes (Alaimo 2010). Used as an ecoGothic tool to explore this fictional narrative, Swamp Thing is conceived when nature and human merge at a molecular level; a material reminder of the porous boundary of the human body as Alex's identity is erased through what Karen Houle (2011) calls "becoming-plant". In discussing the philosophical notion of becoming-plant, Houle offers a deeper look at Deleuze and Guattari's rhizome theory to suggest that becoming-plant involves more than a shared experience, yet "[v]ery little attention has been devoted to imagining what these unique expressions of plant-livings might actually be" (2011, 97). To understand "the unique qualities of plants or plant-lives", she continues, "*becoming-plant* would involve our extension and ideas entering into composition with *something else*" (Houle 2011, 97–98, italics in original). In becoming-plant or becoming-swamp, Alex not only physically merges with the swamp vegetation but is afforded a vegetal insight through his transformation into Swamp Thing.

For Simon C. Estok (2009), nature overpowering the human body through a mutation creates horror based on ecophobia. Furthermore, the horror of ecoGothic stems from a deep-seated fear of nature's power, its ability to defy control and an uncertainty of our own human instincts, driving fears "about the transience of our corporeal materiality" that Swamp Thing embodies within its plant-human admixture (Estok 2014, 131). However, Alex's failure to reconcile his human and vegetal composition within his new form as Swamp Thing becomes evident when the creature fixates on killing his former friend in revenge, which is a very human characteristic. It is clear that Alex remains the controlling force and authority in this plant-human combination to some extent. Yet, Swamp Thing is "[u]nable to communicate or to convince Linda [his wife] he is actually Alex" before accepting his lot and disappearing into the swamp (Smith 2015, 368). The plant part of the Alex-hybrid renders communication impossible, depicting a monster that reflects the environmental activism and American conservative populism's "silent majority" politics of the late 1960s and early 1970s.

This original monster story was DC's best-selling issue in the summer of 1971 and prompted the launch of the character's own comic series, *Swamp Thing* (1972–1976). The series contained 24 issues and was "DC's first major attempt to publish a horror-themed comic with a recurring protagonist" (Gray 2013, 44). The renamed scientist Alec Holland, "is now working on a secret 'bio-restorative formula' to end world hunger, and the explosion is set by mysterious corporate forces [for] their somewhat vague but nefarious business interests" (Smith 2015, 368). The storyline principally "revolved around Holland's futile attempts to regain his lost humanity" until the series petered out due to declining interest (Gray 2013, 44). Perceived as a gothic monster through an amalgam of swamp plants and man seeking to return to his former human self only serves to underline contemporary ecophobia despite the growing environmental movement. Philosopher Michael Marder (2014) suggests that our inability to empathize with our environment derives from a long tradition of Western philosophy to dispel or control the vegetative nature of the human condition, providing a basis for ecophobia. "Imagining the power and the danger of nonhuman agency often means imagining threats to human control", remarks Estok, hence "ecophobia turns nature into a fearsome object in need of our control" (2014, 135). Throughout the series, Swamp Thing is pursued as an uncanny, murderous monster by former head of the lab's security detail Lt. Matthew Cable, enacting a militaristic ecophobic attitude. In fact, Cable is persistently but imperceptibly protected by Swamp Thing throughout from those of nefarious intent lurking in the swamp of both human and nonhuman varieties. It is within this series that Swamp Thing's ambiguity challenges ecophobic associations. Depicted invariable as a monstrous Other through his species hybridity and Holland's perceived loss of humanity, Swamp Thing's eco-centric empathy and determination to protect Cable and other innocents as well as the swamp-life situates him far from supervillainy or nature-revenge concepts.

A Vegetal Posthuman

Revived cinematically by Wes Craven with *Swamp Thing* (1982), DC's ambiguous plant-human hybrid figure follows the original quite closely and Swamp Thing is the result of a bio-engineering sabotage that engages with growing environmental concerns. With overt eco-horror, at a top-secret bio-engineering laboratory in the heart of American South swampland, Dr Alec Holland (Ray Wise) and sibling Dr Linda Holland (Nannette Brown) are working on separate projects that not only presage events to come but also engage with contemporary gender debates. Linda Holland is exploring a plant-based explosive – a militaristic science usually the reserve of male scientists – that a minor lab accident reveals spawns rapid plant growth, while brother Alec is analyzing his discovery of a hybrid plant-animal cell – a more passive, feminine-style science. Working amidst his vast collection of orchids, which as I have argued elsewhere foreshadows gothic plant horror associated with feminist gender politics (Fitzpatrick 2020), *Swamp Thing* blends masculine and feminine ideals, forming a monstrous creature in a plant/man hybrid that is linked to the liminal space of the swamp; like an ecological *femme fatale*, the swamp is a place of natural beauty but is just as equally dangerous. Many of Craven's films, Kendall R. Phillips notes, are concerned with the fusing of human-science, such as botany in the case of *Swamp Thing*, where any traditional demarcation of boundaries is undermined and where "[t]he swamp is also a decidedly gothic space in which dark secrets … resurface" (2012, 101). Secrets like Holland's murdered/damaged body. The gothic blurring of plant-human is mirrored in the film's aesthetic "bleeding of one type of narrative form into another" (Phillips 2012, 103) with the use of comic book visual techniques and transitional wipes between major scenes in the film.

Alec Holland's transformation into the eponymous Swamp Thing (Dick Durock) is the result of Anton Arcane's (Louis Jordan) paramilitary attack on their laboratory. The

Hollands are murdered, and Alec's body and their research end up in the heart of the swamp where marsh plants and man are fused in a trans-corporeal becoming-plant. While monstrous involvements tend to focus on the technological posthuman hybrid or animal-human confusions, Swamp Thing's uncanny otherness stems from his vegetal liminality that "revolves around our fear of becoming Other" and raises "questions of (human) identity constructions" (Heise-Von der Lippe 2019, 218). When the insurgents kidnap and attempt to drown visiting government official Alice Cable (Adrienne Barbeau) in the swamp, a green human-like creature fights off the henchmen and drags Alice ashore. As the rebels track Alice around the swamp, the marsh monster repeatedly wades in to protect her and other innocents, and she eventually realizes that it is a plant-hybridized Alec. As Swamp Thing, Holland transgresses the boundaries of nature/culture as his material body has commingled with the swamp vegetation to create a liminal being that epitomizes the ambiguously gendered monster. The close association of Nature and women means plants are recurrently configured as monstrously feminine in the popular imagination across fantasy, traditional Gothic and the emerging ecoGothic frameworks.

Despite feminist calls to separate these long-standing associations between nature and women, plant monsters remain entwined with gender. They are integral to a web of entanglements that discard dichotomous boundaries of culture/nature, male/female, human/nonhuman. As protector of the swamp and of those within it, Swamp Thing is only monstrous to the extent of his hybridized disfigured bigendered body. Swamp Thing not only harnesses the swamp's natural propensity for re-growth to restore himself and the innocent victims of Arcane's henchmen, but Holland's hybridity with nature also tempers the creature's monstrosity. Swamp Thing is both plant and Holland, a Green (Wo)Man figure that fuses binary gender categories, being hypermasculine in stature and strength (helped by Durock's brawny physique and hulking 6′ 5″ height), and in harnessing the (feminine) regenerative power of nature. Hypermasculinity as displayed by Craven's Swamp Thing was prevalent in 1980s action-movie heroes, yet his strength comes from the combination of human-plant in a reflection of contemporary gender politics in the era of the "yuppie", where young couples worked collaboratively without recourse to gender-stereotyping roles.

Craven's film focuses on "science's careless intervention into the natural order of things" (Philips 2012, 103), with the battle between Holland/Swamp Thing and Arcane reflecting concerns about uncontrollable conglomerates and their perceived immoral commercialization of nature through science. While Holland is conducting experimental botany, he nevertheless "has a reverence for the natural world in which he works" (Philips 2012, 103). He is enthusiastic and appreciative of his orchids and the swamp; "Arcane, on the other hand, sees both science and nature as merely instruments in his hands" (Philips 2012, 103). Moreover, Swamp Thing's gendered vegetal hybridity allows him to ward off Arcane's predatory scientific villainy, a signifier for patriarchal masculine ideals. Taking Holland's research potion "neat" transforms Arcane into a boar-like creature in a clear Jekyll/Hyde reference to his inner evil, which Swamp Thing must defeat. The ensuing battle between plant-hybrid and purist-science reflects contemporary anxieties about "biomedical reductionism" that James Whorton, MD (2003) identifies as stimulating the rise in alternative medicine during the 1970s and 1980s in response to the loss of confidence in scientific and medical establishments after many new drugs of the 1960s had profound untoward effects. As a posthuman hybrid, Swamp Thing embodies a desired synergy between nature and science, as well as gender (and other) equality, underlined by his inability to separate himself from the swamp vegetation, materially or otherwise. Nevertheless, the marsh monster remains largely human in form and some of Alec Holland's humanity remains deep within the vegetal swamp creature, with his protectiveness of Alice, for instance, demonstrating his human empathy. Unlike his 1970 predecessors, who are eventually overpowered by the vegetal, Craven's character remains a composite figure, with plant and man (nature/culture, male/female) defying categorization in a synergic body. It is, however, language that distinguishes us from the non-human world, according to Graham J. Matthews, who argues that "[p]lant life lacks speech organs and communicates instead through its materiality and its posture" (2016, 125). Yet, Alec/Swamp Thing holds a brief dialogue with Alice before re-joining the swamp; although Alec speaks disjointedly, struggling to make himself understood through the remaining vestiges of his human body.

The monstrousness of Swamp Thing comes, Karen Houle argues, because we "are built from the very carbons of [plants]" (2011, 92). Plant horror stems, it seems, from "the unsettling sense that maybe we are also *like plants*" (Keetley 2016, 16, italics in original), as Holland's fascination with the swamp and his deeper understanding of the environment is apparently what has transformed him into Swamp Thing. Despite the low-budget rubbery suit worn by Durock, Craven's Swamp Thing illustrates the porosity of the human body. The lab explosion re-configures Holland's DNA and exterior as a mass of green swamp vegetation when the formula interacts with man and marsh. While the film suggests science is to blame for mutating plant-human organisms, when Arcane duplicates the formula, Swamp Thing reveals that it amplifies a person's inner qualities, and hence the villains are transformed into rat-like and boar-like hybrid creatures. Craven's protagonist, however, remains an ambiguous figure of the DC world; monstrous in his vegetal merging of human and swamp, but as an environmental posthuman, Swamp Thing embodies changing perceptions toward the natural world, which is underlined by its trans-corporeal conception.

Trans-Corporeal Eco-Hero

Craven's *Swamp Thing* (1982) revived the hero for a comic series called *The Saga of the Swamp Thing*, later *Swamp Thing* (1982–1996). Alan Moore was at the helm between 1984 and 1987, which radically revised the character (Gavaler and Goldberg 2017) in a reflection of Moore's own (and contemporary) environmental politics through "a subtext of wide-ranging environmental destruction" (Gray 2013, 47). In true gothic style, with artists Stephen Bissette and John Totleben, Moore resurrects the dead and dissected creature not as a human Alec inextricably entangled with the swamp, "transformed and tortured [and] forced to live outside of civilization" (Smith 2015, 369), but as "an entirely vegetable entity" (Gray 2013, 47) that only thinks it is the deceased Alec Holland. For McDonald and Vena "this new conceptualization of Swamp Thing repositions the creature as a *thing*" (2016, 198, italics in original) in accordance with its nomenclature, not as a Swamp Creature or Swamp Monster. They argue that "the unintelligible *thingness* of Swamp Thing" in its monstrous material assemblage of plant and man "questions the ontological integrity of the 'human,' insofar as it … provoke[s] a categorical crisis" (McDonald and Vena 2016, 198). Yet, while the creature is generally perceived "as something to be defeated or destroyed precisely because it threatens to amalgamate gendered and sexual boundaries" it also "champions the liberatory potential of the agential unhuman" (McDonald and Vena 2016, 199). Moore's Swamp Thing is "redefined not as a hybrid creature but as an earth elemental" (Gray 2013, 47), which Colin Beineke describes as being "essentially transformed … from a man who happened to be green, to a Green Man—a figure composed of living vines, growing moss, decomposing leaves, and pure earth" (Beineke 2011). While extracting the human from its composition to suggest a sentient vegetal being that communicates with plant-life counters ecophobic attitudes to agential nonhuman nature, doing so also undermines Swamp Thing's ability to effectively challenge categorizations. Exploring Moore's incarnation of Swamp Thing as a trans-corporeal contemporary Green Man, however, allows the creature the scope to not only challenge conceptual binary boundaries as a hybrid eco-monster, but to champion an ecological ethos that moves beyond nature-as-resource toward a deeper understanding of our place in the world of the Anthropocene.

Swamp Thing's trans-corporeality and position as an environmental superhero is highlighted best when compared to his villainous counterpart, the Floronic Man (also revived by Moore). Really botanist Jason Woodrue, who uses an experimental formula in Jekyll/Hyde fashion to bring out the vegetal within, Woodrue's transformation turns his hair into leaves and his skin resembles bark in emulation of a tree. Equally a "plant/human hybrid", Woodrue "remains partially human" so he only "*appear[s]* to be a Green Man" (Beineke 2011, italics in original). Although Floronic Man can also manipulate plant-life, in order to communicate with "the Green" (all plant-life) in the same way Swamp Thing can, he believes he must ingest parts of Swamp Thing's (post-dissection) defunct body-shell. Indeed, eating becomes a chief trans-corporeal component in advocating Moore's environmental message of oneness with nature and the dissolution of culturally constructed boundaries. Swamp Thing and Abigail/Abby's conscious-melding event within "the Green", for example, is also instigated by Abby's consumption of "fruit" from the Swamp Thing's body. Ideas of trans-corporeal entanglements with nature are depicted as bodily integrations across several colorful sequences as boundaries of all kinds (including those of the page) are transgressed and Abby communes with nature. This act of eating, however, both compounds anthropocentric thoughts and disrupts categorizations. If Swamp Thing is pure nature, then its consumption by Abby and Woodrue simply re-enforce notions of nature as resource; eating a trans-corporeal vegetal Holland, however, positions Woodrue in particular, as cannibal, although Abby perhaps less so in her consumption of "fruit" offered by Swamp Thing himself. While human and plant do not physically resemble each other, it is the gothic trans-corporeal "kinship" that invokes a sense of horror. While "metaphors of eating—and notably those of cannibalism—are used to represent relations of power" (Jooma 2001, 58), here it is the dominant intent of the human that skews the relationship Swamp Thing facilitates with the natural world. For Abby, her somewhat reluctant consumption of the "fruit" offered her is an act of her desire to understand her former lover; in contrast, Woodrue consumes random "body-parts" of the vegetal entity for selfish reasons in wanting to commune with "the Green".

However, as a human hybrid rather than a trans-corporeal entity, when Floronic Man attempts to become one with "the Green" through eating parts of Swamp Thing, it drives him insane as his human consciousness devolves into ideas of human domination. Whereas the original Swamp Thing saw Alex Olsen surrender his humanity and succumb to his vegetal state, which suggested that amalgamations of dissolved boundaries cannot survive, Floronic Man's attempts to maintain his anthropocentricity while releasing his vegetal origins produces an unstable kinship with the environment he seeks to tap into. Once he has communed with "the Green", Floronic Man becomes fixated on avenging the polluted environment and intent on obliterating humankind. Woodrue's hybridity embodies the anthropocentric vision of the human/nature divide, with his villainous destruction of cities and human populations a reflection of his revenge-driven human obsession in defense of his apparent kinship with the vegetal world. When Swamp Thing points out to Woodrue/Floronic Man that he is "poisoning the green with human forms of consciousness: 'This … is not … the way … of the wilderness. / This … is the way … of man.'" (Moore, Bissette and Totleben 1984, quoted in Gray 2013, 48), Moore's character emphasizes, as Karen Houle points out, that becoming-plant involves more than a shared experience, but rather is a "heterogenous alliance" with the nonhuman vegetal (2011, 97). Indeed, Gray argues that Moore's *The Saga of Swamp Thing* "stages many of the debates occurring within the contemporary green movement between anthropocentric and biocentric positions, through an exploration of the Gothic trope of monstrosity" (2013, 49), and which is perhaps most evident in the contrasting views of Floronic Man and Swamp Thing.

Chris Gavaler and Nathaniel Goldberg argue that unlike Floronic Man, "Moore's Swamp Thing is somehow triggered by Alec Holland's body, and the stuff of Alec Holland's memories and consciousness are somehow configured into a new plant body" (2017, 239), generating an uncanny manifestation of ecological anxieties and a trans-corporeal recognition of our material position in the planet's ecosystem. Swamp Thing is not so much a human-plant hybrid as a vegetal/swamp entity that has subsumed not just the material substance of Holland's physical form, but the very essence of his being as well. Despite suggestions by Beineke (2011), Gray (2013), McDonald and Vena (2016), and others that Moore's revenant is no longer human or even posthuman but something else entirely, through a material ecoGothic approach, clearly Swamp Thing *is* Alec Holland; no longer as a monstrous hybrid combining human corpse and plant as a (con)fusion of the two, but through a trans-corporeal subsumption of Holland's material and insubstantial being. Potentially because Holland has been so traumatically murdered alongside the unforeseen consequences of the lab pollution of the swamp, the trans-corporeal entanglements are not only advanced, but these also prompt an uncanny s(t)imulation of (non)human agency within a discombobulating form.

Communicating the Environmental Message

Infusing plant-life with a sentience and consciousness reflects the growing contemporary environmental movement, the emergence of ecofeminist theory, and global calls for a better understanding of the interconnectedness of nature and civilization. In fact, Swamp Thing foils Floronic Man's plot to rid the planet of animal and human life by reminding "the Green" that plants also need our carbon dioxide to survive. His ability to commune with vegetal nature provides a voice that advocates ecological harmony between human and nonhuman life, a message that continues to resonate into the 21st century. Moreover, as a gothic trans-corporeal being, Swamp Thing can also communicate with the humans he comes into contact with. In both Craven's film and Moore's graphic novel "Swamp Thing speaks in a manner consistent with his vegetable nature" (Beineke 2011). Craven's Swamp Thing seemingly gasps for air as a result of his injuries and speaks disjointedly which emphasizes his struggle to negotiate his vegetative hybridity with his human vocal cords. The request to protect the research notebooks is a combined message from both Holland and the swamp to protect nature from human misappropriation of his discovery. The disjointed speech similarly reflects the last vestiges of his human form as the swamp DNA begins to take over (much as the environment does when humans abandon sites). Similarly, the speech of Moore's character is emphasized by the frequent use of ellipsis (as seen above) between a few or singular words. Presenting Swamp Thing's communicative powers with "[t]his slowness of speech, reflective of the slow yet steady growth of plant life" (Beineke 2011), suggests it originates with their plant-selves.

The DC Universe television series *Swamp Thing* (Dauberman and Verheiden 2019) is equally ambiguous as it navigates the conflicting anthropocentric and eco-centric ambitions. Released just prior to the COVID-19 pandemic, this story nevertheless concerns a viral mutagen that imbues the Louisiana swamp plant-life with active agency, sparking a "green flu" as local residents are progressively infected, fatally hallucinate and/or are drawn to the swamp where the plants enact their revenge as a consequence of pollution and attempts at land reclamation. In a deviation to the previous iterations, the story follows Dr Abby Arcane, CDC specialist, as the main protagonist, although the core premise remains the same. Here too, the swamp claims the corpse of Alec Holland who trans-corporeally emerges as the eponymous Swamp Thing. Prior to his demise, Holland claims that the swamp has had enough, and the "green flu" is the swamp seeking retribution for the damage humans have caused locally and to the natural world at large, endowing the series with more of a nature-revenge aspect than any superhero genre quality. As Swamp Thing, his mission becomes to protect Abby and other innocents from both human and vegetal dangers. He is also compelled to protect the swamp, as part of his new trans-corporeal self, from the nefarious actions of land-developer Avery Sunderland and bio-geneticist Jason Woodrue. Tapping into the many environmental anxieties of today, DC nevertheless cancelled the series after one season; but clearly, the gothic trans-corporeality associated with the creation of Swamp Thing continues to speak to our ecophobia and make us uncomfortable as we face our Anthropocentric misdemeanors.

Conclusion: Environmental Superhero

Despite his monstrous origins, not least due to his connections with the murky Louisiana swamp, the trans-corporeal, Holland-imbued Swamp Thing engages with a growing awareness in environmental issues that started in the 1960s and resulted in environmental activism throughout the 1970s and 1980s through to present day. Because plants are "very distant from us, alien, to the point that sometimes it's even hard for us to remember they're alive" (Mancuso and Viola 2015, 125), Swamp Thing embodies an agential nature that is often overlooked, unsettles the anthropocentric stance, and obfuscates culturally/socially constructed boundaries. With growing political impetus on environmental issues during the 1980s, and "[r]esearch into plant communications (also called – 'plant signalling')" that also "began in earnest in North America around 1983" (Houle 2011, 98), Swamp Thing became less of an ecoGothic monster as science demystified the plant world. The character's own transformation from a monstrous plant-human hybrid into a trans-corporeal vegetal entity marks a shift in Anthropocentric understanding toward an eco-centric consideration of our responsibilities toward issues such as climate crisis, climate poverty, and conservation. Like Alec Holland, who despite being a biological engineer already had an empathy for nature and an appreciation of the swamp before the incident, the human characters that Swamp Thing protects have an equally eco-centric outlook.

Despite his monstrous ecoGothic form, Swamp Thing is an advocate for his murky, decaying environment. Holland's involuntary trans-corporeal entanglement with the swamp affords him, as Swamp Thing, a greater understanding and appreciation of the vegetal world than he could hope to gain through his scientific research. His newly forged vegetal kinship offers the audience and reader a fresh opportunity to re-evaluate their own anthropocentric attitudes toward the nonhuman and prompts a re-assessment of our place within the natural world. Even as Swamp Thing returns in full CGI-enhanced nature-revenge nightmare for the 21st century in Gary Dauberman and Mark Verheiden's 2019 television version, this trans-corporeal eco-monster is in fact, more akin to DC's superhero Aquaman, "defender of the seas", in that Swamp Thing is defender of "the Green". From this standpoint alone, it is possible to argue for Swamp Thing as an environmental superhero rather than an eco-monster. What initially unsettles us may be Swamp Thing/Holland's trans-corporeal monstrosity and entanglement with the less-than-pristine nature of the bayou, but his environmental credentials disturb us more because he underlines our own anthropocentric guilt.

References

Alaimo, Stacy. 2010. *Bodily Natures: Science, Environment and the Material Self.* Indiana University Press.

Beineke, Colin. 2011. "'Her Guardiner': Alan Moore's Swamp Thing as the Green Man." *ImageText: Interdisciplinary Comics Studies* 5 (4). https://imagetextjournal.com/her-guardiner-alan-moores-swamp-thing-as-the-green-man/.

Craven, Wes. dir. 1982. *Swamp Thing.* Warner Brothers Pictures.

Dauberman, Gary, and Mark Verheiden, dev. 2019. *Swamp Thing.* DC Universe.

Estok, Simon C. 2009. "Theorizing in a Space of Ambivalent Openness: Ecocriticism and Ecophobia." *ISLE: Interdisciplinary Studies in Literature and Environment* 16 (2): 203–235.

Estok, Simon C. 2014. "Painful Material Realities, Tragedy, Ecophobia." In *Material Ecocriticism*, edited by Serenella Iovino and Serpil Oppermann. Indiana University Press.

Fitzpatrick, Teresa. 2020. "Green is the New Black: Plant monsters as ecoGothic Tropes; Vampires and Femmes Fatales." In *EcoGothic Gardens in the Long Nineteenth Century*, edited by Sue Edney. Manchester University Press.

Gavaler, Chris, and Nathaniel Goldberg. 2017. "Alan Moore, Donald Davidson, and the Mind of Swampmen." *The Journal of Popular Culture* 50 (2): 239–258.

Gray, Maggie. 2013. "A Gothic politics: Alan Moore's Swamp Thing and radical ecology." In *Alan Moore and the Gothic Tradition*, edited by Matthew J. A. Green. Manchester University Press.

Heise-von der Lippe, Anya. 2019. "Posthuman Gothic." In *Twenty-First-Century Gothic: An Edinburgh Companion*, edited by Maisha Wester and Xavier Aldana Reyes. Edinburgh University Press.

Houle, Karen L. F. 2011. "Animal, Vegetable, Mineral: Ethics as Extension or Becoming? The Case of Becoming-Plant." *Journal for Critical Animal Studies* IX (1/2): 89–116.

Jooma, Minaz. 2001. "Robinson Crusoe Inc(Orporates): Domestic Economy, Incest, and the Trope of Cannibalism." In *Eating Their Words: Cannibalism and the Boundaries of Cultural Identity*, edited by Kristin Guest. State University of New York Press.

Keetley, Dawn. 2016. "Introduction: Six Theses on Plant Horror; or, Why Are Plants Horrifying?" In *Plant Horror: Approaches to the Monstrous Vegetal in Fiction and Film*, edited by Dawn Keetley and Angela Tenga. Palgrave Macmillan.

Mancuso, Stefano, and Alessandra Viola. 2015. *Brilliant Green: The Surprising History and Science of Plant Intelligence.* Translated by Joan Benham. Island Press.

Marder, Michael. 2014. *The Philosopher's Plant: An Intellectual Herbarium.* Columbia University Press.

Matthews, Graham J. 2016. "What We Think about When We Think about Triffids: The Monstrous Vegetal in Post-war British Science Fiction." In *Plant Horror: Approaches to the Monstrous Vegetal in Fiction and Film*, edited by Dawn Keetley and Angela Tenga. Palgrave Macmillan.

McDonald, Robin Alex, and Dan Vena. 2016. "Monstrous Relationalities: The Horrors of Queer Eroticism and 'Thingness' in Alan Moore and Stephen Bissette's Swamp Thing." In *Plant Horror: Approaches to the Monstrous Vegetal in Fiction and Film*, edited by Dawn Keetley and Angela Tenga. Palgrave Macmillan.

Moore, Alan, Stephen Bissette, and John Totleben. 1984. "Roots." *Swamp Thing* (Volume 2) #24. DC Comics.

Phillips, Kendall R. 2012. *Dark Directions: Romero, Craven, Carpenter, and the Modern Horror Film.* Southern Illinois University Press.

Smith, Michael. 2015. "Embracing Dionysius in Alan Moore's Swamp Thing." *Studies in the Novel* 47 (3): 365–380.

Whorton MD, James. 2003. "Countercultural Healing: A Brief History of Alternative Medicine in America." *PBS.org*, November 4. https://www.pbs.org/wgbh/pages/frontline/shows/altmed/clash/history.html.

40

ANIMAL MAN

The Countercultural Superhero of the Anthropocene

Chris Hall

Subverting the Status Quo

The April 1989 issue of *Animal Man* #10 features a metafictional strategy that would become familiar to readers of the series under writer Grant Morrison. Setting up a series of interlocking narrative frames through which Buddy Baker's Animal Man persona, and the procession of the title's plot, are viewed, Morrison undermines the logical grounding of the series' story, decentering its present tense and its subjective core in Buddy's daily life. The issue begins with Buddy working through a disruption of his powers, which draw upon the abilities of nearby animals, assuming their capacities for flight, agility, regeneration, etc., without his body itself changing. As Buddy flits chaotically around, accidentally assuming the jumping power of fleas when attempting to connect with his dog Skipper, the visual frame shifts and recedes, and the reader views Buddy's family (his wife Ellen, son Cliff, and daughter Maxine) through the glossy bubbles of an alien viewing room. One of these spindly Yellow Aliens suggests, in light of Buddy's condition and the potential disruption of "the continuum," that they might "review the creation of 'Animal Man' as *we* remember it" (Morrison et al. 2002 [#10], 12). What follows is the recounting within Buddy's present tense of his own "creation": a retelling of the September 1965 issue of *Strange Adventures* #180 in which he made his first appearance, entitled "I Was the Man with Animal Powers!"

As the Aliens observe this historical recitation through their metallic lenses, which is complete with the campy dialogue and maudlin overearnestness of its time, their detached commentary ironicizes its energetic sincerity. An Alien watching the mysterious spaceship explosion that infuses Buddy with his powers notes that "It's always been the same on this stratum: radiation, chemical accidents, magic rings. The physical laws under which these people operate are all but incomprehensible!" (Morrison et al. 2002 [#10], 20). Skipping ahead to another of Buddy's early escapades, one remarks: "Saving the world from alien invasion, preserving the status quo from the forces of chaos. It's an almost universal scenario" (23). It is not only that an otherworldly presence has insinuated itself in the storyline here as a device for manufacturing mysteriousness; a glimpse is provided in these pages into the avant-gardism that lends to *Animal Man* a radically countercultural impetus.

 DOI: 10.4324/9781003366911-46

This is hardly *Animal Man* under Morrison at its most experimental. Yet, it serves as a crucial tell for the commitments and implications of a series that are not just formal or generic, but political: "Morrison's metafictional strategies" in *Animal Man* "do not serve only to question the relation between reality and fiction, but also, even primarily, as a way of bringing about a different understanding of ethics" (Mahmutovic et al. 2015–2016). The intervention of Morrison's *Animal Man* series will turn out, above all else, to be into that drive for "preserving the status quo," and its primary means of doing so will be precisely through the metafictional. Under Morrison, the series will involve explicit political agitation for issues such as vegetarianism and animal rights. The project that binds its commitments in nonhuman activism with its formal ones in avant-garde metanarrative, however, is counter-culturalism. It is this complementary drive that undermines the anthropocentric logic lodged within the presumptions of both species hierarchy and narrative order. In its retelling of "I Was the Man with Animal Powers!", *Animal Man* turns toward its own history via a formal remove. This shift allows the comic to comment upon what had previously been its own rhetorically limited remit, replaying and throwing into question its own origin. In a parallel manner, the arc of the series itself under Morrison will coalesce around a multi-pronged determination, not to sooth "the continuum" and reproduce the kind of desire for stability that the comic detects in its own past, but to upend the status quo of a logic of human exceptionalism. This exceptionalism underwrites the ethics of allowable animal violence *and* those of admissible narrative structure. The radically countercultural thrust of Morrison's storytelling resides in its demonstration that these are interwoven concerns.

This chapter, then, analyzes Morrison's stretch on *Animal Man* for its unique experiments with countercultural critiques of the anthropocentrism driving the Anthropocene – an Anthropocene that is as much a matter of the valuation and fallout of human actions as it is one of how stories are told about those actions. As José Alaniz has written, the series is part of a growing body of work in comics analyzing "the place of animals in an age of human-caused ecological destruction (i.e., the Anthropocene) and how the lack of human speech consigns them to subordinate, instrumentalized status, mass extinctions, and unspeakable suffering in industrialized food systems" (2020, 332). Yet, it is not only speech, but also culture and subjectivity from which animals are expelled that has made possible the blighted futures of human dominance. There is a persistent danger, as Joseph Zornado and Sara Reilly point out, that "The conceit of human exceptionalism that makes any superhero fantasy narrative possible also functions as an ideological imperative" for upholding the standards of anthropocentrism (2021, 86). What follows demonstrates how Morrison's countercultural narrative instead identifies and disassembles the key forces contributing to the wanton destructiveness of the Anthropocene, showing how superheroes can and should function as sites for a radical posthuman ethics of remaking our relationships with otherness amid a world in crisis.

Cultures of Anthropocentrism

DC Comics launched *Animal Man* as a distinct title in September 1988, to be helmed by Morrison, penciller Chas Truog, and inker Doug Hazlewood, as part of a push to bring mostly obscure characters from the publisher's past into the spotlight in ways that would expand the boundaries of genre and storytelling for the comics medium (Wallin 2020, 18). Morrison's run on the series, which would continue through the August 1990 issue (#26), marked a crucial moment in superhero politics, establishing what had been a largely unknown character as an insurgent countercultural figure within the comics mainstream by reimagining him as a hero of and for the Anthropocene. Under Morrison, Animal Man becomes occupied with the lives and plight of the animals populating his world and from which he draws his powers, enabling the series to develop as a platform for examining the rights, hunting, abuse, eating, and testing of animals, and for exploring the possibilities of Morrison's avant-garde style. As Jason Wallin writes, Morrison's *Animal Man* takes as a central concern "articulating the problem of the Anthropocene and its referent in anthropocentrism" (2020, 39), examining not only the deplorable ecological conditions of our time but also the logic that makes them possible.

Morrison's *Animal Man* sequence is concerned with the harm being done to animals not in a vacuum or only by particular bad actors. Instead, it links the capitalistic degradation of life and the perverse masculinism of animal cruelty with the biopolitical project of producing "Man" as a purified species. Conjoining all of this on the formal level is Morrison's radically metafictional style, which connects *Animal Man*'s ethical themes to a larger project of undoing the anthropocentric logic of consumerism, which feeds upon animals as the debased fodder for its own self-aggrandizement. Joanna Zylinska posits that ' If the Anthropocene names a period in which the human has become a geological agent,' shaping the present and future of life on a planetary scale through the ecological and logical effects of anthropocentrism, then it becomes necessary in responding to this to "cut through some of the sedimented layers of meaning that have already accrued" alongside this new geology (2018, 7). Undertaking this, as *Animal Man* demonstrates, involves not only articulating the rampant nihilistic violence by which a new ecological epoch constructed upon the premise of human superiority is enacted. Cutting through the "layers of meaning" that shore up the logical presumptions undergirding this superiority entails rewriting the narrative pathways that have made it possible for human beings to tell a story about themselves within which they are the privileged actors and beneficiaries.

Though it might appear counterintuitive, it is for this reason that the most effective rejoinders to the destructiveness of the Anthropocene are found not in the straightforward depictions of its negative effects. Instead, forceful responses exist where the work of imagining ways of living beyond the status quo meets that of thinking, writing, and narrativizing outside of logic. This means they are outside too of that progressive logic within which hierarchies are compiled, heroes identified, and all that remains is to map out strategies for preserving the life of the ordained. The countercultural moves counter-wise to culture by breaking the dichotomous chains of opposition and hierarchy. Anthropocentrism, it might be said, is culture itself: the foundational determinations on who can speak and where, in what way, and within what context, rest upon deeply ingrained assumptions of the fundamental differences between human beings and other forms of life, animals in particular. Where Max Horkheimer and Theodor Adorno famously wrote around the middle of the 20th century of the industrialization of a "Culture today ... infecting everything with sameness" (2002, 94), we might further speak of another sort of cultural ubiquity that has infected the machinery producing the discourses and determinations concerning what counts as life, how it is organized, and what stories can be told about it, in the omnipresent force of anthropocentrism.

Counterculture, from this vantage, would name movements capable of enduringly disturbing the established pathways for thinking and living that endlessly defer to the natural preference for human flourishing above all else. This preference, of course, does not affix itself to all lives deemed "human" in the same manner; there is an incessant negotiation of the terms of proper humanity, excising some entirely while nurturing others, in the machinations of biopower that are constitutive of modernity. The division between human and animal, "as the history of slavery, colonialism, and imperialism well shows—is a discursive resource, not a zoological designation" (Wolfe 2013, 10). A counterculture worthy of the name would be capable of infiltrating the cracks in this edifice. As Timothy Leary once wrote, the "mark of counterculture" is "the evanescence of forms and structures, the dazzling rapidity and flexibility with which they appear, mutate, and morph into one another and disappear" (2005, ix). If what has come to count as culture is the exchange of artifacts and dialogue between those calling themselves human, then the alternative aesthetic, political, and vital forces insubordinate to this industrialized sameness should be thought of as possessing their own countercultural drive. The ultimate form of culture today, the form accruing for itself the lion's share of wealth, land, and epistemological prestige, is found in the strongholds of anthropocentrism. The countercultural, then, is to be discovered in those insurrectional eruptions of living structures capable of destabilizing the logic of biopolitical dominance, turning its foundations to sand.

Countercultural Commitments

It is no coincidence that Morrison's work could be described using Leary's language, as a drama of "the evanescence of forms and structures." Their writing enacts the anarchy of a play which establishes familiar edifices of power only to inject them with a riotousness whereby they come apart and back together strangely and in ways that put their ongoing stability into question. Leary himself receives a shout-out in *Animal Man* #23, alongside fellow countercultural icon Ken Kesey (Morrison 2003, 140). Responding to the anthropocentrism that has made possible the cataclysmic epoch of the Anthropocene, with its staggering pollution, extreme weather, and generalized precarity, entails not only responding to the hierarchical displacement of other animals from the haughty space of the human; countering the edifices of power that have enabled human beings generally (and certain human beings in particular) to run rampant in gobbling up the planet's resources and laying waste to its ecosystems involves also undermining the identarian methods by which anthropocentrism cultivates visions of its favored subject. The full-steam-ahead perspective of Man as engine of progress that has manifested our global ecological plight takes refuge in the illusion of its unassailable security, but this "denial of precarity leads to the drawing of various lines of differentiation such as gender, race, class, or bodily ability" (Zylinska 2018, 57). For Man to survive, it becomes necessary to render all of those forms of life, excepted from its fanciful self-ideal, available for sacrifice.

Early on *Animal Man* evinces resistance to anthropocentrism and the spectral figure of Man. Issue #1 opens not on Buddy, but with a helmeted figure walking down a highway. The first sentence reads: "Ten miles outside the city, the *screaming* begins in earnest […] screaming...the *monkeys* screaming...rattling the bars" (Morrison et al. 1991 [#1], 1). This first scene introduces the blend of dense characterization, animal rights discourse, and estrangement from industrialized modernity that will become the series' calling card. Soon complimentary political themes are added; although in the flashback of issue #10 we see Buddy hunting just before the explosion that gives him his powers, in #1 he tells his friend Roger, who was with him in that earlier (and later) scene, "I had to give all that up when I got my Animal Man powers. I could *feel* it every time I killed something" (16). This is an expression of nonhuman empathy, but it is also one of rejecting the masculinized camaraderie of violence. As David Coughlan writes, although Buddy appears as a conventionally masculine character (2009, 245), he also "softens the hard lines of his heroic profile" in how he positions himself in relation to others (243). Later in issue #1, Buddy is brought in by S.T.A.R. Laboratories to investigate a break-in at their research department, where they had been testing an experimental AIDS vaccine on primates. Buddy uses his powers to take on the scent of smell of a nearby laboratory dog in order to track the perpetrator, but in assuming this canine perspective he also senses, woozily, that the dog is not as healthy as his guide, Dr. Myers, is pretending. And early in issue #5 Ellen will find Buddy throwing out the family's groceries in an effort to have them become vegetarian.

In short, the series quickly takes up a set of counter-positions to the hegemonic anthropocentrism that would find no moral qualms with caging and tormenting animals, killing them for sport, experimenting on them, and consuming them as the output of a globalized industry that converts life into meat. These political commitments should be thought of as countercultural; it is a central premise of contemporary human life that, though it may be distasteful or even painful to acknowledge, it is ultimately necessary that nonhuman animals be subjected to violence, imprisonment, and destruction in service of caring for the race of humanity, whose lives are, it is generally agreed, of an absolute, natural, inarguable magnitude of value exceeding that of the nonhuman. But this assumption does not come from nowhere and is not itself natural. As Jacques Derrida notes, it can be traced in the west back to discourses of humanist metaphysics and religion, which emphasize the need for sacrificeable lives that can be simultaneously expelled and consumed. Such discourses, Derrida argues, "are also 'cultures,'" ones which have set aside a crucial place in their cosmologies for the "ingestion, incorporation, or introjection of the corpse" (1991, 112), particularly the corpses of what goes by the name of "animals." Any discourse, then, that balks at the necessity of preparing particular forms of life for their expulsion from the carefully policed bounds of the human, and subsequently of their reincorporation within those limits as dead fodder for the physiological and ideological perpetuation of the human, is potentially countercultural.

In issue #6, Buddy and Roger meet for a talk about Buddy's career which, to his displeasure, takes place at the zoo. Roger, who has been acting as Buddy's manager, is concerned about the tenor of Buddy's duties as Animal Man: "I thought this Animal Man stuff was strictly business, but it looks like it's becoming an *obsession* [...] all I'm getting is calls from animal rights groups who want you to help them rescue some lab rats!" (Morrison et al. 1991 [#6], 4). Buddy's response: "Tell them I'll do it" (4). Buddy has come to see his role not as economical, but ethical. What Roger diagnoses as a distracting and potentially destructive mania, Buddy has increasingly conceptualized as a radical reconfiguration of his moral duties, and with them his very understanding of species relations and the human: "I hadn't realized the amount of *suffering*," Buddy tells Roger; "Someone's got to *do* something. *I've* got to do something!" (4). Roger's response is predictable and eminently reasonable: "surely it's better for a few rats to die if the research saves one kid" (4). But Buddy rejects this premise: "You're just assuming that a rat's life is somehow less important than a human life. Who's to say that's true?" (4). There's an easy answer to this question, of course: Roger is to say; common sense is to say. And this is precisely the point. When Roger explodes, "This conversation's getting *stupid!*" (5), he's more right than he knows, for what Buddy is putting into practice is of an order of thinking that totally disregards the most fundamental assumptions made by Western subjectivity about how life is to be organized and valued. This is, in other words, just the kind of stupidity necessary for undermining the cultures of anthropocentrism.

A Countercultural Politics of Form

Like other moments of explicit anti-anthropocentrism, such as when Buddy lends his support to an eco-terrorist group combating an annual festival of slaughtering dolphins in issue #15, or joins in on a laboratory break-in to free a group of monkeys from experiments in sight deprivation in #17, Buddy's vegetarianism and his rejection of zoos and animal testing fall directly under the purview of animal rights. And like instances of drug use (as in Buddy's extended peyote trip that dominates issues #18 and #19) and anti-authoritarianism (the murder of Buddy's family late in the series will be ordered by a government panel totally detached from ethical and environmental concerns), which carry a distinct countercultural flavor, these on their own tease a critique of hegemony and posit an adjacency of *Animal Man* to alternative political formations. Nor does the series lack the capacity to extrapolate from anthropocentric anti-ethics to the broader catastrophe now widely known as the Anthropocene. Buddy's early foe (and later ally) B'wana Beast draws the connection quite poignantly in the moment of his defeat and unmasking: "*No!* Don't take the *helmet*...I... can't hear the animals...The world's so...*empty*...without them [...] Don't you understand? They're digging a *grave* for the *world*...and there's no one to...*stop* them" (Morrison et al. 1991 [#4], 15). Losing touch with our animal others means losing the world itself; if we become unable to sense and respond to animals, to feel them as vital to our collective present and future, we are likely to find ourselves without a future world at all.

As Donna Haraway has pointed out, the concept of the Anthropocene carries its own dangers, perhaps most notably that of replicating the anthropocentrism it is generally leveraged to critique by again placing Man at the narrative center:

> The story of Species Man as the agent of the Anthropocene is an almost laughable rerun of the great phallic humanizing and modernizing Adventure, where man, made in the image of a vanished god, takes on superpowers in his secular-sacred ascent, only to end in tragic detumescence, once again.
>
> *(2016, 47)*

In responding to this critique Haraway poses a set of other naming stratagems that highlight more specific (and less anthropocentric) aspects of the eco-crisis (Capitalocene, Plantationocene), pointing the way toward more responsive and responsible futures without surrendering to the apocalyptic temptations of the Anthropocene's endgame. This is fully apparent in her concept naming "a kind of timeplace for learning to stay with the trouble of living and dying in response-ability on a damaged earth": the Chthulucene (2). Crucial throughout the conceptual subversions Haraway introduces into the anthropocentrism of the Anthropocene is seeking out other means of storytelling, of unmaking the calcified narrative logics of human importance.

Haraway's experimental theorizing, which rewires language and thinking to practice its ethical and activist arguments on the level of meaning-making finds its kin in *Animal Man*. Timothy Morton is right to point out that, in fact, "*'Anthropocene' is the first fully antianthropocentric concept*" (2018, 24), and what makes Morrison's series most enduringly effective as itself a counter-Anthropocene artifact is not only its willingness to collect a diverse set of countercultural lifeways and activist impulses under one heading, but its capacity for refracting its critiques through the lens of a formal avant-gardism. During Buddy's peyote trip, for instance, he is gifted a revelation about his powers: it is not, in fact, by drawing upon various animals in nearby proximity that he is able to access nonhuman abilities. Rather he realizes, as his companion for the adventure Jim Highwater puts it, that he is "hooked up to the morpho-genetic field" (Morrison et al. 2003 [#18], 22); he can tap into the spectrum of life itself in a way that amplifies a preexisting affinity with all animals. In this moment of epiphany, a countercultural predilection for consciousness expansion coincides with an avant-gardism of form and ethics that is thoroughly posthuman. The scene's reconfiguration of Buddy's relationship to himself and his world, breaking it free of its bounded assumptions and revealing his radical plurality, makes possible the viscerally metafictional scenarios of the following issue (#19), in which, the trip still ongoing, Buddy bears witness to a slideshow-style history of his own backstory, meets another version of himself, turns to confront the reader, and escapes from the confines of the panel entirely, swimming through the page's white space as he attempts to reach out to Highwater.

As the series builds toward a climax of style, plot, and ethics all at once, it takes its primary site of intervention as the lived edifice at the center of anthropocentrism itself: the integrity of the human subject. "I don't think I can stand the stress," Buddy muses, in the sudden awareness of his impossible interrelationality with all of the living creatures of the world; "All these presences. These animal essences. I'm connected. Streaming out. I'm part of them" (Morrison et al. 2003 [#18], 21). He feels, suddenly, the leakiness of his subjectivity, not as a loss, or the ascendant bliss of a pure transcendence, but as the blinding presence of an infinite fullness. This is a cacophony of life, necessitating an endless interchange with the folds of extra-human alterity, in a process shot through with ambivalence, to be at once endlessly promising and ceaselessly troubling. This is a rigorous reimagining of environmental ethics as involving, but not being limited to, the liberation of subjugated animals and the rectifying of environmental degradation, along the lines by which Félix Guattari refocused ecology in a sense that "questions the whole of subjectivity and capitalistic power formations" as an elemental aim (2017, 35). The very position and composition of the human subject is exploded in the culmination of Buddy's countercultural retreat from superhero business as usual, as *Animal Man*'s metafictional counterculturalism finds itself allied with speculative comics which, Mike Frangos argues, "are particularly suited to Anthropocene visualization" based on their capacity to envelop us in the messiness of extra-humanity (2024, 237). From here it will not be possible to retreat back to the cozy imaginary of human sovereignty over body and world. Instead, the series' narrative will increasingly trespass upon the boundaries of body and page until each finally appears as what they are: fictions.

A Sign from the Other

For Buddy, the basic conditions of living and survival for the animals around him take the shape of superpowers. The semi-allegorical implications of this, the means by which the series converts animals into essences (or, occasionally, vice versa), is far from elevating Buddy to a privileged position within a network of nonhuman relations only to be marveled at. Instead, Morrison's thoroughgoing envelopment of Buddy in the field of nonhuman lifeways evinces a theory of human-animal relations to match the activist practice of the series' commitments to animal rights and ecology, a form of "zoomorphism" occupied with "defamiliarizing the human" (Herman 2011, 174). Here Haraway's point above, that under the shadow of the Anthropocene Man "takes on superpowers in his secular-sacred ascent" (2016, 47), acquires an entirely new valence. The function of the superhero, Buddy's function, is indeed to assume the fantasies of humanity in fully public view, to put the masculinity and muscularity of Man on display in all its joy and tragedy, its absurdity and seriousness, in a manner that renders them available for reflection and critique.

This is unashamedly a tale "made in the image of a vanished god" (Haraway 2016, 47). As the narrative's participants demonstrate an increasingly metafictional cognizance of their place as "just a character in a story" (Morrison et al. 2003 [#25], 186), they refer explicitly to their creators and readers as gods. But these are not benevolent gods; they are gods with "sick minds" ([#24] 169), who "want to see people *hurting* each other" (161). Morrison here renders literal, and farcical, the reactionary proclivities of comic book creators, who too frequently take to "reveling in the shameless exploitation of the enormous, divine-like powers the genre bestows to them" (Angelis 2013, 26). The world of the superhero, in *Animal Man*, is an arena for staging the violence and barbarism contained in the second term of Buddy's assumed name, which matches that of so many other superheroes. Confronting this, though, makes it possible that *other* stories might be told. It is, in an ironic twist on Haraway, in this case precisely by taking on the secular-sacred superpowers of Man that humanity itself might be deflated and packed away.

As the series builds to its conclusion under Morrison's writership in issue #26, its formal structure ruptures in increasingly explosive ways, the generic conventions of the comics medium trembling as the distinction between narrative and reality collapses entirely. Having entered the comic as the god-like, or, as Morrison puts it, "demiurgic" (2003, 208), Writer the character Buddy has been seeking, it is Morrison "himself" (the character, unlike the author in the present day, uses masculine pronouns) who explains to Buddy that this is his "*last* story"; he'll soon have to turn things over to "your new writer" (217). Alternately ironic, combative, and deeply heartfelt, most of this final issue consists in a long talk between Buddy and Morrison, punctuated by various inconsequential scuffles transparently included, as Morrison's character says, "just to keep people interested" (211). Morrison lays out the situation to Buddy: "I'm the evil mastermind behind the scenes. I'm the wicked puppeteer who pulls the strings" (207). "I can make you say and do *anything*," he tells Buddy (208); "I *wrote* your grief and your rage *and* your acceptance," he says of Buddy's mourning process over the murder of his family in issue #19, as Buddy peruses a copy of the issue (212). "*I'm* a vegetarian" Morrison says, in explanation of Buddy's dietary choices (217), and as for Buddy's deep-seated empathy for animals: "You care about animals because *I* wanted to use you to draw people's attention to what's *happening* in the world" (218). Summoning a couple of other characters appropriate to Buddy's animal theme to fight with him, at the suggestion of readers Morrison adds, he buys time to give the series' acknowledgements, thanking by name his fellow artists and colleagues. It is just as chaotic as it sounds, though distinctly more impactful than any description can convey.

The extremity to which this sequence stretches the series' longstanding inclinations to metacommentary could easily flatten itself into a caricature of postmodern nihilism: meaning is constructed, consequential action is hopeless, everything is immaterial and there is only the aesthetics of endless self-referentiality. And yet it does *not* become this, for at the same time as the issue is being ruthlessly self-deprecating and playfully malevolent it is also wrenchingly earnest. Morrison's character asks "*anyone* who cares about animal abuse to join *PETA*," giving the organization's address, and decidedly not in jest (222). He speaks of his cat Jarmara, who passed away the previous year, bitterly, cynically, touchingly. He tells Buddy his family is gone, he can't bring them back, "It wouldn't be *realistic*" (218), and then, as their conversation concludes and Morrison disappears into the rough sketch of an incomplete draft,

Buddy finds himself home again, and his family is there. The series finishes with Morrison's character recreating a scene from his childhood, walking out to the top of Angus Oval, in Glasgow, shining a flashlight for Foxy, his imaginary friend, and waiting for a response. There isn't one. Morrison turns and leaves but for two more frames we watch. And then, the light appears; the series ends.

It isn't so much the specifics of Foxy's imagined life that lend this closing its emotional and moral weight, that "he lived in a vast underground kingdom. A *utopia* ruled over by peaceful and intelligent foxes" (228). It's the gift it gives of the mystery with which it ends, the appearance of the light that only we can see, that is lost to the presumptive form of the "realistic" human intruding upon the fantasy. This is a light that comes from elsewhere, from the nostalgia of wide-eyed memory and the spectacular imaginary of a mystical Scotland, but most of all from an animal, from an other, from out of the murky, twisting layers of a storytelling of what might be between humans and animals; of the possibility of there being a response and the lingering question of what responsibility that might entail. And so, though the series ends with Morrison taking on a suddenly direct narrative dominance and just as sudden disappearance, this is not a work that is about character or author. It is also not simply, in its countercultural leanings, "about" psychedelia, or the comics medium, or even animal rights. It is an experiment concerning the departure of the human and the flashing into life of something impossible, something animal, but beyond representation. Ethics after the Anthropocene can happen only here, at a place where the human subject has departed and we are left to wonder at how we might relate to the specter of an animality allowed to remain wholly other.

References

Alaniz, José. 2020. "Animals in Graphic Narrative." In *The Oxford Handbook of Comic Book Studies*, edited by Frederick Luis Aldama. Oxford University Press.

Angelis, Valerio Massimo De. 2013. "Super-Pop Culture: With Great Power, a Greater Irresponsibility." *RSA Journal* 24: 13–31.

Coughlan, David. 2009. "The Naked Hero and Model Man: Costumed Identity in Comic Book Narratives." In *Heroes of Film, Comics and American Culture: Essays on Real and Fictional Defenders of Home*, edited by Lisa M. DeTora. McFarland and Company.

Derrida, Jacques, and Jean-Luc Nancy. 1991. "'Eating Well,' or the Calculation of the Subject: An Interview with Jacques Derrida." In *Who Comes after the Subject?* edited by Eduardo Cadava, Peter Connor, and Jean-Luc Nancy, translated by Peter Connor and Avital Ronell. Routledge.

Frangos, Mike Classon. 2024. "Comics Anthropocenes: Visualizing Multiple Space-Times in Anglophone Speculative Comics." *Journal of Graphic Novels and Comics* 15 (2): 236–251.

Guattari, Félix. 2017. *The Three Ecologies.* Translated by Ian Pindar and Paul Sutton. Bloomsbury.

Haraway, Donna J. 2016. *Staying with the Trouble: Making Kin in the Chthulucene.* Duke University Press.

Herman, David. 2011. "Storyworld/Umwelt: Nonhuman Experiences in Graphic Narratives." *SubStance* 40 (1): 156–181.

Horkheimer, Max, and Theodor W. Adorno. 2002. *"Dialectic of Enlightenment: Philosophical Fragments."* edited by Gunzelin Schmid Noerr, translated by Edmund Jephcott. Stanford University Press.

Leary, Timothy. 2005. "Foreword." In *Counterculture through the Ages: From Abraham to Acid House*, edited by Ken Goffman and Dan Joy. Villard Books.

Mahmutovic, Adnan, David Coughlan, and Stephen Blake Ervin. 2015–2016. "*Ecce Animot*: Or, The Animal Man That Therefore I Am." *ImageTexT* 8 (2): https://imagetextjournal.com/ecce-animot-or-the-animal-man-that-therefore-i-am/.

Morrison, Grant, Chas Truog, Doug Hazlewood, and Tom Grummett. 1991. *Animal Man.* Volume 1. Vertigo.

Morrison, Grant, Chas Truog, Doug Hazlewood, Paris Cullins, Mark Farmer, and Steve Montano. 2003. *Animal Man: Deus Ex Machina*. Volume 3. Vertigo.

Morrison, Grant, Chas Truog, Doug Hazlewood, Tom Grummett, Steve Montano, and Mark McKenna. 2002. *Animal Man: Origin of the Species*. Volume 2. DC Comics/Vertigo.

Morton, Timothy. 2018. *Dark Ecology: For a Logic of Future Coexistence*. Columbia University Press.

Wallin, Jason. 2020. "Evolve or Die!: Enmeshment and Extinction in DC's *Animal Man*." *Closure* 7: 18–42.

Wolfe, Cary. 2013. *Before the Law: Humans and Other Animals in a Biopolitical Frame*. University of Chicago Press.

Zornado, Joseph, and Sara Reilly. 2021. *The Cinematic Superhero as Social Practice*. Palgrave Macmillan.

Zylinska, Joanna. 2018. *The End of Man: A Feminist Counterapocalypse*. University of Minnesota Press.

41

WAKANDA AND TECHNOLOGY IN THE ANTHROPOCENE

Black Panther's Lesson on What a Sustainable Coexistence Looks Like

Siobhain Lash

Introduction

In recent years, Artificial Intelligence (AI) and climate change impacts have dominated the media headlines, but they have done so separately. Discussions about AI include a wide array of topics, ranging from implicit bias to national security. Meanwhile, climate change discussions center on unpredictable weather patterns to the increase in vector-borne diseases in a warming world. Lately, some experts have shifted their research to examine AI's carbon footprint (Bolle 2024; Heikkilä 2023; Tomlinson et al. 2024), while others have focused on AI's capabilities to aid in climate mitigation and adaptation methods. This chapter attempts to bridge these discussions by explicitly viewing AI in a context of the Anthropocene. Considering AI through this lens allows for an exploration of AI in relation to our impact on the earth, a perspective often overshadowed by AI's technological capabilities.

In this chapter, I argue that the technological advancements and environmental stewardship the Wakandan society shows in the films *Black Panther* (2018) and *Black Panther: Wakanda Forever* (2022) provide various examples of what a sustainable coexistence can look like with emerging AI technology. Section 1 briefly discusses the historical context of resource extraction, inequitable distribution of resources, and the consequences of technological advancements on society and the environment during the Industrial and Technological Revolutions. Section 2 analyzes policy lessons from the Wakandan society. Section 3 examines the ethical considerations arising from the Wakandan society's approach to balancing technological advancements with environmental stewardship.

Policy Lessons from the Industrial Revolution

Brief Historical Context of Resource Extraction

During the Industrial Revolution, resource extraction informed by colonialism dominated business practices that included the agricultural, mining, chemical, and textile industries. Resource extraction primarily encompasses the extraction of finite or non-renewable materials, such as oil, gas, and minerals through various methods (e.g., drilling, mining, and

DOI: 10.4324/9781003366911-47

deforestation). During this period, experts and scientists observed palpable impacts of human extractive practices, marking the start of the Anthropocene. As a geological framing, the Anthropocene denotes a significant disturbance of the planetary system from the previous Holocene epoch. In the article "The Concept of the Anthropocene," Yadvinder Malhi explores the history and origin of the Anthropocene. In their article, Malhi states:

> Other key features of the Anthropocene often include emphasis on (a) the global and pervasive nature of the change; (b) the multifaceted nature of global change beyond just climate change, including biodiversity decline and species mixing across continents, alteration of global biogeochemical cycles and large-scale resource extraction and waste production; (c) the two-way interactions between humans and the rest of the natural world, such that there can be feedbacks at a planetary scale such as climate change; and (d) a sense of a current or imminent fundamental shift in the functioning of our planet as a whole.
>
> *(2017, 79)*

Malhi's definition captures the various features of the Anthropocene that help us to understand its complexity. Specifically, it makes it clear that the change that marks the Anthropocene drastically differs from previous epochs, such as in relation to the decline in biodiversity and the subsequent migration of species seeking refuge in undisturbed regions. In particular, extractive methods like mining and deforestation not only contributed to the decline in biodiversity but also in the increase in industrial and hazardous waste.

By the 1950s, the harms caused by these newer business practices became more obvious during a time period called the Great Acceleration. In the article, "From Anthropocene to Noosphere: The Great Acceleration," Boris Shoshitaishvili states, "The Anthropocene paradigm interprets the Great Acceleration as a world-historical shift in which humanity becomes a technologically empowered and primarily material planetary force, signaling the start of a new geological epoch" (2020, 1–2). This period marked a significant transformation in the impact of mankind's increase in technological advancements. Unlike previous eras, human activity caused perceptible environmental problems (e.g., pollution and waste).

(In)Equitable Distribution of Resources

The reluctance of Western governments and societies to address the harms caused by their business practices and policies, including slavery, stems from the significant wealth that they generate (Ndlovu-Gatsheni 2021). As such, they continue(d) to prioritize economic growth over externalities, such as social and environmental concerns in developing economies. However, in 2001, the United Nations (n.d.) adopted the Durban Declaration and Programme of Action (DDPA) during the World Conference Against Racism that addressed the harms by colonialism, racism, xenophobia, and discrimination globally. The DDPA serves as the United Nations' framework for addressing the ongoing harms caused by colonialism. In 2023, at the 54th regular session of the Human Rights Council, the United Nations Office of the High Commissioner for Human Rights (OHCHR), used the DDPA to stress the current harms against the Global South, African nations, people of African and Asian descent, indigenous peoples, and the legacy of colonialism. Chair of the Committee on the Elimination of Racial Discrimination, Verene Shepherd referenced the DDPA as, "a milestone in articulating the harms of colonialism, both historically and in the present" (Office of the High Commissioner for Human Rights. n.d.).

Since the conception of the DDPA, Western governments have made efforts to reframe and reevaluate their economic assessment methods concerning the harms of their industrial practices in post-colonial regions. However, these efforts have been criticized by climate-impacted countries for their lack of substantive action (Gathara 2022). Furthermore, this delay continues to result in the inequitable distribution of resources between advanced economies and less economically robust and regulated societies. This includes the disproportionate amount of pollution and civil and human rights violations that occur in relation to foreign operations in these countries (U.S. Global Leadership Coalition 2021).

The OHCHR's advocacy for the continued regional decolonization as a way to achieve economic and social growth, and stability, aligns with recent challenges of earlier understandings of the Great Acceleration. Previously, scientists viewed the Great Acceleration as a global phenomenon. However, Organization for Economic Co-Operation and Development (OECD) nations have emerged as the primary contributors. In their article, "The trajectory of the Anthropocene: The Great Acceleration," Will Steffen, Wendy Broadgate, Lisa Deutsch, Owen Gaffney and Cornelia Ludwig (2015) stress the point that not all countries equally contributed to the Great Acceleration. Steffen et al. (2015) found a palpable socio-economic distinction between countries under the OECD, wealthy countries, and those outside of the OECD.

Steffen et al. found that developing economies, or BRICS (Brazil, Russia, India, China, and South Africa), contributed the least amount to the Great Acceleration, while the advanced economies contributed the most. Steffen et al. state, "This points to the profound scale of global inequality, which distorts the distribution of the benefits of the Great Acceleration and confounds efforts to deal with its impacts on the Earth System" (2015, 91). What their findings highlight here is that originally the Great Acceleration implied an equal and global contribution to these negative impacts, when this is not the case. In their article, "Co2 Emissions: How much CO2 does the world emit? Which countries emit the most?", Hannah Ritchie and Max Roser (2024) support the claim that OECD countries emitted the most emissions in the 20th Century. Ritchie and Roser (2024) state,

> We see that until well into the 20th century, global emissions were dominated by Europe and the United States. In 1900, more than 90% of emissions were produced in Europe or the US; even by 1950, they accounted for more than 85% of emissions each year.

Ritchie and Roser also acknowledge present trends that continue toward China, India, and the United States as the leading contributors. However, the sharp increase in emissions in developing economies does not necessarily point to an increase in emissions from the country. Rather, it points to the ongoing use of colonial practices by advanced economies to continue offshoring their energy and resource-intensive methods of production in developing economies.

The Consequences of Technological Advancements on Society and the Environment

During the late 20th century, the world experienced an explosion in technological advancements, marking the Technology Revolution. Since the 1980s, the global focus shifted to innovations in technology, often times at the expense of environmental and societal impacts. For example, technology from just a few years ago quickly becomes outdated because of how rapidly our technology is progressing. As a result, this rapid turnover has significantly increased electronic-waste (e-waste) worldwide, as consumers update their electronic devices (World Health Organization 2024). This surge in technological advancements has brought renewed attention to the implications and use of AI. However, in general, our current energy infrastructure cannot handle the strain of the AI boom (Solman and Holmes 2024; Cohen 2024). As a result, due to the amount of energy needed for data centers to store and cool down the processing systems, there is a growing call for "green regulation" (Popkova and Sergi 2024). Other policy proposals include a focus on transparent practices like requiring a company and their data center to disclose the use of local water and energy (Berreby 2024).

Currently, the use of generative AI by consumers requires ten times more energy than a traditional internet search (Gantz and Trudell 2024). Likewise, training these generative AI systems requires intensive energy use (Kumar and Davenport 2023; Solman and Holmes 2024). Accordingly, this puts a strain on local community water and energy systems. Moreover, AI usage and engagement is starting to put a strain on power grids across the globe (CNBC Television 2024). In their 2024 report, "Electricity 2024: Analysis and forecast to 2026," the International Energy Agency (IEA) projects that data centers could consume up to 1,000 terawatt-hours (TWh), which is more than double of their current 460 TWh usage (2024, 8). The IEA continues, "This demand is roughly equivalent to the electricity consumption of Japan" (2024, 8). Therefore, the growing energy consumption of Big Tech's data centers for emerging AI technologies, coupled with inadequate e-waste disposal, also echo extractive practices reminiscent from the previous revolutions.

Consequently, as emerging AI technology requires an increase in energy usage and demand, this will contribute to climate change and a warming of the earth. As the earth warms, Greenland's ice sheets continue to melt into the North Atlantic Ocean. This increase in freshwater impacts the dynamics of the Atlantic Meridional Overturning Circulation (AMOC). As more ice sheets melt, they disrupt the distribution of salt and heat throughout the ocean currents (Berwyn 2024). Subsequently, as salinity levels decrease, the water becomes less dense and stops sinking (NASA Science Editorial Team 2023). As a result, the AMOC currents slow as less and less water sinks. This has raised concerns regarding the AMOC weakening and projections of it partially or fully collapsing (Intergovernmental Panel on Climate Change 2023, 39). Because the AMOC serves as an equilibrium for Earth's weather, its collapse could be catastrophic and significantly cause abrupt changes in weather patterns across the globe. Thus, if the AMOC slows or collapses, scientists predict that not only will that make hot areas hotter and cold areas colder, but it would also cause a strengthening of storms.

Already, the effects of these weather disruptions and atmospheric changes are becoming increasingly evident. Recently, a highly publicized incident occurred in May 2024 when Singapore Airlines experienced severe clear-air turbulence (CAT), causing the plane to plummet 178 feet, killing one passenger (Thorsberg 2024). The flight experienced the dramatic fall due to CAT or invisible turbulence. According to the National Weather Service (n.d.), CAT occurs above altitudes of 15,000 feet and is not limited to cloudless skies. Attributed to temperature inversions, CAT typically manifests in patches and occurs more frequently in winter. The growing intensity and frequency of CAT have renewed the discussions in public discourse of the impacts of climate change on atmospheric temperatures and flight safety. Experts (Copley and Hersher 2024; Poynting 2024; Thiem 2024; Thompson 2024) anticipate climate change exacerbating a number of similar unprecedent current events (e.g., Hurricane Beryl).

A further illustration of the mounting repercussions of the impact that humans have on the earth includes the recent rapid intensification of Hurricane Beryl. On June 28, 2024, Hurricane Beryl first formed as storm, but within 48 hours it had rapidly intensified into a Category 4 hurricane. According to the National Oceanic and Atmospheric Administration (NOAA) (Thiem 2024), Beryl is the first ever Category 4 hurricane to form in the month of June. Similar to the increase in severe CAT incidents, Beryl's rapid intensification spurred discussions of natural disasters like hurricanes in relation to the climate warming, and what their intensity, frequency, and rapid development means for the future (Thompson 2024; Poynting 2024; Copley and Hersher 2024). Thus, the consequences of technological advancements on society and the environment within our current colonial framing are already severe.

Policy Lessons from Wakanda

In Wakandan society, vibranium is the powerful metal from which Wakanda builds its infrastructure and technology. In the movie *Black Panther* the audience gets introduced to the origin and use of vibranium. Vibranium formed from a meteorite that struck Wakanda prior to the settlement of men. It impacted the earth around it, producing a heart-shaped herb that, once ingested by an individual, gives them "superhuman strength, speed and instincts" (Coogler 2018, 00:00:23). Once men occupied Wakanda, they developed five tribes, that suffered from ongoing and prolonged wars with one another. Civil unrest between the tribes persisted until a warrior shaman received a vision from the Panther Goddess, Bast. In the vision, Bast shows the warrior shaman where to locate the herb. After the shaman found the vibranium and ingested the herb, four of the five tribes established the first Black Panther king and protector, to bring peace to Wakanda. This allowed the Wakandan society to become one of the most technologically advanced countries in the world. Because of the strength of vibranium, Wakandan society decided to shield itself from the rest of the world and keep it and vibranium secret, away from the chaos and unrest of the rest of the world.

An integral feature of Wakanda's utilization of vibranium includes using its power-enhancing qualities for important ceremonial rituals. During the ritual, the newly appointed Black Panther drinks the liquified version of the herb. His advisors then bury him in sand so he will join the ancestral plane. There, the Black Panther seeks advice and guidance from their ancestors. The ritual is essential in connecting the king to his heritage and roots, to inform his ruling as both Wakanda's ruler and spiritual leader (Coogler 2018, 00:28:36). Wakanda's incorporation of looking to the ancestors for guidance resembles the decolonized customs and frameworks many Indigenous, Black, and African communities use to inform their business practices.

Decolonized Practices

Wakanda's incorporation of ancestral customs, such as seeking for guidance from past rulers, informs their management of vibranium that aligns with decolonized methods. In her book, *Decolonizing Methodologies: Research and Indigenous Peoples*, Linda Tuhiwai Smith states, "it is about centering our concerns and world views and then coming to know and understand theory and research from our own perspectives and for our own purposes" (1999, 39). According to Smith's view, decolonization includes the centering of world and individual views to help inform our understanding of theory and experiences. Some decolonized practices include approaches like the Nguni concept of ubuntu. In their book, "Hunhuism or Ubuntuism: A Zimbabwean Indigenous Political Philosophy," Stanlake John Thompson Samkange and Tommie Marie Samkange define ubuntu. Samkange and Samkange state, "The attention one human being gives to another: the kindness, courtesy, consideration and friendliness in the relationship between people; a code of behaviour, an attitude to other people and to life, is embodied in hunhu or ubuntu" (1980, 39). Ubuntu is a relational ethics rooted in an African philosophy that scholars consider the antithesis of colonization. In the article, "Ubuntu," Munyaradzi Felix Murove states, "The argument for the reconstruction of an African identity through Ubuntu becomes an antithesis of colonial values such as those enshrined in the doctrine of atomic individualism" (2012, 45). In essence, ubuntu emphasizes the interconnectedness of humans and their relationship with one another. Unlike colonial individualism, a personal responsibility to behave in a way that not only augments the well-being of oneself but society is integral in ubuntu ethics.

Wakanda reflects ubuntu ethics through their centering of human connectedness with the environment and each other. This includes their integration of spirituality that allows for future practices to better balance between human behavior and the health of their immediate environment. For example, Wakandan society develops their policies and centers technological advances from resourcing vibranium responsibly. They emphasize the ethical extraction of vibranium, which informs their fierce protectiveness of its resources from the rest of the world. The viewer sees clips of this throughout the film. For example, in *Black Panther*, while Zuri and T'Challa discuss N' Jobu's death, the viewer sees Zuri gently tending to the heart-shaped-vibranium-infused herb. In this scene, the viewer sees the careful ways in which vibranium is tended to and harvested (Coogler 2018, 01:05:18). In a later scene, agent Ross wakes up in Shuri's lab after she heals his bullet wound (Coogler 2018, 01:10:14). He discovers that he is in Wakanda and that Shuri's lab is amongst where Wakanda mines its vibranium. Shuri explains the mining operations and the technology used for transporting and stabilizing vibranium. She explains that they transport the vibranium through magnetic levitation and stabilize it through sonic stabilizers to temporarily destabilize it for safe handling.

Another example includes the scene when N'Jobu's son, Erik Killmonger, challenges and beats T'Challa for the throne (Coogler 2018, 01:28:35). Killmonger wakes up from visiting the ancestral plane and demands that the Dora Milaje warriors destroy and burn all of the heart-shaped herbs. One of the warriors tries to impart the importance of the herb in Wakandan tradition, specifically for future kings. He asks, "the heart-shaped herb did that? This all of it." The Dora Milaje warrior responds, "Yes. So when it comes time for another king, we will be ready." Killmonger responds, "Another king? Yeah, go ahead and burn all that." The Dora Milaje warrior responds, "My king, we cannot do that. It is our tradition." He responds by attacking the warrior, saying, "When I tell you to do something, I mean that shit." Then, when he releases her, he demands, "Burn it all!" During this exchange, we see Nakia sneak into the burial place and take a piece of the heart-shaped herb. Killmonger's directive to burn the heart-shaped herb is the first departure from Wakanda's ubuntu and communal practices.

While these scenes more explicitly highlight resource management and technological advancements in Wakanda, they also underscore the communal approach to resource management and ethical considerations in sourcing vibranium. In the scene with Zuri, Zuri is careful in the way he is harvesting the heart-shaped herb, tending to it gently, to ensure both the herb and environment remain unharmed. This is an embodiment of ubuntu, because he ensures his handling of the herb is careful and in a way that safeguard's both the immediate environment and the herb. Similarly, when the Dora Milaje warriors attempt to prevent Killmonger from burning all the herbs, their protests are not simply against the deviation of tradition but also because it is harming the environment and future Wakandans more generally. Killmonger's focus on individual gain contradicts and violates Wakanda's interconnectedness and communal commitment to the responsible stewardship of resources for the benefit of both the community and environment.

Equitable Distribution of Resources

In the *Black Panther* film, T'Challa captures arms dealer Ulysses Klaue. During his interview with agent Ross, T'Challa learns that Klaue has been revealing Wakanda's secret to outsiders. While listening in on the interrogation, the viewer sees T'Challa struggle with this decision to safeguard Wakanda's secret. Thus far, Wakanda successfully hides behind allowing advanced economies to confirm their own prejudices and biases against countries in Africa. This subterfuge allows Wakanda to maintain its distribution of resources within the Wakandan society and avoid possible exploitation by Western countries.

While agent Ross interrogates Klaue, Klaue asks agent Ross, "What do you actually know about Wakanda?" Agent Ross responds, "Um…Shepherds, textiles, cool outfits." Klaue interrupts him and says,

> It's all a front. Explorers searched for it for centuries. El Dorado, the Golden City. They thought they could find it in South America but it was in Africa the whole time. A technological marvel. All because it was built on a mound of the most valuable metal known to man. *Isipho*, they call it. The gift. Vibranium.

Agent Ross, incredulously responds, "Vibranium, yeah, the strongest metal on earth." Klaue continues, "It's not just a metal. They sew it into their clothes. It powers their city, their tech, their weapons." Agent Ross, asks, "Weapons?" Klaue laughs, and says, "Yeah. Makes my arm cannon look like a leaf blower." Still unconvinced, agent Ross responds, "That's a nice fairy tale, but Wakanda is a third-world country and you stole all their vibranium." Seeing agent Ross's disbelief, Klaue challenges agent Ross to ask T'Challa what is in his suit and claws (Coogler 2018, 00:56:02).

Wakanda sharing its resources with the rest of the world is a repeated and central theme in the film with Nakia also challenging T'Challa to share Wakanda's resources and technology with oppressed populations and taking in refugees (Coogler 2018, 00:34:00). T'Challa becomes further conflicted when he learns that his father, T'Chaka, killed his uncle, N'Jobu, for supplying oppressed and marginalized populations with vibranium-enhanced weapons. Even though T'Chaka intended to take his brother back to Wakanda to be tried by the elders, N'Jobu was killed for attacking the king's friend, Zuri. In order to "maintain the lie," T'Chaka left N'Jobu's body in the United States along with his child, Erik Killmonger (Coogler 2018, 01:07:21).

Later, when the viewer sees Killmonger at the throne, he continues to disrupt tradition by sending vibranium to arm oppressed people across the world. He proclaims,

> We got spies embedded in every nation on Earth. Already in place. I know how colonizers think. So we're gonna use their own strategy against 'em. We're gonna send vibranium weapons out to our War Dogs. They'll arm oppressed people all over the

world so they can finally rise up and kill those in power. And their children. And anyone else who takes their side. It's time they know the truth about us! We're warriors! The world's gonna start over, and this time, we're on top. The sun will never set on the Wakandan empire.

This initiates a discussion amongst the elders and leaders of Wakanda about whether they should implement Killmonger's suggestion. W'kabi agrees with Killmonger's plan and states, "The outside world is catching up and soon it will be the conquerors or the conquered. I'd rather be the former" (Coogler 2018, 01:30:14). W'kabi's concern reflects Wakanda's recognition of the unequal distribution of resources caused by colonization. Killmonger's break from tradition and adoption of the "colonizer's" methods creates civil unrest in Wakanda. There are some who are hesitant to adopt his new policies and departure from tradition due to their awareness of the world's treatment of resource-rich countries. Then, there are those, like Nakia, who take a more optimistic approach insofar as believing the good of sharing their technology and knowledge with others.

The Benefits of Technological Advancements on Society and the Environment

Although never explicitly shown or discussed, there are many ways in which Wakandans incorporate AI into their existing technologies. One of the featured ways is the vibranium-powered kimoyo bead, which is multifunctional. It serves as a communication device, medical monitor, data storage unit, weapon, navigation tool, and emergency medicine aid. Their benefits include an interoperability with other Wakanda systems and devices, allowing its user to have access to information and users at all time. Another example of their integration of AI into their infrastructure is seen at the beginning of *Black Panther: Wakanda Forever* (Coogler 2022, 00:00:18). There, the audience meets Shuri's AI assistant, Griot. Initially, Griot assists Shuri in finding a way to use the heart-shaped herb to save T'Challa. However, over the course of the film, Griot assists Shuri in both her civilian and military research efforts, including helping her in armed conflict. As a part of this process, Shuri continues to introduce and integrate AI into Wakanda's existing technology and infrastructure.

Ethical Insights from Wakanda in Nature and Tech

The *Black Panther* films stress the tension between decolonized stewardship and colonial exploitation. This comparison between the two approaches reveals the ethical dilemma that Wakanda faces. For example, in both *Black Panther* and *Black Panther: Wakanda Forever*, Wakanda must reconcile these disparate approaches and find a middle ground with the rest of the world. At the end of *Black Panther*, T'Challa demonstrates his strategy in integrating tradition with engagement with the rest of the world (Coogler 2018, 02:01:37). He introduces the first Wakandan International Outreach Center located in Oakland. Later, T'Challa gives a speech to the United Nations in which he proclaims,

And for the first time in our history, we will be sharing their knowledge and resources with the outside world. Wakanda will no longer watch from the shadows. We cannot. We must not. We will work to be an example of how we as brothers and sisters on this earth should treat each other. Now, more than ever the illusions of division threaten our very existence. We all know the truth. More connects us than separates us. But in times of crisis, the wise build bridges, while the foolish build barriers. We must find a way to look after one another as if we were one, single tribe.

(Coogler 2018, 02:05:11)

In his speech, T'Challa commits to Wakandans' wishes while balancing the benefits and harms of sharing both knowledge and technology with the rest of the world.

This tension between the colonized and decolonized approach to natural resources is further explored in *Black Panther: Wakanda Forever*. At the beginning of the film, a UN session convenes over the use of vibranium. In the scene, the member states discuss the use of vibranium as a weapon of mass destruction and its overall undetectability by standard security systems and metal detectors. In response to their worries, Queen Ramonda points out that the danger is not the vibranium. The true danger is the member states. Queen Ramonda says, "It has always been our policy to never trade vibranium under any circumstance. Not because of the dangerous potential of vibranium, but because of the dangerous potential of you" (Coogler 2022, 00:07:50). Queen Ramonda continues,

You perform civility here. But we know what you whisper in your halls of leadership and in your military facilities. 'The King is dead. The Black Panther is gone. They have lost their protector. Now is our time to strike.

(Coogler 2022, 00:08:50)

After T'Challa's death, the attempt by Western governments to take Wakanda's resources by force confirms Wakanda's fear; they anticipated advanced economies resorting to violence instead of using more collaborative and transparent methods to gain access to vibranium.

The Upshot

Overall, the colonial approach is inherently unsustainable because it relies on extractive and violent methods that exploit resource-rich countries and their people (Murove 2012, 41). A colonial approach cannot accommodate major deviations from its status quo, such as emerging technologies and climate change. We are seeing this failure and inability to meet these challenges in the present day. As climate change advances, more billion-dollar weather events continue to test and pressure our current business practices and policies informed by colonialism.

For example, a study by the NOAA National Centers for Environmental Information found that the United States experienced 391 $1 billion-dollar weather and climate disasters since 1980 with a total cost exceeding $2.755 trillion (National Centers for Environmental Information 2024). If we continue this trajectory with emerging AI technology and do not learn more sustainable practices, then we risk even more costly mistakes and further climate breakdown. However, we can learn from Wakanda's decolonized methods and make the shift from rigid and extractive colonial methods. This will be especially crucial as we are already witnessing the harmful impacts of AI.

Conclusion

In summary, the AI Revolution in the Anthropocene raises significant sustainability concerns about balancing new emerging technologies with environmental stewardship and we can better understand AI's impact on the earth through this lens. Our current dominant extractive practices, informed by colonialism, have contributed to significant environmental degradation and to the rapid intensification of natural disasters like hurricanes. However, the *Black Panther* films highlight how decolonized practices can serve as a model for achieving a more sustainable future. Despite the irreparable damage to the environment, we can use Wakanda's approaches as a guide toward a more sustainable future.

References

Berreby, David. 2024. "As Use of A.I. Soars, So Does the Energy and Water It Requires." *Yale E360*, February 6. https://e360.yale.edu/features/artificial-intelligence-climate-energy-emissions.

Berwyn, Bob. 2024. "Extreme Climate Impacts from Collapse of a Key Atlantic Ocean Current Could Be Worse Than Expected, a New Study Warns." *Inside Climate News*, February 9. https://insideclimatenews.org/news/09022024/climate-impacts-from-collapse-of-atlantic-meridional-overturning-current-could-be-worse-than-expected/.

Bolle, Monica de. 2024. *"AI's Carbon Footprint Appears Likely to Be Alarming."* Peterson Institute for International Economics, February 29. https://www.piie.com/blogs/realtime-economics/2024/ais-carbon-footprint-appears-likely-be-alarming.

CNBC Television, dir. *AI Drives Energy Consumption*. Uploaded July 3, 2024 on YouTube. https://www.youtube.com/watch?v=AmbYUofQOpQ.

Cohen, Ariel. 2024. "AI Is Pushing The World Toward An Energy Crisis." *Forbes*, May 24. https://www.forbes.com/sites/arielcohen/2024/05/23/ai-is-pushing-the-world-towards-an-energy-crisis/.

Coogler, Ryan, dir. 2018. *Black Panther*. Walt Disney Studios, 2020. Disney+.

Coogler, Ryan, dir. 2022. *Black Panther: Wakanda Forever*. Walt Disney Studios, 2023. Disney+.

Copley, Michael, and Rebecca Hersher. 2024. "Climate Change Makes Hurricanes like Beryl More Dangerous." *National Public Radio*, July 4. https://www.npr.org/2024/07/04/nx-s1-5026730/hurricane-beryl-climate-change.

Gantz, Rachel, and Tim Trudell. 2024. "EPRI Study: Data Centers Could Consume up to 9% of U.S. Electricity Generation by 2030." Electric Power Research Institute, May 29. https://www.epri.com/about/media-resources/press-release/q5vU86fr8TKxATfX8IHf1U48Vw4r1DZF.

Gathara, Patrick. 2022. "The West Will Not Act on Climate Change until It Feels Its Pain." *AlJazeera*, November 19. https://www.aljazeera.com/opinions/2022/11/19/global-south-pleas-wont-get-the-west-to-act-on-climate-change.

Heikkilä, Melissa. 2023. "AI's Carbon Footprint Is Bigger Than You Think." *MIT Technology Review*, December 5. https://www.technologyreview.com/2023/12/05/1084417/ais-carbon-footprint-is-bigger-than-you-think/.

Intergovernmental Panel on Climate Change. 2023. *Climate Change 2021 – The Physical Science Basis: Working Group I Contribution to the Sixth Assessment Report of the Intergovernmental Panel on Climate Change*. Cambridge University Press. https://doi.org/10.1017/9781009157896.

International Energy Agency. 2024. "Electricity 2024 – Analysis and Forecast to 2026." Hosted on ManagEnergy, January 26. https://managenergy.ec.europa.eu/publications/electricity-2024-analysis-and-forecast-2026_en.

Kumar, Ajay, and Tom Davenport. 2023. "How to Make Generative AI Greener." *Harvard Business Review*, July 20. https://hbr.org/2023/07/how-to-make-generative-ai-greener.

Malhi, Yadvinder. 2017. "The Concept of the Anthropocene." *Annual Review of Environment and Resources* 42 (1): 77–104. https://doi.org/10.1146/annurev-environ-102016-060854

Murove, Munyaradzi Felix. 2012. "Ubuntu." *Diogenes* 59 (3–4): 36–47. https://doi.org/10.1177/0392192113493737

NASA Science Editorial Team. 2023. "Slowdown of the Motion of the Ocean." NASA, June 5. https://science.nasa.gov/earth/earth-atmosphere/slowdown-of-the-motion-of-the-ocean/.

National Centers for Environmental Information. 2024. "Decades of Data on a Changing Atlantic Circulation." April 24. https://www.ncei.noaa.gov/news/decades-data-changing-atlantic-circulation.

National Weather Service. n.d. "Turbulence." Accessed February 4, 2025. https //www.weather.gov/source/zhu/ZHU_Training_Page/turbulence_stuff/turbulence/turbulence.htm.

Ndlovu-Gatsheni, Sabelo J. 2021. "'Moral Evil, Economic Good': Whitewashing the Sins of Colonialism." *AlJazeera*, February 26. https://www.aljazeera.com/opinions/2021/2/26/colonialism-in-africa-empire-was-not-ethical.

Office of the High Commissioner for Human Rights. n.d. "Racism, Discrimination Are Legacies of Colonialism." Accessed February 4, 2025. https://www.ohchr.org/en/get-involved/stories/racism-discrimination-are-legacies-colonialism.

Popkova, Elena G, and Bruno S. Sergi. 2024. "Energy Infrastructure: Investment, Sustainability and AI." *Resources Policy* 91 (April):104807. https://doi.org/10.1016/j.resourpol.2024.104807.

Poynting, Mark. 2024. "How Record-Breaking Hurricane Beryl Is a Sign of a Warming World." *BBC News*, July 4. https://www.bbc.com/news/articles/c9r3g572lrno.

Ritchie, Hannah, and Max Roser. 2024. "CO_2 Emissions." *Our World in Data*, January. https://ourworldindata.org/co2-emissions.

Samkange, Stanlake John Thompson, and Tommie Marie Samkange. 1980. *Hunhuism or Ubuntuism: A Zimbabwean Indigenous Political Philosophy*. Graham Publishing.

Shoshitaishvili, Boris. 2020. "From Anthropocene to Noosphere: The Great Acceleration." *Earth's Future* 9 (2): e2020EF001917. https://doi.org/10.1029/2020EF001917.

Smith, Linda Tuhiwai. 1999. *Decolonizing Methodologies: Research and Indigenous Peoples*. Zed Books Ltd.

Solman, Paul, and Ryan Connelly Holmes. 2024. "AI and the Energy Required to Power It Fuel New Climate Concerns." *PBS News*, July 4. https://www.pbs.org/newshour/show/ai-and-the-energy-required-to-power-it-fuel-new-climate-concerns.

Steffen, Will, Wendy Broadgate, Lisa Deutsch, Owen Gaffney, and Cornelia Ludwig. 2015. "The Trajectory of the Anthropocene: The Great Acceleration." *The Anthropocene Review* 2 (1): 81–98. https://doi.org/10.1177/2053019614564785.

Thiem, Haley. 2024. "Category 5 Hurricane Beryl Makes Explosive Start to 2024 Atlantic Season." Climate.gov, July 3. https://www.climate.gov/news-features/event-tracker/category-5-hurricane-beryl-makes-explosive-start-2024-atlantic-season.

Thompson, Andrea. 2024. "Meteorologists Have Never Seen Anything like Hurricane Beryl." *Scientific American*, July 4. https://www.scientificamerican.com/article/why-hurricane-beryl-underwent-unprecedented-rapid-intensification/.

Thorsberg, Christian. 2024. "Climate Change Is Making Airplane Turbulence More Common and Severe, Scientists Say." *Smithsonian Magazine*, May 31. https://www.smithsonianmag.com/smart-news/climate-change-is-making-airplane-turbulence-more-common-and-severe-scientists-say-180984440/.

Tomlinson, Bill, Rebecca W. Black, Donald J. Patterson, and Andrew W. Torrance. 2024. "The Carbon Emissions of Writing and Illustrating Are Lower for AI than for Humans." *Scientific Reports* 14 (1): 3732. https://doi.org/10.1038/s41598-024-54271-x.

U.S. Global Leadership Coalition. 2021. "Climate Change and the Developing World: A Disproportionate Impact." https://www.usglc.org/blog/climate-change-and-the-developing-world-a-disproportionate-impact/#:~:text=While%20global%20leadership%20on%20climate,most%20vulnerable%20including%20women%20and.

World Health Organization. 2024. "Electronic Waste (e-Waste)." October 1. https://www.who.int/news-room/fact-sheets/detail/electronic-waste-(e-waste).

42

GREEN LANTERN, STRUCTURAL RACISM, AND N.K. JEMISIN'S *FAR SECTOR*

Christopher Roman

As Sheena C. Howard and Ronald L. Jackson write in their introduction to *Black Comics: Politics of Race and Representation,* "the fantastical worlds of comic strips, cartoons, and comic books have the powerful potential to weave imaginary narratives that offer possibilities for seeing black heroism" (2013, 1). N.K. Jemisin's (writer) and Jamal Campbell's (artist) *Far Sector* (2020–2021) centers black heroism and its challenges in this Green Lantern story about Sojourner "Jo" Mullein: a black, queer, and female member of the Green Lantern Corp, assigned to a "far sector" of space. Jemisin holds up a mirror to contemporary society, as she draws Jo into the difficult racial tensions in The City Enduring.

While seemingly remote from the political issues of contemporary America, this chapter will examine the parallel social justice issues shown in the recent Green Lantern comic. Furthermore, the chapter will situate *Far Sector* in line with other Green Lantern stories that have dealt with social issues, such as the 1970–1971 *Green Lantern* arc that guest-starred Green Arrow, written by Dennis "Denny" O'Neil with art by Neal Adams. *Green Lantern co-starring Green Arrow* attempts to critique the Green Lantern Corp as a police force through its relation to social ills. But, while trying to examine social problems, this comic suffers from the problem of the superhero; in other words, the superhero is the single (male) individual to right all the wrongs of society. *Far Sector* is part of a genealogy of these kinds of Green Lantern superhero stories, but Jemisin does not rely on the individual to fix everything; rather, she outlines how systemic changes need to be made in order to redress injustice and invokes contemporary social events to comment on systemic racism and social class conflicts.

This chapter will use scholarship on systemic racism in order to address how Jemisin represents systemic change by reimagining the Green Lanterns, who are analogues for the police, as a force that undermines traditional (brutal) policing for a role that supports community and serves the oppressed. *Far Sector* utilizes contemporary politics to inform the backstory of its Green Lantern, Sojourner Mullein, through references to the Black Lives Matter movement, as well as, issues of police brutality. By examining the Green Lantern Corp as a universal police force, one that assigns a Green Lantern or two to each section of the universe, Jemisin is also suggesting, through the utopic-thinking of comic books, of how policing can be rethought as an institution, moving away from reducing crime as a

DOI: 10.4324/9781003366911-48

thrust of its purpose, toward an institution that helps connect the voiceless with those in power positions.

As Joe R. Feagin writes, systemic racism

> encompasses a broad range of white-racist dimensions: the racist ideology, attitudes, emotions, habits, actions, and institutions of whites in this society. Thus, systemic racism is far more than a matter of racial prejudice and individual bigotry. It is a material, social, and ideological reality that is well-imbedded in major U.S. institutions.
>
> *(Feagin 2006, 2)*

Older models of addressing racism often point to the individual as the cause of continued racism in society, however, taking a systemic approach to the problem of racism uncovers the ways systems such as economics, housing, joblessness, law, and policing have been built to favor white citizens to the detriment of the black population. Thus, as Feagin writes, "this mainstream approach, tends to view persisting racial-ethnic concerns and conflicts today as being matters of prejudice and stereotyping or of individual and small-group discrimination" (Feagin 2006, 4). Feagin contrasts the "mainstream approach" against that of the "systemic racism" approach as a way to redress the real institutional biases that exist to keep black people as second-class to white power. These disparate approaches to racism are evident in early *Green Lantern* comics where the answer to racism is pointing out individual oppressors while leaving the fundamental system intact. As I will discuss below, we see this in Denny O'Neil's and Neal Adam's *Green Lantern/Green Arrow* story. Jemisin's work, attempts to address race systemically through her Afro-futurist space story.

Sojourner "Jo" Mullein is a Green Lantern assigned to a sector of space so distant that it does not have a number. She is the first black, queer women in the Green Lantern Corps' history. As Deborah Elizabeth Whaley writes, "sequential art [is] a viable form for understanding how popular literature and visual culture reflects the real and imagined place of women of African descent in nation making, politics, and cultural production" (2016, 8). This is significant for the complex story of *Far Sector* as she brings her intersectional identity to bear on solving the crimes of The City Enduring and reimagines her role as a Green Lantern along the way. We are given her backstory in issue #5 of the 12-issue story. Sojourner is an Earth woman, and N.K. Jemisin situates her childhood in New York City during the early 2000s. Sojourner is the oldest of three girls. We meet her and her sisters in a panel with her family, where her mother, entering the door, announces she was passed over for a promotion again. She explains to her husband that the white man, who got the promotion for the job she was already doing, threatened her: "he warned HR he'd sue for discrimination against white men if I got it… every person in that office is a white guy except me" (Jemisin and Campbell 2020d, 10). Jemisin begins to set up the structural injustices at work in Sojourner's world with claims of "reverse racism" and a workforce where a black woman cannot get ahead.

The next few pages of issue #5 of *Far Sector* move forward in time, revealing Sojourner's parents' divorce. While Sojourner escorts her father from Divorce Court, they see the Twin Towers in flames. The events of 9/11 inspire Sojourner to eventually join the Army on the same day she receives an acceptance letter to Princeton University. She does a tour of duty in Iraq where she sees the US Military as causing harm to the civilian population, emblematized by a child on the side of the road who is missing an arm. Sojourner then tries Princeton before enrolling in the police academy. In a pivotal panel that echoes throughout the book, her police partner beats an unarmed black man (Jemisin and Campbell 2020d, 12–14). The panel we see in *Far Sector* #5 depicts a close-up of the butt of the gun drenched in blood while Sojourner looks on horrified (13). She reports her partner to the "higher-ups," but she is fired from her job for a "social media violation;" a friend has tagged her in Black Lives Matter post. As she laments to the disguised Guardian who is recruiting her to be a Green Lantern, "not my photo, not my tag, but it counted as a 'social media policy violation'" (19). This is the moment when the Guardian of Oa, who up to this point had appeared as a tall, flirtatious black woman, reveals herself to offer Sojourner a Green Lantern ring.

As can be seen from her backstory, Sojourner Mullein and *Far Sector* are steeped in contemporary politics. From issues such as the difficulties that black women face in majority white workplaces, to the War in Iraq, to police brutality, and Black Lives Matter; each of these systemic issues disproportionately affects the black population. Her white police partner may be charged for his brutality and crimes, but the immediate penalty is meted out on Sojourner. N.K. Jemisin provides the reader with a backstory that shows how Sojourner has tried to work within the systems in order to better her life (family, school, military, police) but each of the institutions lead to a failed sense of justice or equity. What she sees and what is represented to us is how these systems are inherently broken.

Green Lantern/Green Arrow and Liberal Approaches to Racism

Before exploring the world of *Far Sector* in terms of systemic racism, it is important to place Jemisin's Green Lantern story in a genealogy with other Green Lantern stories, especially as they highlight social justice issues and center a black Green Lantern. By introducing these stories, the chapter will point out the ways that they fall into the "mainstream approach" that Feagin addresses above. While, for their time, they addressed racism and other social justice issues, turning the comic book into a space to address real-world issues such as drug addiction or feminism, they fall into the trap of blaming the singular "villain" as the center of prejudice while ignoring larger systemic problems. In 1970, Denny O'Neil (writer) and Neal Adams (artist) created *Green Lantern co-starring Green Arrow,* which is often referred to as *Green Lantern/Green Arrow,* beginning with *Green Lantern* #76 (1970). The premise of the comics is that the more conservative Green Lantern, Hal Jordan, takes a road trip across the country with the more anarchic Green Arrow, Oliver Queen, as they explore the problems of America. As Denny O'Neil writes in the introduction to the collected edition,

> Green Lantern was, in effect, a cop. An incorruptible cop, to be sure, with noble intentions, but still a cop, a crypto-fascist; he took orders, he committed violence at the behest of commanders whose authority he did not question. If you showed him a law being broken, his instincts would be to strike at the lawbreaker without asking any whys.
>
> *(O'Neil and Adams 2004a, 5)*

The thrust of the comics was to educate the "crypto-fascist" Hal Jordan to a more leftist way of thinking about American society's ills.

Green Lantern #76 sets up the problem of Hal Jordan's approach to crime. The story opens with Hal Jordan coming across a "punk attacking" an older man (O'Neil and Adams 2004a, 11). Two men confront the older man pushing him to the ground. Jordan comments, "No respect for law and order. None" (11). Jordan breaks up the skirmish but is soon pelted by garbage coming from the occupants of the building. Green Arrow then confronts Hal and gets him to see that Jordan is backing the wrong side. It turns out that the man in the suit is a slum lord who is about to evict everyone in the building to put in a parking lot. Hal Jordan attempts to defend himself by saying, "I have a job... I do it" (14). Green Arrow retorts, "Seems I've heard that line before... at the Nazi War Trials" (14). In the next panel, Green Lantern is confronted by an older black man and resident of the building:

> I been readin' about you... how you work for the blue skins... and how on a planet someplace you helped out the orange skins... and you done considerable for the purple skins! Only there's skins you never bother with... the black skins. I want to know how come?
>
> (15)

Green Lantern hangs his head in shame and cannot answer the charges.

The rest of the issue involves trying to catch the slum lord for his crimes. The slum lord, Jubal Slade, argues that he has "law on my side. I can do anything I want with that property" (O'Neil and Adams 2004a, 17). Eventually Slade is captured after admitting to a disguised Hal Jordan that he took out a hit on Green Arrow. In true comic book fashion, the crook is captured. However, it is unclear what the fate of the evicted tenants will be as the comic does not return to them. The narrative shifts to plans for the road trip across America with Green Lantern, Green Arrow, and a representative for Oa so that Hal can address his white guilt. The bad guy is captured; however, the system of housing inequity and injustice has barely been touched. As Jesse T. Moore comments, "The *Green Lantern/Green Arrow* comic series calls for a reordering of America's political affairs, while simultaneously urging a reform of the consciousness of its citizens" (Moore 2003, 267). As Moore suggests, this is an important comic, steeped in the politics of the New Left. However, perhaps tethered by its time, it often leaves the system to take care of itself, as if by simply catching one bad apple the entire apple cart can be liberated.

Yet, we can see the roots of Jemisin and Campbell's *Far Sector* here, especially in Hal Jordan's appeal to "law and order" and the critique of the Green Lanterns as universal cops who merely follow orders. One might argue then, that O'Neil and Adam's story is steeped more in liberal thinking (the individual can change things) than a thinking that considers systems and the ways those systems create inequality and oppression. However, these stories do highlight the problematic role that Green Lanterns play as a universal police force. If Green Lanterns are merely concerned with law and order, then they simply perpetuate the same injustices.

These series of comics are also important in introducing the first black Green Lantern, John Stewart. In *Green Lantern* #87 (1972), the Guardians of Oa chose John Stewart to be the second Green Lantern for Earth despite Hal's objections that Stewart is too angry: "he has a chip on his shoulder the size of the Rock of Gibraltar" (O'Neil and Adams 2004b, 106). Despite Hal's bias toward the "angry black man," the Guardians task Hal with training John Stewart. Their first mission is to save a crowd from a wayward oil tanker as they are welcoming the arrival of Senator Jeremiah Clutcher from his airplane. While Jordan herds the crowd out of harm's way, John stops the oil tanker before it hits the airplane, though letting a little spurt of oil fall onto the Senator. When the Senator complains that "it's an outrage! Someone will pay" (110), Stewart comments to his black-oiled face, "Haven't I seen you picking cotton somewhere?" (114). Stewart's comment highlights Hal Jordan's ignorance of the situation, as in the next few pages the reader learns that Clutcher is a racist. The comic shifts to a rally that the Senator is holding where he says to the crowd, "understand I've nothing against the darkies, but it's scientific fact their brains are smaller than normal... they can't appreciate the finer things" (111). While Stewart calls outs Clutcher on his racism and his provocation to the crowd, Hal chalks Clutcher's speech up to the price of free speech. The tensions of the rally are further heightened when a black assassin attempts to gun down the Senator. Stewart once again sees the truth of the situation. The assassin was hired to shoot blanks at the Senator. Stewart explains that he had seen the man with the Senator that morning and further that the attempt makes "it look like the blacks are on a rampage... and Clutcher is everyone's hero" (114). In his first adventure as a Green Lantern, John Stewart proves to be a more astute Green Lantern, noting the trouble that the Senator is causing through his racist rhetoric. As William Evans and Omar Holdman point out, "Hal Jordan is someone who usually sees things in black and white, whereas John Stewart is the type of person who sees the gray areas" (2021, 75). While the assassin is black, it is Stewart who notices him, as if Hal Jordan is "color-blind." Issue #87 ends tidily enough, however, with Hal trusting that the Senator's "colleagues in Congress will bounce you where you belong" (O'Neil and Adams 2004b, 114). Once again, Jordan trusts that the system will take care of the Senator (who, oddly, is not arrested for inciting a riot in the stadium or faking an assassination attempt). The liberal response in O'Neil's comics, even with a black Green Lantern and the introduction of the themes of racism and politics, is similar to the end of the slum lord story; once the single "villain" has been apprehended, it would seem that the problem has been resolved. In reality, the system of both unfair housing practices and a racist political system remain in place.

A bobblehead of John Stewart appears on the cover of *Far Sector* #2 (Jemisin and Campbell 2020a) indicating the ways that Jemisin is creating connections to John Stewart's influence and history. Going further, the *Green Lantern/Green Arrow* stories serve as genealogical roots for *Far Sector*. With their introduction of a black Green Lantern, and the addressing of social ills, the *Green Lantern/Green Arrow* series serve as a foundation to the systemic problems that Jemisin will address offering the reader a new way to think about the power of the comic book and its grappling with contemporary politics.

Far Sector and Systemic Oppression

To begin to explore the systemic problems of The City Enduring, it is key to understand their governmental structure. As Feagin writes, examining the structures of institutions is a key way to address racial oppression:

> (1) it should indicate clearly the major features – both the structures and the counterforces – of the social phenomenon being studies; (2) it should show the relationships between the importance structures and forces, and (3) it should assist in understanding both the patterns of social change and the lack of social change.
>
> *(2006, 7)*

This city/planet is made up of three races called the Trilogy and comprises 20 billion citizens. The Nah are the most human-like of the races except they have wings with venomous tips and tails. The @At are a digital species who mostly live in the networks (like the internet), but they can upload themselves (at a price) to the organic world. The keh-Topli are a race of carnivorous plant-like beings that look like Venus fly-traps but with humanoid heads. These races can coexist peacefully because upon birth they are given what is called the Emotion Exploit which shuts down emotional responses. It is believed by shutting off emotions they can avoid a renewed catastrophic war that resulted in them coming to The City Enduring in the first place. There is one hitch to this seemingly peaceful city; there is a black-market drug called Switchoff that suppresses the Emotion Exploit and allows the user to feel emotion. *Far Sector* begins with the first murder the planet has experienced in 500 years. A keh-Topli has murdered a Nah; this murder reveals the systemic problems underneath The City Enduring.

The "structures and counterforces" of The City Enduring involve the Peace Office, akin to our police, who answer to the Council. The Council is made up of one representative from each race. Social class is a key element to this story, as the reigning members of The Council come from important families. As Sojourner comments, "The Council has unrestricted authority. Councilors serve lifetime appointments until they choose otherwise. In theory, a referendum can recall any councilor, but it's never happened. Never. Not once in a thousand years" (Jemisin and Campbell 2021a, 2). The problem of the Emotion Exploit and the sale of Switchoff leads to other city-wide problems involving the exploitation of the @At and their use of Switchoff to create "memes" (digital products that also provide sustenance for the @At). Even though the Emotion Exploit is made to quell any racial disharmony, the majority of @At's are exploited, unable to afford physical manifestation for themselves, and only able to contribute to society through the creation of underground intellectual property.

The City Enduring is rife with hidden sweatshops that create intellectual property (in the form of memes). These sweatshops keep citizens hooked on Switchoff in order to make music, jokes, and dance moves – creative works that only emotional people could make (as the comic argues). By keeping the "residents" on Switchoff and, ostensibly not allowing them to leave the compounds, The City Enduring uses trafficked people in order to create content that is bought and sold on The City Enduring's version of the internet. Captive, the sweatshop victims are made to become addicted content creators in a world that values the novel. The only way to enjoy these creative goods, however, is to take Switchoff (Jemisin 2021b, #10). In this way, the system feeds on itself.

This cannibalistic-revelation works to solve the first murder. The keh-Topli librarian, Meile Thorn, was given money in order to fund her vegetarianism (keh-Topli are carnivorous); the bargain was that she would be taken to a sweatshop to create content. Hooked on Switchoff, Meile escaped. So that she did not reveal what was done to her, Meile was then mind-hijacked by @At operatives (who can download themselves into biological beings) where she murdered the Nah. Meile was then herself killed in the police station so that she could not uncover the whole sweatshop operation. When Sojourner captures the three @At who hijacked the librarian, one of them reports that they were being paid in Earth memes which would allow him to "get back on his feet" (Jemisin and Campbell 2020e, 14). The poverty of the @At keeps the engine of the sweatshops moving.

Drug use, exploitation, sweatshops; as Sojourner digs, she uncovers the complicated problems of The City Enduring. These are not just individual "bad guys," rather, the problem with the City Enduring is systemic; the citizens, specifically the @At, resort to crime only because the system will not allow them a way out of poverty. The initial murder also results in the population rising up to demand a referendum to end the Emotion Exploit. It is perhaps the protest that resonates most with the Black Lives Movement and the problems of police brutality. The family of the original murdered Nah organizes a protest demanding the referendum. Because of the Exploit, the widow comments that she is unable to grieve (Jemisin and Campbell 2020c, 12). The protestors are met by counter-protestors who want the council to arrest Switchoff addicts. Green Lantern Mullein is charged with protecting the protestors even though the peace officers have been ordered to open fire on the protestors in order to dispel the crowd. Sojourner, meanwhile, offers to take a list of written demands to the council. The protestors are surprised she would suggest this solution or that someone would even listen to their wants.

Here, Jemisin re-envisions what the police are for; Jo offers to help voice those who feel they are voiceless as a way to change the system. While initiating this systemic solution, one of the protestors disagrees, arguing that Sojourner must not believe in "law and order" (Jemisin and Campbell 2020b, 24). Jemisin asks the reader to consider the difference between justice and "law and order" in the following panel. The panel contains overlayed images all based on the arguments, distortion, and injustice that the phrase "law and order" leads to. As Rebecca Wanzo points out:

> the gutter demonstrates the role of comics in reimagining the kind of temporal narra-
> tive we tell about racism. If 'post-race' discourse insists on placing racism in the past,
> comics is a medium that insists on placing the past, present, and future on the same
> page, and demonstrating the relationship between space and temporality.
>
> *(2020, 65)*

Right below the protestor's appeal to "law and order" in Issue #3, Campbell creates a panel that evokes the misuse of this phrase by those in power by overlaying historic images with the present (Jemisin and Campbell 2020b, 24). On the left of the panel is an image of the Manzanar War Relocation Center where Japanese-Americans were relocated after the Japanese bombed Pearl Harbor. In the name of "law and order" and fears that Japanese-Americans, some of who were third-generation and had never been to Japan, would be spies for the Japanese government, Japanese-American citizens were rounded up and sent to relocation centers scattered throughout the West and Midwest. They lost jobs, money, and land because of the racist fears of government officials. In the middle of the panel is a political button for Richard Nixon and Spiro Agnew's 1968 political campaign. They ran on a platform of "law and order" in response to student protests over the Vietnam War and black protests over segregation and oppression that marked the 1950s and 1960s. By appealing to white, older American's fears, Nixon and Agnew won the 1968 election. At the top right of the panel is a paraphrased version of the 1989 advertisement that Donald Trump paid for in New York City newspapers. The advertisement in *Far Sector* reads "Bring Back Law and Order. Bring Back Our Cops" (24). The advertisement used by Trump reads "Bring Back the Death Penalty. Bring Back Our Police." Jamal Campbell uses the same font and shape of the document to refer to Trump's advertisement. Trump was provoking public opinion calling for the *execution* of the so-called Central Park Five. The Central Park Five were five young teenagers of color accused of raping a white woman in Central Park. None of the DNA collected from her matched the DNA of the teenagers, but they were accused and tried. After serving out their sentences maintaining their innocence, a fellow inmate confessed he had raped the woman. The Five later sued for malicious prosecution, racial discrimination, and emotional distress, and New York City settled their suit for 21 million dollars.

In Darieck Scott's meditation on black comics and fantasy, he writes that "the hero who is you, the reader, becomes fantastical by having to internalize and endeavor to domesticate the inhuman or alien perspective formerly produced by the old fantasy genre's aim to represent the transcendent" (2022, 231). In the final image in the panel, the viewer is directly engaged in internalizing the fears invoked by "law and order" as it takes up the bottom half of the panel. There is a black woman with her back to the reader standing with her hands up. A squadron of military-style dressed police aim their firearms at her and, by extension, the reader. In the name of "law and order," it is unclear why these cops are terrorizing an unarmed civilian. She has a purse slung over one shoulder and her hands are in the air. She is not holding a sign nor is she with a crowd. One reading is that she is a part of a Black Lives Matter protest, and the cops are trying to maintain "order." Another reading would indicate the danger that black citizens face even walking down the street when the police are in the mood to maintain "law and order." The next page contrasts with this image in that it includes a fuller panel of the incident with Sojourner's white police partner from *Far Sector* #5. He is beating a suspect with the butt of his gun. The policeman says, "Stop resisting. We are gonna have order goddamit" (Jemisin and Campbell 2020b, 25). The suspect tries to shield himself from the blow, weakly saying "Help. Stop" (25). Sojourner is behind them, frozen in shock.

All of these images work to critique the concept of "law and order" which unjustly affects people of color and minorities in the name of (white) law and (white) order. When "law and order" is invoked, it is usually those in power who are threatened by demands for justice. For Jemisin, "law and order" functions to oppress the voices of those treated unfairly. Thus, Sojourner's solution is to have the protestors voice their concerns to those in power: claims of "law and order" silence the people. Using her privilege as a Green Lantern to get oppressed voices heard is a systemic answer to the claims of "law and order."

Jemisin creates a world in which an alternative to policing exists through contrasting Sojourner's use of the Green Lantern personae with that of the peace officers in The City Enduring. As Blount-Hill et al. point out, a change in policing involves the "police to work toward not only changing their own relationships to marginalized peoples but also challenging structured and systemic processes of dominance subordination throughout the larger society that are said to represent" (2023, 18). Sojourner challenges the systemic oppression found in The City Enduring. As Sojourner comments, "the police can't become the public's enemy. We're supposed to help" (Jemisin and Campbell 2020b, 26). Sojourner becomes a figure of police *service*.

The peace officers of The City Enduring, on the order of councilor Marth, open fire on the crowd killing dozens of protestors. Sojourner attacks the peace officers stopping them from continuing to fire, but there are protestors who are killed. Sojourner cannot completely stop the violence. Despite the killings, and because of Sojourner's influence as an alternative to typical policing, the council decides that they will, after all, hold a referendum on the Emotion Exploit in which the citizens can vote for its removal. The protestors are ultimately skeptical, however, that the council will abide by the vote. While Sojourner is able to use superhero techniques, using the power ring to separate protestors from anti-protestors or knocking down the peace offices who are firing into the crowd, Jemisin is suggesting that the role of the police is not to harm citizens or act on orders that are unethical, but rather to help citizens navigate the tricky world of a government bureaucracy whose systems are purposefully opaque.

Systemic oppression keeps the @At in poverty and exploitable. As Sojourner's @At assistant points out to her after their trip to Atville: "you saw Atville. My people have been living like that for centuries. Starving. Do you think any of us would vote to keep the Emotion Exploit?" (Jemisin and Campbell 2021a, 4). For Feagin, "racial oppression involves the social construction of a material reality... this racialized exploitation has always involved hierarchical social relationships, with an exploiting class and an exploited class" (2006, 267). By exploiting the capital that the @At produce, a hierarchical relationship ensues keeping them "starving" and unable to be full citizens in The City Enduring.

The crisis of The City Enduring is solved through understanding the racist systems used by those in power and slowly dismantling it through a people's revolution. Jemisin builds a slow case through these 12 issues for the reader (and Sojourner) to understand how the system is unjust. When Sojourner uncovers that the sweatshop she breaks up is owned by one of the councilors (Marth), who had sent her there, the ways that The City Enduring truly runs on illegal emotion become more and more apparent. The Council's investment in the system becomes clear as councilor @At Glory arrests Marth for his sweatshop. She then turns the city's defenses on itself in the hope of destroying all biologicals (Nah and keh-Topli) while, at the same time, disallowing @At's to vote electronically. @At Glory knows her fellow @Ats will vote the Emotion Exploit down as they cannot afford to physically manifest; they must vote online. Eventually, @At Glory's plan unravels, the referendum can take place, and the Emotion Exploit is voted down. With the Emotion Exploit removed, a new vote for Councilors also occurs, and the city peace officers have to begin "trust-building" with its citizens (Jemisin and Campbell 2021c, 11).

As Jonathan Gray writes in his entry on "Race" within *Keywords for Comics Studies*, "comics scholarship has to this point been dominated by a diacritic formalism that directs undue attention to the logics that inform the marks on the page while granting less attention to the politics of what is represented there" (2021, 179). As this comic grapples with police brutality, systemic racism, and capitalist exploitation, Jemisin comments on our contemporary moment and it is paramount to see the ways in which she grapples with American politics through the mirror of The City Enduring. The key to solving these issues is not found in the single villain who is locked away while the system continues, but with understanding the often-complicated interlocking systems at work that continue to perpetuate racist oppression and social class hierarchies. While early Green Lantern stories were invested in more liberal approaches to the ills of society, putting the root of the cause at the feet of the individual, Jemisin's *Far Sector* emphasizes the ways that systems are pernicious, in the ways they continue to perpetuate oppression, and it points out how citizen-led change can untangle and subvert those systems.

References

Blount-Hill, Kwan-Lamar, Kate C. McLean, and Michael J. Jenkins. 2023. "The Reform Story: Shifting Narratives from Mistrust to Collaboration, Defensiveness to Service." In *Justice and Legitimacy in Policing: Transforming the Institution*, edited by Miltonette Olivia Craig and Kwan-Lamar Blount-Hill. Routledge.

Evans, William, and Omar Holman. 2021. *Black Nerd Problems*. Gallery Books.

Feagin, Joe R. 2006. *Systemic Racism: A Theory of Oppression*. Routledge.

Gray, Jonathan. 2021. "Race." In *Keywords for Comics Studies*, edited by Ramzi Fawaz, Shelley Streeby and Deborah Elizabeth Whaley. New York University Press.

Howard, Sheena C. and Ronald Jackson III. 2013. "Introduction." In *Black Comics: Politics of Race and Representation*, edited by Sheena C. Howard and Ronald Jackson III. Bloomsbury.

Jemisin, N.K. and Jamal Campbell. 2020a. *Far Sector* #2. DC Comics.

Jemisin, N.K. and Jamal Campbell. 2020b. *Far Sector* #3. DC Comics.

Jemisin, N.K. and Jamal Campbell. 2020c. *Far Sector* #4. DC Comics.

Jemisin, N.K. and Jamal Campbell. 2020d. *Far Sector* #5. DC Comics.

Jemisin, N.K. and Jamal Campbell. 2020e. *Far Sector* #8. DC Comics.

Jemisin, N.K. and Jamal Campbell. 2021a. *Far Sector* #9. DC Comics.

Jemisin, N.K. and Jamal Campbell. 2020b. *Far Sector* #10. DC Comics.

Jemisin, N.K. and Jamal Campbell. 2020c. *Far Sector* #12. DC Comics.

Moore, Jesse T. 2003. "The Education of Green Lantern: Culture and Ideology." *The Journal of American Culture* 26.2: 263–278.

O'Neil, Dennis, and Neal Adams. 2004a. *Green Lantern/Green Arrow*. Volume 1. DC Comics.

O'Neil, Dennis, and Neal Adams. 2004b. *Green Lantern/Green Arrow*. Volume 2. DC Comics.

Scott, Darieck. 2022. *Keeping it Unreal: Black Queer Fantasy and Superhero Comics*. New York University Press.

Wanzo, Rebecca. 2020. *The Content of Our Caricature: African American Comic Art and Political Belonging*. New York University Press.

Whaley, Deborah Elizabeth. 2016. *Black Women in Sequence: Re-Inking Comics, Graphic Novels, and Anime*. University of Washington Press.

43

THE SHIELD OR THE SKULL

The Civil-Military Gap, the Militarized Superhero, and Veteran Stereotypes in American Myth and Memory

Christina M. Knopf

As worldwide war loomed in the late 1930s, the nascent comic book industry was one of the most prominent, and powerful, voices for US involvement. Costumed superheroes and paramilitary groups combatted Axis forces at home and abroad and, later, encouraged readers to support the war by recycling and buying bonds. Captain America even recruited fans to the "Sentinels of Liberty," enlisting them to fight domestic espionage (Kimble and Goodnow 2016). This was arguably the beginning of a symbiotic relationship between American superheroes and the US military, with the blurring of comic book fantasy and military reality found in the US Army's advertising relationship with Marvel, trends of banal militarism in media, military cooperation with superhero films, and nanotechnology developments (Bickford 2020; Lecker 2013; Stahl 2010; Cocca 2021; Milburn 2005). But, the military-superhero connection is not simply one of propaganda, publicity, or promotion; it is often an integral part of narrative and character development. Thus, if we accept that superheroes are symbols of particular geopolitical identities and environments, modeling community values, public virtues, and proper civic behaviors (Dittmer 2013; Deis 2013; Wanzo 2009; Coogan 2013; Round 2008; Devarenne 2008), we may assume that cultural ideas about civil-military relations are embedded in these characters. (For another example of lessons of civil-military relations in superhero media, see Saideman 2023).

Militarized and war-born superheroes abound in comics, ranging from well-known figures, such as DC's Hal Jordan, who was a US fighter pilot before taking up the mantle of the Green Lantern, to newer characters like Frank Adams in Bliss on Tap's *I Play the Bad Guy* (2014–2015), who was part of an experimental military program during the Cold War. Within this narrative tradition, Marvel Comics is notable with its claim that "the Marvel Universe has always reflected the 'world outside your window' – from the moment Captain America charged into battle in World War II" (Beazley 2019, back cover). As Michael J. Lecker argues, Marvel Comics often blur the lines between "hero" and "soldier" by repeatedly having "US soldiers take on the mantel of superhero and having superheroes joining paramilitary or military organizations" (2013, 231). Marvel's "super-soldiers'" include not only Captain America, who famously enlisted in the Army to serve in World War II (WWII), but also Iron Man, whose embodiment of American individualism, capitalistic enterprise, and weapons technology is representative of the US military-industrial complex (Thomas

2009; Chambliss 2013); Captain Marvel/Carol Danvers, who serves as a model for female empowerment by joining the Air Force to better herself and pay for college (Cocca 2021); and Punisher, whose service as a US Marine in the Vietnam War has made him a symbol of PTSD and "moral wounds" (Gruszczyk 2020). This chapter focuses on Captain America and Punisher, fictional veterans of two defining wars in American myth, as representatives of how the US public remembers its wars and those who fought them.

Captain America, a product of WWII, and Punisher, a product of the Vietnam era (and both iconic heroes in modern media products) provide excellent cases for a consideration of what Katherine Kinney describes as "the ambivalent battle between the imagery and narratives of World War II and the Vietnam War – between the good war and its other," as US society reimagines itself in the 21st century (2005, 129). Captain America, appearing in 1941, is the personification of patriotism with a strong moral code: a hero born from the apparent clarity of purpose of WWII. He is an anachronistic "man out of time," a nostalgic relic of an extinct way of life (Dubose 2007, 927). Punisher, appearing in 1974, is a traumatized killer, broken by the failings of his government – a disturbed figure born from the violence and anxieties surrounding America's involvement in Vietnam. He is a symbol of a "dystopic America," alienated and cynical (Scott 2012, loc. 2255). Each character is thus more than just a representative of the wars that inspired them; they have also become the embodiment of the US public's contradictory views of military veterans, who are caught between misguided hero worship and social stigmatization.

The chapter proceeds with an overview of underlying cultural myths that shape civil-military relations in the US. It then offers a brief discussion of WWII and Vietnam in US culture and collective memory, with attention to how Captain America and Punisher have been read and developed in light of the public perception of those wars. Following this, the chapter takes a closer look at how the characters of Captain America and Punisher contribute to American cultural myths and media stereotypes of veterans. While the wartime service of both characters is featured throughout their various stories in comics, film, and television, in important and often complementary ways, the discussion here focuses on the three-part comic *Punisher/Captain America: Blood and Glory* (1992). This comic was published in the aftermath of Operation Desert Storm (aka Gulf War I), which was symbolically used as a salve for the national wound left by Vietnam (Kendrick 1994). The story brings experiences and sentiments of WWII and the war in Vietnam into conversation with each other, as Cap and Punisher each reflect on their military background.

Soldiers and Supers

In his review of the research on military-related journalism, Hans Schmidt (2020) found that news coverage of veterans and service members is positive overall, even during unpopular wars but that news and entertainment tend to trade in stereotypes, which can be problematic. Schmidt summarized the positive stereotypes found in the research as framing service members as stoic, heroic, patriotic, dedicated, hypermasculine, or even superhuman. The sentimentalizing or glorifying of veterans often limits them within the confines of traditional masculinity and makes their individuality and vulnerabilities invisible. Furthermore, not all media frames for service members and veterans are positive, and they may also be stereotyped as charity cases, victimized, broken, disabled, traumatized, at-risk, suicidal, or dangerous. Such negative portrayals may have positive effects in raising awareness of veteran issues, but they also narrow the public's understanding of veterans and contribute to a gap between how veterans and civilians characterize military service, complicating some veterans' return to civilian life.

This break between civilian understanding of military service and veteran perception of military service is one manifestation of a civil-military gap. Civil-military relations are the interaction of the military with the public it serves, from formalized governmental control to public opinion in the widest range of civil society (Nelson 2002). Relational tensions exist in part because there is not a continuum stretching from military to civilian ethos; the military's values are relatively static and universal in comparison to civilian values that vary individually (Huntington 1957; Young 2006). Thus, military service and civilian experience are often polarized, alienating the military from civilian leadership and society (Higate 2001; Hawkins 2001). This is especially true with an all-volunteer force, viewed as "expensive specialists" (Cohen 2008, 252). Poor media coverage and unrealistic fiction about the military is believed to contribute to this gap (Wiegand and Paletz 2001; Kinney 2005).

Moreover, the military is often romanticized, yet ostracized, for its patriotic sacrifices on behalf of its community. Carolyn Marvin and David W. Ingle argue that in American patriotic myth, the military serves as a "sacrificial, border-creating class through whose death [the community] purifies itself. Since violence is contagious, death-touching soldiers must be set apart. Living separately, dressing differently, they observe an ascetic vocation" (1999, 100). Their separation is a "sign of submission, it designates the holy. The lonely hero volunteers to bear sacrificial burdens for the group. The flag he carries signifies his willingness to be expelled from the group, to cross the border" (74). Meanwhile, "the community regards ambivalently the soldiers they gave up for dead, who were sent to die but did not. Soldiers likewise mistrust the community that sent them to die" (122), further contributing to the civil-military gap. Here, similarities between the figure of the veteran and that of the superhero emerge. Both wear, either literally or metaphorically, the flag of their country, with superheroes often having nationalistic costumes, as epitomized by the flag-styled attire of Captain America, Captain Britain, Captain Canuck, and Wonder Woman (Dittmer 2013). And yet, both are outsiders to their communities because of their vocation, skills, and/or ideology (Shugart 2009).

Remembered Wars

In their study of how regional news publications in the 50 states represented veterans on Twitter, Parrott et al. (2018) identified three prominent news frames: charity case, hero, and victim. News stories of heroism contained references to honor and pride, and were usually focused on veterans of WWII, the smallest population of veterans still living in the US, whereas veterans of Korea and Vietnam were mostly omitted from the hero frame, despite comprising nearly half of the living veterans in the US at the time of the study. Charity and victim frames emphasized the negative outcomes of military service and the gap between military and civilian cultures. Victimization particularly highlighted the mistreatment of veterans by the military and/or society, mental health issues, and politics, in sharp contrast to the values ingrained in military personnel, including stoicism, physical and mental toughness, and self-reliance. The contrast between Hero and Victim captures the narrative sentiments of WWII and the war in Vietnam, respectively, in collective memory (Huebner 2008). Captain America and Punisher serve as embodiments of those narratives.

WWII in American cultural memory is a moment of unity around "mythical images of a powerful nation and righteous citizen-soldiers" (Bodnar 2010, 1; also Kinney 2005). Captain

America, Cord Scott notes, is symbolic of this idea because he "keeps the mythos of a righteous, moral America alive" (2009, 126). His origin story, as defined in the *Marvel Encyclopedia,* is that a young, aspiring artist, named Steve Rogers attempted to enlist in the military but was classified as 4-F (unfit for service) because of physical frailty. He was then recruited for the experimental Project: Rebirth program, designed to develop a battalion of supreme fighting men to be a bulwark against Nazi aggression. Once given the revolutionary Super-Soldier Serum, Rogers was instantly transformed into the pinnacle of physical perfection. He was subsequently equipped with a virtually unbreakable red, white, and blue shield, trained in combat, espionage, and strategy and rechristened Captain America, quickly becoming a symbol for the US fighting forces and a formidable foe of the Axis powers (Brevoort and Teitelbaum 2014; also see Crowe 2011). As part of the enduring media narrative that has shaped collective memory of WWII as "the good war," Cap functions as a symbol for an idealized America: a nostalgic yearning for ideas of moral clarity, national unity, and justice (McClancy 2018; Dittmer 2013; for constructs of the "good war" see Polenberg 1992).

Vietnam challenged the popular image of American fortitude and patriotism engendered by WWII (Stolor 2011). Thomas Doherty argues, "The disrepute of the interminable war transformed military action into a code phrase for legalized atrocities and made the soldier the butt of comedy, condescension, and contempt" (1993, 282). Thus, the soldier of Vietnam is often reductively remembered as being lost to the trauma of war, typically beyond rescue because their sacrifice had no purpose (Morag 2006; Kinney 2005; Rasmussen and Downey 1991). Collective memory could not ignore the graphic reality of a televised war to romanticize the soldier as it had in the past (Aichinger 1975). And Punisher is symbolic of the resulting American outrage and cynicism (Scott 2012). As described in the *Marvel Encyclopedia*, Marine Captain Frank Castle was a skilled combat veteran and decorated hero of the war in Vietnam, until, while on leave in New York, Castle's wife and two children were killed by the mob. After the loss of his family, he became Punisher, a vengeful vigilante on a one-man crusade against crime (Teitelbaum and Forbeck 2014). His reliance on lethal force against all kinds of criminals is represented by the large white skull – the death's head – on his costume. Kent Worcester writes, Punisher's "life story, and his comic book stories, offers a firm rebuke to the idea that post-Vietnam America could ever hope to achieve 'a more perfect union'" (2012, 330).

The Hero's Shield and the Victim's Skull

Punisher/Captain America: Blood and Glory is a three-issue mini-series, published in 1992, featuring a story about weapons sales, narcotics, and terrorism as a means of gaining political influence in Washington, DC. It reflected national uncertainties about post-Cold War domestic politics and international relations. The story begins with Captain America and Punisher independently pursuing a drugs-for-guns conspiracy linked to a shadowy governmental agency, organized crime, and a South American dictator. Punisher's investigation begins in New York City, following the drugs, while Cap is on the trail in Texas, following the weapons. Their paths soon cross as adversaries and then as uneasy allies as they work to bring down a foreign dictator and prevent an international catastrophe. Along the way, they confront their moral codes of justice and vengeance, shaped in combat, and the sacrifices required to protect the greater good.

The story immediately situates Cap and Punisher within cultural narratives of "the good war" and a divisive war, respectively, as each character is introduced in *Blood and Glory #1* through inner monologues. In his introduction, Cap recalls learning to use his shield and how he instinctively "knew that all that had to be done was let it fly, to be part of the **war**, the fight for the **right** and the **just**" (Janson et al. 1992a, 5). He then confirms that he himself is a product of that war, as he reflects, "There's no such thing as **a just war** – unless maybe the one that **made me** what I am. 'The Good War', 'The Necessary War' we called it" (8). Like the sacrificial hero of American myth, Cap carries his nation's flag as a signifier of his willingness to die for the community. He notes that "a **good soldier** needs his **cause**, to anchor himself to what he is," and says, "I **wear** my **cause**. It's woven into the very chain mail of my **uniform**. The **stars** and **stripes** of freedom and justice" (12). In contrast, Punisher recalls "we left so many things **hanging** because of that **other fight** in that **Asian jungle** -- ...so many **used** and **abused** by the powers that betrayed" (27). He further reflects, in *Blood and Glory #2*, that he, too, began as the sacrificial hero of American myth, saying, "I fought for the **flag** once. Before it **betrayed** us in that jungle war" (Janson et al. 1992b, 10). His words reinforce the view that the soldiers of Vietnam were, as Carl Boggs and Tom Pollard write, at best, "noble grunts, innocent and often illiterate kids just struggling for survival in the hot, dense, menacing jungles of an alien country" (2007, 90). If they engaged in the horrors and atrocities of the conflict, they were either part of an abnormal minority or were doing so at the behest of a corrupt Pentagon, CIA, or White House (Boggs and Pollard 2007; Doherty 1993).

Moreover, the story illustrates the mythologized distance between the WWII veteran and the Vietnam veteran in the American public psyche. In *Blood and Glory #1*, Punisher recalls,

> **They** came home from the Second World War to **parades** and **open arms**. I stepped down **off** the **plane** from 'Nam, a woman threw **blood** in my **face** and called me a **baby-killer. A call to duty** turned to **damnation**.
>
> *(Janson et al. 1992a, 47)*

And the hero worship Cap continues to receive decades later underscores the difference in public consciousness. Watching tributes to Captain America on TV, in *Blood and Glory #2*, one disaffected Vietnam vet comments, "All you World War II guys got it all – parades, medals, welcomes-home! What'd **we** get? A pat on the back 20 years later 'cause some boys go sunbathin' in an Arabian desert" (Janson et al. 1992b, 10). The man's remark not only contrasts the hero worship connected to WWII veterans with the victimization and vilification of Vietnam veterans, but also alludes to how support of the troops in Gulf War I was a symbolic atonement for the estrangement of Vietnam veterans (Tuleja 1997).

Significantly, these perceptions of those who fought in WWII and the war in Vietnam, are more myth than reality. The soldiers of WWII often enlisted for practical, rather than patriotic, reasons, seeking personal security more than global peace (Aichinger 1975). And despite the common view of Vietnam veterans as betrayed, neglected, and disrespected, evidence indicates that they readjusted to civilian life quite well and that their myriad problems were grossly exaggerated by media narratives (Dean 1992). Captain America and Punisher are both products of, and agents in, this mythologizing, dealing in stereotypes that contribute to the civil-military gap.

In the opening monologues of *Blood and Glory #1* that set up both the historical roots and moral orientations of the characters, Cap observes that in the "last days of the Second World War," strategy succumbed to "**raw intensification. Courage** and **imagination** became **casualties** to overwhelming force... while **daring** and **intelligence** were killed off in favor of getting the job over" (Janson et al. 1992a, 9). Punisher demonstrates this kind of approach in his detached delineation of how to "**destroy** [the enemy] **completely**" and to "kill without joy" (18), as he dispassionately lists, and follows, the three principles of wartime strategy: "**Start** the **bleeding**. **Stop** the **breathing**. **Promote** established **shock**" (20). This kind of characterization reinforces some of the problematic stereotypes that veterans face in real life. Research by Shepherd et al. found that veterans are morally typecast as agentic – as "'doers' who can plan, take action, and get things done" (2019, 75), but who lack emotional experience and volition – much like Cap's observations that imagination, intelligence, and courage were lost in war's relentless drive to finish the job. This view of the veteran as emotionless may perpetuate the even more negative stereotype of the dangerous veteran, which is typically associated with PTSD. Moreover, veterans with PTSD are more likely to induce fear, being perceived as more dangerous than civilians with PTSD, resulting in increased social alienation for veterans (Correll et al. 2021; Hipes and Gemoets 2019).

Though the US Department of Veteran Affairs reports that only 7% of veterans will experience PTSD, compared to 6% of adults in the general population (Schnurr 2024), the association of PTSD with veterans is reinforced through both Cap and Punisher. Not only have both characters been read as having PTSD throughout their media histories (see analyses in Gillen 2009; Weiner 2009; Gruszczyk 2020), but both experience symptomatic flashbacks in *Blood and Glory*. While navigating a jungle of South America in *Blood and Glory #3*, Punisher recalls taking similar walks through the jungles of Vietnam. "I'm back in the jungle again," he observes. "Back among the warm rot. The moist decay. Platoons died in a place like this" (Janson et al. 1992c, 4). While these words draw attention, again, to the corruption and death engendered by the war in Vietnam, his own violent war memories eventually overlap with those of the murder of his family. In two parallel columns of panels, scenes of a deadly walk through a Vietnamese jungle are compared, step for step, with the scenes of the fatal walk through Central Park with his son (28). For Cap, a siege on a South American city in *Blood and Glory #3* recalls the war in Europe. He says, "The night screams, horribly familiar. I saw in the newsreels of 1937 before living with it for an entire world at war" (31). Additionally, both Punisher and Cap are depicted as being capable of violence. Punisher expresses his rage not only through frequent use of lethal force, but also by noting, in *Blood and Glory #1*, that "**rage** [is] the perfect weapon. The **soldier's ally**" (Janson et al. 1992a, 24). Cap experiences such rage in *Blood and Glory #3* when he confronts the US Attorney General who has been complicit in the drugs-for-weapons conspiracy, brutally beating the man for his failure to uphold the laws of the country (Janson et al. 1992c, 43–45). The combination of flashbacks with the capacity for violence perpetuates the stereotypes of veterans as traumatized and dangerous. Exposure to these kinds of stereotypes leads the public to perceive an increased likelihood of PTSD and violence among veterans, decreasing civilian desire to be socially close with them (Parrott et al. 2022; Parrott et al. 2023).

The civil-military gap, particularly a perceived lack of understanding of civilians for their military, is expressed in *Blood and Glory #1* through Punisher's belief that "**civilians** need a constant **reminder** of how **ugly** the **war** is" (Janson et al. 1992a, 35). But, knowledge of, and attention to, that ugliness appears to contribute to the distance between veterans and civilians, creating an image of the modern veteran as victimized and broken. Likewise, the continued valorizing of war that Cap engages in, as when he tells Punisher in *Blood and Glory #2*, "Sometimes **wars** aren't right, but **reasons** always are" (Janson et al. 1992b, 34), and romanticizing of soldiers, as when, in *Blood and Glory #3*, he recalls WWII propaganda that proclaimed, "We're going to do our part… and we'll win because we're on God's side"

(Janson et al. 1992c, 25), also contributes to civil-military distance, by perpetuating the narrow views of veterans as patriotic and superhuman.

Conclusion

Cap observes, of his interaction with Punisher in *Blood and Glory* #2, "There's a **dichotomy** between us – more than the **wars** that made us what we are! A **divergence** of **ideals**" (Janson et al. 1992b, 41). In this, *Blood and Glory* participates in the public memory of WWII as a noble endeavor where teamwork triumphed, and of the war in Vietnam as a failed enterprise at the cost of individual soldiers (Huebner 2008). But these memories are incomplete and the contrast between good soldiers and damaged soldiers is oversimplified. When these myths and stereotypes are distilled in and embodied by two well-known superheroes – figures that model community norms and civic ideals – they exacerbate the civil-military gap, which has real-life implications for real-life veterans seeking education, employment, mental and physical healthcare, and social belonging. Additionally, in being defined as *products* of the military and "wars that *made*" them what they are, Cap and Punisher contribute to a growing, and yet often ignored, portrayal of soldiers as specialized worker-warriors, which may have an influence on military spending, policies, and engagements.

Blood and Glory #3 concludes with Punisher and Cap saluting each other in the rain at Arlington National Cemetery, a burial ground for the US military. A monologue that could belong to either man closes the story: "In that silent moment, there are no 'super heroes.' No sanctioned patriot and hunted vigilante. We are only soldiers fighting the same fight for the country we both hold so dear. Each of us but one among equals" (Janson et al. 1992c, 49).

In these final scenes, Cap and Punisher shake off the national myths and media narratives that have otherwise defined them in, and beyond, *Blood and Glory*. Here, they are not a heroic soldier from a good war or a victimized soldier of a bad war, they are just two soldiers among many who sacrificed for their country; but, still, they stand apart from the civilian community for which they served.

References

Aichinger, Peter. 1975. *The American Soldier in Fiction, 1880–1963: A History of Attitudes toward Warfare and the Military Establishment*. Iowa State University Press.

Beazley, Mark D., ed. 2019. *Marvel Comics: The World Outside Your Window*. Marvel Entertainment.

Bickford, Andrew. 2020. "The 'Superman' Solution 'Super Soldiers' and 'Superheroes' in the United States military." *Anthropology Today* 36(5): 14–17.

Bodnar, John. 2010. *The "Good War" in American Memory*. The Johns Hopkins University Press.

Boggs, Carl, and Tom Pollard. 2007. *The Hollywood War Machine: U.S. Militarism and Popular Culture*. Paradigm Publishers.

Brevoort, Tom, and Michael Teitelbaum. 2014. "Captain America: Living Legend of World War II." In *Marvel Encyclopedia: The Definitive Guide to the Characters of the Marvel Universe, updated and expanded*, edited by Tom DeFalco. DK Publishing.

Chambliss, Julian. 2013. "Upgrading the Cold War Framework: Iron Man, the Military Industrial Complex, and American Defense." In *Ages of Heroes, Eras of Men: Superheroes and the American Experience*, edited by Julian Chambliss, William Svitasky, and Thomas Donaldson. Cambridge Scholars Publishing.

Cocca, Carolyn. 2021. *Wonder Woman and Captain Marvel: Militarism and Feminism in Comics and Film*. Routledge.

Cohen, Eliot. 2008. "The Military." In *Understanding America: The Anatomy of an Exceptional Nation*, edited by Peter H. Schuck and James Q. Wilson. Public Affairs.

Coogan, Peter. 2013. "The Hero Defines the Genre, the Genre Defines the Hero." In *What Is a Superhero?* edited by Robin S. Rosenberg and Peter Coogan. Oxford University Press.

Correll, Danielle N., Krista M. Engle, Shayne S.H. Lin, Andrew Lac, and Kristin W. Samuelson. 2021. "The Effects of Military Status and Gender on Public Stigma toward Posttraumatic Stress Disorder." *Stigma and Health* 6(2): 134–42.

Crowe, Lori A. 2011. "Superheroes or Super-Soldiers? The Militarization of Our Modern-Day Heroes." In *The Militarization of Childhood: Thinking Beyond the Global South*, edited by J. Marshall Beier. Palgrave Macmillan.

Dean, Jr., Eric T. 1992. "The Myth of the Troubled and Scorned Vietnam Veteran." *Journal of American Studies* 26(1): 59–74.

Deis, Chris. 2013. "The Subjective Politics of the Supervillain." In *What Is a Superhero?* edited by Robin S. Rosenberg and Peter Coogan. Oxford University Press.

Devarenne, Nicole. 2008. "'A Language Heroically Commensurate with His Body': Nationalism, Fascism, and the Language of the Superhero." *International Journal of Comic Art* 10(1): 48–54.

Dittmer, Jason. 2013. *Captain America and the Nationalist Superhero: Metaphors, Narratives, and Geopolitics.* Temple University Press.

Doherty, Thomas. 1993. *Projections of War: Hollywood, American Culture, and World War II.* Columbia University Press.

Dubose, Mike S. 2007. "Holding Out for a Hero: Reaganism, Comic Book Vigilantes, and Captain America." *Journal of Popular Culture* 40(6): 915–35.

Gillen, Shawn. 2009. "Captain America, Post-Traumatic Stress Syndrome, and the Vietnam Era." In *Captain America and the Struggle of the Superhero*, edited by Robert G. Weiner. McFarland & Company.

Gruszczyk, Aleksandra. 2020. "The Punisher: A Cultural Image of the 'Moral Wound.'" *Cultural Analysis* 17(2): 24–50.

Hawkins, John P. 2001. *Army of Hope, Army of Alienation.* University of Alabama Press.

Higate, Paul Richard. 2001. "Theorizing Continuity: From Military to Civilian Life." *Armed Forces & Society* 27(3): 443–60.

Hipes, Crosby, and Darren Gemoets. 2019. "Stigmatization of War Veterans with Posttraumatic Stress Disorder (PTSD): Stereotyping and Social Distance Findings." *Society and Mental Health* 9(2): 243–58.

Huebner, Andrew J. 2008. *The Warrior Image: Soldiers in American Culture from the Second World War to the Vietnam Era.* University of North Carolina Press.

Huntington, Samuel P. 1957. *The Soldier and the State: The Theory and Politics of Civil-Military Relations.* Belknap/Harvard.

Janson, Klaus, D.G. Chichester, and Margaret Clark. 1992a. *Punisher/Captain America: Blood and Glory #1.* Marvel. Marvel Unlimited, 2020.

Janson, Klaus, D.G. Chichester, and Margaret Clark. 1992b. *Punisher/Captain America: Blood and Glory #2.* Marvel. Marvel Unlimited, 2020.

Janson, Klaus, D.G. Chichester, and Margaret Clark. 1992c. *Punisher/Captain America: Blood and Glory #3.* Marvel. Marvel Unlimited, 2020.

Kendrick, Michelle. 1994. "The Never again Narratives: Political Promise and the Videos of Operation Desert Storm." *Cultural Critique* 28: 129–47.

Kimble, James J., and Trischa Goodnow. 2016. "Introduction." In *The 10 Cent War: Comic Books, Propaganda, and World War II*, edited by Trischa Goodnow and James J. Kimble. University Press of Mississippi.

Kinney, Katherine. 2005. "The Good War and its Other: Beyond Private Ryan." In *War Narratives and American Culture*, edited by Giles Gunn and Carl Guierrez-Jones. American Cultures and Global Contexts Center at the University of California.

Lecker, Michael J. 2013. "Superhero Fantasy in a Post-9/11 World: Marvel Comics and Army Recruitment." In *Ages of Heroes, Eras of Men: Superheroes and the American Experience*, edited by Julian Chambliss, William Svitasky, and Thomas Donaldson. Cambridge Scholars Publishing.

Marvin, Carolyn, and David W. Ingle. 1999. *Blood Sacrifice and the Nation: Totem Rituals and the American Flag.* Cambridge University Press.

McClancy, Kathleen. 2018. "Winter Soldiers and Sunshine Patriots: World War II and the Cold War in Captain America." *ImageTexT* 9(3). https://imagetextjournal.com/winter-soldiers-and-sunshine-patriots-world-war-ii-and-the-cold-war-in-captain-america.

Milburn, Colin. 2005. "Nanowarriors: Military Nanotechnology and Comic Books." *Interexts* 9(1): 77–103.

Morag, Raya. 2006. "Defeated Masculinity: Post-Traumatic Cinema in the Aftermath of the Vietnam War." *The Communication Review* 9: 189–216.

Nelson, Daniel N. 2002. "Definition, Diagnosis, Therapy: A Civil-Military Critique." *Defense & Security Analysis* 18(2): 157–70.

Parrott, Scott, David L. Albright, Caitlin Dyche, and Haley Grace Steele. 2018. "Hero, Charity Case, and Victim: How US News Media Frame Military Veterans on Twitter." *Armed Forces & Society* 45(4): 702–22.

Parrott, Scott, David L. Albright, and Nicholas Eckhart. 2022. "Veterans and Media: The Effects of News Exposure on Thoughts, Attitudes, and Support of Military Veterans." *Armed Forces & Society* 48(3), 503–21.

Parrott, Scott, David L. Albright, Nicholas Eckhart, and Kirsten Laha-Walsh. 2023. "U.S. Veterans and Civilians Describe Military News Coverage as Mediocre, Think Stories Affect Others More Than Themselves." *Armed Forces & Society* 49(3): 713–28.

Polenberg, Richard. 1992. "The Good War? A Reappraisal of How World War II Affected American Society." *The Virginia Magazine of History and Biography* 100(3): 295–322.

Rasmussen, Karen, and Sharon D. Downey. 1991. "Dialectical Disorientation in Vietnam War Films: Subversion of the Mythology of War." *Quarterly Journal of Speech* 77: 176–95.

Round, Julia. 2008. "London's Calling: Alternate Worlds and the City as Superhero in Contemporary British-American Comics." *International Journal of Comic Art* 10(1): 24–31.

Saideman, Stephen M. 2023. "Civilian Control of Superheroes: Applying What We Know from Civil-Military Relations." In *The Politics of the Marvel Cinematic Universe*, edited by Nichoas Carnes and Lilly J. Goren. University Press of Kansas.

Scott, Cord. 2009. "The Alpha and the Omega: Captain America and the Punisher." In *Captain America and the Struggle of the Superhero*, edited by Robert G. Weiner. McFarland & Company.

Scott, Cord A. 2012. "Anti-Heroes: Spider-Man and the Punisher." In *Web-Spinning Heroics: Critical Essays on the History and Meaning of Spider-Man*, edited by Robert Moses Peaslee and Robert G. Weinder. McFarland & Company.

Schmidt, Hans. 2020. "'Hero-Worship' or 'Manipulative and Oversimplifying': How America's Current and Former Military Service Members Perceive Military-Related News Reporting." *Journal of Veterans Studies* 6(1): 13–24.

Schnurr, Paula P. 2024. "Epidemiology and Impact of PTSD." *U.S. Department of Veterans Affairs.* Last updated December 20. https://www.ptsd.va.gov/professional/treat/essentials/epidemiology.asp.

Shepherd, Steven, Aaron C. Kay, and Kurt Gray. 2019. "Military Veterans Are Morally Typecast as Agentic but Unfeeling: Implications for Veteran Employment." *Organizational Behavior and Human Decision Processes* 153 (July): 75–88.

Shugart, Helene. 2009. "Supermarginal." *Communication and Critical/Cultural Studies* 6(1): 98–102.

Stahl, Roger. 2010. *Militainment, Inc: War, Media and Popular Culture.* Routledge.

Stolor, Mark A. 2001. "The Second World War in U.S. History and Memory." *Diplomatic History* 25(3): 383–92.

Teitelbaum, Michael, and Matt Forbeck. 2014. "Punisher: War hero turned vengeful vigilante." In *Marvel Encyclopedia: The Definitive Guide to the Characters of the Marvel Universe*, updated and expanded, edited by Tom DeFalco. DK Publishing.

Thomas, Jr., Ronald C. 2009. "Hero of the Military-Industrial Complex: Reading Iron Man through Burke's Dramatism." In *Heroes of Film, Comics and American Culture: Essays on Real and Fictional Defenders of Home*, edited by Lisa M. Detora. McFarland & Company.

Tuleja, Tad. 1997. "Closing the Circle: Yellow Ribbons and the Redemption of the Past." In *Usable Pasts: Traditions and Group Expressions in North America*, edited by Tad Tuleja. University Press of Colorado and Utah State University Press.

Wanzo, Rebecca. 2009. "The Superhero: Meditations on Surveillance, Salvation, and Desire." *Communication and Critical/Cultural Studies* 6(2): 93–97.

Weiner, Robert G. 2009. "Sixty-Five Years of Guilt over the Death of Bucky." In *Captain America and the Struggle of the Superhero*, edited by Robert G. Weiner. McFarland & Company.

Wiegand, Krista E., and David L. Paletz. 2001. "The Elite Media and the Military-Civilian Culture Gap." *Armed Forces & Society* 27(2): 183–204.

Worcester, Kent. 2012. "The Punisher and the Politics of Retributive Justice." *Justice Framed: Law in Comics and Graphic Novel* 16: 329–52.

Young, Thomas-Durell. 2006. "Military Professionalism in a Democracy." In *Who Guards the Guardians and How: Democratic Civil-Military Relations*, edited by Thomas C. Bruneau and Scott D. Tollefson. University of Texas Press.

44

TRAUMA IN SUPERHERO FILMS

The Case of Tim Burton's *Batman* (1989) and *Batman Returns* (1992)

Sean Travers

Introduction

Trauma is defined as an experience involving "actual or threatened death or serious injury, or a physical threat to the physical integrity of the self," including wars, accidents, or other extreme "stressor" events, resulting in certain clusters of symptoms (Luckhurst 2008, 1). Trauma has become a central paradigm for reading contemporary American culture. Since the early 1980s, an extensive range of genres increasingly feature traumatized protagonists and center on traumatic events. In particular, trauma has become an important facet of contemporary American popular culture. As trauma scholars Lucy Bond and Stef Craps observe, "today, trauma is a big business" (2019, 3). Indeed, trauma is a frequent trigger for a turn to superheroics in Hollywood blockbusters, major US television series recurrently center on catastrophic apocalyptic events, while American video games increasingly use trauma as a short-hand to fill in character backstories and motivations.

The following will examine trauma representation in Tim Burton's Batman films: *Batman* (1989) and *Batman Returns* (1992). Much scholarship is written on the trauma themes in *Batman* comics, cinematic adaptations, and reboots. However, this scholarship largely focuses on the traumatic past of The Dark Knight, with Gotham's "villains" receiving significantly less scholarly attention in terms of trauma analysis. Also, this scholarship overlooks how trauma representation in Batman texts is gendered and potentially subverts dominant concepts of trauma. This chapter, then, expands existing scholarship by analyzing Burton's films in relation to the following topics:

- How Burton represents Batman and Catwoman's trauma, and how these representations differ.
- How the representation of Catwoman's trauma is significant in terms of gender, particularly feminist trauma theory.
- How the representation of Catwoman's trauma challenges and subverts conventional trauma representation more widely, specifically the dominant, "event-based" trauma model that Batman's trauma representation appears to stem from.

DOI: 10.4324/9781003366911-50

Before conducting this analysis, it is first necessary to outline this chapter's definition of terms and their cultural contexts, including the event-based trauma model and feminist trauma theory.

Trauma Theory

Rehearsing a full genealogy of trauma and post-traumatic stress disorder (PTSD) is beyond the scope of this chapter and already covered in existing criticism. In summary, since the 1980s, PTSD and trauma have reached far into culture, effecting "the rise of what is becoming almost a new theoretical orthodoxy" (Radstone 2001, 10). PTSD was first designed through its inclusion in the 1980 third edition of the American Psychiatric Association's *Diagnostic and Statistical Manual of Mental Disorders* (*DSM-III*) (1980). The dominant trauma theorist Cathy Caruth has also been very influential. Essentially, Caruth's trauma theory (1995) draws upon Holocaust Studies, post-structuralism, Sigmund Freud, and the roots of PTSD as a concept in the experience of Vietnam veterans. Indeed, while PTSD was defined in 1980, the condition was discussed much earlier, such as, for example, in Freudian reports of shellshock during 1920 after World War I. Allan Young, for instance, notes that traumatic memory "originates in the scientific and clinical discourses of the nineteenth century; before that time there is unhappiness, despair, and disturbing recollections" (1997, 141). Ben Shephard also asserts that Vietnam "helped to create a new 'consciousness of trauma' in Western society" (2001, 355).

Regarding Caruth's definition of trauma: Caruth claims that trauma is belated, meaning that a traumatic event is so overwhelming it cannot be assimilated into memory at the time of the event and is instead repressed and returns in the form of flashbacks and nightmares (1995, 4). This idea stems from Freud's notion of *Nachträglichkeit* ("belatedness" or "afterwardness"). Gibbs, for example, refers to the belatedness model of trauma as the "Freudian-Caruthian model" (2014, 33). Caruth also defines trauma as comprising the experience of a sudden, overwhelming event that is "outside the range of usual human experience," an idea which stems from the 1980 diagnostic definition of PTSD (1995, 3). Therefore, while Caruth's theory was formulated after texts such as *Batman Returns*, the Freudian theory she draws upon was popular during the time this chapter's selected texts were produced.

Feminist Trauma Theory

The Freudian-Caruthian conceptualization of trauma has long been considered a requirement for entry into the canon of valued trauma literature. Examples include D. Salinger, Joseph Heller, Kurt Vonnegut, Robin Moore, Philip Caputo, William Lederer, and Eugene Burdick. These texts are frequently presented from a white American androcentric perspective, and focus on singular traumatic events. However, the model has come under criticism by feminist trauma scholars, because it applies mainly to straight white men and does not account for the types of trauma frequently experienced by gender, racial/ethnic, and sexual minorities (indeed, canonical trauma representations are frequently phallocentric). This is in part due to Caruth's definition of trauma as a sudden, overwhelming event "outside the range of usual human experience" (1995, 3). The type of trauma minorities experience tends to be the more insidious, "everyday" traumas resulting from ongoing distress related to domestic violence, child abuse, poverty, and "repeated forms of traumatising violence such as sexism, racism and colonialism" (Rothberg 2009, 89). For instance, according to Laura S. Brown:

> the range of human experience becomes the range of what is normal and usual in lives of men of the dominant class; white, young, able-bodied, educated, middle-class, Christian men. Trauma is that which disrupts these particular lives, but no other.
>
> *(1995, 104)*

Likewise, postcolonial critics, including Stef Craps and Gert Buelens, highlight "the chronic psychic suffering produced by the structural violence of racial, gender, sexual, class, and other inequities" as potential causes of trauma (2008, 3–4). Similarly, Judith Lewis Herman asserts that "there is a spectrum of traumatic disorders, ranging from the effects of a single overwhelming event to the more complicated effects of prolonged and repeated abuse" (1981, 3). Feminist trauma theory, then, demonstrates that trauma can be ongoing and very much a part of an individual's usual human experience.

Batman (1989) and Trauma: Conventional Trauma Representation

Eschewing the campness of the 1960s television series, Burton's live-action *Batman* franchise put forth a darker, ostensibly more serious version of the character in line with that of Frank Miller's noir *Batman: Year One* comic book arc, published in 1987 (*Batman* #404–#407). Similar to Miller's prequel story, which reinvents a Batman origin myth by revamping Bruce Wayne's violent traumatic past and giving Batman a motive for his actions, Burton foregrounds Batman's traumatic origins (Duquette 2010, 2). Burton fashions a more "psychological" (Salisbury 2008, xiv) story for the Caped Crusader that plays up the character's disturbed, split personality, and foregrounds his traumatic origins. In superhero media generally, trauma is a frequent trigger for a turn to super-heroics.

According to Janet K. Halfyard:

> A theme of the [superhero] film is that these characters are in many respects… people who have suffered some great trauma and as a result have developed an animal alter ego who either rises above the trauma to fight for good or becomes a vengeful, embittered, and possibly insane villain, this being a classic comic-book convention.
>
> *(2004, 30)*

This trope aligns with the Freudian-Caruthian belatedness model in the way such characters are either instigated by a sudden traumatic event to *use* their abilities to fight crime or are shown to *obtain* their powers via a sudden traumatic incident. This kind of narrative is evident across a range of contemporary comic book heroes, including Spider-Man, Daredevil, Deadpool, and Luke Cage. For example, the murder of Peter Parker's uncle drives him to fight subsequent crimes in New York City; Matt Murdock obtains his powers having been blinded by a radioactive substance that falls from an oncoming vehicle; Wade Wilson and Luke Cage obtain their abilities through involuntary experimentation.

Burton's Bruce Wayne (Michael Keaton) is in a number of ways a typical trauma protagonist. Wayne is an affluent, straight white male character who continues a tradition of "upper-class heroes" (Heldenfels 2015, 98). He lives in a mansion so vast that there are rooms he claims to have never been in before. Wayne has been affected by a singular trau-matic event: the murder of his parents by a street thug when he was a child. The event is both unexpected and overwhelmingly violent. An unidentified criminal approaches the Wayne family in a dark alley outside the theater and fatally shoots Thomas and Martha Wayne, leaving child Wayne alone beside his parents' lifeless bodies and unable to grasp the event. According to Kelly Duquette, whose thesis examines Frank Miller's *Batman: Year One*, Wayne's "inability to comprehend the experience not only establishes this initial episode of the history of Batman" but also "guarantees a structural basis for Bruce Wayne to begin and carry on life as the Caped Crusader of the Batman canon" (2010, 4). Wayne experi-ences clichéd symptoms accordingly, such as dissociation in the form of his dual identity and flashbacks of the incident. For instance, Wayne experiences a flashback of his parents' murder when he sees Jack Napier/the Joker (Jack Nicholson) with his make-up removed because in Burton's adaptation, Napier killed Wayne's parents. This flashback scene is significant because while Wayne experiences flashbacks of this incident throughout the Batman canon, the Joker and the original mugger are unrelated in the comics and previous adaptations. Burton's adaptation is thereby analogous to the dominant Freudian/Caruthian concept of trauma, specifically the idea of associative flashbacks and the "increased arousal to… stimuli recall-ing the event" (Caruth 1995, 4). Wayne's exposure to something "remotely associated with the traumatic event" (Vickroy 2002, 31), in this case, Napier's grimacing visage, triggers in Wayne a memory of Thomas and Martha's murder.

Moreover, this new origin story for the Joker devised by Burton, in revealing him to be the killer of Thomas and Martha Wayne, further foregrounds the traumatic origins of Bat-man, as it establishes that Wayne's decision to assume the Batman identity and fight crime is, fundamentally, a response generated by his childhood trauma (Duquette 2010, 14). Wayne dons this disguise to protect the people of Gotham from the same fate that befell his parents, to avenge their deaths by both preventing the tragedy of his parents' murders from happen-ing to others and defeating the Joker, their killer, at the end of the film. Wayne's assumption of the Batman persona can also be described as the character attempting to, in the Freud-ian/Caruthian sense of the term, fully grasp the traumatic experience, specifically the way in which trauma is understood as a mental wound that "is experienced too soon, too unexpect-edly to be fully known and is therefore not available to consciousness until it imposes itself again, repeatedly, in the nightmares and *repetitive actions of the survivor*" (Caruth 1995, 4). This is evident in how, as Duquette observes, Wayne's crime-fighting persona is not merely a means of avenging his parents' murders but provides him with multiple "opportunities to (re)grasp" this traumatic event and re-enact this trauma repeatedly (2010, 16). This is evident in the film's opening scene in that it closely parallels with the flashback of the Wayne murders we see later in the narrative: a couple with their son are held at gunpoint and robbed in a dark alleyway. This time, however, Bruce as Batman manages to successfully confront the muggers. In so doing, Bruce creates an alter ego who is driven to assuage the guilt of his childhood self who could not save his parents (Halfyard 2004, 50).

Wayne's dual identity as millionaire philanthropist and masked crime fighter is also analo-gous to dissociation or splitting, a symptom of trauma whereby an individual splits off a part of their consciousness from a traumatic experience and remembers it as occurring to some-one else, thereby creating an "alter personality" (Herman 1997, 103). This trauma concept was popular during the time Burton's *Batman* was produced and continued to be so in dominant Caruthian trauma theory. Burton's adaptation of *Batman* "play[s] up" this aspect of the Dark Knight in particular, that is, Batman's "disturbed, alienated, split-personality"

(Salisbury 2008, 70). In an interview conducted by Mark Salisbury, Burton states: "while I was never a big comic book fan, I loved Batman, the split personality,... which is really what I think the movie's all about" (2008, 71). According to Duquette, "Wayne's assumption of the Batman image situates a new, post-traumatic ego for Bruce Wayne" (2010, 17). Burton continues this tradition in Batman. However, Burton's film suggests that Batman is the true identity while Bruce Wayne, the millionaire playboy, is the disguise. Notably, Burton's film introduces Batman *before* Bruce Wayne. In the opening scene where he confronts the muggers, the character triumphantly declares "I'm Batman." By contrast, in the fundraiser scene which introduces Bruce Wayne to the audience, the character seems uncertain of his own identity. The reporter Vicki Vale (Kim Basinger) asks Wayne "Could you tell me which one of these guys is Bruce Wayne?" to which he responds "I'm not sure."

This is in stark contrast to other interpretations of the character, such as that of Christopher Nolan's in *Batman Begins* (2005), because Nolan's Batman (Christian Bale), while traumatized, nevertheless seems to harbor the hope of recovery. Nolan's Wayne states that he "doesn't want to do this forever." For Burton's Wayne, however, the Batman persona is an essential part of his character; for example, he is shown in *Batman* to sleep upside down. For the duration of Burton's film, Wayne spends his days either isolated in his mansion or underground Batcave. When the character is introduced, the city flashes the bat-signal into the sky and the film cuts to a shot of Wayne in the Batcave sitting in an armchair, as though waiting to don the Batman persona. When presenting as Bruce Wayne, the character is passive and conspicuous. He does not fit into Gotham's social scene or society at large, exhibiting socially awkward behavior. Burton describes Wayne as an introvert "who always wants to remain in the shadows, to remain hidden" (Salisbury 2008, 72), to the extent that the film was criticized for having its hero overshadowed by characters such as the Joker, resulting in Batman being "forced to take a back seat" in the narrative (Salisbury 2008, 103).

Batman Returns and Trauma: Feminist Trauma Representation

Halfyard asserts that the principal characters of *Batman Returns* are linked in that they are all "dual personality characters... people who have suffered some great trauma" (2004, 30). Burton says that what he likes about *Batman*'s characters include their "duality" and "the fact that they're all fucked-up characters, the villains and Batman" (Salisbury 2008, 103). Whereas Burton's *Batman* is in many ways a conventional representation of trauma, its sequel *Batman Returns* takes a more innovative direction regarding Catwoman's trauma narrative. Burton's Catwoman experiences a number of ongoing traumatic events, resulting from both physical violence and everyday experiences of inequality and oppression. Primarily, Catwoman's narrative foregrounds the more insidious, ongoing trauma of patriarchal domination. According to Brown, such insidious trauma is "the traumatic effects of oppression that are not necessarily overtly violent or threatening to bodily well-being at the given moment but that do violence to the soul and spirit" (1995, 107). As Melanie Bates points out: "Batman's neuroses are brought on by his own personal trauma and the failures of his benevolent capitalism, Catwoman's by the constant trauma of the male oppression typified by those things" (2016).

For example, Selina Kyle (Michelle Pfeiffer) is continuously subject to the sexism of her boss, Max Shreck (Christopher Walken), the owner of a multi-million-dollar department store and business empire. It is evident that Kyle is an ambitious, competent worker and intelligent individual: she is the first to discover Shreck's illegal activities by figuring out the password to his computer, and she acts and describes herself as an executive assistant rather than a secretary by assuming additional tasks which include bringing Shreck the speech he wishes to read to Gotham City on Christmas Eve. Despite Kyle's attempts to move up in the corporate world and become part of the patriarchy, Shreck has her perform menial tasks such as making coffee for his fellow male corporate executives, and responds mockingly to Kyle's suggestion at an all-male board meeting, firmly re-establishing traditional gender roles: "I'm afraid we haven't properly housebroken Miss Kyle. In the plus column though, she makes a hell of a cup of coffee." In his implication that men should make the executive suggestions while women should make the coffee, Shreck is drawing upon the sexist public/private dichotomy to exclude Kyle from the capitalist world she strives to be a part of, suggesting that men belong in the public sphere of corporate capitalism, while women should remain in the private sphere of domestic chores. When Kyle attempts to make a suggestion, she asserts: "Um, I have a suggestion." The men appear taken aback and Kyle rephrases and hedges her words, no longer speaking in the same language as her male colleagues but employing the language professional women are instructed to use in order to avoid appearing "too abrasive": "Well, actually, really, just more like a question." The composition of this shot makes Kyle appear smaller and insignificant in comparison to Shreck and the other men in this scene. The scene then cuts to a long shot of the men turning in their chairs to face Kyle. They look at her (and the camera) skeptically, as Kyle is shot from over the shoulders. Her feelings of intimidation are emphasized here as the viewer shares her perspective. When Shreck and his colleagues depart, Kyle appears frustrated from her constant exclusion in the workplace and rebuking herself for the way she phrased her idea: "Oh God. 'Actually, it's more of a question,'" she says in a high-pitched mimicking tone, then sighing, "You stupid corndog! Oh, God. Corndog! Corndog!"

Kyle's return from work also shows her experiencing the "chronic psychic suffering produced by the structural violence of… gender… inequities" (Craps and Buelens 3–4, 2008). Societal pressures and challenges faced by women are overtly foregrounded, such as pressures to marry when Kyle enthusiastically greets her empty apartment with "Honey, I'm home!", then disappointedly "Oh, I forgot. I'm not married" (instead, a neon sign upon her wall lights to read "Hello There"). Kyle's exhausted appearance together with her concerns about paying rent indicate the low pay received by women and the undervaluing of their contribution to the workplace: "I seem pathetic, but I'm a working girl, gotta pay the rent." Kyle's messages on her answering machine lists varying, ongoing struggles of women, in line with what Brown calls "'normal' traumatic events" (1995, 101), that is, how women's experiences are "daily blighted by abusive situations that, while part of their everyday life, are nevertheless traumatic" (Gibbs 2014, 16). These messages include the expectation for women to care for elderly family members rather than pursue careers. Kyle's mother says "I'm disappointed that you're not coming home for Christmas. We must discuss why you insist on languishing in Gotham City as some lowly secretary." Kyle corrects her mother's description of her as secretary to "executive assistant." The message from Kyle's boyfriend, who ends their relationship because she beat him at a game of racquetball, also highlight gender inequities in relationships. Highlighting male fears of female competence, Kyle says, "I guess I should have let him win." Kyle's boyfriend insensitively ends their relationship via an answering machine, the reason being, he claims, is that his therapist advises him "to be his own person and not an appendage." As Bates notes, this is "[a] cruel joke given that Selina clearly needs emotional support and another signifier of men's [dismissal] of women in this world" (2016). The third message is from Shreck's store, which emphasizes women's role as erotic object: "Gotham Lady Perfume. It makes women feel like women and the men have no complaints either." Further underscoring the menial nature of her job, the final message is Kyle reminding herself to collect Shreck's files. Kyle is subsequently murdered by Shreck at the office when she discovers his illegal activities. Shreck and his all-male team plan to construct a Power Plant for Gotham City, but Shreck plans to use this plant to suck power from the city rather than generate or restore it. Before Shreck kills Kyle, Kyle tries to appease Shreck by establishing gender roles in a similar manner to how he did in the board meeting previously and her mother in the phone message, emphasizing how Kyle is a "secretary" and "meaningless":

Shreck: What did curiosity do to the cat?
Kyle: I'm no cat. I'm just an assistant. *A secretary.*
Shreck: And a very good one.
Kyle: Too good? Listen. It's our secret. Honest.

[Shreck approaches her menacingly]

Kyle: How can you be so mean to someone so meaningless?

Shreck then pushes Kyle from the office skyscraper window, an act of violence which instigates her transformation into Catwoman. When Kyle lands in the snow, numerous cats emerge from an alleyway and mysteriously resurrect Kyle by scratching and chewing on her lifeless body.

While Shreck's attempted murder of Kyle presents the kind of sudden, punctual trauma in line with the Freudian-Caruthian model, the trauma that instigates the creation of Catwoman aligns more with the prolonged, insidious suffering produced by gender inequities, evident in the lengthy scenes that show Kyle as gradually traumatized by sexism and corporate patriarchy. Moreover, as with *Batman*'s Joker, this is a new origin story for Catwoman, with the misogynistic business mogul Shreck being a new addition to the *Batman* canon. The character has never appeared in the comics or previous Batman adaptations. That Catwoman character has suffered from trauma, or has been a victim of some kind of abuse, is canonical. For instance, in the early comics, Kyle is introduced as an amnesiac flight attendant in *Batman* #62 (1950), which in *The Brave and the Bold* #197 (1983) is later revealed to be a cover story for her escape from an abusive husband from whom she stole jewelry, launching her career as a cat burglar. Her origin story was revised in Frank Miller's *Batman: Year One*; in this interpretation, Kyle is portrayed as a prostitute who aims to break away from her abusive pimp and former boyfriend. Similarly, the four issue *Catwoman* (1989) limited series written by Mindy Newell explores Kyle's early years in prostitution and eventual murder of her pimp for abusing her sister Maggie, in addition to a number traumatic events from Kyle's childhood, which include her mother's suicide, her father's alcoholism, and her subsequent experiences of living on the streets and later the juvenile hall. In selecting workplace harassment and "the constant trauma of male oppression" (Bates 2016) as the source of Kyle's trauma in his film, Burton once again reinvents a character's origins to suit his particular psychological approach to Batman, this time to foreground sexism and the chronic psychic suffering produced by this structural violence of gender inequities.

As Kyle suggests that Shreck let her in on his activities before her 'murder', she is murdered specifically because she attempts to become part of the patriarchy. Also, it is suggested that Kyle is murdered by Shreck not only because she attempts to become part of the patriarchy but also because she does so in favor of the more traditional feminine role as love interest or erotic object. When Kyle re-enters her apartment post-resurrection, Kyle/Catwoman receives another message from Shreck's department store which guarantees that wearing their perfume will attract the attention of one's boss: "One whiff of this at the office and your boss will be asking you to stay after work for a candlelight staff meeting for two. Gotham Lady Perfume. Exclusively at Shreck's Department Store." By contrast, Kyle pursues a working or professional relationship with her boss rather than a romantic one as suggested by the perfume advertisement. Patriarchal conditions, then, give Kyle concrete motivation as Catwoman, her mission being to disrupt the patriarchy that oppressed her and take revenge on Shreck. In contrast to The Joker, who is usually depicted as a terrorist or insane bank robber, Catwoman's first mission is not an act of random terrorism but to blow up Shreck's department store. When Kyle hears the message from Shreck's department store, she pours milk onto her phone and smashes it. That Kyle's traumatization and transformation into Catwoman stems from patriarchal oppression is further suggested when she proceeds to vandalize her entire apartment and destroys all signifiers of femininity. She breaks the paintings and mirrors upon her walls with a frying pan; rips up her stuffed animals and shoves them into the waste-disposal grinder; and spray-paints black lines across her pink walls and pastel-colored clothes. The frying pan in particular can be read as symbolic of oppressed femininity, whereas the Catwoman costume Kyle creates is evocative of feminist elements of punk, as it is made from an old PVC jacket hanging in her closet. Kyle also smashes the sign that reads "Hello There" so that it reads instead "Hell Here," and repeats the phrase "Honey, I'm home. Oh, I forgot. I'm not married," but this time in a flat, parodic way of how she said it earlier. In contrast to Wayne in *Batman* and his conventional belated trauma then, the trauma that instigates the creation of Kyle's alter-ego aligns with the more prolonged, insidious suffering produced by gender inequities. Certain critics, such as Halfyard (2004), for example, argue that Catwoman's trauma was merely "physical" rather than psychological, that her trauma was solely triggered by Shreck's attempted murder. While Shreck's attempted murder of Kyle presents the kind of sudden, punctual trauma in line with the Freudian-Caruthian model (and that which is covered by earlier definitions of PTSD), this is not the case as the film includes lengthy scenes that clearly foreground the ongoing sexism and corporate patriarchy that Kyle is subject to.

Further foregrounding women's ongoing trauma, Catwoman, rescues a woman from rape. When she spots the attacker dragging the civilian into a dark alleyway, Catwoman emerges from the shadows and beats the man unconscious: "I just love a big, strong man who's not afraid to show it with someone half his size… I am Catwoman, hear me roar." This act of heroism mirrors that of Batman in the opening scene of *Batman* where he confronts the two muggers robbing a family. Catwoman's scene in *Batman Returns* also takes place at night in an alleyway and, having rescued the civilian from danger, Catwoman proclaims her heroic identity in a similar fashion to the Dark Knight: "I'm Batman"/ "I am Catwoman." In having Catwoman rescue a woman from rape, the ongoing trauma suffered by women is again at the forefront in this scene. Rape is a constant fear that plagues women and makes every day experiences traumatic, such as commuting to and from work. For instance, Susan Brownmiller describes rape as "nothing more or less than a conscious process of intimidation by which *all* men keep *all* women in a state of fear" (1993, 13). Further emphasizing the "ordinariness" and perhaps overlooking of women's traumatic experience is the fact that the woman who is attacked is shown walking in a crowded area when she is grabbed; we see a brief glimpse of a couple walking in close proximity to her seconds before she is assaulted. Superhero narratives and adaptations generally depict the "origin" of their title hero, that is, they show how the hero obtained their powers and also their initial experimentation with these powers via performance of (in terms of plot) minor heroic acts such as preventing local crimes and rescuing random civilians. In Sam Raimi's Spider-Man (2002), for example, Peter Parker (Tobey Maguire) is shown obtaining his superpowers when he is bitten by a radioactive spider, and testing out these abilities by climbing skyscrapers, confronting school bullies and preventing robberies and muggings. Again, Burton appears to rework superhero tropes to suit his particular feminist approach to Batman and trauma.

As well as conforming to feminist trauma theory, *Batman Returns* also subverts and literalizes the concept of repeated, prolonged trauma. Catwoman is "killed" eight times in the film. In addition to Shreck pushing Kyle from a window, both Batman and The Penguin throw her off a building, and she "dies" when electrocuting Shreck at the end of the film. Shreck also shoots Catwoman four times in this scene, to which she remarks: "You killed me. The Penguin killed me. Batman killed me. That's three lives down. You got enough in there to finish me off?" In having Catwoman murdered by Shreck, Batman, and The Penguin, the character is killed each time by one of the main representative members of the patriarchy within the film. Indeed, Batman, like Shreck, and The Penguin, is a member of the corporate patriarchy. As with Shreck, Catwoman is "killed" precisely at moments when the character refuses to fulfill the traditional feminine roles assigned to her by the men in the film. Batman and The Penguin also kill Catwoman for refusing traditional feminine roles of love interest and submissive damsel. Batman pushes Catwoman off the building when she chastises him for his rescue and refuses to play his damsel in distress. When fighting with Batman on a rooftop, Catwoman loses the fight and begins to fall from the building. Batman saves her from falling, but this gesture angers her and she stabs him in the stomach with her claws. He then pushes her from the building and she lands in a truck full of cat litter. Similarly, The Penguin kills Catwoman for rejecting his sexual advances, exclaiming: "You lousy minx! I ought to have you spayed! You send out all the signals! And I don't think I like you anymore!" The Penguin proceeds to throw Catwoman off the building they stand upon and she crash-lands on a bed of flowers in a nearby green house, seemingly dead. Refusing to be killed off and silenced, however, Catwoman rises from the earth and screams so loudly the glass walls of the greenhouse shatter to pieces. The shattering of the greenhouse evokes the concept of the "glass ceiling": an unacknowledged and illegal barrier to career advancement for women and people of color. Catwoman literally emerging from dirt- and ash-like substances (flowers in earth, cat litter) further drives home the image of the character dying and being resurrected.

This chapter has analyzed trauma representation in Burton's Batman films, specifically how these representations are gendered, as well as conform to, challenge, and subvert both conventional and feminist trauma theory. In analyzing how Burton's films subvert trauma concepts, new ways of representing trauma are uncovered. Furthermore, Burton conforming to dominant Freudian-Caruthian trauma theory in his interpretation of Bruce Wayne/Batman and feminist theory for Selina Kyle's/Catwoman's trauma representation demonstrates the limitations of dominant trauma theory during the time *Batman* was produced. While diversity in pop cultural trauma representation has certainly improved since, the Freudian-Caruthian model has retained a hold upon much cultural trauma theory and representation. This chapter, then, both adds to existing Batman scholarship as well as current trauma discourse.

References

American Psychiatric Association. 1980. *Diagnostic and Statistical Manual of Mental Disorders: DSM-5.* American Psychiatric Association Publishing.

Bates, Melanie. 2016. "On *Batman Returns*." The Progressive Democrat, March 16. https://mjshochat 723.wordpress.com/2016/03/14/on-batman-returns/.

Bond, Lucy, and Stef Craps. 2019. *Trauma.* Taylor and Francis Group.

Brown, Laura S. 1995. "Not Outside the Range: One Feminist Perspective on Psychic Trauma." In *Trauma: Explorations in Memory*, edited by Cathy Caruth. Johns Hopkins University Press.

Brownmiller, Susan. 1993. *Against Our Will: Men, Women, and Rape.* Fawcett Books.

Burton, Tim, dir. 1989. *Batman.* Warner Bros.

Burton, Tim, dir. 1992. *Batman Returns.* Warner Bros.

Caruth, Cathy. 1995 "Trauma and Experience: Introduction." In *Trauma: Explorations in Memory*, edited by Cathy Caruth. Johns Hopkins University Press.

Craps, Stef, and Gert Buelens. 2008. "Introduction: Postcolonial Trauma Novels." *Studies in the Novel* 40, no. 1 & 2: 1–12.

Duquette, Kelly. 2010. "Bruce Wayne's Traumatic Past and Batman's New History: Ego-ideal and Ideal Ego in the Batman Origin Myth." MA Thesis, College of Liberal Arts and Sciences.

Gibbs, Alan. 2014. *Contemporary American Trauma Narratives.* Edinburgh University Press.

Halfyard, Janet K. 2004. *Danny Elfman's Batman: A Film Score Guide.* Scarecrow Press.

Heldenfels, Richard D. 2015. "More Than the Hood Was Red: The Joker as Marxist." In *The Joker: A Serious Study of the Clown Prince of Crime*, edited by Robert Moses Peaslee and Robert G. Weiner. University Press of Mississippi.

Herman, Judith Lewis. 1997. *Trauma and Recovery.* BasicBooks.

Luckhurst, Roger. 2008. The Trauma Question. Routledge.

Miller, Frank, and David Mazzucchelli. 1987. *Batman #404–407.* DC Comics.

Nolan, Christopher, dir. 2005. *Batman Begins.* Warner Bros. Pictures.

Radstone, Susannah. 2001. "Trauma and Screen Studies: Opening the Debate." *Screen* 42, no. 2: 188–193.

Rothberg, Michael. 2009. *Multidirectional Memory: Remembering the Holocaust in the Age of Decolonisation.* Stanford University Press.

Salisbury, Mark, ed. 2008. *Burton on Burton.* Faber & Faber.

Sam Raimi., dir. 2002. *Spider-Man.* Columbia Pictures.

Shephard, Ben. 2001. *A War of Nerves: Soldiers and Psychiatrists in the Twentieth Century.* Harvard University Press.

Vickroy, Laurie. 2002. *Trauma and Survival in Contemporary Fiction.* University of Virginia Press.

Young, Allan. 1997. *The Harmony of Illusions: Inventing Post-Traumatic Stress Disorder.* Princeton University Press.

45

THE PHOENIX AND DARK PHOENIX SAGAS

Moral Ambiguity, Disagreement, and the Superhero Mission

Justin F. Martin

Building on recent work explicating the potential of superhero narratives to interrogate morally relevant concepts (Martin 2021, 28–33; 2023a, 76–82; 2023b, 23–30; Martin et al. 2023, 219–223), this chapter explores how the *Phoenix* and *Dark Phoenix* sagas, as told in *X-Men: The Animated Series* (1992–1997), afford opportunities for such interrogation. By centering two features of social interactions considered by Social Cognitive Domain Theory (SCDT) to be important for understanding the nature of, and relations between, morally relevant concepts (Turiel et al. 1987, 178–182), the *Phoenix* sagas demonstrate how beliefs can inform people's treatment of others. These features pertain to frequent ambiguities surrounding social events and the various disagreements that tend to follow when trying to make sense of these events. Scholars have highlighted complex themes within these narratives in other areas, such as the implications of Jean's struggle with the Phoenix Force for thinking about the relationship between individual moral decision-making and broader economic and political structures (Fawaz 2016, 206–207, 224). This chapter contributes to this literature through employing a constructivist lens to examine the role of ambiguity and disagreement in navigating social relations.

These ambiguities and disagreements occur against the backdrop of two shifts. One involves Jean initially being mostly in control of the Phoenix Force, to the "control" question being more ambiguous, to eventually the Phoenix being mostly in control. Another concerns the nature of the Phoenix Force itself, specifically the shift between the Phoenix being an entity in service of the Shi'ar Empire to an entity that exists only to experience new (dark) sensations and emotions.

The Sagas: Power, Purpose, and Ambiguity

Arguably one of the most important storylines in the X-Men universe (Fawaz 2016, 155), the *Phoenix Saga*, told across five episodes in season three of *X-Men: The Animated Series*, tells the story of the X-Men's efforts to thwart a galactic catastrophe when D'Ken, emperor of the Shi'ar Empire, tries to harness the power of the M'Kraan crystal to use it as a weapon. Understanding the power of the crystal and the immense threat to all sentient life posed

DOI: 10.4324/9781003366911-51

by her brother's actions, Princess Lilandra steals the crystal from her brother and contacts Professor X telepathically for help. During their efforts to help, the X-Men, and more specifically Jean Grey, encounter the Phoenix Force, an entity of immense power that according to Shi'ar myth is the guardian of the crystal. The Phoenix inhabits Jean's body and Jean, using her empathic abilities, is able to work with the Phoenix to stop D'Ken and keep the crystal away from sentient life.

In addition to the complexity within the Phoenix Force itself – evident through its simultaneous representations of death, destruction, and rebirth (O'Rourke and O'Rourke 2014, 229) – the narrative is characterized by multiple ambiguities and associated disagreements. An important source of ambiguity established in the saga's first episode concerns Professor X. Sensing the gravity of the telepathic messages he is receiving but unable to fully understand their meaning, Professor X sends his X-Men into space with very limited information yet clearly articulating the moral significance of their mission. The focal character across the sagas, Jean, experiences similar ambiguities concerning her new powers and the associated psychological changes, as well as the full extent of what she will need to do to prevent the destruction of all living things. And even at the narrative's conclusion, Professor X expresses concern over the implications of Jean's merger with the Phoenix and subsequent heroic actions: "But at what cost?" (Houston 1994d, 00:17:35).

The *Dark Phoenix Saga*, told across four episodes later in season three explores the implications of the Phoenix Force merging with Jean, both in terms of Jean's ability to control the Phoenix and in terms of the threat it still poses to sentient life while using Jean as the host. Despite psycho-neural therapy being able to calm Jean's mind, the Phoenix Force remains inside of Jean despite completing their mission. Once a group of powerful mutants known as the Inner Circle learns of the Phoenix force, they set out to control the Phoenix Force in accordance with tradition. To do this, they attempt to manipulate Jean's mind and by doing so, control the Phoenix.

The X-Men intervene, and over the next three episodes, the X-Men try to save Jean and all sentient life while wrestling with whether they are capable of doing either. They also learn that the reason the Phoenix refuses to leave Jean's body is because the merger, combined with the Inner Circle's manipulations, caused the Phoenix Force to experience intense, dark human emotions, altering the Force in the process as it now only seeks to satisfy dark desires concerning power and destruction. Once the Phoenix appears to have taken over Jean's psyche for good, Professor X agrees with now emperor Lilandra that Jean must be killed lest this "dark" Phoenix destroys all life in the universe. Once the Shi'ar successfully kills Jean, the Phoenix returns to its true nature and informs the X-Men that if they are each willing to sacrifice part of their own life forces, those portions can transfer to Jean's body, resurrecting her. They agree, and Jean is saved.

As with the *Phoenix*, the *Dark Phoenix* is characterized by ambiguities and disagreements. But they appear to serve a more central role in this narrative compared to its predecessor. This is evidenced by the varied contexts in which these ambiguities and disagreements unfold. *Intra*personally, there is a dynamic relationship between Jean and the Phoenix Force, whether they are constantly jockeying for control, even up to the point of Jean's initial death. *Inter*personally, superheroes and supervillains often have conflicting views related to the Phoenix. These include disagreements concerning the nature of the Phoenix, whether Jean Grey has sufficient psychological control, and the proper response to the threat it poses. For instance, all the X-Men did not agree on who had ultimate psychological control or whether the High Council of the Shi'ar Empire was justified in determining that Jean needed to die for the sake of the universe. Moreover, the Inner Circle doubted whether Mastermind was powerful enough to control the Phoenix Force through manipulating Jean.

Social Cognitive Domain Theory: Superhero Life is Complicated

According to SCDT, the social lives of children, adolescents, and adults are complex, consisting of social interactions varying in both number and kind (Turiel et al. 1987, 167–182; Smetana et al. 2014, 24–27). Concerning differences in kind, SCDT posits that individuals construct meanings of these diverse social interactions that become more elaborated with age. These meanings are best characterized as belonging to three conceptual domains. Based on the unique features of social interactions, people construct distinctions between those that are *moral, societal*, and *psychological* in nature. These distinctions account for both differences in degree (e.g., severity or deservingness of punishment judgments) and kind (e.g., concepts used in justifications and responses to criterion judgment questions), as relying on the former is insufficient (e.g., sometimes a societal violation is viewed as more wrong or deserving of punishment than a moral violation).

Moral acts are usually understood to be generalizable, not based on rules, authority, or local context, and not up to individual discretion. Main concepts or considerations (henceforth used interchangeably) include those pertaining to harm/welfare, justice/fairness, human rights, and civil liberties. Typical real-life examples include hitting someone (harm/welfare), refusing to hire someone for reasons other than their qualifications (justice/fairness), and subjecting someone to slavery or torture (human rights). Some potentially analogous examples across the sagas include Cyclops using his optic blast to temporarily incapacitate astronauts so the X-Men can replace them aboard the space shuttle Starcore (Houston 1994a, 00:08:12; harm/welfare), The Shi'ar High Council's decision to kill Jean Grey for acts committed by the Phoenix (Houston 1994h, 00:17:14; justice/fairness), and Mastermind and Emma Frost's attempts to manipulate Jean's mind to control the Phoenix (human rights).

As important as morality is to social relations, moral considerations – and the acts influenced by them – exist alongside many nonmoral considerations that people also deem important. One set of considerations belongs to the societal domain and includes concepts concerning adherence to authority, rules, laws, tradition, customs, and norms. Unlike moral acts, societal acts are usually not generalizable, are rule, authority, or local context dependent, and are not up to individual discretion. Real-life examples include players following a coach's directives, teams abiding by game rules, laws pertaining to when one can obtain a driver's license, cultures with distinct rites of passage ceremonies (tradition), and communities that vary in terms of child play and supervision norms or expectations (e.g., how long children are left without adult supervision; norms). Potentially analogous examples from *Phoenix* and *Dark Phoenix* include the X-Men following Professor X's orders to find a way onto the space shuttle Starcore so they could go to the Eagle One Space station to investigate the threat (adherence to authority; Houston 1994a, 00:05:25); Gladiator, as a member of the Imperial Guard and subject to the authority of Emperor D'Ken, attempting to retrieve Lilandra on D'Ken's orders (adherence to authority; Houston 1994b, 00:07:21); The Inner Circle seeking to gain control of the Phoenix because tradition dictates that they wield such power (Houston 1994e, 00:10:16); and Professor X invoking Shi'ar law, which dictates that they cannot refuse combat challenges in the name of honor, in an effort to save Jean from being killed (Houston 1994h, 00:02:05).

Lastly, there is the psychological domain. These acts are usually understood to not be generalizable or determined by rules, authority, or local context, but are up to the individual to decide. Relevant concepts include those pertaining to autonomy, choice, desires, privacy, preferences, and prerogative rights. Common examples include choosing one's attire and friends, and preferring certain foods, films, and music genres over others. Potentially analogous examples across the sagas include D'Ken's desire to use the crystal as a weapon, Cyclops and Professor X's desires to maintain their intimate connections with Jean and Lilandra, respectively, and the Phoenix's refusal to leave Jean's body because it wants to continue experiencing (dark) human emotions.

In addition to social interactions (and people's attempts to understand them) varying based on their features, social interactions are multifaceted. In other words, people's social lives often include situations that, instead of primarily being understood through one concept (e.g., harm/welfare) and domain (e.g., moral), include multiple concepts and/or domains. In general, SCDT asserts that multifaceted social interactions tend to include one or more of the following: second-order domain combinations, between-domain combinations, within-domain combinations, or ambiguous features (Smetana et al. 2014, 26–27; Turiel 1983, 55, 114–129; Turiel et al. 1987, 187–188).

A second-order domain combination is evident in situations where an act committed in one domain has implications for another domain. As an example, take a social context where it is well established that shaking one's hands is the interpersonal greeting norm. In the abstract, or without considering concepts within other domains, one would be expected, upon entering said context, to greet others by shaking their hands. But let's imagine that this individual is carrying a serious disease that can spread by shaking hands. Let's further assume that this person is aware of the harmful nature of the disease they possess, how it is transmitted, and is presently unable to thoroughly clean or sanitize their hands. Now, adhering to this norm has moral implications, as doing so could lead to others experiencing bodily harm. The initial act, in and of itself, is still societal according to SCDT. But the implications of the act extend well past the societal domain and into the moral domain. As leaders and thus responsible for giving commands and instituting norms and policies governing the X-Men, Professor Xavier and various team leaders over the years (Cyclops, Storm, Rogue, etc.) have often made decisions from positions of authority that had moral implications for fellow X-Men, villains, and non-mutant humans. Usually, these decisions pertain to the use or non-use of a mutant's powers in particular contexts, the sanctioning of particularly violent teams like X-Force, and how close to work with the government.

In these and other situations (e.g., consider the potential moral implications of violating traffic laws), the initial act still conceptually resides in its "host" domain. But adding additional features associated with the act affects the context, and this could *conceptually alter the meaning* of the (total) event (e.g., which includes the act, the knowledge possessed by the perpetrator, and its consequences). This ability of narratives like the *Phoenix* and *Dark Phoenix* sagas to frequently present events that can be conceptually altered by the addition or modification of relevant features makes for compelling storytelling. It also affords opportunities to (critically) interrogate the relationship between moral and nonmoral considerations within superhero narratives (for related analyses concerning the superheroes Black Panther and Luke Cage, see Martin 2021, 28–29; 2023a, 65, 73–75; Martin et al. 2023, 208–215).

For this chapter, morally relevant considerations are broadly construed to include considerations tied to acts committed within the moral domain (e.g., the intentional use of violence toward another) and acts "housed" in a nonmoral domain (e.g., commanding someone to intentionally harm another). Concerning the former, examples include the Phoenix commit-ting violent acts against others and the Shi'ar's attempts to hold her accountable and seek justice for victims. Concerning the latter, Jean's attempts to assert her autonomy or psycho-logical control over the Phoenix has many moral implications. Insofar as she is successful, her control has implications for human welfare (a harm consideration) and accountability (a justice consideration). If she is unsuccessful, sentient life will be destroyed on earth and throughout the galaxy. Further, whether the X-Men considered Jean culpable has implications for their views of the legitimacy of Shi'ar law, as when Beast criticizes the Shi'ar law dictating they must accept battle challenges on the moral grounds that Jean should not be held accountable for the Phoenix's actions: "Such a trial is no contest of reason, it is a war. Such a position mocks justice. Lilandra is wrong" (Houston 1994h, 00:05:18). Collectively, examples like these highlight the multifaceted nature of the sagas by frequently "connecting" moral and nonmoral considera-tions in attempts to understand an ambiguous entity in the Phoenix.

The next two types of complex social interactions – those involving between-domain and within-domain combinations – tend to include clearly competing concepts or domain-relevant considerations. Examples of between-domain and within-domain combinations, respectively, include situations involving (1) a conflict between adhering to a family curfew rule (rule, societal) or helping a friend who has been physically hurt (harm/welfare, moral) and (2) breaking a promise made to one friend (justice/fairness, moral) to uphold a promise made to another friend. Research suggests that in these kinds of situations, it is important to account for the extent individuals are attempting to weigh these competing considerations while resolving the complexity or ambiguity through a process known as coordination. Take the following example of coordination (Nucci et al. 2017, 320). Youth of various ages were presented with a situation where a person must decide whether to stop and help someone in pain, knowing that doing so means they will be late to soccer practice and thus cut from the team. Scholars found age differences concerning coordination. Older youth tended to believe that the person should stop and help while also understanding that the person has the autonomy to choose to do what they want, reasoning as follows: "she has the ability to not help, but I don't think she has the justified right to not help the girl … it's her choice … but I think she's more right to help the little girl." In this example, the respondent acknowledges the legitimacy of the nonmoral viewpoint while still prioritizing the moral viewpoint. It is worth noting that this example is a brief snapshot of more elaborate responses and is thus not meant to capture the fullness of the coordination process.

Although different contexts and not assessed using SCDT criteria, one may be justified in wondering if Professor X, when discussing recent developments concerning Jean and their implications for what may come next, also engages in some form of coordination. One exchange with Cyclops goes as follows:

Cyclops: "As long as Jean is alive, we can't stop trying,"
Professor X: "Of course, Scott, but we must also be honest with ourselves about the depth of the problem. Unless the Phoenix agrees to leave Jean's body, I see no way to save our friend!"

(Houston 1994g, 00:10:16)

In both examples, individuals appear to be weighing competing considerations. In the study excerpt, the dilemma is between helping someone who was hurt (moral) and pursuing a per-sonal goal of wanting to be on the soccer team (psychological). For Professor X, the dilemma is between saving Jean (moral) or saving life across the galaxy (moral). One might further argue that his description of Jean as "friend" suggests another consideration bearing on the situation: personal friendship (psychological).

As discussed, second order, between-domain and within-domain social interactions can contribute to notable differences in opinion insofar as people construe the relevant features of social events in different ways. Nevertheless, the fourth type of social interactions, ambiguous situations, is of particular interest given its representation in the *Phoenix* and *Dark Phoenix* sagas. Whereas the previous three types usually involve clear domain-relevant considerations, in ambiguous situations the relevant considerations are usually unclear. The result is that when people try to evaluate, understand, or determine how to act, they vary in their domain attributions (Turiel 1983, 55). A common example of an ambiguous event is abortion, but, as polling data suggests (Pew Research Center 2021a,b), issues related to matters like gun policy, or COVID-19 vaccines may also include ambiguous elements.

Part of the reason for people's varying views concerning these and similar matters, according to SCDT, stems from their informational assumptions. Sometimes varying across social dimensions (e.g., race/ethnicity, culture, religions) and other times varying in knowledge, these are divergent beliefs individuals hold concerning the nature of physical, social, and psychological reality (Turiel et al. 1987, 189–191; Smetana Jambon and Ball 2014, 26–27). One way to view this relationship between ambiguous events and informational assumptions, is that because individuals construct meaning through social interactions (Turiel et al. 1987, 182–186), ambiguous events can create sufficiently wide enough "conceptual" gaps that are filled by various means (beliefs) as people seek to attribute meaning to their experiences and relations between persons. To the extent such an interpretation is plausible, analogous examples across the sagas are apparent. For instance, multiple characters hold divergent beliefs concerning the nature of the Phoenix (Is the Phoenix a myth or real? Can it be controlled or manipulated?) and its relation to Jean (Is Jean or the Phoenix in control?). As a result, disagreements abound concerning whether Jean is morally responsible for the actions caused by the Phoenix.

What We Tell Ourselves: Narratives Concerning Harming Others

SCDT's constructivist approach to the development of social and moral understanding centers the relationship between an act's unique features and people's conceptual understanding of the act. Many social interactions are not easily conceptualized, and thus processes of weighing and reflecting on concepts, sometimes against a backdrop of broader assumptions about physical, social, or psychological reality, influence how people navigate these complex or ambiguous situations. Such an interactive view of social and moral development implies, in certain situations, that disagreements are normal given people's interpretative capacities.

Building on this idea, some scholars investigate the role of interpretations in the context of youth's concrete experiences with harm. Specifically, Cecilia Wainryb et al. (2005) assessed the narrated accounts of children and adolescents (preschool, first grade, fifth grade, and tenth grade) of a time when they harmed a peer (as a perpetrator) and a time when they were harmed by a peer (as a victim). The authors contend that analyzing the harm narratives of children and adolescents from perpetrator and victim perspectives affords opportunities to better understand both how they evaluate the acts and how they come to construct meanings around, and interpret, those acts (Wainryb et al. 2005, 19). Moreover, through centering children's interpretations of concrete social interactions involving moral conflict, harm narratives can make salient features of social interactions that are constitutive of subsequent moral development and understanding. And although children's varying interpretations of social reality do not determine their development of moral understanding, they represent the context through which the relationship between social interactions and moral development plays out (Wainryb et al. 2005, 19, 70). Clarifying this point, they note: "Children develop moral concepts and understandings by abstracting and reflecting on features of social interactions that bear on harm and justice. Children's construals of situations surrounding moral conflict serve to illustrate this process well" (Wainryb et al. 2005, 70). Given the myriad disagreements superheroes and supervillains have concerning the nature of the Phoenix Force and how to respond to it, the sagas provide many opportunities for viewers to engage in similar processes of abstraction and reflection.

The following analysis aims to highlight the potential for the sagas to allow for an examination of the relationship between social interactions, conceptual understandings, and diverse interpretations in at least three ways. One is through the ambiguity surrounding Jean Grey as both perpetrator and victim. The other is through complicating the relationship between (moral) judgment (e.g., the general belief it is wrong to cause others harm) and (immoral) behavior (e.g., the realization that one's actions caused others harm). This tension is considered a core element of harm narratives (Wainryb et al. 2005, 62). The third examination is through the varying disagreements experienced by the characters, which, considering the work of Wainryb et al., may be suggestive of different construals of the same events. After briefly discussing some general findings from their research, broad connections are drawn between certain events across the sagas. Only a few are mentioned for the sake of brevity.

Three findings revealed across all ages (preschool, first grade, fifth grade, and tenth grade) and perspectives (victim and perpetrator) bear on the aims of the chapter. One is the centrality of harm as evident in the number of times the perpetrator's harmful acts were mentioned. Second, most of the youth believed that the perpetrator's actions as told through their narratives were wrong. Third, youth referenced the victim's emotions more frequently than the perpetrator's emotions. When the youth themselves were victims, they referenced their own emotions more than when they were perpetrators. And when the other youth in the narrative was a victim, they referenced the other youth's emotions more than when the other youth was a perpetrator (Wainryb et al. 2005, 51–52, 62).

As mentioned above, the combination of the possibility of Phoenix causing galactic scale harm and ambiguity surrounding its nature drive the narratives of *Phoenix* and *Dark Phoenix*. For Cyclops, who in many ways can be viewed as a central character across the arcs given his dual obligations as Jean's romantic partner and the leader of the X-Men, this combination proved particularly challenging. For instance, upon boarding Starcore he shoots the crew members, telling them that he may have saved their life if the professor's concerns bear out. In addition, across the sagas he is often at odds with Professor X, as they are frequently seen clashing, with Cyclops either wanting more information or disagreeing about whether Jean Grey still maintains (some) psychological control over the Phoenix. But Cyclops is by no means alone. Jean Grey, believing that her powers give them the best chance to land the shuttle once they encounter unexpected danger, uses her powers to render Cyclops unconscious so he cannot switch places with her (Houston 1994a, 00:19:47). And a few episodes later, after merging with the Phoenix, she tells Cyclops that there is much she must do alone yet also much she does not know (Houston 1994c, 00:04:00).

The *Dark Phoenix* saga in particular affords opportunities to interrogate the role of emotions when understanding victims of harmful acts, as the ambiguity surrounding who has psychological control over Jean's body plays out against the backdrop of the relation between more positively and negatively valenced emotions. On the one hand, Jean's strong empathic abilities proved useful in the *Phoenix* saga and appears to be one of the reasons she is able to momentarily intervene at critical moments to save lives. Notable examples are when she intervenes to save Cyclops from Mastermind, Wolverine from Phoenix and, presumably, the Universe from Phoenix (Houston 1994f, 00:12:00). On the other hand, without the pull of Jean's empathy toward others, the Phoenix would not have inhabited Jean's body in the first place. As told in *Dark Phoenix*, this process revealed a vulnerability of sorts, such that the Phoenix, with the help of Mastermind and Emma Frost, was able to experience equally strong, negatively valenced, or dark emotions related to power and destruction. Moreover, one could argue that for different reasons, both Jean and Phoenix were victims whose emotions were altered, co-opted, or manipulated for different ends (for heroic ends in *Phoenix* and villainous ends in *Dark Phoenix*).

Wainryb et al. also found that even though most youth across perspectives evaluated the perpetrator's actions negatively, narrative perspective still mattered. For instance, when narrating as a victim, the perpetrator's actions were evaluated more negatively than when narrating as a perpetrator. Second, across all ages, references to intentions were more common in perpetrator versus victim narratives. Lastly, whereas youth overwhelmingly focused on their own experience with the harmful event when providing a victim narrative, they shifted between their own experience and that of the victim when providing a perpetrator narrative (Wainryb et al. 2005, 51, 62, 74).

The events surrounding the *Phoenix* and *Dark Phoenix* sagas parallel the overarching theme from both the findings and the relationship between ambiguous events and divergent beliefs. In some cases, the meaning people attribute to an event may be influenced by the perspective and underlying assumptions they bring to the event. Despite the sagas occurring across five and four episodes respectively, there is only so much that can be depicted in an episode, let alone one targeted toward children ages seven and older. Nevertheless, the sagas provide opportunities to examine people's diverse perspectives about others and their morally relevant actions. For brevity, the following discussion is limited to a particular context: the nature of the Phoenix and whether Jean or the Phoenix Force should be held responsible for the harm caused.

While Professor X was struggling to make sense of the telepathic messages he was receiving and the nature of the threat they would ultimately face, members of the Shi'ar empire, aware of the Phoenix Force, were still unclear on its nature. Whereas Lilandra and Gladiator encountered the Phoenix through Jean and believe that the legend about the protector of the M'Kraan crystal is true, D'Ken, who has yet to encounter the Phoenix, still believes the legend to be a myth (Houston 1994c, 00:09:58). Given the moral implications of D'Ken's quest to weaponize the crystal and his sister Lilandra's attempts to stop him, it is worth considering how their differing perspectives on the existence of the Phoenix Force informed subsequent narrative events. For instance, maybe D'Ken never obtains and unleashes the crystal's power if he believes in the existence of the Phoenix from the beginning, the Phoenix Force never "binds" with Jean's empathic connections to the X-Men in order to contain the crystal's power, the Dark Phoenix never emerges, and the Shi'ar and X-Men never grapple with whether Jean should die so the universe can be spared.

As the nature of the threat D'Ken poses to the universe becomes clearer and Jean becomes more intertwined with the Phoenix, questions around psychological control and moral culpability become more ambiguous. *Dark Phoenix* explores this ambiguity in more detail, often presenting characters, heroes and villains alike, articulating different and often competing perspectives on one or both matters. Consistent with the findings that victim narratives tend to focus more on the harmful consequences of events and evaluate the actions of the perpetrator more negatively, *Dark Phoenix*, through centering the perspectives of the actual and potential victims, highlights the importance of harm considerations, and people's general prohibitions against harming others. Actual victims pertain to those attacked/harmed by Jean/Phoenix and potential victims include the countless lives throughout the galaxy at risk if the Phoenix embarks on a path of destruction.

Moreover, it is worth noting that given the danger presented by the Phoenix, differences in perspectives between and within major groups in the *Dark Phoenix* narrative (X-Men, the Inner Circle, and the Shi'ar Empire) are frequently represented throughout the saga. The fact these perspectives are frequently articulated and debated by a diverse array of characters with respect to their motivations and relational proximity to Jean attests to the saga's effective use of ambiguous events to interrogate morally relevant actions and the beliefs that may undergird them. Examples of perspectives differing between groups include the X-Men and Inner Circle differing on whether the Phoenix (and by extension, Jean) should be manipulated to serve selfish ends, and the X-Men and Shi'ar disagreeing on whether Jean Grey should be held morally culpable for the Phoenix's actions (i.e., whether Jean and Phoenix have become one and the same).

These depictions of group-level perspectives notwithstanding, differences within each group were also prevalent. Examples include Storm and Beast disagreeing over the legitimacy of the Shi'ar honor battle (Houston 1994h, 00:04:53), Gambit raising the possibility to Wolverine that Lilandra is right about the Jean/Phoenix being too powerful to remain alive (00:05:34), and Jean disagreeing with Cyclops concerning her ability to psychologically control the Phoenix (00:16:29). Second, prior to the Inner Circle unintentionally helping unleash a more power-hungry, destructive version of the Phoenix, Sebastian Shaw, Emma Frost, and Mastermind debated the efficacy of Mastermind's powers for sufficiently controlling the Phoenix (Houston 1994f, 00:07:00). Particularly illustrative of the uncertainty surrounding their ability to control the Phoenix, Emma, after aiding Mastermind in controlling the Phoenix, was unsure how long it would last, stating "We can't control and deceive the Phoenix forever. Someday she'll discover the truth, and turn against the Inner Circle" (Houston 1994f, 00:06:29). As expected with narratives characterized by morally relevant actions occurring against the backdrop of profound uncertainty, conflicts and disagreements are common.

Lessons from Xavier's School

Collectively, findings from the narrative study suggest that experiences involving harm and injustice are common among the social lives of youth (Wainryb et al. 2005, 82). And as Cecilia Wainryb and Monisha Pasupathi assert, since the meaning individuals attribute to an event is tied to the "ways facts are combined with the psychological and broader context, the same facts … can reflect different meanings when told by different narrators who report different emotions, goals, and beliefs … or when combined with different facts" (2018, 106). This chapter argues that through centering ambiguity and disagreement, the *Phoenix* and *Dark Phoenix* sagas highlight the ability of certain narratives to interrogate morally complex themes in a manner broadly consistent with the central claims of SCDT and related research on the (re)construction of harm narratives in youths. These narratives thus provide opportunities to reflect on how people's interpretations of events can influence both how they evaluate and apply their moral and nonmoral concepts to understanding them. Insofar as this may be the case, then we can learn something from the students of Xavier's school.

Bibliography

Fawaz, Ramzi. 2016. *The New Mutants: Superheroes and the Radical Imagination of American Comics*. New York University.

Houston, Larry, dir. X-Men: The Animated Series. Season 3, episode 3, "The Phoenix Saga, Part I: Sacrifice." *Written by Michael Edens, Bob Harras, and Eric Lewald*. Aired, September 5th, 1994a, on Fox Kids.

Houston, Larry, dir. X-Men: The Animated Series. Season 3, episode 5, "The Phoenix Saga, Part III: Cry of the Banshee." *Written by Michael Edens, Bob Harras, and Eric Lewald*. Aired, September 7th, 1994b, on Fox Kids.

Houston, Larry, dir. X-Men: The Animated Series. Season 3, episode 6, "The Phoenix Saga, Part IV: Starjammers." *Written by Michael Edens, Bob Harras, and Eric Lewald*. Aired, September 8th, 1994c, on Fox Kids.

Houston, Larry, dir. X-Men: The Animated Series. Season 3, episode 7, "The Phoenix Saga, Part V: Child of Light." *Written by Michael Edens, Bob Harras, and Eric Lewald*. Aired, September 9th, 1994d, on Fox Kids.

Houston, Larry, dir. X-Men: The Animated Series. Season 3, episode 11, "The Dark Phoenix Saga, Part I: Dazzled." *Written by Jan Strnad, Bob Harras, and Eric Lewald*. Aired, November 12th, 1994e, on Fox Kids.

Houston, Larry, dir. X-Men: The Animated Series. Season 3, episode 12, "The Dark Phoenix Saga, Part II: The Inner Circle." *Written by Steven Levy, Bob Harras, and Eric Lewald*. Aired, November 12th, 1994f, on Fox Kids.

Houston, Larry, dir. X-Men: The Animated Series. Season 3, episode 13, "The Dark Phoenix Saga, Part III: The Dark Phoenix." *Written by Larry Parr, Bob Harras, and Eric Lewald*. Aired, November 19th, 1994g, on Fox Kids.

Houston, Larry, dir. X-Men: The Animated Series. Season 3, episode 14, "The Dark Phoenix Saga, Part IV: The Fate of the Phoenix." *Written by Brooks Wachtel, Bob Harras, and Eric Lewald*. Aired, November 26th, 1994h, on Fox Kids.

Martin, Justin F. 2021. "The Many Ways of Wakanda: Viewpoint Diversity in Black Panther and Its Implications for Civics Education." *Dialogue: The Interdisciplinary Journal of Popular Culture and Pedagogy* 8, no. 1: 24–36.

Martin, Justin F. 2023a. "Harlem's Superhero: Social Interaction, Heterogeneity of Thought, and the Superhero Mission in Marvel's Luke Cage." *Popular Culture Review* 34, no. 2: 43–89.

Martin, Justin. 2023b. "Superhero Media as a Potential Context for Investigating Children's Understanding of Morally Relevant Events." *Libri & Liberi* 12, no. 1: 11–35.

Martin, Justin. F., Mark Killian, and Angelo Letizia. 2023. "Comics and Community: Exploring the Relationship Between Society, Education, and Citizenship." In *Exploring Comics and Graphic Novels in the Classroom*, edited by Jason D. DeHart. IGI Global.

Nucci, Larry, Elliot Turiel, and Alona D. Roded. 2017. "Continuities and Discontinuities in the Development of Moral Judgments." *Human Development* 60, no. 6: 279–341.

O'Rourke, Morgan B, and Daniel J. O'Rourke. 2014. "Prophet of Hope and Change: The Mutant Minority in the Age of Obama." In *The Ages of the X-Men: Essays on the Children of the Atom in Changing Times*, edited by Joseph J. Darowski. McFarland & Company.

Pew Research Center. 2021a. "Amid a Series of Mass Shootings in the U.S., Gun Policy Remains Deeply Divisive." April 20. https://www.pewresearch.org/politics/2021/04/20/amid-a-series-of-mass-shootings-in-the-u-s-gun-policy-remains-deeply-divisive/.

Pew Research Center. 2021b. "Majority in U.S. Says Public Health Benefits of COVID-19 Restrictions Worth the Costs, Even as Large Shares Also See Downsides." September 15. https://www.pewresearch.org/science/2021/09/15/majority-in-u-s-says-public-health-benefits-of-covid-19-restrictions-worth-the-costs-even-as-large-shares-also-see-downsides/.

Smetana, Judith. G., Marc Jambon, and Courtney Ball. 2014. "The Social Domain Approach to Children's Moral and Social Judgments." In *Handbook of Moral Development*, 2nd ed., edited by Melanie Killen and Judith. G. Smetana. Psychology Press.

Turiel, Elliot. 1983. The Development of Social Knowledge: Morality and Convention. Cambridge University.

Turiel, Elliot, Melanie Killen, and Charles C. Helwig. 1987 "Morality: Its Structure, Function, and Vagaries." In *The Emergence of Morality in Young Children*, edited by Jerome Kagan and Sharon Lamb. University of Chicago Press.

Wainryb, Cecilia, Beverly A. Brehl, and Sonia Matwin. 2005. "Being Hurt and Hurting Others: Children's Narrative Accounts and Moral Judgments of Their Own Interpersonal Conflicts." *Monographs of the Society for Research in Child Development* 70, no. 3: 1–114.

Wainryb, Cecilia, and Monisha Pasupathi. 2018. "'I Hurt Him': From Morally-Relevant Actions to Moral Development, by Way of Narrative." In *New Perspectives on Moral Development*, edited by Charles C. Helwig. Routledge.

46

THE UNBELIEVABLE GWENPOOL AND THE LIMITS OF EMPATHY

Devon Keyes

In April 2018, millions across the world witnessed an unprecedented event: without warning, half of all life in the universe was suddenly and unexpectedly erased from existence. Lives were lost, families were torn apart, and futures were irrevocably changed as nearly every institutional structure governing everyday life was, in an instant, upset across a global scale. Amid the wake of this harrowing moment, a new world emerged: one defined by an insurmountable absence with which every individual around the world struggled to cope for years to come.

And Then the Credits Rolled

It was over. The danger witnessed extended no further than the boundaries of thousands of theater screens across the planet, all of which were screening *Avengers: Infinity War*, the first of the epic two-part culmination of Marvel Studios' then ten-year cinematic saga, bringing fan-favorite characters from across all its products together for audiences on an unprecedented scale. In the years that followed, those same audiences would continue to tune into Marvel Studios' cinematic universe as it dealt with the ramifications of Thanos' catastrophic "correction" of a universe deemed broken, eager to be entertained despite the Mad Titan's harrowing effects. A world died, and everyone moved on as if nothing happened.

This is, of course, because audiences engage with the many fictive worlds in comics media as just that: nothing but fiction. Cognizant of their artificiality, comic book readers and moviegoers engage with the narrative ramifications of those sprawling storyworlds at a conceptual distance which rarely demands from its audiences an emotional response akin to those often reserved for real-life tragedy, despite those very texts often encouraging us otherwise. Indeed, if the question "do fictional characters deserve our empathy?" lies at the heart of these texts, the answer, more often than not, is a resounding "no."

This particular question is one often raised by Gwendolyn Poole, a recent addition to Marvel's canon since her debut in 2015. Gwendolyn's unique origins as an ordinary person from the "real" world who is suddenly transported into the Marvel Comics' fictional universe, bringing her knowledge and love of comics with her, forces both the character and her audience to reconsider just how quickly one might answer questions around empathy. As

 DOI: 10.4324/9781003366911-52

Gwendolyn engages with the many moral complexities inherent to her new home, and to her role in it as the superhero Gwenpool, so too must she confront the inherent incompatibility of a moral system she applies to a world she once exclusively approached as fictional, but with which she must now engage as if it were not.

Such is the central tension that lies at the heart of Gwenpool's migration from her original reality (often billed and presented as the "real world") to the fictional reality maintained by Marvel Comics, charted across her initial appearance in *Howard the Duck* (2015–2016) and her debut solo series, *The Unbelievable Gwenpool* (2016–2018), both written by author Christopher Hastings. As Gwenpool learns to acclimate to her new reality, Hastings leverages this tension to explore the complex processes by which individuals form and reform the boundaries of the moral systems required to interact with the world around them, and the challenges faced if and when those systems prove unsuitable should that world change. By examining how Gwenpool negotiates her new subjectivity, her unique relationship with violence, her process of moralization, and her engagement with the Marvel Universe through fantasy and play, this chapter holds that Gwenpool ultimately reckons with an unstable and incompatible moral framework which she must redress by revisiting the question of "do fictional characters deserve our empathy?" in a universe where those very characters are now given a say in the matter.

Morality and Fictive Subjectivity

One significant component informing Gwenpool's moral framework and its need for reconstruction after entering the Marvel Universe (hereafter cited as MU) is her unique subjectivity as a perceived "real person" operating in a perceived fictive space. As a character with the ability to see, interact with, and (in some cases literally) break the fourth wall, Gwenpool's actions frequently draw attention to the MU's nature as artificially constructed: a universe managed and maintained, influenced by fan demand and character popularity, and highly resistant to radical change. Consequently, Gwenpool's interactions with the various heroes, villains, and citizens she encounters initially prioritize their status less as people and more as characters, who exist solely to further the plot. This tension is one Ira Newman marks in *Virtual People: Fictional Characters through the Frames of Reality* as essential to understanding the "fictive imagination" as a space of duality, beholden to both internal (story-as-realized-world) and external (story-as-constructed-narrative) perspectives (2009, 75). Newman contends that audiences who enter into fictional spaces must engage with a cyclical meaning-making process by which real-world concerns (such as moral and ethical frameworks) are projected onto the storyworld in order to impart them with a sense of realism; in turn, those concerns are filtered and changed through those fictional narratives, and then projected back onto the real world in order to use the unique perspectives afforded by fiction to better engage with real-world problems (80).

Many of Gwenpool's actions, however, suggest an interruption of this process: though she has gained physical access to storyworld, she struggles to engage with it conceptually, primarily due to her constant awareness of it as a fictional space. The consequences of this interruption are shown almost immediately across Gwenpool's brief narrative history, as her three-part origin story in Christopher Hastings' run of *Howard the Duck* (2015–2016) casts her status as a superhero into doubt thanks in part to her inability to see characters beyond their narrative utility. While attempting to chase down and kill Howard after he is hired by Felicia Hardy (antihero Black Cat) to find her, Gwenpool interrupts her own search for Howard through an abandoned building to launch into a flashback detailing how she obtained her signature white and pink costume, noting that she "[needed] the costume" because, in the world she now lives, "if you're not wearing a mask or a cape…you're just an extra" (Hastings 2016, 19). The urgency at the heart of Gwenpool's remarks suggests that her initial moral framework is not one rooted in issues of goodness or badness, but rather in issues of narrative purpose; this results in a hierarchy of character value that positions costumed individuals (superheroes and villains alike) at the top, and renders "extras" (secondary, supporting, or background characters with little to no influence on the MU) at the bottom.

Such a hierarchical worldview, which reduces the value of life down to pure functionality, drastically influences the way Gwenpool often interacts with the characters around her after her arrival to the MU. Gwenpool herself boasts about this worldview in the opening pages of *The Unbelievable Gwenpool* (2016–2018), during which her attempts to open a bank account and establish legal residence are interrupted by an impromptu robbery. In an aside during the robbery, Gwenpool tells the reader that she understands why the other denizens in the bank are scared, since "if [she] were one of these random extras in this scene, [she'd] be freaked out, too. Who cares about the extras?" (Hastings 2016, 49). In this particular case, the "extras" to which Gwenpool is carelessly referring are mere bystanders, who take a more or less passive role in a text that ultimately positions them as victims. However, Gwenpool's worldview also extends to extras that take a more active role in the development of the narrative as well. Later on in the series, Gwenpool assembles a super team to rid New York City of a race of alien invaders who seek revenge against Gwenpool for killing one of their own. To stop them, Gwenpool proposes luring the aliens to Times Square using herself as bait, at which point she will eliminate them all in one fell swoop. One member of her team, Batroc the Leaper (reimagined in *The Unbelievable Gwenpool* [2016–2018] as less of a villain and more of an antihero), takes issue with the recklessness of her plan, noting its potential to place the lives of innocent police officers at risk. In response, Gwenpool again reveals her inability to engage with the internal fictional world on its own logical terms, opting to remind Batroc (and the reader) that, in a world such as theirs, police officers "are just another plot device to further the existence of super heroes," and thus their deaths would come at no great narrative loss (Hastings 2017a, 81). In both cases, Hastings positions Gwenpool as a figure initially unable to negotiate with both halves of Newman's internal/external storyworld construction, ultimately giving more weight to MU as a constructed narrative; as such, her worldview better serves her immediate goals. As a result, perhaps as an inevitability, Gwenpool's interaction with those "extras" across *Howard the Duck* (2015–2016) and *The Unbelievable Gwenpool* (2016–2018) suggests a perspective that dismisses the very figures superheroes are charged to protect, as they are beneath her time, her attention, and her interest, highlighting the boundaries of her empathy as worryingly narrow for the very citizens who likely need it the most. This narrow moral framework often impedes Gwenpool's ability to establish herself as a genuine hero within the MU, as her initial motivations to become a superhero frequently prioritizes satisfying the demands of the narrative as if from above, rather than from within.

This fraught relationship with the characters around her presupposes in Gwenpool's careless attitude that empathy expressed toward fictional characters is not a "genuine instance" of that emotion, and as such is not comparable to similar emotions expressed for real-world individuals (Sankowski 1988, 51). Throughout her journey, Gwenpool struggles to express genuine empathy for characters with which she frequently interacts precisely because the value of their lives rarely supersedes their status as fictional characters, often preventing her from emotionally connecting with those around her, *especially* those "extras" who she struggles to view as anything more than mere narrative fodder. This empathetic failure serves to reinforce the conceptual distance between herself and her peers, further highlighting the incompatibility of the moral framework that she brings into the MU. Hastings capitalizes on this incompatibility frequently across his tenure with the character, as is evidenced in his one-shot *Gwenpool Holiday Special #1* (2015): alone for the holidays, Gwenpool accepts a contract to kill the sword-bearing supervillain Orto, responsible for the murder of her unnamed client's brother. While disclosing details on the job itself, the client attempts to empathize with Gwenpool, who admits that she is unable to spend the holidays with friends and family since they are in an entirely different universe. When the client attempts to sympathize with her circumstances, Gwenpool quickly dismisses his sympathy, instead encouraging him to disclose more details about his job offer, namely because it gives her "something to do tonight" along with an excuse to purchase more weapons (Hastings 2016, 36). Though it certainly may be argued that Gwenpool's eagerness to accept the job is a way of avoiding a potentially tense conversation, the continuous rebuffs of her client's sympathies as they chat ultimately implies that her desire stems less from a need to avoid her anxieties and more from a need to alleviate her boredom. This notion is furthered by the additional distance Gwenpool erects between herself and the client during that very same conversation, in which she spends the majority of the time engaged by her phone rather than listening to his story. Much like in *Howard the Duck* (2015–2016) and *The Unbelievable Gwenpool* (2016–2018), Gwenpool's actions in *Gwenpool Holiday Special #1* (2015) similarly reflect a fundamental detachment not only from the "extra" that has hired her, whose existence she views as only important in staging the narrative that follows, but also from the dangers posed by the job itself.

Repeatedly, Hastings forces Gwenpool to confront the state of her own unique subjectivity in the MU as a means through which larger conversations around empathy and morality can be made manifest. As Gwenpool settles into her new reality, her specific understandings of what it means to be a superhero, to engage in a fictive universe as a "real" person, and to negotiate the proper level of empathy for fictional "extras" all ultimately highlight the moral framework Gwenpool brings with her into the MU, and suggests through her exploits the spaces where that framework is rendered incompatible with her new reality.

Morality and Fictive Violence

In addition to highlighting how Gwenpool's unique subjectivity renders her initial moral framework incompatible with the MU, Hastings further destabilizes that framework through Gwenpool's newfound relationship with (and quick adoption of) superhero violence and spectacle. Superheroes are, of course, no strangers to violence. Indeed, superheroes often justify their varied acts of violence and destruction as necessary to uphold the systems of justice at the heart of decades of interlocking superhero narratives. Gwenpool, an avid comic book reader herself, is no stranger to this particular narrative rationale. Yet her initial participation with that violence as a *reader* rather than its potential *subject* further strains the moral and ethical frameworks Gwenpool initially imposes on the MU, thanks to an interest in comics media (books, tv shows, video games, films, forums, fanfiction, etc.) that frequently engages with violence as both a locus of moral discussion and a form of desirable entertainment. Reflected across her struggle to engage with the MU (and its "extras") beyond its narrative mode, the superhero-violence-as-entertainment perspective she initially privileges further destabilizes Gwenpool's moral framework. It presents a relationship with violence that mirrors the spectacle she reads in comic books, yet remains divorced from its potential ramifications or consequences. Such a depiction ultimately debuts Gwenpool as a superhero who favors violence in ways that are highly theatrical, but only ostensibly heroic.

The potential pitfalls of Gwenpool's unique relationship with violence and its effects on her moral framework are made clear in her very first appearance, in which Gwenpool drives a motorcycle into an ongoing scene, steals a sample of a deadly virus from a group of unnamed cultists, and disarms a nearby guard by stabbing him through the hand with a pen (Hastings 2016, 8). Though the violence on the display in this moment is, as mentioned, not uncommon across superhero comics, this debut effectively underscores Gwenpool's relationship with violence as one initially marked by carelessness, recklessness, and impulsivity, framed by her experience with the MU as a product of commercial entertainment. Ironically, Hastings presents Gwenpool's very first act as a superhero as one that is slightly villainous: full of impartial, indiscriminate violence, with little regard for what may be happening, who might be in danger, or what might be at stake, all factors irrelevant to a world that is fiction, filled with "extras" that are expendable, entangled with violence designed to entertain.

Throughout her series, Gwenpool firmly establishes herself as a figure whose unique relationship with violence is tempered by a history with comics that often demands from that violence some degree of extravagance and spectacle. Consequently, the moral and ethical structures she initially considers are again rendered incompatible for a world where violence holds a variety of conflicting demands, many of which she must simultaneously negotiate. This incompatible framework initially encourages her to prioritize a need for immediate legitimacy as a superhero (by the readers, by her peers, by Marvel's editors and publishers) over a desire to do good, again highlighting Gwenpool's initial struggle to develop an ethical framework more suitable for her new reality.

Morality and Fictive Disengagement

Informed by her awareness of the fictive nature of the world she comes to inhabit, which in turn prompts her to prioritize acts of violence as spectacle, Gwenpool's unique subjectivity and relationship to violence reflects a moral system characterized by what Albert Bandura terms *moral disengagement*: a process by which individuals actively relinquish moral agency from harmful actions in order to absolve responsibility for those actions. Bandura is quick to note that moral disengagement does not necessarily translate to an *absence* of moral justification; rather, moral disengagement speaks to a process by which personal responsibility for violent acts are relocated outside of the subject's moral purview:

> People do not usually engage in harmful conduct until they have justified to themselves the morality of their actions. Social and moral justifications sanctify harmful practices by investing them with honorable purposes. Righteous and worthy ends are used to justify harmful means. The moral imperative enables people to preserve their sense of self-worth even as they inflict harm on others.
>
> *(Bandura 2016, 49)*

Bandura maintains that moral disengagement often involves shifting moral responsibility for harmful actions in order to deem those actions more justifiable. Frequently, that responsibility is anchored to institutional apparatuses (religious organizations, political parties, cultural structures, military units, terrorist sects, etc.) reassigning moral responsibility to a "legitimate authority [who] accepts responsibility for the effects of their conduct" (58). Unsurprisingly, superhero comics frequently contend with the extent, limits, and consequences of moral disengagement through characters who often relinquish personal responsibility for their actions across ideological lines (represented by superhero teams such as the Avengers, the X-Men, and the Fantastic Four), political lines (represented by state-affiliated figures such as Captain America and the Black Panther), and spiritual lines (represented by religious figures such as the catholic superhero Daredevil, or the Jewish superhero Moon Knight). What makes Gwenpool's specific construction of moral disengagement so distinctive, however, is that she frequently eschews relinquishing responsibility across ideological, political, or spiritual lines, and instead initially abstracts responsibility for her (often violent) actions along *narratological* lines, leveraging her awareness of the medium in which she resides to render any action on her part as self-reflexively permissible.

Again, Hastings immediately foregrounds Gwenpool's process of disengagement directly in her debut in *Howard the Duck* (2015–2016). After Felicia hires him to recover the stolen virus sample, Howard is cornered by Gwenpool and begins to beg for his life. Curiously, a puzzled Gwenpool asks Howard why a character who repeatedly falls out of print is worried about being killed, signaling exactly where she has shifted responsibility for her actions: "What's the big deal if you die? You've disappeared from publication for months—*years* at a time. You'll just come back again eventually" (Hastings 2016, 16). Aware of the nigh immortality often afforded to recognizable (and thus lucrative) comic book characters, Gwenpool initially disengages with the morality of her actions by diluting their significance at the meta-narrative layer, waging that even an act as violent as murder will eventually (perhaps even inevitably) be narratively undone and is thus of little ethical consequence. This expression of moral disengagement, achieved by her unique relationship to the narrative in which she operates, further reinforces Gwenpool's struggle to establish a functional system of ethics that properly considers her newfound role in the MU, as one of its new inhabitants, as a part of its many chains of events, and as someone responsible for her many choices.

In addition to dismissing moral responsibility for acts of violence directed toward recognizable characters, Hastings further highlights Gwenpool's incompatible morality in the acts of violence she often directs toward those she deems inconsequential to the narrative. Shortly after meeting Miles Morales (Spider-Man) in *The Unbelievable Gwenpool* (2016–2018), the two superheroes investigate a bombing at Miles' school that injures a handful of students. Once the two discover the perpetrator, Spider-Man elects to apprehend the suspect and leave them for the authorities, an action more reflective of a conventional superhero moral framework. Gwenpool, however, attempts an alternative tactic wholly reflective of her unique relationship to the MU: she decides to execute the culprit to prevent any more harm. In this moment, Hastings reflects the moral disengagement at the core of Gwenpool's ethical framework and suggests that such disengagement is what renders her initially incompatible with her new role. Gwenpool externalizes this disengagement to a shocked Spider-Man by claiming that the culprit "wasn't important! He was a plot device! A B-Story!" This again reflects Gwenpool's relationship with the "extras" around her as narratively insignificant to her, and any need for empathy by her unnecessary, thus rendering any act of violence inconsequential (Hastings 2017a, 38).

Crucially, Gwenpool's deliberate application of narrative jargon ("plot device," "B-Story") reinforces her moral disengagement and echoes Bandura's assertion that acts of violence are frequently diluted through language meant to lessen their overall impact to make those acts more permissible. Rather than a person, Gwenpool positions the culprit as no more than a narrative object, beholden to the rules governing the narrative, and thus less worthy of remorse or empathy. Similar to her attempt to delegitimize New York City's police officers, Gwenpool effectively weaponizes her unique knowledge base to "extract every ounce of humanity" from her adversaries in order to relinquish any moral responsibility for the violence her actions might incur (Bandura 2016, 53). This practice of linguistic dehumanization is one that Gwenpool employs frequently throughout her series, often as a means through which narrative convention itself shoulders sole responsibility for her violent deeds. When in a stalemate with a malfunctioning clone of the supervillain Doctor Doom, who takes her friends hostage in issue #10 of *The Unbelievable Gwenpool* (2016–2018), Gwenpool threatens to "off [two] background characters" to which the malfunctioning clone has grown close (Hastings 2017a, 117). Gwenpool again justifies her violence by emphasizing the conceptual distance between herself and the world around her, using her unique subjectivity as a means through which she disengages with any conception of morality that might require her to empathize with characters perceived as inconsequential to the narrative. To Gwenpool, the logic follows clearly: she is the protagonist of the story; Doctor Doom is the villain of the story; her friends are in life-threatening danger; her actions will only affect "background" characters; thus, any violence against such characters is admissible.

As evidenced by both her resistance to engage with the MU beyond its status as a fictive storyworld, and a unique relationship with violence informed by role of comics as an entertaining spectacle, Hastings repeatedly highlights the active ethical disengagement that underpins the moral framework Gwenpool brings to the MU. This stance continuously proves incompatible with the new relationship she maintains with her new reality, and is one that she spends the majority of *The Unbelievable Gwenpool* (2016–2018) ultimately attempting to reconcile.

Morality and Fictive Play

Throughout both *Howard the Duck* (2015–2016) and *The Unbelievable Gwenpool* (2016–2018), Hastings repeatedly highlights the incompatible moral framework Gwenpool brings to the MU, which challenges the boundaries of her empathy due to a variety of factors: the unique subjectivity afforded by her status as a "real" character in a fictional world; the influence of her prior engagement with the MU as an entertainment product; and the ongoing process of moral disengagement she frequently employs to absolve any violent actions therein. Each of these pieces contributes to the initial instability of her moral framework and serves as one of the central tensions she confronts as her narrative progresses. However, Hastings also includes one final point of complication, which further renders Gwenpool's ethical framework unstable: her engagement with the MU as less of a realized world and more as a place of creative play and fantasy fulfillment.

As mentioned, Gwenpool's initial relationship with the MU was one filtered through comics media, beholden to various exigencies (financial, narrative, editorial, etc.) that govern its shape as commercial entertainment. Yet, in addition to merely *consuming* such content, Gwenpool is an avid *producer* as well, having been a fanfiction writer in her original reality prior to becoming a superhero in the MU (Hastings 2018a, 17). Such a history with fanfiction further informs Gwenpool's perception of the MU as one of constant, active construction and participation; for Gwenpool, it's not enough to simply *read* about the MU, her passions drive her to contribute to it as well, in her own way, always with the goal to validate the superhero fantasy she holds dear. (Those same passions in the real world, I suspect, led to the creation of this very Companion). Indeed, Gwenpool makes this drive clear while arguing with her parents in her original reality near the end of *The Unbelievable Gwenpool* (2016–2018): after her father complains about the amount of time she spends writing instead of looking for a job, Gwenpool defends her occupation by acknowledging the importance of "fantasizing about a better world than this one" (Hastings 2018a, 18). The need to both create and consume that fantasy in order to perpetuate it is certainly not one unique to Gwenpool; Hastings deliberately positions her alongside the many other teenagers who escape into comics, video games, and other media as a way to avoid an otherwise difficult home life. Thus, when given the opportunity to escape directly into the MU, her understandable instinct is to maintain that fantasy as much as possible with her at its center, fulfilling what Scott McCloud defines as superhero comics' primary function: the act of "role-playing—becoming the character" (McCloud 2000, 118).

It is this very understanding of her new home as merely a fantasy to be fulfilled, however, that contributes to Gwenpool's difficulties engaging with the MU on its own internal terms, further complicating the moral framework she employs to maintain that fantasy. Her desire to claim a superhero costume and distinguish herself from the MU's "extras," for instance, is a clear example of that fantasy-fulfillment mindset. This mindset is at its most explicit in the third volume of *The Unbelievable Gwenpool* (2016–2018), in which the supervillain Arcade traps Gwenpool and her team in one of his iconic murderworlds: a mechanical labyrinth designed to kill its victims in increasingly elaborate ways. Gwenpool pieces together that her murderworld is modeled after a sword-and-sorcery-themed video game, so to facilitate her escape, she quickly acclimates to her new climate, referring to Mega Tony (her team's chief scientist) as a "cleric" and "healer," and to the lower basement of the murderworld as "level one" (Hastings 2017b, 32). When the two encounter a potential fight, she bemoans that she didn't "roll a rogue," again suggesting both a subordination to genre conventions and a framing of those around her through their presumed narrative utility (Hastings 2017b, 33). Gwenpool later literalizes this MU-as-play mindset while visualizing her murderworld as a tabletop board game, with her as its game master and her team as its player pieces (Hastings 2017b, 52). In the same way she ultimately leads her team to safety by assuming the role of the game master within the issue, Gwenpool frequently positions herself as "game master" of the MU itself, claiming inheritance to the title by way of her extensive in-universe knowledge. This role encourages Gwenpool to maximize the fantastical potential of the narrative, yet simultaneously devalues those around her into game pieces under her control, further distancing Gwenpool from any ethical ramifications as she plays.

By having her continually prioritize the fantastic potential of the MU over its everyday realities, Hastings further demonstrates how Gwenpool's incompatible moral framework limits the extent of her empathy for those she often sees as game pieces in a world she often sees as a game. Gwenpool expresses her engagement with the MU fantasy most literally while in Arcade's murderworld; however, when her team later criticizes her leadership after she abandons them to spend more time with Spider-Man, she perhaps expresses this sentiment at its most emotional, simply stating in lieu of an apology: "this isn't fun" (Hastings 2017a, 45). Similarly, in *Howard the Duck* (2015–2016), Gwenpool admits that she ultimately sold the stolen virus to the terrorist organization Hydra because it was "not very fun or Cosmic Cube-y or Merlin Stone-y," again suggesting that if the "game" insufficiently fulfills the fantasy, if the pieces aren't good enough, aren't *fun* enough, they are unworthy of her attention, and the consequences of her actions are beneath her concern (Hastings 2016, 21).

By detailing how Gwenpool's fantasy-fulfillment approach to the MU influences her motivations and priorities, Hastings exposes a tension inherent in Gwenpool's character, born from the conflicting demands of the many fantasy-fulfillment roles she adopts (the comic reader, the fanfic writer, the superhero, the story protagonist, the self-insert character). What unfolds across Gwenpool's journey, then, is a desire to reconcile these varying roles as best she can, in ways that ultimately help her redress the complex moral framework at the heart of such a uniquely positioned figure.

Through Gwenpool's central desire for fantasy fulfillment, Hastings presents a character whose closest narrative approximate is not a superhero, but rather a Skrull: a figure that strategically imitates superhero archetypes in order to successfully pass among their ranks. This imitation, this *performance*, is reinforced by the unique subjectivity afforded by Gwenpool's love of comics, through which she gains the tools to maximize the fantasy's potential upon entry. But the irony that Gwenpool realizes throughout *Howard the Duck* (2015–2016) and *The Unbelievable Gwenpool* (2016–2018) is that her desire to fulfill the fantasy at all costs is ultimately the very thing that prevents her from becoming the very superhero she so repeatedly, albeit quite earnestly, imitates.

Beyond the Moral Wall

Given the often conflicting and contradictory terms that comprise many of Gwenpool's subjectivities, positionalities, motivations, and drives, it comes as no surprise that Christopher Hastings presents Gwenpool's journey to establish a moral framework best suited for her new environment as one with no clear answers. Her unique role within Marvel's canon, along with the many perspectives such a role brings, ultimately shapes her character into one in part defined by a state of constant flux. And, as Gwenpool learns to acclimate to her new world, so too must she learn to come to terms with who she is, what it means for someone like her to be a hero, and what parts of her old life must be reconfigured as she embraces her new one. In her attempt to connect with legends and icons she's idolized since childhood, she is often unable to see them beyond their status as characters beholden to narrative conventions; in her attempt to take up arms against evil, she struggles to acknowledge the effects and consequences of her violent actions beyond their value as entertaining spectacle; in her attempt to maximize the joy of being in a world that brings her more pleasure than her previous one, she is challenged to engage with that world beyond its status as mere fantasy. These tensions culminate in a character whose journey routinely reflects the need to grapple with the varied demands of each layer of her fictive environment, from the White Space downward.

Though I maintain that such a unique character is governed in part by her engagement with a conundrum with no clear answers, this is not to say that Gwenpool remains fixed in place because of those challenging existential circumstances. Indeed, much of Hastings' effort near the end of *The Unbelievable Gwenpool* (2016–2018) highlights how Gwenpool begins to acknowledge the gravity of her abilities, her circumstances, and her newfound role. It is through this process that Gwenpool begins to fully settle into the MU and address the ethical framework she carries with her; it is also through this process that she ultimately sacrifices herself for the safety of those around her, electing to end her own story and erase herself from existence rather than continue down a path she discovers will inevitably turn her into a villain (Hastings 2018b, 92).

Yet, like so much franchise superhero storytelling, the work continues; the work *always* continues. Many of the moral complexities Hastings seeds in his own stories continue to be explored throughout Gwenpool's many successive appearances, including her brief stint with the West Coast Avengers, as well across the entirety of her second major solo series, *Gwenpool*

493

Strikes Back (2019), written by Leah Williams. As Gwenpool continues to utilize her time in the Marvel Universe, to further address the central question at the heart of this chapter – "do fictional characters deserve our empathy?" – given her personal expertise on both sides of the page, perhaps it might be a question best left for her to answer.

References

Bandura, Albert. 2016. *Moral Disengagement: How People Do Harm and Live With Themselves*. Worth Publishers.

Hastings, Christopher. 2016. *The Unbelievable Gwenpool: Believe It*. Marvel Comics.

Hastings, Christopher. 2017a. *The Unbelievable Gwenpool: Head of M.O.D.O.K.* Marvel Comics.

Hastings, Christopher. 2017b. *The Unbelievable Gwenpool: Totally in Continuity*. Marvel Comics.

Hastings, Christopher. 2018a. *The Unbelievable Gwenpool: Beyond the Fourth Wall*. Marvel Comics.

Hastings, Christopher. 2018b. *The Unbelievable Gwenpool: Lost in the Plot*. Marvel Comics.

McCloud, Scott. 2000. *Reinventing Comics*. HarperCollins Publishers Inc.

Newman, Ira. 2009. "Virtual People: Fictional Characters through the Frames of Reality." *The Journal of Aesthetics and Art Criticism* 67 (1): 73–82. https://doi.org/10.1111/j.1540-6245.2008.01336.x.

Sankowski, Edward. 1988. "Blame, Fictional Characters, and Morality." *Journal of Aesthetic Education* 22 (3): 49–61. https://doi.org/10.2307/3333050.

47

LEGACY, MEMORY, AND FATHERHOOD IN *ALL-STAR SUPERMAN* (2005)

Owen Farrington

Introduction

Superman has remained one of the most instantly recognizable fictional characters worldwide since his legendary first appearance in *Action Comics* #1 (1938). Throughout his 80-plus year existence, the Man of Steel has become the archetypal superhero, representing the best that comic books have to offer. Alongside being the longest-running superhero in print media, Superman has been the subject of much scholarly analysis over the past century. Umberto Eco's *The Myth of Superman* (1972[1962]) inspired decades of academic study into the Last Son of Krypton. From Les Daniels' chronicling of the hero's publication history (1998), Tom De Haven's exploration of Superman's continued popularity amongst audiences and status as one of America's most prominent characters (2010), and Daniel Peretti's research into Superman's relationship with folklore and myth (2017), there is an ever-growing field of scholarship around DC's flagship hero.

However, one aspect of Superman's mythos that has yet to be fully explored is his relationship to legacy and memory. More so than any of his fellow heroes, Superman represents a vital component of the superhero myth; despite his immense power and fantastical nature, Clark Kent's empathy, reliability, and humanity remain his greatest traits. For all his near-endless abilities, vast rogues' gallery, and otherworldly allies, through both the inhabitants of Metropolis and the generations of real-world fans who avidly follow his adventures, Superman maintains a deep connection to humanity. Despite being born on an alien planet, Superman is, at his core, as human and ordinary as anyone else; he shares the same hopes and fears as those around him. When asked about the challenges that arise when attempting to tell relatable Superman stories, Grant Morrison (writer of *All-Star Superman* and several other Superman stories) remarked that

> The great thing with Superman is that even when you juggle stars, Lois Lane can undermine [you] with one cruel word. And that was what was powerful about it for me. That's why we made him even more powerful than ever, because everybody kept saying, 'You can't make a Superman story because if he can do anything, then what

DOI: 10.4324/9781003366911-53

conflicts are there?' And I thought, 'Well, emotional conflicts, the biggest ones, the things we all understand'.

(Warner Bros. Entertainment 2012, 00:10:53)

Despite his extraordinary abilities, Superman is not indestructible. While bullets may not pierce his skin, he remains helpless to the same insecurities, concerns, and vulnerabilities as anyone else. Superman is an everyman hero, and as such, the legacy his actions leave behind has been considered by multiple comic book writers. Over the previous eight decades, many stories have discussed Superman's legacy and humanity through his relationship to specific characters, with perhaps the most notable examples being Jeph Loeb and Tim Sale's *Superman: For All Seasons* (1998), which spotlights Clark's relationships with Jonathan Kent, Lois Lane, Lex Luthor, and Lana Lang; and Alan Moore and Curt Swan's *Whatever Happened to the Man of Tomorrow?* (1986), which imagines how the world remembers Superman ten years after he mysteriously disappears. However, few accomplish this feat with more nuance and complexity than *All-Star Superman*, the 12-issue limited series released between November 2005 and October 2008, written by Grant Morrison and drawn by Frank Quitley.

All-Star Superman is an insightful study of the importance of superhero fiction in the modern world and the extent to which the trials and tribulations of these remarkable characters shape our media, ethics, and morals. Written following the loss of their father, Morrison depicts Superman's final year on Earth as he faces impending death due to overexposure to solar radiation. With this tragic fate looming large, *All-Star Superman* highlights Superman's importance by questioning how the world would cope with his demise and, by extension, what the legacy of such an exceptional hero would be. This chapter will examine how *All-Star Superman* uses themes of legacy and memory to analyze Superman's status as the flagship superhero, the role of superheroes in broader popular culture, and how we remember and honor those who make a difference in our lives.

"A Faster, Stronger, Better Idea": The Origin of *All-Star Superman*

All-Star Superman was published as part of the new All-Star initiative by DC Comics, which aimed to pair their flagship characters with celebrated writers and artists on unique, out-of-continuity stories. Morrison, who had pitched an ambitious Superman relaunch in the late 1990s before leaving to work on *New X-Men* for Marvel, was tasked with writing a 12-part series to showcase the essential elements of the Man of Steel and create a timeless and quintessential depiction of Superman. When conceptualizing *All-Star Superman*, Morrison drew influence from several notable sources, including the work of Mort Weisinger, John Byrne, and the character's creators, Jerry Siegel and Joe Shuster. Taking elements from each of these creators, who wrote Superman during different decades and eras, Morrison aimed to create a version of Clark Kent that was the "ideal paragon of human physical, intellectual, and moral development that Siegel and Shuster had originally imagined," accessible to new readers but familiar to avid Superman fans (Morrison 2012, 409). As Morrison described it, the All-Star imprint aimed to "distil everything we like about the characters into one simple package that's very much aimed at a more mainstream pop audience" (Offenberger 2005).

While these influences are worth mentioning, *All-Star Superman*'s most significant source of inspiration came outside the printed page and in Morrison's personal life and history; in both its themes and story, the work draws heavily from the death of Grant's father, Walter Morrison, in February 2004. As Morrison explains:

> I started to work on what became *All-Star Superman* after my return to DC in 2003. The story I had planned was to deal with Superman's mortality, depicting his final days, and the twelve heroic labors he would perform for the benefit of all humankind. When my dad died the following year, he gave a part of his spirit to the book.
>
> *(Morrison 2012, 405)*

Morrison's decision to examine Superman's relationship to fatherhood is not an approach without historical context. It is worth noting that Superman's co-creator, Jerry Siegel, lost his father after he was attacked by a shoplifter, suffering a fatal heart attack. According to Brad Ricca, this incident, which occurred six years before the character debuted, had a notable influence on Superman's creation: it created a hero who was impervious to bullets and who could be a father figure to a generation of children living in a world on the brink of world war (2013, 301). Brad Meltzer notes similarly, stating that "your father dies in a robbery, and you invent a bulletproof man who becomes the world's greatest hero …there's a story there" (Elsworth 2008). Meltzer continues, stating, "America did not get Superman from our greatest legends, but because a boy lost his father …Superman came not out of our strength but out of our vulnerability" (Elsworth 2008). Morrison's reasoning for writing *All-Star Superman* is similar to Siegel's inspiration for creating Superman. Similarly to how Siegel's grief impacted the character's conception, Morrison uses the Man of Tomorrow to discuss their feelings of grief, loss, and vulnerability.

Nevertheless, understanding the extent to which Morrison was personally and professionally shaped by their father is critical to identifying how the themes of legacy and memory manifest in *All-Star Superman*. In several interviews, Morrison has discussed how their father shaped their worldview and career. When speaking with *The Scotsman*, Grant described Walter as a "genuine superhero" (2019). Recalling his time as a member of the anti-nuclear organization, Committee of 100, they state that "he was really clever. I saw him going out on campaigns, going up against the police, breaking into bases and taking photographs to get information out to working class people" (The Newsroom 2011). Walter's anti-nuclear activism greatly impacted Grant's childhood, shaping their understanding and love of superheroes. Growing up only four miles away from RNAD Coulport (home of the UK's Trident-missile-armed nuclear submarine force) during the Cold War, the fear of nuclear annihilation loomed large in Grant's mind. Morrison notes that even though their childhood was dominated by the anxiety of "the Bomb…killing everybody and everything," superheroes provided an escape from these concerns (2012, xiii). As they explain,

> Superheroes laughed at the Atom Bomb. Superman could walk on the surface of the sun and barely register a tan…Before it was a Bomb, the Bomb was an Idea. Superman, however, was a Faster, Stronger, Better Idea
>
> *(Morrison 2012, xv)*

Muireann O'Sullivan highlights how Morrison uses "the comics form to articulate this sense of impending destruction, in order to create a more emotionally tangible forum in which to engage with and interrogate these fears" throughout their career (2015, 184). This approach is evident throughout *All-Star Superman*. Discussing the climax of the series, which sees Superman battle Solaris, O'Sullivan states that

> Morrison's incarnation of Superman is designed not only to save society and lead it away from the destructive powers of radiation, as the sun is almost destroyed, but also to subvert the personification of nuclear disaster, which is Solaris, by capturing the tyrant sun to provide an opportunity to provide positive change.
>
> *(O'Sullivan 2015, 192)*

This aspect of *All-Star* is heavily influenced by Grant's childhood and their father's activism, but Walter's fingerprints on this story do not end here. Explaining how Walter's passing influenced the creation of the series, Morrison notes that:

> [I]f you want to tell stories that are about real things, then you have to make your inspiration real …it was just after my father had died, so those kind of feelings went into the story because, as a writer, that's the only way you've got to articulate these feelings…all of the inspiration for Superman, for Batman, for all of these characters comes from things that happen in real life, and just from trying to make sense of the way people deal with each other and, you know, the things that we all have to deal with as we go through life.
>
> *(DC 2011, 00:00:04)*

Morrison constructed *All-Star Superman* to pay tribute to their father's legacy, processing their memories of Walter throughout their life and the grief they felt in the months following his passing. Through the prism of telling a Superman story that considers how the hero would grapple with his own mortality, *All-Star Superman* exists as a poignant and heartfelt homage to the "genuine superhero[es]" that inspired Morrison. (Morrison 2012, 410–11).

"It All Comes Out Right in the End": The Legacy of Fatherhood

Throughout *All-Star Superman*, Morrison explores the relationship between fatherhood and the comic's overarching themes of legacy and memories. Not only was the writer inspired to tell the story after the loss of their father, but Superman's memories of Jonathan Kent (his adopted father) and Jor-El (his biological father) form an integral part of the narrative, as Clark reflects on the loss of both fathers as he processes his own mortality. This theme even extends to Superman himself, who could be viewed as the father of the superhero archetype and a father figure to those who idolize and look up to him.

As Superman faces his impending death, the comic shows him reflecting on the lessons he learned from his fathers, and at the same time, we see the world that idolizes the Man of Tomorrow contemplate how they will remember him once he is gone. This concept is best encapsulated by Jor-El's message to Superman in *All-Star Superman* #12 (2008), where Superman, as his condition worsens, experiences a vision of his father on Krypton before its destruction. Here, Clark can speak to his father for the first time, expressing his concerns about the legacy he will leave behind on Earth. Upon hearing these worries, Jor-El tells his son,

> You will give the people of Earth an ideal to strive towards. They will race behind you, they will stumble, they will fall. But in time, they will join you in the sun, Kal. In time, you will help them accomplish wonders.
>
> *(Morrison and Quitely 2009, 138)*

This quote is pivotal to understanding how Morrison considers legacy and memory throughout *All-Star Superman*. Jor-El's speech, which encourages Superman to reawaken, defeat Luthor, and save all of humanity by repairing the sun, emphasizes how the people of Earth view Superman as a father figure. Just like Clark turns to his fathers for wisdom and guidance, humanity seeks inspiration from Superman. Jor-El states that, after stumbling and falling like a child learning to walk, they eventually follow in his footsteps, learning to walk with their beloved hero as equals.

The final moments of the comic reinforce this notion. Superman is believed to be dead after flying into the sun's core, and the people of Earth maintain his legacy in three distinct ways. First, a statue is erected in the center of Metropolis to commemorate his heroics, which Jimmy Olsen states that thousands of people visit to pay their respects. Second, Dr. Quintum unveils his Superman-2 project, suggesting that he, and, by extension, humanity, will create a new Superman to continue Clark's mission in his absence. Third, as the world remembers Superman, they choose to carry with them the principles and values that he stood for, with each person touched by the Man of Tomorrow carrying a piece of his legacy. Jor-El's proclamation that Clark "will help them accomplish wonders" encapsulates this idea and suggests that Superman's actions will inspire those around him to become the best versions of themselves. In his absence, it is hoped that the world will collectively become Superman, transforming their memory of the Man of Steel into a collective sense of compassion, kindness, and empathy. As Dan Phillips comments, "central to this final issue of Morrison and Frank Quitely's story is the simple idea of Superman as a pure ideal that the entire human race should try to achieve – the literal and figurative Man of Tomorrow" (2008). In *All-Star Superman*, the hero's ultimate legacy is leaving behind a better and kinder world, inspired by his selfless acts and unwavering dedication to helping others. However, it is also the legacy of Jor-El and Jonathan Kent, the fathers who taught Clark these values and encouraged him to use his abilities to inspire those around him.

Jor-El plays a crucial role in *All-Star Superman* #12, and this issue mirrors *All-Star Superman* #6 (2007), which chronicles Jonathan Kent's fatal heart attack and Superman's memory of his adopted father. Superman returns to the day of Jonathan's death through a sci-fi-infused time-travel plot. Disguising himself in bandages, Clark comforts his adopted father in his final moments, saying goodbye to Jonathan as they approach their last days. This heartfelt exchange is intercut with a young Clark Kent encountering the monstrous, time-consuming Chronovore. Unlike the future Superman, who accepts that he cannot save Jonathan and instead chooses to keep him company during his last moments, the young Clark frantically races home upon sensing his father's heart attack. However, the Chronovore eats the exact time it would take for Clark to return home, meaning he cannot return in time to prevent his father's death. This issue raises several intriguing points about legacy and memory. The younger Clark is forced to accept the limitations of his powers and that he cannot save everyone, while the adult Clark gains closure in his father's last moments as he processes the looming death. Although the Chronovore is a literal antagonist in this story, the main villain of *All-Star Superman* #6 is time. Each of the main characters in the issue (young Clark, adult Clark, and Jonathan) is limited by their lack of time, and it is only through accepting that time is beyond one's control that Superman makes peace and learns from this tragic moment. As Ashley V. Robinson highlights, "The emotional core that runs underneath All-Star Superman #6 is the most deeply human truth to our shared experience. The death of our parents is something that we all know is coming …yet can never prepare for" (2018). Although Clark has immense power, he cannot save Jonathan and must deal with his loss, acknowledging that despite his extraordinary abilities, even Superman cannot defeat time. As Morrison forces the hero to confront this inevitability, they demonstrate Superman's humanity and the importance of remembering and celebrating the lives of those who have passed away.

All-Star Superman #6 also contains numerous comparisons to Morrison's personal experiences with their father's passing. Much like Superman, Morrison was forced to process the grief of their father's loss, accepting their inability to save him, and instead chose to remember and honor their father after his passing. Whereas *All-Star Superman* is a testament to Walter Morrison's legacy, Superman, and what he becomes at the finale of the story, is Jonathan Kent's true legacy within the story. As the young Clark explains at Jonathan's funeral,

> Jonathan Kent taught me that the strong have to stand up for the weak and that bullies don't like being bullied back. He taught me that a good heart is worth more than all the money in the bank …He taught me that the measure of a man lies not in what he says but what he does.
>
> *(Morrison and Quitely 2008, 150–51)*

This concept of Superman existing as Jonathan Kent's legacy is reinforced in the issue's conclusion, with several Supermen from different points in time paying their respects at Jonathan's grave. One, a gold-skinned Superman from the far future, leaves an indestructible flower next to the headstone, proclaiming, "For him, from all of us. In remembrance of all that we are. And all that we will be" (Morrison and Quitely 2008, 153). This golden Superman is explained as the protagonist's final form, travelling back from the future once his mission to repair the sun is complete, and this moment demonstrates that Superman's ultimate act of heroism is not just Clark's legacy but the legacy of Jonathan Kent, Jor-El, and all those who encouraged Superman to use his powers for good.

"In Love and War": Superman through the Eyes of Lois Lane and Lex Luthor

Morrison's examination of legacy and memory in *All-Star Superman* is not limited to the concept of fatherhood. Although this concept is integral to the story, Morrison also explores how Superman will be remembered by examining his relationships with Lois Lane and Lex Luthor. *All-Star Superman* #2 (2006) and *All-Star Superman* #3 (2006) spotlight Clark's relationship with Lois and highlight how their love will carry Superman's legacy after the hero is presumed dead. Following Superman's diagnosis at the end of *All-Star Superman* #1 2005), he creates a formula that allows someone to gain his powers for a day. On Lois's birthday, he reveals his secret identity and gifts her the formula, and then the couple soar through the skies and fight crime together. Not only does this serve as a heartfelt moment between the pair, but it also connects to the series' overarching themes. Given Superman's first actions after learning of his fate is to create this formula and gift it to Lois, it suggests that for the first time he wants to share this aspect of his life with the woman he loves, shedding the "bumbling, oafish Clark Kent" disguise to allow Lois to experience the life Clark lives outside the Daily Planet (Morrison and Quitely 2008, 49). Superman's mortality forces him to let his guard down and show his true self to Lois Lane. Moreover, by giving Lois his powers and embarking on adventures together, Clark wants her to experience the world the way he does every day. This means that, even once he is gone, someone will understand how Superman sees the world around him and why he loves humanity. He chooses Lois due to his love for her, and it is through their love that Superman's memory will be kept alive, especially once Lois has seen the world through his extraordinary eyes. This sentiment is reinforced later in the comic when Clark, writing his will in *All-Star Superman* #10 (2008) proclaims, "To Lois Lane, I leave our future," suggesting that she will be the one to carry Superman's legacy forward and share it with the world after his death (Morrison and Quitely 2009, 103).

While these issues spotlight the love that Clark and Lois share and how this love will carry Superman's legacy after his demise, *All-Star Superman* #5 (2006) flips this dynamic by highlighting how the hero will be remembered by his greatest foe: Lex Luthor. After being incarcerated and sentenced to death for sabotaging Dr. Quintum's mission to the sun and causing Superman's fate, Clark interviews Lex before his execution. During the interview, Luthor boasts about fulfilling his dream of killing Superman. During this issue, the Parasite attacks Stryker's Island, causing Clark and Luthor to escape through an underground tunnel. However, Lex returns to his cell, informing Clark that he no longer fears death now that he has cemented his legacy as the man who killed Superman. Whereas the Lois-focused issues study Superman's memory through the prism of love, this issue focuses on Luthor's disdain toward the Last Son of Krypton. Whereas Superman struggles with realizing that his time is finite, Lex appears calm and unbothered about his pending execution, comforted by the idea that he will be remembered as the man who killed Superman.

This comparison between Superman and Lex and how they process their legacy and mortality is encapsulated by *All-Star Superman* #12 (2008). Here, Superman has significantly deteriorated and cannot use his powers. In contrast, Lex, having escaped prison and taken the formula Clark created for Lois, is now unstoppable, rampaging throughout Metropolis. Whereas Luthor uses his newfound powers to wreak havoc and assert his dominance, Clark, relying on little more than his will and determination, fights Lex and defeats him. After causing the time around Luthor to accelerate (which causes the formula to wear off), Lex admits defeat, proclaiming, "This is how he sees all the time. Like, it's all just us, in here, together. And we're all we've got" (Morrison and Quitely 2009, 147). At this moment, Lex experiences an epiphany: witnessing the world like Superman does, which humbles him and reduces the villain to tears.

Lex's breakdown contrasts Lois's experience when she obtains Clark's powers. Although the reader is not privy to how Lois processes this power, Morrison makes it clear that Superman wants Lois to experience humanity through his eyes; Clark wants Lois to fully understand why he fights for everyone and what the world means to him so that once he is gone, someone will still love and care for those around them much like he did, and share this compassion with the rest of the world. While Lois accepts this role as Superman's true love and confidant, Lex cannot cope with the intensity of these powers and the responsibility that comes with them. Upon hearing millions of voices crying out for help at once, Luthor is broken by the weight of responsibility, subtly accepting that he cannot protect and care for those in need as well as Superman does. Ultimately, this realization enables Superman to defeat Lex and assert his legacy as a symbol for all humans to rally around and aspire to be, sternly telling his longtime foe, "You could have saved the world years ago if it mattered to you, Luthor" (Morrison and Quitely 2009, 148). This moment illustrates that even without his extraordinary abilities, anyone can be Superman by practicing kindness, empathy, and compassion.

Metatextual Legacy

Although Morrison primarily examines Superman's legacy and memory via his relationship with several influential figures in his life, *All-Star Superman* also discusses Superman's importance on a metatextual level. Superman is not just an integral figure within the fictional DC Universe but a beloved pop culture icon in the real world. Through the writer's commentary on Superman's legacy, Morrison examines how both realities perceive and idolize the Man of Steel. This approach is prevalent throughout *All-Star Superman* #10, which details Superman's final labors of heroism as he writes his will. Throughout this issue, Clark discusses the memories of those closest to him and how he seeks to be remembered by them while solving as many of the world's problems as possible before his death.

Superman ponders how Earth will fare once he is gone, and uses a "nano-optical transfusion of solar energy" to create a new world without any trace of the Last Son of Krypton (Morrison and Quitely 2009, 105). Labeled Earth-Q, this world develops at a hyper-accelerated rate. While Superman performs his daily duties, Morrison and Quitely intercut the narrative by showing Earth-Q's development. Heavily implied to be the real world (or a close recreation of it), Earth-Q evolves through multiple stages of human history in a single day. Throughout *All-Star Superman* #10, Morrison showcases different stages of human civilization and the mythologies created in each era. For instance, real-world philosophers Giovanni Pico della Mirandola and Friedrich Nietzsche are shown to exist within Earth-Q. The inclusion of these two philosophers within *All-Star Superman*'s narrative is no coincidence, as their theories and worldviews are of great relevance to Morrison's interpretation of Superman. Mirandola, in his 1,486 declaration, *Oration on the Dignity of Man*, argues that humanity's desire for knowledge will bring them closer to God and that humans are God's final and greatest creation (Borghesi and Massimo 2012, 67). In contrast, Nietzsche, in his 1883 book *Thus Spake Zarathustra*, rejects the role of God and instead proposes the existence of the Übermensch, a heroic figure "capable of feats far beyond those of mortal men" and "the end goal for all humanity" to aspire to (Bogaerts 2013, 88).

Morrison includes Mirandola and Nietzsche within Earth-Q to suggest that Superman represents aspects of their philosophies. The writer has previously expressed admiration of Mirandola's work and described their portrayal of Superman as a "Renaissance idea of the ideal man, perfect in mind, body and intention," directly citing the *Oration on the Dignity of Man* as an essential text in forming their version of the hero (Babcock 2018; Morrison 2012, ix). By referencing Mirandola directly in *All-Star Superman* #10, Morrison suggests that humanity's advancements over centuries eventually led to the creation of Superman and the superhero myth. Similar to Jor-El's declaration, Morrison believes that those who believe in Superman (in both the real and fictional worlds) can become kinder and more compassionate by following his example. The parallels between Nietzsche and Superman are more overt. Roy Schwartz argues that Siegel and Shuster's original Superman mirrors Nietzsche's

Übermensch, describing the Golden Age Superman as a "true embodiment of Nietzsche's concept" (2021, 169). Schwartz states that this early Superman "symbolised power and superiority," often dispensed "his own brand of justice under no authority other than his unchallenged might" and had both "the might to do the right thing" and assurance "about what the right thing is," traits that reflect Nietzsche's Übermensch (2021, 169). In addition to this, Christopher Knowles states that Siegel likely took the name Superman from the English translation of *Thus Spake Zarathustra*, which saw "Übermensch" become "Superman" (2007, 56).

Morrison includes Nietzsche in *All-Star Superman* to suggest that his philosophy advances and furthers Mirandola's concepts, developing the notion of humanity becoming its own savior and the concept of the Übermensch. This belief is expanded upon in *All-Star Superman* #10's climax, when the comic returns to Earth-Q and introduces readers to Jerry Siegel and Joe Shuster, Superman's real-world creators. On the issue's penultimate page, the pair create the first sketch of their new character, proclaiming, "Third time lucky. This is the one… this is going to change everything" (Morrison and Quitely 2009, 105). Siegel and Shuster's inclusion suggests that Morrison believes their work represents the next stage of philosophy previously advanced by Mirandola and Nietzsche, building upon their concepts and resulting in the creation of humanity's finest achievement: the superhero. Additionally, their inclusion contributes to *All-Star Superman*'s focus on legacy, particularly concerning fatherhood. Siegel and Shuster can be interpreted as Superman's literal fathers, creating the hero from nothing but their individual experiences and imagination. Therefore, like Jor-El and Jonathan Kent, they are acknowledged as pivotal figures in Superman's development, both as the imagined superhero and a myth that inspires the worlds of fact and fiction. In addition, Siegel and Shuster's inclusion in *All-Star Superman* furthers the implication that Earth-Q is not simply a reality created by Superman as an experiment but that it is actually the real world. To quote Timothy Callahan, Morrison includes these real-world figures to signify "the connection between the fictional reality of the DC Universe and the reality of the world of its creators" and proposes that "Superman isn't a concept that humans created, humanity is a concept that Superman created" (2008). Earth-Q's role in *All-Star Superman* is to contend that Superman's myth is powerful in both realities and that the hero's legacy embodies the philosophies and imagination of those who contributed to his creation or decades of adventures.

Through this interpretation, Jor-El's speech in *All-Star Superman* #12 carries a more metatextual definition. Superman's legacy is quantified by his impact in two distinct worlds: the imagined DC Universe and the real world that thought him into existence. Morrison's interpretation of Superman in this series is heavily rooted in metatextuality. In a 2009 interview, they reflected on *All-Star Superman* and remarked, "[s]omewhere, in our darkest night, we made up the story of a man who will never let us down and that seemed worth investigating" (Thill 2009).

The relationship between how these two worlds perceive and remember Superman is an intrinsic part of *All-Star Superman*'s narrative. Within the imagined DC Universe, he serves as the unwavering symbol of heroism whose sacrifice inspires its inhabitants to continue his work by becoming kinder, more caring, and more compassionate. Meanwhile, he is a fictional character in Earth-Q who will likely inspire generations of comic book readers. Superman's status in Earth-Q parallels his role in the real world as a beloved character that many (including Morrison themselves) found inspiration in during dark periods of their lives. Superman serves an essential function in each reality. *All-Star Superman* contends that Superman's legacy goes beyond the printed page and rests in the hearts of those he has comforted and entertained throughout his 80 years of existence.

"If You Seek his Monument, Look around You": The Idea of Superman

All-Star Superman's metatextual approach to examining Superman's legacy is taken one step further in *All-Star Superman* #12. The final issue reflects this notion of Superman's true legacy by highlighting how he inspired humankind. Here, Superman flies into space to repair the sun after Solaris damaged it, a task that will take multiple lifetimes and transform Superman into a solar being (resulting in him becoming the gold-skinned hero that appeared in *All-Star Superman* #6). Faced with wondering how Earth will fare without its greatest hero, the final page reveals Dr. Quintum's latest project: a door containing the number two in the style of Superman's shield. Although the exact nature of this project is left unanswered, it is implied, as it was in the conclusion of *All-Star Superman* #10, that humanity will create their own Superman to continue in Clark's absence. Siegel and Shuster created their Superman within Earth-Q, who would go on to embolden generations of readers, and Quintum's project will likely do the same: create a new, man-made Superman who will represent Kal-El's values and ideals in the hero's wake. The implication of Quintum creating a man-made Superman echoes Nietzsche's concept of the Übermensch. In *Thus Spake Zarathustra*, Nietzsche declared, 'You could create the Superman. Perhaps not you yourselves …But into fathers and forefathers of the Superman you could re-create yourselves: and may this be your best creation!' (Nietzsche 2003, 62). This notion is explored literally in *All-Star Superman*'s ending, with Quintum seemingly building a new Superman to continue its predecessor's work and carry on his legacy.

Morrison's thesis on Superman's legacy is that he is an idea, one faster and stronger than any bomb or man-made construct, and one that will continue to inspire the world for centuries (Morrison 2012, xv). As Krypton's Last Son becomes the heart of the sun in *All-Star Superman*'s climax, Morrison declares that Superman's purpose lies at the center of the universe, both literally existing at the Sun's core, and figuratively, within the hearts of those who carry with them the ideas that he represents truth, justice, and a better tomorrow. According to Phillips, once Superman transcends his physical form in the comic's final page, he evolves into a "pure ideal that the entire human race should try to achieve," guiding humanity into a brighter future through the legacy he leaves behind (2008). Whether through Quintum's mysterious project, Siegel and Shuster's creation, or the memory of Superman carried by Lois Lane and the rest of humankind, the idea of Superman will transcend Clark Kent and live on for generations.

References

Babcock, Jay. 2018. "'The Astronaut or the Gangster': Grant Morrison on Superman, the Enlightenment, Humanism and the Magic Word." *Arthur Magazine*, September 28. https://arthurmag.com/2008/10/28/grant-morrison-on-superman-the-enlightenment-humanism-and-the-magic-word.

Bogaerts, Arno. 2013. "Rediscovering Nietzsche's Ubermensch in Superman as a Heroic Ideal." In *Superman and Philosophy*, edited by Mark D. White. Wiley-Blackwell. ePub. https://www.perlego.com/book/1003911/superman-and-philosophy-what-would-the-man-of-steel-do-pdf

Borghesi, Francesco, and Massimo Riva. 2012. "Overview of the Text." In *Oration on the Dignity of Man: A New Translation and Commentary*, edited by Francesco Borghesi, Michael Papio and Massimo Riva. Cambridge University Press.

Callahan, Timothy. 2008. "All-Star Superman #10." *Comic Book Resources*, March 29. https://www.cbr.com/all-star-superman-10.

Daniels, Les. 1998. *Superman: The Complete History: The Life and Times of the Man of Steel.* Chronicle.

DC. "Grant Morrison on Superman #4." Uploaded August 26, 2011, on YouTube. https://www.youtube.com/watch?v=jF-C7yv0vvc

De Haven, Tom. 2010. *Our Hero: Superman on Earth.* Yale University Press.

Eco, Umberto. 1972[1962]. "The Myth of Superman." *Translated by Natalie Chilton. Diacritics* 2: 14–22.

Elsworth, Catherine. 2008. "The tragic real story behind Superman's birth." *The Telegraph*, August 27. https://www.telegraph.co.uk/news/celebritynews/2628733/The-tragic-real-story-behind-Supermans-birth.html.

Knowles, Christopher. 2007. *Our Gods Wear Spandex: The Secret History of Comic Book Heroes.* Weiser.

Morrison, Grant. 2012. *Supergods: Our World in the Age of the Superhero.* Vintage.

Morrison, Grant, and Frank Quitely. 2008. *All-Star Superman: Volume 1.* DC Comics.

Morrison, Grant, and Frank Quitely. 2009. *All-Star Superman: Volume 2.* DC Comics.

Nietzsche, Friedrich. 2003. *Thus Spake Zarathustra.* Translated by Thomas Wayne. Algora.

Offenberger, Rik. 2005. "Comic Book Biography: GRANT MORRISON." *First Comics News*, September 6. https://www.firstcomicsnews.com/uniquely-original-grant-morrison.

O'Sullivan, Muireann. 2015. "Fallout Boys: Paranoia, Power and Control in Morrison's Cold War Superheroes." In *Grant Morrison and the Superhero Renaissance*, edited by Darragh Greene and Kate Roddy. McFarland & Company.

Peretti, Daniel. 2017. *Superman in Myth and Folklore.* University Press of Mississippi.

Phillips, Dan. 2008. "All-Star Superman #12 Review." *IGN*, September 18. https://www.ign.com/articles/2008/09/18/all-star-superman-12-review.

Ricca, Brad. 2013. *Super Boys: The Amazing Adventures of Jerry Siegel and Joe Shuster – The Creators of Superman.* St. Martin's Press.

Robinson, Ashley V. 2018. "All-Star Superman 6 May Be the Greatest Superman Comic Ever Written." *DC*, April 16. https://www.dc.com/blog/2018/04/16/all-star-superman-6-may-be-the-greatest-superman-comic-ever-written

Schwartz, Roy. 2021. *Is Superman Circumcised? The Complete Jewish History of the World's Greatest Hero.* McFarland & Company.

Thill, Scott. 2009. "Grant Morrison Talks Brainy Comics, Sexy Apocalypse." *Wired*, March 19. https://www.wired.com/2009/03/mid-life-crisis.

The Newsroom. 2011. "'Interview: Grant Morrison, comic book writer." *The Scotsman*, July 24. https://www.scotsman.com/news/interview-grant-morrison-comic-book-writer-2463755.

Warner Bros. Entertainment. "All-Star Superman | Featurette: 'Now' | Warner Bros. Entertainment." Uploaded November 19, 2012, on YouTube. https://www.youtube.com/watch?v=6VO9505oVkM.

INDEX

For Product Safety Concerns and Information please contact our EU representative GPSR@taylorandfrancis.com Taylor & Francis Verlag GmbH, Kaufingerstraße 24, 80331 München, Germany

Printed and bound by CPI Group (UK) Ltd, Croydon, CR0 4YY

06/01/2026

02029729-0005